Shaeli of Purple Leaf

R.L.Aiken

Copyright © 2016 R.L.Aiken

All rights reserved.

ISBN

978-0-6485683-0-8

For Philip

ACKNOWLEDGMENTS

There are many people to thank in bringing this book to you: the members of my writers group who read this for me and gave me inspiration and help when I was just a newbie at this game; Carrolline, who read the very first pages; Gill, the LOTR devotee; Diane, Lisa, Sara and Suzanne, and all the other members who shared my journey. Friends and family who read it and loved it and gave me such encouragement. Annie for getting it out there, at last; to our daughters, who had to wait for me to finish "this bit" before they had dinner. And to my wonderful husband, my best friend, my number one fan in every way, as I am his, for his unfailing belief in me.

My thanks and love to you all... xxx

The World of the Traders

PROLOGUE

Tenelon lay dying, and he had been a long time about it. The long Winterings of his reign had been peaceful, prosperous ones, and he would be mourned by many. His death was also anticipated, with secret joy, by a few.

Small knots of people, voices hushed, faces shadowed, gathered in corners of the room, and the scent of burning herbs and oils hung palpably; an odorous mist which only served to make the stench of Green Fever more revolting.

Snatches of conversation drifted past the lady seated by the bed, making little more impression than the heavy fragrances moving sluggishly around her head.

"...*never* seen it attack so viciously..."

"I was sure the callow-root would work. It seemed to, for a while..."

"...and the kingdom will falter, when this evil thing..."

Quiet weeping came from the corner where the women took comfort from each other. Queen Irinesta took scant notice of these either.

"...remember how they danced at the Spring Ball? My Lady was so happy."

"How could we know?"

Ahh... it comes again...

The queen gave no outward sign of the racking pain that struck like a blade in her back, only a slight sheen rose upon her forehead, and a tooth pierced her tongue as she bit it.

"...she shouldn't sit there again tonight. It's too much."

That was E'Nith, always worrying – this time, perhaps, with reason – but sit here she would, as long as she had to.

"Leave her, E'Nith, she has little time left to sit beside him."

"But..."

"No, E'Nith." Lady Arinola's voice was firm, yet softened at the hurt in the old woman's face. "I will bring her myself if it becomes too much." A plump white hand reached out to touch the weathered one. The voice lowered. "It will miss its father's face by almost a Moon, but she is strong this time, even with what she endures. Go now. Do not worry."

A smile as the hand was removed, but E'Nith had no choice but to leave. She had been dismissed, kindly, but dismissed all the same. With an anxious glance toward her mistress, she left the room.

Irinesta glanced at her friend before turning back to her husband, lest the Lady Arinola see something amiss in her face; a face which should show grief and loss, yes, but no sign of pain. No. No one must know.

Ten days had passed since the inception of the plan she had devised, a frightening plan because, once set in place, there would be no turning back; no recourse but to leave everything in the hands of the gods and virtual strangers. And worst of all, never to know... never to see... But that didn't bear thinking about – it must be enough to know that their long-awaited child would be safe. She was no longer as naive as some believed, and she knew there were those who craved power and all that went with it. Too many people had access to a babe in a castle the size of Great Court, and she could not know what lay ahead, did not even know why she felt as she did, but she would not risk this new life. Better it claim the throne when fully grown... and it would grow up free, and with honour...

Her reverie was broken as the pain came again. The salty taste of blood filled her mouth for the second time and she struggled to keep her face from betraying her. She took hold of her husband's remaining hand – the other was gone, along with the arm, removed almost to the shoulder in a bid to stop the Fever spreading. The king had calmly halted the desperate attempts to save his life, knowing that soon the Fever would reach his brain and he would no longer have the will left to stop them. He had been right. She had not heard his voice in eleven days.

She pressed her lips to his fingers, remembering the thousands of times they had brushed her cheek, entwined in her hair. She thought, too, of the many times she had joyfully conceived, only to have the joy torn from her with the bloody voiding of the tiny beings they had so wanted. That he would never touch her hair or face again, nor touch the face of the one inside her – the one who was, even now, trying to be born – was almost too much to bear.

The pain passed and tears ran down her face, but that was alright, that was acceptable. Tears were expected of her, and no one need know just how many things she grieved for.

Her mind sought for diversion, and she thrust it back, far into the past, to the first time she had met the king. He had seemed so old from afar, and, besides, she had thought Sir Vulcan of Conroi much more dashing, and not *quite* as old. Tenelon had, in actuality, just turned four-and-thirty, but it had been all the same to an innocent girl of sixteen. Ancient.

She had come to Zirrus with her father for the Spring Carnival, and although she was accompanied everywhere by E'Nith, formerly her nurse, now her maid, it was her first foray into the world of her adulthood, for she would not be returning home to Romynn with her father, but remain here with E'Nith to learn the ways of Court. It was an honour to be chosen; the old queen, Vermona, held little power and ruled the ladies of the Court with an iron smile, surrounding herself with beauty and elegance but having little herself – or so it was said, for Irinesta had yet to see Queen Vermona, Second Mother to the King, Mother to the Princess Virrisian.

Another shaft of pain ripped through her, and she fought to keep her mind in the past and away from the torment of the present. Where had she been? *Ah…Virrisian…*

Virrisian had despised her in the beginning. At their first meeting she had wrested a brush from Virrisian's hand, a brush being used to beat a young apprentice until blood flowed. The others had stood watching stupidly, open-mouthed, doing nothing; this was their king's sister, a princess of the Realm, and if she chose to punish a Faunist's apprentice, reason or no, what right had they to interfere? The young Irinesta had no such qualms, she saw only an injustice being done, and flew to the defence of the child. The grown Irinesta sitting beside the bed almost smiled at the memory. She *had* been naive.

Wresting the hairbrush from Virrisian's hand as it hovered, poised for another blow, Irinesta flung it across the room, demanding Virrisian *stop*, stop it at *once*. Virrisian was four Winters younger than Irinesta, but she stood a full head taller, and was already bigger in bust and hip than Irinesta would ever be, and she turned with a look of such hatred that Irinesta lost her nerve. The child apprentice, Mareesha, slumped into a tearful heap, and Irinesta shrunk back against the door-frame waiting for the coming blow, yet the blow never came. The king appeared in the doorway, saw the blood on the face of the weeping young Faunist, Irinesta cowering before Virrisian's upraised hand, the silent, grim women watching. He rebuked his half-sister and Virrisian veiled her expression, at once contrite.

The king saw to Mareesha first, then he looked to Irinesta and helped her from her curtsey. He asked if she was harmed and smiled gently, and Irinesta blushed, curtsied again, smiled back. It began then. The glamorous Sir Vulcan was instantly forgotten. She was mesmerised by eyes as blue as summer sky, and as warm. Her hands burned with sudden heat where he touched them, her heart trembled, and she couldn't seem to catch her breath…

Just three Moons later, on their wedding eve, when he confessed to those same feelings, she had laughed, amazed. She'd learnt his character in the days since they'd met, known by mid-spring that he was the kindest of men, and when he'd asked for her hand on the first day of summer, she'd known that she could never leave him.

Irinesta was drawn reluctantly back to the present by a flurry at the door. Cold winds ruffled the tapestries on the walls. Another Wintering was beginning. The World seemed also to mourn the passing of the king.

Virrisian swept into the room, her entourage following meekly behind. At seven-and-thirty, as yet unmarried, she had become a striking woman. Coal-black hair hung past her waist, braided with pearls and gold thread, slate-grey eyes bore into everything and everyone. She had learned to contain her temper to the occasional outburst, and was known for her witty repartee and lavish parties. Her prowess on the war-fields made her a favourite, championed particularly by the knights she so regularly bested on the field – *and* in her chambers, or so it was whispered.

Tenelon and Virrisian shared the same father, the late King Tarkon, but were borne of different mothers. Tarkon had married Vermona fourteen Winters after Tenelon's mother had died bearing him, their only child, and eight more Winters had passed before Virrisian was born.

Virrisian's mother had chastised her for her public display of temper on the day Tenelon and Irinesta met. The lecture had been pointed, and predictable; it was beneath a princess to beat a common apprentice, Vermona had said. "Think of our image. Remember who you are."

The Court had buzzed with the news. Many people thought it high time; a haughty young miss, they said, too big for her satin slippers, but all was quickly forgotten when, ten days later, Vermona died in her sleep. Her daughter had wished her goodnight, the maids said, and she'd taken her evening toddy as usual, chatting to them as she readied for bed, yet next morning she was found cold and staring at the window. A grand funeral was held, and the Princess Virrisian drew many fine words as she walked with great dignity behind the coffin, her face streaming tears. Queen Vermona would have been proud.

This was followed, three Moons later, by the wedding of King Tenelon of Zirrus to the beautiful, young Lady Irinesta of Romynn.

Prosperity had reigned most of the days of Tenelon's rule, as it had in Tarkon's; a few scuffles over land; outlaws on the roads; the short, murderous rampage by the half-elf, Periqol, and his band; a rare uprising by several Wokkii nobles. All quickly settled, nothing really to mar the general peace. The Moons had passed into seasons, the seasons into years – each year marked by the passage of the Wintering across the Lands – and Zirrus had thrived. Tenelon had thrived with it, until one small wound at the Autumn's Eve Hunt had brought him to this... this *torture*.

Three Moons to happiness, Queen Irinesta thought. *Three Moons to sorrow.* Three Moons from meeting to marrying her king; three Moons waxing and waning as Tenelon fought death. And such a trivial wound, a misfired arrow, a mere graze, yet despite the proper cleansing, it had quickly become apparent that Green Fever was present.

Irinesta cursed inwardly as another pain began to build in the base of her spine. *Not now,* her mind pleaded. *Not* now*!* The mound of her belly tightened and there was a wetness between her thighs as Virrisian moved towards the bed, hands outstretched. *I must rise. I must speak with her*, Irinesta thought, but her body seemed unwilling to obey.

A movement from the bed saved her. She turned as Tenelon's eyes flew open and Virrisian gasped behind her. One of the women let out a cry and was quickly hushed.

The king's Faunist came forward and peered into Tenelon's face, studying his dull eyes. "My Lord?" she spoke calmly. "Do you hear me, my Lord?" A bell struck somewhere. No other sound was heard as the Faunist straightened and spoke regretfully. "I'm sorry, my Lady, 'tis just the Fever, I fear. He does not see, nor hear me."

The contraction had passed while the room was silent, and Irinesta looked from the Faunist's retreating back to her husband. She stood and examined his face.

"My Lord. My love. Do you know me?" Aware of those around her, around *them,* she leaned closer, her body awkward in its fullness. She peered into the once-bright eyes, now muddy and sightless, then put her cheek to his. "Hear me now, dearest, they will keep the child safe, I promise you. No one shall harm it." She whispered intensely, her anguish brushing his ear. "Please know, please, hear me, our child will be held safe." She wanted him to know... *needed* him to know. It was all she could do for him, now.

Was there some flicker of recognition? A glimmer of the man she knew? But no, there was only blankness. No light, no life. Perhaps the Faunist was right; perhaps it was only the Fever.

Irinesta sighed as she stood, her free hand going to her back. The other still held the remaining hand of Tenelon as she turned to face her sister-by-law.

Virrisian again held out her hand to Irinesta, dipping her knee just enough for good manners, apparently unruffled by her brother's staring eyes which only moments before had left her gasping. She was flushed with youth and vitality; Tenelon lay with the life seeping out of him, consumed by an enemy none could stop. As time had dragged on, Irinesta had increasingly resented Virrisian for her continuing, perfect health. Why should *she* be untouched by sickness or sorrow? Irinesta knew it was irrational to begrudge Virrisian her good health, even childish. She did not care. She forced a tight smile, moved her hand from her back, and took the proffered fingers in formal greeting. Unconsciously, her hand returned to rest upon the swell of her stomach. She almost wished this were over, so she could go to her room. The Glade Room. Sanctuary.

Irinesta blinked. Virrisian had spoken to her. *What did she say?* Then she remembered. Virrisian asked the same question every evening: *How is my brother, the king, this day?* Irinesta began to reply with her usual answer, but it seemed a farce.

"The Fever will take him this day, Virrisian. How do *you* think he is?" Sarcasm curdled her voice and she heard bitterness there too, but also a calm she did not feel.

If Virrisian was taken aback by Irinesta's words she gave no sign, she merely kissed Irinesta's flushed cheek with cool, dry lips. It was the last time Irinesta would ever feel that kiss.

"I do not desire to upset you, Irinesta. Concern only was my intention." Virrisian's voice, like her lips, was dry and cool. "Please, sit down. I would not tire you."

Irinesta was suddenly ashamed and smiled sadly. "No, it's I who am sorry, sister. My nerves are on edge with this waiting, and you're right, I am tired."

"Sit then, and we shall wait together. Perhaps we can give him some comfort, and we can talk." Irinesta shifted uncomfortably, but she kept her face still as Virrisian continued. "Unfortunately, there are pressing matters of state that must be decided upon before this is…" she glanced towards the bed, "…before this is over," she said.

Something in Virrisian's voice made Irinesta look closely at her, but Virrisian's face showed only the concern she spoke of. *Is it my imagination?* Irinesta thought. *Am I frightened of shadows?* She shivered, though it was warm in the room, and she knew her instincts were right, knew she had chosen the right path.

As she turned to sit, good-fortune deserted her; the pain came again, and this time she could not stop a small cry from escaping her. She compressed her lips, clutching at Tenelon's hand, but Virrisian had noticed. She noticed everything.

"What is it, Irinesta? Not the child already?" Again that odd note. Anticipation?

"No. It's... it's..." Irinesta stammered, striving for control. A sudden pressure on her hand shifted her attention to the bed.

Tenelon lay as before, but he was calmly staring at her. Not *through* her, blankly, lifelessly, as before, but *at* her. *His eyes. His eyes. Thank the gods.*

Her knees went weak, her back and belly filled with fire. The baby fluttered within her. Her voice came from far away. "Tenelon?"

He spoke one hesitant word. "Irinesta."

"I'm here, dearest. I'm beside you." She bent and kissed him as his image shimmered through her tears.

"As always, my love, when I have need of you, you are there. I must speak with you." His voice, though weak, rose slightly and carried throughout the room. "I would speak with you all."

There was utter silence. The Faunist hovered as uselessly as a moth. Every face was turned to the king. With one abrupt move Tenelon sat up, gripping Irinesta's hand so tightly the rings crushed into her fingers. His face grew animated, his voice grew stronger.

"The child *will* be held safe, Irinesta, do not worry. Its brother and sister will save it." He spoke eagerly, almost joyfully. "I have seen it. The birds will rescue them. There will be light again after the darkness."

Irinesta became frightened. His words made no sense. Their child had no brothers or sisters. Darkness and birds? It made no *sense*.

The voice of the king rose again. It rolled as thunder through the room. "Let those who would rule know that their time is short, they will not succeed." The words came faster. "The others run with the wind. Metal birds seek them. Thrice will my child be saved by its sister." Tenelon spoke urgently, but with unmistakable assurance, power in every syllable. "The old one knows the way in, seek for her on Xyros. *The child will rule!*" The words echoed through the room as he fell back against the pillows and his voice dropped to a whisper. "Worry not, dearest Irinesta." She leant closer, laying her hand against his fevered cheek, and he kissed her tenderly, reluctantly, knowing it would be for the last time. "My only love, you have always been everything to me. Worry no more about our blessed child, the gods protect it now." Tenelon sighed once as he let go of her hand, his eyes fusing with her own, even as he died.

Tears seared her lids as she kissed his forehead, his cheeks, his lips. She closed his staring eyes, studied his face, one last time. She stood. Turned.

A sea of faces surround her, mouths moving, but she hears nothing. People pluck at her, Virrisian, Vulcan, the Faunist. All of them, smothering her, drowning her.

"Leave me," she screams. "*Leave me!*"

She pushes past them, finds the door, sweeps down a hall. Someone is behind her, calling her name. She stops, turns. Arinola – a few others clustered behind. She stares at Arinola, falls upon her shoulder, sobbing, screaming. Drowning.

Arinola holds her, murmuring soft, meaningless words until the pain comes again, dragging her back, unwillingly, to her senses. This time the flow of liquid between her thighs is increased. It soaks hotly into her petticoats.

"The Glade Room, Arinola, help me."

Then she is there, shutting them out, all of them, despite their many protests. Insisting, commanding. *Leave me, oh, just leave me. GO!* And they're gone, Arinola, E'Nith, all, the door bolted behind them. No one to see, or hear. Only the Glade as witness.

Pain. Blinding pain. Face in a cushion to stifle the screams. *I can't.*

You can. Try harder. Tenelon's voice. One last time.

She can, and does. Finally.

Is it alright?

Yes! It breathes. It cries.

She severs the cord that binds it to her, wipes it, examining every perfectly formed limb. Wraps it, holds it to her breast. One time it will suckle there as her womb finishes its work. A small interlude in which to fit a lifetime of love.

Hush, sweet one. Hush.

She lies back, exhausted, but she must not rest; time is at its fleetest when one wishes it to linger most. She looks into the sweet face, memorising every curve, every feature. The father's dark brows; the mother's eyes, perhaps?

Tenelon's words return to her. The child... thrice saved... a sister. Birds. The old one... Safe.

I don't understand, but I believe.

She dresses again, throws her soiled garments and the sheet wrapped around the evidence of birth onto the fire. She takes up a bundle and hugs the child to her, determined, but so afraid.

"Always know I love you." Her voice breaks. "I'm sorry I cannot protect you here, but I will be in your heart every day, and in your dreams at night." She kisses the tiny head, her tears mingling with the soft, dark hair that has already dried into feathery curls. "Come, precious one. It is time."

* * *

CHAPTER ONE

Shaeli peered over the side, leaning as far out as she dared, holding tightly to the rail with one hand. The other, encumbered by the elbow wrapped around a taught rope, waved at three people in a small boat as they swept past.

She was not supposed to lean over – her father would be angry, she knew, if he saw her – but, oh, it was exciting to watch the water rush by beneath her and feel the wind in her hair. And she was careful, *very* careful. She didn't like too much *down*.

Besides they were all too busy to notice; hurrying to reach Cave before the Wintering began; Eenis sick again; and the new babies, two new babies, sisters at last – no more just her and the boys – and Da said they were all well, just tired, and she could see them this evening.

She squinted at the sun hanging just above the horizon, huge and deep gold. It nearly *was* evening. Good. She hadn't seen Mam with her big round belly since yesterday afternoon when she'd told her that the baby was on its way and she would soon be a big sister. That was good, too. She was tired of being the littlest.

Shaeli had gone to sleep last night listening to the sounds from the next room where her mother laboured, curious, and a little afraid, because Mam had made funny groaning noises every now and then. Mam had said that she needed no one but Da to help her, assuring Eenis that she would wake her if the need arose. Shaeli had lain awake for a long time before she slept, the soft murmurs of her parents' voices and the occasional peep of a night bird in M'Zen'sclahr Forest the only sounds to be heard, and when she'd finally drifted away, her dreams were a jumble of unremembered pictures.

She had her own little room, hardly bigger than her bed, with a tiny round window where she could sit and watch the clouds and the mountains go by, and see the stars as she lay in bed. She'd woken later in the night with the stars' eyes upon her, and what hour it was she didn't know, only that it was still dark and very cold. The Wintering was close, and yesterday when they had moored near the forest, Shaeli had heard her father muttering about the lateness of the season as he eyed the dark clouds massing over the Land.

She had drowsed as the stars began to lose their glow to the sunrise hours. Awareness faded in and out as she floated, almost asleep again, listening to the night's soft sounds... Mam's voice, quiet now... A funny noise, like birds far away... Da's deep voice... Another voice, soft, urgent... Whose?

She concentrated on the words to see who the voice belonged to, but it was unfamiliar and she couldn't work out what they were talking about. After a while she did not pay much attention, though the wall was thin and she could hear almost every word... Mam said it wasn't nice to drop-eaves, and she didn't understand anyway. She was sleepy, and perhaps she would see the elf, Williver, in her dreams again tonight.

The boys had teased her when she'd confided that an elf told her tales while she slept, embarrassing her so badly that she'd never spoken directly of the dreams again – although a few times she had told her father some of the "stories". He had listened patiently, smiling, and once he'd even laughed out loud, ruffling her brown sun-streaked hair and wondering at her "clever mind".

She was brought roughly back from her daydreaming as hands grabbed one of her ankles and lifted it from the crate on which she was perched. Shaeli squealed, struggled, kicked backwards, and someone let out a cry of pain and her ankle was released. She turned and jumped down.

Her cousin, Dari, was sprawled on the deck, rubbing his chin, a dazed look on his face. His brother, Andos, and her brother, Tarkoda, were bent over in gales of laughter behind him.

Shaeli's temper rose in direct proportion to her level of fright. She stamped her foot. "You little sneak, Dari. That was dang'rous." Her small voice rose. "And you *scared* me."

"Good," her cousin shouted back. "You know we're not allowed to lean over. And you kicked me."

"I'll do it again, if you ever do *that* again." She thrust out her pointy little chin. "Sneak. Toad, *pig*."

"That'll do, Shaeli," said her brother. "You weren't in danger, I was watching, and Dari's right. Da would give you fury and you know it." Tarkoda spoke quietly and stood casually, but his blue eyes were serious. He pushed hair that was three shades darker than his sister's from his face and looked calmly at her.

Shaeli bit down on her anger. It tasted sour on her tongue, but she listened. People always listened to Tarkoda. Da said he spoke sense, even if he was only a boy of seven Winters.

"I'm sorry, 'Koda," she said. "But he *did* scare me, and I love to see the waves, you know I do, and I *was* holding tight to the rope. We'll be at Cave soon and we won't see any water but the spring-stream, or much of anything for *ages*." She took a breath and smiled disarmingly. She didn't like Tarkoda to be mad at her.

He wasn't. "Just be careful, Mouse. It's a long way down to your beloved water." Like Da, he never called her Mouse when he was mad. "A very long way," he said, and looked up. "About as far down as the top of the balloon is *up*."

Shaeli looked up too. Above them soared a great balloon, the underside far out of reach, the balloon towering high into the sky, as big as a house. It was not a round balloon, like a child's toy given Lift by a second-rate Warlock at a fair, but elongated, like an enormous patterned sausage; a green-and-purple cloud cutting swiftly through the air. It was bright colour splashed against the blue sky; enormous green leaves scattered on a rich, purple background, and from this pattern, their balloon received its name: Purple Leaf.

The balloon obscured a huge chunk of sky and was puckered with many ropes. The rigging of thick hemp rope was anchored in many places to the railing and the deck upon which they stood, securely lashing the balloon to the ship-like dwelling that hung beneath it. The main deck was broad, the railings about them thick and unbroken, save for a seam which showed where the landing-gate lay, and another deck, raised above the main deck, filled the small triangular space at the front of the vessel, reached by a flight of steep steps on the same side as the gate. At the back, along the rear railing, lay a tiny hen house, water barrels that serviced the kitchen beneath, and beside them sheets flapped from a line. The rippling balloon rode the sky proudly in the strong wind, flying easily through the cold afternoon, high above the dark surface of the lake, guided by their Zoi.

They were traders, an ancient profession. Their home and their family's livelihood were carried in the wooden vessel hanging beneath the huge balloon, and the deck became a market in the cities, towns and villages they visited on their annual journeys. They carried much needed supplies and transported goods on the Trader, and Mam healed the ailments of the People and their animals with her Faunist skills. A flag fluttered at the back of the ship – the Faunist's symbol of a white hand on a green background – and the lack of Faunists in the smaller villages always kept Mam busy. Often, there was a girl or two after a hair potion; perhaps a young wife in need of advice about how to become pregnant – or how *not* to; always an old person wanting Mam's famous bone ointment to warm ancient joints during the Wintering.

Shaeli couldn't imagine living in the same place all the time, seeing the same people and things every day, never seeing the other Lands, or the Seas, or the Lakes. They flew over the greatest of the lakes now, Lake Marnis, its midnight-blue surface chopped with small waves, and before long it would be dotted with ice as the Wintering took hold of the World. The lights of Marnissi had begun to twinkle astern, and the last rays of the sun sent fingers of gold into the pink clouds behind the city. Soon Marnissi would be left far behind, for they would fly past nightfall and rest the Zoi tomorrow on the far side. One more day to play by the waves, and although it wasn't warm enough to swim, Shaeli didn't mind; there was always so much to look at – pretty shells and driftwood to add to her collection, or she might even find another crystal to put in her amulet. She put her hand on the small pouch that hung from her belt, the sourness of her anger gone, happy at the thought. She looked at Tarkoda and grinned.

Her brother marvelled at the way it changed her. Her pointy little face lit up, the grey-sometimes-blue eyes positively beamed, transforming his plain sister into a bewitching child. No wonder she could talk Da and Jeth into almost anything – him, too, when she wanted something. Not quite in her fifth Winter and already she knew how to charm. Tarkoda frowned; best she not know *that*.

"Anyway, Da wants you. You can see Mam now," he said. He turned away, dismissing her, but Shaeli did not notice. She was already skipping off to see Mam. And the new babies.

* * *

They lay in the big bed, the three of them, all together. Da was sitting on the edge, holding Mam's hand when Shaeli came to the half-open door and shyly tapped.

"Come in, but not too long," Da said. "Mam's tired." Then he smiled. "You got your wish, Shaeli. Another girl on board."

"*Two* more girls, Jarris," Mam said quietly. Her round face was soft with weariness, but her eyes shone as brightly as always.

Shaeli thought how different Mam looked, lying in bed with her thick black hair in two braids, instead of bustling around the kitchen with her hair tucked tightly into its lace-covered bun, and she looked flatter, somehow. After a moment Shaeli knew why – Mam had lost the big, round belly which had stolen her lap, and she hoped she would be able to sit there again now.

Mam smiled. "Come and meet the twins, big sister."

"Twins, of course. I'm not used to the idea of having two, yet," Jarris grinned. "We never had two at once before." He lifted Shaeli up onto the bed and Mam moved back a little so Shaeli could see the bundles beside her.

Two faces appeared, hardly bigger than the face of Shaeli's favourite doll. Two little faces with skins flushed pink like the petals of a rose, tiny hands, fingers curled into fists beneath the bumps of future chins. Shadows of eyebrows, ears like pink shells, clouds of dark hair. Both were sleeping soundly.

"Oh, the darlings," Shaeli whispered, "the little darlings." She looked at her mother, eyes round with wonder. "Mam, can I touch them?"

Her mother laughed softly. "Wouldn't you like a cuddle instead?"

"Could I really?" Shaeli's eyes grew rounder. "Cuddle both?"

"I don't see why not. I'll help, and I know you'll be careful."

"I will, Mam. So careful."

Shaeli barely breathed as her mother laid a bundle of baby in each arm, propping them safely with pillows and showing her how to support their heads, and as Shaeli looked from one to the other, she was overwhelmed with love. All the things they would do together went through her mind; the games they would play, stories she would tell them, things she could show them, but more than that she felt a need to look after them. They were so tiny, and Shaeli suddenly felt so big. A big sister at last.

She studied their faces, breathed in their warm, fresh scent, like powder and spring blossoms. What would they look like with their eyes open? As if in reply the baby in her left arm yawned, squirmed and opened her eyes. They were darkest blue, like the night-sky just before the sun touches it.

"Look, Mam, one's awake," Shaeli whispered. "She's *looking* at me." She had never been so thrilled.

The baby looked calmly up at her and yawned again, then she screwed up her face, opened her mouth and screamed, long and loud.

Shaeli looked at her mother, aghast. "What's the *matter* with her?"

The baby's face was turning crimson with effort.

"Nothing. She's just hungry, that's all," Mam laughed.

She took the baby, opened her gown and guided the mouth to her breast. The baby's cries ceased instantly, and Shaeli looked down at the babe lying in the crook of her right arm. She was surprised to see that this baby was also awake, but she was lying quietly, looking up at her. Her eyes were also an intensely deep blue.

"This one's awake, too, Mam," she whispered.

"Good. You cuddle her until this one finishes."

Shaeli and the babe sat quietly looking at each other. Grey eyes regarded depthless blue. Outside, a Zoi cried out.

Shaeli looked back at her mother, regarding the baby she held, considering. "My one's littler than yours, isn't she, Mam?"

"Yes, there's usually one bigger, when it's twins. Your one," Mam smiled, using Shaeli's terms, "your one *is* littler, but she's pretty, don't you think? And she'll soon grow."

"I think they're both pretty. This little one is so cute, and her hair's longer." She looked at the dark head nestled against Mam's bosom. "And your one is really *noisy*." Her father stifled his laughter and another thought occurred to her. "Was I this little? When I was a baby?"

Jarris answered. "You were, and just as pretty. Come on, give that baby to Mam for her feed, and then we had better let them all sleep."

He took the baby from Shaeli's arms, and handed her to his wife. A moment of silence descended as they stared at each other, locked in silent communication, and Shaeli looked from one face to the other, all but forgotten, until her father grinned, scooped her up from the bed and threw her up so she squealed.

"I am a lucky man to have three such pretty daughters," he said. He bent and kissed Mam, holding Shaeli so she could kiss her mother's cheek, too. "And such a brave, loyal wife. Beautiful, too."

"Go on, silly man, let us rest," Mam said, yet she gave him a look that belied her words. "I'll sleep when I've fed this little babe." She looked down at the two dark heads within the circle of her arms, and kissed each one. When she looked up, her eyes were bright. "Silly man," she said again.

Jarris looked back at her from the doorway. "May your dreams be bright and peaceful," he said, the formal goodnight spoken with infinite tenderness. "Sleep well, Mareesha."

* * *

They passed Eenis at the bottom of the stairs. Her pinched, pale face peered up at them, her eyes red as they always were when her head ached, but Shaeli didn't think her aunt looked quite as imposing from up here with her father's arms safely around her.

Eenis taught them reading and numbers during the morning hours, and even though Shaeli had just started to sit with the boys and was learning quickly, Eenis often found fault with her work or manners. Shaeli had begun to dread the lessons she had so wanted to begin. She snuggled closer to her father.

"Glad to see you're feeling better, Eenis," he said pleasantly. "Did Mareesha's herbs help?"

"A little, thank you, Jarris, but someone must make supper and clean up." Her mouth tightened. "And someone must wash the linen." The way she said *someone must*, you knew she meant *she* must. "It is unclean to leave birthing sheets too long."

"No need, Eenis. I have attended to it already, and they are hanging to dry." He smiled at the doubtful expression on her face. "Have no fear. Mareesha told me which herbs to use to cleanse them properly."

"Yes, well, I suppose that's alright, if Mareesha told you how." Eenis had no qualms about Mareesha's skills; she was proud of their reputation for having a Faunist more skilled than any other in the Fleet.

Jarris looked down at Shaeli, and deftly changed the subject. "Supper sounds good though, doesn't it, Mouse?"

"Yes, Da. I'm hungry." She was, but she knew Eenis' supper would be plain and flavourless compared to her mother's. Her aunt believed that too much of anything was a corruption to the soul, even to the flavour of her food, and she had an abhorrence of strong herbs and spices.

"Supper will be on the table directly after sunset." Eenis looked at Shaeli for the first time. "Tell the boys," she said shortly.

"Yes, Eenis." Shaeli replied quietly. They all knew that meant *exactly* directly after sunset. No one would be late.

"I shall make a tray for Mareesha, too. No doubt she'll be hungry."

"I thank you, Eenis. She'll appreciate it, I'm sure."

Shaeli snuggled closer to her father's shoulder. He was always patient with his brother's wife, as he was with most people. He said she'd had a hard life before coming to live on their Trader, and if she was sometimes sick or difficult it wasn't entirely her fault.

"I'll see you at supper, then." Eenis turned abruptly, her tall frame with its greying, scraped-back bun disappearing into the shadows of one of the passages that led to the kitchen.

* * *

Up on deck, Jarris put Shaeli down and she ran off to tell the boys about supper. He looked back across Lake Marnis to the lights of Marnissi, still visible on the horizon. His brow furrowed and his blue eyes grew dark.

No trace of colour was left in the sky. Here and there a star peeked through a rip in the clouds as if to reassure itself that the World still sailed beneath, and the sight of the stars relaxed him. He, like all traders, could tell where he was by seeing just one, and he was calmed by their familiar patterns.

They were making good time and Jarris was glad of it. Cave was still five or six days journey, the Wintering was very close, and he worried about pushing the Zoi. Still, he was an optimistic man, the wind was with them, and he had faith that all would be well, despite the lateness of the season.

The events of last night echoed through his mind; Mareesha's strained face and sweaty brow; the relief when the babe was delivered safely. He had become an adept midwife with the births of their children; his mother, Wyshka – the best midwife any Trader could offer – had still lived on Purple Leaf when Tarkoda and Shaeli were born, and she had insisted Jarris take part and learn all he could, and his brother, Jeth, had also assisted with the births of his two boys, Andos and Dari. It was three Winters now since Wyshka had tired of travel and trading and said she wanted to stay at Cave with the other old ones, to sit and talk in the sun, with nowhere to go. It would please Jarris greatly to see her face this Wintering.

He wondered why Mareesha had agreed to this strange plan. Surely she was overreacting to the changes that must come following the impending death of the king. Why should they be the disastrous changes she predicted? He believed things would remain basically the same, no matter who sat on the throne. They met many people in their travels, of diverse fortune and face, and almost everywhere they were contented, untroubled people. There had been peace and good fortune in the Four Lands for many decades, why should anyone change that? Still, even with her stubborn nature Mareesha had seldom insisted on anything as adamantly as she had on this. He had, in the end, reluctantly agreed to what she had asked of him, though he had not understood the need... but last night he had wanted to change his mind.

Mareesha's frantic manoeuvring of the past days had almost amused him, and he had taken her to where she said she must be, knowing of, and agreeing to, her intention. How the task was to be achieved she would not tell him, and so inconceivable was it that he supposed he had not taken it as seriously as he should – he had not given the matter proper fore-thought, at least, not until their visitor this morning in the small hours before dawn. The magnitude of what he had agreed to struck him then like a hammer-blow, and as he smuggled the woman aboard, sure they would be seen, looking furtively over his shoulder, terrified by every sound, the consequences suddenly overwhelmed him and he tried desperately to dissuade them from such a drastic scheme. To deceive the Court? The entire Realm? Was there no other way?

They insisted. There *was* no other option.

Jarris finally acquiesced when the noble lady fell to her knees, weeping softly and pleading with him, clutching the bundle in her arms tightly to her breast, her tears falling upon it. It shamed him to see her there before him, so fearful, so obviously at the end of her strength; she, so revered, so dignified, kneeling at his feet, and he a humble trader. With an agonised look at his wife he drew the lady to her feet, kissed her hand and begged forgiveness – and he gave her the promise she so desperately craved.

Relief flooded her face, and she kissed his hands in return, embarrassing him all the more. Her tears kept falling as she kissed Mareesha and lay the bundle in her arms, hugging them both fiercely as she and Mareesha held a whispered exchange which Jarris had been unable to hear. A small, strangled cry escaped her as she turned and fled the room, and Jarris followed silently, reaching her as she crossed the deck. He supported her to the ground and along the shadowed path to the forest's edge, for she was in great need of support, yet she would allow him no further than the wall of trees and he did not argue. He had no wish to enter the dark confines of the forest.

Her last words to him were a reminder to never forget his promise. It was a sacred trust, she said, tears streaming unheeded down her cheeks. Tortured eyes bored into his; everything depended upon him and Mareesha, she said, he *must* understand: his task was vital.

The desperation in her voice did nothing to lessen his fears, but he solemnly repeated his oath, and she seemed satisfied. She opened her mouth as if to add something more, hesitated, then just blessed them all and turned her back on him. She had melted quickly into the dark forest, exhaustion like a cloak upon her shoulders, the sound of her grief drifting back to him for a moment, and then that, too, disappeared. He would remember her eyes often during the coming Winters, beautiful eyes, the colour of the dew-wet leaves that hung like tears from the trees. Emerald eyes.

He'd hurried back to Mareesha then, eager for the sight of her. His wife, too, had green eyes, but so different from those of the other lady; deep and warm green were Mareesha's eyes, like clover in summer sun. He had been unaware of the sharp eyes that had watched his return to the Trader, just as they had curiously watched his departure with the stumbling, shrouded lady.

Jarris resolved now, as he stood looking back at the fading lights of Marnissi, to look only towards the future, and not ponder overmuch on this past night. Their course was fixed, as surely as the Wintering followed the year. The past was unchangeable. What lay ahead would come as it would.

Jarris sighed, and went to find Jeth for supper.

* * *

CHAPTER TWO

It was quiet at the table that night; even the three boys were unusually subdued. Jarris and Jeth discussed the best way to Cave, though both knew what route they would take, they just talked to break the silence.

Jeth was the older of the two, yet he was not as tall as his brother, nor were his shoulders as broad. His features were similar, yet less distinct, his beard thinner, his blue eyes more faded, his chin less firm. They were a good team, both patient, quiet men, and they were good friends.

After dinner, Tarkoda and Andos played a board game at one end of the table. The cousins, too, were good friends, and both favoured their fathers in looks. Tarkoda had Jarris' firm features, determined chin and blue eyes, coupled with his mother's high cheekbones and thick hair. Andos was like his father, Jeth, but a softer, blurrier version, and his nature was even milder than his father's.

Dari, the image of his thin-lipped, thin-haired mother, was made to read by the big lamp near the stove with Eenis – something he was finding difficult to grasp, and thoroughly detestable. Shaeli had already surpassed him. To her delight the letters had made sense to her quickly, and she wondered again why Dari disliked her for it. He was better with numbers than her, yet did she care? No. It seemed silly to mind about something like that. Some people were just cleverer at things, like her mother with cooking, but Eenis sewed the most beautiful tapestries and her embroidered handkerchiefs were sought by the most refined ladies. And her father always consulted Jeth about matters of navi... navi...? about where they were going; he said it was as if his brother could smell east, like the Zoi, and he was *proud* of that, it didn't make him mad, so she didn't understand why Dari became annoyed when she read aloud. Shaeli shrugged off those thoughts, snuggled down in her father's big chair and opened her drawing pad. No reading for her tonight, she would draw a picture for her mother and the babies.

The room where they sat held the main living quarters. It filled the rear half of the Trader and was nearly big enough to fit all the bedrooms inside. A large table dominated the centre of the back wall, and on one side a sink stood in the corner surrounded by benches and cupboards. A tin bath was tucked behind a screen nearby, for the kitchen area was the only place fed with running water by the barrels on deck. The large stove near the sink served both cooking and heating needs, and had an ingenious flue system, leading the smoke out through a long chimney far behind, so no stray spark had a chance to fly near the balloon. The material of the enormous balloon was protected by the Warlock's magic, but fire and lightning remained the trader's chief concerns. Open flame was not permitted in the bedrooms, the storerooms or the Zoi nests, and the small covered lamps they used shed only dim light, but here Mareesha's two glass lamps shed light into every corner; beautiful, elegant lamps – a gift from the queen herself.

Any important work was carried out in this communal place, referred to as either the kitchen or the big room, depending on one's task. Mareesha sometimes called it her workroom, for she prepared her potions and tonics on the benches in the corner opposite the kitchen area. Eenis sewed here, Jarris and Jeth pored over their books and charts, and the children took lessons at the table, unless it was a nice day and Eenis was feeling generous and they had lessons on deck. Thick windows ranged the walls to let in natural light and fresh air, but tonight they were closed tightly and the curtains drawn. The wind howled about the Trader, hunting for a crevice through which to poke its icy fingers.

Two passageways led off the kitchen, and the families had their bedrooms on the outer side of these passageways. Both were identical; three doorways set in the outside walls, the inside walls solid wood, and both passageways joined the broad hall that bisected the front of the ship where the main stairwell led up to emerge beneath the fore-deck. The section in between the rectangle of passageways was devoted to the storage of their cargo and supplies, and was accessed by a big door opposite the stairwell. Underneath their feet, below the stout, wooden boards, lay more storerooms, and a larger area where the Zoi nested.

Shaeli heard footfalls overhead, where Jarris and Jeth were back on deck checking the rigging and making sure that the Zoi were coping with the long haul, for they would not stop until Lake Marnis was crossed; for all its likeness to a ship, the Trader would not float long upon water. Shaeli had heard her father say they would make good time with this wind behind them, and she knew she would wake tomorrow at a Landing on the other side.

She finished her drawing and put it aside to give to her mother in the morning. The boys were packing up their game, and Dari had been released from his torture. Eenis had finished cleaning away the remains of the meal and sat before her latest tapestry. Several of her works hung about the walls, pictures of birds and flowers, Eenis favoured that style, but Shaeli preferred the kind she worked on tonight, a beautiful lady talking with a hovering fairy and a tall elf beside a stream, and Shaeli wished that one day she might meet a fairy. The tapestry was an order for a rich nobleman in Romynn, and would be delivered next summer by one of the Fleet. Shaeli wondered if *she* would be good at sewing when the time came, and she decided she could wait and see. Eenis would teach her, in addition to the usual lessons. She stifled a yawn, but Eenis saw it anyway.

"Best you get ready for bed, miss, and be sure you don't disturb your mam. She needs rest." Her tone made no argument possible and, as always, her aunt was as economical in her speech as she was in everything else. "You boys can go, too. We have a long journey ahead. Go and sleep." She turned back to her sewing.

Shaeli gathered her things, ignoring the accusatory looks from the boys. She couldn't *help* yawning. Andos and Dari kissed their mother's thin cheek, said a cheery goodnight to Tarkoda, completely ignored Shaeli and went up their hallway, past the door of their parent's room to the bedroom they shared. Their room lay under the landing-gate, and the view from their window was always obscured by whatever Landing they were moored at. The last door at the junction of this passage held the modest privy, which had a small shuttered window set high in the wall.

Shaeli's family slept on the other side of the Trader, Tarkoda closest to the big room, then her parents' bedroom, and last lay her little room, tucked away in the corner of the two hallways nearest the stairs. She strained to hear something from the babies as she crept past her mother's room, but, disappointingly, all was quiet. She went and changed into her nightgown in near darkness, a feat not easily accomplished, but she had no wish to go back and trouble Eenis for a lamp.

It was cold in her bed, so she put her head under the quilt for a while to warm it with her breath, making a cosy pocket of air to snuggle into, wishing her mother would come and tuck her in as she usually did.

As she lay listening to the sounds of the Trader, she thought of the Wintering at Cave; the games with the other children, the stories to be heard, and all the things she would tell Kirrit, her best friend. She couldn't wait for Kirrit to see her new sisters, but she was unsure what Kirrit's reaction would be. Kirrit had *so* many brothers and sisters – twins even, though they were boys – and perhaps she wouldn't be interested in the babies.

The last thought to occur to Shaeli before sleep claimed her was that she hadn't asked what the babies' names were.

* * *

"That Shaeli," frowned Dari, pulling his pyjamas over his head. "Always ruining stuff."

Andos yawned. "It's not as if Mam would have let us stay up much longer anyway," he said.

"Doesn't matter," said Dari, climbing into his bed. "She just likes to wreck stuff. Nearly as much as she likes showing off."

"She's only little," said Andos. "*And* a girl."

"That's no excuse," said Dari, and he turned his face to the wall.

* * *

Shaeli woke with the sun on her face. She yawned, stretched and squinted up at the window. Sunshine spilled through the glass, the patch of sky framed within it pale blue and cloudless. This late in the season, every drop of warmth was to be savoured, so she dressed quickly and raced up on deck. She found her father leaning against the rail, drinking a steaming cup of tezz, a warm, sweet beverage, ground from the seeds of the terrezza tree, and a staple part of the diet in every Land. She climbed up onto some stacked baskets to sit beside him.

The sun was not yet high in the sky. Bands of colour streaked the horizon and the mountains were black silhouettes between tassels of pale sunlight. The thunderheads of last night lay banked behind the Trader, but the sky to the east was clear and bright above the mountains for which they were headed. The tip of *their* mountain rose higher than the rest, covered in a cap of perpetual snow and unusually free of cloud, and Shaeli knew they must be safe at Cave before the first snowstorms began. Traders had been known to Winter outside in desperate circumstances, but almost never had the Zoi survived the Wintering unprotected by the Cave, and a trader was lost without his Zoi.

The Zoi were the lifeblood of the traders, their sense of direction was stronger than any other creature's, and they and the Traders kept the Four Lands, the Starisles, and their people from much hardship. Supplies to the smaller towns, villages and islands were delivered almost wholly by Trader; deliveries by road were slow and at the mercy of the weather, road conditions, and raiders, though they were few. Traders transported all manner of goods across their own and other Lands, and some Traders spent much of the year carrying passengers as well as supplies. Without the Zoi all this would be impossible. The Traders could still fly, for flight was achieved with the balloon by the Lift spell cast upon it by the Fleet Warlocks, but without the Zoi they were virtually directionless, at the mercy of the winds, or lack thereof, like a ship with no rudder to steer by.

The Zoi were birds, though unlike any other bird; comparing Zoi to common birds was like comparing a twig to a terrezza tree, or a rock to a mountain. They stood taller than three men, and their wing span was more than twice their height. Heavy oval bodies, long slim necks holding aloft proud heads, huge, black-patterned eyes which missed nothing and held rich emotion. Pearl-white feathers covered them, and only in flight could their colours be seen; iridescent rainbows rippling along the underside of their wings and tails, ever-changing and wonderful to see.

No one knew how or why the Zoi had chosen to serve, the reasons were lost even to trader legend, but serve they did, faithfully and with great dignity. Families of Zoi served families of traders, generation after generation, and just as Jarris and Jeth had inherited the Trader from their father, Povann, and he from his father, so had the Zoi passed down their guiding responsibilities to their offspring. This family of

Zoi had been with Jarris' ancestors since time immemorial, and each must consider the well-being of the other if they were to prosper, and, at times, even survive.

Zoi mated for life, and were long-lived – the lead birds on Purple Leaf were older than Jarris – yet their offspring were few, born during a decade when the birds reached their prime, and chicks were considered a blessing, celebrated by the whole Fleet; their courtship rituals and the births of the chicks, unseen by any man, took place in a private cavern at Cave.

People everywhere were in awe of the great birds, and with good reason. Although they most closely resembled the giant swans of the Lakes country, their noble demeanour was the antithesis of their vain and flighty cousins, and no swan ever possessed the long, curved razor-sharp beak of the Zoi, nor the deadly spike tucked into the heel of talons more like those of an eagle than a water bird. Seldom was a Zoi provoked into using its defences, they patiently bore with crowds and the petting of small children, but when the safety of a mate or offspring was at risk, any creature foolish enough to threaten them found a deadly adversary. More often than not the foolish creature lost its life, especially when attacked by a mature female, for she, when greatly roused, secreted a fatal poison from the spike in her heel.

The birds were sheltered when they were moored in a large nesting space in the bottom of the Trader. Each Trader had a ladder or two lashed underneath their ship, used to reach the Zoi nests and storage spaces, for the Trader itself never touched ground, and releasing the Zoi from their harnesses and opening their doors were always the first tasks after a landing. The giant birds were fed grain and strips of raw meat, and they would often fly off to forage in surrounding woods and fields.

A Trader could, at any given time, have five to ten Zoi, but they were such powerful birds that three could pull a Trader if the need arose. They flew in V-shaped groups, the younger birds at the rear, always the mature, mated couple as lead birds, the male at the head of the V to provide strength and direction, the lead female behind his right shoulder, giving her expertise to landings and lifts, and supplying occasional melodic encouragement to the younger birds, often their offspring.

The marvellous voice of the Zoi, raised in its harmonic call, chimed on many different levels, and blended into a chord of such beauty that most who heard it felt joy, for the chord seemed to resonate as much in the soul as it did in the air. The cry of a mature female was particularly harmonious, a full, rich chord, achingly beautiful, but seldom did the People hear it; only the traders were truly familiar with the remarkable sound, yet even they never failed to be moved by its plaintive echoes.

Shaeli and Jarris sat in companionable silence for a while, listening to the soft calls of the birds below and watching the pale sky deepen to indigo, sharing the last of the tezz and soaking up the warmth from the sun's weak rays. Shaeli sighed. She would miss the World over the Wintering. She liked seeing the other traders, and her grandmother, of course, and it was the only time she could spend days talking with Kirrit. This year there would be the twins to play with too, but she *would* miss the World.

She wondered how the People fared during the Wintering without a big Cave to protect them and so little company. There were those with grand houses and castles who must be secure and have cheerful company, and most towns had a Wintering Hall to protect them from the strongest blizzards, but it would be very lonely in the smallest villages and on the farms. Shaeli felt a little sorry for everyone who did not have the good fortune to be born into a trading family. Theirs was a well-respected Trader, too, with Jarris on the Trader's Council, and Mareesha the highest ranking Faunist on any ship. Only the Fleet's Head Faunist, Sahli'en, ranked higher, yet she no longer flew on a Trader, but stayed at Cave with the other old ones.

Remembering her last, sleepy thought from the night before, Shaeli looked up at her father, studying his profile, the proud lift of the bearded chin, the heavy brows shadowed by thick brown hair – sun-streaked like her own – the creases around his eyes.

"Da," she said. "What are we calling them?"

It seemed Jarris knew what she meant, despite the obscure reference, and he smiled down at her, his pale blue eyes twinkling.

"I expect Mam has that figured out. Shall we take her a cup of tezz and ask her?" He glanced up at the sun. "I have some time before I go and tend to the Zoi, and Mam should be awake by now." He took Shaeli's hand and helped her down from her perch, and as they walked across to the stairwell beneath the upper deck, he grinned down at her. "I think Wyshka is a fine name, don't you? After your grandmother."

"Wyshka? *No.*" Shaeli was indignant. "That's an old lady name. They need pretty names."

"And who's to say Wyshka is not a pretty name? Don't you think my mother is beautiful, Mouse?"

Shaeli looked up at him, her arched eyebrows riding high, her up-tilted eyes – blue in the morning sun – wide open. Her hair flew as she shook her head.

"No, Da," she said, seriously. "She has a kind face, it makes me want to hug her, but I don't think she's beautiful. Not like a princess or an elf or a fairy. They're beautiful. Granny Wyshka is too... too *saggy* to be beautiful."

Jarris laughed and after a moment Shaeli joined in. She didn't know what was so funny, but she liked to laugh with her father. He had such a nice, *big* laugh.

They crossed to the wide doorway underneath the foredeck, and descended into the chilly shadow below, their feet finding the treads until their eyes adjusted to the darkness.

Wide steps led down to a landing, where a small door led to another storage area under the triangular upper deck, and to the left, around a sharp corner, the stairs continued down. Jarris was still chuckling as they reached the bottom.

"Ah, you have such a way with words, my girl," he said, as he stopped outside her door. "Say it as you see it, just like your Mam, though she's learnt some diplomacy." He squinted down at her. "Best duck in and brush your hair while I get the tezz, or Mam will be after us, and there'll be no diplomacy in that."

Shaeli didn't know what diplomacy was, but she knew how her mother felt about messy hair and she went into her room while Jarris went on down the passageway. She brushed her hair, took the drawing she'd made last night, and went back out. She knocked gently when she saw him coming back, a tray in his hands, and she opened the door for him.

Mareesha looked up at them as they entered, smiled and said good morning, then went back to changing the napkin of the baby lying on the bed before her.

"A lovely morning this morning," she said, as she re-wrapped the baby and lay her over one shoulder. She leant down and kissed Shaeli, admiring the drawing.

The other baby lay sleeping in the big cot on the far side of the bed, and Shaeli could just see the little round face amid the padding and blankets.

"This babe," said Mareesha, gently rubbing the back of the baby over her shoulder. "This babe slept through much of the night. I had to wake her up to feed her. That one," she poked her head at the cot. "That one wanted feeding every time she moved."

"I know." Jarris kissed his wife and lay the tray on the bed. "I heard her."

"I didn't." Shaeli said, then frowned at the polite untruth. "Well, not much, anyway."

"You're lucky." Jarris said. "She has the voice of one of those seagulls you so admire. Not very pretty in the sunrise hours."

Mareesha smiled at him. "You'll soon learn to ignore it, my dearest. You have before."

"Who me?" Jarris asked with pretended surprise. "Ignore a hungry baby? Never." He turned to Shaeli. "Can you remember me ignoring you, Mouse?"

"No, Da, but..."

"You see, Mareesha." Jarris spread his hands before her, his face striving for innocence. "It never happened."

"But, Da..." Shaeli began again.

Jarris pretended not to hear. "Now, Mareesha, let Shaeli hold that babe for you. Then you can drink your tezz before it gets cold, and eat the breakfast Eenis has made."

Mareesha was still laughing as Shaeli sat in the rocking chair by the window. Jarris carried the baby over to her and tucked a pillow under her arm.

There was a light tap at the door and Tarkoda opened it and came in grinning. Mareesha suggested he find her brush and do something about his hair, which stuck up in unhappy tufts on his head. She said it looked like battered sheaves of wheat.

Shaeli looked at her father. "No 'plomacy in that," she said, and they both erupted into laughter, much to the puzzlement of Mareesha and Tarkoda.

A burst of warmth filled Shaeli as she looked from one face to the other, smiling as they continued their gentle banter. The most important people in her world were in this room, and now two little sisters. She looked down at the warm bundle in her arms, content.

It seemed this little sister was also well content. She was almost asleep, a drop of milk still on her bottom lip; creamy-white against the rose. Shaeli rocked gently until the huge, dark eyes closed and the tight fists relaxed, and when the baby slept, she slipped one finger between the five little ones and the tiny hand blossomed open like a flower. Shaeli softly stroked the faint lines on the miniature palm, amazed that it was such a perfect hand, nails so small you could hardly see them, so perfect and round. She kissed the tips of the fingers, one by one.

"Shaeli was wondering what their names were to be, Mam. She thought we should call one after Wyshka." Jarris sat on the bed, helping himself to Mareesha's toast.

"I did *not*," Shaeli spluttered, deeply offended. "*I* said something pretty."

"I know well it's your Da that likes that name, Shaeli," said Mareesha, smiling. "He wanted to call you Wyshka, but I had set my heart on Shaeli, yet he did try."

Shaeli looked relieved. "Thank you, Mam, I'm glad you didn't let him," she said, and her mother laughed. Shaeli's mind leapt on. "What if I were a boy, what would I have been called?"

"That's easy," Jarris spoke around the toast. "You were to be called after my father. Povann."

"Povann? Lucky I *was* a girl then."

Shaeli spoke with such relief that both her parents roared, and Tarkoda almost fell off the bed, giggling so hard his eyes watered. Again, Shaeli was puzzled, she had only spoken the truth; Povann was an awful name. She shook her head. People were odd sometimes.

"But, Mam," she persisted. "What *are* their names? We can't just call them 'the babies'."

"No, we can't, and I've been thinking about it. I like Roshanna and Reneesha. What do you think, Jarris?"

Tarkoda snorted his opinion, but they ignored him.

"Well, they're not Wyshka, but nice enough names, I guess. Maybe a bit long."

"We can shorten them. 'Shanna and 'Neesha for everyday. Please, think about it. Shanna and Neesha. Alright?"

Shaeli knew that's what their names would be – Mam could talk Da into almost anything. Pretty names, too. "They could be Rosh and Ren, too, Mam. For short," she said.

"That's right, Shaeli, but which shall be which?"

"Reneesha for that noisy one," Jarris said, pointing over at the cot. "And the softer name for the quiet babe with Shaeli. Roshanna."

Shaeli looked down at the sleeping bundle in her arms. "Roshanna," she whispered. "Did you hear that, baby? Now you've got names. Shanna and Neesha of Purple Leaf Trader, and we'll take good care of you both."

She did not see the suddenly serious look that passed between her parents, but she felt a small chill run up her spine. She shivered, and hugged the baby against her thin chest.

* * *

CHAPTER THREE

The Landing at which they were moored lay on the south-eastern shore of Lake Marnis, within sight of the low foothills that edged the mountain range which marched down the east coast of Zirrus. The mountains began far to the north and ran down to Zirrus' southern tip, hugging the coastline for hundreds of leagues, unforgivingly rugged and all but impassable.

They had flown through half the night, Jeth and Jarris taking turns at watch and mooring in near-darkness, and they would be away again before lunch, as soon as the Zoi were fed and rested.

The Landing was small, but big enough for the trading purposes of the village that lay out of sight over the brow of a hill. It was one of hundreds of Landings scattered throughout the Four Lands and the Starisles for the use of traders, who needed a solid base to moor their ships as well as easy access for their customers. The larger towns and the cities incorporated their Landings into squares within the town, ensuring the Traders had adequate space to land and lift; smaller towns and villages had their Landings on the outskirts, usually in a field close by. Some Landings, near great castles or in the cities, were elaborately ornate, decorated and roofed for the comfort of the rich and the high-born, with comfortable couches or ante-rooms for buyers to inspect wares at their leisure; other Landings were little more than a rough ladder ascending to a stage-like platform. This Landing was closer to the latter. A small covered platform lay at the top of a plain wooden staircase, and Eenis had already had several buyers this morning, the villagers overjoyed with this unexpected chance to stock up on forgotten items or last-minute supplies.

Eenis turned away a few who wanted Faunist skills, and the disappointed villagers found themselves buying or bargaining for things they had not known they needed, a particular skill of Eenis'. She had secured a side of bacon, a length of thick velvet and a small barrel of butter, as well as some coin. Already a good morning's trade.

After breakfast and her few chores, Shaeli sought permission to go down to the shore for a walk. There would be no lessons until they reached Cave, and the boys had already run off somewhere to explore. Jarris agreed, but told her to stay in sight of the Landing, for they would be leaving soon and she was still too young to go far by herself. Shaeli grinned and ran over to where the Trader met the Landing.

Halfway along the side of the ship, a wide gap interrupted the solid railing. The missing piece was hinged and swung inward, and this opening gave access to the Landing and its stairs. The deck and the Landing were on the same level, and the Trader was tied tightly, but there was a gap between them where Shaeli could see all the way down to the ground. She was always scared as she stepped across the gap.

She thought her father and Jeth extremely brave the way they leapt back and forth when they were landing and lifting. When they weren't tethered, the gap between the Trader and the Landing was sometimes a huge span, or so it seemed to Shaeli, but it was as if it was nothing to them, just a step. She imagined the long fall – and the crash at the end.

Once, she had lain on the deck, inching forward until her chin rested on the edge of the gap and she could see the ground. The sensation had made her light-headed, while at the same time a dark weight had settled into the pit of her stomach, and then, though there was barely room for it, she had dropped an egg through the gap. It seemed to take forever to hit the ground, falling end over end as if in slow motion, but then it had suddenly exploded, and with such violence that her heart had tried to leap from her chest. She'd felt it bump on the deck beneath her. She had gone down the Landing steps, her stomach rolling, and studied the crushed remains; the splashes of yellow egg-blood spread on the grass, the shattered shell.

She always held her breath and kept a tight grip on the rail as she crossed from Trader to Landing, she never ran, like the boys, and Mareesha said she was sensible. Her mother didn't know that she was terrified of heights, no one did, except Tarkoda. Shaeli was ashamed of herself. Traders weren't scared of heights; they *lived* high. It was ridiculous, but there it was.

It didn't bother her when they were flying. She had confidence in Jeth and her father, the balloon and the Zoi. Flying over the hills and the trees, seeing the birds fly past, so relaxed and free, she felt safe, somehow part of the wind and the sky, but when they were moored, it was different, she was all too aware of the distance to the ground, she heard again the sickening *pop* as the egg disintegrated into messy oblivion.

One thing had cemented in Shaeli a fear of falling. This last summer, the boys had let her tag along with them one golden morning to collect seeds for the tezz, and she'd skipped along beside them, her seed basket bouncing against her hip to the stand of trees. Andos and Dari climbed quickly into two tall trees and Tarkoda had boosted Shaeli into another, told her to stay near the bottom, and climbed into a tree nearby.

Terrezza trees have wrinkled bronze trunks, their branches beginning close to the ground and growing at regular intervals, like out-flung arms; trees made for climbing. Shaeli had set to, picking the brown seed pods, climbing higher and higher despite Tarkoda's warning, eager to fill her basket. When he had called to her that they had enough, and to come down, Shaeli had suddenly realised just how high she had climbed. She looked down at Tarkoda, his face a pale dot between the branches. It seemed to be at the end of a long tunnel. The World began to spin. Fear clamped black claws into her stomach. She'd frozen where she was, closing her eyes and gripping the trunk with all her might. A sweat broke out over her body.

She was so *high*.

There was so much... *down*.

Nothing was holding her *up*.

Tarkoda had had to climb up and prise her fingers from the tree, gently talking to her, guiding her hands and feet until she was safely down. Dari had started to tease Shaeli on the way home, and Koda had hushed him, helping her carry her basket, showing Mareesha how many pods she had picked, but never mentioning her terror in the tree. Shaeli had clumsily tried to thank him, but he had brushed her thanks aside, saying only that she had best keep her feet where they felt safe, and he hadn't spoken of it since. She remembered the incident with a strange mixture of terror and gratitude, and she admired Tarkoda all the more because of it. It was a small, unspoken bond between them. Not long after, she had dropped the egg through the gap.

Now, she shivered as she stepped across, walked to the stairs and went down. She breathed a big sigh as her feet touched solid earth below, and she stopped for a moment to look around.

Things looked so different from down here on the ground, taller, yes, but smaller at the same time. You couldn't see very far, not like when they were flying, yet everything seemed more *there*. Bigger, but more *closed*.

Shaeli moved off as an old woman approached the Landing, a coarse grey shawl wrapped tightly about her head. She had no wish to waste time with questions or pinched cheeks. There was something about old ladies, always wanting to pinch your cheeks, or worse, kiss them and then pinch them. Some even had hair above their lips, like her father. She thought the twins would be getting their share of pinched cheeks soon, and wouldn't Wyshka be surprised to have two to cuddle? The thought made Shaeli smile, and she was still smiling when she reached the shoreline, stopping with her boots at the edge of the water.

Lake Marnis was large enough to be a small sea, though it was fresh water. It stretched before her, far to the north and west, the water as blue as a sapphire, flat and calm. Tall green reeds around its edges whispered to the wind, and long-legged grey birds waded amongst them.

Shaeli breathed deeply, the sharp tang of cold air filling her lungs. When she breathed out, it puffed in steamy clouds that disappeared a hand's length from her mouth, and she experimented with it for a few moments, enjoying the ability. Dragon weather, she called it in her head. Breathe in, breathe out, mist, almost like magic. Her pointy nose turned pink as she stood there, making little white clouds out of the cold air and her warm breath and wondering where the dragons had gone.

She looked back over her shoulder. She couldn't see much of the stairs, they were hidden by a slight rise in the ground, but the Landing and the Trader were clearly visible, the colours of the balloon shimmering in the late-autumn sun. She could see Eenis talking with the old woman, and her father behind them, up on the fore-deck. Jeth was just disappearing out of sight down the stairs; he would be going down to feed the Zoi and ready them for the next leg of the journey. She'd heard him say that he thought they were eager to reach Cave too, and that they disliked the smell of snow. Shaeli thought hard about that. Could you *smell* snow?

She wandered slowly along the water's edge, eyes to the ground. She stopped once or twice, squatting down for closer examination, but then abandoning the find as not special enough, for she was very fussy about what she added to her collection. Her most prized possession was the perfectly formed purple crystal, found one day near a creek on the north-eastern tip of Zirrus, a special find, for amethyst crystals were one of the stones used by the elves for their wands, and Shaeli had begun her collection with it. Her treasures hung in a small pouch from her belt, and she seldom went anywhere without her amulet. She would feel the objects through the soft leather when she was agitated or concentrating, comforted by their familiar shapes. At night she would take them out and examine them, marvelling at the amethyst, the shell turned by time into rock, the pebble with a streak of gold running through the middle, and the black stone from Wokk. Long ago, Jarris had told her, Wokk had been one island, but it had been blown apart by the burning mountain which had been its centre, and her black stone was part of that mountain.

She turned around, checking the distance to the Landing. She had come far enough, but she hadn't found anything. A little bit further wouldn't hurt. She wandered on, oblivious to the billowing clouds scudding towards her and the way the wind was rising, her eyes on the ground.

Up ahead, a small overgrown creek met the lake, and when she reached it, she looked back. All she could see of the Trader was the very top of the balloon, and guilt twinged in her chest. She had come too far, but her eyes were drawn to the little creek. You could find things in creeks. They came from the mountains, where pretty stones grew, like her amethyst. And she could still see the Trader – sort of.

The wind tugged at her hair, and she noticed how quiet it suddenly was, how the birds no longer stalked the shallows or called to each other. She looked at the sky, at the clouds moving closer every moment, her eyes narrowed. She took one last look at the green and purple patch over the hill, then she turned her back on it and plunged into the undergrowth beside the creek.

It was dark in there, but quiet, the wind on the shore rattled the trees overhead, and yet here there was only the trickle of the creek and the crunch of her boots as she walked along the rocky edge. She walked quickly, eyes searching for anything shiny, moving higher up the creek, unmindful of the thickening of the undergrowth or the way the banks rose steadily on either side. She ignored the guilty twinge in her chest until a clap of thunder shattered above, and she jumped and spun around.

She was in a tunnel, a dark tangle of a tunnel, the wind ripping at the branches somewhere far above, and the way out was a small hole between ugly bushes. She couldn't see the lake, and her heart beat harder as she realised how far she'd come, how angry her father would be, and she started back.

She had taken only a few steps when, high on the bank above, a branch cracked. She froze, looking up, thinking there must be someone there, but no other sounds followed. She sighed and turned to go on, but she saw something sticking out of the bank, under a little overhang. She went over for a closer look, and almost dismissed it, thinking it was only a bit of wood. She poked her finger at the dirt holding it in place. What was poking out appeared to be only a portion of what lay still buried, so she picked up a stick and scraped around the edges. She did not hear the low growl from the bank above, or the crackle in the undergrowth higher up the creek.

Her scratchings revealed what looked like metal beneath the dirt, and she grabbed the end, wrinkling her nose as mud oozed through her fingers, and pulled hard. She wobbled the stick back and forth, and pulled again. At first it moved only a little, but as she dug more from around the base, it began to work free, and the dirt scratched off along one side. It *was* metal that lay beneath the dirt, not wood. She began to dig faster.

She almost had it free when she heard it, the soft splash in the water behind her. She turned her head slowly, and there, eyes gleaming in the tunnel, was a jenka. The mottled cat bristled, but did not move, and Shaeli scanned the banks. Jenka were small, but they hunted in groups, and on the far bank she saw another, crouched beneath the bushes, the end of its tail twitching. Thunder cracked again, almost overhead, but the jenka did not flinch. Where there were two, there would be more, and Shaeli's heart beat a faster rhythm. Grasping the treasure-stick in both hands, eyes on the closest jenka, she put one foot against the bank and gave a huge pull.

It came with a soggy, sucking noise, resisting until the last, and then it came so suddenly that Shaeli almost fell over backwards. She staggered and one foot went into the creek, soaking it instantly. Both jenka jumped, and one growled in the back of its throat. Her hands tingled strangely, but she barely noticed. She turned and ran.

She heard the one in the creek splashing behind her, and the other one on the opposite bank, but it was the crackle from the bushes above her that frightened her most. One or two jenka she thought she could handle, standing up, but if there were more, and they knocked her over...

She heard a shrill whistle as the tunnel began to widen – her father calling for her – and as the lake appeared through the hole in the undergrowth, she glanced over her shoulder, gulping huge breaths of air. They were nearly upon her. She ran harder, and as she burst out onto the shore, she spun around, swinging the muddy stick in a wide arc. She caught the cat behind her in mid-leap, smacking it across the shoulders as it came at her, claws outstretched. She screamed and the cat screeched, and she kept on swinging. There were six of them now.

The wind was gusting hard, and the World had grown dim as nightfall, but she ignored the storm, her eyes on the circling cats, her heels almost in the lake. Another jenka darted at her, and her stick connected with its head, and Shaeli screamed again, but her voice was swept away with the wind. Again she felt a strange tingling in her hands, but she paid little attention, concentrating only on swinging the muddy stick back and forth. She heard the whistle again, but she dare not turn; did not dare take her eyes off the growling jenka.

She kept on swinging, the wind tearing at her hair as the storm moved closer and closer. Again and again one of the jenka leapt at her, but she swung the treasure-stick, hitting each cat as it leapt at her, until finally, one by one, they began to back away, slinking into the undergrowth around the creek. She gulped some more air, and looked at the thing she had pulled from the bank.

It was heavy and longer than her arm, but so covered in grime that she could not tell what lay underneath. She glanced back at the creek, saw the gleam of several pairs of eyes staring back at her, and she bolted around the lake. One foot squelched inside its sodden shoe, giving her steps an odd rhythm, step, *squish,* step, *squish,* step. The wet stocking clung to her ankle, the dampness soaking its way up towards her knee.

The wind was still rising and black clouds were thick across the sky, turning the surface of the lake to leaden grey. White-caps began to dance on waves that had been non-existent before.

Her father whistled again from the Landing as she neared and she waved at him. He yelled something she could not hear, but he was clearly impatient.

She turned back to the lake, even her father's anger secondary now to finding out exactly what it was she had pulled from the mud. The panic of her encounter with the jenka was fading, and curiosity bloomed in its place as she rinsed the find and her hands in the freezing lake. She held the slimy treasure out before her, and then shook it backwards and forwards under the water again. The mud wasn't only slimy, it smelt pretty bad too.

As Shaeli washed away the last clots of mud, she became excited. She took the treasure out of the water and rubbed it with the edge of her shawl. It brightened with each passing stroke as the metal appeared, dirt streaked, but shining, and there were even a few jewels encrusted to the shaft. Her excitement increased. She rubbed harder, scratching at stubborn bits with a fingernail, then stood it in front of her, studying it intently.

It wasn't gold, the metal was too pale – almost pink – and the top was as thick as her wrist. There was an open claw where it had once held something in its grasp, and under the claw the haft tapered down to a slim point. The metal was plaited, twisting and turning in an intricate braid and etched with illegible writings, and she counted six stones of different colours and sizes embedded in the shaft, and the places where once had rested at least a dozen more. She held it out in the air before her, its weight making it wobble in her small fist. She drew in a deep breath, overcome with the magnitude of her find. Shaeli knew she had found something special, but *this*...

She was suddenly sure what it was.

A wand. An elfin wand.

* * *

The old woman was scurrying away up the road to the village as Shaeli raced up the stairs, for once not caring about the drop. Her only thought was to show her father. She found him up on the triangular foredeck, checking the ropes to the Zoi harness.

"Da, I found something at the lake," she cried, holding the wand out before her like a pungent offering.

"Not now, we're just about to cast off," he said, clearly unhappy at being distracted. "I'll look after lift." He glanced at her. "When we decide what your punishment is for disobeying me."

"But, Da..." she began. He had not even looked at her find.

"Not now, Shaeli. After lift."

He returned to his task, and Shaeli turned away, disappointed. She knew that tone in her father's voice. It was no use arguing.

She wandered down and tucked herself in beneath the stairs to the upper deck, beside the doorway that led below, where she could see out, but was not easily seen. She wrapped her treasure in her shawl – it was filthy anyway – and waited.

She could hear Jarris moving about on the deck above, shouting occasionally down to Jeth, who was on the ground with the Zoi, ready to cast off the lower ropes.

There were anchor ropes on the ground and more on the Landing, and she knew by the sudden lurch when Jeth let go the back anchors. The front would be next, a moment before her father untied the ropes on the top deck, then Jarris raced down to the gate as Jeth was racing up the stairs of the Landing. Shaeli could hear the ruffle of sound from the Zoi's wings.

Only one rope tethered them to the Landing now, the one next to the open gate. Jarris untied it and Jeth leapt across the widening gap, closing and latching the gate behind him as Jarris bounded back up the stairs to the top deck. The open space became solid again. The tiny Landing drifted away. It was over.

They rose quickly, clearing the few trees and the low hills, the Zoi guiding them infallibly into a clear stream of air, heading east. Thunder rumbled and Shaeli turned her face up to the storm that hovered over them. A mass of mountainous black-hearted clouds surrounded the balloon and it would rain before long, so she sent a prayer to U'ee, the god of storms, to keep the lightning away. Across the vast expanse of deck, behind the Trader, a plume of smoke trailed them like a cloudy tail. It would be warm down in the big room, but she stayed where she was, determined to make her father look.

The storm caught them, the first, fat drops of rain began to fall, dappling the worn wood. The balloon shivered in anticipation.

Her father appeared. "Come with me," he said, as she came out from under the stairs.

He didn't even glance at her, but led her downstairs to their room. The door was closed. It had been closed a lot, lately, and, somewhere in the back of her mind, Shaeli wondered about that.

"Let's see what Mam has to say about you running off and coming back covered in filth," he said. He looked down at her and shook his head. "'Tis a sight you are."

Shaeli looked down at herself. She *was* a mess; streaky with mud, shoes wet, one stocking drying in brown stains.

Jarris opened the door and Mareesha gasped at the sight of Shaeli. Jarris began to bluster about wandering off, disobeying orders as Shaeli went in, head hanging, unsure of what to say, or how to begin, but when there was a break in the blustering, she unravelled the wand and held it out in both hands.

"I found this," she said, and placed it in her father's hands. She stepped back to see what he would say, the ruined shawl dangling from her hand.

It seemed Jarris would say nothing. His eyebrows lifted, his mouth opened, then abruptly closed. He blew a long stream of air from his lips, turned to Mareesha, opened his mouth again, closed it, and shook his head. He gingerly handed the wand to Mareesha, obviously at a loss. He looked at Shaeli, then at the wand, at Mareesha's face, and then back at Shaeli. He completed the circle of looking twice more, and Shaeli saw with surprise that he was awe-struck and she a source of wonder. Rain began to thrum on the sides of the Trader, but for once Jarris did not notice. Finally, he spoke.

"Is this what you wanted to show me before?" he said. His voice, though hushed, sounded almost normal.

Shaeli nodded.

"You found it in the lake?"

She nodded again. Her throat began to feel tight. "In the mud. *Near* the lake." Her eyebrows met. "It was dirtier then, and smelly. I cleaned it." She looked at her mother and swallowed at the tightness in her throat. "That's how I got so dirty and wet. I didn't mean to get so dirty, Mam, I'm sorry." Shaeli's voice and bottom lip had begun to wobble in unison.

"Of course you didn't," Mareesha said. "There now, don't cry. You've found a wonderful thing, Shaeli, a wonderful, special thing." She smiled encouragingly.

Shaeli's eyes had filled with tears. One slipped over and ran slowly down her cheek, leaving a thin streak in the grime. She sniffed and walked over to Jarris, slipped her small hand into his big, rough one, and looked up at him.

"You're not mad, then?"

Jarris looked down. He knelt and hugged the thin little body to him, overwhelmed with stark amazement. He stroked her messy hair, tipped her chin up and wiped away the stray tear.

"Well, yes, my little mouse, I am mad about you running off, it was dangerous, and you're filthy, but I'm sorry I didn't pay more attention to that smelly old stick earlier."

He grinned and Shaeli grinned back. He had noticed after all.

"I thought it was a stick at first, too, Da," she said. "But it clunked and I started wondering, so I dug it out." She took a breath and raised her chin. "And then some jenka chased me, and I whacked them with it."

Her mother gasped.

Jarris' brows rose. "Jenka? Chased you?" He closed his eyes, and shook his head.

"Oh, Shaeli," said Mareesha. "They could have killed you." Her face had paled, her eyes grown wide.

"Your mother's right," said Jarris. "You're very lucky, and you'll not leave this Trader alone again until I think you've found a bit more sense, but..." He looked at the wand. "But your curious nose has led you to a treasure indeed this time. Now, you tell us exactly how you found this... thing."

So she told them everything that had happened, *exactly*, just as her father said. When she was finished, she sat quietly, waiting to hear what they would say. Apart from Mareesha being sure it *was* a wand – and probably elfin – she was disappointed.

They needed to discuss it, they said. They had to clean it properly and take a close look at it. They would tell Shaeli tomorrow what was to be done, and it was best she not mention it to anyone until then. Mareesha would be up in the morning and she could show it to the rest of the family, but now she was to go and get clean and help in the big room until dinner. Her father had work to do. He'd finally noticed the rain drumming a constant beat outside.

Shaeli frowned, but knowing better than to argue she turned to leave the room. She stopped with her hand on the knob, looking back over her shoulder.

"Mam?"

"Yes, love?"

"Do you think there's any magic left in it?"

Jarris' eyebrows leapt skyward and Mareesha laughed at the look on his face.

"No, Shaeli," she said. "I think any magic this wand possessed has long since been lost, along with most of its gems. Off you go, now, I'll see you in the morning. And Shaeli?"

"Yes, Mam?"

"You did the right thing, bringing it to us. We love you." She blew a kiss and Shaeli pretended to catch it.

"Love you, too. See you in the morning."

She turned and left the room, closing the door behind her. The smile faded as she walked down the hall. She supposed she would change and help set the table for lunch. There was nothing else to do, now. She had *so* wanted to show off her treasure to those smarty boys, and to not even be able to tell them was too cruel, yet she tried not to brood for too long. She would do her gloating in the morning.

* * *

Shaeli woke to the sound of bells and rain beating against her window. Looking out, she could see little. Her room faced away from the Landing, but she knew that they were moored. She could feel it.

It was bitterly cold and she could hear voices on deck, and she pulled a coat on over her nightgown and hurried up the stairs to see what was going on. She hadn't thought they were near any towns big enough to have a Wintering Hall with bells.

She found the boys clustered at the top of the stairs, Mareesha and Eenis standing with their shawls wrapped over their heads just outside, under the overhang of the top deck, the rain falling in torrents before them. Even beneath the shelter of the balloon the deck was wet.

Shaeli could see little past the rail, but the bells were even louder up here, different tones and rhythms, lots of them. She picked out one, chiming furiously, as if the ringer shook the bell with all his might, then it faded a little and she heard another, closer, this one deep-toned and slow – a joyless sound. She crept over to Tarkoda and took his hand.

"What's happening?" she asked.

Her voice sounded small in her ears. The voice of the rain spoke too loudly, drowning sound from the World. All sound but the bells.

"I'm not sure," her brother answered, his face grim. He made no move to release her hand. "But, I think…" he swallowed. "I think King Tenelon is dead. Da and Jeth have gone to see."

Shaeli pondered on this information, staring out into the grey morning, then she looked back up at her brother. "Where are we?"

"Cransbey."

Shaeli nodded. "Those bells are creepy."

"Yes."

They stood, hand in hand, the rain blowing in fitful gusts beneath the balloon. Tiny droplets of water drifted in until they were covered with rain as light as mist, dusting their hair and eyebrows with white, settling softly on shawls and shoulders. Shaeli thought it looked like fairy-dust.

When Jarris and Jeth came up the steps their faces were bleak. Eenis began to weep even before they spoke. They all knew what had happened; it lay plainly upon their faces. King Tenelon was dead.

"When did it happen?" Mareesha asked, her face pale, eyes dark.

Jarris took her hand. "Three nights ago, when we were moored beside M'Zen'sclahr Forest. The news reached here in the sunrise hours this morning."

"Three nights ago? Then..." she swayed and leant against him, eyes closed. Her hand touched the small scar above her left eyebrow. "Jarris, that means..."

"Hush, Mareesha, don't think of it now. Downstairs with you, you're still weak." He looked at them, tears standing in his eyes. "Everybody, downstairs and dry off. I think we could all do with a cup of hot tezz, eh, Eenis?"

"Yes, yes, certainly. Come children." She dabbed at her eyes with the edge of her shawl. "Such sad, terrible news. Such a good and noble king." She sighed and went down the stairs, followed by Andos and Dari.

Jarris looked at his brother. "I'll just see Mareesha to bed and we'll leave. Best feed the Zoi, and ready them."

"They are tired, Jarris, they flew all afternoon yesterday and into the night. Is it not best to rest them?" Jeth spoke as if he, too, were very tired, but his brother's voice was brisk.

"They will be alright, Jeth. We are making good time, and at this rate we will be there in three days instead of five. We'll fly while the light holds and rest the Zoi tonight. If we fly up-river, and keep close above the water, we should make Cronnus Landing by nightfall."

"Yes," Jeth considered, stroking his short beard. "Yes, I guess we can. If we stay down near the river the wind won't be as strong. Thank the gods there is no lightning with this rain." He turned and went back across the deck.

Shaeli and Tarkoda followed their parents downstairs. Jarris still had an arm around Mareesha's waist and she leant heavily against him.

"Can I do anything, Da?" Tarkoda asked, his face anxious.

"Yes, son. See your sister gets dried off, then bring Mam some tezz. She's had a bad shock. Then bring some up for me and Jeth, too."

"Alright, Da. I won't be long."

As the door closed them out again, they heard Mareesha say, "Oh, Jarris, she never said a word," and then she began to cry.

Jarris hushed her, the same way he hushed Shaeli when she woke from a bad dream. Tarkoda and Shaeli stood outside the door for a moment, and Shaeli looked up at her brother.

"Mam was friends with King Tenelon, wasn't she, Koda?"

He nodded. "She lived a long time at Great Court," he said.

They walked slowly down the hall, still holding hands, the smell of tezz drifting from the kitchen. Shaeli gave her brother's hand a squeeze as they walked through the door. He didn't look at her, but he squeezed back, and she was comforted.

* * *

CHAPTER FOUR

They travelled all that long, dismal day, flying across a wind that grew stronger by the hour, following the path of the river. The rain kept coming in never-ending torrents, and they lit the lamps in mid-afternoon because it grew so dark they could hardly see. Shaeli forgot all about gloating that day. It was a day filled with hushed tones and sadness. A sombre day. A day of mourning.

Eenis kept the children busy in the storeroom and kitchen, stowing away anything that could fall and break. Mareesha kept to her bed, so Shaeli had no chance to ask about the wand, or to see the babies, although she heard one cry every now and then.

Jarris and Jeth took turns on deck, expecting the Zoi to tire, but they flew unerringly on through the rain-filled day, not straying from their course, seemingly unperturbed by the buffeting they and the Trader were receiving. They flew low over the River Armez, keeping watch on the Zoi and the river ahead, the death of the king weighing more heavily upon them than the leaden skies.

* * *

Mareesha heard a Zoi cry out above the drumming of the rain as she sat in her room, yet the sound brought her no joy. Her mind was weary from the torment of her thoughts, her eyes swollen with the weight of unshed tears. The voice of the female Zoi seemed to mirror the ache in her soul, as if the Zoi, too, were grieving the loss of King Tenelon.

Mareesha's sorrow sat heavily upon her. The loss of the king, coupled with concern for the queen, what she must be feeling – *concealing* – filled her mind with turmoil. Twice she had almost decided to contact Irinesta, to lend comfort and strength; the second time she had even gone so far as readying the means. She knew Jarris was safely on deck and she would not be disturbed, yet, as she began, she suddenly knew the risk was too great. She was enveloped by fear, and abandoned the idea. She'd dismantled and locked the tools again in their small box, meaning to tuck it back in the hole beneath the boards, but instead she sat with it on her knee, feeling the anguish of her friend across the long distance. She closed her eyes against the grief and let her brain drift, trying to shut out the thoughts that tortured her.

When she opened her eyes again she felt strangely disconnected. Her vision was foggy, her mind the same. She was unaware of how long she'd sat with the box upon her knee – seeing nothing, hearing nothing. She could not remember her name.

A persistent rapping filtered through, bringing the room vaguely back, yet it was without focus, as if she was looking through a veil of dark shadow. With the sound of the knocking came some peripheral awareness of a baby crying – long, hitching sobs, far away. The sound of rain whispered too, somewhere.

She shook her head and stood, one hand rubbing at the tiny scar above her left eye. The box fell unheeded to the floor. She croaked, unaware of what she said. She took two shaky steps across the room and stopped, unsure. She was disorientated and her head pounded. Something dragged at her mind. A black wind roared in her ears. Time moved as sluggishly as her body.

A little girl was suddenly beside her, tugging at her sleeve, shaking her arm, calling to her, but she could not answer, could only stare stupidly at the babbling child. She had some memory of the girl, and her mind groped at it. Her hand moved with her mind, groping at the air before her face for understanding.

The girl went to a cot and looked down. She reached in with one hand. Colour fled from her face in an instant; the ash-white of panic replaced it. The girl ran back and grabbed her by the arm, pulling at her and screaming.

"The *baby*," she was shouting. "The baby, Mam. Quick, Mam."

But a shadow still lay over Mareesha's mind. She stared blankly down, recognition lost in a dark, empty space. The child's face was stricken, but Mareesha could not help her.

Shaeli gave a final shake, desperation wringing at her voice, not knowing what was wrong with her mother, but only that she was needed, needed *now*. She stepped back and kicked her mother on the shin with all the strength she could muster.

"Wake up, Mam," Shaeli screamed. She kicked again. "Wake up, *please*."

Awareness hit Mareesha as the bolt of pain shot through her. She blinked. Her eyes finally took on focus.

Shaeli was crying now, but still pulling her mother towards the cot. Mareesha tottered the few steps, shook free and leant over, peering groggily inside.

There were two babies in the cot. One babe cried still, yet her cries were fewer, her face red from effort, her eyes fixing on Mareesha as she looked down. One tiny arm lifted. The other babe was lying still and pale, her lips rimmed with blue.

"Oh, the gods," Mareesha cried, full sense rushing her brain in a torrent. She scooped the babe up, put an ear to her mouth, blew in her face, rubbed her tiny chest.

What had happened? Why had she not heard the crying? How could she not know something was amiss? So much depended on her. A thousand thoughts shot through her mind in a moment, but that one horrified question echoed ceaselessly: what had *happened?*

Mareesha turned to the child standing ashen-faced behind her. "Shaeli, tell Eenis to bring my bag. *Hurry*, child."

She carried the limp bundle to the bed and lay the baby upon it, peering intently into the tiny face. Shaeli turned and fled the room.

* * *

Jarris found her, much later, curled up on some old blankets at the back of the storeroom. She'd moaned softly as he entered, and it had been his only clue to her whereabouts. They had all been searching for her, and this was the third time he had checked the storeroom; Jeth had been in here twice. He clambered over piled baskets and knelt down.

Shaeli lay under a shelf, an old blanket drawn about her, her pointy face tear-streaked and grimy. She slept, but her brows were drawn together, and her breathing was shallow. She drew a long, hitching breath as he watched, and her bottom lip trembled. The sight of her brought tears to his eyes.

Mareesha had told him what had happened, plainly at a loss to explain her disconnection, or what she called "the dragging at her mind". All her attention had been turned to the babe, whose heart had been beating so slowly that she'd had trouble breathing. Shaeli, after running frantically to Eenis and delivering her message, had disappeared.

Jarris leant in beneath the shelf and gently brushed a strand of hair off Shaeli's cheek. He touched her shoulder, softly calling her name. She woke with tears in her eyes and upon seeing him, threw herself against his chest, sobbing.

He held her as she spent her misery, stroking her head and hushing her, feeling his shirt dampen with her tears. When she quieted, he sat her up, lifting her chin until she looked at his face. Her eyes were huge and darkly grey. The fresh tears had cut clean streaks through the dirt on her cheeks. He cupped her face with one large, rough hand and kissed her forehead.

"Oh, Da," she said, her voice trembling, "the baby... Mam..." She could go no further. Her voice broke and more tears welled in her eyes.

"She's *alright*, Shaeli. The babe is alright, thanks to you." He spoke so gently that the tears still fell, but relief brightened her eyes. "Mam reached her in time and she is sleeping soundly beside her..." he hesitated for just a moment, "...her sister. She's fine now. Mam is very grateful, Shaeli, and is anxious to see you. We were worried when we couldn't find you. Everyone has been searching."

"Da," she said, her voice soft and trembling. "I was so frightened. I heard a baby crying for the longest time from my room and I thought something might be wrong. I knocked and knocked but Mam didn't answer, so I went in. One was still crying... but... but the other was so white and... and Mam looked so *strange*, like she couldn't see me, or hear me."

The words came quickly now, falling out in a rush. She knew her sister was alright, her mother was alright, and her terror began to fade. Jarris could see her relaxing as she spoke, though her hands still clutched the little amulet on her belt.

"I called and pulled at her, and one was still crying and I thought... you know... I thought that the other was..." She left the sentence unfinished, and looked down, swallowing a sob. Her eyebrows drew together, she took a deep breath, and spoke so quietly he could barely hear her. "So I kicked her." She looked back up at him, frowning and tense, but bravely repeating her confession. "I kicked Mam, Da. *Hard*. Hard as I could." Her bottom lip trembled. "Two times I kicked her. I *had* to. I couldn't think what else to do. She couldn't hear me, and the baby..." She stopped again, and pursed her lips. "I kicked her real hard, Da."

She pressed her face against his chest, afraid of what he would say, and Jarris was glad of it. He had to try very hard not to laugh, though tears pressed hotly against the backs of his eyes. He held her tightly until he had command of his face and his voice again.

"Mam told me," he said gently. "And she isn't angry with you." She looked up at him again, her eyes hopeful, and he smiled. "She understands that you had to do it," he added.

"Truly, Da?"

"Truly."

Shaeli frowned. "But what happened to Mam? Why couldn't she hear me, or the baby crying? I tried to make her. I called, and pulled at her, but she just wasn't... *there*."

Jarris shook his head. "I don't know, and neither does Mam. She was frightened, too." Shaeli looked faintly surprised, and Jarris smiled again. "In fact she's grateful you kicked her. It brought her back, she said." His smile widened. "Not that you should make a habit of kicking your mother, mind."

The corners of her mouth lifted, just the tiniest bit. "I won't, Da," she said. "Promise."

"But *this* time you did the right thing." He spoke seriously again. "Exactly the right thing. You probably saved your sister's life today, Shaeli." He took her face in both hands, staring intently into her eyes. "I'm very, very proud of you. You couldn't have done better if you were fully grown." Shaeli's face beamed in the warmth of this high praise and Jarris lifted her up, hugged her tightly and carried her to the door. "Now I think that Mam will want to see you, and I shall tell the others to stop searching."

"You're *sure* she's not mad, Da?"

"I'm sure. If anything she's mad at herself, but she's so proud of you, she's fit to burst with it, and she's been so worried about you."

Shaeli smiled her relief as he set her down outside their bedroom door and opened it. Mareesha stood at the cot, looking down, her face lined with weariness and worry.

"Here she is, Mam, safe and well."

Mareesha turned and her face broke into a smile even as the tears formed in her eyes. She opened her arms. Shaeli ran into them, and was enfolded.

Jarris left them like that, hugging and crying together. He closed the door softly behind him.

* * *

After the long, eventful day it was a relief when they reached Cronnus Landing at dusk. The bells solemnly tolled the death of the king there, too.

After the Zoi were fed and nested for the night, the whole family gathered at the table for dinner, and even though Mareesha was exhausted, she insisted on being there. She would not let the babies out of her sight, so they too were there, snuggled together in a big, round basket beside the table, swaddled in blankets and supervised by their proud, tired sister.

They ate a quiet dinner; the emotions of the day had wearied them all, and there was little conversation, each of them occupied by their own thoughts. Shaeli imagined that if you could see thoughts they would run silkily around the room like shiny spider's webs, curling and twisting and whispering together in corners.

After the dishes had been cleared, Mareesha set a glass from her bridal set before each of them, and took her prized wine from the cupboard. She filled the adults' glasses with the thick crimson liqueur, gave the children each a drop, and they all drank to King Tenelon and kept a moment's silence in remembrance of their monarch. The children listened as the adults talked about the great things accomplished by Tenelon, and Mareesha told of the time she had lived at Great Court, and how kind King Tenelon and Queen Irinesta had always been to her. She looked at the beautiful lamps shedding their warm glow throughout the room, and tears stood in her eyes as she proposed they drink also to Queen Irinesta, and give thought to her in her time of grief. When Eenis asked they also drink to the health of the unborn heir, the eyes of Jarris and Mareesha met over the rims of their glasses, and they drank a private toast.

Then Mareesha said she had another announcement to make and she left the room, returning moments later carrying a mysterious bundle. There were baffled looks around the table, except from Jarris, who knew what was coming, and from Shaeli, who had, with growing excitement, guessed.

Mareesha lay the bundle on the table, but did not unwrap it. She looked at each of them, her eyes lingering on Shaeli, and she began to speak.

"You all know what happened today with the babies," she said, her eyes shifting to the basket where the babies slept, and back to the table. Jarris took her hand and she took a deep breath and continued "I... well, I don't know what happened to me, I cannot explain, but what I *do* know is that Shaeli brought me back, and she is to be congratulated. I want her to know how grateful I am that she thought to kick me." She looked at her smiling daughter and raised her glass. "To Shaeli. How lucky the twins are to have her for their big sister."

They all raised their glasses, and said "to Shaeli", and then the boys began elbowing each other, giggling and whispering, "you ask", "no, you", until Tarkoda blurted out, "Mam, can we see the bruise?"

There was laughter around the table, and then gasps as Mareesha put her leg up on the chair and rolled down her stocking. A large, oval bruise was revealed on her shin, black and purple in the middle, red-pink at the edges. The boys admired it thoroughly, Eenis made tut-tutting noises, and a blushing Shaeli endured some good-natured ribbing.

Mareesha rolled her stocking up and put her foot back down, laying a hand on the bundle before her, a slight smile playing about her mouth. Shaeli thought she would burst with anticipation.

"Now, what you don't know is that yesterday morning, Shaeli also made a discovery. An amazing discovery," Mareesha said. She looked at Shaeli. "Da and I have decided to show your treasure to the High Warlock and the old ones when we reach Cave, just to be sure." A look of alarm crossed Shaeli's face, and she reached over and patted her daughter's cheek reassuringly. "Don't worry, I'm sure they'll see that it holds no threat, and it will be yours. No magic could endure in it without its gemstones, and it will not work unless held by the one it was made for."

Shaeli was relieved and the others were obviously intrigued by this talk of magic and danger. Eenis looked vaguely uneasy, and Jarris sat back, arms folded, amused by the scene as Mareesha slowly unwrapped the wand to sounds of amazement from around the table. Shaeli hardly recognised it as the dirty thing she had pulled from the bank, so brightly did it shine, and even though she had known what to expect, she too, was amazed. Mareesha had cleaned every bit of mud encrusted to its surface and polished it, and the wand sparkled, the gems still embedded in the metal twinkling where the lamplight hit them. Every facet of the intricate braiding could be clearly seen, and the tiny writing was revealed, starting at the top where the empty claw began and continuing on down the length in a strange, unfamiliar script. The faintly-pink metal glowed with a hidden warmth, and Shaeli almost convinced herself that she felt something distinctly magical coming from that glow.

The boys and Jeth gathered round, voices raised in wonder, touching the wand, tentatively at first, then taking turns holding it and pointing out details to each other, excited. Tarkoda and Andos kept looking at Shaeli with admiration and more than a little envy, and Dari was as interested as the others, and as envious, but his forehead was furrowed as he looked at the wand.

Tarkoda slapped her on the back, congratulating her with such enthusiasm that she blushed anew. Andos asked her how she found it and she quickly recited the story. There was excited conversation around the table; after the distressing day this was a welcome diversion – until Eenis spoke from the end of the table where she'd sat with one hand over her mouth, a growing look of horror upon her face, her voice red-rimmed with harshness.

"I cannot believe you would have this... this *abomination* in our home, Mareesha, let alone allow the child to keep it." Her hand fluttered around her mouth as if ready to stop the flood of words that poured forth. "Andos, Dari, do not touch it. Evil things never lose their power."

Dari pulled his hand back, but Andos seemed merely surprised by his mother's outburst. Dari looked at Shaeli, eyes narrowed, as his mother raved on.

"And this thing *is* evil, made by evil little hands for evil purposes, bewitching and controlling, spreading wickedness among good people. The stink of corruption lies upon everything they touch. Their magic is heartless and cruel." Eenis' voice rose shrilly, her eyes were glazed. She was clearly angry – and terrified. "No good will come of it, it is evil, I tell you. I cannot bear to look at it. I can *smell* the foulness seeping from it. Take it away." She looked imploringly at Mareesha. "Please, take it away, Mareesha, I cannot bear it." The hovering hand leapt again to cover her mouth. Her thin face seemed paler than ever, shadows and fear hollowing her cheeks.

Jeth moved around the table to her, his face, like those of Jarris and Mareesha, showing his concern. The children looked bewildered by the flood of words from the tight-lipped Eenis.

"Now, Eenis, don't be frightened," Jeth said, gently. "Mareesha says there's nothing to fear from it. 'Tis only an old bit of metal, it has no magic now, evil or otherwise."

"Mareesha says she does not know, Jeth, and you cannot tell me *not* to fear it. You have not seen the destruction these things can cause." She spat the words between hovering fingers, her eyes narrowing. "*I* have, and I can promise you it *is* frightening, and evil."

Jeth put an arm about her. "I know you have reason, but that has nothing to do with Shaeli's wand. You cannot know what or who it was made for. You need not fear it, I'm sure." He met Jarris' eye, and his brother nodded imperceptibly. "But if it upsets you so, we shall put it away." He looked across the table, appealing for understanding. "Won't we, Mareesha?"

Mareesha smiled. "Of course we will. I'm sorry, Eenis, I did not think. I would not have brought it out if I'd known it would upset you so, or if I thought there was any danger in it." She handed the cloth to Shaeli. "Wrap it up, now. I shall mind it until the old ones and the High Warlock can see it and make sure it's safe." She leant down and kissed Shaeli's forehead, adding quietly, "I'm sure it will be fine. Don't worry."

Eenis looked mildly placated. "I would feel better if Almarnoch and Navez declared it safe," she mumbled stiffly. Her hand moved from her mouth to rub at the centre of her forehead. "I apologise for upsetting you all."

Jeth patted her shoulder.

Shaeli slowly re-wrapped her treasure, studying the tiny lettering underneath the claw as she did so, but making no sense of it. She wanted to see every detail, spend time marvelling at the braiding – she thought she could see tiny figures hidden in it – but she could delay no longer. She reluctantly finished and handed the bundle back to her mother, stifling her disappointment.

She went to bed then, going without complaint to her room, for she was very tired. It seemed forever since this morning when she had stood in the rain holding Tarkoda's hand, hearing the news of the dead king; an eternity since she had kicked her mother. Dari's narrow eyes and thin mouth followed her to the door.

Her mother took her to her room, tucking her in for the first time since the babies had come. Mareesha reassured Shaeli again that the old ones would think as she did, that the wand was harmless, then she sat on the edge of the bed and spoke gravely about how thankful she was Shaeli had come into her room when she heard the baby crying. Her voice began to tremble as she hugged Shaeli tightly to her.

Shaeli was proud, but a bit embarrassed, and she hugged back, patting her mother protectively on the shoulder. "It's all right, now, Mam. It's all over," she said.

Mareesha laughed, tears shining brightly in her green eyes. She kissed Shaeli goodnight and stood, wishing her bright and peaceful dreams as she shut the door behind her.

Shaeli lay in the dark, contentment washing over her. A little part of her mind wondered why Eenis was so afraid of elves and their magic, but mostly she just wanted to sleep. As she slipped into dreams, she fancied she heard a lullaby on the breeze, but then Williver was taking her floating on the clouds in a crisp blue sky, and she was telling him about the wand she had found stuck in a bank near Lake Marnis.

* * *

CHAPTER FIVE

At the very edge of the World, far to the north, a boy of ten sat by a small fire. He stared into the flames, wrapped in a blanket he had brought from the old stone hut behind him. The hut, shrouded in evening shadows, seemed almost a part of the rocky hill at whose foot it huddled.

He could not venture far, for the old woman might need him, and unless his father was home, he seldom went further than the sound of her bell. She was his responsibility now; his responsibility since his Mam had died last spring. He felt a twinge at the thought of his gentle, brown-eyed mother. He missed her still.

Out here on the beach he could hear the tinkling of the old woman's gold bell, yet he knew she slept soundly after dinner, at least for a while, then she would wake and want her evening tezz.

He shivered a little, pulling the blanket more closely around shoulders that were broad for his age, strengthened by hard work. He looked out across the dark sea to where he knew Zirrus lay hidden somewhere under a mountain of cloud far to the south, the Wintering almost upon it. Flashes of lightning lit the clouds along the horizon, heralding the coming storms that would isolate those on the larger islands; on the Four Lands, even the simplest journey could be a nightmare during the Wintering, and he smiled smugly to himself. Here on the Starisles there was no need to be segregated; it became bitterly cold, but there was little real snow, only sleety rain and ice. Occasionally hail fell in stony sheets, causing great damage and even a few deaths, yet generally the Wintering was as joyful a thing to the Starislanders as it was a misery to those on Zirrus, Ashkanna, Romynn and Wokk.

On the Starisles, the cold was a small respite in a year of constant heat and humidity; a time when little work was done, and people took time to visit and relax. He'd heard that sometimes, on islands close to each other, huge bands of ice would form a bridge, and the people could walk back and forth across the frozen water, but here they were almost alone. Just a few small, scattered islands far out on the eastern edge of the Starisles.

The boy didn't see many people, mostly just the members of the families on the neighbouring islands – he could see their lights twinkling low across the water to the west. Occasionally a passing fisherman would come ashore for fresh water, and the boy would eagerly chat to him or her, but that was all, except when his father was home. Of course, there was always the old woman, shuffling around the hut, sitting on the bench outside in the sun, mumbling to herself over her big books and drinking endless cups of tezz.

He had no idea just how old the old woman was, but he knew she had been around a long time. Even his grandmother had called her "the old woman" before she had died, five Winters before. The people nearby treated her with great respect, and supplied her with the few things her family could not, but they required little. Milk they had from the old cow in the lean-to; wax and honey from the hives on the hill; seafood and salt from the sea surrounding them; fruit and a few vegetables from their small garden. His father brought home whatever else they needed, as well as an occasional gift.

He held such a gift now. A beautiful wooden flute rested upon his crossed legs, the firelight reflecting russetly upon its varnished surface, and he took up the instrument and played a quick scale, happy with his progress. He'd only had the flute these last two Moons, but he practised every moment he could, and was now master of several simple tunes. He played a lullaby his mother had sung to him, luxuriating in the way the music drifted off across the water, imagining it floating on and on, reaching the ears of someone on Zirrus or Ashkanna, and he smiled to himself, his brown eyes bright with pleasure.

He heard the old woman's bell as the last note drifted away, and he sighed and stood, brushing the white sand from his clothes. He shook hair that was the same dappled mahogany as the flute from his eyes.

Taking the blanket and flute, he headed for the hut to prepare tezz and some of the soft honey-cakes she enjoyed so much, then there would be a short lesson of some kind – he never knew what it would be; history, numerology, reading – depending on the old woman's whim.

During daylight hours were the lessons he enjoyed most, archery and fencing. Surprisingly, she was an amazingly successful teacher of these, though she hardly ever moved from her chair. He had become very adept, at least in theory, for he rarely had a real person to practise with, unless the boys from the nearby islands came over. The boy looked forward to the Wintering, for that meant more time practising with a real opponent. Occasionally, and privately, she showed him small feats of magic, little more than tricks really, but he enjoyed them enormously.

As he walked up the path he looked back over his shoulder, watching the flames send tiny sparks up into the night sky. He knew his father would be able to see the small beacon should he be sailing for home tonight, and he would keep the fire burning most of the night, and every night from now until his father returned. He would be home soon – even now he would be on his way back from Romynn – and the boy was glad. His father would be here for the Wintering, and together they would prepare the kelp beds for the coming year and ready the harvest for the spring markets, and he would be able to spend some time alone, or row over to visit the neighbours, and not always have to stay within bell-range. Not that he minded so much about having to stay here all the time. Of course, he dreamed of sailing away with his father, visiting the places he had heard so much about, but he knew it was right that he should be here. After all, the old woman needed him, and he loved her wizened little soul dearly. She was a joy and a bother, funny, strict almost to a fault, exasperating – and kinder than anyone he knew. *And* it seemed that she knew everything. He could ask her any question – why, or who, or where – and she always had an answer. She could remember when such-and-such a thing had happened, or she had met so-and-so, or their brother or cousin or grandson. She had travelled to every part of the Four Lands, even into the Drell Mountains, and she would paint so bright a picture for him that he learned many things without even knowing it.

He wondered, not for the first time, what would happen to them if his father never came back. It happened, sometimes, boats never coming home, a storm, pirates. The thought stopped him. He turned at the top of the path, anxiously scanning the dark horizon, but there was nothing to see, only the waves and the silvery splash of a solitary fish. Fear crept into his heart, yet it left instantly as the old woman's voice reached him. It chimed like her golden bell from inside the little hut, and he smiled. Her voice was the only thing she still possessed that was young – an audible reminder of a long-gone youth.

"It will be a day or two, yet, Zeb," she said, from inside the shadows. "Worry not. He is safe."

He was not surprised she had guessed his thoughts – she often did, and he was used to it. He supposed it was because she knew him so well.

"Come, shut the door, boy. I smell the Wintering, and this year its scent is oddly sour." He could hear the smile in her voice. "It must be time for some tezz, eh?"

His smile broadened, and he went inside, shutting out the dark and the smell of the Wintering as he closed the door behind him.

* * *

On Zirrus, in the village of Boccra on the shores of the Bay of Islands, Fezzik did not smell the Wintering, but he sensed it creeping up from the south and he felt the bite of it on the breeze coming off the bay. Soon it would be time to close up the forge and prepare for the blizzards, yet this year he did not mind the times they would be shut in the close confines of the Wintering Hall; this year he looked forward to those times. He grinned to himself, and, as if on some unseen cue, the reason for his grinning came out of the house behind him. A thick shawl was wrapped around her shoulders, but her head was bare and her hair shone like corn silk in the moonlight. She walked up the path to where he stood at the little gate between the garden and the forge, looking expectantly past the darkened structure to the street beyond, as if there would be someone there. When all she saw was the dark forge and the silent street she looked up at him, craning her neck to look into his eyes.

"Why do you stand out here, grinning at the dark night, my husband?" Verlie asked him.

"I was thinking of the wedlock room we shall be sharing in the Wintering Hall," Fezzik said, and he grinned harder at the pink blush which spread so prettily across her cheeks.

They had been married only a few days, and the smug grin had been a fixture on his face ever since. It had been the cause of much amusement to the villagers, and although the old ones gleefully told him it would soon wear off, he couldn't imagine such a thing; he had all he wanted now. He wrapped his arms about her and kissed the spot where the blush ran into the curve of her throat, feeling her laugh tremble beneath his lips before it reached his ears.

"Let me go, Fezzik," she said, struggling uselessly in his huge arms. "Come inside, the dinner is nearly ready."

He held her a moment longer, liking the feel of her against his chest, and then he released her. They walked towards the square of light shining on the path, their arms about each other.

"The wedlock room could not be nearly as nice as our own little home," Verlie said, stopping with her shoes touching the edge of the light, looking up at their house.

Fezzik had built the house for her, two rooms up, two down, with wide verandas at the back that looked down over the River Clahren, with space to expand should they need more rooms – a statement which always made Verlie blush. Behind them was the forge, facing out into the street, and beside it the house where Fezzik had grown up, and where his parents lived. They had offered to share it with the newly-weds, but Fezzik and Verlie had wanted their own home, and Fezzik's father had given him the field that ran behind the forge on which to build it.

Verlie looked from the lamp-lit windows into his eyes. "There will be so many people in the Wintering Hall, and here we are all alone."

Her dark eyes and the curve of her lips smouldered somewhere in his chest and he pulled her to him again. This time there was no resistance, her mouth met his eagerly, and when he released her she stroked his beard with a touch so light it sent shivers to his very toes.

"Yet here there is work to be done, my love," he said. "The forge, the wood, the rails on the veranda." He ran his hand down the braid that reached her waist; it felt like satin beneath his rough fingers. "While the Wintering does its worst, there will only be time to spend with you. In the wedlock room, as is tradition."

She smiled that smile again, the one that smouldered inside him. "Well, we shouldn't fight tradition, I suppose," she said, standing on her toes and turning her mouth to him.

"I suppose not," he said, leaning to meet her.

Their kiss was interrupted by a clatter from the street; a horse galloping through the town, the rider uncaring of the horse's hooves on the cobblestones. The horse, a glimpse only of a cloaked figure upon it, thundered past, a bell ringing in his fist. Moments later another bell peeled loudly from the square in the village. Fezzik's father called out to him from beside the forge, and the two went to see what had happened.

When they returned, Verlie was waiting with Fezzik's mother in a puddle of light in the street. Fezzik's father spoke. He was a big man, like his son, but his massive shoulders were slumped, his usually florid face grey in the moonlight.

"Our good king is dead," he said, the words flat and lifeless. "Dead these three days."

Fezzik's mother began to cry. "Oh, the poor queen," she said. "The poor, poor queen." Her face went pink and she began to wobble all over as she wept. "The poor fatherless babe."

Her husband stared at her blankly, as if her distress was beyond him.

Fezzik and Verlie looked at each other. Three days. King Tenelon had died on the same day as they were wed.

Nobody said it, but none of them thought it a very good omen.

* * *

At Great Court, Irinesta sat huddled in blankets beside the fire. E'Nith was making her a broth, but Irinesta already knew she would not be able to eat it. She'd barely eaten anything since Tenelon died. Her eyes roamed the room, tears rolling down her cheeks. Here in the Glade Room was the only place she felt any peace at all, and now it was even more precious.

Tenelon had presented it to her as a wedding gift. Knowing she would miss the warmth of her native Romynn, he had redecorated the round turret room which had once been his mother's; except, of course, the part that held the Glade.

The Glade. A mural so magnificent it was hard to believe there was not a small, green clearing surrounded by forest in the secluded tower room. It was a cunning illusion, created to enchant the viewer, painted with meticulous attention to detail. As old as it was, no sign of decay could be seen. The colours were as fresh as daybreak, the shadows dark velvet.

The small, painted glade was lush and filled with expectation, the trees surrounding it seemed as old as the Land itself – a thick forest soaring above in a myriad of greens and greys, crowding the perimeter as if trying to see in to some great spectacle. Sunlight streamed down, highlighting the tiny, painted clearing so each blade of grass was clearly seen; small lizards and insects crept through the grass; tiny winged creatures and fairies fluttered amongst hundreds of blushing blooms laying scattered like gifts around the feet of the trees. Scores of butterflies hung in the air – sapphire blue, satin red, saffron yellow – but the clearing was empty of any larger forms of life. In the brightness of its perpetual sunshine, the glade seemed to wait for someone to stroll within its arms, to spend time in its quiet warmth, but from the forest behind the empty glade, scores of eyes looked out. The painted forest surrounding the glade was braided with life. Birds, elves, drell, and dozens of other creatures hid in the branches and between the trunks of the thick trees, faces indistinct, forms melting into shadows. Serpents entwined within leafy forks; birds crowded the branches; spiders spun intricate webs; hares peeked from burrows as mottled jenka stalked them; elfin faces smiled from behind thick trunks; here hid the tiny face of a jevvi, there the wet-brown eyes of a huni-deer; hawks hovered in lacy clouds – or were they dragons framed against the soft blue sky?

In the gnarled, ancient trunks of the trees themselves were the faces of people and animals, most showing rapturous delight at being captured by an ancient giant; some with agony upon their tortured faces.

The forest surrounding the empty glade hid layer upon layer of painted life, each form unique, each set of eyes staring out into the room. The mural was a masterpiece of imagination, impossible to recall in detail, only the magnificence of it remained in the memory. The Glade enchanted all who saw it, though some said they saw strange things lurking in the dim background, between the trees where the slanting shafts of painted sunlight did not reach, and Irinesta had often laughed with Tenelon at the rumours about the mural, secretly amused at the fearful glances of the very superstitious. She had never seen ominous things within it, although she had, at times, imagined she felt soft tendrils of magic reach tentatively into the room, as if testing their welcome.

She loved being at the top of the turret, the sweeping view of the Bay of Islands, the private, inaccessible balcony. Warm and sunny on all but the coldest Winter's day, the windows of the tower framed in coloured glass and crystals faced north to catch the sun, the crystals capturing the sunlight and casting dancing rainbows throughout the room; miniature spectrums waltzing with the sun, and yet, as beautiful as the room was, most of all she loved The Glade. In five-and-twenty Winters she had never tired of looking at its beauty, nor had its soothing green magic ever failed to calm and comfort her when she was troubled.

She had spent the first nights after her wedding eve in the round room, and had always been comforted by the serenity in the eyes looking out from the mural – eyes that seemed follow her as she moved about the room. She and Tenelon had shared many nights under the gaze of the ancient trees, preferring to sleep in the Glade Room rather than the more formal room where he had died. Tenelon had told her of things in the Glade Room which she had scarcely believed; secrets of the Realm; hidden passages throughout the castle; tales of magic, dragons and fairies; the deeds of kings, Warlocks, elves and Ammerr in Winters long past...

Irinesta jumped as E'Nith put a bowl of broth down beside her.

"I'm sorry," said E'Nith. "I did not mean to startle you."

Irinesta smiled. "That's alright," she said. "I was just thinking."

"I know," said E'Nith with a sad smile. She patted her mistress's hand. "He loved you very much, you know."

"I know," said Irinesta. She blinked hard as the tears prickled her eyes again. She cleared her throat. "Will you be leaving soon?"

E'Nith nodded. "As soon as you finish that broth," she said.

Irinesta sighed and took up the bowl. E'Nith would be disappointed if she did not try.

She had told her old nurse everything. She'd had to. She had one more task to complete, and she needed E'Nith's help to do it, yet even though she needed her badly, she was frightened for her maid, but E'Nith had not baulked at what her queen had asked of her. Indeed, she had smiled grimly.

"I know just what to do," she'd said.

It was E'Nith's custom to visit an old friend from Romynn down in Palveron every few evenings, and this had become central to their plans. There was no guarantee they would find what they sought, but Irinesta, as always, trusted in the gods.

E'Nith gathered her things while Irinesta took what she could of the broth. She had just put down the half-empty bowl when the door flew open. Virrisian stood there, a tall dark-haired man Irinesta had never seen before standing behind her. Virrisian strode into the room and came over to stand before Irinesta's chair. E'Nith stood beside the bed, her shawl in her hands.

"How do you fare, sister?" Virrisian said, leaning forward and peering into Irinesta's face.

Irinesta stood, her hand moving to rest upon the swell of her belly. It felt so different than it had just a few short days ago, but E'Nith had done a good job of it. No one had noticed that she was no longer pregnant.

"Well, thank you, Virrisian," she replied. "As well as can be expected, at least."

Virrisian nodded. "And the child," she said. "No sign of it yet?"

"No," Irinesta said. "It will be some days yet, I think."

Virrisian looked at her, eyes boring into her. Irinesta met those eyes unflinchingly.

"Well," Virrisian said at last. "We shall see it soon, I hope."

"Yes," said Irinesta. "The gods willing."

Virrisian turned and strode from the room. The dark-haired man, his face expressionless, looked at them a moment and then he followed Princess Virrisian.

E'Nith shut the door, then hurried over to Irinesta.

"What did she want?" she said.

"I don't know," said Irinesta. "But we must be careful. Very careful."

* * *

"Forgive me, but was there a point to all that?"

"Of course," said Virrisian. She stopped and looked at the man beside her. "There is a reason for everything I do, Azeron."

"May I ask the reason?"

Virrisian sighed. "You were sent here to obey me, Sir Azeron, to obey me and to serve me in whatever way I ask, *not* to question me," she said, her lip curling. "But I shall indulge you. You please me." She lowered her voice. "I have information that my dear sister has plans. That she may try to take the child from the castle."

Azeron shrugged. "We are watching them. Nothing comes out of that room that I don't know about. We will know when the babe comes, she cannot hide it."

"It may be that she has already given birth."

Azeron frowned at her words. "Is that possible?"

"All things are possible," she said. "Yet I have people searching, and the chances are slim at best that she has managed such a thing. She has been watched for a long time, and I think we will wait a few days yet to see the brat, as she said."

Virrisian walked on and Azeron followed.

"What do you intend on doing when it does come?" he asked.

She did not speak for a long time and Azeron thought she would not answer him, yet finally she spoke, her voice as edged as a blade.

"Tenelon's child will not live a Moon," Virrisian said. "I will be queen before the new year begins." She tossed her head. "As it has been promised."

***

CHAPTER SIX

Jarris and Jeth had Purple Leaf underway before sunrise. The sky lay dull and grey above them and the wind had dropped to a chilly breeze. The Zoi pulled them on through the dullness of the day, and they moored at the Landing in the town of Vellyn in the late afternoon. They spent a gloomy night and left soon after daybreak, reaching Zerrin Crossing mid-morning.

The river was wide and flowed swiftly. Many smaller streams converged on it both above and below this crossing, but it was here that the River Zerrin truly began, flowing from the mountains all the way across Zirrus to the Sea of Aa'liu. Shaeli liked to imagine that the snow that fell on their mountain, Zerrinius, would melt into the small streams that fed the river, and flow across the whole Land. Across the river the mountains loomed, Mount Zerrinius largest of all. On this side stood a huddle of ramshackle buildings, the strong smell of horse drifting across to the Landing.

Shaeli sat on the small, triangular top deck, her legs hanging through the rails, her face pressed between them, watching the flurry of landing. It was just the same as a lift, really, but in reverse.

The Zoi brought the Trader down, skimming over the trees and flying low across the clearing. Jeth had the gate open, a huge hook in his hands, and as they approached the Landing, he sunk the hook into an enormous post embedded in the ground a short distance from the Landing, throwing out the attached rope. The rope was tied to the rear of the Trader and anchored them to the landing post as Jeth leapt across to the Landing, a second rope in his hands. As the Zoi flew past the Landing they put their feet down, lowering their huge bodies and setting up a terrific backdraft, great wings beating furiously, and Shaeli listened to the curious humming sound that accompanied this manoeuvre. To her left, her father threw down another rope, and then he leapt down the short flight of stairs, raced across the deck, jumped across the gap, then straight on down the steps of the Landing to secure the forward ropes to another landing post. The ropes tightened, Jeth strained at the rope he had wrapped around a pole at the gate, pulling until there was only a small gap between the Trader and the Landing – the one that frightened Shaeli so much. She knew in her *mind* that it was impossible to fall through the gap, it was just that her mind had forgotten to tell her stomach.

It had been an easy landing; the wind had dwindled to a whisper, and the clouds hung leaden and still above. Sometimes, if the wind was strong, it could be difficult to land, and it was not unknown for a Trader to have to make the attempt two or three times if conditions were bad.

Shaeli knew they could have kept going on over the wide, rushing river, and even though they wished to make good time, there was no question that they would stop, for it was an unbroken courtesy for a Trader to carry those in need across the River Zerrin. There was a barge that crossed the distance, yet its journeys were erratic, undertaken only when enough paying customers made it worth the owner's while, and when conditions were favourable – the two coinciding at irregular intervals – so each Trader stopped at the Crossing. While this relieved the barge owner of the need to make the unpredictable passage, thus depriving him of some coin, his business also included the tavern, boarding house, and stables that were the only buildings at the Crossing, so he was not overly troubled; while people waited to cross, they must wait – and spend – in at least one of his establishments.

Shaeli stayed where she was after the landing, for she was not allowed to leave the Trader. She had to content herself with watching people climb the stairs, smiles on their faces as they carried up their bundles, their children, their baskets, their chickens; even a small, squealing piglet in the case of one toothless old man. Each one thanked Jarris, who stood near the Landing, and Eenis, who stood below Shaeli's dangling feet. They spoke loudly of their good fortune, settling themselves upon the deck, looking up at the great balloon in wonder, thanking everyone again, filling the deck with colour and chatter like a flock of bright, noisy birds. More than a dozen people climbed the stairs, and Shaeli counted seven children accompanying them.

One grubby little face peered up at her, its small fist clutching a dripping wad of honeycomb. She waved at the child, who continued to stare up, expressionless, honey dribbling between the dirty fingers, and then the sticky hand waved slightly. A small tongue popped out and began licking at the honey, the eyes still fixed unblinkingly upon Shaeli.

A young man in the king's colours was holding an animated conversation with Jarris at the top of the stairs. Her father called for Jeth to join them, and the discussion continued. Jarris and Jeth finally nodded, and the young knight bowed and disappeared at a run back down the stairs.

Shaeli had little time to wonder about him; her attention was taken by the appearance on the Landing of the barge, tavern, boarding-house, and stable owner. A more vast difference to the knight he had replaced at the top of the stairs could not be imagined. Where the young knight had been tall, thin and dark, this man was short, grossly obese, and red as an overripe tomato. The flush on his cheeks continued up past his forehead to slide over the top of his balding head, and he puffed his huge bulk across the deck to Eenis, wiping his sweaty face with a voluminous handkerchief.

"Ah, mistress, your arrival is indeed timely," he panted. "Very timely." He stopped to wheeze some more. "I am in need of several items urgently, and we have not seen a Trader since before the Full."

Eenis spoke coolly, her countenance stiffer even, than usual. Shaeli guessed she did not like the fat tavern-keeper very much.

"Have you a list, Savic?" Eenis asked impatiently. "We are anxious to leave as quickly as possible." She glanced at the sky.

"Of course, of course," Savic replied, producing a greasy scrap of paper from beneath his dirty robe. "A few necessary items. Nothing too much, I think?" he inquired.

As Eenis looked over the list, a smile hovered upon Savic's red face. Shaeli supposed the smile was meant to be pleasant, but it was merely hideous – as if the muscles in his cheeks were unused to stretching into such positions and didn't quite know what to do with themselves; a seldom-used smile.

"I'll do what I can." Eenis nodded. "Wait here." She turned and disappeared below deck.

Savic looked up and saw Shaeli peering down at him.

"Hello, little mistress," he said. "You're a pretty one, aren't you?" Then, horribly, he directed that awful smile at *her*. He had green things stuck between his teeth.

Something in his eyes and his thick lips made Shaeli vaguely uncomfortable, so she took a cue from the honeycomb-sucking urchin and said nothing, just stared back at him. She knew it was rude, but she didn't care. The fat-red man was awful.

"Where's that pretty Mam of yours today?" he asked, and Shaeli couldn't help answering that.

"Downstairs," she said, a little boastfully. "With the new babies."

"Babies, is it?" he looked surprised. "How many? Five?"

Shaeli giggled. "No," she answered. "Just two." He didn't look so bad when he wasn't smiling, but he was *so* fat. And he smelled bad, too. Even from up here.

"Two?" said Savic. "And where did you find them? Palveron?"

"We didn't *find* them," Shaeli said scornfully. She thought he must be quite stupid as well as smelly. "They were *borned*."

"I see," he said. "Where were they 'borned'?"

"Across Lake Marnis," she said. "I forget the town."

Savic nodded, and started to say something else, but a commotion from the Landing drew his attention.

Shaeli could see nothing at first, people had gathered at the railing, but a curious clattering reached her ears. The sound grew louder, and suddenly a horse appeared at the top of the stairs, nostrils flaring, ears hard back. The young knight was at its head, one hand holding a cloth over the animal's eyes, the other gripping tightly to its bridle. At the top of the Landing, its rump brushed the wooden railing, and it tossed its head uneasily, yet the knight held on and led it quickly across the gap and onto the deck, whispering softly to it the whole time. He led it to a spot opposite the Landing, tying the magnificent, jet-black horse to the rail and rubbing its high neck, soothing the skittish beast. He removed the cloth from the horse's eyes and it tossed its head again, its ears pricking back and forth. It stamped a hoof, nostrils blowing hard as it took in its surroundings.

Eenis had reappeared during the horse's arrival. She passed Savic his bundle and accepted payment without comment, her eyes fixed on the strange sight of a horse on deck. Savic saw her surprise and was only too happy to gossip upon its source.

"The young Sir Brudloc will go nowhere without his horse. They say he will ride no other. Went to all the trouble of bringing it from Romynn, you know. Wouldn't have a Zirrus nag." His voice was scornful. "But then, he *is* a cousin to the queen, *and* from Romynn," he said, as if that explained everything. "I must be going. A good Wintering to you all." He waddled to the Landing and began to heave his way down the stairs.

"And to you," Eenis murmured absently, still staring at the horse.

Sir Brudloc had calmed the horse and was still speaking softly to it as he unsaddled it. He took a brush from his bags and began to brush the horse's dark coat. The animal relaxed with the familiar routine, and despite the people surrounding them, it began to playfully nuzzle its young master. It pushed at his shoulder with its dark head until Sir Brudloc pulled a carrot from his pocket. The horse delicately took the offering and stood chewing while the knight finished its grooming. Its coat shone like ebony underwater.

Shaeli looked down at the top of Eenis' head, wondering if her aunt would be upset with her father and Jeth for allowing a horse on board, but when Eenis finally spoke, her voice was as soft and wondrous as a girl's.

"Magnificent," she breathed. "Beautiful, beautiful creature."

As the amazed Shaeli watched, Eenis almost floated across to the young knight and shyly asked if she could stroke his horse. Upon gaining his permission, Eenis reached out a hand and ran her fingers along the smooth jet flank, smiling in a way that Shaeli had rarely seen.

Well, she thought, *Da always says wonders will happen every day, if you look for them, and there's a real wonder.*

It continued to unfold as Eenis introduced herself and Sir Brudloc gave his name, and said he was on his way to Ashkanna. He bowed low over Eenis' hand and she blushed – Shaeli could see the pink run up Eenis' neck and over her cheek, and Shaeli shook her head, and then, to further add to the wonder, she heard her aunt request his presence at dinner that evening after they reached Serrat. *And* Sir Brudloc graciously accepted.

Andos, Dari and Tarkoda appeared on the Landing. They had been making a quick exploration of the Crossing and had not seen the horse arrive, and their excitement was plain. As

Eenis turned to them, smiling still, a gust of wind swept across the deck; a muttering followed it. People peered out from beneath the balloon, pointing fearfully at the sky. The clouds had undergone a rapid change in the short time they had been at Zerrin Crossing, condensing into ominous black thunderheads, and flashes of lightning had appeared to the south.

Jarris and Eenis called for people to sit as Jeth raced down the stairs to release the hook from the rear landing post, and rapidly the frenzy of the lift began. The people watched nervously as the traders ran back and forth, and they gave a collective shudder as the Landing moved away and the balloon began to rise. The great black horse jumped and shivered.

As they rose, Shaeli saw the fat Savic disappearing into the shabby tavern. A few gaudily dressed women waved from windows like blank eyes in the paintless face of the building, then another gust hit them hard, and they were pushed over the rushing river. It became apparent that it would be a race to reach the safety of Serrat before the full fury of the storm hit them.

* * *

Savic went through the tavern and across the dusty ground to the stables. A lofty man waited for him, his hand on the bridle of a horse. His thin, white-blond hair was tied at the nape, and he pierced the fat man with ice-blue eyes as Savic came around the corner.

"Well?" he said.

"Twins," said Savic. "But they do not come from anywhere near the city. They came over Marnis."

"And you believe this is the truth?"

"A child told me," Savic shrugged. "She wasn't lying."

"Good," said the man, tossing a bag of coin to Savic. He mounted his horse and rode away, into the path of the storm.

Savic watched him go, wondering why a nobleman from Wokk was so interested in the children of traders.

* * *

It had rarely been as crowded in the big room as it was that afternoon. As the wind and rain buffeted the windows and the Trader rocked with rising gusts, the passengers murmured nervously. Mareesha and Eenis moved amongst them, reassuring them with soothing words, and people smiled and nodded, but as soon as the women moved away they resumed their anxious mutterings and fearful glances at the ceiling.

Shaeli noticed that it was the poorer people who were the most nervous. Two well-dressed merchants who sat at the table teaching Andos and Tarkoda some sleight-of-hand appeared largely unconcerned with the storm, enquiring only about their expected time of arrival in Serrat and then settling themselves to spend the afternoon as comfortably as possible. The two boys were happy to provide a diversion, but Dari had gone to his room; he hated storms and complained they made his head ache. Shaeli thought he was just plain scared.

She was called from her place by the twins' basket to take tezz to the men left sitting on the steps below the main doors. Eenis did not mind people taking shelter downstairs, but she drew the line at animals in their kitchen.

The old man with the piglet smiled gummily at her as she gave him the tezz, and she smiled back as she put down the tray. She was relieved she had not spilt any on her wobbly walk down the passageway, and pleased with the destination of the remaining cup. She carried it carefully up the stairs, past several baskets of fluttering chickens, to where Sir Brudloc sheltered with the black horse.

The animal stood just outside the doors under the overhang of the top deck, sheltered from rain-filled gusts blowing in beneath the balloon. The horse's great bulk filled most of the space outside the door, and it stood with a feed-bag over its neck, munching contentedly. Amazingly, it had one of Eenis' best quilts draped over it, and her face must have proclaimed her surprise, for she heard a chuckle to her left, and turned to see the young knight sitting in the corner.

"I thought it was a bit much, too, but the good lady insisted," Sir Brudloc smiled. "I had not the heart to refuse her."

"It looks nice on him," Shaeli said, moving a little further away from the horse's lofty rump.

"We both thank you for that, miss, don't we, Rhom?" he asked the horse.

Rhom regarded him with a huge black eye, tossed his head, blew loudly into the feed-bag and returned to his meal. Shaeli and the knight looked at one another and burst out laughing.

"You see," Sir Brudloc chuckled. "He is well content."

Shaeli remembered the cup in her hands, and held it out to him. "Would you like some *tezz?*"

"That I would, miss," he said, but as he reached out his hand a sudden gust hit them and the Trader lurched.

Shaeli stumbled forward, and would have fallen, but Sir Brudloc grabbed her arm and kept her upright, yet half the tezz was spilt on his sleeve in the process.

"Oh, I'm sorry," she cried, as he pulled a kerchief from his pocket and dabbed at the wet patch. "Is it hurting? Shall I fetch Mam?"

"No, miss, there's no harm done," he smiled. He took the cup from her and downed the remains in one swallow. "It is warm only."

"I'll fetch you some more," she said.

"No, lass," he said. "I shall be fine until I reach Serrat. I'd be happier for you to give it to me at dinner." Then he asked her name, and they talked for a while, every now and then hearing muffled sounds and voices from Jeth and Jarris on the deck above them.

Shaeli spoke shyly at first, but soon relaxed as they discussed the storm, the horse, and the Trader. She told him of the fears of the people downstairs, and he nodded, and said that this chance trip on the Trader would probably be the only one most of them would take in their whole lives.

"People are often nervous with the unfamiliar, Shaeli," he said, and then he said something that she never forgot. "The more familiar one becomes with imagined fears, the less frightening they become. Fear comes from the not *knowing*, I think. Doing something often, making it familiar, can often take the fear away."

Shaeli pondered his words for a while, then rose. "I'd better go and collect the cups," she said.

"Well, then, I shall see you at dinner," he said, rising gallantly. "And I'll expect the food on the plate, rather than on my clothes, shall I?"

"Of course," she blushed. "I am sorry."

"No, miss, *I'm* sorry. I'm jesting at your expense," he smiled. "A joke between new friends, only. Truly, there's no harm done."

Shaeli smiled, took his cup and returned downstairs, impressed by her first encounter with a real knight, a cousin to Queen Irinesta.

* * *

The Zoi worked harder that afternoon than they had for a long time. Lightning streaked the sky, rain battered them, but the Zoi flew inexorably on, straining at their harnesses, pulling Purple Leaf through the grey World.

The vest-like harnesses the birds wore were attached to strong ropes above the Zoi's broad shoulders. The lead bird had two lines attached to his harness, so each arm of the V was connected to him, and these fine strong ropes led through the flock, linking each bird to a central ring in two lines. Strong hemp ropes connected the giant ring to both the balloon and the Trader, so the two were pulled together.

The central ring linking the birds to the ship was one of the most crucial points on a Trader, but the smaller ring welded to the top of it was even more essential. Through the eye of this smaller ring ran the finest, toughest rope, linking the lead bird to the Trader. The rope ran in an unbroken line to the lead Zoi, and with this link the trader used different combinations of signals to communicate directions, or to indicate a landing. The birds often seemed inherently to know which route to take, but the ability to communicate directly was imperative. This day they needed no such guidance; the River Zerrin lay behind them and the safety of Serrat lay ahead.

Serrat was built at the base of a craggy mountain, enfolded in a valley between two of the mountain's arms. The buildings were large and stately, their blocks hewn from the mountain towering above, and it was a thriving town, on the main route between Zirrus and Ashkanna and boasting a huge central square. It was also the closest town to Cave, with a Landing big enough to moor six Traders, and as Serrat was protected from the harshest weather, it made it one of the safest Landings on Zirrus. It was for this safety that they were headed.

The storm had caught them in its fist. Bolts of lightning crackled frighteningly close, rain pelted them from every direction; the Trader rolled in time with the thunder.

The people gathered on the inside stairs, some looking out past the black form of Rhom, others huddled on the small landing below, eyes closed, silent prayers to the god U'ee trembling between white lips. One of the watching farmers, braver than the rest, stood outside. He let out a cry as he sighted the huge ridge that was one of the arms enclosing Serrat, and the others echoed his relief. Their cry was drowned by a deafening thunderclap and a flash of lightning directly overhead.

On the deck above, Jeth peered through the driving rain at his brother. Their eyes were thin slits, faces red and stinging from rain that hit like needles.

"That was close," he shouted.

Jarris nodded, but kept his eyes on the ridge looming ahead. As they passed over it he tugged subtly on the lead rope and the Zoi swept them down close to the ground. The wind lessened instantly, and the lights of Serrat appeared ahead, but he kept his relief in check until they were moored at the Landing, then he sighed and looked up past the balloon at the boiling mass above their heads.

Lightning bolts still raged and the wind struggled to tear holes in the churning cloud, rain fell heavily on his upturned face still, but they were safe, the storm could not reach them here. The wind howled at the loss of its prey and Jarris smiled. He liked to outwit the skies.

* * *

Night gathered quickly, and the great lamps were lit early. Rhom had been safely disembarked and was stabled comfortably; the people had dissipated quickly, but with gratitude at reaching Serrat safely.

They were a merry group at supper that evening. Mareesha and Eenis had prepared a feast in celebration of reaching Serrat, in honour of Sir Brudloc, and in relief that one more day would see them at Cave.

Their friends, Billit, a baker, and his family, joined them, and there was much talk around the table; of the storm, the town, the year's trade, but mostly they talked about the passing of King Tenelon, and what it meant to Zirrus and the other Lands.

Sir Brudloc spoke knowledgeably for one so young, and the others listened closely. It was Sir Brudloc's mission to Winter in Ashkanna, and then escort Queen Elenes back to Great Court for King Tenelon's funeral after first thaw. He had left Great Court in nervous uproar, he said, and the mood could only remain unsettled until the birth of the queen's child. Mareesha shifted uncomfortably in her seat as they spoke of the child.

The boys were on deck with the sons of Billit and his wife, and Shaeli sat with their daughter Meri, stringing beads in Mareesha's room, in case one of the babies woke. Meri was close to Shaeli's age and the two were good friends, though they met only twice a year, and they sat close together, sharing popcorn and secrets, importantly checking the twins far more often than was necessary. Shaeli told Meri about the wand, after Meri swore an oath to the goddess Aa'liu to keep the secret, and Meri's eyes grew huge as she heard the story. She looked fearfully over her shoulder as if magic would sneak up and grab her, and later they fell asleep on the big bed as the adults talked long into the night.

Before Sir Brudloc left, Mareesha insisted he come and see the twins. He was a little puzzled, but politely accompanied her. The babies were duly admired, but as he turned to leave, Mareesha stopped him with a hand on his arm.

"Sir Brudloc," she began, her eyes on Shaeli and Meri in her bed. "I wish you to give a message to the queen, when you next see her. I..." she stopped uncertainly, looked at him and started again. "You know, I think, that Irinesta and I were friends many years ago." Sir Brudloc nodded and she continued. "I am greatly concerned for her. I know how much she loved Tenelon, and losing him will be very hard for her."

Sir Brudloc nodded again, and tried to speak reassuringly. "That is so," he said. "Yet she has much support, and the coming babe to sustain her."

Mareesha dropped her eyes. "That is true," she said softly.

"She seemed to be coping when I left. She is pale, but carries her burden well, I think. My worry is that she must wait for the Wintering to be over before the funeral can take place. Every noble in every Land will come, and none may travel until first thaw." His mind turned to the mission ahead. He had scant time to reach Ashkanna before the Wintering. "I will gladly deliver your message, good lady, though I'll not see my cousin until the spring, when the worst of it will be over."

Mareesha mumbled an agreement and then looked back up at the young knight. He had a good, strong face; handsome, the face of a nobleman. His colouring was unusually dark, even for one of the Romynnii, but she could see something of Irinesta in the green of his eyes and the slight copper sheen on his dark hair. It was a good face, a trustworthy face, and Mareesha smiled at it.

"Irinesta will have need of her family and friends in the days to come. Tell her I wish I could be there with her, and am thinking of her. Tell her..." She stopped, unsure of what she should say. There was so much she *wanted* to say. "Just tell her that Mareesha and her family are safe and well. The children, the twins," she glanced at the sleeping babies, "tell her all is well. And Sir Brudloc?"

"Yes?"

She looked piercingly at him. "Protect her. She will have enemies, now."

His eyes narrowed and he frowned. "With my life, good lady. Do not worry. My cousin will be well protected."

Mareesha nodded, and thanked him. She would have to trust that those closest to the queen would keep her safe.

When Sir Brudloc left, she begged he not forget her message. He bowed and gave her his assurance that he would remember. He would leave for Ashkanna before sunrise; like them, he raced the Wintering.

Later, as Mareesha lay in bed, she thought momentarily of more direct contact with Irinesta, but she disregarded the idea. It was too dangerous. The last time she had taken the tools from their box something had invaded her; a black wind that had swept her mind away, and she felt sure the two were somehow connected. She shuddered, remembering the draining, helpless feeling, and she rolled over and huddled against Jarris' back. She thought of the morrow and felt a calm drift through her. *Tomorrow we reach Cave,* she thought. *The gods be praised.*

Mareesha slept more easily that night than she had for a full Moon.

* * *

Midday found them halfway to Cave.

They had breakfasted with Billit at the bakery in the dark, and in the half-grey light of dawn they had lifted. As they flew from Serrat, they heard hoof beats clattering on the road beneath them and the whinny of a horse, and they looked down to see the shadowy figure of Sir Brudloc, arm raised in farewell, and they'd waved back. Eenis had secretly given her precious quilt as a gift, but Sir Brudloc exposed the secret, loudly proclaiming his thanks. She tried to hush him, but they all heard, and felt varying degrees of surprise; Jeth the least, the children the most, and at the end of the thoroughfare they parted ways, Sir Brudloc following the road east to Meoro Pass and the Trader flying north, going where no road lay.

The land between Serrat and Cave was rugged. Enormous boulders lay on the ground, and few trees survived in the harsh conditions. As the afternoon passed, they flew above a wide valley, its centre cut by a tumbling stream, the mountains on each side growing higher with each passing league. The boulders grew more prevalent until they were jammed together and on top of each other, a mass of rock upon rock. This was the Valley of Stones and they were almost home.

It was nearly impossible to traverse this region on foot. During the Wintering, the land lay frozen under a thick blanket of ice and snow, and below the deep drifts treacherous rocks with hungry teeth sat in wait. Walking here even during the year led to countless dead-ends, and trying to clamber over the boulders and rocks was to invite a landslide, a broken limb, or neck. There were tales of strangers arriving at Cave; a lost traveller; a small band of young men testing their courage, but this happened seldom, and once the Wintering set in, any soul unfortunate to be in the mountains would surely perish.

The stream, too, hid countless dangers, boulders hanging their feet in its path, sticking ragged faces from the tumbling waters, or dropping sheerly away, creating falls and gushing rapids. All this created a natural defence for Cave, a defence that had never been needed, yet the traders liked the security and privacy the landscape provided. They saw so many people during the year that it was a comfort to be with only their Fleet family while the Wintering raged across the Land.

Shaeli began to recognise different outcrops as they flew through the Valley of Stones. Some of the rock-falls towered over the Trader, and she and the boys called out the names of the odd-shaped edifices as they were sighted. Shaeli didn't know many of their names, but Tarkoda knew them all; the Bird, the Drell, the Castle, the Horse, the Turtle, the Swan, one long series of rocks named the Dragon; dozens more.

The storm of the night before had swept on, but it had left a heavy sky overhead like a forgotten grey cloak. A light wind blew at their backs, and Mount Zerrinius loomed ahead, filling the sky with gigantic shoulders and a proud, snow-capped head. The ground around them rose up to meet it, and the Trader, too, rose higher. The air grew colder and the sky darkened as the sun dropped heavily to the west beneath the weight of the leaden skies.

They all stood on the top deck as they flew up over the last ridge. It was a huge wall of rock, rising high across the end of the valley, cut in two by a silver knife of waterfall. The Zoi strained at their ropes as they pulled the Trader up and over the ridge.

The Valley of Stones was behind them, and before them lay the Long Lea, a vast field laying like a welcome mat beneath the mouth of Cave. Dark shadows huddled over the meadow, but beyond, at the feet of Mount Zerrinius, the ledge outside Cave was still lit by the sun. The Zoi cried out, their voices echoing across the empty Lea as clouds covered the sun once more.

They cheered and hugged one another, then hurried off to prepare for the final landing of the year, until only Jarris and Shaeli were left on the top deck. They flew silently over the Long Lea, its gardens and grasses dead and brown, watching Cave draw closer as the light faded.

Shaeli wandered over to the stairs and looked back over the Valley of Stones. Another gap opened in the clouds and a few pale rays shone through as Jarris came up behind her, resting a hand on her shoulder, and together they looked at the last sunshine they would probably see for three Full Moons. Suddenly, a black shape flew across the patch of open sky. It was outlined against the sky for only a moment, and then it disappeared into the clouds.

Shaeli felt her father's hand tighten on her shoulder, and she heard him gasp. She turned and looked up at him.

"What was it, Da?" she asked, her voice tiny. "It was so high."

Jarris shook his head. He was lost for an answer. A small knot of fear lodged deep in his chest.

"I don't know, Mouse." He tried to smile reassuringly at her, but was unable to reassure himself. "Perhaps there are some dragons left in the World after all. Let's not worry about it now. Go and tell everyone it is time."

Shaeli shrugged and ran down the steps.

Jarris gave a last look to where the strange thing had disappeared into the clouds. He knew of nothing that flew so high, or so quickly. For all he knew, it may well have been one of the lost dragons. He shook his head again, and cast the sight, for now, from his mind.

The mouth of Cave was upon them.

* * *

CHAPTER SEVEN

It was almost dark inside, but here and there, Warlock light still clung to outcrops. Voices called greetings from the shadows of a small shaft just inside as they flew slowly towards the first curve, the roots of the mountain surrounding them, the soft tinkle of running water below.

The family had gathered once more on the fore-deck, their voices hushed until they rounded the last corner, then the golden light at the end was sighted, the closeness of the tunnel was left behind, and they were surrounded by space and light as Cave opened before them, vast enough to hold a small town comfortably within its stony embrace. Cave stretched its arms wide in greeting and smiled a glittering smile from a thousand flames, the cavern yawning above, its heights shrouded in thick shadow. Scattered throughout were gigantic stalagmites of extraordinary colours, some joined to the stalactites hanging above to form glittering columns, and here and there were other tunnels, most leading into smaller caves used for storage, but one, far down at the back, led to the Wintering cave of the Zoi. A couple more, infinitely mysterious and forbidden to every trader, led into the endless catacombs that lay under Mount Zerrinius.

On their left, a natural spring had created a wide pool. From this spring-pool, a stream ran through a channel across the sandy floor, following the winding tunnel back out to the mouth to fall from the large flat rock into a series of small pools and waterfalls to the Long Lea, where it meandered across the meadow to fall into the Valley of Stones. The knife of waterfall which cut the last ridge before the Lea and the stream which had flowed beneath them in the Valley of Stones began as a spring of cool clear water inside Cave and emptied into the River Zerrin somewhere to the south-west.

Behind the spring-pool was the meeting place, beyond glowed huge pits filled with fire, and huddled on a rise overlooking pool and fire-pits were the Wintering huts of the old ones. A well-worn path separated the meeting place and the huts, and although Cave was filled with activity and warmth, most of all it was filled with the ships of the traders. They were moored row upon row, two to a Landing, different shapes and sizes, each balloon coloured to proclaim the Trader's name; Red Arrow moored with its sister ship, Green Arrow; Golden Eagle, the Head Trader's ship; Blue Dolphin, salty still from its time on the Starisles; Little Moon beside its sister Crescent; Running Bird, Blue Snake, White Star, Sky Lark, Rainbow, Red Feather, Silver Hawk, dozens more of every colour and pattern. This was the Fleet in all its glory, a carnival of colour against the rock backdrop.

Many arms and voices were raised in greeting as the Zoi guided them to their own Landing, and they floated easily to place and moored. The whole family spilled down the stairs, Mareesha and Eenis holding a baby each, and there was much hugging and kissing and slapping of backs as the traders gathered to greet the last of their ballooning family.

The twins were admired, clucked over, congratulated upon their arrival in the World and Shaeli noted that although none of the old women pinched *her* cheek, the twins certainly had a double helping. Neesha set up a loud wailing after one overly affectionate squeeze, and the women laughed and complimented Mareesha on the babe's strong voice. Shanna lay with eyes wide, unaffected by the noise.

Wyshka came through the crowd and hugged them all in turn, smiling as her tall sons leant to kiss her, delightedly admiring the two babies; listening, somehow, as they all spoke to her at once. Kirrit of Red Arrow ran up and hugged Shaeli, grinning widely.

Jeth and Jarris unharnessed the Zoi, and the family went to farewell them. It was time for them to leave for the Wintering with the other birds.

Jarris put a hand on the shoulder of his lead bird, spoke a quiet word of thanks for his loyal service, and he and Jeth went through the birds, touching each one. They came back to stand before the great birds, then went down on one knee and bowed their heads, and the lead bird lowered his head also. The rest of the family knelt and bowed in the traditional farewell, and the other Zoi followed, until each head was bowed gracefully and they faced each other in mutual respect. Then the Zoi straightened, spread their wings, and flew to the back of Cave to the tunnel that led to their own, private cavern. No trader was permitted down this tunnel, and the birds required nothing from the traders during the long frozen Moons. Although everyone wondered what their cave was like and how they sustained themselves, none would think of invading the Wintering cave of the birds who were their livelihood throughout the year.

Joints of meat hung over the fire-pits and the smell of them roasting filled Cave, and after the initial greeting the traders moved to begin preparation for the Winter Feast, traditionally held on the night the last Trader arrived. This year, Purple Leaf was the last to arrive.

Mareesha asked Jarris to bring down the babies' basket, and she left the twins with Wyshka while she and Eenis raided their stores for the tastiest items and a barrel of wine. Tarkoda and Andos ran off to reacquaint themselves with their friends, most of whom they had not seen since the last Wintering, and Dari stood looking around for a while, then wandered off by himself. Shaeli, Kirrit and three other girls sat with Wyshka, looking at the twins, but as they did very little, the girls soon ran off to watch the preparations for the Feast.

Long tables lay behind the fire-pits with low benches framing them, the wood worn smooth by centuries of use. Soon they could not see the wood of the table between the laden bowls and platters that were placed upon them, and as the joints were taken, juices dripping, to a massive, wooden block for carving, the last of the traders gathered for the Feast.

Plates and bowls were filled with the finest foods any Land had to offer and they ate until they could eat no more. As the fire-pits died down, more fire rocks were added until the darkness was held back once more, and the children settled themselves on pillows and blankets as Mareesha opened her last casket of special wine, saved since the day she and Jarris were wed. Voices faded as Taffka, head of the Traders, stood to speak.

He was a tall man, taller, even, than Jarris. His shoulders were broad as a horse's and held as much strength, and his father had been Head Trader before him, but this was not the reason for his leadership. He had a way of speaking softly, saying little, yet his words held great wisdom, and his slow, quiet way belied a quick and cunning mind. His observations were keen, and his dedication to the well-being of the traders unquestioned. It was he who negotiated with the heads of the Lands to determine trader's rights and tariffs; he who knew the cargoes and approximate routes of each balloon; he who would travel to Great Court to represent the Fleet at the funeral of King Tenelon.

The Fleet sat quietly, listening as Taffka spoke of the year's trade, respectfully thanking the gods. He listed the names of those who had died, and of those born since the last Wintering, and Shaeli's family smiled proudly as the names of Reneesha and Roshanna were added to the Lists of Traders. They toasted the closing year and a safe Wintering, and tradition was satisfied, yet Taffka remained standing, as they had known he would. There was more to be said.

Taffka waited, thoughtfully stroking his beard as he looked at them, each face familiar, each character clear to him. Good traders all, loyal and brave almost to the last.

"Two days ago," he began, "Yellow Star brought the news that King Tenelon had died." He waited while expressions of sadness murmured through the crowd. "Sad and grievous news it was, and though we knew that Green Fever had taken hold, I know we had hoped for some miracle that would save our king. But it was not to be. He is gone, and our loss is great." Taffka bowed his head a moment, and when he looked up again he saw the brightness of tears in many eyes, and was not ashamed of his own. Many times had he shared tezz or a meal with King Tenelon, and he felt the loss of a friend as well as a king. "At first thaw, Golden Eagle will travel to Great Court to attend the funeral, and to determine what this tragedy means to us, and to the Realm." Another murmur ran through the assembly, this time of concern. Taffka held up a hand and the voices were hushed. "We shall know of the babe our queen carries by then, and who will guide the Realm in its name."

Again he looked at each anxious face, his eyes lingering on Mareesha, her sorrow painfully obvious. She had known the king even better than he, and he tried to catch her eye to offer some reassurance, yet, oddly, she avoided it. He spoke again.

"Raise your glasses, then, and drink to our fallen king and the health of this most precious babe. Pray the gods keep it safe."

Mareesha drank, and prayed harder than any.

* * *

Later, after the remains of the Feast had been cleared away and sleepy children had been carted off to their beds, the traders drifted into small groups around the fire-pits. They talked of King Tenelon; of who would rule in the name of the child; of who would rule if, by chance, it did not live. The name of the Princess Virrisian was mentioned many times. They talked as the night melted into the earliest hours of the next day; comparing the year's trade; hearing of the year passed at Cave by the old ones and their young companions; the harvest from the gardens on the Long Lea; talking of myths and legends and kings and queens of long ago, until, one by one, the groups diminished, soft voices called goodnight, candles were extinguished, lamps blown out. Darkness crept back to hover stealthily around the edges of the abandoned fire-pits.

Jarris climbed the steps, weary, but content. They had reached the safety of Cave for another Wintering, and those he loved were all under one, cavernous roof. He checked on Shaeli as he passed, crept in to tuck the covers more tightly around her and kiss her forehead.

He expected Mareesha to be sleeping, too, and was surprised to find a lamp still burning beside the bed, yet Mareesha was not upon it. She was sitting in the rocker beside the cot, staring intently at the babies. He was puzzled, and called her name. When she turned towards him, he saw her face was haggard and awash with tears, and, after a moment, he understood. He opened his arms to her and she rose and stumbled into them, weeping anew. He hushed her and held her for a long time, yet he did not know the words that would bring her comfort.

* * *

Dari paused outside his aunt and uncle's door, listening to Mareesha crying before he continued on to the stairs. He did not know what she was crying about and he did not much care. They concerned him as little as he concerned them, and he had other things on his mind.

Shifting the cake he had stolen to his other hand, he felt for the railing to guide him up the stairs to the deck. He enjoyed being the only one up at night, creeping about the Trader while they all slept, sneaking in to steal some food and roam outside.

It bothered him, being in the air all the time. There was so much that could go wrong and they could all be killed in a moment, but he seemed to be the only one made nervous by this fact; his mother had brushed aside his concerns, and his father had laughed at his fear, actually laughed. Storms in particular terrified him, the thunder echoed mockingly in his head, but down on the ground, one had so much more control.

He had seen some interesting things in his dark roamings, made all the more exciting by knowing how much it would frighten his mother, and he grinned to himself as he crossed the Landing and went down the stairs.

There was no one about, but he went from shadow to shadow until he reached the dark place behind the old ones' huts, then he sat down to eat his cake. Stolen food always tasted so much better. He sat and brooded for a while, and when he had finished eating and brooding, he rose and slipped along the line of huts, pausing here and there, listening at doors, stopping to watch an old couple drink tezz in their beds.

He had almost reached the last building, a bigger structure where the Warlocks slept, when he tripped over something. There should have been nothing in his way – he'd hung around here earlier when they were readying for the feast – but something was there now and he sprawled on the path as someone let out an oath. Before he could raise his head, he was pulled to his feet and a hand slapped him hard across the face.

"What are you doing here, boy?" a voice said; a man's voice, but high and petulant. "Why are you sneaking about?"

Dari smelled the sour-fruit smell of stale wine, and the hand holding his collar shook him. He was cuffed again and pushed away.

"Get away before I smite you," said the man.

Dari stumbled, picked himself up and backed away. He bolted around the corner of the Warlocks' hut and did not stop until he was in the shadow beneath Purple Leaf's Landing, his cheek hotly numb from the blows he had been given. When he looked back he saw the man emerge from behind the huts and stagger down to the spring-pool.

It was Garrit, the High Warlock's newest apprentice.

***

CHAPTER EIGHT

When Shaeli opened her eyes the next morning and looked out her window, she was surprised to see the tip of a stalagmite and dark shadows behind it.

Where's the sky? she thought, and then she remembered; they were at Cave, and she was meeting Kirrit after breakfast. She threw off the covers, shivering as she dressed, then took a scarf, jacket and hood from behind the door, tied on her amulet and ran down the hall to the kitchen where the lamps were burning brightly, but Andos and Tarkoda were the only ones there, eating big bowls of creamy porridge. She took a bowl from the warm stove-top and joined them at the table, sprinkling a generous spoonful of brown sugar on top. Her mother had made it, she decided; Eenis' always had lumps. The boys finished and rinsed their bowls.

"See you later," said Tarkoda, picking up a bundle from beside the door.

"Where are you going?" she asked.

"Me and Andos are going fishing at the end of the Lea," he said. "I told Mam. We'll be back for lunch." He grinned. "*With* lunch." He looked at Andos. "Right?"

"Right," he answered.

"Let's go, the others will be waiting," Koda said, and they shouldered their bundles and left.

Shaeli finished her porridge and went upstairs, and as she crossed the gap to the Landing, she thought of what Sir Brudloc had said: the more familiar you were with something, the less you feared it. She turned and looked down at the tiny gap. It was silly, really, to be afraid of something so little. She would not fall, *could not,* even from the Landing, unless she tripped down the steps.

Pink Swan Trader was moored beside theirs, and she looked over to see if anyone was watching, then, holding on to the rail, she boldly stepped over the gap, turned, and stepped back. She let go of the rail, and stepped over, turned, stepped back. Again and again she stepped over, from Trader to Landing to Trader, unafraid for the first time since the day in the terrezza tree. She jumped over one last time, smiling proudly to herself, and then she went down the stairs. She could see Kirrit waiting with Driss, Bonn and Shylo beside the spring-pool.

There were few adults around this morning. Some of the old ones sat drinking tezz close to the warmth of a fire-pit, and she passed a group of mothers sitting on blankets spread beneath a Trader, supervising toddlers and young children. Kirrit's mother, Delphi, a round, buxom lady, sat with them nursing a large, fat baby. Another, about a year older, clung to her knee, shyly watching the other children play, and the bright, copper curls of Kirrit's three-Winters brothers were among the noisiest group. Delphi's family was one of two that included twins in its numbers. Three now, with her new sisters. She stopped to see the baby she remembered as a skinny, wrinkly babe of six weeks.

Tajindi sat on his mother's knee, calmly watching the little crowd. His huge eyes, unbelievably blue, turned to her as she leant down, took his hand and said a soft hello. He regarded her solemnly for a moment and then his chubby face broke into a huge dimpled grin. He reached out a fat fist, patted her cheek and gurgled loudly. Shaeli laughed.

Delphi smiled fondly at him. "It seems Tajindi remembers all those cuddles you gave him last Wintering, Shaeli," she said.

Shaeli smiled broadly – she liked Kirrit's mam – and she chatted to her as Tajindi snuggled against Delphi's generous bosom. The tiny girl, Mimsy, still held tightly to her mother's skirt, and hid her face against Delphi's knee every time Shaeli looked at her.

"You better go, Shaeli," Delphi said after a while, looking over at her second-eldest daughter. "I think Kirrit is about to explode."

Shaeli nodded and said goodbye to the women and Tajindi, who smiled again, showing pearly teeth. She ran over to Kirrit, who stood hands on hips, her head tilted to one side, lips pursed.

"About time," she said. "I thought you were going to play with Mam instead of us."

Shaeli laughed. "Don't be silly. I was looking at Tajindi." She smiled a greeting at the three other girls who stood behind Kirrit. "He *is* nice, Kirrit."

Kirrit's frown faded a little, and she nodded. "*I* know, he's very nice, but we'll be stuck with him all Wintering, once the storms set in." She threw her arms wide. "Let's do something. Outside."

"Fine then. Let's go," Shaeli said, and taking Shylo's arm, she walked around the spring-pool, followed by Driss and Bonn. Kirrit stood still for a moment and then ran to catch up.

The five girls had become good friends during the last Wintering. Driss of Blue Snake Trader was seven and the oldest; her sister, Shylo, Shaeli, Kirrit, and Bonn of Little Moon were all around the same age.

They passed the fire-pit where the old ones sat, Wyshka among them, and she called for Shaeli to come over. The four girls stood watching as Shaeli kissed her grandmother's cheek and held a short conversation, nodding her head vigorously. She waved goodbye as she ran back to join her friends.

"Sorry," she said breathlessly. "Wyshka wants to make us lunch. I said we would."

Driss clapped her hands. "Good for you, Shaeli," she said.

Bonn, her long, blonde plaits swinging, danced around the group. "Wyshka's for lunch," she piped. "But what are we going to do until then?"

"Anything," said Kirrit. "As long as it's *outside*. Let's go." And she turned and led them past the fire-pits and on up the slope.

To their right lay the tiny, wooden huts of the old ones, and to their left was the rocky amphitheatre where formal meetings took place. Shaeli looked back over her shoulder to the mouth of the main tunnel, now far behind them. Only a few Landings lay between the amphitheatre and the main tunnel on this side of Cave, and the Trader's bright balloons were rippling in a breeze not felt on the ground, a breeze brought in by holes high in the roof, small tunnels which led up to the side of the mountain above.

They reached an opening in the rock wall and entered a small tunnel, wide enough for three of them to walk abreast. The golden light of Cave faded behind them and the walls narrowed above, until, in most places, they met overhead, forming a peaked ceiling. Occasionally, the thin cleft between the walls went on and on, up into the darkness, and it was a favourite pastime of the older boys to explore these shadowy crevices. Warlock lights were scattered around the walls to light the way, and once or twice a chilly gust blew down from above and the lights flickered, sending shadows dancing along the walls. This shortcut led in an almost straight line to the main tunnel, only two sharply-angled turns close to the centre marring its course, and from its lightning-bolt shape it took its name, the bolt tunnel.

The tinkling of the spring stream met them as they emerged, and they ran to the entrance and out onto the ledge, looking out across the Long Lea, feeling the harshness of the imminent Wintering on their cheeks after the warmth of Cave. The dull sky hung heavily, and they stood, undecided, sobered by the sight of the weighty clouds, watching the wind wash mournfully across the brown grasses and empty gardens of the Lea, their breath puffing out in little white clouds.

"Dragon breath," murmured Shaeli, and at Kirrit's upraised eyebrows, she gave a demonstration. "See," she said. "Dragon's breath." And they all stood giggling and puffing out steamy "dragon breath".

Three teenage girls came out of the tunnel and walked across the stepping stones studding the spring stream's course beneath the overhang and went on down to the Lea. They watched them go, and then sat down on the ledge, breathless.

"We might have seen a dragon last night," Shaeli said, as casually as she could.

The others exploded with expressions of disbelief.

"Oh, you did not."

"Who did?"

"There's no such thing anymore. Da said they're all gone."

"Where?" This was from Kirrit.

"Out there," said Shaeli, pointing out over the Lea. "Me and Da saw *something*." She frowned and her voice rose. "It was dark, and pointy, and flying right up in the clouds. And it went fast, really fast." Her pointy chin thrust out, her face reddened and her hand went to where her amulet lay under her coat. "Even Da didn't know what it was. He said for all he knew it *might* have been a dragon, so there." She turned and ran back to the tunnel mouth, sitting down with her back to her friends, hands clenched around her knees.

The others were silent for a moment, digesting this – it was clear that Shaeli was serious, and traders, as a general rule, did not lie. Kirrit walked across to Shaeli and squatted down beside her, the other three close behind.

"Sorry, Shaeli," said Kirrit, taking her hand. "We thought you were joking, didn't we?" She looked at the others, who nodded, but Shaeli pulled her hand away and ignored them. "Tell us again," Kirrit soothed. "When was this?"

Shaeli wasn't mollified. "Last night," she said coldly, not looking at them. "Just before we got here." She flapped a hand at the Lea. "Out there. A long way away. But we *saw* it. Me and Da."

"But what did it look like?" asked Bonn, her blue eyes wide.

Shaeli looked at her knees. "Well, it was big and dark, and we only saw it for a moment, but it *might* have been a dragon."

"Imagine," said Kirrit, a gleam in her dark eyes. "Imagine if the dragons came back. Mam said that there were lots living in the northern part of the mountains once." She looked up at the tunnel. "Over behind our mountain somewhere. They had their own cave, just like us."

"Where did they go?" asked Shylo.

Her sister replied. "They just went. A long, long time ago." Driss frowned. "Nobody knows for sure what happened to them, but Da said the elves were angry, 'cause they were friends with the dragons."

"Oh, that's sad," said Shylo. "I would have liked to see a dragon." Then her face brightened. "But maybe it was a dragon, one that's come back, that Shaeli and Jarris saw. That would be so exciting."

"But won't they eat us?" Bonn asked, a little fearfully, her voice trembling, and they giggled. Bonn not only had the dragons alive and well, but hungry for little girls, too.

Shaeli didn't want to laugh with them. She buried her face in her knees.

"There's the boys," Driss said suddenly, pointing down at a dozen, pole-carrying figures approaching a thick stand of willow trees.

The spring-fed stream wandered snake-like across the Lea, joined by other small streams along its course, and not far down its length lay the year-huts of the old ones. Past the year-huts, a large stand of willow trees sheltered a wide pool, and the group of boys disappeared inside the bare branches. Shaeli stood up and walked back outside, her anger fading.

"Koda said they were going fishing at the other end," she said.

Kirrit snorted. "Alvaro won't let them go that far. Not with the sky like it is." Alvaro, her eldest brother, was leading the fishing expedition, and she looked up speculatively. "I expect it'll rain before lunch. Maybe even first snow."

The others eyed the clouds, too; the traders lived so much in the sky that most of the children read the weather as second nature, and they peered knowledgeably at the sky and agreed on the rain, but Driss and Shaeli said they didn't think they would see first snow.

As they waited to see if the boys would emerge from the other side of the willows, Shaeli looked sideways at her friends and decided she would probably forgive them. She asked if they thought you could smell snow and Shylo giggled, her freckled face turning pink, as if she found the question enormously funny. Bonn began to giggle at Shylo and Driss rolled her eyes and shook her head at her younger sister. What Shylo found highly amusing, Driss, invariably, did not. Though the two had identical dark curls and deep brown eyes, their temperaments were very different.

Kirrit was thinking seriously about the question, her head tilted to one side, her eyes on the sky, several red curls which had escaped her hood laying brightly against her pale forehead. A few dark freckles spread across her nose, and in the years ahead the freckles would multiply, gathering together in secretive little clumps across her nose and cheeks. Her creamy complexion was at odds with a nature better suited to her auburn curls, and people often mistook her delicate appearance for a reflection of her personality, but none of the Fleet ever did; the impulsive, boisterous reputation of Red Arrow Trader was well known, and Kirrit was no exception.

"Maybe you *could* smell snow," she said at last. "If you practised. Let's try."

So they stood, chins out, nostrils flared, trying to smell first snow. Shylo giggled absently once or twice, but they soon tired of the game and their noses were starting to freeze.

When the boys didn't come out from the stand of willows, they knew they must have stopped to fish in the wide clear pond in the centre of the rippling branches.

Bonn and Kirrit both had brothers in the fishing expedition. Bonn's two brothers were teenagers approaching Cave year, and Kirrit had three brothers in the group; Wez and Beren, of eight and nine Winters, who were firm friends of Tarkoda and Andos, and Alvaro, fifteen, the eldest of the brood. This gave Kirrit six brothers, and with the three girls – Kirrit, the two year old Mimsy who had been clinging so tightly to Delphi's knee, and another, twelve – gave Red Arrow nine children, all red-heads, and made theirs the largest family in the Fleet. Shaeli wondered at the quiet natures of the youngest two, the sweet Tajindi and the shy, knee-clutching Mimsy, and she supposed that perhaps the family had run out of rowdiness by the time they were born. She looked at her friends and finished forgiving them for their earlier scepticism.

"We could go down and pick the last blackberries," she said innocently, and then laughed at the shocked faces that were turned towards her. "Wyshka told me there's some left in the patch behind the big boulder."

"*Shaeli.*" Kirrit's hands were back on her hips. "Why didn't you say so?"

"Well," she said. "I thought you might think I was joking."

Before they could answer she turned and ran to the stepping stones. Though it wasn't deep, and would barely cover their knees, the spring stream was icy cold, and she went slowly as she stepped from one mammoth rock to another, the surfaces smooth with many Winterings of passing feet. Kirrit's voice was raised in exasperation, and Shaeli grinned as she waited on the other side. They came across in single file, Shylo holding tightly to the back of Bonn's coat, her scarf trailing behind, almost in the water.

On the far side of the ledge, a path led downwards, and Shaeli again looked at the heavy clouds building over the Valley of Stones.

"Let's run," she said, and took off down the hill. Kirrit overtook her quickly, the others trotting behind.

The path fell smoothly, curving down to the right, the ledge above them, the scrubby mountainside to their left. As they reached the bottom, the ridge of mountain petered away, the path widened, and a small field opened out, the grass browned by the frosty air. This space was called first terrace, and a little waterfall spilled from the ledge above into a shallow pond at the end before flowing out the other side.

The girls were not allowed below first terrace, but they had no need to go much farther and Shaeli led the way across the grassy expanse. On the far side, a second path descended down to the Long Lea, but they turned off onto a well-used path and at the end was a boulder of gigantic proportions, behind it a large blackberry bush, bereft of most of its leaves, but showing clumps of ripe, black fruit. When they had finished the fruit that lay within easy reach, and scratched themselves trying to reach the berries higher up, they wandered back to the terrace where several large flat rocks made convenient seats.

They talked for a while of the past year; of sights seen and people met, and Shaeli and Kirrit told of meeting at a fair on Ashkanna; how they had eaten so many candy apples they had almost been too sick to watch the skylights.

The next year they would begin more formal lessons, but throughout this one they had all been taught the rudiments of reading, the ways of the World, the seasons, the names of the brightest stars, and the names and tasks of the gods. They went through the gods together in sing-song voices, the words learned by rote during the year, but holding little meaning yet in their young minds: the goddess Aa'liu, who governed the oceans, rivers and streams, and who understood the feelings of the people; the god of the skies, U'ee, who made the winds and storms and moved change through the World; the god of strength, Ettorr, who ruled the sun and the mountains; his sister, the goddess Arrell, moved the moon and the seasons through the World, and gave endurance to all things. Above them all was Merrom, mother of the World and all the plants and creatures that roamed it. The girls talked of these things and more as the soft breeze rose to a cold wind.

A low rumble stopped their prattle, and at the sight of the obviously impending rain they stood without comment. Voices came from the wider path down the hill, and they waited to see who was coming up.

As heads bobbed into view, and then bodies emerged, it was clear it was a large group. The three girls they had seen earlier were in the company of about fifteen other teenagers and some adults and old ones carrying a variety of tools and boxes.

Kirrit's elder sister, Maize – she had been born above a corn field – was among them. She nodded as she passed, but her attention, and that of the friend she walked arm-in-arm with, was drawn by the two boys who preceded them up the path.

Bonn rushed forward, and they saw the tall figure of her mother walking in the rear of the group. A thick plait, the exact shade as Bonn's, hung over one shoulder and fell to her waist. She leant down to embrace her daughter, and they walked hand-in-hand back up the slope to where the girls waited. Bonn's mother, Perlis, regarded their purple-stained fingers and lips.

"'Tis easy to see what you girls have been doing this morning," she smiled.

Another slow roll of thunder sounded overhead, and as one, each face turned to the sky.

"Where have you been, Mam?" asked Bonn as they followed the group back across first terrace.

Perlis, a Faunist like Mareesha, and daughter to Sahli'en, First Faunist, looked from the sky to her only daughter's face.

"Fixing a roof on one of the cottages, and mending a fence," she said. "We won't have too many chances." She looked up at the sky again. "The Wintering is almost upon us."

"Unfortunately," grumbled Kirrit, and Perlis laughed.

"I felt much the same way at your age, Kirrit," she said. "But now I see the Wintering as time to catch up with things." She smiled. "You wouldn't see much of your friends if it weren't for the Wintering, would you?"

"I guess not," Kirrit agreed. "But that's the *only* good thing."

Perlis laughed again, and as they reached the top of the path, the rest of the group began crossing the stepping stones. Perlis crossed with easy grace and the girls followed her with much less assurance, and as they reached the other side the rain began to fall. It was scant at first, falling in huge, fat drops, painting the ledge with dark spots, then the spots grew more numerous and began to join together, and they left the rain behind and went to see what Wyshka had made for lunch.

* * *

They were sitting at a table below the old one's huts eating portions of meat pie when the boys emerged from the bolt tunnel. They were in high spirits despite being wet and chilled, and Tarkoda proudly held up a big, spotted fish as he passed and Wyshka called her congratulations. The other boys called greetings to the old ones, but the girls were generally ignored and Wyshka chuckled to herself – how different things would be in ten Winters time. Olver caught her eye and winked, and she knew his thoughts mirrored her own, as they so often did.

Shaeli saw her, and smiled. Wyshka had been living with Olver for two Winters now, and they looked happy. Shaeli had heard her father say he worried less about his mother now that she had someone to look out for her and keep her company – and Olver was one of the Fleet's best storytellers, a definite advantage as far as Shaeli was concerned. She looked at the retired trader and he smiled, his sun-faded eyes crinkling at the corners, and she smiled back.

She looked down the table to where the other old ones sat engrossed in quiet conversation, feeling a little in awe of them. Well, not Kozett, so much, but the other three held the highest positions in the Fleet, after Taffka, and were much revered and respected by all.

Cave's First Faunist, Sahli'en, Bonn's grandmother, sat leaning forward, her chin resting on the tips of her long, thin fingers. Her brown eyes were fixed intently upon her spouse, Navez, who headed the Council of old ones, and she nodded her grey-streaked head, in obvious agreement with her husband. Her face, smooth and unlined for her age, was grave as she replied.

The Cave's High Warlock, Almarnoch, sat opposite Sahli'en, his chair pushed back from the table, the remains of his pie in front of him. His eyes were closed, the long, wispy beard and white hair obscuring most of his face, and his chin rested upon his chest. Though he gave every indication that he slept, everyone at the table, including the girls, knew that the High Warlock Almarnoch rarely missed a fraction of what went on around him – and often knew things he had no natural means of knowing. His wizened form held enormous power and his knowledge of Warlock magic was unsurpassed – in the Four Lands and on the Starisles, Almarnoch's name was mentioned among the greatest Warlocks in history, and they continually begged him to come and teach again at the Bay of Islands, but Almarnoch had had enough of teaching and travelling. He had been born a trader and said he would spend his remaining years as one of the Fleet.

The traders had needed a strong Warlock after the long-serving Adz had died, to weave the complicated Lift spell and the spell of protection over the balloons. Almarnoch had been known to say that while the Lift spell was hard work, he had the whole year to recover from it, with nothing more strenuous to do than give lessons and direct the other Warlocks in looking after the orchards. It was also his task to tutor those young traders undergoing their Cave year to see if any had true magical gifts, although few ever exhibited the gift that would enable them to become a Warlock, but Almarnoch kept looking. He said it was time another High Warlock came from trader stock.

As Shaeli studied the old man, his eyes opened and fixed upon her, pale grey and unreadable, the lips a thin line below the long, pointed nose and wispy moustache. She smiled nervously, and the Warlock's features softened and he smiled back. So changed was he that her smile broadened into a genuinely friendly grin, and she giggled when Almarnoch winked at her.

The others had been listening to Olver tell a story about a cluster of fairies he had seen once on Romynn, and Kirrit looked around at Shaeli's giggle, saw she was laughing at the High Warlock, and elbowed her in the ribs, thinking she was being disrespectful.

It was Almarnoch's turn to laugh. "No need for that, young Kirrit," he smiled. "Shaeli and I were merely becoming friends." His eyes twinkled at her, his voice as low as distant thunder. "Weren't we, Shaeli?"

Shaeli nodded, surprised to find it was the truth. She did feel she had found a friend in the old Warlock, and she flicked Kirrit a glowing smile as the Warlock spoke again.

"Tell your mother that the First Faunist and I will be over this evening." He glanced at Sahli'en, who nodded her agreement. "We wish to see your new sisters, and give them our blessings."

Shaeli nodded, powerless to widen her smile further, but Almarnoch's next words turned the smile into an O of surprise.

"Do not be scared at the meeting of the Trader's Council this evening," he said, his voice gentle. "I shall be there to lend strength, and all will be well."

She sat with her mouth hanging open as he settled back into his former position. Before he closed his eyes again, he added one more thing that astonished her even more.

"We shall have much to discuss, you and I," Almarnoch said, "about your wondrous find on the shores of Lake Marnis." He smiled again briefly, and shut his eyes.

Conversation had ceased around the table. Every pair of eyes turned from Almarnoch to Shaeli, who blushed under the scrutiny.

Wyshka saved her by briskly asking her to help clear the table. The old ones tactfully returned to their conversation, but the eyes of Sahli'en followed her as she placed mugs on a tray. She could feel Kirrit's eyes too, boring hotly into her back with unspoken questions.

As she stood with Wyshka in her little kitchen, unloading the tray, she wondered why she would have to attend the meeting, how Almarnoch had known about the wand, and why her grandmother did not ask her anything.

"Wyshka?" said Shaeli, after they'd finished clearing. "Will you be at the meeting tonight?"

"The old ones are always welcome at meetings, Shaeli," she said. "And, yes, I will be there. You may have need of me, too." She smiled and walked back outside.

Shaeli was grateful that her grandmother had not asked questions which she could not answer; her only problem now was how to avoid Kirrit's questions, but Kirrit only looked narrowly at her, and hushed the girls when they wondered aloud at Almarnoch's words. Shaeli squeezed her hand in unspoken thanks, and Kirrit frowned and changed the subject, but Shaeli caught them all looking at her strangely every now and then. It made her self-conscious and uncomfortable; as if she was at fault for something she could not explain. She did not much like the feeling.

* * *

CHAPTER NINE

Perlis found them after lunch as they sat by the spring-pool. They were making soap out by the tunnel mouth during the afternoon, she said, and the girls would be needed to help look after the little ones. Shaeli ran up to Mareesha, who contributed a supply of herbs and oils to perfume the soap, and was disappointed to find she was not going. She thought it was too cold for the twins out near the entrance, and was worried about them catching a chill.

Shaeli looked doubtfully at the tiny, relaxed baby sitting upon her mother's knee. Neesha had just been fed. Her chin rested drunkenly between Mareesha's thumb and forefinger, her eyes half closed, a drop of creamy milk poised to fall from her bottom lip, and Shaeli did not think she had ever seen anyone look less in danger of catching a chill, but she didn't like to say so. The baby suddenly opened her eyes wide and let go of an enormous burp. Shaeli giggled as her mother rubbed Neesha's back and told her she was a good baby.

"You wouldn't say that if *I* made that noise after dinner," Shaeli grinned.

Her mother smiled back. "I know of once or twice when you have, miss, and luckily you remembered your manners."

Shaeli giggled again as her mother carried the almost-sleeping baby to her cot, her arms hanging loosely, head slung back upon Mareesha's palm, her eyes a dark slit. She twitched as Mareesha lay her down, and her eyes closed. Shanna twitched in unison beside her, and her eyes fluttered open.

Mareesha sighed. "So much for *that* cup of tezz," she muttered, scooping out Shanna and handing her to Shaeli to bounce as she gathered the soap perfumes.

As Mareesha moved about the room, Shaeli gave her the message from Almarnoch. Mareesha nodded at the news of Almarnoch's visit with Sahli'en, and smiled when Shaeli told her how he'd hinted at the wand. Mareesha said Jarris had given the Warlock the wand the evening before, and told him where Shaeli had found it, but she shook her head at Shaeli's questions about being called to the meeting, wondering herself at Almarnoch's meaning.

Shaeli and her friends spent a busy afternoon, holding babies and chasing toddlers and singing songs and telling stories with some older girls. By late afternoon, when the last big pot was emptied, the collective patience of the baby-sitters had worn decidedly thin and they were relieved to hand the little ones back to their mothers. As the others disappeared down the bolt tunnel, the five girls hung back.

Shaeli was wondering for the hundredth time why she would be called to the meeting as Almarnoch had said she would; that it would be so, she had no doubt. She supposed it was about her wand, and didn't know whether to be excited or nervous. She peered down into the darkness of the main tunnel and stood up, brushing the sand from her hands.

"Let's walk back the long way," she said, and at their groans of protest, added, "The glow-worms might be out and it's good luck to be first to see them."

The grey light of the afternoon faded as they walked, then withered to a memory, the few Warlock lights dotting the walls as dim as banked embers. To their right, in the last drift of light from the rain-drenched tunnel mouth, there was a black smudge, as if the tunnel wall had been coloured with coal, the entrance to the cavern where their small herd Wintered, the smell of ancient dung drifting from it. The animals were still down on the Lea, but they would soon be brought up and the smell in this part of the tunnel would take on fresh pungency.

The tunnel consisted of three U-shaped bends between lengthy straights, and the sound of the stream on their left and the occasional drip from above accompanied them as they headed for the first of the long-burning oil lamps sitting between the path and the stream. They passed the first lamp, its yellow light making shadow patterns on their faces, and they could see the light of the next around the first of the bends. The second lamp was passed and they walked down the straight to where another lamp shone on the curve of the second bend, and they stopped for a moment, peering up into the darkness, but they couldn't see any sign of the glow-worms.

The glow-worms were an important part of life for the Fleet. At the beginning of the Wintering, eggs secreted deep into crevices of the tunnel roof hatched and the worms emerged to feast on insects, and by the time the Fleet left after first thaw, many of the glow-worms had already begun to weave their cocoons. The five girls had never seen the flying creatures which emerged from them, but they knew that the casings of their cocoons were collected and the fine thread unravelled and spun to be woven for the material of their balloons.

Along the straight, past the fourth lamp, Shaeli kept them amused with a funny tale from one of her Williver dreams. It was about a fairy named Ink who had the misfortune to fall in love with a butterfly, and the girls were giggling as they reached the last, left-hand curve. The light of the next lamp shone dimly around the corner, and then, suddenly, it was gone.

The girls stopped and clutched at each other. They peered into the darkness, then back towards the wavering, far-off light of the last lamp. Footsteps approached the tightly clustered little group and a shadowy figure loomed around the bend. Shylo squeaked, and Kirrit called out, trying to be brave, but her voice trembled.

"Who's there?" she said.

A faint echo rolled eerily around them, and they sighed with relief when a familiar voice rumbled from the dim figure.

"'Tis your father, miss, and what are you doing here, if I may ask?" The face of Baroz appeared behind the voice.

The girls grinned at Kirrit's huge, red-bearded father. Baroz's booming voice and frowning countenance should have been intimidating, but was not; they knew the loudness of his voice was overshadowed by the softness of his heart, and Kirrit walked over and took his large, gnarled hand in her small pale one.

"Hello, Da," she smiled, her head tilting. "We're looking for glow-worms, that's all." She swung the big hand and looked at him sternly. "You gave us a fright, Da, when the light went out."

Baroz laughed, and the echo bounced around the walls. "My apologies, miss, but it must be done. The worms do not love lamp-light. I heard your giggles and silly chatter, and knew it was you coming down our path. Once you walk around the corner, you will see the light of Cave." He straightened his face, and looked down at his daughter. "I fear Mam is looking for you, Kirrit. Something about eggs." Though he tried to look stern, one side of his mouth twitched. "It won't do to keep forgetting them. That's twice since we reached Cave."

Kirrit had the good sense to look suitably chastised and mumble an apology. Her father ruffled her hair, urged them to hurry home, and they watched his broad back until he reached the next lamp and motioned them away. They went round the corner where they could see the light of Cave far ahead, but suddenly Kirrit stopped. Bonn, unable to see properly in the almost-dark, bumped into her back. Shylo giggled.

"What's the matter?" asked Driss. "Why did we stop?"

They could just see Kirrit's pale face floating in its cloud of red hair, disembodied by her dark coat.

"I thought I saw something," she whispered. "Be quiet."

"Where?" asked Bonn.

"Up there," said Kirrit, pointing across the spring-stream and up towards the shrouded roof. "Near the top of that column."

"I can't see anything," complained Shylo. "Let's go."

"Ssh," hissed Shaeli, peering up to where Kirrit pointed. "What did it look like?"

"I'm not sure," Kirrit whispered back. "I only saw it for a moment. But it was *something*."

They squinted up into the darkness, the quiet sound of their breathing and the tinkle from the spring stream all that broke the silence until they gasped in unison. A bright yellow spot of light had appeared just to the left of where Kirrit had pointed. The girls froze. The only movement was Bonn slowly taking Shylo's hand, and Driss' mouth falling open.

They held their breaths as the spot grew and stretched. The colour changed from yellow to deep gold, as the head – for a head it was – dropped from an unseen hole. Its body, thin as a reed but soon to grow thick as a rope, unravelled further and further, lowering the head into the dark tunnel, floating downwards like a slowly falling streamer, and then swaying gently back and forth, the arc of its movement growing wider as more of its glowing body slithered from the hole in a ribbon of colour. It slowly changed from gold to bright orange to a dull, throbbing red, and the tunnel was bathed in an eerie, crimson glow. As it swayed, insects were drawn to its ever-changing light, and the worm snapped at them, chewing with tiny teeth, audibly sucking the juices from the creature's body. The girls shuddered as the worm spat the unwanted bits out onto the ground.

Driss nudged Kirrit and pointed up to where another worm had descended silently above them, this one a blue so dark they had not seen its light. It faded to pale indigo as they turned their faces up, the light mixing with the dull red of the first worm, giving their faces an odd, lilac complexion.

The blue-tinged worm snapped at a large brown moth that was drawn to its luminous body; the moth was captured, sucked in and chewed up, and as the creature spat out the masticated wings and body, the girls realised their danger. They tried to get out of the way, but the blob of rejected insect pulp hit Shylo on the shoulder and she let out a cry of disgust.

The glow-worms instantly stopped their sway and pulled their sinewy bodies back into their holes. The light in the tunnel returned to its former gloom and Shylo was loudly complaining about the chewed moth which clung stickily to her sleeve. The others tried to placate her, but Driss was annoyed and told her she was being a baby. Shylo began to cry softly.

"It wasn't my fault, Driss," she sniffed. "How would *you* like to have moth guts spat on you?"

"I wouldn't make such a fuss, that's for sure." Her sister spat the words, just as the glow-worm had spat the moth, and would have continued the tirade, but Bonn stopped her.

"It doesn't matter," Bonn said. "It's time we went home."

Kirrit nodded, thinking guiltily about the eggs. Shaeli was thinking about the meeting again. She thrust the thought away.

"Let's race to the spring-pool," she said, and she took off down the shadowy tunnel, the others close behind, the argument forgotten. The thudding echoes of their feet faded as the light brightened.

As they passed from the tunnel into Cave, Shaeli and Kirrit were shoulder to shoulder, Driss just two paces ahead. Bonn and Shylo did their best to keep up, but were gradually left behind. Someone called encouragement from a Trader; a woman filling water jugs by the side of the stream was quickly dodged; Kirrit jumped cleanly over the top of a game of marbles being played by three boys. Shaeli tried to keep up, but she was flagging, yet Kirrit ran effortlessly on, overtaking Driss, and shouting loudly to everyone they passed.

"We saw the glow-worms," she chanted. "We saw the glow-worms."

They had almost reached the pool when Shaeli heard a cry from behind. She looked over her shoulder and saw Bonn sprawled on the path, but she was grinning up at Shylo. When Shaeli turned forward again they were both sitting in the path, giggling foolishly.

She turned in time to see Kirrit reach the big flat rock beside the spring-pool, Driss just behind her. A dozen more steps and she was with them, panting as she threw herself down on the rock beside an exhausted Driss. Kirrit stood looking back to where Bonn and Shylo still sat laughing in the path. She was breathing a bit heavily, but generally unaffected by the long run. Kirrit could outrun all of them, even many of the boys, and it amazed Shaeli that her friend could run and run, with hardly a trace of tiredness.

She looked around at the fire-pits glowing brightly, the glow of lamps and candles reaching high up the glittering columns, the balloons floating above the Traders like painted apples in a tub. Groups of people were clustered around the fire-pits and tables, talking or working, small children tumbling around their feet, and a large crowd of teenagers sat laughing at the far end of Cave where the light faded into gloom.

On the other side of the spring-pool, where the floor rose up in a series of four arched terraces, several members of the Council and a few old ones were setting the table for the meeting. A fire-pit lay in the centre of the natural amphitheatre, and Taffka was talking with Sahli'en and Navez by the velvet-draped table where they would sit with Almarnoch tonight. As she watched, her father joined them and they began an earnest conversation, but she had little time to wonder about them. A groan drew her eyes to Kirrit's frowning face.

Delphi was striding towards them, and Shaeli thought she looked different somehow. After a moment she realised it was because she had no babies with her.

"Here you are," Delphi said, stopping in front of Kirrit, her hands moving to her broad hips.

Shaeli was reminded of the way Kirrit had stood this morning; apart from her father's red hair, Kirrit was very much like her mother. Delphi had thick, dark hair falling in a long braid over one shoulder, but her daughter had inherited her translucent skin, and her attitude.

"Yes, Mam, we're here," said Kirrit sweetly, and before her mother could speak she hurried on. "I'm sorry about the eggs, Mam, really I am. I saw Da in the tunnel, and he was pretty mad."

Shaeli raised her eyebrows at the way Kirrit had bent the truth, but Delphi was not fooled.

"You know as well as I do that your father gives no thought to such things. There'll be no going off and playing after dinner tonight, miss, nor any other night that you forget your chores." Delphi looked at her daughter piercingly. "Is that clear?"

Kirrit nodded contritely, and looked at her feet.

"Good," said Delphi. "Now say goodbye and come and help me with the little ones." She turned and walked back to Red Arrow.

With promises to meet in the morning the others ran off, leaving Shaeli sitting alone on the rock. Reluctantly she stood and began to walk towards home, knowing that after dinner the meeting would begin. She feared the thought of speaking before the Council, even if it meant she was allowed to keep her wand.

* * *

Mareesha and Eenis were in the kitchen when she entered, Andos and Tarkoda were sprawled on the rug, playing a game of cards, and Dari sat in a chair watching them. There was a pale bruise on one of his cheeks; apparently he had walked into a wall in the middle of the night on his way to the privy. The twins lay asleep in their big basket by the table and Shaeli wandered over and looked down at them.

They lay face to face, tiny hands entwined, breathing softly. Neesha snuffled and her mouth made sucking motions for a moment before she settled again into deeper sleep. Shanna remained still, only her lashes fluttering slightly against her rosy cheeks. Shaeli smiled at them, and softly stroked the joined hands.

Mareesha walked over and stood behind her, her hand resting on Shaeli's sun-bleached hair. Shaeli looked up at her.

"The babies are alright now, aren't they?" she asked.

Mareesha nodded. "They seem to be."

Shaeli nodded too, then she frowned and took Mareesha's hand.

"And you, Mam," she said quietly. "Are you alright too?"

Mareesha knelt down and hugged her. "I think so," she said, and hugged tighter.

* * *

"'Tis time to pack up your game," Eenis said from the stove a short while later. "Your fathers will be here to eat soon. They'll not want to be late for the meeting."

As she spoke, footsteps were heard on the deck, and by the time Jarris and Jeth entered the room, the table was ready.

Tarkoda was praised on his fine catch, the storm was discussed and the mad scramble up to Cave laughed over. Dari said he was glad he'd stayed inside.

Shaeli sat listening until her father asked her what she had done all day.

"We went down to the terrace. Wyshka told us where to find some berries," she said. She described their encounter with the glow-worms, and the boys regarded her enviously, laughing when she told them of Shylo's unfortunate splattering. She told them where they had seen the giant worms, and they planned to go down after dinner to try their luck.

Jarris and Jeth left soon after they finished the meal. Eenis did not wish to go to the meeting, for she was almost finished with the tapestry for Romynn, and Mareesha would not attend either. The boys hastily helped clear the table and then they also left the room; even Dari was interested in seeing the glow-worms.

Shaeli helped Eenis dry the dishes and then went and sat with her mother, watching as she fed Roshanna and lay her in the basket, the whole time listening for footfalls. She was beginning to think that Almarnoch had, for once, been wrong, and she had almost relaxed when the footsteps came. Her muscles tensed as the steps came down the hall. Shaeli moved closer to her mother.

Jarris smiled at her when he entered. "Shaeli is needed at the meeting, Mam," he said.

Mareesha nodded and patted Shaeli's hand. "There's no need to be nervous," she said. "Just do as your Da says. He'll look after you."

Eenis seemed surprised at the request, but asked no questions, at least not while Shaeli was in the room.

Shaeli took her father's hand, and he squeezed it and smiled. She smiled wanly back, her eyes as pale as her face.

"No need to be scared, Mouse," he said. "They only want to ask a few questions."

Shaeli nodded, but did not speak. She wanted to. She wanted to ask why the Council wanted *her*? Couldn't they just *look* at the wand? But she said nothing. She couldn't. There seemed to be something stuck in her throat. She asked the god Ettorr for strength as she went across the Landing and down the steps, trying to swallow the thing in her throat.

Jarris squeezed her hand again as they passed the spring-pool, and then they were entering the brightly lit space of the amphitheatre. Her courage almost left her as they walked across the floor to stand before the great table. Two huge candelabra cast light over the velvet cloth and the maps and papers scattered upon it.

"Here she is," said Jarris. He let go of her hand, patted her shoulder, and he stepped back a few paces.

Shaeli looked over her shoulder at him, panic in her eyes. She tried again to swallow the thing in her throat, to say something, but she could not. Jarris smiled and nodded encouragingly, and she looked up at the traders seated on the steps of the amphitheatre. Their eyes were all upon her and she felt impossibly small. She gulped and looked back at the table. The faces all looked so severe, so grim – Taffka, Navez, Sahli'en, Almarnoch – and she looked around again, trembling, her hands clutching the small bag of treasures at her waist, her heart drumming against her ribs, her breathing coming in shallow gasps. Every eye was directed at her, every gaze seemed to expect something of her. She felt like she was shrinking under the weight of their eyes.

Oh, if only they would stop staring, she thought. *If only they would* stop.

She looked nervously about, her heart beating in her ears, and she began to see that the faces looking at her were not unfriendly, merely serious. Wyshka and Olver smiled at her from the tier behind the Trader's Council, Kozett and other old ones nearby. The Faunists, all friends of her mother's, sat on the tier behind them, each regarding her kindly. The three Warlocks beside them were solemn and unsmiling, and Shaeli looked back at the old ones and was given many nods of encouragement. Her eyes ranged down to the bottom tier again. She knew all of the Trader's Council by sight, many by name, and Jeth smiled calmly at her as she spied him. Baroz, seated next to him, gave her a hearty wink. Her trembling subsided and she took a deep breath. The lump in her throat shrank a little, and she looked at the table where Sahli'en, Navez, Taffka, and Almarnoch sat. The sight of the Warlock calmed her, and when he smiled she was further reassured, just as he had said she would be.

She had gone over and over the finding of the wand, sure she would be asked to recite the tale of its discovery, so she was totally unprepared for the question that *was* asked of her. Her eyebrows rose, and her surprise was so obvious that Taffka thought she had not understood, and he repeated the question.

"What did you see in the sky last night, Shaeli," he said, "just before you reached Cave?" He spoke gently, and Shaeli answered without thinking.

"It was a dragon, Taffka," she said, and then she blushed as laughter rippled through the crowd. "Well, it might have been," she murmured, but her voice was lost amid the chatter that followed her statement.

She touched the objects in her amulet, and their familiarity gave her confidence. She became annoyed at the titters and amused looks now directed at her. Her brows lowered.

Taffka held up a hand, and the voices faded. Shaeli looked back at him, her lips pursed. In her annoyance she almost forgot to be frightened. Taffka asked her to tell them what it had looked like, so she described it to them, much as she had to her friends earlier that day. Taffka scrutinised every detail.

Yes, it was black. Yes, it was towards Serrat. Yes, it flew as high as an eagle. *Much* higher than Traders did. Round in circles they went, asking questions she did her best to answer, until finally she asked one of her own.

"Why don't you ask Da?" she said. "He was there too."

Taffka chuckled, but it was Almarnoch who answered.

"We have, Shaeli," he said. "Your father has told us all he knows, but there were some who could not quite believe what he said. He is fortunate you were with him, so there is no doubt that he saw something."

Shaeli frowned so hard her eyebrows almost met in the middle. Her annoyance flared from a spark to a flame. As if her father would make it up. Almarnoch smiled and replied as if she'd spoken aloud.

"We do not *disbelieve* him, Shaeli," he said. "'Tis just that such a thing has never been seen before, and we wonder what it could be." He looked up at the gathering. "We are mystified, and will ponder long on this matter."

Taffka thanked her for her help, and then Jarris came forward and took her hand. It was over.

She began to walk with her father back towards the spring-pool, but she stopped and looked back at Almarnoch, and then tugged at Jarris' sleeve. "But, Da," she whispered, "what about the wand?"

"The old ones have it," he said, and began to walk again. "I gave it to Almarnoch yesterday evening, and after studying it, he gave it to the Council, and they gave it to the old ones." He smiled down at her. "They will tell us when they have decided."

Shaeli's face fell. She was bitterly disappointed. The 'dragon' was the reason for her summons, not the wand.

Jarris, proud of the way she had overcome her fear and spoken at the meeting, told her so, and she smiled at him, but her good temper was unrestored. He knew she wanted the question of the wand resolved, and he wanted to find out what the High Warlock and the Council would decide too, yet he soon forgot about it. His thoughts turned quickly back to the thing he had seen in the sky.

* * *

CHAPTER TEN

Later, soon after the meeting had finished, Almarnoch, Sahli'en and Navez arrived at the Trader.

Shaeli sat sleepily in the corner, curled up with a milky tezz, ready for bed. The boys were already asleep, satisfied at seeing a glow worm in the tunnel after dinner.

Mareesha showed Sahli'en the twins, who lay sleeping in the big basket. Sahli'en admired them, and in their features found many similarities with their parents; Jarris' chin here, Mareesha's brows there, perhaps the lips also. Mareesha smiled proudly.

Almarnoch joined the women, and leant down to peer at the babies, his scruffy white brows drawn together. He asked for their names, and spoke them aloud, placing a thumb upon each tiny forehead, his gnarled fingers resting in their soft, dark hair. He spoke the formal blessing quietly, yet everyone in the room heard his voice and was touched by his words. When it was over Mareesha found herself wondering why she had been nervous about this visit.

"They are fine, healthy girls, Mareesha," said Almarnoch without turning. "I see vast differences in their characters, one so thoughtful, the other so impulsive. And something else..." His voice trailed away and he took his hands from their heads and stood, but his eyes did not leave the babies, and his countenance was deeply thoughtful.

Mareesha murmured something, glancing across the room to where Jarris stood, bolstered by his calm, blue eyes. She met Almarnoch's gaze with a composed smile as he turned and took her hands.

"Fine girls indeed," he repeated. He kissed one cheek, then the other, and whispered in her ear before releasing her. He spoke so softly that Sahli'en, who stood close by, could not hear. "The way ahead is dark and I cannot see far. Yet it *is* the right way, do not doubt it." His eyes held hers in a tight grip for an instant, and then he turned away and began searching absently for his tezz, his face serene and smiling as he asked for Shaeli.

Mareesha's composed smile had set like mortar with his words. She blinked, and started when Sahli'en took her elbow, but she recovered quickly, and moved to the table with the graceful Faunist. Only Jarris noticed the tightness of her smile.

Shaeli had watched from her chair, tired, but determined to stay awake, and when Almarnoch called for her she knew it *must* be about the wand. Her stomach filled with a thousand flutters as she stood and walked across the room.

Sure enough, Navez held a long thin bundle across his knees, and she knew it was the wand. She grinned at her father, and then looked expectantly at Almarnoch, yet it was Navez who spoke. She turned to the head of the Council of old ones.

"We have all looked closely at your wand, Shaeli, and found it of much interest," he said, his rough, square face serious, but kind. "You found it near Lake Marnis?"

Shaeli nodded. "Yes, Navez. It was stuck in the bank beside a little creek."

"Did you know what it was?" he asked.

"No. At least, not 'til I'd washed it."

He smiled. "And then?"

"I showed it to Da and Mam."

"That's good, Shaeli," he said. "Do you know why?" She shook her head and he continued. "Because it *is* an elf-wand, and sometimes they may hold danger, and old magic."

Eenis almost groaned. "I knew it," she said. Tension filled her face, and her right hand began to rub at her forehead. Jeth took the hand and held it.

Navez smiled reassuringly. "But that is *not* the case with Shaeli's wand, not the case at all. This one," he said slowly, tapping the bundle on his legs, "this one appears empty of all magic. A wand like this is made for a specific person, an elfin person, and they must be long dead to have lost such a prize." He tapped the bundle again. "And its gems are few. Without the right stones in their proper places, without the right wielder, it has no chance of creating any magic, nor any danger."

"You're sure?" whispered Eenis.

Navez turned to look at her. "Quite sure, Eenis," he said. "There is nothing to fear."

His voice was encouraging, and she was somewhat satisfied, yet she looked to Almarnoch for confirmation.

"I also say there is nothing to fear, Eenis." He looked intently at her. "We have studied it thoroughly. The wand is very old, and bereft of magic."

Eenis seemed finally satisfied. Her thin mouth curved into a miniscule smile.

Navez unwrapped the wand, and it glistened in the light of the lamps. The pale, pinkish metal shone in a hundred places, the gems reflected tiny shimmering prisms which danced on Navez's square face, and then on Shaeli's as he solemnly passed the wand to her. Her delight was plain. She beamed at them, hope shining brightly in her eyes.

"I can keep it?" she breathed. "Truly?"

"Yes, Shaeli," said Navez, smiling. "Truly."

Shaeli looked at the Warlock. Almarnoch nodded too, his eyes twinkling, and her face filled with pleasure. With sudden impulse she kissed his hairy, wrinkled cheek, and hugged Navez. Shaeli kissed them all, even Eenis, and held the wand up over her head.

"Thank you," she cried. "Oh, thank you, so much."

Almarnoch's voice halted her, and though he smiled, he was not yet finished, and she went to stand before him again.

"With possession of such an item comes responsibility, Shaeli," he said, peering intently from beneath wispy, white brows. "You must not take the wand from Cave, nor from Purple Leaf when the year begins again. Many people are greatly superstitious and would be frightened by such as this, and there are also those who would covet its jewels." He held the wand in his hands again, and Shaeli had no idea how it had come to be there. "I would recommend that you show it to no one outside the Fleet." He looked down at the wand and then back into her eyes. "Also," he continued, "we are intrigued by its etchings, and would like to study it further, if you will allow us."

Shaeli was astonished by the request. Imagine, the High Warlock asking *her* for permission. She nodded, dumbfounded.

"Of course," she stammered.

"I thank you," he smiled, "And, in return, with your parent's permission, and also if you desire, you may study elf-lore with us this Wintering."

She nodded again, this time eagerly, and looked at her father.

"I don't see why not," Jarris said, and looked at Mareesha. "As long as Mam agrees."

Mareesha smiled her agreement, and Shaeli clapped her hands and turned to face Almarnoch.

"Thank you, Almarnoch," she said, beaming at the old Warlock.

This was what he had meant this afternoon. She was thrilled, and tried to curtsey, as her mother had been teaching her, and he bowed his head in return, his eyes twinkling.

Soon after, she was taken to bed with her precious treasure wrapped and tucked tightly under her arm. She said goodnight to everyone, and as she skipped from the room, holding tight to Mareesha's hand, she did not notice the troubled eyes of Eenis following her. But of course, Almarnoch did.

* * *

That night, long after she had happily fallen asleep, Williver appeared in her dreams.

She could not remember when she had first begun to dream of the tall elf, and she never knew when he would appear. It seemed that he had always been a part of sleep for her, like night-time or the moon, and though she did not speak of him to anyone, he was a large part of her world. She thought of Williver as she thought of those she loved in the waking world, as real and important as any, and she knew his face as well as she knew her own, the high cheekbones, the slight cleft in his chin, the way his blue eyes crinkled when he smiled.

Tonight she walked with him in a cool, green glade, the edges scattered with dozens of blooms, a deep forest surrounding the bright clearing. They sat together under a gigantic, gnarled tree, and she told Williver about being allowed to keep the wand, and of the thing she had seen in the sky that had looked like a dragon. He listened with interest, his blond hair ruffled by a breeze she could feel in her own hair but not on her face, and then he told her the story of the elf-lady, Shahlita, and her dragon, Wipp.

The Lady Shahlita, he began, his voice drifting through the empty glade, *was famous throughout all the Lands for riding a dragon, and because she had the gift of understanding the animals and birds. Shahlita called all creatures friend, and would often bring an injured animal to your Faunists or our elven healers. She was one of the few who was given the gift of flying with the dragons, in the days when there were many in our mountains. One dragon served her all of her Moons on this World, and the two loved each other dearly.*

Shahlita would call for her dragon, and wherever she was, Wipp would hear, and come. Many adventures they had, and many times they helped those in distress. Often she was seen – by your people and mine – sitting at Wipp's feet, deep in conversation with gatherings of birds and beasts. All were unafraid of the dragon, or of each other, while they talked with Shahlita.

How lovely, said Shaeli, stroking the soft grass. She could feel the prickle of it through the material of her nightdress, and the breeze toyed with her hair, yet she was not cold. *Was she beautiful, Williver?* Shaeli asked. *The Lady Shahlita?*

She was, he said. *Her likeness stands there, if you wish to see it.* He pointed a long, thin finger across the glade.

Where no one had been before, the figure of a tall, lithe woman now stood. Shaeli blinked in surprise. She could see right through her. In the folds of the lady's flowing gown and through her fair skin, Shaeli could faintly see the trees and the shadowed spaces between, but the lady — obviously, beautifully elfin — stood smiling and looking back at them, a proud smile on her face. The bodice and the shoulders of her sleeveless aqua gown were tied with many ribbons of deep green and purple, her long, brown hair fell to her knees and was woven with more ribbons and scattered with tiny, brightly-coloured feathers. Glittering green bands were clasped upon her upper arms, and her eyes were the same shade of glowing green.

Oh, Williver, Shaeli breathed, *she is beautiful.*

She waved, and amazingly, Shahlita lifted a long graceful arm and waved back, the green armbands sparkling as she moved. Shaeli turned to Williver, smiling, and his merry blue eyes crinkled as he smiled back.

She looked at Shahlita again, and was disappointed to find that she was fading away. The hand was raised now in farewell, the green eyes fixed upon Shaeli as first the gown, and then the green-and-purple ribbons disappeared. Shahlita slowly paled to a fine aqua mist and drifted off gently with the breeze.

Williver took Shaeli's hand, his fingers cool in hers, and they stood and walked across the glade to where Shahlita had stood. A tiny feather, caught between the blades of grass was lifted by the breeze and carried into the surrounding forest, and suddenly, momentarily, it felt as if they were not alone among the giant trees. Shaeli thought she saw something moving between the thick gnarled trunks, but when she looked again there was nothing there. Williver did not seem to notice. He looked down at her.

Did you see the armbands the Lady Shahlita wore? he asked. *The green bangles?*

Shaeli nodded. *Yes, Williver. They were pretty.*

Remember them, he said. *One day you may see one – perhaps both. And listen carefully, Shaeli, if you see the armbands, wherever you find them, buy them, or beg them. Anything. But they must be yours.*

Why, Williver? she asked, surprised. *Are they special?*

Yes, very special, he said, his usually lively face serious. *They are made from the scales of Wipp herself.*

Shahlita's dragon?

Yes Shaeli. They are encrusted with gem dust, and were presented to the Lady Shahlita as a gift. You'll remember to look for them?

Yes, Williver, I'll remember.

Good. He took her hand. *And I must ask you not to speak of this quest to look for the bangles. Is that alright?*

Shaeli shrugged and nodded. *Alright, Williver,* she said. She did not speak of Williver to anyone anyway, so the request was easily granted.

Now it's time to go, he said, and smiled at her groan of disappointment.

Will I see you soon? she asked.

Yes, little one. When the time is right, we shall talk again. He scratched the top of one pointed ear. *It seems I have a few stories left to tell you.* He grinned down at her, his arched brows high, his blue eyes gleeful. *And a little magic to show you, perhaps?*

And then he also began to fade, just as Shahlita had, slowly at first, his image shimmering as it softened, and then she could see the trees clearly through him, the green leaves seeming to sprout through his pale hair. He began to dissolve more quickly, his body turning to a mere smudge of colour that drifted like mist onto the grass, and where the light mist fell, a small flower instantly began to grow. It burst from the lush grass, unfolding in moments to yield one perfect, tiny blue blossom, just the colour of Williver's eyes.

Shaeli leant down and breathed in the sweet, light perfume. Williver's voice whispered from the trees.

Dream well, little one.

The leaves trembled, and she knew he was gone. She crouched and picked the tiny blossom, and smelled the light, delicate fragrance. As she stood, the glade began to melt away, to dissolve around her, just as Williver and Shahlita had faded and dissolved.

As the glade slipped away, Shaeli saw the face of another lady between the trees. Not an elfin face, as before, but the face of one of the People, her eyes as green as the leaves on the trees in the disappearing glade. Before darkness took her, Shaeli wondered why the lady looked so sad.

* * *

Next morning when she woke, she found the scent of the tiny flower still in her nostrils, sweetly fragrant, a perfume as blue as Williver's eyes. She sniffed at it as she dressed – not knowing that smelling that small flower would alter her sense of smell in a most unusual way – and she thought of Williver, and of the looks on her friend's faces when she showed them her wand.

She was not disappointed. Their faces blossomed with awe. Bonn's eyes grew and grew until Shaeli wondered how wide they could possibly grow, but once Kirrit touched it, excitement overcame amazement, and they crowded round and took turns holding it up and studying the few small gems, showing each other the different patterns and pictures. There were cries of envy when Shaeli told them she would be studying elf-lore in return for allowing Almarnoch and the Warlocks to study her wand, and it was agreed that Shaeli must be the luckiest girl in the Fleet.

They spent the morning pretending to be dragons and fairies and elves on the deck of Purple Leaf, taking turns with the wand. Many times someone interrupted their games; word had spread of Shaeli's find, and the wand was admired by half the Fleet during the morning. Shaeli wrapped it back in its cloth before they had lunch, and in the afternoon the clouds pulled back, the sun shone, and they played on the terrace outside.

It seemed most were out in the sun that afternoon. Old ones warmed themselves on the ledge beside the spring stream, and not a child was to be seen inside Cave. Many of the Fleet went down to the Lea, despite the mushiness of the ground after so much rain, to bring the small herd of cattle up from their stables. They were led up the slope, looking dumbly surprised at being escorted by such a large, noisy group.

As evening began to brush the edges of the few stray clouds with grey, the traders regretfully started to move inside. They were chilled, for the air was lined with ice, but all were warmed in their hearts by the gift of sunshine. Shaeli, face to the paling sky in search of the first star, noticed an odd smell in the air, although no one else could smell it.

The next day dawned clear and freezing cold, but despite the bitterness, many again ventured out. Shaeli still thought she could smell something as she played on first terrace with the others and fancied it might be first snow, but there was not a cloud in the sky.

The next morning also dawned cloudless, the sky a high, clean blue, but in the afternoon enormous thunderheads began to build up beyond the Valley of Stones and the children were warned not to leave the ledge. Shaeli sat with a large group of silent, watchful children just outside the tunnel mouth, eyes on the mountain of cloud rolling closer to their mountain of rock, knowing they would see little of the World when the blizzards began. Their world would contract to Cave, and the Four Lands and the Starisles may as well not exist.

She smelt the odd smell again as the breeze died and the Long Lea grew silent below them; a sweet smell, fresh and clean as cut-grass far away, but with a twist of sourness, as if the grass had begun to rot, just a little. The wind suddenly rose, gusting down the Lea and whistling across the ledge, and the rumble of thunder began to the south. The children rose, took a last look at the World, and went inside to the warmth of Cave. First snow was upon them.

* * *

Far across the Land, Irinesta watched the blizzard roll in from the Bastinian Ocean, and although the room was warm, she shivered as the city below became invisible. Passage down to Palveron would be impossible now, at least until the first storms had passed, but there was no reason to leave the castle; they had what they needed. E'Nith had been lucky; she had brought it back a few days before, and it lay in a frozen bundle on the balcony. They were lucky it was so cold.

Her stomach clenched every time she thought of it, poor thing, yet E'Nith was ever practical.

"I will do everything," she soothed over and over. "And it will have a better resting place than it would have had, amongst kings and queens. Do not worry."

They would wait only a few days, she could not bear it longer than that, but it would be enough. It would have to be enough. Then the waiting would begin.

* * *

In another turret at Great Court, Princess Virrisian sat alone in her room, oblivious to the Winterings first blizzard covering the city. She was speaking intently.

"You told me you *had* this mind. You said it was filled with Irinesta and the babe. You said you could find it."

"I said the link was tenuous at best, but that I would try," replied a harsh voice. "I have found no sign of it."

"You're sure they have a stone?"

"Oh, yes, that much was clear."

"But not where they were?"

"That I cannot know. A ship I think, they were surrounded by water. I could hear the rain in the mind. It was a small room, and I felt the presence of children, one of which I had a link to before the connection was broken." The voice spoke even more harshly. "But you know this. I can do no more without knowing where to look."

"Then I will watch Irinesta closely." Virrisian smiled, unaffected by the rough tone. "She goes nowhere that I do not know about. She has barely left the Glade Room since Tenelon died." The smile left her face. "I thought the child would come that night, she looked so strange, but no one entered the room, and she did not leave it."

"Yet still you check ships for newborns." The voice held a mocking note now. "Even the traders are suspect, even though none were near the city since before Tenelon died."

"You told me there were thoughts of Tenelon's child in the mind you captured," she replied. "I thought it best to be sure, seeing as you have such feeble information. If she has already given birth, I will know about it. If not, then time will give me what I need." She gave a snort of impatience. "I cannot believe you are unable to see what she's thinking for yourself. What's so special about *her* mind?"

"It is not her *mind* I cannot enter, it is the *room*," said the voice. "It holds more ancient spells than even I know, but worry not." The voice softened, as if its owner were smiling. "Worry not, the child will soon arrive. It cannot be more than a few days, and then... well, you know what to do."

"Yes," said Virrisian, smiling again. "I know what to do."

* * *

On the other side of the bay, Fezzik was helping close the shutters of the Wintering Hall. The voices of the men were whipped away on the rising wind, the sky to the south boiled with dark cloud, and the bay was shrinking as the storm closed in on them. In a few days the Clahren would be frozen, the town would be covered in snow drifts, and they would keep to the warm confines of the hall. First snow always held the worst blizzards, and he would not see their little house for many days, perhaps even a whole Moon.

He stopped on the steps to take one final look at Boccra and the World beyond, and he heard a dull clattering. Two horses appeared, the riders low over the horses' necks. Past the Wintering Hall they galloped, neither glancing at the big, bearded man standing on its steps. They were from Wokk – Fezzik could tell by their white-blond hair – and they had ridden through the village almost before he had time to wonder at them. He could imagine little that would send a man into the path of first snow. He shook his head, and went inside to find Verlie, leaving Zirrus to be engulfed by the dark cloud of the Wintering.

* * *

CHAPTER ELEVEN

With first snow the routine of Winter began in earnest. Lessons for the children were held every morning in the amphitheatre beside the spring pool where they sat in groups and were taught a broad range of subjects. Every few days after lunch, Shaeli took the elf-wand to Almarnoch's little hut to learn elf-lore, something few Traders were interested in.

The first time she went, she had been nervous, unsure of what to expect. The three lesser Warlocks shared a hut at the end of the row where the old ones Wintered, but Almarnoch's hut lay far past the huts and the Traders, off by itself at the back of Cave, far from the brightness surrounding the spring-pool. It sat shrouded in shadow, a thick column to the right reflecting the red of the distant fire-pits, only one small window shining light into the inky blackness behind the building – a place of monster-shapes and blank-faced voids. She had almost turned and run back to the safety of Purple Leaf, but then she had heard Almarnoch laugh from inside, and she felt suddenly calm and the light about her seemed a little brighter. The door was opened a moment after her timid knock by Llevvis, the first apprentice, who was still chuckling at whatever had caused Almarnoch to laugh so loudly. Llevvis' long, plain face shone with warmth as he called back over his shoulder to announce her.

The one room of the little hut was lit with many Warlock lights, and a huge lamp shone over a centre table. Book-filled shelves lined every scrap of available wall right up to the low ceiling, other books lay scattered on tables and dozens more were precariously stacked in tall piles around the room. Their musty, old-book smell filled the small space and made Shaeli's nose twitch.

A green curtain embroidered with gold stars closed off one corner – she supposed that was where Almarnoch slept – and a fire burned in a small grate opposite. Shaeli was not surprised to see that although there was no chimney, the fire burned without smoking, for it was stacked with rocks the same as those that filled the fire-pits outside. Only Warlocks could light the rocks, which burned hot and smokeless for days, and without them it would be impossible to keep the Wintering at bay.

Almarnoch greeted her just as warmly as Llevvis had, and the other two Warlocks, Garrit and Demeris, nodded and smiled.

The Warlocks were all very different. Demeris, a widower these last three Winterings, was old, and although he was not as old as Almarnoch, there was little but grey in his hair and beard, and he had served at Cave for many years. He had a round bland face, old patched robes, and a gentle smile.

Garrit beside him could not have been more opposite. His face was clean-shaven, his hair combed neatly over his wide forehead, his robes perfectly tailored to enhance his lithe frame, yet the smile on his face did not reach his indifferent eyes. He reminded Shaeli of a river-rat, all sleek and sneaky, and she tried not to dislike the second apprentice as much as she wanted to.

Llevvis she liked instantly. The first apprentice was a tall man, not very young, she thought, yet not very old either, with a long face and broad smile. He had no beard and no hair, and his head looked like a shiny brown egg in the lamplight. Both Llevvis and Garrit had yet to attend their final years at the Warlock's island in the bay below Great Court.

She was led to the cluttered table which filled the middle of the room, and beneath the light of the hanging lamp, Shaeli unwrapped the wand and stood proudly as they examined it, and then she was given tezz and she sat with Llevvis on a little couch by the fire to look through the books of elf-lore. Llevvis' interest in all things elfin matched Shaeli's own, and from that first day they spent many hours together on the little couch, poring over Almarnoch's books while the other three made endless drawings of the wand and tried to interpret its writings. Almarnoch possessed a wonderful tool, a thick glass disc set into a silver ring which magnified the intricate script covering the wand, allowing the Warlocks to transcribe the writings and tiny figures to paper.

On her free afternoons, she retold the best elfin stories to her friends as they went about the business of being children. Sometimes they went down the bolt tunnel to the Cave mouth and had snowball fights, or made castles and people from the great mounds of snow which were blown in by the blizzards. Once they had gone up the bolt tunnel to find the exit blocked by a wall of snow, and they spent the rest of the day helping to unblock the small tunnel by dumping buckets of ice in the spring stream.

Shaeli's fifth birth-day came and went early in the Wintering. She was given a party around the spring-pool, and received many small gifts from her family and friends; a pillow filled with Zoi down; a pencil box; a slightly misshapen wall-hanging from her friends. Eenis had made a new belt for Shaeli's amulet, cunningly tied with impossibly small knots, with a pattern of tiny stars running down its length, and after she'd helped Shaeli thread it through the amulet and tie it around her thin waist, she brushed aside Shaeli's thanks, brusquely muttering something about keeping one's treasures safe.

Almarnoch gave her a small book, full of the most beautiful elfin pictures and poems, and Llevvis presented her with a drawing of her wand, worked on by all the Warlocks. They had been allowed to stay up very late after the birth-day dinner, and Olver had kept them amused with stories far into the night.

One day, halfway through the Wintering, Shaeli and Llevvis were sitting on the little couch by the fire studying a huge leather-bound book. When he had taken it from the shelf and opened it, the dust made Shaeli sneeze, but she soon forgot the smell, for the book was filled with fabulous pictures of elfin lords and ladies; a history of one branch of elfin royalty. Many pages were covered with tiny elfin script, the rudiments of which she was just beginning to learn, but there were also pages filled with beautiful, coloured drawings. Shaeli thought they were similar to those in the little book given her by Almarnoch for her birth-day, and Llevvis told her that they had been drawn by the same artist, the famous Ref'el, over two hundred Winter's before. Shaeli found she suddenly viewed her poem-and-picture book in a very different light, and she looked over to where Almarnoch sat at the table, surprised that he had given her such a special gift. She turned back again just as Llevvis turned the page, and there was a picture showing a tall elfin lady wearing a flowing aqua gown. She was beribboned with green and purple, and tiny feathers were braided through her hair.

"Oh, it's Shahlita," exclaimed Shaeli. "Is there a picture of Wipp?" she asked, looking up at the young Warlock.

But Llevvis was not looking at her. He was looking at Almarnoch, who was putting put down his pen. Almarnoch stood, and came over, and Llevvis rose from Shaeli's side as the High Warlock crossed the room.

"How do you know of Shahlita, child?" Almarnoch said. He asked the question gently as he stopped before her, but his face held a strange look, one Shaeli had not seen before.

She frowned, unsure of what to tell him. Although she had promised Williver not to speak of the bangles, he had never forbidden her to speak of him or his dream-time visits, she had merely been embarrassed out of doing so. She looked doubtfully into Almarnoch's clear grey eyes, and was met with such genuine curiosity and trust that she knew here, at last, was someone to whom she could tell the truth.

"I dreamed about her," she said softly, and looked quickly down at her hands, waiting to hear what he would say. Would he laugh?

He did not. He placed a hand over her folded ones, and she raised her eyes to find him smiling. Llevvis stood behind him, looking surprised, but not disbelieving. Garrit and Demeris sat at the table, pens hovering, watching silently.

"Tell me about it," Almarnoch said, sitting down beside her.

The words came out slowly at first, and then in a torrent; it was a relief to speak aloud of things which occupied her thoughts so much. She told them about Williver and the stories he had told her, or shown her, including that of Shahlita, and how she had seen her image, in a glade, in a dream. Almarnoch asked a few questions, but on the whole remained silent and just let her speak.

When she had finished, there was silence in the room. All eyes were turned to the inscrutable face of Almarnoch, who sat holding Shaeli's hand, his thoughts in an unknown realm.

At last he turned back to Shaeli, who had grown apprehensive as time passed, yet Almarnoch's eyes were animated, and his brows bristled with enthusiasm.

"I see we have more to discuss than even I first thought, Shaeli," he said. "Tell me, have you told anyone else about your dreams?"

She shook her head. The blonde streaks, almost lost back into the brown by the time at Cave, were highlighted by the lamplight. Her grey-blue eyes were fixed on Almarnoch, her free hand clutching her amulet.

"I tried once, to tell the boys, but they just laughed," she said, her lips pursing at the memory. "I've told Da and the girls some of the stories," she lowered her eyes. "But they think I made them up."

Almarnoch chuckled, and Shaeli looked back up at him and smiled.

"I think it best they continue to do so, child. The dreams you share with Williver are... unusual, a most uncommon thing, and you were wise to stay silent." He patted her hands and then sat back and folded his own upon his lap. "Now tell me more of Shahlita, for she is one of your dreams, as you see, that is not a story. And she has always been one of my favourites."

So Shaeli told him all that Williver had told her, except for the dragon-scale armbands, and they weren't in the picture anyway. She looked at the book, her head on one side, considering.

"Shahlita's hair was longer," she said. "It was almost down to her knees."

Garrit suddenly threw down his pen and stood, his face incredulous. "I cannot believe you put credence in the dreams of a child, Almarnoch," he said. "'Tis nothing but childish fantasy, surely?"

"I think not, Garrit," said Almarnoch smoothly. "Perhaps some of Shaeli's dreams are just dreams, but she is correct when she says Shahlita's hair was longer. It is chronicled in later books."

He looked sternly at Garrit, but the young Warlock was not put off. A stubborn frown settled on his forehead, and Shaeli thought it looked at home there.

"Surely it is only that she has heard the story elsewhere and it has been re*membered* in a dream." His voice was reasonable now, despite the sullen look on his face. "Some story of Olver's, perhaps."

Almarnoch nodded. "That could be so. I suppose it *is* possible she could have heard the story of Shahlita, though not from Olver, for he is not versed in elf history. Few are." He glanced at Shaeli. "And although the sharing of dreams is very rare, and is not encouraged, nevertheless, it is not impossible."

He looked up at Garrit, and smiled, yet the gaze held steel, and Garrit looked back at him for only a moment before he dropped his eyes.

"As you say," he murmured, and he turned back to the table, his hand moving to rest upon the wand.

Almarnoch looked back at the child beside him and smiled. His eyebrows quivered, and he chuckled to himself. He looked at Shaeli as if he'd found a gift he had not expected. Serendipity happened so seldom.

Shaeli decided it was fun to surprise the old Warlock, and for the rest of the afternoon she sat with Almarnoch and Llevvis, talking of Williver to her heart's content, yet she shifted uneasily whenever the sullen eye of Garrit fell upon her.

* * *

The Wintering raged outside, storm after fierce storm buffeted the Lea and the mountains, and the traders were forced to spend their time inside Cave. On the rare, sunny days, many ventured out, pushing a path through the snowdrifts to build snow-figures on the terrace, or slide down the wide path to the Lea on toboggans, or just enjoy the fresh air. Those who had passed their Cave year were allowed to don snow-shoes and explore the frozen Lea, and the younger children built castles out of snow boulders and had snowball wars, their faces growing red and their eyes bright with the brilliance of the cold air. Invariably the storm clouds would build up over the Valley of Stones and a bitter wind would send them inside, confining them again to the warmth of Cave.

As the Moons waxed and waned unseen behind the blanket of the Wintering, every Trader received repairs. New paint was applied, ropes were replaced, the huge webs of rigging checked and checked again. During their yearly travels, most of the balloons received some injury; a small tear from a tree branch; a collision with an unfortunate bird; a split in a worn seam, yet it took a huge rent to fell a Trader. Small splits and tears were repaired as they flew, with the tailors climbing the rigging and mending the tears as they dangled precariously above the decks, but sometimes the damage was great, and this Winter two Traders, White Star and Sky Lark, were in need of major repairs. White Star had been blown into a tree by a sudden gust after a lift, but they had been nearing Cave for the Wintering after a good year of trade, and they'd had little trouble flying home.

Sky Lark had not been so lucky. They had been caught in a storm on Wokk in early summer, and one seam had been torn along half its length. They had limped home to Cave, a loss in Lift forcing them to take a circuitous route by roads and open fields, and the journey across the open waters had, by all accounts, been a nightmare, the Zoi exhausted by the time they reached Zirrus. It had taken two Moons for them to reach the foothills, and autumn had begun by the time they reached Cave. There had been little trade for them last year.

The whole Fleet gathered to watch the High Warlock remove the Lift spell. The two balloons, moored together at the back of Cave, began to deflate and pucker before the outstretched arms of the tiny Warlock. Almarnoch stood in front of the ships, murmuring meaningless words, his staff glowing as the balloons fell gracefully until they lay limp and lifeless, the ships sinking slowly to the ground as the magic evaporated from the balloon, sitting crookedly upon the ladders lashed to their bottoms.

Sky Lark was first; the webbing of rope was removed and the huge bulk of limp balloon was lifted by every available pair of hands, carried from the Trader and laid out on newly-swept ground.

Lunn and his wife Tylo, of Sky Lark Trader, stood anxiously watching as the great balloon was carried across the floor, Lunn leaning heavily on a cane, his face pinched, frustrated by his inability to help. He had sustained a broken leg in the same storm which had crippled his Trader, and though it had healed, it had been clumsily set by a Faunist on Wokk, and he walked with a limp. Lunn and Tylo had a daughter about Shaeli's age, and four sons, the eldest just married, the youngest approaching his Cave year, so they had ample help, yet Lunn mourned the loss of his agility.

As the enormous rent in the seam was repaired, Tylo and others, Eenis among them, crawled about on the pale pink material sewing glittering beads to the eyes of the blue-green birds which gave the Trader its name. Tylo was pleased with the effect, but Lunn stood solemnly by, watching the proceedings, saying little.

When they had finished, the balloon was rolled and carried back up to the deck of the Trader, and then it was White Star's turn. The jagged rent was quickly repaired and a new line of white stars were sewn on to strengthen the new seam. Both balloons would be given Lift again the next day with the other Traders, for the Wintering was drawing to an end.

That night a feast of sorts was held. Supplies had begun to run low, but Wyshka brought out from one of the small caves a store of preserves, and everyone had a helping of deliciously sweet fruit floating in thick syrup.

Talk of balloon repairs turned to trading disasters past; vicious storms outrun; Traders downed, or worse, vanished completely. They talked also of what had passed at Great Court while the Wintering raged, and the new king or queen was spoken of with hope. While the talk of politics sent the children sleepily to their beds, many of the adults stayed up long hours talking of what the death of King Tenelon would mean to the Four Lands. Some thought that things would change little, that good sense and peace would prevail; others hinted darkly at power struggles and unrest. No conclusion was reached, yet they kept talking, going over and over already covered ground, tamping it down, inspecting every blade of grass on the vast field of it. Speculating. Wondering.

* * *

Dari watched them talking late into the night. He sat far back from the fire-pits, out of reach of the light, waiting for them all to go, and then he would sneak over and see if anybody had dropped anything interesting or if there was anything left to eat. His mother never let him eat enough to satisfy his hunger. She thought he was in bed, but he'd snuck out as soon as he knew Andos was asleep. He was careful though, much more careful since his encounter with the second apprentice.

When finally they all drifted away, he went closer, slipping around the edges of the fire-pits, looking around until he found half a jar of preserves beneath a bench, and he sat down in the shadows to eat them. He was almost finished when a darker shadow fell across him. He looked up and froze. Garrit was standing over him.

"I thought I might find you out here," Garrit said. "May I sit down?"

Dari nodded, his eyes wide, his mouth hanging open as Garrit sat beside him.

"Any preserves left?"

Dari passed the jar to Garrit, sitting silently as Garrit finished off the last of the fruit, watching carefully. When Garrit was done, he put the jar down and leant back, looking around.

"I enjoy the silence too," he said, his voice smooth, intimate. "Can't stand all those people all the time."

Dari smiled tentatively.

"I've been meaning to talk to you for a while, to apologise for that time, you know, behind the huts."

Dari nodded.

"You startled me, that's all."

Another nod. "That's alright," Dari said.

"I'd like to make it up to you," Garrit said. "And I think we should be friends, if that's alright with you."

Dari looked back at him for a moment, and then his smile widened.

* * *

Everyone was tired next morning, but they all gathered to watch the Warlocks cast the Lift and Protection spells. First thaw was not far away, and they had left repairs until now, when Almarnoch could encompass all the Traders in the intricate spells.

Almost every light had been extinguished; only the small lamps on the prow of each Trader remained shining as the Warlocks emerged from the depths of Cave, walking solemnly towards the gathered Fleet, dappled in crimson light from the fire-pits. Almarnoch looked stately in his white, star-embroidered robe, the other Warlocks in dark robes behind him. They stopped at the head of the spring-pool before a small table draped in purple velvet. Upon the table were two candles in golden holders, an enormous, vaguely-purple crystal ball, and a thick book.

The traders stood in family groups in front of their ships, the old ones, too, standing with their families, waiting for Almarnoch to begin. The air of Cave trembled with anticipation.

Almarnoch stood with his head lowered; a white speck amid the vastness of Cave. He concentrated on the page of the open book before him, leaning upon his staff, his lips moving as he read, but they could not hear his voice. The crystal, set on a low pedestal in front of the book, began to glow brighter with his unheard words and tiny sparks appeared and began to fly around inside it, dark purple in the lavender sphere. Almarnoch, too, began to glow. The whiteness of his robe grew brighter, his skin and hair filled with radiance until it was blinding. Brighter the crystal ball grew, whiter and brighter grew Almarnoch, and just when it seemed he would burst with it, the light began to emanate from his body. The line between Warlock and light blurred, his body became indistinct as he glowed; white fire engulfed him. He was the light. The light was him.

The lesser Warlocks standing behind him emanated their own light, a less clean light, tinged with gold, light that spiralled toward the glowing figure of Almarnoch and joined with the brightness surrounding him, making it grow bigger, brighter. Many of the Traders veiled their eyes with their hands, squinting into the brilliance. Somewhere, a child began to cry.

The crystal ball became a frenzied mass of shooting purple sparks in the centre of the white light. The sparks, caught tightly within their crystal prison, exploded into pin-points of light against the walls of the sphere.

The High Warlock within the white fire stood tall, and his arms opened wide. They could hear his voice now, hear the words of the spell he wove, though they could not understand them. He raised the long staff and brought it down hard against the floor. The thud echoed through Cave and the staff blazed into gold-white light. In an instant the staff became a torch that leapt to the very roof of Cave, illuminating everything in its beam.

Almarnoch grew with the light that reached to fill the cavern, grew until he and his staff towered over everyone, and his voice grew with him. It fell like a waterfall about them, and at the climax of his words he struck the staff once more on the floor with a resounding thud and the blinding, white-gold light splintered from the staff and showered down upon the Fleet. Every balloon filled with light until they glowed with it, each straining against their ropes and shivering, white sparks surrounding them. The two balloons which had been repaired rippled and glowed more brightly than the rest, their skins filling quickly with the radiant light of the Lift spell.

As the white light at last began to wane and each balloon swelled with new magic, the crystal ball reached its frantic zenith, and with another mighty crack from the High Warlock's staff, the dark purple sparks leapt from the sphere, free at last from their crystal prison. Thousands of glimmering sparks flew around Cave, darting and spinning through the air, crashing into each other and joining, growing bigger and bigger until enormous balls of spinning, deep-purple light hovered above each balloon. With a last command from Almarnoch, the purple spheres exploded as one, surrounding each of the Traders in a shower of violet sparks.

The children, and many adults, were entranced by the show of the Protection spell. It was like standing in a shower of purple raindrops, and a murmur of appreciation rippled through the crowd as the sparks drifted down around the Fleet.

The lights began to fade. The light from the small lamps and fire-pits came back into focus, pale and weak compared with the light of magic.

Almarnoch slumped and tottered, leaning heavily upon his staff, one hand going to the table before him. The towering majesty of the Lift and Protection spells were gone and he had again become a wizened old man, and with a sigh he leant over and closed the great book. The crystal ball faded back into a nondescript purple.

Behind Almarnoch, the Warlocks also showed signs of fatigue. Garrit was on his knees, Demeris standing wearily beside him, urging him to his feet. Llevvis stumbled across to take the arm of Almarnoch and carry the heavy crystal, Sahli'en moved to take Almarnoch's other arm, and together they walked with the exhausted Warlock back to the little hut at the end of the light.

The traders stood in small groups, looking up at the resplendent balloons, their colours shining more brightly than they had before the magic of Almarnoch had touched them, and brighter than they would for the whole year ahead; the reds richer, the blues brighter, the yellows dazzling.

Almarnoch, though the ceremony had not taken long, was put into his bed, to sleep the better part of three days and nights. All felt the lack of his energy in the air.

Shaeli missed him while he was abed. Llevvis was also too listless to talk much with her, so she spent the days with her friends and entertaining the twins, who favoured her with fat-cheeked smiles and gurgles of delight. The Moons of the Wintering had seen the girls grow and thrive, and they were now plump, pink babies, eternally bundled to repel the cold. Reneesha remained the larger of the two, but Roshanna matched her roll by fat roll, and Shaeli delighted in tickling their first giggles out of them.

With first thaw fast approaching, Shaeli knew she would have to discard her lessons on elf-lore and she would miss the High Warlock and the plain, friendly face of Llevvis when they left Cave. The year seemed a long time to wait to see them or the scores of wonderful books that lined the shelves of the little hut, yet when Almarnoch finally woke from his slumber and she spoke of these things to him, he waved her sentiments aside and said that time took care of all things missed. She was not consoled, until she remembered how much she had begrudged coming to Cave, and yet she had hardly thought of the World during the Wintering.

A few days later, a current of warm air blew down from the north, and the icicles that lined the mouth of the great tunnel like pointed teeth began to drip. The ice clinging to the edges of the spring stream began to break off in lumps and fall over the edge to melt in the tumbling waterfall. First thaw had begun.

At the Full of the Moon, the Zoi emerged from their cave. Each family knelt low, bowing to the birds in the traditional greeting as they emerged from the tunnel, and the birds separated into their usual groups. Half a dozen ships welcomed chicks aboard, the pearlescent feathers still showing signs of downy fuzz, and that night Last Feast was prepared. Next day the Fleet would begin to leave.

Golden Eagle was the first to go, heading for the belated funeral of King Tenelon, who would at last be laid to rest with his ancestors on the Island of Dead Kings in the bay below Great Court. Rafi, Taffka's son, stood waving with the others as Golden Eagle disappeared into the main tunnel, and then he ran up the bolt tunnel to stand on the ledge and watch as the Zoi drew the Trader into a warm south-bound current. Rafi's mother, Renn, stood with her father, Ennan, and Taffka at the railing, waving back at her son, calling endless good-byes and instructions to take care. Rafi waved until Golden Eagle disappeared over the edge of the Lea into the Valley of Stones, and then he turned and wordlessly disappeared back inside. The separations of Cave year were hard on the young, the first days strongly felt by both the leavers and the left.

A few days later, it was the turn of Kirrit's brother, Alvaro, to wave farewell to Red Arrow. While he appeared to take it well, Shaeli, who stood nearby sadly waving to Kirrit, thought she saw a tear fall from his eye as he turned, but she pretended not to notice.

One by one, the Traders negotiated their way up the long, winding tunnel to disappear over the edge of the Lea and back into the World. Purple Leaf was one of the last to leave and Shaeli thought that Cave looked strangely lonely without the bright balloons filling the vast space.

Only a score of Traders were left as Purple Leaf entered the tunnel, and when they passed into the bright sunshine and fresh air, the Zoi let out their marvellous, resounding cry. Shaeli gave one more wave to the dwindling figures of the old ones and the teenagers with lost faces who stood with them, and before she turned to look ahead she saw Almarnoch raise his staff in farewell. She blew back a kiss that she hoped his old eyes would see.

They dropped over the edge of the Lea into the Valley of Stones, and Cave was gone until the next Wintering. Another year had begun.

* * *

CHAPTER TWELVE

They spent one night at Serrat, and then they followed the road taken by Sir Brudloc before the Wintering to Meoro Pass. There had been no word from the outside world at Serrat, but at Meoro Village at the far end of the pass, it was hoped there would be news of events in the Land during the Wintering.

They were all on deck as they passed the rough land leading to the Valley of Stones, and then the way to Cave was left behind as they flew between the two mountain arms which sheltered Serrat. The road beneath them led past a little village where children waved from the tiny Landing, and then it wound down into the natural river-made valley that was the main passage through the rugged mountain range.

They flew east between mountains covered with drifts of white snow and trees decorated with snowy lace and dripping icicles. Below ran the river, still iced at the edges, small floes breaking impulsively away and racing towards destruction in the waters of the Nebillonia Straits. Far to the south, the last banks of the Wintering's clouds were being pushed back by warm northern winds.

Shaeli stood on a box beside her father and the boys on the top deck, hands gripped tightly to the railing, elbow wrapped around a rope, drinking in the sights around her, tasting the crispness of the World on her palate. Her nostrils filled with familiar scents, her ears with the sounds of birds and the wind ruffling the balloon above, and she drank deeply of these too.

They passed a group of huni-deer in a clearing, pawing at the ground to uncover the fresh new shoots of grass, their luxuriously thick brown Winter coats white-tipped to match the snow. The small creatures turned up their pretty, triangular faces to watch the Trader pass, the males tossing their curling antlers in defiance, the females turning docilely back to paw at the soft snow. Just past the clearing, a striped cat was slinking furtively towards where the huni-deer grazed, and Shaeli wanted to warn the deer of their danger. The memory of her encounter with the jenka when she found the wand was brought starkly back at the sight of the cat stalking the deer just as they had stalked her, and she clutched the rope tighter. The mottled jenka was not a large cat, but it was a fierce hunter, and Jarris pointed out two more creeping through the snow behind the first, yet they were swiftly left behind, the fate of the huni-deer forever unknown.

The day was filled with wonders. Birds and animals she saw in plenty, and dozens of bright butterflies flitted in the air, dancing joyously with each other and then floating off with the breeze. There were a few early flowers in sun-warmed corners, the colours shining brightly against the white; tiny pink and blue smiles promising spring. The sun was shining, weakly, but shining nonetheless, small puffs of cloud scudding on the high winds like white dolphins riding wind-waves in the surf of the sky.

Meoro Pass was a wide valley, the little river thickening as it gathered smaller streams along the way, and beside the river ran the broad road they had followed from Serrat. Often they passed groups of people, walking or riding upon horses or in wagons, and once they passed a huge open carriage, pulled by six horses and filled with stylish people.

Shaeli spent the day alternating between the left, watching the road, and the right, where the little forest crept along on the other side of the river. The boys spent the morning with her, but by afternoon they had tired of the sport, and they spent their time lying in the sun seeing who could tell the biggest lie. Dari was particularly adept at this game.

Afternoon brought them to a Landing halfway down Meoro Pass, and they moored for the night watched by the occupants of three wagons who were setting up camp nearby. The travellers called a friendly greeting and an invitation to dinner, which was gratefully accepted, for the stores aboard Purple Leaf were sorely in need of replenishment. Some supplies could be found when they reached Meoro Village, but everyone coveted something special from the towns of Ashkanna where they would fill the storerooms.

The sun fell quickly behind the mountain range, dusk was short, and by the time darkness had hidden the river and the bank opposite, they were sitting around an open fire, enjoying plates of thick stew with the families from the wagons.

They were three brothers, their wives, and an assortment of small children, and they were on their way to relocate to the far side of Zirrus. They were unsure of their exact destination; somewhere near the great lakes or the warmer climes on the Sea of Aa'liu. They seemed unperturbed by the journey ahead, likely to take the entire year to complete, and if the Wintering caught them still unsettled they were confident that they would find a haven in which to spend the frozen Moons.

They were a merry family; the brothers tall and bearded, all with the same warm brown eyes, their wives young and excited about the adventure before them. Meoro Village where they'd grown up held little fascination, and they were all eager for a new life. The travellers gained much knowledge from the traders that night, about the best routes to follow and the most pleasant villages on the other side of Zirrus. Mareesha told them of a lovely town on a small bay on the north-east coast, where warm winds crossed the sea from Romynn.

Shaeli was befriended by the youngest of the wives, Ellirra, a beautiful girl with the dark skin of one of the fabled race who had come from far across the sea, the Irikai. These black-eyed people had been wrecked off the Starisles more than a hundred years before, their ship crowded with scores of people whose skins were the colour of tezz seeds. Since their arrival, the Irikai had spread throughout the Starisles and the

Four Lands, revelling in the peace they found in the southern lands so far from their war-ravaged home. Their descendants were numerous, their blood joined with the people of every Land, yet they did not love the colder Lands and most Irikai still lived on the Starisles, where the bones of their great ship could be seen upon the reef that had destroyed it.

Ellirra took Shaeli into her wagon after dinner, and showed her some of the things she had collected to begin a new life; boxes stacked with finely embroidered linen; dishes wrapped in soft tissue paper; pots and pans for her future kitchen swinging on hooks from the roof. With the blush of a dusky rose, she showed Shaeli tiny white baby clothes and patted her small, swollen belly, and spoke of the baby who would be born before summer's end.

They talked for a while, and then Ellirra took out a small wooden box which shone like a mirror, and she sat down on the floor of the wagon. Her huge, dark eyes reflected the light of the candle, and Shaeli was reminded of the eyes of a huni-deer. She sat in front of Ellirra, legs crossed, waiting expectantly to see what was inside the pretty box, but Ellirra seemed in no hurry to open it. She sat stroking the shining wood, her eyes fixed on something far away while Shaeli sat quietly, feeling the shapes in her amulet. Ellirra took a breath and looked at her.

"Long ago, my people came from far across the sea," Ellirra began, her voice low.

Shaeli nodded. She could smell a story. It had a sweet, musty smell, like the inside of Almarnoch's hut.

"When the mother of my grandmother was a young girl," Ellirra continued, "she travelled with *her* mother, and others of their race, the Irikai, to seek for the great Land in the south which was spoken of in legend. There was much turmoil in their land, a place far to the north under a white-hot sky. Her father had been killed in the Eternal War, and her mother wanted peace and took the chance on the great ship."

Ellirra's voice held the pitch of retelling an often-heard story, but Shaeli was entranced.

"After long Moons of travel and many hardships, at last they reached the edge of these great Lands. They could see green islands rising from the shining sea and they rejoiced, for they had lost many of their number and much of their hope during the journey, yet as they drew closer and could see the fruit ripe upon the trees, the great ship was dashed upon reefs that lay like knives beneath the waves.

"When the great Mother Ship was broken on the rocks of the Starisles, some of her Children were lost to the sea. The mother of my grandmother saw her small brother washed from the arms of their mother, and he was never seen again." Ellirra stopped for effect. "Yet most gained the land, and as they lay upon the white sand, others with skin as pale as honey came from the sea on small craft. More came, these with hair like the sun, and pointed ears, and so the Children of the Mother Ship were saved."

"Elves," breathed Shaeli, and Ellirra nodded solemnly.

"The mother of my grandmother was one of the last to be taken from the island with the reefs of teeth. As she waited, she wandered along the shore, searching through the debris from the Mother Ship; searching for anything from her homeland far to the north. At last she found one small bag belonging to her mother, but as she turned to leave the beach she heard a cry, and she walked again among the drifts of shattered ship, searching for the source of the cry.

"Beneath a pile of splintered timber, in a basket covered with seaweed, she found a babe, a tiny girl of her race who had survived the sea and been washed to safety. She took the babe, basket and all to her mother, and they searched for the parents of the child, but none were ever found, and so the child stayed with them and was brought up as a sister, a gift of life from the sea to replace the one taken. In the basket with her were a few small items of jewellery, and three gold coins." Ellirra paused again, savouring the tale like well-aged wine. "When the babe was grown into a woman, she left our family to go into the World, but before she left, she gave one of the coins and a piece of the jewellery to my grandmother's mother, to be kept and passed down to the youngest daughter in each generation." The voice of Ellirra dropped even lower and Shaeli leant forward. "It is told in my family that in a time of great need there will come one who seeks for the jewellery, and it is to be given without question. It is said that whoever holds them will know to whom it is to be given." Ellirra paused once more with great effect. "It will be told in a dream." She sat up and her voice rose to normal. She entirely destroyed the mysterious mood with a bright girlish giggle as she opened the lid of the box. "It is my turn to hold them until that day, and it's such fun. I do hope something happens while I have them. Don't you think that would be exciting?"

Shaeli grinned, nodded and leant forward to see what was in the box.

From among the ribbons and cheap earrings, Ellirra drew a small bundle. She unwrapped the material and produced a small gold coin as thick as three buttons, with a crescent moon stamped upon it. She passed it to Shaeli, who dutifully marvelled at it, amazed by the weight of so small a disc, and she handed it back to Ellirra, who tucked it away. Then, with a flourish, Ellirra drew something else from the material and held it out.

"And this," Ellirra said proudly. "This is the bracelet."

Shaeli could say nothing. The grin was frozen on her face. The blue of her eyes drained away, leaving only smoke-coloured grey behind. She tried to speak but her voice was stuck in her throat. She stared at what dangled before her eyes.

It was Shahlita's bangle. The dragon-scale bangle.

* * *

Shaeli barely noticed when they arrived at Meoro Village the next day. She took no notice of the busy streets, nor of the ships that filled the harbour. The sights and sounds of the bustling port village at the bottom of Meoro Pass held no delight for her.

She was worried. About the bangle. About Williver. She had gone to sleep last night expecting to dream of him, to explain why she didn't have the bangle, and she didn't know what to say, only that she couldn't have asked Ellirra for the grandmother's bangle. Even if she'd explained about Williver and the dreams, she didn't think Ellirra would believe her. Certainly not enough to give her the bangle. She wondered what Williver would say, but it didn't matter now, anyway. Ellirra and the bangle were headed in the opposite direction, and she didn't know where they were going. *They* didn't know where they were going.

She was distracted for a while by a small assortment of people who came aboard to ask about passage to Ashkanna, but there was no one of any great interest, just a couple of nobles and a few merchants. Mareesha came up to speak to them, asking if there had been any news from Great Court, and one of the merchants shook his head, but said that a huge procession had gone through the Pass three days before; the Royal party from Ashkanna, bound for Great Court and the funeral of King Tenelon. Shaeli wished she'd seen them – she could have waved to Sir Brudloc.

She didn't want to go to bed that night. She told her mother she wanted to wait until after lift, but was taken to her room anyway. Lift was a long time away, Mareesha said, but when she woke the waters of Nebillonia Straits would be below them.

Shaeli tried to stay awake, but it was no good. She drifted. She struggled. She drifted again. She slept. She dreamed. And Williver came. Smiling.

They walked hand in hand near the Landing on Meoro Pass. Bright morning sunshine fell on their faces, and

Williver's hand was warm as he held hers. They stopped beside the river, and he pointed down the road.

Purple Leaf was disappearing around a bend further down the Pass, yet the sight did not alarm her. She saw with amazement that she could see herself waving from the railing as she had this morning, when they had flown to Meoro Village. She had been waving good-bye to...

Ellirra. She turned and there stood Ellirra, her arm raised. She dropped it and walked towards the group around the wagons, her eyes sweeping across the place where they stood. Shaeli looked up at Williver, surprised.

She didn't see us.

No, little one. We are made of dreams, and you cannot see dreams.

But it was real this morning, she said. *It wasn't a dream then.*

This morning is now part of the memory of the World, Williver answered. *All things that happen leave an imprint upon the World, things past and things present. We are merely visiting this morning's memory in the dreamworld.*

She nodded. It was enough.

Why are we here, Williver? she asked.

To watch, he said. *And to listen.*

He looked towards the little group, and Shaeli followed his gaze. One of the brothers was speaking and she could not hear a word, but then Williver waved his hand before them and the conversation of the travellers was suddenly clear, as if a door had been opened.

So it is settled then, the man was saying. *We head for the top corner, for the town on the bay that Mareesha spoke of.* He looked around, and one by one the others nodded. *Good.* He smiled. *We head for Trilby. With luck we shall reach it before the Wintering. Let's go.*

They began to clamber onto the wagons, and as Ellirra was hoisted up she spoke gaily to her husband.

It is nice to know where we are going, Iden. It sounds a nice place. Trilby.

Iden smiled, picked up the reins, and in moments they were gone. Shaeli and Williver were left standing alone in the slushy roadway. Williver turned to her.

You heard where they go, Shaeli? he said.

Trilby, she nodded. *We were there in summer.*

Good girl, Williver said, smiling. *It matters not that Ellirra holds Shahlita's bangle. You have found the first one, and you shall know where it is when it is needed.*

Shaeli looked doubtful. *But will she give it to me, Williver?*

Yes, little one, he laughed. *I will make sure she dreams of it, when the time comes. Worry no more about it. You have found the first,* he repeated. *Seek the other.*

Shaeli nodded and smiled, and then she knew nothing more. She woke the next morning with the sun streaming in her little window and Williver's voice echoing in her ears.

You have found the first. Seek the other.

* * *

CHAPTER THIRTEEN

After breakfast, Shaeli ran up on deck to see where they were.

The mountains of Zirrus lay behind them, snow-covered and beautiful in the morning light. The waters of the Straits of Nebillonia rocked below them and a clear, pale sky stretched its arms above. A cloudless, lovely morning. They were almost halfway across the Straits, and the hills of Ashkanna could be seen lying low on the horizon ahead, the early mists smudging its shores.

Shaeli went aft to feed the chickens and collect their eggs, and the hens scrambled from their perches as she opened the little door, crowding around her feet for the kitchen scraps and seed she'd brought. She took the eggs from the warm nests and backed out the door while the chickens were still eating. She always felt a bit guilty about taking their eggs.

The day passed quickly. Morning lessons began again, and the afternoon was spent watching the shores of Ashkanna creep closer.

The Zoi flew strongly, eager to stretch their wings after the Wintering, and soon the trees on the shore could be seen. They flew north along the coast, and as afternoon turned to dusk, the lights of a port town began to flicker over the water, and as darkness fell, they moored at Djelda.

Djelda was a big town. Long fingers of wharf stretched into the waters of a huge, teardrop-shaped bay, and many ships were moored along them; more were moored in the bay.

Ashkanna was renowned for its produce and its fabulous textiles, and the Ashkannii were extremely fashionable, devoting whole industries to dressing the more style-challenged – in their eyes, all those on other Lands. Many were the clothes shops and warehouses devoted to clothing, almost as many as those devoted to fine produce, and much of the wealth of Ashkanna passed through Djelda in one way or another. The city gushed people, oozed fine wares, and saw an eternal tide of visitors. The buildings crowded the shoreline so as not to miss any of the fun.

Further along the bay, warehouses and shops gave way to houses, with larger, grander homes lining the gently sloping shores at the plump end of the bay. Private wharves led to most of these big houses, and small lights bobbed at the end of each little wharf, reflecting like miniature moons on the water.

The town had two Landings. The one where they moored was in the central square beside the wharves, and it was a large plain edifice, built for practical purposes. The other was at the far end of the bay among the largest houses in a smaller, but much grander square. Purple Leaf had moored here first to collect supplies, but they would also visit the other Landing before they left Djelda.

After dinner Jarris suggested they go and have honey-cakes and syrup at an inn down on the waterfront, and although Mareesha tried to excuse herself, she was persuaded to bundle up the twins and join the party.

The air outside was crisp and clean, and Shaeli could taste the tang of salt on her tongue as she ran with Andos and Tarkoda across the cobbled square to the waterfront, leaning over the low sandstone wall to watch the dark water of the bay slap against the rock. Dari walked sedately along beside his mother as the others ran ahead, his eyes on the dark alleys around the wharves. Eenis put an arm around his shoulders and smiled fondly at him.

They wandered along the waterfront until they reached a brightly lit building. A sign with a picture of two fish dressed in fine clothes, dancing together, hung outside, and Shaeli sounded the words written below inside her head: *The Dancing Fish*. The courtyard in front was filled with tables of chatting people, and small fires in iron cauldrons were scattered between the tables, for the spring air still held a bite of frost.

They made their way to a table in the corner of the courtyard, Mareesha and Jarris each holding a baby. Shanna was soundly asleep, snuggled against Mareesha's breast, but Neesha was awake and gurgled at the people around them, entranced by everything she saw.

Jeth went inside the inn and soon the table was filled with a mountain of tiny honey-cakes, a jug of warm syrup and a bowl of clotted cream. Neesha made unsteady grabs at anything that came near, watching as Jarris spooned piles of cakes into his mouth, her own tiny mouth working in time with his, and Jarris smuggled her bits of cream on the end of his finger when Mareesha wasn't looking. She said they were too young, yet, to eat such things, but Neesha sucked greedily at every bit of the forbidden food until Mareesha caught Jarris with a clump of cream poised to enter the babe's mouth. Shaeli stifled a giggle as her father looked abashed, but Reneesha wailed as the morsel hanging so tantalisingly close was removed. Mareesha handed Shanna to Eenis, rolled her eyes at Jarris, took Neesha from him and hushed her at the breast.

They were watching the moon rise when there came a sudden tolling of bells from the square, and people began to murmur as questions flew around the courtyard like leaves on a breeze of curiosity. The questions were met by shrugs. A few of the more inquisitive left and began to hurry towards the square. Jarris met Mareesha's eyes across the table.

Eenis added her terse voice to the questioning ones around them. "What is it, do you think?" she asked Jeth.

He shook his head. "I don't know," he said. "Probably news from Great Court."

Everywhere, people had been waiting for the heralds to bring news from Court, and Jeth's words fluttered through the crowd. More people left their tables and headed for the square.

"We should go too," said Jarris. "Whatever is happening, we'll have a better view from the Trader." He looked at Mareesha. "Are you ready?"

She nodded and stood, settling a now-sleeping Neesha over her shoulder. "Yes, Jarris," she said. She took a deep breath and lifted her chin. "I'm ready."

* * *

When they reached the square they found it almost full of people, with more arriving. They made their way across to the Landing, surprised to see another Trader had moored in their absence. It must have come in low, and from the south, or they would have seen it.

Jarris was puzzled. He knew Silver Hawk had been headed for Wokk, and he hurried up the steps. The Landing was filled with people, too, and Jarris took Shaeli's hand and guided her through the crowd to Purple Leaf. He looked back over his shoulder at Jeth.

"Find out why Silver Hawk is here," he said, and Jeth nodded and disappeared through the crowd.

The others went up to the top deck, Eenis holding Dari tightly by the hand until he complained that she was hurting his fingers. She let the hand drop, and clutched Shanna to her breast instead.

The torches that rimmed the square and the dais opposite the Landing had been lit. The crowd below surged and murmured like an anxious sea. The dais was empty, but every face was turned expectantly towards it. The bells still tolled.

Jeth bounded up the steps. "Kaplan said they came upon the royal herald at the top of Meoro Pass. His horse had broken its neck and he needed to cross the Straits with all haste. He has news which he would not impart until he reached Ashkanna, and obviously flying was the quickest way." Jeth shrugged. "So they brought him. Their Zoi are worn out. They've been flying since yesterday morning. They only just managed to get them nested before the bells began."

Jarris was about to reply, but the bells abruptly ceased, creating an eerie silence. He turned to see Djelda's governor mount the steps of the dais, followed by a herald in the colours of King Tenelon. The crowd shivered expectantly.

The herald looked exhausted, even across the distance. His shoulders were slumped and his head hung so low his chin almost rested upon his chest. As he reached the top of the stairs, he raised his head and attempted to straighten his shoulders. His right arm hung in a sling and there was a graze upon his forehead.

Mareesha's free hand rubbed at the scar above her eyebrow. Jarris moved closer, and she leant back against him.

There was utter silence from the crowd. The governor did not speak, merely motioned the herald forward. They all knew he brought news from Great Court. The man walked to the edge of the dais. Everyone heard him draw breath as he clumsily unrolled a scroll and began to read.

"Let it be known throughout the Four Lands and The Starisles that a Royal Coronation was held at Mid-Winter." The people rustled uncomfortably as the herald continued, his strong voice rolling across the gathering like a wave across the bay. "Queen Virrisian, Ruler of all Zirrus, Lady Regent of Romynn, Wokk and Ashkanna, Princess of The Starisles, sends her greetings and regards, and vows to work for the benefit of all." The herald paused again. "Lady Irinesta of Romynn, queen of the late King Tenelon, was delivered of a stillborn son two days after first snow."

A ripple of disquiet swept the crowd. It became a tide as full knowledge reached the edge of the throng. Indignation lapped at the sides of the Traders, people swelled against the base of the dais, shouting questions that the embarrassed herald was unable to answer.

For Virrisian to be crowned before Tenelon was even buried, the babe barely cold, was grave insult indeed. Her right to the throne was not in question, but her method of taking it showed enormous disregard for the traditions of the Realm, and lack of respect for the dead. As the tide of disquiet ebbed, someone at the edge of the crowd began to chant.

"Hail, the new Queen of Zirrus. Hail, Queen Virrisian!"

The cry was begrudgingly taken up, and throughout the square, voices were raised to the new queen, though the faces were still bewildered, still angry. The children aboard the Trader cried out with the rest.

"Hail, Queen Virrisian."

Mareesha remained silent. She looked at Shanna nestled against Eenis' thin chest, and down at the sleeping Neesha in her own arms. She slumped against Jarris, and he put his arms around her and the child. After a moment she straightened and turned to face him, placing the baby in his arms. The green of her eyes was as hard as slate in the torch light.

"I must fetch my bag and see if the herald has need of a Faunist," she said.

"But, Mareesha," Jarris said, "surely he is in good hands? There is no need."

"There *is* a need, Jarris," she answered. "I know him. His name is Gremon and he was in Tenelon's service for many years. He will surely want the comfort of a friendly face to heal his wounds." She silenced his protests with a pointed look. "He has come from Great Court, Jarris, and he knows me," she said, and he understood.

He kissed her cheek and she turned and went below. In moments she was back with her tapestry bag in her hand, and she kissed the children and left the Trader. The square was emptying of people as she made her way across it, and they watched her until she disappeared up the street leading to the house of the governor.

The Landing had almost cleared as the children were ushered downstairs, and Jarris hailed those on Silver Hawk and asked them over for tezz. Kaplan and his sister, Teila, accepted, but Kaplan's wife, Narla, excused herself; she also had children to put to bed.

When Mareesha returned hours later, Kaplan and Teila still sat at the table in the big room, talking quietly with Jarris. Teila stood as Mareesha entered the room.

"Come Kaplan, the hour is late," she said.

"So it is, sister," Kaplan replied. "And it is a long way yet to Wokk."

"You'll leave tomorrow?" asked Jarris.

Kaplan shook his head. "The day after. The Zoi will be more rested and we may as well load some supplies here and travel down the coastline."

Teila looked at Mareesha. "How is the herald?" she asked. "Did he speak of the mood at Great Court?"

"Gremon does well, Teila, and sends his thanks to Silver Hawk," Mareesha said. "His arm is broken, as you know, but not badly." She smiled tiredly at the younger woman. "You set it well."

"Thank you, Mareesha." Teila smiled back, brushing a curl from her forehead. "I'm no Faunist, but I didn't think it was too bad, although he was in pain, much as he tried not to show it." Her voice softened. "And things at Court?" she prodded again. "How go they?"

Mareesha's smile faltered. "Unsettled. Gremon said that many were displeased at Virrisian's taking the crown so hastily. She is rightly heir," Mareesha shifted uncomfortably, "but she would not be persuaded to postpone the coronation, though everyone advised her to. She has dismissed over half of Tenelon's advisors, his Faunists, and his guard, and replaced them with her own, yet apparently she insists little will change within the kingdom. Sir Vulcan is said to have her ear, and most value his opinion and wait to see what will happen." She shrugged. "More than that I do not know."

"And Queen Irinesta, how does she fare?" asked Teila gently.

Mareesha's face set firm. "There is little news of her," she said. "She is said to be in seclusion in the tower of the Glade."

Teila shook her head. "Poor woman. To lose a husband and a child within the same Moon must be a burden indeed."

She and Kaplan said their goodnights and left. Jarris walked them up, and when he returned he found Mareesha in their bedroom, standing by the cot, staring down at the sleeping babies. When he put his hand upon her shoulder, she leant back against him as she had when they'd listened to the first decree from their new queen.

"No one has seen Irinesta since before the coronation, Jarris." She turned to him, her eyes dark and hollow beneath her brows. "I am frightened for her," she said, and she buried her face in his shoulder and wept.

Jarris stroked her head, knowing her strength would return with the shedding of her tears, and he spoke words to bring her comfort, though dread grew inside his chest no matter how he tried to quiet it.

"Irinesta has many friends at Court," he said, "and the People will expect to see her. She will be alright. If she feels unsafe, surely she will go to Romynn?"

Mareesha looked up at him, and nodded. She wiped her eyes. She could help Irinesta only one way. She turned and tucked a blanket around the twins. They lay face to face, breathing softly, and she leant down and kissed the warm heads. She straightened and took Jarris' hand.

"Let's go to bed," she said, her eyes warm and still wet from her tears.

* * *

In the village of Boccra, Verlie was shedding tears too. Fezzik tried to comfort her, but the right words would not come. They had heard of the coronation of the new queen a few days before and there had been anger in the village just as there had been throughout the rest of the Land. Koak at the Orange Duck had forbidden anyone to toast the queen in his establishment. Fezzik's father and the others who gathered at the forge had railed against the injustice, the dishonour, the plain lack of common decency.

"Hush, Verlie, hush," Fezzik said. "There, now. Think of the babe."

"I am thinking of the baby," she said. "I *am* thinking of the little life growing inside me. How much I already love it… how much I love you. And every time I think of poor Queen Irinesta, how awful it must have been for her… to lose the king and then that little baby so soon after. My heart breaks for her."

"I know," he said. "But you must try to look after yourself. It is very late and you must get some sleep. Come, I'll make you some tezz."

"Alright," she said, sniffing and wiping her eyes. "And then can we go outside and ask Aa'liu and Arrell to look after Queen Irinesta? To pray Merrom and the gods will watch over her?"

"Of course we can," Fezzik replied, as he set the water on to boil. "Of course, my love."

* * *

Irinesta woke from the dream bolt upright, perspiration like a clammy hand upon her forehead.

She had been in a rowboat with Tenelon, drifting on calm water in the Bay of Islands, the sun warm on their laughing faces, but birds of prey circled overhead instead of gulls. The Island of Dead Kings lay nearby, the ancient trees hiding the statues and mausoleums. Tenelon had kissed her and dived over the side, but when she'd looked into the water he was gone and the limp form of a tiny baby floated like a rag in his place. The sky had grown instantly dark, the waves enormous, and the boat had been dashed onto the rocks of the island. She had been thrown by a wave onto a little beach, and when she'd dragged herself up, beside her on the sand was the body of the babe, white and shrivelled, and it had been crying…

She shuddered and pulled the blankets more closely about her. Across the room, E'Nith snored softly, and Irinesta was glad she had caught the scream which had been in her throat before it had been given voice. She had no wish to wake her maid. The old woman had been through so much already.

Irinesta sighed and lay back down, though she knew it would be a long time before she slept again. These dreams came often; Tenelon; the poor dead babe; the island. Sometimes she relived the night they had told the soldiers outside the door to fetch water, that the baby was coming. She saw again the unwrapping of the tiny frozen body; the warming of it in a basin of heated water; the throwing of a lump of meat onto the fire before opening the door to declare the child stillborn. E'Nith had done these things; Irinesta had only to lay on the bed looking pale and grief-stricken. It had not been hard. Every time she thought of the dead baby E'Nith had smuggled up from Palveron beneath her clothes she wanted to weep. Knowing he was to be buried with royalty on the Island of Dead Kings instead of in some pauper's grave, unloved and unwanted, brought her no comfort. She had used him. Used his little body to protect her own child, and she could not blame him for disturbing her dreams. It seemed fitting.

She knew every detail of that night had been reported to Virrisian; the water; the noises; the afterbirth burning in the grate; every word, every action, had been judged. She knew too that the child had been examined by Virrisian's Faunists, but she also knew that they could not determine when the child had died. Virrisian would have said something.

The new queen was still visiting the Glade Room whenever the mood took her, and Irinesta was always on edge, expecting her to stride through the door and make some snide remark full of innuendo, or tease E'Nith about her speech. She knew that Virrisian had suspicions, and although Irinesta was sure she had no proof, she also knew Virrisian would not stop looking.

Tomorrow she would leave the Glade Room for Tenelon's funeral. She had watched the ships sail into the harbour, the carriages bringing nobles up to the castle, the Trader fly in from the east, knowing that she would soon accompany her husband on his final journey to the place of her nightmares, the Island of Dead Kings. The casket holding the dead baby boy would be laid beside him, honoured as a child of the Realm. She would wear a dark veil to hide her face, and she would speak to no one. She would then return to the Glade Room, to her "seclusion". She did not have a choice. She would not oppose Virrisian again. Once had been enough.

She had been shocked when she'd heard the news of Virrisian's Mid-Winter coronation; shocked and furious, and she had rushed to First Tower. The princess had been with her advisors when Irinesta had burst in and demanded Virrisian give her answers. Virrisian had calmly dismissed everyone and then turned to Irinesta.

"Why, sister," she'd smiled. "I had not realised that my coronation would upset you so. It *is* only a mere formality, after all."

"Upset me, Virrisian?" Irinesta seethed. "With Tenelon not even interred or decently mourned? The boy dead less than a Moon? How could you think this would *not* upset me?"

Virrisian shrugged deliberately. "Tenelon is dead. The throne is mine." The smile disappeared. "And as for the babe..." She let the words hang for a moment and fear clutched at Irinesta's heart. "I have my doubts about the babe."

Irinesta kept her face still. "Doubts? What doubts, Virrisian?"

Virrisian looked closely at Irinesta, her ice-grey eyes narrow.

"Oh, just *doubts*." She shook her head, and her cool smile reappeared. "You had him embalmed and in his casket so *swiftly*, Irinesta. Within a day of his unhappy death."

"It was over, Virrisian. I saw no reason to prolong it."

"Over. Yes, over." Virrisian came closer until Irinesta could have touched her. "I wonder about that, sister."

"What do you mean?"

Virrisian shrugged again, the cold smile still on her face. It seemed suddenly very out of place.

"One hears things," she said. "One can make inquiries. Easily, if they are queen." The smile was gone and Virrisian snatched Irinesta's wrist. "One never knows what one may find. 'Tis said to be easy to find a babe, if one has coin. Alive *or* dead." The cold hand gripped tighter. "Easy to hide one, change one for another."

Virrisian's face was close. Irinesta could feel her breath. It smelled of cloves and threats.

"Do not cross me, *sister*," Virrisian said softly. "Not about my *rightful* coronation, or anything else, or those you care for will be truly sorry. I would hate for anything to befall Sir Vulcan or Lady Arinola. Your faithful old maid. Some accident. An illness." The grey, almost lashless eyes filled Irinesta's vision. "And if I find evidence of what I seek, then…" that careful shrug again. The cold in Virrisian's eyes mirrored the chill in Irinesta's heart.

She suspects, cried Irinesta's mind. Her heart was beating hard against her ribs, but she stayed calm, and kept her face merely angry. Virrisian could prove nothing. Find nothing. Know nothing. Irinesta took the offensive.

"Are you *mad*, Virrisian?" she cried, wrenching her wrist from Virrisian's grip. "You talk nonsense. My husband and child are *both* lost to me." It was not a lie, and her voice cracked as she spoke the words. "You speak out of turn, Virrisian, and with no compassion. When did you become so cold, so cruel?" She turned to sweep from the room. "You have not heard the last of this. I shall speak to the Court. You shall not win in the matter of the coronation."

"Oh, but I will win," said Virrisian, so quietly that Irinesta stopped and turned. "I will *always* win. This is only the beginning. I advise you to stay in your precious tower." The cold little half-smile appeared again. "You would do well to consider retirement. Seclusion. If you are sensible. Heed me, Irinesta."

But Irinesta had not heeded, not then, yet seven days later she had been forced to heed, and heed well. She had spent those days talking and lobbying for a postponement to Virrisian's coronation, and she had drawn much support. Many were those who thought as she did; the crowning of Virrisian was untimely and disrespectful.

Then, one night, she was woken from sleep by her door banging open. The moon was a thin crescent, but there had been enough light to see two black-clad figures thrust something through the door and slam it shut.

Irinesta had leapt from the bed and hurried to light a candle as the bundle moaned. She found E'Nith lying on the floor, blood covering her face and clothes. The tip of her tongue had been cut off, and she had cried as Irinesta took her in her arms, her own eyes brimming.

E'Nith began shaking her grey head, moaning, clutching at a note pinned to her bodice. Blood smeared the crudely written words. E'Nith clutched her arm, trying to speak.

"I know," soothed Irinesta. "I know you told them nothing. Hush, now. Hush." She held the weeping old woman tightly. "They shall not hurt you again," she whispered. "I'll not make them hurt anyone again."

Only the beginning, the note pinned to the old woman's chest had read. They were Virrisian's words, repeated on paper, just as she had spoken them to Irinesta in First Tower.

Only the beginning.

***

CHAPTER FOURTEEN

The next morning was a busy one on Purple Leaf. Those from Silver Hawk came over for breakfast and the kitchen was filled with noise and activity. Mareesha and Jarris made mountains of pancakes, and after breakfast the boys went with the adults to order supplies at the warehouses along the bay. Dari had to be prised from his bed; he had wanted to stay asleep, and Eenis worried that he was ill and kept feeling his forehead.

Mareesha and Narla stayed aboard with the younger children. Kaplan and Narla had two children; a boy, Kahn, not much older than the twins, and a daughter, two Winter's younger than Shaeli, and they spent a quiet morning until the others arrived back in a flurry of laughter, their arms full of purchases; even Eenis was almost cheerful, having struck many a fine bargain with the Djeldan merchants. They had brought a variety of exotic foods with them for lunch, and then they transferred their goods to the Traders' storerooms.

The local merchants carted goods to the Landing, and each Trader had a boom opposite the landing gate. The boom swung out, a hemp net was lowered, filled with goods, raised up and swung back on deck. Everybody helped with the unloading, and even the babies were propped up to watch in a basket on deck.

Next morning, Kaplan and Teila lifted Silver Hawk smoothly from her moorings to begin their belated journey to Wokk, and then Purple Leaf lifted also and flew down the bay to the smaller Landing amid the grand houses of Djelda. The houses had lush lawns sloping down to the water, and in the garden of one enormous white-columned house, several children played. They stopped their game as the Trader flew past and ran to the water's edge to wave, and Shaeli waved back, admiring the lovely, port-wine coloured cape worn by one of the girls. The girl stood at the front of the group, her blonde curls falling from her hood, and she yelled something up to them, but Shaeli couldn't hear what she said.

They moored at the Landing in a garden-like square, and several people arrived for Faunist's treatment, drawn by the flag fluttering at the rear of the Trader, a white hand on a green background. Though there were many Faunists in Djelda, there were those who liked to try someone new as well as those who came specifically to see Mareesha.

The Landing was one of the more ornate ones, the wood carved with small waves and fishes, one end enclosed to create a small private room, and Mareesha saw people in this anteroom, crossing to Purple Leaf to prepare medications or tonics.

Shaeli was sitting on deck when a carriage pulled up at the bottom of the Landing, and the girl with the beautiful cape stepped down from it, a small basket in one hand. The man who helped her down had hair the same curling blonde as the child's. The girl smiled when she saw Shaeli looking over the rail.

"I told you I'd see you here," she said, her accent rich with the cultured note of a well-bred Ashkannii. "As soon as I saw you I told Father he must bring me." She looked up at the man beside her. "We need to see the Faunist, don't we?" she asked, and he smiled back down at her and nodded.

"It seems so, Crissita," he said. "Snowflake is not getting any better, is she? And no Faunist in Djelda has managed to find the cause."

Crissita began to say something else when a harsh cough stopped her, and she covered her mouth as her father patted her back. When the fit had passed, she shook her head again and smiled at Shaeli through tear-filled eyes.

"I'm terribly sorry," she apologised. "This silly cough comes every year." She cleared her throat and looked around. "Where is the Faunist?"

Shaeli opened her mouth to answer, and jumped as a voice spoke from behind her.

"She's downstairs making a tonic for someone, but she won't be long."

It was Tarkoda. He had come up behind Shaeli and she turned to look at him, but he was looking past her at Crissita with a peculiar grin on his face.

"I'll tell her you want to see her," he said, and he turned and raced below.

Shaeli shook her head at this odd behaviour, and turned back to Crissita.

"Who's Snowflake?" she asked.

Crissita motioned her over and Shaeli crossed to the Landing. Crissita put the basket on the bench and pulled back the cover.

"This is Snowflake," she whispered.

The smallest, fluffiest jevvi Shaeli had ever seen lay asleep in the basket, its long tail curled all the way around it. Jevvies, tiny native marsupials, were a favourite pet of the rich on Ashkanna. They grew no bigger than a slipper, were extremely intelligent and easily tamed. Their gentle nature made them a favourite with children, and Shaeli had seen them before, sitting on the shoulders of their masters, long, fluffy tails hanging down, huge, round eyes and pointed ears alert to everything.

Shaeli sighed at Crissita's little jevvi. She'd never seen a white one before, only pale grey and brown ones, and they'd all looked so lively that it was easy to see this one was ill. It lay shivering and snoring, one paw over its eyes.

"Oh," said Shaeli, "poor little thing." She reached out a hand and stroked the soft fur. "Don't worry Snowflake, Mam will fix you," she whispered.

Crissita softly stroked the jevvi's ears and it snuggled against her hand.

"Is your mam the Faunist?" she asked, and Shaeli nodded. Crissita covered the basket again, and asked Shaeli what it was like to travel around in a Trader. "I've always thought it looked like such fun," she said, looking admiringly up at the balloon.

They sat talking while Crissita's father stood nearby, gazing out at the bay, his hand tapping a light rhythm against the rail, until Mareesha came across the deck, closely followed by Tarkoda. When Mareesha crossed to the Landing, Shaeli took Crissita's hand and stood up.

"Crissita's jevvi is sick, Mam," she said. "You'll fix it, won't you?"

To Shaeli's surprise, her mother dropped into a low curtsey, and bowed her head. Shaeli looked at Tarkoda, and saw her own surprise mirrored on his face, but only for a moment. His eyes moved back to Crissita, and they glazed slightly as he stared at her, his mouth slack. Shaeli was more surprised than ever. She had only ever seen that look on her brother's face once before.

Last spring, he'd stood with Andos gazing for hours through a window at a knife in a shop on Wokk. The knife had had five different blades, each folding cunningly into the elaborate handle, and there had been a place to engrave the owner's name on the side. Only on Wokk could such an ingenious knife be found, and Tarkoda and Andos had talked of nothing else the whole time they were there and for a full Moon after. Now he looked at Crissita the same way he'd looked at the knife, part awe, part longing.

Mareesha rose from her curtsey, and smiled at Crissita and her father. "I will be happy to look at your jevvi, princess," she said.

Shaeli looked at the girl beside her, her mouth hanging open as Mareesha smiled at Crissita's father.

"I will be but a moment, Prince Davron," Mareesha said, "and then you may bring them in." She bobbed again at his nod and went into the anteroom.

Shaeli looked down and found she was still holding Crissita's hand, and she dropped it, closed her mouth, and stared uncomfortably at her feet. A princess? And she'd been sitting there babbling about silly things, just as if Crissita were an everyday person. She was horribly embarrassed.

Crissita appeared not to notice Shaeli's discomfort, and she dimpled at Tarkoda, who hung over the rail staring. He smiled foolishly and Shaeli thought she'd never seen him look so silly – or so restrained. He was usually relaxed and confident, and had vast numbers of acquaintances in towns everywhere, and it was strange to see him struck dumb by anyone, especially a girl. He didn't usually have much time for girls.

Shaeli looked back at Crissita, who was peering into the basket. She *was* pretty, and Shaeli guessed she was about Koda's age, but she couldn't see why he would act so strangely.

Andos walked up behind Tarkoda and asked him what he was doing. He had been waiting for Tarkoda on the top deck, and loudly inquired about what had kept him. Tarkoda muttered he'd gone to find his mother, and then whispered that Crissita was a princess. Andos regarded her for a moment, then shrugged, unimpressed, and urged him to come and finish their game. Tarkoda trailed his cousin across the deck, looking regretfully back over his shoulder.

Mareesha opened the door of the anteroom, and an elegantly dressed woman stepped out. She saw Crissita and her father, dropped into a curtsey and murmured a greeting, then thanked Mareesha and swept down the stairs.

Crissita rose to her feet, the little basket in her hand, and was racked by another harsh cough. Her father rubbed her back, and Mareesha's brow wrinkled in concern. The fit passed quickly and Crissita apologised and followed Mareesha to the door. She stopped and looked back at Shaeli.

"Do you want to come?" Crissita asked.

Shaeli looked at her mother, who smiled and nodded slightly. Shaeli grinned and eagerly followed them through the door and closed it behind her.

Crissita placed the basket on the table in the centre of the room. She dropped the hood of her cape and shook her blonde curls before pulling off the cover of the basket. Her father took a seat, appearing content to let the child speak, and Crissita was obviously used to making herself understood.

She and Mareesha held a short, concise discussion on Snowflake's condition, the length of her illness, her diet and habits. Mareesha then took the animal gently out of the basket and examined her. She felt the belly of the jevvi, peered into her mouth and eyes, even smelt her breath. She asked Crissita more questions about Snowflake's diet, and then nodded.

Mareesha managed to keep her smile in check as she explained what was the matter: Snowflake was drunk. It seemed that she had a habit of sneaking into Crissita's mother's rooms and helping herself to the brandy-soaked plums which were kept there. How many times a day she was stealing the heavily laced fruit was not known, but it was obviously too many. They were evidently greatly favoured by the jevvi as well as Crissita's mother, and Mareesha, her laughter at last sneaking past her lips, prescribed a strict diet and advised the brandy-plums be kept well out of reach.

She handed the jevvi back to Crissita, who held her up to eye level and scolded her. Snowflake yawned and put a paw over her huge brown eyes and fell asleep. They all laughed as Crissita bundled the jevvi back into its basket, and covered her. Crissita's laughter turned into another coughing spasm, and Mareesha looked in concern at the child.

"How long have you been ill, my lady?" she asked.

Crissita shook her head. "Oh, I am not ill. I have this cough every spring. It always passes." She looked up at Prince Davron. "Doesn't it, Father?"

"Yes, Crissita, it does." He looked thoughtful for a moment. "And yet, it seems this year it is worse."

Mareesha looked at him. "Will you permit me to examine her, Prince Davron?" she asked.

He looked down at his daughter's face, pink from effort, her eyes watery, as breathless as though she'd been running. He looked back at Mareesha and nodded.

Mareesha asked Crissita to take off her cape, and Shaeli sat with it upon her lap, stroking the rich, wine-red velvet as Crissita sat upon the table and Mareesha asked her questions, similar to those she'd asked about the jevvi. Then she took a short, hollow cylinder from her bag and went behind Crissita, placing one end under the girl's shoulder blade and her ear on the other, and she asked Crissita to breathe deeply. As Crissita did so, Mareesha began moving the cylinder around her back, listening intently. On her fifth breath Crissita began to cough again, and Mareesha stood, nodded and placed the cylinder back in her bag.

"Your daughter has a very slight weakness of the chest, Prince Davron," she said. "But I think it shall be easily remedied, and she'll cough no more." She smiled down at Crissita. "You will need all your energy to keep that little jevvi from eating any more brandy-plums."

"Do I have to take a tonic?" Crissita asked suspiciously.

Though she smiled still, it was a smile born of good manners only, and did not touch her narrowed eyes. Shaeli was surprised at the change in her.

Mareesha laughed. "No, Princess, no tonics. Just breathing steam and special herbs, a few times a day. Alright?"

Crissita nodded. This time her answering smile was genuine, her good humour instantly restored. She jumped off the table and gathered up the basket containing the jevvi. "Thank you," she said.

"You are most welcome, Princess Crissita," replied Mareesha, bobbing back. She looked smilingly at Prince Davron. "Will you wait a moment while I prepare the herbs?"

He nodded and they walked back outside. Shaeli trailed along behind, still carrying the cape.

Mareesha crossed to the Trader and disappeared below deck, returning quickly with a package of herbs, and instructions for their use were given.

"If the cough returns, and you have need of more herbs, the Lady Chi'alon has the same condition, and always has a great supply," said Mareesha.

The prince nodded. "Lady Chi'alon, the lady who just left?"

Mareesha nodded, and looked down at Crissita. "Swimming is also good for you, when the weather warms."

"I swim now," said Crissita. "We have a warm pool at home. Our Warlock keeps it so. It is inside, so we can swim during the Wintering." She looked to Shaeli. "You can come and visit, if you'd care to."

Shaeli turned eagerly to her mother.

"Perhaps," Mareesha said, but Shaeli could tell that her mother wasn't enthusiastic about the idea.

Prince Davron turned to leave, and Shaeli held out the cape, but Crissita shook her head.

"You can have it, if you'd like," she said. "It's getting a bit short, and I've dozens more."

Shaeli once again looked to her mother, who in turn looked to Prince Davron, who shrugged. Mareesha smiled at Shaeli and nodded, and Shaeli hugged the cape to her chest. Mareesha waved away the coin Prince Davron offered her. Looking at Shaeli's joyful face, she assured him it had been her pleasure.

Shaeli thanked Crissita again and again, her eyes shining. Crissita looked as if she couldn't understand what the fuss was about – indeed, now she seemed bored, and anxious to be off.

As they drove off in the carriage, Shaeli took Mareesha's hand and they crossed over to the Trader. She looked up at the gently bobbing balloon, and wondered for the first time what it would be like to be someone else. She'd thought about the people who weren't traders, of course, and been glad that she was one, but to *be* someone else, have *dozens* of velvet capes, and a warm pool, inside. She shook her head and nuzzled at the cape, let go of Mareesha's hand and spread the cape over her shoulders. Mareesha knelt down and helped her with the tie, and pulled the hood up. It had a band of black fur around the edge that tickled her cheek.

"How come she's a princess, Mam?" Shaeli asked.

Mareesha finished with the hood and stood up. "Prince Davron is brother to Queen Elenes," she said.

Shaeli nodded, and looked thoughtful. "They only have queens on Ashkanna, don't they?"

"Yes, and Queen Elenes has many brothers. Princess Crissita is one of only a few girls born to their lineage, and so is one of those in line for the throne, after Elenes' own baby daughter."

"Can I visit Crissita, Mam, and see the pool inside?"

"Perhaps Shaeli," she said. "We shall see."

But again Shaeli had the feeling that the idea didn't appeal to her mother. "Don't you like them, Mam?" she asked.

Mareesha thought for a moment before answering. "I like them well enough, Shaeli. 'Tis only that I think she'll not remember. The princess has many... distractions, and I think that it is unlikely she will recall the invitation." *Or even your face when next she sees you*, Mareesha thought to herself.

Djeldan nobles were noted for their pursuit of pleasures and dislike of anything serious, and she doubted a child of the vague, self-indulgent Prince Davron, and his vain, elegant wife would be very much different.

But she was wrong. The next morning a runner came from the house of Prince Davron, requesting not only Shaeli, but the boys, too, come for lunch with Crissita. The children begged to be allowed to go, Tarkoda even more vocal than Shaeli, and they were given permission. Even Dari was enthusiastic about the idea.

For Shaeli the morning dragged. She played impatiently with the twins and wandered the length of the Trader, willing the time to pass. When at last it had, Jarris escorted the four of them, dressed in their best clothes, to the high gates surrounding the white-columned house.

They spent a wonderful afternoon after a lunch that could have fed twenty children; they swam in the warm pool and played on the lawn where they had first seen Crissita. The bay sparkled, and Shaeli tried to imagine what the Trader had looked like from down here, with her waving, up there.

They also played with the jevvi, who exhibited no sign of her stupor of the previous day. Crissita had half a dozen of the little creatures, and Snowflake kept them amused finding nuts hidden by the children, locating even the most cunningly concealed.

Shaeli's day was only marred, and then just a little, by Crissita's slightly condescending manner. It was she who determined what they did and where they did it, and when Crissita was bored they did something else, but it was all such fun, and so different to their everyday life, that it hardly mattered. When Jarris collected them late in the afternoon, they were full of the wonders they had seen, the size of the house, and Dari's pockets bulged with the lollies he had taken from every bowl he'd seen.

The big Trader seemed very cramped that night, and as Shaeli lay in bed, the velvet cloak draped over her, she thought how glad she was that her mother had been wrong, and Crissita had remembered her, after all.

* * *

But, in the end, Mareesha was right.

Three Winters later, when Purple Leaf was again in the city of Djelda, Shaeli saw Crissita in the streets and rushed to greet her, smiling broadly.

Crissita looked puzzled, and merely nodded absently as she passed by. Shaeli, her feelings hurt, frowned at the retreating, stylish figure. Crissita glanced back over her shoulder and then whispered in the ear of her equally well-dressed companion. The two giggled and Shaeli's face burned. She was sure the remark had not been pleasant, and it had been directed at her. Mareesha tugged gently on her hand, and they continued on, but Shaeli remembered that slight for a very long time.

* * *

It had been a quiet three years. Despite an initial uneasiness with the new Queen Virrisian, the people had relaxed into her reign, and the Four Lands and the Starisles had continued to run much as they had before. The new colours of the Queen's guard, black and scarlet, were to be seen throughout the Lands, but they were unobtrusive, and soon taken for granted. A sigh of relief seemed to breathe across Zirrus.

Purple Leaf had traded mostly on Ashkanna and Zirrus the first two years, but last year they had flown across to Wokk, spending half the year there before flying up to Ashkanna.

Wokk was rich in ore, and the Wokkii were masters of metal-craft, makers of fine weapons, kitchenware and jewellery. It was a land of contradictions, lush plains and valleys to the north, rocky open spaces to the south, mountains thick with rainforest and majestic rivers in between, yet it was also a dangerous land, dotted with mountains holding fire deep inside their bellies. They had seen one of the smoking mountains far off on the western coast, another across a black, uninhabited plain, and her father had told her that Wokk was sometimes affected by earth tremors, where the ground would shake, and the buildings could be toppled and people killed.

Many and strange were the creatures of Wokk; odd birds; tiny jenka; marsupials whose call was like the sound of children giggling in the trees at night; others that inhabited the plains, making enormous mounds to live in, dirt castles to keep them cool in the summer and protected during the harsh Wokk Wintering. Yet what made the creatures of Wokk the strangest of all the Lands was that there, some had grown big. Very big. The chickens were the best known, as dull as chickens everywhere and easy to farm, yet they were the size of small boulders. There were huge insects; dragonflies the size of dinner plates; butterflies like flying pillowcases; caterpillars as thick as a child's waist and as long as a landing post; and in the sea there were the whales, ever the largest of creatures, but also starfish as big as blankets, and seahorses almost the size of their cousins on land. There were also the Qotarr.

The Land was made up of four main islands and dozens of lesser isles, and one of these lesser isles, off the coast of the largest eastern island, was the home of the Qotarr. On the way from Wokk to Ashkanna, Purple Leaf had flown over the island.

It was a big island, thickly forested around its rim, with stony beaches falling into deep blue water. In the middle, the land rose sharply, sheer ragged cliffs raising the centre up into a high plateau that was half covered with forest, and half of the remains of a mountain, its sides black and rocky, its centre a deep crater. One thin line of smoke drifted up from the crater into the sky as Purple Leaf flew towards it beneath the early morning sun, and Jarris told them the top of the mountain had blown off many decades before, and the land around it was only now recovering. He flew the Trader around the edge of the decapitated mountain, and down across the thick trees of the plateau. As the land dropped away abruptly beneath them, he took the ship down.

Tarkoda was the first to see one. He shouted, his arm flying out like an arrow as he pointed into the trees below. A giant lizard lay on a rocky outcrop, sunning itself. Its back was studded with two rows of gigantic spines, its tail showing rows of lesser spikes, long and sharp as swords, and ending in a spiky ball. It raised its massive head as the Trader flew over, opened its mouth and hissed at them. Shaeli had never seen anything so frightening in her whole life, and she clutched at her father's arm as she looked down into the mouth of the giant, shuddering at the blue-grey tongue, the black gaping hole rimmed by yellow teeth.

Along a rocky beach they saw another, as long as a Wintering Hall, lumbering back into the forest. They followed the coast around, and along the edge of a bay, six more Qotarr roamed, some looking up at the Trader and hissing, others laying on the rocks, indifferent to the intrusion. One was accompanied by two young, as long as carts, the spines on their backs mere nubs, watching from the water's edge as their mother waded in the bay. She snapped at something beneath the water as they flew over, coming up with a large stingray, its grey wings and tail flapping uselessly as she carried it back to her waiting children. They pounced on it as she came from the water, tearing shreds from the writhing creature. Further along the bay, another Qotarr swam in deeper water, its tail snaking along behind it. Shaeli looked over at the big island to the west.

"Do they ever swim over and eat the people there?" she asked, and Jarris smiled and tousled her hair.

"The Qotarr are good fishers," he said, "but they can't swim far. The people of Wokk are safe, though sometimes, I hear young men with more courage than sense sail over and try to rope one of the beasts."

"I heard of someone capturing a baby once," Jeth said, "and taking it back to the mainland."

They circled the bay, watching the baby Qotarr squabbling over the remains of the stingray, and then they flew to Ashkanna for the rest of the year.

The last Wintering had passed quickly, and they had flown again to Ashkanna after first thaw. Mareesha would gather Faunist supplies, but then they would be heading much further north into the warmth of the spring. This year, they were going to the Starisles.

* * *

Dari spent their last night in Djelda roaming the streets around the Landing. He looked in windows and wandered into alleys around the docks; he broke the heads off flowers in well-kept gardens and watched the women standing beneath lampposts call to the sailors leaving the taverns. One checked doorhandle revealed an open office, and he helped himself to the coins he found in a drawer and a set of fine quills that he thought Garrit would like.

He had become good friends with Garrit over the last few years, and Garrit wasn't horrified by Dari's wanderings as others would be, he advised only that Dari keep them short, and that he be careful not to miss too much sleep.

Garrit was envious of Dari's travels. He loved a city, speaking often of the fine foods and wines, the pleasant, witty company; he abhorred Cave, and while he revelled in the prestige that being taught by Almarnoch would give him, he could not wait to go back out into "cultured society".

Dari had looked at most of the cities they'd been to, alone and in the dark, but only a few of the towns, and sometimes, if he was in the mood, he would go and open gates in flock-filled fields or the doors on chicken coops. Wokk had been fun for that; giant chickens were easily spooked and almost as stupid as his brother.

Here in Djelda there was always something of interest, the docks, the taverns, the fights outside when the sailors had drunk too much, and Dari was already bored with the thought of the Starisles. He imagined that the only good thing about it would be telling Garrit how awful it was when he got back to Cave for the Wintering. He saw them laughing together over the dullness of the islanders and the trivial lives of his family. It always amused Garrit, hearing about the dullards of the World, and if there was anything which gave Dari joy, it was amusing Garrit.

* * *

CHAPTER FIFTEEN

Mareesha crossed from the cool shade of the stairwell into the brightness of the day. She scanned the expanse of deck for her daughters, and then walked up the short flight to the top deck. Jarris was there coiling rope, and she asked him if he had seen the girls.

He peered across the deck. "I believe there was some excitement about new chicks," he said, his blue eyes crinkling in amusement.

Mareesha smiled at him, went back down the steps, and crossed to the small coop at the far end of the deck. As she neared, she heard hushed voices and soft clucks from the chickens, and she leant down and peered through the partly open door.

Shaeli and the twins sat on an old sack in the centre of the small coop, half a dozen hens roosting about them. Three new chicks sat in the pocket of skirt that hung between Shaeli's crossed legs. Roshanna and Reneesha sat on either side of her, stroking the fluffy yellow down.

Neesha saw her mother peering in the door and jumped to her knees. "Look Mam," she cried. "Chicken's had babies."

Her cry sent the chicks scurrying off Shaeli's knee and under the breast of their nearby mother. Shaeli rolled her eyes at her sister.

"Oh, Neesha," she said. "You frightened them."

"I didn't fright them, Shaeli," Neesha said, in her strong, baby voice. "Mam did."

Shaeli and Mareesha laughed, and Shaeli stood up and ushered the girls out the door, pulling it closed behind her. Shanna pulled at Shaeli's skirt, and Shaeli looked down at her.

"It *was* Neesha frighted them," Shanna said softly. "Wasn't it?"

Shaeli nodded, her lips curving. She smoothed the dark hair off Shanna's forehead, took her hand, and began to walk back towards the stairwell. It was time for an embroidery lesson and Eenis would be waiting for her. Shaeli walked slowly. She disliked sewing more than she had ever thought possible. Tapestry was fine, but embroidery escaped her entirely.

Neesha came and took her other hand and Mareesha watched the three from behind.

Shaeli, eight this last Wintering, had proved an invaluable help with the twins. At three, they had become inquisitive and lively toddlers.

Reneesha had thick brown hair, a square chin, and deep-green eyes. She had talked early, exercised her voice at every opportunity, and her cries of indignation or distress could be heard throughout the ship. All Wintering she had dominated the group of small children at Cave with her loud voice and bossy ways, and yet they all adored her.

Roshanna, too, had green eyes, but her hair was almost black, similar in colour to Mareesha's. Her heart-shaped face reflected a nature that was much gentler than her sister's, but she could be extremely stubborn when the need arose, and was inclined to sulk, which Jarris joked had been inherited from Shaeli. Though Shanna, too, had learned to speak early, she used her voice only when she needed, preferring mostly to watch all that went on around her. Both girls adored their brother and cousins, yet Shaeli was their idol and they shadowed her everywhere.

"When will we be in the Starisles, Mam?" asked Shaeli, as they walked downstairs.

"We shall be there by the Full, and when the moon is dark we'll see the skylights at the Spring Festival on Pa'laidiz." Mareesha stopped outside her bedroom door. "These girls are having their rest, Shaeli, and Eenis is waiting for you."

Shaeli nodded and headed towards the big room, Neesha's loud voice complaining about having to lie down followed her down the hall.

Despite the embroidery lesson, Shaeli was excited. She couldn't remember ever going to the Starisles, though Mareesha assured her that they had been there five Winters before, when she was about the twins' age. Mareesha's herb cupboard was filled to overflowing with the produce from the fields of Ashkanna, and the storage space at the bottom of the stairs was filled with callow-root. Mareesha would grind it during the journey north into the fine, antiseptic powder so highly prized by Faunists everywhere.

They had left Djelda the day before and Shaeli was not sorry to leave it behind. Embarrassment still burned her cheeks when she recalled her meeting with Princess Crissita on the street a few days before, and she longed to put the incident as far from herself as she could. They flew over Ashkanna soil still, but it would not be long until the waters of Nebillonia Straits would be beneath them. They would cross to the first of the islands, Xenel, in the strait between Zirrus and Ashkanna, and then visit Argon and the other small islands on their journey north. Xenel Island, though small, was a popular stopover point for both Traders and ships travelling the northern waters, and the islanders traded well. It was fruitless to cross to Zirrus before Xenel. The waters of Zirrus' shoreline between Meoro Pass and Xenel Island were inhospitable, filled with sharp reefs and treacherous rocks, and the mountains loomed above, high and forbidding, hugging much of the jagged coastline for hundreds of leagues.

As Mareesha had said, before the full of the moon they had reached the northernmost tip of Zirrus, mooring in the large coastal town of Conroi, a bustling port city eternally busy with travellers. On a high bluff overlooking the town were the bones of a new outpost for the queen's guard, and although the trade in Conroi was brisk, they stayed only one night before flying to the Starisles.

It was a long haul across to the first of the Starisles, Irojadis, a half-circle island with white sand and tall palm trees. It was, like Conroi and Xenel Island, a place of transience, and they stayed there for three days, resting the Zoi after their journey over the Estrellan Sea.

The Starisles was almost another world. It was ruled by a council of people from all over the islands, the Starcluster, and it stood apart from the Four Lands. Hundreds of islands were scattered through the northern sea, some mere mounds of sand, others wide and verdant with peaked mountains towering over thick forests and rich fields; islands every shape and size in between. Sweet, natural springs abounded, some with amazingly warm waters bubbling up from the ground which the people captured and fed into long tiled pools. The people of the Starisles cultivated the surrounding oceans, and their kelp, salt and fish produce, their mastery of jewel-craft, made for strong trade and ties with the Four Lands.

Purple Leaf took the journey to the main island slowly, stopping at many of the smaller islands along the way. As the mountains of the main island drew near, the enthusiasm aboard Purple Leaf grew, and even the adults were infected by the growing excitement.

Pa'laidiz was a huge island of soaring green mountains and tangled valleys of rich rainforest. It was a wild and beautiful place, the city renowned for its elegance and charm, the people admired for their warmth and love of life. Hundreds of lesser islands lay scattered around Pa'laidiz like handfuls of bright pebbles in the northern sea.

Scores of boats filled Pa'laidiz harbour, craft big and small rode the water, throngs of people milled along the shoreline, and the streets were wide and lined with flowering trees in shades of pink and mauve. Graceful turrets and gabled buildings overlooked the harbour in a rainbow of colours; blue peaks, pink columns, lacy yellow verandas, lilac-framed windows, blending with the drifts of trees and flower-filled gardens to create a feeling of light and harmony. The mountains behind provided a perfect dappled-green backdrop for the pastel city.

They landed easily at the big Landing beside the harbour where mysteriously draped stalls filled much of the square, but the children were not allowed to explore that afternoon; there was much to do before the next day, a market day.

Another Trader was moored at the big Landing, its white-dolphins-on-blue balloon bobbing gently in the breeze. Blue Dolphin came to the Starisles every year, to transport vast cargoes of salt back to the mainland. It was said at Cave that by the time Blue Dolphin lost its salty smell, the Wintering was over and it was time for them to fly back to the Starisles. Larby and his son, Bryl, hung in the rigging and waved as Purple Leaf moored. Bia and her daughter, Betka, stood on the deck, and called greetings across the Landing, and the two families chatted until the fading light sent them below decks.

The next day was filled with activity and good things to eat. The stalls in the square opened early, the drapes pulled back to reveal a huge array of goods, and when the children had eaten too much and inspected every stall, they retired to the Landing to watch the bright throng milling below. At the end of the day the stalls were draped again, and only a few would open for trade before the Spring Festival.

The days before the festival were spent exploring the town and lazing on the white sands of the beaches strung like strands of pearls around the harbour. Shaeli, Tarkoda and Andos built castles which the twins delighted in knocking over, the adults sat in the shade of the flowering trees, and Dari just lazed in the sun. They swam for hours in the sheltered waters; Shaeli, a proficient swimmer, had developed a smooth clean stroke and she practised diving from a big flat rock and explored the little pools at the edge of the beaches.

One day as she squatted by a pool, sifting through the sand in search of shells, she saw a small fishing boat sailing around the point. A boy sat on the prow, leaning forward, his eyes fixed eagerly on the approaching city. The man at the tiller called something to him, and the boy turned, grinning widely and replying before facing forward again. Shaeli couldn't hear what they said, the wind stole the words away, but they both looked so happy that she smiled across the water at them. The boy glanced toward the shore, his brown hair ruffling in the breeze, and then he looked ahead again.

Suddenly, a seabird dropped to the sand beside her, shaking its head and cawing loudly. She jumped in fright, and then froze, staring at the long-legged bird.

It was a pretty bird, cool grey with a crisp white throat and black streaks around its eyes, but it was croaking and shaking its head, rolling its eyes at her. Puzzled by its odd behaviour, she sat unmoving as the bird shook its head, bent its long neck forward in a kind of bow, and closed its eyes. It struggled for a while, coughing and cawing, webbed feet scratching at the sand, then, with a final shake of its head and a strangled squawk, the bird hacked an object onto the sand. It fixed Shaeli with one shiny black eye, and flew off, loudly crying its relief.

Shaeli walked over to the thing that lay in the sand, and understood the bird's distress. At her feet lay a tangled ball of fishing line, as big as a plum. She poked at the lump with her toe. Enmeshed in the core was something solid, and she squatted down and peered at it. A small pear-shaped stone, the remains of a strand of leather wrapped around the smaller end, was tangled inside the clump of line, and she picked up the tangle between two fingers and carried it over to a rock pool and dropped it in. When any remains of what might be found in a seabird's throat had been washed away, she began to untangle the fishing line from around the stone. It took a long time, and then she rinsed the stone again and held it up to the sun.

It was a flattened pear, big as a coin, but light between her fingers, and it was a lovely colour; a pale, burnt honey, perfectly clear, with a smooth, shiny finish. The stone was like a drop of sun-warmed ale, complete with tiny bubbles trapped in its centre.

The strand of leather proved difficult to remove, and she walked back up the beach to where Mareesha sat watching the twins chasing small waves, and showed her the stone and told her how she had found it. Mareesha shook her head in amazement and said the stone was amber and that they were sometimes used in the casting of lesser spells. Shaeli tucked the amber-stone inside her amulet, greatly pleased; it was the most interesting thing she'd found since discovering the wand near Lake Marnissi.

Two days after she'd found the amber, when the moon had turned her face from the World, the market in the square was again full of people. The Spring Festival was to be held that night, and hundreds of people wandered the streets and foreshores around the harbour. As the sun sank into the ocean, the last rays turned the floating clouds to pink and deep crimson, silhouetting the western islands. In the square, on the Landing, and along the shoreline, great crowds waited expectantly for the first star to appear.

As the crimson clouds paled to rose and then grey and the blue of the sky deepened to darkest sapphire, the first star thrust its head into the sky. With its twinkle the crowd cheered, and then a hush settled over them as an orchestra began the strains of a melody. Darkness draped the harbour as softly as a feather falls.

The orchestra was on a barge on the harbour, and the lilting melody drifted across the water like a breeze. The music was beautiful, a simple, gently-flowing melody that sent Shaeli's skin into a shiver of prickles as the music flowed through her, filling her chest with warmth as she breathed in time with the melody. It was like listening to bells and waterfalls; like listening to snow fall, to flowers blossom; like listening to leaves change colour in the autumn.

The melody changed, became livelier. The music began to tap its feet and sway its hips. It grew fuller, enriched with more instruments, and with the first beat of the drum, the sky exploded.

Shaeli jumped as a shower of silver filled the sky. The sparks floated down, disappearing as they reached the dark water below, but before they faded they were replaced with coloured stars that shot across the sky, exploding into each other and forming an enormous rainbow. The rainbow dissolved into a waterfall, small yellow and red fishes swam up it and flew off into the sky, and then the waterfall was gone and there were trees growing in its place. The skylights flew in time with the music, and as the tempo quickened its pace and the melody danced gaily along with it, the skylights followed. Towers of light appeared in the sky; great round spheres blossomed and grew into garlands of flowers; golden balls appeared from nowhere and turned into a flock of birds. Next came a dragon, swooping across the water and dissolving as it reached the shore, turning into raindrops of red light, all brilliantly mirrored in the bay below. Bright colours burst forth into the night sky again and again; more trees grew, flowers blossomed on their branches; red, green, purple arrows leapt into the air trailing rainbows; tiny balls of fire changed colour as they chased each other across the sky – and always the music flowed with the skylights, or they with it, in time and volume. The bright stars hung their heads like dismal relations.

Shaeli was entranced as she stood on the Trader. While the music was building and the sky was filled with light and colour she was aware of nothing else, not the whooping boys behind her, nor the twins standing beside her on boxes, their hands gripping the rail, their eyes like green mushrooms. She did not see the crowds bathed in light and colour, the golds and blues reflecting on the faces of her family; she did not hear the cries of delight from the thousands of voices lining the harbour. The music and the spectacle before her drowned her other senses, all was lost to the skylights, for nothing else could possibly exist in the World. As the orchestra hit the crescendo, the sky blazed with colour in a final burst of celebration, yet she almost felt like crying, because she knew it was over.

The last lights floated gently down onto the waters of the bay, and the music slowed and became the lovely, simple, haunting melody that had begun the skylights. She sighed deeply and leant against the rail, reluctant for the strange mixture of feelings to end.

"Oh, Mam," she breathed, "how do they *do* that?"

"Skylights are magic, Shaeli," Mareesha said. "A special kind of magic."

"Who does them?" Shaeli asked. "Is it elves?"

Eenis snorted and turned away.

"No, Shaeli, not elves," Mareesha said. "The gift for this kind of magic is usually elfin, but not always. Occasionally one of the People will be given the ability to create skylights, and every year some of them come to Pa'laidiz to perform."

"But how do they get the magic?" Shaeli said.

"It is just in them," Mareesha said. "Like the colour of hair, or the shape of a chin. Some families carry more magic than others, but such gifts can come to anyone."

"Is there any magic in our family?" Shaeli's eagerness was plain.

Jarris laughed. "Barely," he said. "Though I think we had an uncle, a long time ago, who was a Warlock, didn't we, Jeth?"

Jeth nodded. "On Wyshka's side," he said. "A great, great uncle."

"Really, Da?" said Dari. "A Warlock?"

Jeth nodded. "So they tell me," he said.

"What about in your family, Mam," asked Tarkoda. "Is there any magic?"

"Not much, though we abound with Faunistry," she smiled. "My mother told me once that her grandmother could light a candle with her finger."

"But *where* does it come from?" Shaeli persisted. "Why do some people have magic and not others? There must be a reason."

"For gifts such as these, there does not need to be a reason," Mareesha smiled. "You may as well ask why someone has a beautiful voice or can paint fabulous portraits, or any such gift. Why is Warlock magic given to one and not the other? It is not for us to ask, but for the gods to give," she said. "Come on now, time to go below."

They went downstairs for tezz, and Shaeli trailed the rest of the family down. She found the big room overly bright and too full of activity, and she asked to take her tezz back up on deck.

"Alright, Shaeli," said Mareesha. "But run and fetch your cape first."

"And don't go further than the Landing, Mouse," added Jarris. "The city will be celebrating until morning."

Crissita's cape was too short now, and growing a little threadbare over the shoulders, but Shaeli still loved to wear it, even despite Crissita's recent snub. She tucked it tightly about her as she sat on the stairs to the top deck, the warm mug in her hands, enjoying the solitude and savouring the memory of the skylights and the music.

As she drained her mug, the sound of a flute began somewhere close by, picking out, tentatively at first, and then with growing confidence, the melody played by the orchestra at the beginning and end of the skylights.

Shaeli stood and placed her mug on the step. She went down and crossed to the Landing, peering into the darkness. A few people were strolling down along the waterfront, but the crowds had quickly dispersed to other parts of the city. Music and laughter spilled from one of the taverns across the square, but the flute was closer, almost under her feet. She put a foot on the top stair, and then stopped and looked back. Her father had told her not to wander away. She mentally promised to go no further than the bottom of the Landing stairs.

She padded down, and as she neared the bottom it became easier to see, for there was a small lamp lighting the base of the stairs. She realised the music was now coming from somewhere behind her, and she sat down and peered through the treads.

A boy stood beneath the Landing, gazing out at the waters of the bay, playing a flute. Shaeli could only see him from behind, but his brown hair seemed familiar to her. He held the flute out before him, his fingers caressing the holes, and when he turned his head she saw his profile, and realised it was the boy she had seen in the fishing boat just before she had found the amber. When he finished the melody, she clapped her hands and then laughed as he jumped and swung around in surprise.

His eyes narrowed. "Where did you come from?" he asked, his brows contracting into a surly frown.

"Up there," said Shaeli, pointing. "I was on deck and heard you." She grinned at him. "Didn't you just love that melody?" she said, her face softening with the memory. "You did it well, once you'd worked it out." Shaeli smiled. "It was beautiful."

The face of the boy relaxed, and his brown eyes filled with veiled eagerness. "You recognised it," he said.

"Of course," she nodded. "It made me feel like smiling, but *inside*, you know?"

He studied her before he returned the smile. It was only a moment of a smile, as veiled as his eagerness, but she saw it just the same, and then he nodded, just once.

"Yes, I know what you mean," he said, and although the smile was gone from his face, she could hear the remains of it in his voice.

Just then Jarris called from the Trader, and Shaeli scrambled to her feet. She leant back down and smiled through the stairs.

"See you," she said, and she hurried back up the steps.

* * *

Zeb watched her feet and the hem of her velvet cape flash between the treads, and listened to the fall of her feet on the Landing above. He heard her greet the man who had called, and his answering murmur, and then all sound of them faded. He turned and went to find his father, the smile still lingering around his mouth.

* * *

Purple Leaf spent the rest of the spring and the summer on the Starisles, visiting dozens of islands, even flying over the skeleton of the great Mother Ship laying on the reefs of the northernmost island; the ship that had brought Ellirra's people, the Irikai, from over the sea.

Some of the tinier islands rarely saw Traders, and a few did not even have a proper Landing, just landing posts in open fields. A rope ladder was lowered on these occasions, and Shaeli was terrified every time she had to use it, much preferring to be lowered down in a net from the boom with the twins – looking after them, she'd say – but she loved her time on the Starisles and was saddened as the time came for them to begin the long journey back to Cave.

Their last night before they began the journey back to Zirrus was spent on one of the farthest eastern islands, collecting a supply of a medicinal kelp which Mareesha would dry and grind to powder on the journey home. There were few islands between this one and the Endless Sea, and Shaeli wandered the shoreline looking out at them and the vast, empty ocean beyond, shivering a little at the infinite distance that lay beyond the last tiny island, just a small hump in the flat, shining sea. She could see a faint curl of blue smoke drifting above the island, and she wondered about the people who lived there, and whether they liked living at the edge of the World. She sighed and turned back towards the Trader; tomorrow they would leave, and the warmth of the Starisles would be left behind. They would spend the autumn trading in the towns on Zirrus, heading slowly back to Cave for the Wintering.

* * *

At sunrise the next morning, Zeb waded in the shallow water along the beach. He wanted to finish his chores early so he could practise on the new flute his father had bought him on their trip to Pa'laidiz. It had been his first trip to the main island for two Winters, and the excitement had not yet worn off, but what amused him most was that as eager as he had been to leave the island, and with the knowledge that she was well cared for, he had worried about the old woman the whole time they had been away. He had spent most of the coin his father had given him on treats for her, and planned to surprise her with them during the quiet Moons ahead when his father was back at sea.

The new flute delighted him, and he looked forward to the hours he would spend learning to master it. M'zena had been pleased with it, too. She said its tone reminded her of a suitor she'd had once. Zeb found it hard to imagine such a thing.

He squinted against the light reflecting off the water, and saw the Trader leaving the Landing on Arenz, four islands to the west. The purple and green of the balloon glowed in the morning sun, and as it flew across the sea he heard a call from one of the wondrous birds who pulled it south. He watched it glide over the glassy ocean until it was a speck in the distance.

He thought of the little trader in the wine-velvet cape who had listened to him playing his flute, smiling as he remembered her pointy face and bright eyes. What had she said? The music had made her feel like smiling, but inside. He chuckled quietly as he left the water and walked back to the little hut, knowing that M'zena would be up and wanting her breakfast.

***

CHAPTER SIXTEEN

Fezzik also saw the green and purple balloon that year. Summer was long past and autumn hung thickly across the Land the day he saw the Trader rise up from the Landing on the other side of Boccra and fly east. It was early morning, but he knew the day would be hot, especially in the forge. He imagined the cool breeze on the Trader, and the cooler waters of the bay beneath it, and he sighed; t'would be a nice life, he thought, travelling through the skies. Boccra was a little close, sometimes; too many noses dripping with other people's business far too often for his liking. He liked to keep to himself, but during the day there were always those who gathered at the forge to gossip like old women, encouraged by his father, who often stopped working to make his point of view known while Fezzik sweated over the fire.

Their current topic concerned the building of a garrison for the queen's guard upriver, on the big bluff above the bridge that crossed the Clahren a few leagues above Boccra. Yesterday they had debated the meaning of the thing as if, Fezzik thought, it was somehow meaningful to their *own* lives. He expected the same gossip today, and he would be right.

He threw the dregs of his tezz onto the grass, took a last look at the dwindling spot that was the Trader, and he took his cup into the kitchen where Verlie was singing softly to herself. He kissed the back of her neck and she squirmed and laughed, taking the cup from his hand and putting it on the table. She turned her face up to his and he leant to kiss her. The small belly bumped against him and he ran his hand over it. Their first child, the one they had waited these years for, would come this Wintering. He was as overjoyed as she, and studiously ignored his anxiety, just as Verlie ignored hers.

She *had* been blushingly pregnant after that first Wintering when he had been so eager to share the wedlock room with her, he so proud the buttons on his shirt struggled to contain the swelling of his chest, but before the ground had thawed she had lost the child, and it had taken a long time for her to become pregnant again. There had been those who whispered about bad luck, about the omen of old King Tenelon dying on the same day as they'd wed. Publicly, Fezzik and Verlie had ignored these just as studiously as they now ignored their anxiety over her swelling stomach, yet privately they had laughed bravely with each other about the talk and "silly superstition". Fezzik had kept his anger at these rumours to himself.

Verlie had kept busy during the years helping in the forge, tying her silken hair up in a scarf and working the smaller bellows, learning to make small intricate items, belt buckles, knives, arrowheads. She repaired reins and pots, sharpened swords and axes, and kept the gossiping men somewhat polite with her quiet presence. Fezzik had proudly supervised her burgeoning skills, but soon there was little either he or his father could teach her about these things. Many a time he had heard someone comment on her knack for balancing a knife or an arrowhead, and the women unfailingly declared their pots as good as new after Verlie had finished with them. Since she had been with child she worked only the morning hours, and despite his better judgement, the midwives, the Faunist, and Verlie herself all thought the exercise good for her, but he had insisted she take the afternoons to rest, and she had agreed. She pulled her scarf from its peg now and followed him out the door, tying up her hair as they walked up the path.

The forge was on the northern edge of Boccra, where the town ran down into countryside. It stood close beside the road, with a courtyard on one side and Fezzik's parents' house on the other. Fezzik and Verlie's house was behind it, where the land began to slope down to the river flats, facing north to catch the best of the sun. The little house now stood in a garden, with young trees already reaching as high as the eaves and flowers beside the paths. They had a fine view of the road that led north and the Clahren River running through the line of trees off to the right.

Boccra was built on a low, flat hill that grew like a mushroom in the corner of land where the Clahren River met the Bay of Islands. Though it was not a large town, it was on the main road that ran from Palveron to the northern parts of the Land, and the townsfolk did brisk business with the passing trade, the forge seeing its share of visitors as well as servicing the needs of the town and the outlying farms.

The southern side of the town had at least two score of houses used purely for holiday cottages, several on the shores of the bay itself, which were rented by the Palveron elite to escape the confines of the city during the year. Most of the shops, the square, and the Landing were all on that side, taking advantage of the marvellous view over the river and the Bay of Islands, and the town looked very picturesque when seen from that side, but the northern approach was somewhat plainer, with the forge on one side of the road and a few homes on the other. The tavern and boarding house down the road was a happier sight to many travellers, but for those with a broken wheel or a horse who'd thrown a shoe, the forge was a most welcome sight. Fezzik's father was always pleased when travellers called first at the forge, for then he heard the rumours from the north before Koak at the Orange Duck Tavern, something he took particular delight in.

His father was already in the forge and had stoked the fires when Fezzik and Verlie arrived, and before mid-morning there were three men there chatting to him. The talk, as Fezzik had known it would be, was of the new garrison.

"What do they want to build it here for?" asked Bort, a farmer waiting for Fezzik to shoe his horse. He slapped his hat against his knee as he spoke, causing a small dust cloud to engulf him. The dirt of his fields was ingrained into his hands and the lines of his face as much as it was ground into the seams of his clothes.

"To watch the roads," said Fezzik's father, Fedor. He was working on a fire-grate, his back bent with the years of toiling over his trade, his knuckles hard little lumps beneath the skin. "They can watch the bridge and the crossroads from that bluff."

"Watch for *what*, Fedor?" asked Kimbel, the baker. His apron was covered with flour as thickly as Bort's clothes were covered in dust. Verlie was repairing some racks from his ovens.

"Don't know," Fedor said with a shrug. "Not a lot to see, really, is there? River, bridge, a road or three. Perhaps they're setting up a summer house for Her Majesty." He wheezed a laugh out through a gap-toothed grin and spat into the fire.

"They'll have a reason, you see if they don't," said Pelazarus, yawning and stretching his arms in a patch of sunlight. He was a tall man, his brown hair tied at the nape, his mouth perpetually curved as if he knew a secret joke. His horse stood out in the courtyard, waiting for Fezzik to finish with Bort's horse.

"It's a fine spot up there, overlooking the river," said Kimbel the baker. "Bit of a waste, giving it to the guard."

"It'd be well defended, not that they have need for it, but those old cliffs are straight up and down," said Bort. "You can only get up there on the southern side. That hill's right steep, but they're building a wall across. Saw the footings this morning."

"We'd get up there, wouldn't we, Fez?" asked Pelazarus, winking one bright blue eye at Fezzik.

"That we would," Fezzik agreed. "Be a tight squeeze now, though."

Fezzik and Pelazarus laughed loudly as the other three men looked at them, unsure of the joke. Verlie looked over from where she was mending Kimbel's oven racks. She raised one side of her mouth at her husband, twinkled at him, and returned to her work.

"What do you two find so funny?" asked Fedor, suspicion in every syllable. "Verlie," he called. "What are they laughin' at?"

Verlie shook her head, the half-smile still on her face, the twinkle blindingly obvious to Fezzik if not to the others.

"I'm sure I don't know," she said.

"It's nothing, Da," said Fezzik quickly, turning his dark eyes away from Verlie's twinkle in case he laughed again. "Just an old joke, that's all." He caught Pelazarus' eye briefly, found him still smirking, and turned back to the horse, hiding the smile behind his thick beard. It was not an old joke at all. It was an old secret.

He and Pelazarus had been friends since childhood, and one summer, along with Fezzik's elder brother, Fozar, they had taken a small boat and rowed upriver. They had a tent and food packed for several days, and felt terribly brave and grown up on their first unsupervised trip away from home. Fezzik and Pelazarus had been fourteen Winters; Fozar sixteen. They'd planned to row up the Clahren, imagining they could row all the way to the River Zerrin far to the north, camping each night on the riverbank.

They'd left early one morning, their mothers waving them off from the riverbank and eyeing the sky. It had started to rain before Boccra was out of sight, but it was fine rain, the day was warm, and they could see the sun still shining on the water downriver where the Clahren met the Bay of Islands. A sun-shower, they told each other, and went on, safe in the knowledge that all their gear was dry at least. The three boys took turns rowing while the rain grew heavier and the clouds thicker. The sun appeared sporadically, but only in the distance.

They made it to the bridge that crossed the Clahren and sheltered underneath, eating some of their supplies as the rain drowned the view on either side. They sat morosely, barely able to speak with the sound of it, soaking wet, until a cart clattered across the bridge, and then suddenly the rain stopped and the sun appeared. They rowed out to see the cart bumping away on the eastern side of the river and the sun looking at them through holes in the clouds. They rowed harder, sure their adventure would see blue skies from now on.

As they rowed by the base of the tall bluff just upstream, the moment of sunshine passed and the drizzle began again. They groaned and looked at each other, none of them wanting to be the first to complain, and that was when Fezzik saw something in the cliff. They rowed closer and saw a spout of water coming from a hole just above the waterline. It was not a large hole, but when Fozar stuck his head in it, he said it seemed to go on a long way, that the water must be coming from somewhere, and did they want to explore it? They rowed around the base of the bluff looking for something to tie the boat to.

The bluff stuck out into the river, its point upstream, and there was a long backwater between it and the willow-lined bank. Around the point they found a deep overhang in the rock, almost a small cave, high enough for them to row into if they ducked their heads. Inside was a thin shelf of rock with a boulder at one end to tether the boat to, and then they slipped into the water to swim back around to the hole.

The backwater was deep, but there was little current until they swam around the point of the bluff into the river proper. The current there grew stronger, but the hole was just around the point and they pulled themselves up into it with little trouble. They were broad-shouldered lads, and the tunnel was small, but they climbed into the dark hole one by one. It led off to the right at a steep angle, the water coming down as if there was a tap running higher up, and they crawled up, the grey hole dwindling behind them.

"Can you see anything?" asked Fezzik. He was at the back and he kept getting his hands in the way of Pelazarus' big feet.

"There's light ahead," said Fozar from in front, "but not much. It looks like the tunnel gets a bit bigger, too."

"Good," said Pelazarus. "That's the third time I've bumped my head."

"And the fourth you've trodden on my hand," said Fezzik.

An oath from Fozar stopped them.

"Don't let Mam catch you saying things like that," said Fezzik, with a chuckle.

"Well, if I ever almost fall through a hole in a rocky tunnel when she's around I think she'll probably forgive me," said Fozar. "Be careful going over this part, it's easy to misjudge the edge in the dark. It's almost too small to fall through, but you could do yourself an injury. And you can see the boat."

"What do you mean?" asked Pelazarus.

"You'll see," said Fozar. He made a few odd lurching movements and then went on up the tunnel.

Fezzik saw what he meant after Pelazarus had moved forward, stopped for a moment, made the same odd lumbering movement as Fozar and gone on. With the removal of Pelazarus' bulk, a weak grey light filtered into the tunnel, and although there was a weaker, almost non-existent light around the shape of Pelazarus ahead, most of the light was coming from somewhere near the floor. He crawled forward and looked into the hole, inching his hands towards it because its edges were hard to see, as Fozar had said. The hole was on the right-hand side, the water flowing past it in a wide channel worn into the rock, and beneath him was the overhang where they'd left the boat. The hole was almost directly above the ledge where they'd moored, and the boat bobbed below, hardly moving in the stillness of the backwater, their fishing rods lying on the bundle of their gear. He put one hand on the far side of the gap, lumbered over it as the others had, and followed them up the tunnel.

The tunnel widened above the hole, and with the wider base, the water's flow decreased so that it ran over their knuckles instead of almost to their wrists and they crawled on for a while until, again, the strange procession stopped. There was still some light filtering in and Fezzik avoided running into Pelazarus' rear end.

"What now?" he called.

"It forks," Fozar called. "Left or right?"

"Which way is the light coming from?" said Fezzik.

"Both," said Fozar.

"Which is bigger?" asked Fezzik.

"The right," said Fozar.

"Right, then," said Pelazarus. "We'll look left later."

On they went, the tunnel widening a bit more, and in moments the tunnel opened around them and the light brightened.

They were in a cave, small, but almost high enough to stand up. Water ran through a hole in the roof just inside the entrance, puddling a bit before running back down through the tunnel, but the rest of the floor was dry and covered with fine sand. A wide hole in the cliff-face opposite the tunnel was like a low window, and they had to stoop to see through, looking over the backwater to the road and the fields beyond. They pulled in their heads, looked around at the snug cave, and in unspoken agreement they decided to camp there for the night. They grinned at each other. The row upriver could wait.

They went back down the tunnel, and Pelazarus and Fezzik waited by the hole above the boat while Fozar went down, swam around to the overhang, and pulled himself up onto the ledge, squinting into the shadows until he found the two pale faces staring at him. The hole was wide enough to fit their bedrolls and packs through, and Fozar passed them up and the others carried them in an awkward, one-armed crawl to keep them out of the water. When they had all they needed they looked around the cave, found shelf-like pockets up near the roof where they could store supplies and sit candles, and several more above the window that went through to the outside. Fozar thought if they had a fire that the holes would draw the smoke outside, yet they did not stay long. They left their packs bundled on one side of the cave and went out to explore the other branch of the tunnel.

They went in the same formation as they had before, crawling back down to the fork and taking the other tunnel that led towards the river side of the bluff. The water running down this side was deeper than the side that held the cave, the tunnel was a little steeper, and it was darker. There was a little light from behind them, but barely any ahead, and for a while they crawled on in near-darkness, the only sounds the splashing of the water and the occasional grunt as someone bumped their head or grazed a knuckle. The light grew slightly brighter, and then Fozar stopped again.

"Another hole here," he said. "But it's in the wall. Nice view," he added. They waited while he admired it, ribbing him for his fine sensibilities, and then he crawled on.

When Fezzik reached it, he had to agree on the view. It was a small hole, providing what light the drizzly day allowed into the tunnel, and they were on the other side of the bluff, looking out over the Clahren, the bridge downstream and the fields on the far side. There were cows in one, huddling together beneath the trees, but they were the only creatures to be seen in the colourless day. Fezzik stuck his head out through the hole, and far below he could see the water pouring from the hole where they had crawled in.

Beyond the hole the way grew steeper, the water tumbling down like a waterfall, and then the tunnel narrowed so much that they had to lie flat and squeeze through the gap, but they could see the light brightened beyond, and they ignored the oppressive weight of the rock and the cold water running past them. On the other side, the tunnel opened out enough so they could crawl again, but it was much steeper, and for a moment

Fezzik felt like he was climbing a ladder. He heard his brother utter another oath, yet this was not an oath of pain, but of wonder. Then Fozar disappeared. Pelazarus also made an oath of surprise, and then he too was gone.

Fezzik was suddenly alone in the tunnel, and it was much brighter, and there *was* no more tunnel, for it ended a short way ahead. He crawled up and light was shining weakly from above, rain fell softly on his face, and he could see the low clouds covering the sky. The others were clambering up huge rocks above him, and water was streaming from the rocks into the tunnel. Fezzik stood up, found a hand hold, and hoisted himself out of the hole.

The rocks above were huge chunky boulders, dark grey and running with water, but they were gritty rocks and it was easy to find purchase for their bare feet. The drizzle was heavier now and they were doused anew by the time they'd climbed to the top.

They were near the peak of the point, standing atop the enormous pile of boulders crowning the bluff, and they could see in every direction. The Clahren meandered towards them and strolled past to meet the waters of the Bay of Islands; Boccra sat on its little hill beside the river, the pall of smoke sitting above it in the rain-soaked day, the houses scattered around it like toys. Farmland spread out on either side of the river, dotted with hills and pockets of forest, the land beyond fuzzy and indistinct. Directly below them the bluff was flat, but then it ran down a steep rocky slope, and beneath them lay the road that led to the bridge, branching off from the larger road that wound north and south, another lesser road running west through the fields. They had a perfect view of this crossroad, the bridge and the river, the bay and the town; they could see for leagues around them, even with the rain-filled day. The rock pile they stood on was a great jumble of a thing, and they clambered down carefully to explore the bluff itself.

On the slope below the flat top were a few stands of straggly trees, and when they'd finished looking around they scavenged underneath them to find some wood. They bundled kindling and a couple of stubby branches together, tied them with their belts and carried them back up the hill.

The pile of boulders looked even more impressive from below, but when they clambered back up, the rocks all looked the same, and it took them a long time to find the place where they had emerged. Up and down boulder valleys they climbed until Fezzik finally found the hole that led back into the tunnel below. They pushed their faggots in, keeping them out of the water as best they could, passing them through the place where they had to get down on their bellies, and crawling back to their cave. They groaned with relief when they finally got there, stripping off their clothes and hanging them over the 'windowsill', as Pelazarus called it. They propped the wood up to let it dry and delved into their packs for food. The rain increased as they sat eating, and for a while the only sound they could hear was the watery voice of the goddess Aa'liu.

Later in the afternoon, the rain stopped and the sun came out, steaming the last of the dampness from their clothes. It grew hot in the little cave and they pulled on shorts and crawled down the tunnel, diving into the river below, the hole still streaming with the run-off from the rocks far above. They swam around to the boat and rowed it across the backwater, tied it to the willow trees, and they fished until the sun started to go down. Only Pelazarus caught one, and they rowed back under the overhang and swam around to the hole. It was very dark in the tunnel and the last rays were shining into the little cave when they reached it, but Fozar had a small fire going before the sun disappeared entirely and the smoke drifted up through the holes and out into the night just as he'd thought it would. They fried the fish and added some of their supplies, and they talked until the fire died to embers, and then they wrapped themselves in their bedrolls and slept.

The next morning dawned fine and clear, but the row to the higher reaches of the Clahren was abandoned in favour of staying right where they were. They fished and swam and rowed upriver and explored the bluff, and each afternoon they crawled back up to their cave, cooked over a small fire and slept with the stars staring at them through the window. They bundled wood in piles and rowed it over to the cliff, where one of them would lower a rope and pull the bundle back up to the cave. It rained a few times, but they just filled their flasks with the clear water that fell through the roof in the cave and went on with whatever they were doing, for they spent most of their time shirtless and wet anyway. The days were sultry, they had a fire and a few stubby candles to push back the shadows at night, and the hardest thing they had to do was decide what they were going to do next. By unspoken agreement they hid every time someone came close enough to see them, ducking behind a tree or boulder, or swimming beneath the little overhang, for they wanted to keep this place to themselves.

They stayed five nights in the little cave, and as they rowed back down to Boccra that last afternoon, they swore to keep the place a secret. They'd gone there many times over the next Winterings, before their lives had become too busy with the burden of adulthood. Fezzik remembered the place fondly, but he had broken his vow and told Verlie about it soon after they'd married.

He looked at Pelazarus now, wondering if either of them would be able to squeeze through the tunnel up to the cave. They had both grown into large men, Pelazarus only slightly shorter and less broad in the shoulders than Fezzik, and despite the passing of the years – they were now nearing their thirtieth Wintering – they were still the best of friends.

Pelazarus ran a fowl farm to the north-west of Boccra, and he had wed the year before; his wife Pemba had already given birth to their first daughter, and she and Verlie were also firm friends.

Fozar had moved further south a few Winterings before, close to the place where their older half-sister lived. She was the child of their father's first marriage, and had been like a second mother to Fozar and Fezzik when they were small boys. She was long married and her eldest child was only a few Winterings younger than Fezzik, and Fozar lived a few towns away from her, both of them only half a day's ride away from Boccra. Fozar barely ever mentioned their little cave in the bluff above the bridge, but when he did it was with undisguised longing.

The bluff was the place where Queen Virrisian's guard were now building their garrison, using the grey stone piled at the peak for the walls, cutting it into great bricks. The colours of the queen had grown more prevalent in the Land over the last year, and Boccra saw guard passing through most days on their way to unknown duties. Fezzik supposed it made sense to have somewhere for them to shelter along the road.

Pelazarus winked again at Fezzik, and he knew they were both wondering the same thing: would the queen's guard find the tunnel between the boulders that led down to the little cave? Yet even if they did, Fezzik thought, it could hardly matter.

By the time Fezzik had finished shoeing Bort's horse, the talk had turned to the new taxes which had just been announced, and Kimbel and Bort both had a lot to say about the new tariffs on flour and grains. Kimbel's prices would have to rise and so would other merchants be forced to raise theirs to cover the costs.

"She'll be putting a tax on hemp next," Kimbel said. "You watch if she doesn't."

"Tenelon would never have done it," said Fedor. "But then, he never had a ball every half a Moon like her. She has to pay for those gowns somehow, I suppose." He spat into his fire again.

"Pity old Queen Vermona isn't still around," said Bort. "She would have made her daughter listen to reason. Old King Tarkon too."

"When did King Tarkon marry Vermona?" asked Verlie.

"Oh, Tenelon would have been about fourteen, I guess," said Fedor. "That's right, isn't it, Bort?"

"Aye," said Bort. "There was another woman before her. One of them Irikai. Everyone thought he'd marry her, but she went by the wayside. Then he met Vermona. Some say she bewitched him, but he seemed happy enough."

"'Twas rumoured her father was a Warlock, I seem to remember," said Fedor. "But you're right, old Tarkon seemed content enough. He was heartbroken when his first wife died in childbirth, Tenelon that was, but he was proud when Vermona had young Virrisian, though it took a few Winters. Tenelon was more than twenty by then."

"And not even twenty-five when Tarkon gave him the crown," said Kimbel. "Pity Tarkon died, he wasn't that old. Virrisian was still only a maid."

"She was six, I think," said Bort. "Had tezz with him the night he died, they said. She'd just gone to bed when he fell, clutching his chest." He shook his head. "He was a good king."

"So was Tenelon," said Fedor. "And we couldn't have had a finer queen than Irinesta. Better than her that's up at Great Court now. Power hungry she is, and that's a fact."

"Never would've seen Queen Irinesta wasting money like that," agreed Kimbel.

"No chance," said Bort, who seemed in no hurry to return to his fields. "A fine lady she was. She still up in that tower?"

"So they say," said Kimbel.

"It's a wonder she doesn't go home to Romynn," said Pelazarus. "She was Romynnii before she wed old Tenelon, wasn't she?"

"That she was, lad," said Fedor. "And I've wondered myself why she hasn't. She must still have plenty of kin there."

"Perhaps she wants to be near him," said Verlie. She looked at Fezzik. "If it was me, I'd want to stay close."

"But you wouldn't stay in seclusion, Verlie," said Fedor. "You'd get out in the World."

"Maybe," said Verlie. "But if I was Queen Irinesta, and their love was as great as everyone says, I might want to hide away, too." She looked again at Fezzik, whose heart swelled with the look on her face. "I might want to stay close. I might just want to sit and look out across the bay, across to the Island of Dead Kings, to where he lies waiting."

* * *

In the Tower of the Glade, Irinesta did indeed spend much time gazing across the bay. She had also thought about returning to Romynn, and she thought that Virrisian might even allow it, yet Virrisian took only slight interest in Irinesta these days, coming seldom to the tower, and lately even her taunts had become half-hearted. Irinesta dreamt of Romynn's warm lands, the grape-laden fields, the sunny beaches, the high, blue sky. The next time Virrisian came to her room, Irinesta was determined to ask.

Her opportunity came late one night. The door opened as Irinesta was getting ready for bed. E'Nith was already asleep behind her curtain, and Irinesta was glad of it. A waft of spirits came through the door with Virrisian, and it usually made her nasty, but tonight she seemed happy enough as she came in babbling about her plans to refurbish the ballroom. Her now-constant companion, the man called Sir Azeron, stood on the landing outside chatting with the guard who always stood there. Irinesta smiled at Virrisian, nodding at her ideas, internally appalled at the expensive proposition.

"And after that, I think I shall build my guard some more quarters," Virrisian said. "There are so many young people wishing to serve me. It is so gratifying."

"How are you to finance these things?" asked Irinesta, feigning interest to cover the disgust.

"I leave that to Orm of the treasury," said Virrisian. "He finds new and interesting ways to fill the coffers." She laughed.

"Taxes, I suppose," Irinesta said, striving to keep her voice light. She remembered Orm as a whiny underling, clever, but barely tolerated by Tenelon's advisors.

"Of course," Virrisian said. "I have many plans and the People will pay for them. One way or another." She laughed again.

Irinesta squirmed at the look on her face, but she pressed on, determined.

"I wonder," she began. "I wonder if I might take E'Nith and return to Romynn?" she said, keeping her voice light, reasonable. "I have a longing to see my homeland, and I know E'Nith feels the same. You have no use for me here, Virrisian. You have your kingdom. Let us go."

Virrisian was in front of her in a moment. The bejewelled hand reached out and grabbed hers, twisting the wrist backwards. Irinesta fell to her knees as she felt one of the bones in her fingers snap. She screamed in agony. Sir Azeron and the guard turned to watch. She heard E'Nith cry out from behind her curtain.

"Why, Irinesta?" Virrisian thrust her face into Irinesta's. "What do you plan?"

"Nothing, Virrisian," cried Irinesta. "Nothing, I swear. My hand. Please."

"You'll not go *anywhere*," Virrisian snarled. "Not *now*, not *ever*." With every word emphasised, she twisted Irinesta's wrist until Irinesta grew afraid her arm would break. "I may have a use for you one day, and you will stay. You will do as I wish." With a final wrench, Virrisian thrust Irinesta away. "They will *all* do as I wish," Virrisian said.

She turned and left the room, leaving Irinesta on the floor cradling her broken hand, and E'Nith kneeling beside her, crying.

* * *

CHAPTER SEVENTEEN

Four Winters later, the mood in the Lands had changed. On Zirrus, the people were becoming restless and confused, and everywhere small knots of people mumbled under their breaths about the strain being felt throughout the kingdom. Scores of new taxes and decrees had been ordered by Queen Virrisian, taxes which affected not only those on Zirrus, but flowed on to all the other Lands. These new taxes and tariffs on formerly untaxed staples had begun with just a trickle of minor changes a few Winterings after Tenelon's death, and by the time people began to feel it, the trickle had become a tide, an outgoing tide, a drain through which their profits were being sucked at ever-increasing speed. As prices rose on Zirrus, so did they also on the Lands surrounding it; transport costs rose, food prices rose, wages struggled to compete. New laws, many without apparent application, had been sent out by herald with almost every Moon during the past year. The size of Virrisian's guard had grown dramatically, their colours seen in almost every town on Zirrus, and they kept strongholds on all the other Lands. Raids along quiet roads and on isolated farmhouses were becoming more prevalent as people became more desperate, and the queen's guard seemed unable to stop them. Across the Land, people were nervous and increasingly indignant with the widely reported extravagance of Queen Virrisian's court.

The traders held a special meeting at the end of the Wintering to discuss the new decree which directly affected them. Virrisian had ordered the running of all Landings on Zirrus be given over to private ownership, leased by the Crown. Traders were to be charged for the privilege of using the Landings, and the "owners" in turn would pay the Crown for the privilege of renting the Landing.

Already, before the Wintering, small huts had begun to spring up near Landings, some in totally inappropriate positions that made landing difficult, a fact which several of the Fleet had tried to point out to the inexperienced new owners. Green Arrow had even knocked the chimney off one hastily built edifice that lay directly in its flight path – something chuckled over at Cave because the only injury was to the chimney – but it spoke of future problems. What might they find after the Wintering near their once-familiar Landings?

They also had to wonder how most of these "landingholders" were to make a living; the sum they proposed to charge the Fleet for the privilege of landing was small, and many places saw Traders only a handful of times a year – and yet for the trader, the payment asked would add up considerably when paid every time they moored.

The traders knew the feeling among the People was with them, and none of the other Lands had followed suit, but the more pessimistic felt it was only a matter of time before they did. The political power of Zirrus was immense, and the reliance of the other Lands on Virrisian's good favour was considerable.

Shaeli had looked forward to their arrival at Cave this Wintering more than usual. Tarkoda and Andos had stayed behind for their Cave year when Purple Leaf had left last spring, and Shaeli had felt their loss throughout the year. The twins, who had turned seven as they had flown to Cave, had filled much of her time during the year, but she was often lonely for her brother's company and the cheerful face of Andos. Dari was a poor substitute for either good company or good cheer; he and Shaeli had never been close and seldom paid enough attention to each other to even argue very much.

It had been a lonely year, the only highlight being that of meeting Red Arrow on the Starisles at the Spring Festival. She had been ecstatic at having Kirrit there to swim and explore and watch the skylights with, and Shaeli had been as mesmerised with the skylights as she had been the first time she'd seen them. She and Kirrit had spent a lovely week together before Red Arrow left, but Shaeli had been doubly lonely after their departure.

When they had flown across the Long Lea on a late autumn day, Tarkoda and Andos were standing on the ledge outside the yawning mouth of the tunnel, jumping up and down, whistling and waving frantically at their approach. Though Andos was a little older than Tarkoda, and he a little young for Cave year, they had begged to be allowed to do it together, and had happily waved goodbye from the same spot at the beginning of the year. Now, at the end of their Cave year, they called excited greetings to their family as the Zoi pulled the Trader over the ledge. When Purple Leaf flew into the mouth of the tunnel, the two boys followed it inside and disappeared at a run up the bolt tunnel.

They were waiting on the Landing and jumped across to Purple Leaf as it glided up beside them. Andos leapt across before Jeth had even jumped with the mooring rope, and he grabbed his startled mother and swung her around, much to her embarrassment and delight. There was much exclaiming on the growth of both boys and the deepness of their voices, and Shaeli was the happy recipient of a rough kiss and a hug from each. She felt almost shy in front of the boys, so grown and self-assured did they seem, and she stood quietly, grinning at the happy scene. Neesha clamoured forward, loudly demanding to be kissed, but Shanna stayed shyly behind her mother's skirt, peeping out at the boys until Koda knelt down and spoke gently to her. Then she smiled and rushed forward, hugging him around the neck, and she did not leave his side for the rest of the day.

The Wintering had passed quickly, and this year it was Dari's turn to remain behind for his Cave year, yet he did not look forward to it as his brother and cousin had. Although he too was a little early for it, at thirteen his parents thought he was somewhat immature; he seldom left the Trader, showed little interest in anything, and they thought an early Cave year would benefit him. Dari resented it and was sullen and moody.

Tonight, when the others were full of preparations for their departure, he moped about, wandering disconsolately around the big room, getting in everyone's way.

Jarris, Eenis, Mareesha and Jeth had returned from the meeting to discuss the new tariffs on Landings, and their faces were grave. After the children had gone to bed, they sat up late discussing what had been decided, and how it affected them.

They had agreed that Purple Leaf would trade solely on Zirrus this year. Coin paid out for landings would be reimbursed by the Traders' Council, so the entire burden did not fall upon the individual Trader. Though this had been readily accepted as the most economical way for the Fleet to handle the tariffs, there were still some who refused to contemplate handing over coin to moor, so Purple Leaf, for one, had volunteered to stay on Zirrus. It was Jarris' feeling that the tariffs would not be in place long; people disliked the idea as much as the traders, and delegations had been sent to protest against them. Others were not so sure. The queen's growing hunger for filling her coffers and maintaining control over everything were fast becoming legend throughout the Lands.

Over the past Winters, stories had filtered down from Great Court about endless banquets and vast refurbishment of the castle. The queen had ordered her guard were to be accommodated in all their needs, at her expense, wherever they were, and by all accounts her soldiers took every advantage of the situation, yet it was said to be difficult to claim reimbursement.

Virrisian's love of clothes, too, was much talked about, and she refused to wear the same gown twice in public, hence her wardrobes reportedly were vast; seldom visited and used less, except for storing more elaborate gowns.

Of the old queen, Irinesta, there was little news: she was never seen in public, and even those at Great Court saw her seldom, and then only on the balcony of the Glade Room. After Tenelon's funeral, where she had appeared black-gowned and veiled, she had retired from public life, living in seclusion in the turret of the Glade, and seeing no one except her maid, the ancient E'Nith.

Mareesha thought of her often, but had never tried to contact her, yet she knew they would visit Great Court's surrounding city, Palveron, at some point during the year. She hoped that perhaps there was a chance she could send a message to Irinesta, as old friends are wont to do.

* * *

Shaeli lay in her room, unable to sleep. She was impatient for the year to begin. She sat up and peered out the little round window into the half-light of Cave.

The fire-pits cast a dull red glow. The shadows were thick as treacle under the Traders and around the huts of the old ones. She could see a small light coming from far down the Cave and she smiled to herself. Almarnoch would be awake still. He complained often about his insomnia, and even after the Lift spell several days ago, he had rested, exhausted, but said he slept little.

Shaeli still spent many hours with him and the other Warlocks, and had become fluent in the common elf language, and was learning the intricacies of the more formal languages. She was a quick learner and her enthusiasm endeared her to the old Warlock.

The bond between pupil and teacher had grown in the past Winters. They were often seen, the twelve-Winters girl and the wizened Warlock, wandering about deep in conversation. While Shaeli had been growing these years, Almarnoch seemed to have shrunk, and it would not be long before Shaeli was standing eye to eye with the old man, yet as his stature diminished, so his power grew, and sometimes Shaeli could feel the magic emanating from him, just as she used to imagine it came from her wand.

She still had the wand, but took it out seldom. She had discovered a wonderful hiding spot, the year after she'd found it. A small square of wood had worked loose behind the head of her bed, and when she'd pried it off, she saw it hid a dusty, narrow place between the wall and the outer skin of the Trader. There was a big beam running all the way forward just beneath the lip of the hole, and when she peered in she saw nothing but a few cobwebs, but guessed the gap went on until it reached the wall of the storerooms under the stairs. It was here that she hid her wand, and any other treasure that did not fit in the amulet she still wore about her waist. The wand was wrapped now in the Princess Crissita's old wine-velvet cape, long since outgrown, its seams thin, the velvet worn through in places, but still soft and perfect for keeping the dust from her treasured wand.

The amulet at her waist had grown heavier with passing years and new finds; a silver shell found in a street on the Starisles; a tiny triangular green stone she'd found while picking berries on Ashkanna the year after her ninth birth-day; a pretty piece of faceted quartz as long as her finger from a dry creek-bed near Cave; and a wonderful stone of a purple so deep it was almost black, thick and shaped like a half-opened fan, its depths shining with tiny silver and deep-violet sparkles, as if a miniature skylight had burst inside. She had found this purple-black stone close by the Drell Mountains as they'd travelled along the coast last summer, but no one could tell her what kind of stone it was, not even Almarnoch and Llevvis, though Llevvis thought he'd once seen some in a noblewoman's necklace.

She sighed as she gazed out at the dim Cave, ready to lie down again, but a movement by the fire-pits attracted her attention. She saw with surprise that it was Dari who was out so late, and she watched as his silhouette passed the next fire-pit and became a vague shadow as he slipped past the huts, heading towards the bolt tunnel.

His behaviour was strange, even his gait had seemed hesitant; he walked hunched over as if he was injured. She watched, wondering if she should wake someone, but after a while she saw him come back into the light of the fire-pit, though she had not seen him emerge from the shadows near the bolt tunnel. Dari sat on the big rock beside the spring-pool, and Shaeli decided she'd let him be. He was probably upset by their departure tomorrow, and could not sleep either.

She lay down, yawned, and was soon asleep.

* * *

Williver stood on the steps of the Landing, a slight wind ruffling his hair. Shaeli thought it strange; there was no breeze inside Cave.

Come with me, Shaeli, Williver said, and he held out his hand.

She crossed to the Landing, her nightgown fluttering about her knees, her hair blowing out behind her, though she could not feel the breeze on her face. She took his hand and they walked down the stairs and across to the spring-pool. Dari still sat there, but Shaeli was not surprised when he did not see them.

They stopped beside him and Williver looked at her, his blue eyes intent.

He has taken something from you, he said.

Shaeli was puzzled and would have asked a question, but Williver led her on. They walked past the huts of the old ones, and on towards the entrance of the bolt tunnel, and Shaeli thought they would go in, but Williver turned to the right, and led her along the wall of the Cave. Beside them the backs of the old one's huts sat like squatting trolls, and as they passed one Shaeli heard a rumbling snore from inside and she giggled.

Williver walked past the huts of the old ones, and on past the hut of the Warlocks. He stopped beside an outcrop of rock and knelt at the base. The rock looked like a large nose protruding from the wall, and Shaeli squatted down beside the elf. At the base of the rock was a thin crevice. Williver peered inside, and then looked at Shaeli

He has hidden it here, Williver said, speaking quickly, his brow creased. *You must come back before Cave awakes. Remember this spot, and return to retrieve your wand in the waking world.*

My wand? Shaeli was shocked, and then her eyes narrowed in anger. *That Dari. He always was a sneak.*

Williver sadly shook his head. *Anger is not the way, Shaeli. Your cousin is dispirited, and has little understanding of his own actions. 'Twas not his idea, though he thinks it was.* He stood and began to walk back the way they had come.

Shaeli looked over her shoulder. *Can't I take it now?* she asked, but as she spoke the words, she knew what he would say.

Williver smiled. *You know we are of dreams, little one, and dreams cannot touch things of the waking world.* His face became mischievous, his arched brows quivered, and all seriousness was forgotten. *There are many things which those of the dreamworld may not touch; many things they may not do, but there is one thing we* can *do in our dreams which is denied us in the waking world.* He took her hand. *We can fly,* he said, and their feet lifted from the ground.

Shaeli squealed and clutched at Williver's arm, looking down at the dusty floor of Cave as it moved beneath their floating feet. They drifted around the corner of the huts, floating above the path to the spring pool and hovering directly over it. Dari sat there no longer.

Shaeli was enjoying herself now, and was unafraid as long as she held the elf's cool hand. Williver lifted them up, higher and higher, until they looked down on the tops of the balloons, the material puckered from the ropes like water-logged skin. The fire-pits shrank to small red spots, and when Shaeli put her free hand up, her fingertips brushed the dry, cool ceiling of Cave. One of the air-vents lay close by, a darker smudge on the blackness, a pair of tiny, glittering eyes regarded her from the opening and Shaeli gripped tighter to Williver's hand.

They drifted down again slowly, gliding between the balloons to Purple Leaf's mooring, landing smoothly on the platform beside the Trader. Williver kissed her lightly on the forehead, said goodbye, and then he floated up and away again, fading and shrinking, until he was nothing but a blue spark shining like a tiny star against the darkness of the roof. The spark glittered once and went out; the unfelt breeze ceased at the same moment. Shaeli's hair fell to her shoulders, and her nightgown whispered against her legs. She stood on the Landing for a moment, then turned to cross to the Trader, yet her feet never reached the deck.

* * *

While Shaeli was dreaming of flying through Cave, Dari was sitting on the fore-deck. He would not be able to sleep, he knew that, though he was tired and his head ached. Tomorrow they would abandon him here at Cave, unwanted, friend to no one but Garrit.

Garrit had not been as enthusiastic about Dari's Cave year as Dari thought he would be. He said he would be very busy, and for Dari this was almost worse than his parents' betrayal of dumping him here early. But Dari had thought of something that would please Garrit. A few days ago they had been talking about Llevvis, who would go to Palveron with Golden Eagle this year to complete his training on the Warlock Island in the bay.

"The great oaf," Garrit had said. "He will return here as soon as he finishes his training. Says he never anticipated working anywhere else."

"How long will he be gone?" asked Dari.

"He won't be back for two years," said Garrit. "The Wintering after next. And by then it should be my turn."

"You won't come back to Cave though, will you?"

"No," Garrit said. "Though I worry how I'll afford to live as I'd like. New Warlocks earn very little." He looked over at Dari. "If I had some inheritance, or had the luck to stumble over something as valuable as your cousin did, I'd be content. I could work for who I please and establish a fine house, room enough for my dearest friends." He nudged Dari. "Especially those who wish to escape a tiresome existence, eh?" He chuckled and went on in that quiet confidential way he had, as if he was including Dari in some secret. "What a wonderful time we would have."

Dari frowned. "You think it's worth all that?" he asked.

"Oh, indeed," said Garrit. "But let's not dwell over such things. Let's talk about you. Your mother is still unmoved?"

"Yes," Dari snorted. "She doesn't care that I don't want to stay here this year. She doesn't care that everyone staying here this year is awful. Thank goodness you'll be here. It's the only thing keeping it from being a total disaster."

"I thank you," Garrit said, smiling his smooth smile. "Yet you know I'll be busy, what with Llevvis being gone, I may not have much time to spend with you." His eyes grew hazy. "Soon it will be my turn to go to the Bay of Islands, and then I shall find my place in the World. Something important, where my talents are appreciated."

It was then that Dari realised that when Garrit left the Fleet, he would lose his only friend. It was then that he had come to the conclusion that he could do something about it.

* * *

Shaeli woke with a start, the strands of her dream braiding slowly together. When the full plait of memory returned she sat bolt upright, pulled off her covers and began to dress.

She crept in stockinged feet up the stairs, across the deck, and sat on the top step of the Landing where last night Williver had taken her hand. She laced up her boots and padded down the stairs.

It was very early and no one moved across the huge expanse of the Cave. The air was a dull red, lit by the glow of the fire-pits. The soft shine of a lamp shone from inside a few Traders, and down the row of huts she saw one of the old ones sitting in shadow, sipping at a steaming cup. She walked as casually as possible towards the bolt tunnel, and when she reached the entrance she glanced over her shoulder. There was no one to be seen and she hurried to the nose-shaped rock, making sure to be especially quiet as she passed behind the hut of the sleepless old one.

She knelt and peered into the crack under the protruding rock, then put her hand in. She had to reach in past her elbow before her fingers brushed against the velvet, and she pulled slowly at the bundle, laying down full length to have better reach. When it finally came out, she unwrapped it, ensuring it was undamaged. Relieved, she covered it again and tucked the bundle into her coat.

She reached her room unseen, and again she unravelled the wand. It lay in its velvet wrap, shining and beautiful, and she re-wrapped it and hid it back in the space behind her bed. Today they were leaving Cave, and Dari would stay behind. She would find another spot before the year was over. She sat wondering why Dari had taken the wand and how had he known where to look? She did not know he'd often stopped outside her door, peering in through a crack. More than once he'd seen her prise open the square behind her bed and pull out the wand.

When she went to set the table for breakfast, Dari sat nearby but he avoided her eye. She would say nothing about the incident; Williver had redeemed the situation, and she could not reveal how she had known where to find the wand without lying, yet she would tell Almarnoch, and after breakfast she ran down to see him. After breathlessly relating the tale, he agreed it was best kept quiet, and said he would keep a watchful eye on Dari. She felt guilty about being relieved that Dari would not be aboard this year, and wondered what he would think when he found the wand gone.

When Purple Leaf sailed out over the ledge, Dari stood beside Wyshka, one hand held at shoulder height in a token wave. Wyshka had one arm about his shoulders and Olver stood beside him, but it was plain to see he drew no comfort from their presence. His face wore the same pinched look that his mother's had at the beginning of one of her headaches.

He was a small, sullen rock, and Shaeli hoped he would find some happiness during his Cave year.

* * *

Late that night, after the Fleet had gone to sleep, Dari snuck out of Wyshka and Olver's little hut. He crept down to the Warlock's hut and waited until Garrit came out. He led him to the nose-shaped rock, knelt down and thrust his hand inside. His face was pale when he pulled his arm out. His hand was empty.

"It was here," he whispered. "It's gone."

Garrit's lip curled in contempt. "That does me no good at all," he said, and he turned and stalked away.

***

CHAPTER EIGHTEEN

Purple Leaf flew west. Drifts of snow lay upon the ground in sheltered corners, and the streams tumbled over themselves, racing towards the River Zerrin.

At the Landing at Zerrin Crossing, a grinning and apologetic Savic took the tariff from Jarris, his fat fingers tucking the coin quickly into a purse around his pendulous stomach. It was one of only a few times they were charged on their journey to Marnissi; many Landings as yet had no landingholder, and they flew by way of smaller villages who were less likely to ask a tariff and be more in need of supplies, but as they flew into Marnissi, they saw a cabin had been built behind the Landing and knew they would be asked for coin. They stayed only long enough to order and load supplies before they continued their journey across the Land.

It was much the same throughout the north-west, many places had no landingholder, but often they heard that Queen Virrisian's guard were in the area scouting for someone willing to run the Landings. It was said that the queen wanted all Landings utilised by the next Wintering, and her soldiers, as always, hastened to do her bidding. The guard were also recruiting many of the young men and women as they scouted for landingholders; idealistic youth eager for adventure.

Purple Leaf flew a slow meandering route west, the Land below stretching the spring from its arms and raising its head to the summer. They passed over fields and forests oozing life; saw creatures and people busily working and thriving under thick sunshine and scudding storms, and once they flew over the mighty karabool, the shy, odd-looking creatures that lived around the lakes. The mob of karabool, enormous and intimidating, with horns curved forward like massive coils, were as skittish as all their kind. They were startled by the sudden appearance of the Trader over a rise and took off, bounding away to safety, their disproportionately large back legs and tail pushing them enormous distances across the ground, their bearded triangular faces turned away from the perceived danger, enormous ears stretching back.

They reached Lake Oliss on the first day of summer. The western end of the lake opened into the Sea of Aa'liu, the only one of the great lakes that was salt water, and the port town of Orrellis spread out along Oliss' north-western shore, nestled between the lake and the sea. The lake was teeming with bird life, and small fishing and pleasure craft dotted the blue-green surface as the Trader flew overhead, its shadow rippling beneath. The children lined the deck, watching the sprawling town draw closer.

The twins stood perched on boxes, Tarkoda on one side, Andos on the other, each with an arm about the waist of an enthusiastically waving girl. Shanna showed no sign of shyness as she waved at each boat they passed. Here, on the safety of the Trader, she laughed and called out to the tiny figures below with a confidence she would never have had if she met those same people face to face.

Neesha would have no such qualms. She was boisterously confident in any situation, her brash manner delighted people wherever they went, and she often spoke for them both when Shanna was too shy. For all that, it was Neesha who was the most easily frightened. It was she who was scared to go to the privy alone at night, a confident Shanna who accompanied her and stood fearlessly waiting outside the door. Reneesha would often ask her sister to check for creatures under her bed at night, which Roshanna did without any trace of uneasiness. Neesha was troubled by dreams she could never remember; Shanna dreamt of butterflies and pretty ladies. Neesha would scream hysterically if a worm, grasshopper or spider came near her; Shanna would calmly shepherd the creature away, and soothe her sister's nerves when the thing was out of sight.

Neesha suffered from a fear of abandonment; Shanna was unwaveringly secure.

The two were the best of friends, adoring of, and adored by, each other. They were happily sharing Tarkoda's room again this year while he bunked with Andos during Dari's Cave year, and they would spend hours playing there, their bright voices and infectious giggles echoing up the halls and bringing smiles to those that heard them.

Often, Neesha's impulsive nature led them into trouble. Commonsense made Shanna somewhat doubtful of many of her sister's daring plans, but loyalty overcame her reservations and she generally followed wherever Neesha led. Both were excited about their stay at Orrellis and the promise of the Summer Fair to be held there.

The Landing at Orrellis was in a large parkland adjoining the lake, close to the town centre. A small hut had been built under a tree close by, and they knew they would have to pay as long as they stayed, yet it was a lovely place, there was good trading to be had, and the Summer Fair was only a few days away.

The fair was to be held in the parkland next to the Landing, and already the skeletons of stalls were springing up around the edges of the vast field. At the far end of the grassy expanse, a tumbling stream rushed down a big, wooded hill into Lake Oliss, and from the trees along its bank hung a variety of swings. A dozen children swung from the swaying branches, their voices echoing across the field to the Trader, imploring the children to go and join them. Shaeli took the impatient twins across and pushed them both together on one big swing until her arms ached.

Next morning they woke to leaden skies, and before breakfast the storm broke. It rained with unrelenting force, drumming on the sides of the Trader with such intensity that conversation was nearly impossible. Every time a bolt of lightning seared the sky, the nervous, upturned faces of the traders were lit with a blue-white glow and the Zoi moved about restlessly beneath their feet.

When the lightning and thunder rumbled slowly out to sea, the vibrations could still be felt in the air and bones long after the last bolt had pierced the half-darkness. Thick, lead-coloured clouds blanketed the sky, rain still fell from them as if they were being wrung by giant hands, but they all breathed a sigh of relief; Almarnoch's spell had protected the balloon again from the deadly lightning bolts.

The rain continued to pound the Trader and Orrellis throughout the night and the next morning before abruptly stopping as they sat at lunch. The sun broke through clouds that scattered before the rising wind like birds before an eagle, and a glittering land was left behind. The trees dripped shining crystals onto jewel-green grass, and the little stream at the edge of the grassland boiled between its banks, a blur of eddies and leaping foam.

The children burst from the Trader just as the stream yearned to burst from its banks. Steam rose from the sodden ground and by mid-afternoon the wind had gone and the moisture-laden heat was oppressive.

Scores of children gathered in the park. Tarkoda and Andos joined a group of older boys and a few brave girls who rode the rapids of the little creek on wine barrels cut in half lengthwise. They rode their wax-rubbed craft down the rushing stream into the lake, and then paddled back and dragged the barrels up the hill again. Those without barrels rode thin curved slabs of wood, and one boy had two dried, inflated cow bladders tied together. He lay between the bladders, had a pliable triangle of wood tied to each of his vigorously kicking feet, and his strange craft was the fastest of all. Tarkoda and Andos were lent barrels and boards, and even had a turn at the bladder-raft each.

Shaeli and the twins stood with a large group of younger children, cheering as each rider swept past. Shanna and

Neesha ran up and down the bank, screaming and waving every time the boys rode by, and Shaeli itched to have a turn, it looked so exciting, but she was scared to try. Some of the boys overturned or were washed off on the rush down, and one boy disappeared right in front of them, sucked under by the current. His head popped up moments later downstream, but his barrel sunk.

When they tired of watching, Shaeli took the girls down to the edge of Lake Oliss. They took off their mud-encrusted boots, Shaeli tucked her amulet into the toe of her boot, and they waded in the water. The lake was shallow a long way out, except for where the entrance of the rushing stream had gouged a hole into the lake bed, and they could wade far out in the lake before it became too deep to stand. The wading turned to running, the running to splashing, and soon they were so wet they swam.

The twins were not the proficient swimmers that Shaeli had been at seven. They could paddle short distances, but were content to just sit up to their necks and splash each other, enjoying the novelty of swimming in their clothes, but Shaeli kept looking guiltily over at the Trader, wondering what her mother would have to say.

They waded back towards the mouth of the stream, skirting the edge of the deep hole at the stream's exit on the way to the bank. Andos and Tarkoda sat there with some of their new friends, basking in the late sunshine, and Shaeli left the girls with them while she ran back to pick up the discarded boots. When she returned, the boys had swum out onto the lake, and only Tarkoda was left, his head leaning against a barrel, his eyes closed against the sun.

"Where are the girls?" Shaeli asked.

"Went for a swing," he answered, without opening his eyes.

Shaeli sighed, and squinted at the sun. "I'd better go and find them. It's time we went home."

"See you there," Tarkoda murmured, unmoving.

She walked up to the stand of trees where a few children swung in slow, drowsy rhythms, but Shanna and Neesha were not among them. Shaeli frowned and looked around, wondering where they'd gone. She was about to leave, thinking they must have gone home, when a loud, familiar squeal spun her around.

The twins were sweeping down the little creek towards her, jammed together in a barrel they must have found and dragged up the hill. How they'd managed to launch themselves, Shaeli didn't know, but as they drew level with her, she had a fleeting glimpse of their faces.

Neesha sat in the front, hands gripping the corners of the barrel, her eyes huge, her mouth open, screaming in excitement and fear. Shanna huddled behind, her hands around her sister's waist, her head against the straining shoulder in front, eyes tightly shut. She opened them as they drew level with their horrified sister, and her eyes locked beseechingly with Shaeli's for a fleeting, terrifying moment, and then they were gone.

Shaeli dropped the boots and began to run, screaming Tarkoda's name.

She almost caught up with the barrel as they came out of the trees, but a trailing root tripped her and she fell heavily to her knees. Nearby sat two men, staring in surprise at the barrelful of screaming girls. Shaeli yelled at them.

"Fetch my Da," she yelled, as she scrambled up and started to run again. "*Please*, fetch Da." She didn't even have time to be astounded when she realised that one of the men was a drell; she just shouted back over her shoulder. "On the Trader. *Hurry*."

She looked ahead once more as the tall man leapt to his feet and began to lope towards the Trader. The drell, after a moment's hesitation, began to jog after Shaeli.

Shaeli rushed headlong beside the stream, the barrel bobbing just ahead. She was almost out of breath, when mercifully, the barrel hit an eddy that stopped it mid-stream and sent it spinning. The twins screamed.

Shaeli caught up and yelled across the water. "Hang on tight. We'll get you."

She began to run again as the barrel broke free and rushed forward. Neesha looked over at her sister, now fully aware of their danger.

"*Shaeli*," she screamed. "Shaeli. *Help*."

Shaeli ran with them, her side aching, her knees streaming blood. She was level with the barrel and they were nearing the lake, and she knew the roughest part of the rapids was at the bottom, where the stream narrowed and jagged rocks lay below the surface. She began to scream for Tarkoda again, and as she neared the little beach, he poked his head up and rubbed sleepily at his eyes. The eyes widened and he leapt to his feet and looked over his shoulder to where the other boys swam, far out on the lake. He let out a piercing whistle as Shaeli reached him, then he grabbed her hand and they ran to the bank above where the stream met the lake.

How the girls ever made it upright through that gap of boiling stream, Shaeli never knew, and the scene played over and over in her head for a long time afterwards; clear memories that came unbidden and unwanted, leaving her as breathless as she was at that moment when she stood on the bank watching her sisters rush below, foaming white-water all about them, their screams echoing in her ears.

It seemed to Shaeli that time slowed. The barrel leapt and dove, tossed on the raging waters like a bird caught in a gale, until it spat out the other side, the twins still upright when the barrel hit the rocking waters of the lake, and yet they were far from safe. The water was deep and the force of the stream was carrying them out onto the lake, more quickly, it seemed, than any of the boys had gone, and much further.

Shaeli could see Andos and the other boys swimming towards them, and she glanced over her shoulder and saw her father and Jeth flying down the stairs of the Landing, the tall man and Mareesha close behind. The drell was puffing towards them, but they were all still so far away.

A loud splash snapped her head forward. Tarkoda had dived off into the water, and was swimming towards the girls. In their fright they had started the barrel rocking and Neesha was wailing loudly.

"Keep *still*," Shaeli commanded in a voice which rang so loudly across the water that she hardly recognised it as her own. She followed her brother into the water in a smooth clean dive that took her far from the bank.

When she surfaced she swam hard, the stream's current helping her and soon she neared Tarkoda. Her legs felt heavy and her knees stung, and each time she looked the girls seemed no closer. She was so frightened of seeing them tip over that she put her head down and just swam. She could feel Tarkoda straining beside her and together, just when she thought she could go no further, they reached the barrel. Neesha clutched at her, her face white. Shanna still held her sister around the waist, but her green eyes fixed on Shaeli, her terror visible, her whole body trembling.

"It's alright," Shaeli gasped, tearing air into her lungs. "S'alright. Be still."

Her fingers tingled strangely, but she took a grip on one side of the barrel, Tarkoda took the other and spoke soothingly to the girls, urging them to hang on tight. He nodded at Shaeli and in wordless understanding they began to kick back towards the shore. The barrel wobbled and the twins screamed, but they kept going.

Shaeli looked at the bank. It seemed so far away, and her breath was coming in ragged gasps. She saw Jarris and Jeth throw themselves into the water and begin to swim towards them. Andos and the boys were a little closer, but she and Koda had to move the girls nearer to shore – they were still in danger of the barrel tipping over, and if they overturned here, Shaeli doubted she could hold one of them above the water.

Her legs were leaden, but she forced them to move, kicking in time with Tarkoda and dragging at the water with her free arm. Koda reassured her as much as the twins as he swam, saying over and over, "It's alright, we're alright, nearly there," in a calm voice.

As she knew she could not go on, Tarkoda yelled something to her. It took a moment to register what he was saying.

"Stand up, Shaeli," he repeated, breathing hard. "Stand up."

She let her legs drop and gratefully felt sand beneath her feet. She threw her arms around both shivering girls, the salt of her tears mingling with the lake water on her pale face.

They were on a small sand bar, and soon Andos and his friends reached them, and many hands steadied the barrel, then Jarris and Jeth were there and everyone was talking, but Shaeli couldn't make out the words.

They began to swim the barrel across the channel to where Mareesha stood to her waist in the lake, her arms outstretched, her skirts billowing in the water.

Jarris asked Shaeli if she was alright to swim, and she nodded and slipped into the water, her teeth chattering. She trailed the barrel to shore, her limbs aching, her light summer skirt a weight clinging to her thighs. Tarkoda swam beside her until they felt sand beneath their feet again.

The last wade to the shore was the hardest. The water dragged at her legs as if unwilling to let her go, her fingers were numb, her lips tinged with blue, and she could not catch her breath. She saw Mareesha scoop the twins from the barrel and hug them possessively to her, berating them, kissing them and crying, all at the same time.

Shaeli felt light-headed and her vision narrowed, framing the picture of her mother and the twins in thick dark lines. The black-framed world shimmered and lost focus. She slipped into darkness.

* * *

When she woke she was lying on a couch in the big room, wrapped in a warm blanket, but still in her damp clothes. Mareesha was leaning over her, her father stood at the foot of the couch, and Tarkoda sat on the floor holding her hand. Jeth, Eenis and Andos stood together in the kitchen. Eenis had her arm tightly around Andos' shoulders.

"Here she is," Mareesha murmured, and helped her to sit up.

Shaeli shook her head. Memory thudded painfully back into her mind like a boulder dropped from a great height.

"The girls," she whispered. "Are the twins alright?"

"See for yourself," said Mareesha, and leant back.

The two girls sat on the floor, cups of tezz in their hands. They were snuggled in blankets, their hair clinging in strings to their faces. They smiled shyly, and Shaeli frowned at them.

"Little monsters," she said. "Scaring me like that." She closed her eyes against their fading smiles and hurt faces.

She sat frowning, eyes closed, the fear and resentment coiled in a hard ball in her stomach until she could stand it no longer. She opened her eyes, threw off the blankets, rushed across the room and kissed both the bewildered girls, hugging them so hard they pleaded for release, their smiles restored.

Mareesha took Shaeli's hand and led her up the hall to her room. She sat Shaeli on the bed, and began to rummage about for dry clothes.

"Just find me a nightgown please, Mam," said Shaeli in a slurred, weary voice. "I want to go to bed."

When Mareesha turned around, Shaeli's face was awash with tears, and she sat down and held her daughter until the hitching breaths stopped and the tears had run out. Shaeli said again in a quiet, cracked voice that she wanted to go to bed. She had never felt so tired.

Mareesha helped her change, something she had not had to do for a long time, and washed her grazed knees with a horrible smelling liquid. It stung for a moment, and then soothed the ache, and Mareesha tucked her in bed. She asked if Shaeli wanted some tezz, but she shook her head, and closed her eyes. Her breathing eased and she slept within moments.

Mareesha sat for a long time, stroking Shaeli's damp, sun-bleached hair, wondering at the courage and strength held within the thin, twelve-Winters frame of her eldest daughter. Tarkoda, too, had earned much praise for his quick thinking and stamina, yet if it had not been for Shaeli's warning, well... Mareesha shuddered. She rubbed at the white scar above her brow, and sighed.

It was time to give the twins a firm lecture on their behaviour this day; and to thank the gods their lives had been spared.

* * *

CHAPTER NINETEEN

The first thing Shaeli was aware of when she woke next morning was a throbbing stiffness in her knees. She pulled back the blankets to inspect the pale thin scabs that had formed over the grazes, and the huge bruise which had come up on her shin.

She dressed slowly, surprised to see bright sunlight pouring through her window. Her mother must have let her sleep in. She yawned as she brushed her hair, and suddenly the day before rushed back. Her injured knees trembled, and she had to sit down.

When she wandered into the kitchen, the whole family was there with the tall man from the day before, and he was again accompanied by the drell. She tried not to stare at the drell as she thanked them for their help.

"Ah, 'twas nothing lass," said the man who had run to fetch Jarris. "We were just saying 'tis you who were the hero of the piece, weren't we Blenny?" He looked at the drell, who nodded.

"We were, Spotjaw," Blenny agreed. "So we were."

Shaeli thought Blenny's face looked like a bowl of porridge; round and pale and lumpy. Like all drell, his eyes were brown and wide-set, with curiously red-rimmed irises, like balls of tezz circled by fire, and, like all drell, each eye could move independently, like those of a frog, and when Blenny fixed one eye on whoever he was speaking to, the other looked about the room. His fingers were longer than any she had ever seen and they had no knuckles, but were sinuous, jointed all the way like the body of a snake, and as he talked they waved about like thick worms. The twins were fascinated by them.

Drell lived on the western side of the Drell Mountains, the rocky mountain range that lay between the great forest of M'Zen'sclahr and the Estrellan Sea to the north, and they were seldom seen by anyone. In the distant past they had been feared by the common people and ostracised, even hunted, by some, and their numbers had dwindled, but the hunting of drell had been outlawed long ago, and with time, people learned not to fear them, yet the drell had never forgotten their fear of the People. It was said they lived a primitive life in the forbidding mountains, keeping to themselves and venturing little into the World. Blenny was obviously an exception, and Shaeli smiled at him, wondering why he had left his people. He smiled back with a smile as round and full as his stubby body, and Shaeli liked him at once.

"Never seen anyone run so fast," Blenny continued, his deep voice full of admiration. "And that dive…" He shook his head, whistled, and made an arcing movement with his hand. "I can't swim a stroke, drell don't, you know, and she's like a fish. Caught up to you in a flash, didn't she, lad?" He poked Tarkoda in the ribs, and Koda readily agreed, grinning broadly.

Shaeli blushed with delight. "I'm not really a fast runner," she said. "You should see my friend Kirrit. She can race the wind."

"But a fine swimmer you are, lass, so you are," Blenny said.

One eye kept wandering over to the twins and winking, while the other stayed fixed on Shaeli. Neesha giggled, and Shanna sat wide-eyed with amazement.

Spotjaw looked at Shaeli, his face full of concern. "How's the knees, lass?" he asked, and said to Mareesha. "Took quite a fall, she did, but straight up and running again," he clicked his fingers, "just like that. Yelling all the while."

His long, string-bean face folded in upon itself in a crooked smile. His jovial manner seemed a bit forced, but Shaeli smiled back, and assured him her knees were fine, just a bit sore.

Mareesha took a look, clicking her tongue against her teeth at the size of the grazes and the colour of the bruise.

"Blenny and Spotjaw brought your boots back," Tarkoda said.

"Oh, thank goodness," Shaeli said, going over and fishing her amulet out of the toe of her boot.

"And they've asked us to their show tonight," her father added.

"Show?" asked Shaeli, shaking her head as she tied the pouch around her waist.

Neesha answered her, going round the table and climbing up on Blenny's knee as she spoke, obviously already on good terms with the drell.

"They do tricks and tumbling, and make all the people laugh, don't you, Blenny?" she said.

"Hopefully we do, lass," he chuckled, producing a wrapped lolly from somewhere in her hair, and presenting it to her.

She clapped her hands, took the offering, opened it and popped it in her mouth, grinning over at Shanna, who sat staring enviously from Jarris' knee. Blenny leant across the table, gently touched her hair with his long waving fingers, and when they came away, there was a lolly in his amazing hand for her, too. She thanked him in a shy voice.

"'Tis a pleasure, lass," he said, his brown eyes twinkling. "I'm thankful you're both alright, so I am." He looked from Tarkoda to Shaeli, and then back to Shanna. "You're lucky to have such a brave brother and sister," he said softly.

Shanna nodded gravely, and gave him a rare, sweet smile.

Shaeli had only seen one drell before, long ago in a village somewhere to the north, maybe even the Starisles, she couldn't remember exactly where. The old drell woman had brought a supply of strange herbs to the Trader, and Mareesha had exclaimed over the rare herbs, willingly paying the drell woman what she'd asked. As the smiling, shrivelled drell had left the Trader, she'd stopped before a staring Shaeli and touched her cheek with long, worm-like fingers. She was tiny, her features puddled by age, and her big eyes were like warm mud as she studied Shaeli's face, their rims fire-red. Shaeli couldn't remember much of the conversation, but she did remember the intense gaze the woman had fixed her with, how it had lasted and lasted, as if the woman was seeing into her mind, and she remembered her final words.

Learn to swim, lass, she had said at last, her voice as cracked as an old vase. *And learn well. Ye shall need it, one day, so ye shall.* And she had turned and left.

Shaeli remembered the words now as she looked at Blenny. *Learn to swim; ye shall need it.*

The drell looked at her and winked. "Good advice, I'd say," he whispered.

No one else heard, and Shaeli's brows rose with astonishment. She had heard some drell had the gift of second-sight, and this was another reason they kept to their own kind, deep in the rocky mountains near the great forest.

Spotjaw and Blenny left soon afterwards to prepare for their performance. Shaeli was fed a huge meal by her indulgent mother, and then she wandered up on deck and found a quiet spot in the shadow of the balloon.

The field below was filling with tents and stalls. The Summer Fair was the next day, and a sense of anticipation hovered over the park. Shaeli watched for a while, leaning against the rail, looking down on the bustle, enjoying the atmosphere and her detachment from it. She could see Blenny and Spotjaw setting out benches around a ring, a small tent under a tree close by, and two horses cropping at the grass beside a wagon. Lots of children roamed the field, Tarkoda and Andos amongst them, but Shaeli had no wish to join them. She wanted only to sit still and be peaceful. Mareesha had enforced a quiet day on the twins, too, and they were downstairs painting. Even Neesha had not protested too much at being kept inside.

Shaeli sat down in the shade on a cushion she'd brought up, and opened a book on elf-lore given to her by Almarnoch. Written in formal elf, it was hard going, but Almarnoch would be sure to ask her about it when they returned to Cave and she was determined to finish it, as much to please the old man as anything else.

As the afternoon wore on and the sun began to creep into the shady place, Shaeli began to yawn. The sunlight crawled up her shins and over her knees, and the higher the warmth crept up her body, the more she yawned. By the time it reached her waist she was asleep. She floated, warmed by golden light.

Williver spoke softly in her ear, and she opened her eyes. He sat beside her, his bright, blue eyes twinkling at a joke only he knew. She smiled sleepily at him.

Hello, Williver, she said, reaching out to hold his hand.

Hello, little one, he answered, his cool hand taking her warm one. *You've had quite an adventure, haven't you?*

I guess so, she said uncomfortably. *But it was no fun. How did you know?*

Your dreams were filled with it last night. And adventures are rarely fun, Shaeli, but they are almost always important. Your adventure was no exception. He stroked her hair. *Shahlita herself could have done no better,* he said, and Shaeli smiled happily, pleased by the comparison between herself and the beautiful elfin lady of old.

I could have done with a dragon, she said. *Wipp would have been a great help.*

She would indeed, said Williver. *Wipp was fond of children.* He grinned. *But not in the way most might imagine.*

They laughed together, and then Williver smoothed his face into more serious lines. He stood and pulled Shaeli to her feet. They walked to the rail and looked down into the field. Shaeli looked over her shoulder and was only mildly surprised to see herself still curled up on her cushion, fast asleep.

Look down there, Shaeli, Williver said, and she turned back, her eyes following the line his long finger made.

A small, unpainted wagon was entering the far side of the field. It was pulled by a bedraggled pair of horses, heads hanging low, tails dragging the ground. Sitting on the dusty wagon, reins in hand, was an equally dishevelled man. Shaeli thought he resembled his horses in more than his scruffy appearance; his hair was the same nondescript brown as their coats and was tied and hung down his back, just like the horse's tails. Shaeli almost expected it to start swishing at the flies hanging around a face endowed with a huge equine nose and heavy brows, and she giggled.

Who is he, Williver? she asked. *He looks funny.*

He is far from funny, little one, said Williver, so sadly that Shaeli's smile instantly faded.

Why? What's the matter with him?

Williver was rarely unhappy, and Shaeli looked more closely at the man in the field. He had halted his wagon a short distance away, yet he did not descend, he merely sat staring across the lake. His face, even over the distance, was filled with such sadness that Shaeli pitied him.

Why does he look so sad, Williver? she asked, looking up at the tall elf.

He lost something very precious to him, a long time ago, and now he has no joy. Williver turned to face Shaeli. *He has not smiled in ten Winters.* His tilted eyes held her blue-grey ones as gently and earnestly as his hands held hers. *You shall find what he has lost, and return it to him. He will be very grateful.*

Shaeli was puzzled. *What has he lost, Williver? And where shall I find it?*

Not it, Shaeli. Them.

Them?

Yes. That which he has lost is his family. He was separated from them when the ship which was carrying them from

Romynn foundered off the coast. He believed they were drowned, and has wandered aimlessly and alone ever since.

No wonder he looks so sad. She glanced down at the field, and back to Williver. *But they weren't drowned?*

No. They were saved by the Ammerr, and thought he was *gone. They have settled here in Orrellis, close by the sea.*

The Ammerr, *Williver? The sea people?* Shaeli leapt at the word she had only heard in legend. *I thought they were just stories.*

The legends said that the Ammerr, the fabled people who roamed the seas as easily as they roamed the World, had disappeared so long ago that even the elves were supposed to have forgotten them. Williver was obviously an exception.

Williver shook his head. *That's what they like people to think,* he said, the corners of his mouth lifting. *But they are there.*

And this family has seen them? she asked, excitedly.

Williver nodded. *They have, but it would do no good to ask them of it, for they do not remember. Now it is up to you to restore the joy to all their lives. Tomorrow you must find the lost family and bring them here to reunite with this man.*

Shaeli gaped. *But how, Williver?*

I will tell you where to seek, for I know where they live.

Did the Ammerr tell you?

Something like that, he smiled. *Now listen. Take the sea road to the last village at the farthest edge of Orrellis. There by the sea, you shall find them. Look for a small, green house. A rose bush blooms in the garden beside a small well. Will you remember?*

Shaeli nodded and Williver smiled and released her hands. He looked down at the man, who had at last descended from the wagon, and as they watched he leant his head against the neck of one of the scruffy horses. He remained standing motionless, leaning against the horse for a long time. Shaeli looked at Williver.

I'll find them, she said, determination upon her face, her eyes glistening. *I'll find them and make them come.*

It may not be easy, he said. *They may not want to listen.* He pointed to a tree stump on the water's edge. *Look within the hollow, and take what you find there with you. Show it to them, and they will believe.*

Shaeli looked down, and back at Williver. She nodded. *I'll find them,* she repeated. *Don't worry.*

I know you will, Williver smiled. He leant down and kissed her cheek. Then he touched her forehead. *Now sleep again.*

Shaeli's eyes closed, and when she woke, the sun shone upon her face and she was hot and sweating. She blinked and rubbed at her eyes, the dream clearer than her sight. She stood and went to the railing.

The wagon with the horse-faced man was below in the field, as it had been in her dream – as she had known it would be. The horses were tethered nearby, and the man sat leaning against a wheel, staring across the lake.

She ran down the stairs, past the man and his wagon to the stump beside the water. It lay just above the tide line, ancient and gnarled, and she looked inside the dark hollow. Something glittered, and she put in her hand and pulled out the object. On a tangled chain was a locket, green with rust, a small flower barely visible on its scarred surface.

She put it in her pocket and walked slowly back to the Trader. As she passed, Shaeli felt the wave of sadness rolling from the sad man, and she noticed how people skirted his wagon, parting and re-forming like water around a rock. They averted their eyes as they passed the dirty wagon as if his sadness was contagious, their discomfort worn as plainly as a jacket. Tears filled her eyes.

"Don't worry," she whispered. "Tomorrow I'll find them."

* * *

By mid-morning Shaeli was halfway across Orrellis, sweating in the hot sun.

She had asked the landingholder where the sea road began, and he had directed her to the town square not far from the park; on the far side began the road that ran west to the sea. She had hurried away through the already-crowded park before anyone saw her; Mareesha thought she was at the fair, and with luck she would be back before anyone missed her.

She squinted at the road ahead beneath the brim of her straw hat. She had left the crowded, house-filled streets of inner Orrellis behind, and here small farms had begun to appear. The sea road shimmered in the heat, distorting the trees and the few houses she could see ahead. Her knees hurt below the barely-formed scabs, and her shoes kicked up tiny clouds of dust as she walked. Her footfalls and the creaking voices of insects were the only sounds to be heard in the summer morning, and she went over Williver's directions again and again; a green house close to the sea; a rose bush and a well.

She had seen few people since she'd left the cobbled streets of the town centre. She supposed most were at the Summer Fair, or inside out of the sun, and she thought with regret of what she was missing at the fair and in the cool water of Lake Oliss. The twins' barrel-ride had not influenced her love of the water and she longed for a swim, yet she was determined to find those she sought and take them back to Orrellis with her. She smiled to herself, anticipating the reunion of the sad man and his family, and she thought if she hurried, she might be back in time to see some of the fair, but she would miss Blenny and Spotjaw's midday performance.

She grinned, remembering their show last night. They'd sat on the benches that Blenny and Spotjaw had arranged around a small fire, the area lit by tall torches, and the two had performed amazing feats of tumbling and had juggled with an incredible array of items; plates and knives and eggs; shoes and hats stolen from the laughing audience; flaming torches, tossing the spinning brands to each other as if they were harmless sticks. Shaeli's admiration for them had grown with each toss, and she'd shaken her head in amazement, even as she laughed, for Blenny and Spotjaw had kept a hilarious dialogue running the whole time they juggled and tumbled around the ring. She had laughed until her cheeks ached with the effort.

When the juggling was over, Spotjaw had moved about the circle putting out most the torches, changing the brightly lit ring into a mysterious, shadowed arena for the second half of the show. Blenny had followed him around, throwing a powder onto the few torches left alight. The powder crackled on the torches and the flames turned a deep, intense crimson, instantly hushing the crowd. When the drell walked to the central fire and threw a handful of the fine dust upon it, a surge of crimson flame shot upwards, and the smoke drifting into the sky turned a dusky pink. The audience drew a collective breath. Their faces grew soft in the red light, mouths slackened, eyes glazed.

Blenny sat cross-legged in front of the flames. He closed his eyes and lowered his head, his body a dark silhouette against the fire. Spotjaw spoke from behind him, his voice low, his long face patterned with crimson and shadow.

"Behold the gift of Blenn," he intoned, with no trace of his broad country accent. "He brings messages from the Dark Beyond."

Shaeli shivered and looked at Blenny. The small drell appeared to grow, and when he raised his head, she was struck by the sudden majesty upon his plain, round face. His features were lit by the fire and the red-flamed torches, his huge eyes unfathomable as they ranged the crowd, the rims of his irises glowing as redly as the flames. His voice was unrecognisable as it flowed from him, depthless and grave.

He looked into the drift of faintly pink smoke above the fire, and then back out at the crowd. His gaze settled upon an old woman in the front row. "You shall be a grandmother again before the moon has reached the Full," he told her. "'Tis a fine, healthy boy."

The old woman's brows rose and she looked at the shrunken man beside her. Then she smiled, her lined face creasing with happiness.

Shaeli noticed the sad man from the wagon standing at the back of the crowd beneath the deeper shadows of a thick tree. His face was carved granite, and she missed what Blenny said next as she studied him. She turned her attention back as the drell spoke to a third person, a small boy who sat at the front.

"Your nightmares will end if you tell your mother what *really* happened to the preserves she thought stolen," Blenny said sternly, and the crowd laughed as the boy looked guiltily towards a woman seated nearby. The woman pursed her lips and folded her arms across her breast, and the boy's face grew as red as the fire.

Blenny continued, his eyes searching the gathering, their red rims reflecting the red flames, moving between the fire and the crowd, seeking out one person after another, bringing smiles to some, frowns to others. His predictions were mostly harmless, or fun – a new job here, a secret crush there, a wedding predicted, a lost item's whereabouts revealed – and the crowd murmured quiet appreciation, and smiled at the more amusing of his prophesies. Tarkoda and Andos fell into gales of laughter when Blenny told them they would one day sit at table with the queen at Great Court. The last person Blenny spoke to was the sad man who hid in the shadows at the edge of the crowd.

"Soon you shall find what was lost to you," the drell said. "And there will be laughter again."

The man stared at Blenny for a moment, then abruptly turned and strode into the darkness, his shoulders drawn tightly around him.

Spotjaw had ended the show there, throwing a substance onto the fire which shot bright yellow flames aloft. The crowd fluttered, blinked, and smiled as if waking from a dream. Eyes took on focus, expressions grew firmer. As they were rising, Spotjaw went among them, a small basket in his hand which soon tinkled with coin. Blenny remained before the fire, another basket before him, and most of those he had spoken to came forward and dropped something into it – even the mother of the small boy who had eaten her preserves.

Jarris gave Shaeli some coins and she ran forward and dropped them into Blenny's basket, his face once again pale and sedate, no trace of majesty remaining. Shaeli had grinned at him, and he'd winked back, first one eye, then the other.

She smiled now as she walked down the dusty road, and she wondered how Blenny had known about the sad man and the others, even though she thought it unlikely her brother and Andos would ever dine with the queen. She shook the memory away; she could smell salt, and hear the familiar rush of the ocean. She must be getting close.

The road rose gradually before disappearing over the brow of a hill, and there were several houses scattered along it. There was a green house halfway up the slope, and she hurried towards it, but then realised that it had no rose bush.

When she reached the top of the rise, she stopped in the middle of the dusty road. Her shoulders slumped. Before her was a small crowded hamlet, obviously a fishing village, two headlands hugging a smooth blue bay. Small boats were pulled up on the beach, bigger boats were anchored in the bay, nets hung in almost every yard, and in the distance she could see a few men on the beach standing around an upturned boat. The village was a part of Orrellis outflung from the centre, like an arm in sleep.

The sea road wound down the slope and ended on the sandy beach. At least a dozen thin lanes branched off on either side, and each tiny lane was lined with houses. The houses were clumped together, filling the hillside between where she stood and the beach below. At least half of them were green.

She sat down on a rock beside the road, dismayed. It would take a long time to search every street for every green house, and she had to be back before her mother missed her. She squinted at the sun. It was almost directly overhead, and her shadow was a puddle around her feet. She frowned at her misfortune, pretty as it was, then stood up and started down the hill.

Up and down the streets and lanes of the little village she walked, hot and dusty, the sun creeping past its zenith and falling slowly downwards. She passed lots of green houses, some with roses, others with wells, some with both. A few times she knocked on doors and was turned away. The later it grew, the faster the sun seemed to fall, and in the end she gave up, becoming more and more worried about her mother as the day passed. She trudged back up the hill in defeat, tired and hungry, and she sat down on the rock where she'd sat earlier, her shoulders drooping, a sense of failure clinging to her like a cloud. She could not do it. She had let Williver down. She had resigned the sad man and his family to their loneliness. Maybe for ever. She was miserable.

She stood up and turned her back on the village. The World wobbled and jumped before her, she felt suddenly light-headed, and she sat back down, almost falling off the rock. She closed her eyes and saw an image of Williver's face, warm and smiling, and her hand went to her pocket. She pulled out the rusty locket and held it in her fist, eyes still tightly shut. The locket warmed in her hand, she opened her eyes and the World shimmered. The quality of light shifted, became more golden, the colours grew brighter. She drew a deep breath, stood up again, and set off down the hill for the second time.

She passed the first lane and the locket was still warm in her palm, yet as she passed the second, it abruptly cooled. She stopped, and turned around. Again the locket heated her palm with a burst of warmth, and she retraced her steps and took the second turnoff. It lay just below and opposite the first, and led along the shoulder of the hill towards the southern headland. Halfway along, the lane forked and she stood hesitating. She set off down the lower fork and knew immediately she had chosen the wrong way. The locket cooled instantly, and again she retraced her steps and set off along the upper lane.

    She began to look anxiously at every dwelling. Small huts, sprawling homes, drying nets, the smell of fish and salt, and always that lovely light, enriching the colours of everything it touched.

    The lane curved around the hill and came to an end a short distance ahead. To her right sat a small, green house with a huge spray of sunburnt-pink roses clambering over the roof, but it was obviously empty. The door and windows were boarded up, the front steps were gone, and the roof sagged inwards with the weight of the roses. Across the lane, now little more than a dusty track, a bottle green house hung from the slope above, the fingers of its foundations clinging desperately to the ground. Though it appeared as if a soft rain would wash it down the hill, curtains blew at the open windows, flowers grew in a well-tended bed, and Shaeli could hear someone singing loudly and discordantly from inside.

    Shaeli looked ahead at the half dozen houses left. She had gone no further than here on her first search of the village; there was no sign of a well and the houses all looked neglected and scruffy. There was an air of dishevelment about the silent lane, and she had been too nervous to go further before.

    Only one other house was green. It was the last on the dusty lane, separated slightly from those before it by overgrown, empty land and a fenced-off space where a brown cow chewed its cud in the sun. The box of a house was shadowed by a huge gnarled tree, and it huddled between the side of the hill and the little headland which tumbled into the sea below. A pocket-sized veranda tacked to the front of the building sagged forlornly in the middle, grey-green paint was peeling in long strips from the walls, but faded curtains hung at the glassless windows, and a thin wisp of smoke hovered above the stone chimney. The chimney had lost some of its rocks, and the blackened holes puffed smoke like the mouths of toothless old men.

As Shaeli hurried down the lane, she saw a girl come from the darkness of the doorway. The girl held a bucket in her hand and she walked across the sun-patterned grass. A small well appeared on the far side of the immense tree, hidden until now by the house and the tree. Into the branches grew a climbing rose, studded with tiny, blood-red blooms. Long tendrils of green and ruby hung down, framing the well and the girl drawing water from it.

Shaeli's heart leapt. She didn't need the hot pulse of the locket in her hand to tell her she had found the right place. She began to run.

The girl looked up, continuing to wind the handle on the well, and Shaeli slowed again to a walk, suddenly aware of how odd she must look. Her heart pounded as she crossed the grass and she smiled awkwardly, unsure of what to say. The golden light which had filled the World faded with the warmth of the locket; the rich colours became duller, as if the sun had gone behind a cloud. She looked at the silent girl, and smiled again.

"A lovely spot you have here," she said, for it was true. Apart from the air of neglect surrounding the house, it was a beautiful place.

The girl nodded in doubtful reply, grasped the brimming bucket she had drawn from the well and tipped it into the one she had carried from the house. She looked up at Shaeli from beneath a thick brown fringe cut straight above her eyes.

"Would you like a drink?" she asked.

Shaeli nodded. A cup hung from a hook beside the well, and the girl filled it from her bucket and passed it to her.

Shaeli thanked her and drank deeply, then asked for the cup be filled again. The long walk had made her very thirsty, but it also gave her more time to think about what she was going to say. She studied the girl over the rim of her cup.

She was a little younger than Shaeli, her brown hair tied back and hanging to her waist. She had heavy, dark brows over deep, brown eyes, and Shaeli thought she could see something of the sad man in her face.

"What's your name?" she asked

"Noola," said the girl. "What's yours?"

"Shaeli. Is your mam home, Noola?"

Noola looked towards the house. "She's inside," she said. "Do you want to see her?"

Shaeli nodded, and Noola picked up the bucket and they walked towards the house. Noola led the way, obviously curious, yet she asked no questions, she merely told Shaeli to wait and disappeared through the doorway.

Shaeli had slipped the locket back into her pocket and she touched it again as she waited. No warmth came from it now, it had done its work. The rest was up to her.

Noola came out of the house, followed by a woman not much taller than herself, and she introduced Shaeli to her mother.

"Good day to you, ma'am," said Shaeli brightly.

Noola's mother, Gwyll, stood on the veranda, her eyes focused on the horizon, her shoulders stooped and drawn. Shaeli could imagine her standing there many times in the past, looking out at the sea, and she fancied the crooked veranda had developed its sag by the weight on the woman's shoulders.

"I thank you for seeing me," Shaeli tried again. "I was sent to find you."

Gwyll dragged her gaze from the sea and looked at Shaeli disinterestedly. Her deeply lined eyes remained distant as she stared, and Shaeli became uncomfortable.

"I... ah... I have a friend," she stammered. "He told me you were separated from your husband a long time ago."

The woman eyes narrowed instantly, lost the remote stare, and focused sharply. Shaeli hurried on, nervously toying with her amulet. She turned to Noola.

"You must have been just a baby," she said.

Noola's eyes had grown wide. "How did you know that?" she whispered.

Gwyll frowned at Shaeli. "Noola's father drowned," she said angrily. Her voice was hoarse, and tears stood in her eyes. "We were *not* separated. He would never leave us." She put her arm around Noola's shoulders.

Shaeli felt the sadness wrap around Gwyll just as she had wrapped her arm about her daughter.

"But he thought *you* were drowned," she blurted. "And he hasn't smiled since."

But the woman's face had closed to her, and she heard nothing but her own anger. She turned to go inside. "Come Noola," Gwyll said. "Enough of this nonsense." She looked back over her shoulder at Shaeli. "You're lucky my sons aren't here, for they'd give you fury for telling such lies. You're a wicked, terrible girl to come here saying these things."

Shaeli *felt* wicked and terrible. "I'm sorry," she cried. "But I'm not lying, truly." She thrust her hand in her pocket and pulled out the locket. "Wait," she called at the retreating backs. "Please wait. Look. There's this."

The woman turned and squinted at her. She opened her mouth to continue her tirade, but when she saw what Shaeli held, her face paled. She stood as if frozen for a long moment, staring at the object hanging from Shaeli's fist, then she suddenly rushed forward and snatched the locket from Shaeli's hand.

"Where did you get this?" she demanded. "It is mine, and was lost to the sea." Her hoarse voice had risen and hysteria burned behind her eyes. "It was a wedding gift from my husband. *Tell me where you found it.*"

Shaeli gulped. "My... my friend gave it to me," she said. "He said it would help you believe."

Gwyll turned to Noola. "Fetch your brothers," she said. "*Hurry.*" Noola looked blankly at her mother, and Gwyll prodded her in the back, pushing her forward. "*Run*, girl," she said, and Noola ran, her eyes still wide, across the lane and down a track between the wind-blown trees. "Where is he?" Gwyll commanded, grabbing Shaeli's arm. "Where is Nol?"

"Orrellis," Shaeli stammered. "At the Summer Fair. He has a wagon and two horses," she added uselessly.

"Wait here," Gwyll said, and she disappeared inside.

Again Shaeli waited outside the little house. She wandered over to the well, drew up a bucket, and had another drink of the cool water. She did not have long to wait.

Gwyll came out of the house, a bundle of clothes across her arm, a hat atop her thin hair, and she walked swiftly to the end of the road. Shaeli could hear her talking urgently to someone out of sight down the hill, and in moments she was joined by two boys, obviously Noola's brothers. Shaeli thought they looked about the same ages as Tarkoda and Andos, and both were shirtless and wore wide-brimmed hats above wet hair. The boys stopped before their mother and she spoke quickly, thrusting a shirt at each of them, gesturing to where Shaeli waited beside the well. Noola appeared breathlessly behind them as Gwyll was showing them what she held in her hand. The eldest boy took the locket from her, looked at it a moment, and then walked across the lane to where Shaeli stood beside the well. She moved forward to meet him, and saw a face very like that of the horse-faced man. She smiled.

"You look like your Da," she said, and he stopped, staring at her.

"That's what Mam always says," he breathed. He shook his head as if to clear it, and then he turned to look at his family. The young man took his mother's hand, and looked back at Shaeli. "Let's go," he said.

* * *

It was very late in the afternoon when they reached the park. It had been a long walk and their shadows stretched out beside them, their hats making them tall shadow-mushrooms, but Noola's family showed no sign of tiredness as they crossed the edge of the field. The face of Gwyll had grown flushed as they walked, and her eyes were no longer dull with disinterest, but shining with eagerness. On the walk to Orrellis she had wrung every detail – scant as they were – from Shaeli about her husband and how she'd found them, and Shaeli was hard-pressed not to lie outright. She was thankful when they reached the fair; her knees ached and her stomach grumbled loudly. Many people wandered about the stalls, and from their colourful ranks emerged Tarkoda.

"There you are," he said, heading straight for Shaeli. "Where've you been? Mam's been looking for you since lunch."

"I'll go and see her now," said Shaeli. She motioned to the family behind her, and began to weave her way through the crush before Koda could ask any more questions. He was lost in the crowd behind them, puzzlement etched on his sun-brown face.

As they neared the Trader at the field's far edge, the crowd thinned. Shaeli stopped and looked at Gwyll. She pointed to the little wagon and the two brown horses tethered nearby.

"He's over there," she said.

The family stared at the wagon, blinking as if waking from an unhappy dream; Noola even rubbed at her brown eyes. Gwyll stared long and hard, and then she took a deep breath. She turned to Shaeli and kissed her cheek, hugging her hard.

"Thank you, child," she whispered. "May the gods bless you." She took Noola's hand, and walked purposefully toward the wagon, the boys a pace behind.

Shaeli ran up the Landing steps and looked back down.

As the four reached the wagon, the sad man came from inside, his shoulders slumped. He looked up, saw the people before him and stopped abruptly. They stood staring at each other for a long time.

The man saw ghosts standing before him. He wiped a hand across his eyes, and looked again, his eyes drinking in the faces before him. His legs gave way, and he fell to his knees, open-mouthed. One arm lifted, the hand reached out, his mouth worked, and then Gwyll rushed forward with a cry, and threw her arms about him.

Shaeli's skin began to prickle. The face of the sad man was sad no more. Joy surged through it as he held first his wife, then his children, and then his wife again. He scooped Noola up and swung her around. Shaeli saw him wiping tears from his face, but as he cried, he was smiling.

* * *

She had managed to evade her mother's questions about where she'd been all day, but the next morning she thought it best that she stay close to home. She made herself useful, much to Mareesha's satisfaction, but at last she had told Shaeli to leave the Trader, insisting that she go out and swim.

Tarkoda's questions had not been so easy to avoid, and she had squirmed under his gaze. In the end, he only shook his head and made her promise to tell him sometime. She had promised, and as she walked across the deck she thought she would ask Almarnoch if she could tell her brother about Williver. She thought he'd believe her now.

Noola was waiting at the bottom of the stairs when she went down.

"My... my Da wants to see you," she said, her tongue tripping over the unfamiliar word. She took Shaeli's hand and began to drag her towards the wagon.

"How did you know where to find me?" Shaeli asked.

"I saw you on the steps yesterday," answered Noola. "Mam was pleased I noticed. She was too busy crying to see where you went." She tugged harder at Shaeli's hand. "Come on."

Shaeli went reluctantly with her, and when they reached the wagon, she was surprised to see Blenny was there. Her face must have proclaimed it, and Blenny laughed at her.

"Hello, lass," he said. "You did a great thing yesterday, so you did."

"Blenny," Shaeli said. "What are you doing here?"

"Nol wished to thank me also, before they leave," Blenny said. "And Gwyll has kindly offered us the use of their field before we continue our travels."

"Thank you, too?" Shaeli asked, shaking her head in confusion.

"Yes, Shaeli," said Nol. "After their show, the night before last, I was packing to leave." He looked at Blenny and smiled. "Our nosy friend persuaded me to stay one more night, though it took some doing. I had no wish to hear him. I could not even recall what made me come to Orrellis in the first place, but Blenny was determined I stay for the fair." He looked then at Gwyll. "Thanks to the gods, I listened."

"Thanks to the gods, and to Blenny," said Gwyll. "But most of the thanks go to Shaeli."

Shaeli stood looking at her feet, blushing under her tanned skin as Nol's family thanked her again and again. Blenny leant against the wagon wheel, smoking a pipe and watching until Shaeli became so embarrassed she begged them to stop.

She barely recognised Nol as the sad man of a few days before, so transformed was he. He was dressed neatly, his manner light, his eyes glowing with pleasure. He laughed and joked with his sons and kept reaching out to touch his beaming wife, as if afraid she was a dream. Even the plain brown horses seemed happier, pawing the ground and tossing their manes.

Gwyll's face shone. Like Nol, if Shaeli had not seen it for herself she would have sworn the woman on the crooked veranda yesterday was no relation to the bright woman in Orrellis today. Her voice was no longer hoarse, and the lurking hysteria had been erased from behind her eyes.

Noola seemed overwhelmed. She did not remember her father, yet the change in her distracted, withdrawn mother was enough to keep a bewildered smile on her face.

Nol proudly told Shaeli they were leaving soon for the little green house by the sea, then he went inside the wagon and when he returned he was carrying a small, battered box. He grew solemn as he faced Shaeli, and though he spoke unwaveringly, it was obvious every word was painful to him. His family grew sombre and moved close to him. Blenny watched silently. The sound of the Summer Fair being dismantled faded into the background.

"When I woke," Nol began, slowly. "When I woke, alone, on a desolate beach ten Winters ago, beside me on the sand lay this small box. I searched for my family through long days and endless nights, but I could never find any sign of them. I was told there had been no survivors but myself from the ship that had carried us." His wife took his hand and Nol held tightly to it, yet his eyes did not leave Shaeli's face. "I thought my world had ended," he continued, "and I kept this as a reminder of the storm which had stolen my life." He looked at Gwyll then, tears standing in both their eyes, and then he turned back to Shaeli. "You have restored my life to me," he said. "And I would like you to have this now, so you will always remember how happy you have made us."

He held out the box, and Shaeli took it, but his face held so much peace that she thrust the scratched box back to him. "I don't want anything," she said. "And I'll not forget you. I'm just happy I could help."

Nol refused to accept its return, shaking his head and holding up his hands. "Perhaps your friend would like it," he said, practising his rusty smile. "I would like to meet him, and give him our thanks also."

Shaeli's thoughts leapt to Williver. "Oh," she said, quickly. "You can't meet him. He's not here in Orrellis." At least it was not a lie.

"Well, then," said Gwyll in a voice very unlike the one she had been using only yesterday. "You'll give him our gratitude then, Shaeli? And tell him we are forever in his debt."

Shaeli nodded and thanked them, wondering what was inside. She opened the lid.

I should have guessed, she thought, and closed the box again. She tried a smile. It felt rustier than Nol's.

Shaeli thanked them again, her face hot, her heart racing. She wished them luck, and was kissed and blessed by every one. Gwyll hugged her hard, Noola begged her to come and visit. Shaeli said goodbye and ran back to the Trader and up the Landing steps, the box tucked under her arm. She stood on deck, waving as the wagon drove from the field, then she went down to her room and shut the door. She opened the box and sat staring at the object inside. Tentatively she took it out, admiring the glittering blue-green cast. She slipped it over her arm, where it hung heavily, much too big. Too big even when she pushed it up past her elbow. She smiled to herself, and placed Shahlita's bangle back in its box.

* * *

CHAPTER TWENTY

Summer was fading as Purple Leaf approached Great Court. They would spend at least ten days in the vast city of Palveron that surrounded the castle, but they would do little trading – the city held almost everything anyone could ever need – yet they would fill the storerooms for the autumn journey back to Cave. They had relatives in Palveron too, and Tarkoda would celebrate his birth-day near the end of summer, and while they would not stay for the Autumn's Eve Hunt, the promise of a party for him added to the excitement of the visit.

They had flown down the coast after leaving Orrellis, visiting many of the small coastal towns along the way. When they crossed the place where the River Zerrin met the Sea of Aa'liu, Shaeli had been rapt. Inland, the ribbon of river thinned and melted into the distant plain, and beneath the Trader the sweet water of the river tumbled over a wide fall to meet the salt of the sea. She imagined the water dashing so excitedly beneath Purple Leaf had travelled all the way from Mount Zerrinius, and she was sorry to leave the river to fly inland across the grassy plains to Palveron.

* * *

Mareesha hid the uneasiness simmering inside. Her sister, Asheen, also a Faunist, lived with her family in the city, and while the prospect of seeing them was delightful, she was apprehensive. She had not been in Palveron in over eight Winters, and the desire to try and see Irinesta while she was there was almost irresistible – and that meant going to Great Court. She had rarely been inside the castle in over sixteen Winters, since she had wed Jarris and become a trader.

Great Court could be seen rising against the sky for leagues around, its towers etched against the blue. It dominated the horizon just as Zirrus dominated the Lands.

Built on the point of a massive headland, Great Court overlooked the Bay of Islands and the city. The bay shimmered in the afternoon sun, the islands fading into the distance. On the southern side of Great Court, several lesser bluffs pushed out into the bay, and beyond a long hilly point of land, the waters of the Bastinian Ocean began.

The headland rose high above the surrounding plains, surging from the earth and pushing out into the bay, the castle at its peak a mass of turrets and pale stone walls, the sun gleaming on the windows. The five main turrets rose high into the sky, the dozen smaller towers blending together across the distance, but the great road cutting a stark line up the centre of the headland and the thick stone wall running across the slope were clearly visible. The gardens and fields above the wall looked like green handkerchiefs laying before the golden castle, and as the Zoi pulled them closer and Great Court filled Mareesha's sight, memories of it filled her mind.

She was able to locate achingly familiar landmarks; the stone buildings which housed those who served Great Court; the many elaborate gardens and private courtyards; the Faunist and Warlock Houses outside the inner wall surrounding the castle. She had once called Great Court home, and Jarris had asked for her hand in one of those secluded gardens.

The high wall which marched across the bluff beneath Great Court effectively cut the headland in two, and Palveron itself began beneath it, spilling down the slope and sprawling around the headland, filling the surrounding plain and the shores of the bay for leagues around. The most highly ranked and the richest of the merchants had their mansions below the wall and their opulent homes flourished like flowers down the slope.

The road cutting straight up through the centre of the bluff was wide enough for twenty horses to ride abreast, and was the same road above which Purple Leaf flew. It unrolled before them into a grand square in the centre of the city, and from the square it continued straight up the face of the headland, through the outer wall and the gardens, up to the courtyard of the castle high above. Mareesha looked from the castle to the excited faces of the children. They, at least, were thrilled with the visit.

* * *

Shaeli's head ached from trying to imagine all the people that lived in the huge city. As always when they approached a new city or town they watched from the rails, and she stood next to her mother gazing at the city and the castle rising above it, the twins beside her, their eyes on stalks. Andos and Tarkoda pointed to landmarks vaguely remembered from their last trip, and though Shaeli had thought she had no memories of the city, the sight of Great Court was oddly familiar.

They followed the broad thoroughfare to the city square, and Shaeli soaked in the sights, her excitement growing. When they flew down into the square towards the hugest Landing she had ever seen, her rapture was complete. Four other Traders were moored at the Landing, Taffka's Trader, Golden Eagle, amongst them, but beside it lay Red Arrow. Kirrit was here!

Tarkoda let out an ear-piercing whistle, and within moments the deck of Red Arrow was filled with waving red-headed children. Baroz came up behind his brood and crossed to the Landing to catch the rope tossed by Jeth, the Zoi pulled them smoothly into place behind Red Arrow, and soon the Landing was awash with smiling traders. The boys rushed to leap upon Kirrit's brothers, Wez and Beren, who had shared Cave year with them, and Kirrit's dark red curls blended with Shaeli's sun-streaked brown as they hugged each other. Shanna and Neesha were swept into the wave of children, Tajindi grinning at them, for he and the twins were as firmly friends as Shaeli and Kirrit had been at their ages. Tajindi drew them to one side, and the three began talking and giggling.

Taffka, the Head Trader, his wife, Renn, and their son, Rafi, came from Golden Eagle, and those from the other Traders, Sky Wing and its sister ship, Dragon Wing, joined them too, and the afternoon passed in a blur of conversation and laughter. When darkness fell, the traders held a feast on the deck of Golden Eagle, and the children, over twenty in all, ran from Trader to Trader and explored the enormous Landing.

It was a massive structure, big enough to moor ten Traders, with staircases at either end and six private rooms in the centre surrounded by a covered area filled with benches and potted ferns. The children explored each room, ran round and round the central structure, and played hide-n-seek between the pots and benches, calling loudly to each other until they were summoned to dinner.

Afterwards, a little subdued by excitement, exercise and food, they sat on the steps of the Landing, watching the people down in the square. Shaeli told Kirrit about the twins' ride down the rapids, and Kirrit's little sister, Mimsy, hid her face against her sister's chest as Shaeli told of the barrel going through the last rocky passage into the lake. Tajindi, sitting with the twins on the step behind them, listened open-mouthed, then he looked at an embarrassed Neesha, shaking his head.

"What are you looking at *me* for?" she cried. "Shanna was there too."

Tajindi raised an eyebrow and Shaeli stifled a giggle. He looked just like Delphi when she was mad at Kirrit.

"I'm sure," he said loftily, "I'm sure it was *not* Shanna's idea."

Neesha pursed her lips, lowered her head, and said nothing. Shanna looked uncomfortable and sought for a distraction. She saw an unexpected one. She jumped to her feet and pointed across the square.

"Look, it's Blenny," she cried.

Shaeli looked across the square and saw the drell disappearing up a side street. He was walking quickly, his head down, and was soon lost in the crowd.

"I don't think he saw us," she said lamely.

The others looked at her as if she had seriously misplaced her wits. Kirrit stated the obvious.

"You can't *miss* a Trader, Shaeli," she said, dryly.

Neesha called up to Tarkoda, who sat on the steps above with a substantial group of boys. "Koda, did you see Blenny?"

He looked down and shook his head. "Where was he?" he asked.

"Across the square," said Shaeli. "He must have been busy."

Tarkoda nodded and turned back to the boys, and Shaeli explained to Kirrit about Blenny and Spotjaw, and how they were there on the day of the barrel-ride. Kirrit asked many questions, for she had never seen a drell, and she kept scanning the square in search of him.

Shaeli told her everything; well, *almost* everything. She thought she would burst with the need to tell someone of Nol and his family, but until she could see Almarnoch and mention Williver, she would have to be content to tell Kirrit about the drell and the show he and Spotjaw had performed.

* * *

Up on Golden Eagle, Mareesha was telling Delphi of the barrel ride too, and Delphi's face and feelings mirrored those of her youngest son's.

"It'd be no wager to guess who thought that up," she said.

Mareesha sighed. "I know," she said. "But I think it may have scared some caution into her. She's been rather quiet ever since."

Delphi nodded. "'T'would be no bad thing, either," she said, and changed the subject. "And you'll see your sister tomorrow?"

"Yes," Mareesha smiled. "And I haven't sent word we're coming. I wanted to surprise her."

She hugged the thought to her and looked across the city to Great Court. Yes, it would be good to see Asheen. She had missed her elder sister.

* * *

The next day Mareesha dressed her children in their best, and she and Jarris took them in a hired carriage to her sister's house, all of them excited by the visit and the novelty of riding in a carriage. Jarris, who could find his way from one end of any Land to the other, was lost in the vast city the moment they left the square, yet Mareesha knew every street in Palveron and her face was flushed with pleasure as she gave him directions.

Shaeli and Tarkoda sat in front with Jarris, calling behind to the girls and Mareesha as they spotted a new marvel ahead. The twins sat on their knees in the rear seat on either side of their mother, ogling at the people and shops they passed.

The streets were a carnival of colour and activity, new sights and smells surrounded them, and people from all Lands walked by. Grand carriages, humble carts, and riders on horseback crammed every thoroughfare, and the buildings crowded the streets, some with towers and gables, others with blank, square faces looking down on the throng. Scores of food shops offered all manner of culinary delights, and tables filled with people overflowed onto pathways and elaborate verandas above their heads. They saw a group of elves sitting on one balcony, and they all stared at the rare sight of elves in the World, even Mareesha and Jarris.

Mareesha guided Jarris through the busy streets towards the Bay of Islands. It opened out before them between the trunks of a tree-lined avenue, the islands floating in a haze of blue. They stopped for a while, admiring the sight, and then they followed the road as it wound along the shores of the bay. Behind them rose the great headland and the castle, and even after they turned along the bay road, Mareesha could feel the sight of it on the back of her neck. She directed Jarris around the last corner, and leant forward as her sister's house came into sight.

It was the last on the street, a long, low, white house, surrounded by broad verandas and willow trees. Four great chimneys rose from the roof, and green storm shutters at every window were testament to the harsh Wintering it weathered, but now a multitude of flowers coloured the garden with bright splashes, and a fruit-laden vine wound along the veranda rail. A wide lawn sloped down to meet the waters of the bay where white birds swam like soft clouds.

Mareesha leapt out as Jarris pulled the carriage to a halt in the driveway, and by the time they were out of the carriage she was up the stairs and knocking on the door. It was opened almost instantly by Asheen's husband, Lord Zander, and before he could speak Mareesha rushed at him and threw her arms around him.

If he was taken aback, he did not show it. His arms went round Mareesha, and he kissed her cheek, welcomed her and then Jarris, clasping him in the same warm manner. Two tall young men and a girl came to the door behind him, and Mareesha exclaimed over them, hugged each one, asking Jarris all the while if he could believe how they had grown. He smilingly answered several times that he could not, meeting Zander's eye in amusement as Mareesha ushered her children forward and proudly introduced them to their cousins.

Shaeli thought she remembered her cousin Iyri. Iyri was seventeen, and almost as tall as her older brothers. She had a soft, sweet face and hair the exact shade as Shaeli's, and she gave Shaeli and the twins a warm hug, and smilingly shook hands with Tarkoda, welcoming them all on behalf of her mother. Zander explained that Asheen was on Faunist duty at Great Court, and Mareesha's face fell.

Zander smiled into his dark, grey-streaked beard, his brown eyes twinkling. "But her Moon ends today, Mareesha, and I was leaving to pick her up, just as you knocked at the door."

Mareesha spoke without thinking. "Let me go, Zander," she said. "It would be such a surprise."

He laughingly agreed, and while Mareesha was surprised at herself, she felt unafraid and filled suddenly with a sense of purpose. Shaeli tugged at her sleeve, the twins close behind her.

"Can we come, too, Mam?" Shaeli asked.

Mareesha hesitated for just a moment, then she smiled as Iyri volunteered to accompany them. "Alright," she nodded.

Jarris and Tarkoda were happy to stay at the house, and in a short while they were headed back down the bay road in the little carriage. Iyri sat in the back and she soon had the twins talking, and Shaeli sat with her mother, amazed at the ease with which Mareesha handled the horses and wove the carriage through the streets.

As they neared the promontory the road began to rise, the slope on their left grew steeper and then dropped away altogether, becoming the ragged cliff which made the headland impenetrable from the water. Shaeli could see the waves crashing onto jagged rocks below, and was relieved when her mother turned the carriage inland and the streets closed around them again. Soon they turned back onto the wide road which ran from the square up to the castle, and Mareesha drove up the busy thoroughfare with a sure hand, for there was once a time when she had driven this route almost every day.

Her mother had been appointed second Faunist to King Tenelon when Mareesha was barely five, and they had lived at Great Court for many years. She had been apprenticed young, at seven Winters, the same time as Asheen, who was fourteen, a more usual age for apprenticeship.

Their mother, Sha'rem, seeing the natural aptitude in the young Mareesha, had consented to the child's desire to begin training. She had never been disappointed. Mareesha had soaked up knowledge, and Asheen had been barely able to keep up with her younger sister. At just seventeen Winters, after Asheen's marriage to Zander, Mareesha had taken her sister's place as her mother's second.

Only one incident had marred her time at Court. Her hand rubbed at the tiny scar above her brow as she remembered Virrisian's blow, but that awful incident in her eighth Winter had led to her friendship with Irinesta, and the blow had been a small price to pay for such a gift.

Irinesta had favoured Mareesha from that time on, and when she became queen she did not forget the child who had been instrumental in giving her Tenelon. The two had become friends as Mareesha learned the ways of a Faunist and Irinesta learned the ways of Court, and when Mareesha had returned from her time on Faunist Island, the bond between them had grown stronger. Together they shared many things, and Mareesha was always a source of honesty and comfort to her queen, particularly through the many miscarriages Irinesta had endured. Irinesta had been heartbroken when Mareesha had told her she was to wed Jarris and leave Great Court, and she had given her a gift that ensured they could speak to each other, however much distance separated them. Mareesha had not used that gift in many Winters. Jarris did not know of its existence.

She slowed the carriage as they neared the castle's wall. A constant stream of traffic moved in both directions through the arch; carts, carriages, people and soldiers on foot or on horseback. She would have to state their business to the guard like everyone else waiting to enter the castle grounds, and as they waited she looked back at the twins. They each wore a strand of Iyri's beads and were sitting quietly, absorbed by the sights around them, and Mareesha smiled at Iyri and turned back. Shaeli was looking with amazement up at the wall towering above.

"It's taller than our Trader, that wall, and wider than a house," Mareesha said, putting an arm around her daughter's shoulders. "It was built hundreds of Winters ago, to protect the castle from its enemies. It is said a thousand people could live inside comfortably for many Winters."

Shaeli looked up, largely impressed at the huge sand-coloured edifice. "A Trader could easily fly over, though," she mused.

Mareesha smiled. "That's true," she said. "But only if it was to bring aid to those behind the wall. There's a Landing inside, but no Trader would ever betray its loyalty to Great Court by giving help to an enemy. Cave lies on Zirrus land, and our people are of Zirrus and ruled by its monarch, though we are apart from them." She kissed the top of Shaeli's head and took up the reins.

"Is it our turn now, Mam?" Shaeli asked, and Mareesha nodded and clicked at the horses.

The stone wall arched high over the width of the road, and they moved into the cool shadow under the vastness of it. Soldiers patrolled the top, watching the city below and the castle above, and Shaeli saw one peering down at their carriage as they drove under. Mareesha stopped in the shadow of the great wall, spoke briefly to one of the guard and he waved them on.

Once inside the wall, Shaeli looked over her shoulder at the two giant gates which could seal off the castle. They were wrought iron, clad with slabs of thick tree trunks, with small holes cut through the wood. Mareesha told her that they were for shooting arrows, but the gates had never been closed in her memory.

On either side of the road were the square, storeyed houses of the guard, and many soldiers walked about or sat in the sun outside the buildings. Further on lay dozens more buildings, smaller and squatter, which housed the gardeners and grooms. They passed a forge where sweating men toiled over blazing fires, and the harsh clang of hammer on metal made the twins put their hands to their ears and wrinkle their noses at the grey, burnt-metal smell. Beyond the buildings, soldiers dressed in scarlet and black were training on horseback upon the expansive grassy field which opened out on the right, and behind the field, almost at the cliff edge, horses were being exercised in corrals between vast banks of stables.

Another field mirrored it on the left, reaching right across to the cliff edge. Mareesha pointed to the hawks and falcons soaring overhead, the banks of low buildings which housed the birds in a far corner of the field, and the men on the ground with gloved hands and eyes squinting at the sky, training the birds. There was a small Landing behind the buildings edging this field, but the Landing and the landing posts were the only familiar sight in this amazing place.

The road narrowed slightly and sloped gently upwards, and the wide fields gave way to massive gardens. Men and women worked in huge plots, sowing and harvesting a multitude of plants, and Shaeli could smell the contribution of the horses on the vegetables. The long rows of edible varieties of plants gave way to gardens where hundreds of blossoms flourished, and the mingled scents of the flowers filled her nostrils with more pleasant odours. The air was thick with the sound of bees gathering nectar, and their hives were scattered along the far edge of the gardens beside the wall which rimmed the top of the headland. Within this sheltered part of the bluff, trees opened their arms above the banks of blossoms, pathways wound through burgeoning flower-beds and private courtyards were scattered about, set behind chiselled-stone walls, manicured hedges, or sheltered by vine-covered trellises. Statues of nymphs, cherubs, and fairies peeped out from beneath flowing branches or held white arms up to the sun. Fountains tinkled to the birds that came to drink from their waters.

Beyond the flower gardens the road levelled again, and they were surrounded by soft green lawns. Trees of amazing variety dotted the grassy expanse, and after the massive labyrinth of courtyards and gardens, the open verdant space was calm and peaceful.

The wall surrounding the peak of the headland had grown higher still, protecting the plants from strong sea winds, yet Mareesha told Shaeli that it was the power of the Warlocks which kept the immense gardens as magnificent as they were; without intervention, most of the trees and flowers would not survive a Wintering. So, too, the Warlocks kept the water needs of the castle in an abundant and pure state, for though Great Court had the mightiest protection from attack, it was all meaningless if those under siege had no water – though there had been no siege for more than a century. All the fountains and ponds were tended by the Warlocks, and a huge well sat in the middle of the forecourt inside the castle's inner wall. The well was always as full as a pond, but where the water came from, none knew but the Warlocks themselves.

Great Court towered above everything, filling the sky with gold-dappled walls and high peaked roofs. The five main turrets encircled the smaller ones, two flanking the gates of the second inner wall, the other three ranged behind. At the peak of the headland stood the tallest turret, that which was the domain of the queen. It was thicker than the rest, and flew an enormous black and scarlet flag at its peak. Queen Virrisian's colours flew everywhere, but Mareesha saw that Tenelon's blue-green standard still fluttered from a balcony high up on the turret on the northern side of the gate, and her heart thudded against her ribs. Tenelon and Irinesta had chosen to live in the slightly smaller tower where the Glade Room crowned the turret; the turret where Irinesta was now in seclusion – where Tenelon's flag still flew.

She looked at the well through the archway of the inner wall. This second wall circled the towers and inner buildings, sealing the castle off from the rest of the headland, yet they had no need to pass the armed guard standing at attention at the gate or enter the forecourt where the well lay. The house of the Faunists lay to their left, outside the inner wall, beneath the Tower of the Glade. Mareesha turned the horses into the round gravel courtyard in front of the building.

Beside the immense castle, the building seemed small, yet it was a huge structure, many storeyed, built of the same pale-gold stone as the castle. Across the road lay another building, home of the Warlocks who served the Court. Unlike most Faunists, who served for a Moon, a few times a year – unless they directly served the monarch – Warlocks served and lived for long periods in the house opposite the Faunists.

Mareesha halted the horses, and she and the girls alighted from the carriage, eager to stretch their legs and look up at the castle. Mareesha asked Iyri to watch the girls while she went to find Asheen, for now she was here, she did not want to linger. Her nerves had begun to jump, and she wished she'd come alone. Iyri said they would wait in the herb gardens, and Mareesha hurried off with barely a glance at the tower above.

Iyri led the girls around the left side of the building, and there lay the loveliest garden of herbs that Shaeli had ever seen. The smells tugged at her nostrils, and white stone statues peered down upon the lush plants. There was a small fountain in the centre of the garden, and the girls ran over to splash their faces and drink the cool, sweet water.

Several Faunists walked in the gardens, others were picking the pungent herbs, and nearby a young Warlock sat under a tree, studying a heavy book. They walked through the garden and then sat on a stone bench, watching the people wandering across the lawns and driving along the road. The young Warlock finished his book and stalked back across the road without raising his head, and Neesha unkindly imitated his stride, making Iyri, Shanna and Shaeli laugh.

Shanna stayed close by Shaeli's side, her green eyes staring in wonder at the castle, overwhelmed by the people and pure size of everything, but Neesha loved it. She said good morning to everyone that passed, and engaged a smiling old Faunist in conversation, stating she would come here and be a Faunist too, when she grew up.

Shaeli was wondering where her mother was when Iyri stood and walked towards a woman who emerged from a side door of the Faunist House. Shaeli knew immediately that it was her aunt, for she looked very much like Mareesha. She was a little shorter, and her dark curls were piled high upon her head, but her smile as she hugged Iyri was the same as her mother's, and her voice when she spoke was identical. She came over and hugged the three girls, and Neesha asked her aunt if she and Mareesha were twins like them. Asheen laughed and shook her head, then took Neesha's hand and began to lead them back to the carriage.

"Where's Mam?" asked Shaeli.

"She saw someone she wanted to speak with," said Asheen over her shoulder. "But she will join us soon." She looked at her daughter and lowered her voice. "She tries to speak with E'Nith."

Iyri seemed surprised. "Didn't you tell her that E'Nith will speak to no one?"

Asheen sighed. "I told her, yet your aunt was never one for being told, and she *would* try." She smiled the smile that was very like her younger sister's. "As I knew she would."

Shaeli, walking behind with Shanna, smiled too. She had often heard her father complain about Mareesha's stubborn nature. She wondered who E'Nith was.

As they reached the carriage, Mareesha emerged from the main door of the Faunist House. She looked at Asheen and shook her head.

Asheen embraced her. "She has spoken to no one for a long time, Mareesha, and she is always accompanied by guards," she said. "It saddens many of us, yet it is Irinesta's wish."

"I knew it was impossible," Mareesha said. "I shouldn't have tried. E'Nith barely glanced at me." She sighed. "Does no one see Irinesta?"

Asheen shook her head. "The only time we see her is when she comes out onto the balcony, and that happens seldom." Asheen looked up. "It is the only way we know she is alright."

Mareesha followed her gaze and sighed again, then she looked down at her daughters and smiled. "Come, girls, let's go and have lunch."

Asheen sat in front with Mareesha, so Shaeli sat in the little seat behind them, looking backward. Shanna squeezed in beside her, and Neesha and Iyri sat opposite as Mareesha clicked to the horses and turned onto the road. Shanna suddenly pointed up to the turret above the Faunist House.

"Look, there's a lady up there," she said, and Shaeli looked.

Asheen turned. Neesha and Iyri looked up. Mareesha too, looked over her shoulder, up to the little balcony high above. She pulled at the reins, and the horses slowed until they were barely moving. The black-clad figure on the high ledge stared out across the Bay of Islands, turned her face up to the sun for a moment, and then she looked back down, her gaze fixing upon the horizon.

Mareesha willed her to look down at them, and, oddly, wonderfully, she did. The face of the black-clad figure on the balcony turned down, travelled along the road and came to rest upon the carriage. Across the distance, their eyes locked. The hands of the woman on the balcony went to her mouth, then reached out towards them. For a long moment they stared at each other.

Mareesha looked at her daughters in the carriage below, and then back to the balcony. Time slowed. Mareesha sat straighter, kissed her fingertips and raised them to the lady far above, then she turned her back on Great Court, and urged the horses forward. Beside her, Asheen dropped her head in respect, then she turned and put a comforting arm around Mareesha.

The lady on the balcony gathered her hands to her breast, folding them as if she held a captured bird in her palms. Her eyes followed the little carriage down the wide road until it disappeared under the great wall.

Shaeli and Shanna watched as the figure dwindled and became a black smudge against the pale castle walls. Just before they reached the gate, Shaeli thought she saw an arm raised in farewell.

* * *

Irinesta was on the balcony when E'Nith returned. She had come as quickly as she could, yet she did not want the guard to think she had reason to hurry. Many people still tried to speak with her, to send Irinesta notes and messages, and she did not want the soldiers to think Mareesha was anyone special. She had been shocked when she'd seen her in the Faunist House, and had looked away, pretending not to notice her.

She placed the basket that had just been searched on the table and went out to onto the balcony. Irinesta was looking down at the city, her hands clutched tightly. When she turned to look at the old woman, there were tears in her eyes. Her face crumpled, and E'Nith knew at once what had happened.

"You saw her?" E'Nith said, her stubby tongue stumbling over the words.

Irinesta clutched the old woman and hugged her tightly. The tears fell, yet she was smiling.

"Yes, E'Nith, I saw her," said Irinesta. "I saw her, *and* her children."

* * *

CHAPTER TWENTY ONE

Mareesha was silent on the drive back to Asheen's. She did not feel the warmth of the sun, nor see the sparkles like diamonds on the surface of the bay. She did not hear the chatter from the girls behind, or sense the discerning gaze of her sister beside her.

Asheen spoke little also. Her sister's mood puzzled her, yet in the end she put it down to disappointment, and worry for Irinesta. They had always been such close friends. When they reached the house, Asheen saw her have a hurried whispered conversation with Jarris, and during lunch Mareesha lost her melancholy and was less distracted.

After lunch, the children ran about on the lawn and swam with their cousins in the bay while the adults sat in the shade on the cool veranda watching them and talking.

Mareesha asked after the Lady Arinola, a close friend of Irinesta's, a lady of whom Mareesha often thought. Asheen told her she was well, but away from Palveron. She no longer resided at Great Court, but lived in her family home in Palveron, yet this summer she had gone to Romynn, and would remain there for the Wintering. Mareesha was disappointed; she had thought to visit the forthright Arinola.

Jarris was speaking to Zander about conditions on Zirrus; the new Landing tax and the landingholders, the score of new laws and taxes throughout the country and the growing discomfort of the people with the queen's lavish lifestyle.

Zander nodded. "Here in Palveron there is unrest too," he said. "No one speaks openly, yet everyone knows people are unsettled. Those closest to Virrisian may try to counsel her to more modest ways, yet it appears they have little influence. She pays heed to no one, not even Sir Vulcan of Conroi." He shrugged. "New troops, new arms from Wokk, new clothes."

"Last Wintering, she sent out a troop to try and reach Romynn because she had run out of her favourite wine," said Asheen scornfully. "Not one returned, and the steward who failed to order enough wine disappeared. 'Twas put about he had retired to the Starisles." It was her turn to shrug. "Yet there are rumours. And sending soldiers out in the middle of the Wintering – though it is said they volunteered – was little short of murder."

Mareesha shivered though the day was warm, and took Jarris' hand.

"There are also rumours," said Zander, lowering his voice. "Of strange craft seen in the night sky."

Asheen made a noise of dismissal. "Those rumours I put little credence in, Zander," she said. "It has been spoken of only by Gremon, and he slipped into madness soon after." She turned solemnly to Mareesha. "He was found in his quarters one morning, mindless and dribbling, and he has not uttered an intelligent word since."

Mareesha shook her head, dismayed. She had known the old soldier well, and the last time she had seen him was when he had delivered Queen Virrisian's first proclamation in Djelda, the year after Tenelon died.

"Gremon was always so level headed," she said. "One of the best of Tenelon's guard. He must be nearing sixty?" she asked, and Asheen nodded. Mareesha sighed, remembering the brash, friendly guard. "He often accompanied Irinesta and I into the city. The poor man."

Jarris leant forward. "You say he had seen something in the sky, Zander?" he asked. "What did it look like?"

Something in his manner disturbed Zander and he spoke slowly, eyes on Jarris' face. "He said it flew higher than a hawk, and faster. He insisted it was almost bird shaped, yet black and huge. Blacker than the night sky in which it flew, so Gremon said."

"Where?" said Jarris.

"Off the coast of Wokk," said Zander. "The east coast. When he returned to Palveron, he talked incessantly of it, so they say. I never spoke to him personally, did you, Asheen?" She shook her head and he tried, unsuccessfully, to laugh. "But they are only rumours, Jarris. Gremon went mad soon after."

"But I am not mad, Zander," Jarris said gravely, leaning forward. "And seven Winters ago, I saw this flying ship, too."

Asheen gasped. Her face paled as Jarris told them briefly what he and Shaeli had seen in the sky over Serrat.

Zander leant forward. "Who else knows of this?" he asked.

"The Council. Most of the traders, I'd say," replied Jarris. "It was decided to say nothing of it in the World."

"Good," Zander nodded. "A wise decision. I'd advise that it be kept so." He thought for a moment, his dark eyes on the castle etched against the sky. "There is no doubt now that the rumours are true, that Gremon saw something, and someone of power must know about it." He was quiet again, lost in thought. "And if it *is* true, it is only reasonable to assume that it is a great secret. And perhaps, just perhaps, what happened to Gremon was not as simple as mere madness."

Asheen's hand clutched her husband's arm. "Surely you don't mean someone *made* him that way?" she cried.

"I do mean just that, my dear," he said, covering her hand with his own. "And it goes without saying that we must not mention this to anyone. *Anyone.* Many people are swayed by the queen's magnetism, and you know her spies are everywhere. Promise me you'll not speak of this, Asheen."

"Of course, Zander," she said. "But who has the magic to rob someone of their mind? It cannot be done with Faunistry, not without death following soon after, and I know of no Warlock with such power. Even the power to reach into the mind of another is rare, except amongst the drell or sometimes the elves, and it can never be sustained." She turned to her sister. "Isn't that so, Mareesha?"

Mareesha did not reply for a moment. Her thoughts were back in the time when she had felt *her* mind invaded, pulled from her against her will, yet she decided to say nothing to Asheen and Zander, it would only trouble them more, and so she nodded.

"'Tis true, it is rare to touch someone's mind, and not usually sustainable. *And* I know of no Warlock with such a power," she said. She drew a breath. "Yet that does not mean there *is* no one," she added softly.

* * *

At dusk they travelled home, back through the darkening streets to the square, Mareesha sitting with Jarris, quietly directing him through the still-busy thoroughfares. Tarkoda sat in the back with a drowsy twin on either side, each resting a weary head upon his shoulders. They were broad shoulders now, his voice had changed to the voice of a man, and Shaeli had to crane her neck to look up at him. She sat in the little backward-facing seat, describing the castle and the gardens and Faunist House. He asked for details about the troops and horses, but she had to admit that she had taken little notice, except for their uniforms and that there seemed to be so many of them.

As they neared the city centre, they saw young Warlocks moving along the wide footpaths, lighting the lamps hanging from posts dotting the paths. The lamp-posts burned with a soft light, covering everything in a golden glow the colour of a late summer afternoon, and though they watched closely, neither Tarkoda nor Shaeli could see how the Warlocks lit the lamps. They carried no brand, and the lamps seemed to hold no flame; they merely glowed. They passed close by a young Warlock, just as he was lighting one. He reached up, seemed only to click his fingers and the lamp was alive, and then he walked on, whistling, to the next. Mareesha told them it was the duty of all young Warlocks to light the lamps. It was an easy spell, she said, to *light* the lamp, if one had the Warlock's gift, but harder to keep it going for the required time. She laughed and said one could always tell when there was an apprentice Warlock lighting lamp-posts, for the golden light wavered, blinked, or disappeared completely.

Jeth and Andos were a welcome sight when they entered the big room. Eenis was in bed already with one of her headaches, but Jeth had a light dinner ready, for which they were grateful. The twins were sent to bed soon after, with none of their usual moaning, for it had been a long day. Tarkoda, Andos and Shaeli disappeared over to Red Arrow for a short time, to remind them, they said, about Tarkoda's birth-day feast, and when they came back they also went to their beds.

Jarris told Jeth of the things he had learnt from Asheen and Zander, and though the hour was late, they decided Taffka must be told, and they went over to Golden Eagle.

Mareesha went to bed, to lie sleeplessly until Jarris came back.

* * *

A few days later, on a sunny afternoon, the deck of Purple Leaf was overflowing. The children had spent the morning decorating the rails with paper streamers and multi-coloured lanterns for Tarkoda's party. Eenis had shown them how to make the lanterns so the flames held no danger, putting the tiny candles safely in a bed of sand encased in coloured paper.

Asheen, Zander and the cousins arrived for the feast with the biggest kite that Tarkoda had ever seen, and Tarkoda's only disappointment was that there was nowhere to try it out in the city. Yet as fine a present as it was, he was overwhelmed when he unwrapped his parents' gift. Inside a leather pouch was the long-coveted Wokkii knife, with five different blades and his name engraved on the side. He stared at the knife in his hand, his face flushing redder with each passing moment, and then he flew at his parents. The deep rumble of Baroz's laugh rolled across the deck.

"We spent a lot of time looking at knives on Wokk," he boomed. "If 'tis not right you can blame Alvaro." He laughed again as he gave his eldest son a hearty clap on the back. "Eh, lad?"

Alvaro, now a man grown, grinned back good-naturedly, his thick red beard and broad shoulders a reflection of his father's. He spoke quietly to his sister Maize, and Taffka's son, Rafi, who stood beside him. The two men were good friends and had shared Cave year together.

Rafi, though tall like his father, had the blonde hair and brown eyes of his mother, Renn, who was as tiny as Taffka was tall. Renn stood nearby with the Head Trader. She shared much of Taffka's load, working beside him on the Trader and at Great Court, directing the Zoi in lifts and landings, and she knew every trader by name and relation. She soothed ruffled nerves, cooled hot tempers, and consoled the grieving. For a little woman, it was said in the Fleet, she had very broad shoulders, and her only sorrow was that she had not had more children. Her tiny frame had made Rafi's birth difficult and both had almost died, and the Faunists had aided her in avoiding further pregnancies. Yet she was an optimistic woman, and she already looked forward to the day when Rafi would wed and fill Golden Eagle with children of his own.

The younger boys crowded around Tarkoda as he opened the blades of the knife, each boyish face growing various shades of envy-green as the knife was examined, praised, and examined again. Wez and Beren petitioned their father to buy them one when they returned to Wokk the next year, but Baroz was not anxious to agree.

"We'll see," he said, his usually open face unreadable. "It may depend on how much help you are to your mother and I between now and then."

Delphi held her smile in check. She knew full well that Baroz intended to buy each of them a knife, yet she knew also that now they would have two boys falling over themselves to help on the busy Trader until the next year. She started to mentally compile a list.

Similarly, Jeth covered his mouth with a callused hand, and his eyes met those of Baroz across their sons' heads. Baroz winked and Jeth winked back. Andos' birth-day was near autumn's end, and his knife was already secreted below decks. Eenis, standing by herself on the fringe of the group, did not approve of such things, but Jeth had been firm: the boy had passed his Cave year and was nearly grown. Eenis grieved at the thought, she loathed and feared the idea of her boys growing and perhaps leaving her, but she consented. She knew Jeth was right.

Her thoughts went from Andos to Dari, as they did two dozen times a day. She wondered if he was alright, if he was happy, if he was careful. He could suffer some terrible accident or sickness, and she wouldn't know until they returned for the Wintering. Perhaps even now...

Dari might be dead... and you just don't know it.

Eenis hushed the panicky voice inside her head, pushing down its whimper. She rubbed the place between her eyebrows, the place where her headaches always began, the place where the whimpering voice lived. She caught a flickering from the corner of her eye, and jumped as the voice in her head suddenly screamed.

Elf-light! It's elf-light. Run. Run!

She controlled the hysteria with the voice of reason. The voice she lived in.

It is only a paper streamer, she told herself tersely. *Be still.*

She would never again let that panic-struck, whimpering voice be her own. Never. She hushed the whining voice, willed the ache away, and her face reflected none of the turmoil she felt. She had control of that, too. Yet the headache grew, and she slipped below to take a double dose of the powder Mareesha made for her. It never completely stopped the headache, but if she took it quickly enough the pain was contained to a dull throb behind her eyebrows. And it silenced the voice.

Mareesha saw Eenis go below, and thought momentarily of following her, for she recognised the tight look of pain on Eenis' face. Yet she stayed where she was; Eenis disliked anyone to cosset her, and Mareesha wished to speak with Taffka.

* * *

Mareesha stood silently, trying to read the faces of Taffka and Renn. She had just told them of the time her mind had been swept from her, and both were looking thoughtfully at her.

"Why did you say nothing of this before, Mareesha?" Taffka asked.

"I thought it was me," she said, embarrassed. "It was not until I heard what had happened to Gremon that I began to question it."

"But Jarris had not seen the flying craft then?"

Mareesha looked at Renn, who stared back unblinkingly, her brown eyes unreadable. She shook her head, and shrugged.

"The two things may have nothing to do with each other," she said. "I just thought you should know." She looked around, her eyes flicking across the gathering, and then she smiled at them. "I'd better go and organise the food," she said, and walked away.

Taffka and Renn could both see the smile was forced. They watched her as she walked across the deck.

"There is more to this, Taffka," said Renn quietly, her eyes following Mareesha.

Taffka turned to look down at his wife. "'Tis just what I was thinking."

"Time will give us answers," she said, looking from Mareesha to her husband. "Yet, I fear we may not like the answers it gives us."

* * *

CHAPTER TWENTY TWO

As Mareesha was talking to Taffka and Renn, Eenis was hurrying along the passageway to her room mixing the powder into a glass of water. She downed the acrid brew in one swallow, and lay on the bed, trying to ignore the thudding footfalls above. She willed the whiny voice to cease its jabbering; to stop bringing the past back. She would not remember. She would *not*. And yet the past unravelled in her mind even as her body was drawn into leaden slumber; unwanted, hated memories flooded her dreams, as clear as the days when they were not dreams or memories, but reality. Horrific, terrible reality.

She saw again the burning village. The people running, screaming, dying as the blue bolts of elf-fire struck them. Her own father bursting into blue flame before her eyes.

Her mother had cried out and run towards him. Remembering her cowering daughters she had turned back. Too late. A blast of blue leapt out of the darkness, struck her mid-centre, and in an instant she was engulfed. She had spoken one word as she died, her eyes stretching across the distance, locking with those of her sixteen-Winters daughter.

Run, she had screamed, and Eenis had taken the hand of her younger sister, Illen, and run.

Through the house they ran, the flames outside making the familiar rooms the stuff of nightmares. Grotesque shadows shuddered and wailed along the crimson walls as the girls ran out the back door and across the tiny garden where Eenis had lovingly tended the flowers. She thought how strange they looked with so much fire in the sky. As if they had been dipped in blood.

The house exploded into flame behind them. The face of Illen was suddenly illuminated, terror making her usually serene eyes huge and bright. Her long hair streamed out behind her and it, too, bore a blood-red sheen. Across the clearing behind the garden, Eenis could see the copse that promised sanctuary. She gripped tighter to the trembling hand of Illen, and ran faster.

They were halfway across the clearing when she heard the hooves. Illen heard them too, and tiny moans began to come from her. They had almost reached the trees when an ugly man on an ugly pony swung in front of them, cutting off all hope of escape.

Eenis could smell the leaves and the mouldy smell of rich compost on the forest floor, yet she knew the sanctuary of the trees was lost to them. She expected to die then, but the ugly man waved a dirty sword in their faces and shepherded them back towards the village.

Illen's moans grew louder as they were prodded into the square. They could see their home being consumed by hungry flames and the still-smoking mounds of ash that had been their parents on the street before it. There were many of the little piles of ash on the streets of their village.

A boy, a friend of Illen's, broke cover and ran towards them, perhaps with some futile hope of rescuing them. A blue bolt from their left struck him, and his screams echoed those of the village dying around him. Illen buried her head in Eenis' shoulder, but Eenis looked to the source of the bolt, and saw the form which had given her nightmares ever since.

An elf, absurdly dressed for battle, rode towards them on another of the barrel-shaped ponies, yet as he drew up in front of them, Eenis saw that he was not *entirely* elfin. She had met a few of the elves who lived in the mountains near their village, and none had looked like this. Never had they caused the terror in her that this man did.

He sat astride his scruffy mount with an air of studied belligerence. A cruel sneer curdled his fine elfin mouth, but it was overshadowed by a beaky nose; a nose most definitely *not* elfin. Slivers of eyes bore into her, glittering with malice and something else – something unreadable – yet her flesh crawled under that gaze. His black eyes were hung with thick, dark brows, something elves did not possess, yet she could see the dull points of his ears jutting from his hair. Eenis supposed he must be half-elf, but whatever his parentage, in his hand he held an elfin wand, a short, thick-hafted instrument. It was with this he had decimated their lives.

Fresh screams drew her eyes, and Eenis looked past the half-elf to where three girls were being prodded towards them by more men. They huddled together as others rode up behind, two more girls driven before them, and the terrified knot of girls clutched at each other as the men looked expectantly towards their leader.

"Are they all dead?" he said, his voice harsh venom.

The man who had captured Eenis and Illen nodded. "Yes, my lord Periqol. What your elf-light did not finish, our swords did." He prodded Eenis in the back. "And we have these for our reward."

"Stores? Horses?" Periqol rasped. "What of these, Niv?"

"Stores we have, lord. They are being loaded into the wagons of the village. Enough to keep us fed for a Moon." Niv shrugged apologetically. "But no horses. Only a few ponies."

Periqol's scowl grew deeper. "I must have a *horse*, Niv. I'll not ride this mangy nag much longer." He kicked the sides of the little pony, who grunted, and his voice grew almost petulant. "'Tis not *fitting*."

Niv tried to placate him. "Perhaps in the next village, lord."

But there was no horse in the next village, nor the next, nor the one after that. When the band returned from its latest foray, empty-handed, to the miserable collection of huts they haunted, Periqol's rage was felt by all.

"Thwarted," he screamed. "Thwarted by country fools in a paltry *village*."

"But, lord, there were king's guard among them." Eenis, listening inside the hut, knew the nervous voice belonged to Niv. "They were ready for us."

"No excuse." The voice of Periqol rose higher, jarring the ears of everyone who heard it.

Those inside the squalid dwellings cowered, wondering who would suffer to sate Periqol's wrath. One of the girls in Eenis' hut was so terrified she ran out the door, the rope between her ankles giving her a peculiar gait. She was spotted at once, and the men toyed with her, taunting her as she clambered over the rubble at the back of the narrow valley.

Eenis, hiding in the shadows beside the open doorway, cringed as the girl was dragged screaming back to the central fire and thrown in the dirt in front of the half-elf.

Periqol pulled the girl up by her hair and slit her from throat to belly without a word, a brutal grin smeared across his face. The girl's screams gurgled to a halt, and he dropped her body back into the dust and peered at the silent band, yet for all this brutality his anger was unappeased. He kicked the dead girl lying in a growing pool of scarlet, and strode towards his own shoddy hut.

"Bring me another girl," he roared over his shoulder. He slashed at a pony tethered nearby with his sword and the pony squealed. The blade left a thin red line behind it. "A man of my excellence should not be stuck in such a place," he howled. "I am *better* than this."

His band breathed a sigh of relief as he stalked inside his hut. Niv turned towards the hovels that were prison to the girls taken from the surrounding villages.

Two dozen days had passed since the village of Eenis and Illen had been devastated – the second in the region to have fallen to Periqol. There were other girls in the hut next to their windowless box, and Eenis had crept over and spoken a few words with them when the band was on a raid. More girls had been thrust into the hovels after each rampage.

The days had dragged by, going from bad to worse to horrible as the moon shrank and began to grow again in the night sky. No breeze blew at the bottom of the craggy ravine, and Eenis had rarely felt the sun on her face. Escape was whispered of more as a source of hope than as a plan for reality, for each knew the hopelessness of their situation. The doors were only latched, but their feet were bound together with thick ropes, tied with knots that only grew tighter as you worked at them; they were hobbled more effectively and more cruelly than the ponies. Besides, there was nowhere to escape *to*; they were far back in the mountains and leagues of uninhabited country surrounded them.

Eenis drew back from the door as Niv approached. She tried to shrink into the shadows, into the very *wall,* and make herself unnoticeable. She burned with shame as the hope that someone else would be taken passed through her mind.

In the days spent in captivity, she had, with the others, been beaten and humiliated. They had been sporadically fed, if there were scraps left over, yet the food was so heavily spiced it made many of them ill. Each had also been brutally used by Periqol's band. Eenis had been to the hut of Periqol once, and she did not want to repeat the experience. Her mind shied away from the memory, and she drew herself back further as Niv entered and looked around the room. There were soft scurryings around the miserable hut as each girl tried to make herself invisible. Only Illen was left in the middle of the floor.

She lay in the dirt, her hands wrapped around her wasted body. Niv squinted at her, grabbed her arm, pulled her to her feet, and started dragging her to the door. Illen did not struggle, she only moaned and clutched herself tighter, her dirty hands almost meeting under her thin shoulder blades. Her eyes stared stupidly, sightlessly, as they had ever since she had been taken to Periqol's hut ten days before. It was more than Eenis could bear. She pulled herself from the shadows and stepped into Niv's path.

"Leave her," she said, in the thin, cringing tone which had become her voice. "Leave her and take me. Her mind will stand no more."

Niv stared at her for a moment. "I'd a mind to have you myself this night," he said.

His thick tongue slipped out and ran over his lips and Eenis shivered, then Niv laughed, shrugged, and let go of Illen. He took Eenis' arm, and as he led her out she looked back over her shoulder. Illen lay curled again on the dirt floor. Soft moans escaped from beneath the once-beautiful hair lying matted and filthy over her face.

A tear slid down Eenis' cheek as she walked through the squalor from which she could see no escape. The rocky valley lay far from any village, and she could not see how anyone could find them, or even know of their plight. She averted her eyes from the girl lying on the stones in a congealing pool of blood.

Perhaps tonight Periqol would kill her. Her throat still wore the bruises he had made on their last encounter, and she almost hoped for the release. She shuddered as the shadow of the hut covered her. She longed to feel a breeze on her face and see the sun in a wide, clear sky.

Niv pushed her forward, and she fell to her knees inside the hut of Periqol. She could hear the pleas and screams of the other girls as the band went among them, and there came a cry from outside, very close, and the sharp sound of a hard hand meeting soft flesh. The headache that had been with Eenis for many days – ever since her mother had disintegrated before her eyes – pounded on the centre of her forehead. The grovelling whine that had become her voice seeped from her lips, and she hated herself for it. She had always been the rational one, the serious one, solemn and sensible. Dependable, her Mam had said. *Boring*, Illen had said.

Illen, a Winter younger than Eenis, had been a carefree, sweet child, preferring to lay giggling in the shade of a tree with one of her many friends than do something useful. Eenis had been the helpful one, capable even as a child, generous and even-tempered. And yet here she was, cowering before a half-elf murderer, her voice a hitching whimper. She did not even know what she said, but Periqol slapped the words from her mouth anyway. The pounding in her head grew louder, drowning much of the noise from outside.

Periqol unbuckled a small knife from his belt and put it down beside the silver wand on the rickety table in the centre of the room. Eenis looked with loathing at the stubby wand with its vicious blue stone and the tiny red stones like drops of blood studded around the thick haft.

Periqol turned and slapped her eyes from the wand as he had slapped the words from her mouth. Then he ripped the rags that had once been her bodice from her, pulling her to her feet with his other hand as he did so. She closed her eyes as he pinched the soft flesh on her arm.

"Open your eyes, and look upon the face of your master," he snarled.

He nodded as her eyes flew open, then he lowered his head and bit her shoulder. A cry escaped her, and she felt blood run hotly down her arm. She fought to keep her eyes open as he raised his head, and he nodded again in satisfaction, his mouth curling into a hideous smile.

As he lowered his head for the second time, a strange rose-coloured light flickered outside. It was followed by a scream, yet not the too-familiar scream of a girl, but the cry of a man. Before Periqol had raised his head, another colour, green this time, flared outside. He thrust her to the floor, and strode to the doorway. The setting sun was in his eyes, and the sudden tumult in his camp stopped him for a moment, then he strode back, picked up his wand and ran from the hut.

Eenis quivered where she lay, unable to move, then the thought of Illen lifted her head and she pulled the fragments of her bodice back over her breasts, and crawled to the doorway.

As she knotted a few strands together to hold her shirt in place, she peered around the edge of the door. Her hands stopped moving as the scene sunk into her tortured mind.

There were men on horses, not ugly, barrel-bellied ponies, but *horses*, dozens it seemed, riding through the shabby collection of hovels. Many wore King Tenelon's colours, but others were like the men who used to live in her village; farmers and merchants.

She saw one man on a magnificent white stallion riding after one of Periqol's band, and she watched, fascinated, as he struck the bandit down with a sword that shone red, first with the setting sun and then with the man's blood.

Periqol stood in the centre of the melee, blue elf-fire shooting from his wand. It was met by the rose and the green lights, and Eenis saw another band of riders on the far side of the clearing. They were elves, true elves, and they drew Periqol's fire as men of the People killed his band, one by one.

She turned back into the hut for an instant before rushing out the door, keeping as low to the ground as she could. She reached the door of the hut where Illen still lay curled mindlessly on the floor. Two other girls cowered in a corner, the rest had fled or been dragged away, and Eenis cut the rope between Illen's ankles with the knife she had taken from Periqol's hut, then she cut her own and drew Illen to her feet. She threw the knife across the room and motioned for the others to follow. She peered again around the doorway and scuttled, half dragging Illen, outside and around the corner. She could hear the others behind her, and one of them moved forward and helped her shuffle Illen away, up through the rubble at the back of the ravine and behind a boulder.

They were just in time. For the second time in a Moon, the dwelling behind Eenis shot into flame. She motioned for the others to stay where they were, and crept out to look back down at the site of their captivity.

The bodies of Periqol's bandits lay scattered in the dirt, the ground turning black with their blood, and the elves rode in a circle around Periqol, drawing his fire as the grim men watched. Niv stood at his back, fighting two men. And losing.

Sweat ran from Periqol's brow as he sent his light hurtling at the elves. He stood legs apart, in the beginning confident of his greatness, swinging this way and that, calling taunts and jeers at the riders, his elf-light shattering the sky, yet few of the blue bolts found their mark. One bolt, uncaught by the elves, sent first a hut, and then a nearby tree into flame, yet time and again the blue from his wand was met by the rose light or the green, or both, and Periqol's flame dissolved, as if eaten by the softer colours. The rose and green lights dissipated the blue, engulfed it, disarmed it, and even when the elves missed their mark, their lights faded and died before they hit anything else, as if they had control over their lights even as they flew. The long, thin wands in their hands captured the sun's last rays, sparkling on the great stones at the tips.

Periqol was not so controlled. The half-elf fired without accuracy or discretion again and again, but as each new bolt was caught and dissipated, as his band was cut down, as it became increasingly obvious that he was grossly overmatched, as Niv died at his back, then the face of Periqol at last began to show fear.

Eenis had moved forward, scurrying down to hide behind a stunted tree where she had a wider view. When Niv fell with first one sword, then the other in his chest, she felt little, no relief, no satisfaction, she only turned her attention to Periqol's last moments.

The elves, led by the two wielding the wands of green and rose, tightened the circle around Periqol, riding round and round, drawing his fire and draining his power. The blue flame of Periqol lost its brightness; the rose and green remained strong and were delivered with unerring accuracy. Magic danced in the auras of the elves and their horses, the air around filling with glittering particles until they rode in drifts of shimmering light, but despite the beauty of their magic, their mission was obvious. The circle about Periqol grew tighter. Ringing the inner circle, closing like a whirlpool, were men with faces grimmer than any Eenis had ever seen.

Periqol fired his weakening flame indiscriminately, but each bolt became paler than the last until all power was gone. The blue stone in the tip of the wand cracked and fell into pieces, and he fell to his knees. He uttered a roar of frustration, and picked up the sword which had fallen from Niv's hand.

The circle of men and elves closed as Periqol tried to struggle to his feet, obscuring his last moments from her sight. Only then did Eenis allow herself to feel a tiny glimmer of hope, the hope of release other than death. Yet immediately following this was the knowledge that she had nowhere to go. Her village, her parents, even her sister's mind were gone, and she had nothing, only her longing to see a wide sky above her head, to feel a cool, clean wind wash away the touch of cruel hands. To be held by gentle arms until she felt safe.

She shivered with a mixture of revulsion and longing, then jumped and screamed as something warm and hairy brushed her shoulder. She leapt back, spun around, and her eyes met the gentle brown ones of a huge roan horse. He must have picked his way up through the rocks without her noticing, so focused had she been on Periqol's defeat, and he stood so close to her that she could feel his hot breath blowing against her arm.

They stood regarding each other, and then the horse took a small step towards her. He lay his warm, soft cheek against her arm, pushing ever so gently. Eenis was too startled to move, and she trembled as the horse sniffed at her and stamped a foot. He lifted his head and stared at her, his deep brown eyes reaching into her blue ones. She could see herself reflected in their dark moist depths, and she thought she looked very small.

The horse lifted his head, nickered softly, and took another step forward until his shoulder was almost touching her nose, and yet she felt no fear. The horse seemed so full of compassion that when he lay his head once more upon her shoulder, Eenis threw her arms about his neck and hugged his warm solid frame. All the terror and shame burst forth, and she sobbed until his neck was wet, and her misery had quieted into long heaving breaths.

How long she stood with her arms about the horse's neck she did not know. She knew only that the fear was leaving her, and she felt better. There was a weight still, in her chest and behind her eyes, yet the terror was gone; the hopelessness was replaced with a small glimmer of trust. She hugged the horse in gratitude, and kissed his wet neck, a smile trembling on her lips.

"Dancer has found where he is needed, I see," said a quiet voice from behind her.

Eenis' smile evaporated and she turned around. She saw a man with weary blue eyes regarding her from halfway down the slope. Behind her Dancer nickered again softly, and Eenis saw with surprise that she knew the man.

"I've seen you in our village," she said, and hated herself for the whine in her voice. She cleared her throat and tightened her lips until they were a thin, white line. This time when her voice came out, it was merely terse, and that was infinitely better. "You're a trader," she said.

The man noticed the struggle of the child to contain the emotions that had moments before been naked upon her thin, dirty face. He saw the bruises under the grime on her slender neck, the dark circles under her haunted eyes, but he merely nodded, keeping his own features still.

"Yes, lass," he said, and tried a smile. "I am Povann of Purple Leaf, and we spent time in your village last spring."

She nodded again, and her next words all but broke his heart.

"I remember. There's nobody... There's nothing left there, now." Her eyes filled with tears, yet she would not let them fall. She lifted her head, her mouth tightening again into the thin line; the line that would soon become habit, and rob her adult face of the soft lines that smiling gave. "We are safe, now," she said, and although it was not really a question, he nodded anyway. She stared off into the distance, then looked back at him. "I must get the others," she said in that hard little voice, and she walked away.

Dancer followed her every step, and Eenis looked round at the horse with such gratitude that the heart of Povann also followed the thin girl. She disappeared behind a huge boulder and emerged with three other girls, her arm wrapped around one who came willingly enough but whose eyes held no life.

Dancer whinnied softly, and Eenis stopped so that he could nuzzle Illen, yet whatever magic he had held for Eenis, Illen felt none of it. A thin string of saliva ran from the corner of her mouth, and she seemed unaware of the great horse before her. Eenis' shoulders lifted and fell as she drew a deep breath, and she put out a hand to touch Dancer's nose.

"Thank you," she whispered. "But I fear it will not be so easy for Illen."

Povann heard her words and felt tears close his throat, yet he swallowed hard at them and moved forward to help. Eenis turned her pale blue eyes up to him, and he saw they were almost the same colour as one of his sons'.

"This is my sister," she said brusquely. She turned to Illen and gently wiped away the drool with the hem of her torn skirt. Illen moaned.

Povann reached out and touched Eenis' shoulder. She recoiled and he saw a drying trickle of blood and two half-moon teeth marks, almost hidden by the scraps of cloth she wore. His eyes filled with the tears he could not swallow.

"You poor, wee lass," he whispered, and stroked her matted brown hair.

Eenis tolerated it, but her face remained pinched. He cut the remains of the rope from their legs, and helped Eenis guide Illen down the slope and into the clearing between the smoking remains of Periqol's camp.

Of Periqol and his band there was no sign, only dark patches on the rocky ground where their blood was drying. The body of the girl Periqol had killed had been removed too, and the other girls stood with their rescuers on the far side if the clearing, swathed in blankets, many in relieved tears. Eenis could see two elfin women sewing something into a blanket, and guessed they were preparing the dead girl's body for burial.

One of the elfin women looked up and their eyes met. The green eyes of the elf moved to Illen, who leant against Eenis. She spoke to her companion, who nodded and continued her work, and she rose and walked across the harsh, stony ground as gracefully as if she walked in a cool forest.

"I am Rhi'aan," she said, as she reached them, and held out her hand. Eenis took it after a moment, and Rhi'aan smiled, then her gaze shifted to the two girls who stood behind Eenis. "We will be leaving soon, though 'tis almost night."

It surprised Eenis to see it was barely twilight; it seemed days since the band had ridden back from their failed raid.

"I think you'll not want to spend another night in this place." Rhi'aan continued. "So we shall ride to a place of green, and tomorrow you shall begin to put the past behind you. Homes will be found to shelter you. Many are those who have offered aid in this sad hour." She smiled gently. "Go over with the others and someone will arrange to carry you."

The two girls thanked her, and walked to where the horses were being readied. Eenis began to follow them, but Rhi'aan put a hand on her arm and she stopped, her arm about her sister.

Povann also stayed where he was. Dancer was his mount, lent by a friend who rode with the rescue party, and Dancer stood behind Eenis' shoulder still.

Rhi'aan smiled at Eenis. "What is your name, child?" she asked gently. Eenis told her, and Rhi'aan looked at Illen. "And this is your friend, Eenis?"

"My sister, Lady." Eenis tried to soften her voice, but the tightness remained. It was better than the whine. "This is Illen."

Rhi'aan tilted Illen's blank face up to her own, and for a long moment she studied her eyes. She looked back at Eenis.

"Your sister has suffered grievously," she said. "Her mind has taken refuge."

Eenis nodded, and her arm tightened around the shoulders of Illen.

"There are those amongst the elves who can heal such damage," Rhi'aan said. She gestured to the other elfin lady. "Whynai has special healing gifts, and I, too, would like to help your sister. It is possible to heal such an injury, though it may take some time, by your reckoning."

Rhi'aan's voice soothed Eenis; soft music in her ears after screams and harsh voices, yet she secretly doubted that Illen's mind would ever return. She believed it was shattered, like a fragile mirror, and would never reflect light again, but she nodded numbly, hopeful that this Lady, with hair like molten sunshine and eyes so gentle and green, could help Illen, a task which her practical mind knew was beyond her.

They rode away from the ugly, thin valley in the half-light of dusk, the dying rays of the sun on the peaks of the mountains above, each dazed girl riding before a weary man or elf. The ponies were led behind them in a long line, their heads low. One carried the wrapped body of the girl Periqol had killed.

Eenis rode with Povann, her hands in Dancer's thick mane, and Rhi'aan rode beside them cradling Illen. They stopped at last in a cool glade, and though the hour was late, the two elfin women took the girls to a small pool nearby. Bright stars gleamed high overhead, and the half-moon sailed above the dark trees as they slipped gratefully into the water. When they had cleansed their bodies, Rhi'aan and Whynai gave them light tunics to wear; soft light cloth to cover bruised and broken skin.

Whynai helped Eenis bathe Illen and dress her. She brushed Illen's flowing hair until it shone, and Eenis could see her sister was calmed by the elf's touch. Illen no longer moaned, but her eyes were dull and she drooled stupidly as she was dressed. Eenis wondered if it was possible for the elves to heal her sister, to make her mind whole again. She knew that, for her, the memories would not be washed away by a cold pool. Hate, almost unnoticed, slowly began to leech into her heart. She did not know what she hated, but it began to make her angry. She still felt the tightness of terror in her chest and the voice of panic lying coiled above her eyes, but anger proved to be stronger. In time the panic faded, and Eenis grew accustomed to the strain of keeping the weak, whimpering voice in its place, yet, sadly, her hate grew, and in the end she would turn the ensuing anger against the elves. It was *they* who had bred Periqol; they who had made the tool which had wielded such destruction, and they who had taken her sister from her, for she had never seen Illen again after the elves took her.

She grew to believe – *made* herself believe – that Rhi'aan, with her soft voice and unnaturally green eyes had bewitched her, and taken from her the one thing that remained from her former existence: her sister. She forgot that it was elf-light which had freed her, she remembered only that elf-magic had destroyed her life. She grew terse and frowning, pious and rigid. Few were those who saw the glimpses of softness she allowed, fewer still were ever acquainted with the gentle girl she had once been. Others who grew to know and love her as the years passed recognised the tight facade was merely protection against a harsh World, and saw her gifts beneath the brusqueness, yet most saw merely what she presented; tight lips and a curt manner. Eenis, over the passing Winters, narrowed her mind just as she had narrowed her smile. She kept her thoughts contained, just as she kept the whining voice contained.

Dancer, though, saved her in those first desolate years from complete disheartenment. The horse had continued to lend her strength, and it was the horses who always remained as the heroes in her mind; horses who became the real saviours. It was Dancer who had carried her from that place; Dancer who kept her from being consumed by hate; Dancer who loved her despite all. To the people who cared for her later she felt gratitude, loyalty, and a need to repay them for their care; some she grew to love in her overprotective, narrow way, yet it was Dancer and his kin who were the truly noble ones. On the journey back, and all the days of his life, Dancer was beside her, warming her spirit with his gentle presence. She rode from the mountains with he and Povann, and when they camped each night, he was always to be found a step from her.

Urell, Povann's friend and Dancer's owner, shook his head in wonder, and his eyes were merry when he joked that his horse had been stolen by the young lady. The others shook their heads, and wondered aloud why the horse had chosen to befriend the lass. They declared they had never heard of anything like it.

Eenis smiled with genuine pleasure, and yet some fundamental piece of her had been lost and the smile quickly faded. She found little joy in anything except Dancer and the sky above her head. She buried the hysteria on the long ride through the southern foothills of Zirrus' great mountain range, and when they arrived two days later at Noresh, she found a village so like her own it made her throat hurt, yet she succeeded in keeping her features unmoving as they rode through the streets, her lips white with their tight line. Dancer beneath her, and Povann's gentle arm about her gave her strength, and she did not flinch from the kind, curious stares of the people of Noresh.

Eenis saw the bright green-and-purple balloon above the roofs ahead, and when they reached the Landing in the square, Povann took his arm from around her and waved up at two blue-eyed lads who hailed him from the Trader's railing. Above the balloon, the clear blue sky seemed very wide and very bright. A cool wind touched her face and she almost smiled.

* * *

From the doorway of their room on the Trader, Jeth saw the half-smile on his wife's face, and a smile touched his own. He knew that Mareesha's powders had worked, and the headache had been subdued. Eenis would sleep soundly and wake composed again.

He, too, had seen her go downstairs with the familiar strained look. He had seen that look on her face when she had ridden into Noresh with his father, so many Winters before, and he smiled at the memory of his strong patient father, so protective of the thin girl Eenis had been.

Jeth had watched with his father as the elves had ridden away from Noresh with Illen. Silent tears ran down Eenis' face as her sister, her broken mind uncomprehending, left the village. Eenis had turned, her heart plain upon her face, and, though it was one of the few times he had ever seen it so, Jeth never forgot it. His heart, like his father's, was drawn to her.

As the Winters passed, every year found them visiting the village of Noresh where Eenis lived with Povann's friend, Urell, and his family. She was happy there, seeing Dancer every day, and learning to ride him. Urell had made her a gift of Dancer, and for that Eenis was ever grateful.

The day after Dancer died and the grieving heart of Eenis still lay plain upon her face, Jeth had asked her to wed. She looked at him for such a long time that Jeth had begun to worry. Then she had simply nodded once, and smiled through unfallen tears.

"Yes," she'd said. "Oh, yes. I can think of nothing I'd like more than to live under a wide sky, with a cool breeze in my face and your gentle arm around me."

* * *

CHAPTER TWENTY THREE

The traders were sitting on the deck of Purple Leaf after Tarkoda's party, replete and comfortable. Stars twinkled above, but Shaeli thought they looked somewhat faded, washed of their brightness by the lights of Palveron, the lesser stars lost altogether. The coloured lamps sitting along the rails cast a soft glow upon their faces, and in the distance the windows of Great Court twinkled.

Shaeli and Kirrit lay on the top deck, staring up at the balloon shivering in the cool breeze. The streamers they had tied to the railings whispered in paper voices, and they could hear the voices of the boys as they ran about in the square underneath the Landing. Shaeli sat up suddenly as she heard Tarkoda's voice shout across the square.

"Blenny," she heard him cry. "Blenny and Spotjaw."

Shaeli leapt to her feet and ran to the rail, Kirrit close on her heels.

Across the square walked Blenny and Spotjaw. Blenny looked up and greeted Shaeli, his long fingers waving about like tiny snakes.

"Hello, sea-maid," he called and Shaeli waved back, a wide grin on her face.

"It *is* a drell," Kirrit breathed.

Shaeli laughed. "Of course," she said. "Come on, let's go and see them." She grabbed Kirrit's hand, and together they ran down the stairs and across the deck. "Spotjaw and Blenny are here," she called to her father as they ran past.

As they reached the landing gate, Spotjaw and Blenny were coming up the Landing steps, surrounded by the boys. Blenny had an arm about Tarkoda's shoulders, Koda was grinning, and Shaeli saw the reason why. In his hands he held a slingshot, but not one of the plain wooden kind owned by most boys, this one was some kind of black metal, yet it did not shine in the lamp light, its odd surface seemed not to reflect light, but swallow it.

Tarkoda ran along the Landing to his father, who had crossed over to greet them. Taffka had come with Jarris, and Eenis, arisen from her rest, her face pale still, walked over with Jeth to stand with them.

"Look, Da," Tarkoda cried. "Look what Blenny gave me."

Jarris took the slingshot and examined it, pulling at the springy pouch. He studied the dark surface and pulled again at the supple pouch, and everyone could see how the metal bent with the pressure, as if it were a spring. Jarris handed the slingshot back to his son.

"You are fortunate, Koda," he said. "'Tis drell-made, and a cunning weapon. I have not seen one since I was a lad." He smiled at the drell. "A kindly gift, Blenny. How did you know it was the lad's birth-day?"

Blenny grinned. "I saw it in the crimson smoke, so I did," he said. "And I said to Spotjaw we must come and see our friends, didn't I, Spot?" He looked up at his tall companion.

Spotjaw nodded. "That you did," he answered. "To which I most willingly agreed. He came back to our lodgings a few days ago, full of the news of your arrival. Yet he wanted to wait until this eve to come. A surprise, he said."

"So I did," agreed Blenny.

"But we saw you," said Shaeli. "Across the square. We wondered why you didn't come up."

Blenny looked crestfallen. "So you did see me?" he said. "I hoped you were too busy with your friends to notice." He turned one red-rimmed eye towards Kirrit. "Is this the one who races the wind?" he asked, the other eye still on Shaeli. The one looking at Kirrit winked and she giggled.

"Yes," said Shaeli. "This is Kirrit. She's the fastest at Cave."

Kirrit's pale skin turned an attractive shade of pink. "Only out of the girls. I can't beat *all* the boys," she grinned at the drell. "Yet."

Blenny laughed, and then a loud voice from across the deck attracted their attention.

"Why didn't someone tell me that Blenny and Spotjaw were here?"

Neesha stood under the cover leading to the stairwell. Mareesha, Shanna and Tajindi were coming up behind her. Neesha ran across, pushing between the legs of the adults to stand in front of the visitors.

"Hello," was all she could think of to say when she got there.

"I was wondering where the little barrel-riders were," said Spotjaw.

"We were downstairs," she said, "helping Mam with the cake and tezz." She took Blenny's hand, and smiled up at him. "Are you going to do some tricks?" she asked.

Blenny looked at Spotjaw with one eye, the other rolled up to consult the sky. His long snaky fingers rubbed at his round chin.

"Mm, I'm not sure," he said. "Are we going to do any tricks, Spotjaw?"

"I don't know," Spotjaw answered seriously, shaking his head. "Are we?"

Then Blenny suddenly grabbed Neesha around the waist and swung her legs in the air. Neesha squealed as Spotjaw grabbed her ankles and pulled off her soft shoes. He began to juggle them and Blenny put Neesha down and grabbed one of Tarkoda's legs, lifted it and pulled off his shoe. This he also threw to Spotjaw, who grabbed it, and added it to Neesha's circling ones. Then Blenny chased Tajindi, who giggled and struggled when caught. His shoes too, were added to the ones in the air. Round and round went Blenny, lifting a leg here, tripping over a wide-eyed, red-headed child there, stealing shoes from everywhere and throwing them over to Spotjaw. The tall man unerringly caught every one, his hands blurring with the swift movements, and he added each shoe to the flying shoe circle. He juggled faster and faster as the circle grew, until a dozen, fifteen shoes whirled through the air, then Spotjaw began to toss them to Blenny, and soon the juggling shoes circled above his head.

Everyone laughed and clapped as the jugglers began to toss the shoes between them. Backwards and forwards they flew, and then they started to throw the shoes back to the gathered traders, but Tajindi was tossed Tarkoda's shoe, and Neesha was thrown Wez's, Rafi caught Maize's. There was much laughter as they retrieved their own shoes and put them on again.

Later, after moon-set, Tarkoda, Andos, Kirrit and Shaeli walked Spotjaw and Blenny to the bottom of the Landing stairs. Tarkoda thanked Blenny again for his gift.

Blenny smiled. "'Tis my pleasure, lad," he said. "Be sure you learn to use it." His round face grew serious, and Shaeli was reminded of how he looked when surrounded by the crimson smoke. "Learn to use it wisely," he said, gravely. "Wisely, and well." Then he smiled, the compelling face softening again into its lumpy lines. "We bid you goodnight, and pleasant dreams, so we do."

He dropped into a sweeping bow, Spotjaw did the same, and they set off across the square. The children watched them go; the tall thin man and the short, round drell. Andos looked at Tarkoda.

"Can you use a slingshot wisely?" he grinned

Tarkoda grinned back. "I can try," he said.

"I would try hard if I was you, Koda," said Shaeli. "A drell once told me to learn how to swim."

* * *

Ten days later, Purple Leaf flew above the Bay of Islands, Palveron and Great Court slowly dwindling behind them.

Shaeli sat on a box on deck, her almost-finished book of elf-lore beside her, staring at the green islands sitting serenely in the bay.

The first island, the smallest and the nearest to Palveron, was the resting place of past kings and queens; huge tombs housing the bodies of the dead sat undisturbed beneath ancient trees; immense stone vaults and imposing statues held graceful arms or stone swords up to the sky.

The largest of the islands housed the seminary of Warlocks, where young apprentices spent their final Winters before they became fully fledged Warlocks. Almarnoch had taught there before returning to Cave after old Warlock Adz died, and Shaeli looked curiously at the many dark stone buildings studded amongst the thick trees. Bright yellow smoke drifted from one of the tall chimneys and a group of Warlocks on the bank were pulling spouting geysers from the water, and she wondered whether Llevvis was among them.

The next, slightly smaller island, was given over to the Faunists for the same purpose. Her mother told her it was a beautiful place, filled with pungent herb gardens and graceful trees. Sha'rem, Mareesha and Asheen's mother – her grandmother – lived there and taught apprentices in their final Winters of learning, and Shaeli waved at the Island of Faunists in case Sha'rem was watching. Sha'rem had spent a few days with them when she received word of Purple Leaf's arrival in Palveron, and Shaeli had liked her. She was different from Wyshka, who was always cooking and eager for a game or a joke, there if you needed someone to talk with. Sha'rem was elegant and serious, a smile seldom touching her face, but her eyes held a lovely shine and she always spoke gently and kindly to everyone. Shaeli could see that those shining, green eyes, so like her mother's, held great love and wisdom. Yes, she had liked her other grandmother very much.

The Trader flew over the bay, the Zoi cutting easily through the clean, salty air, the voice of the lead female crying out the joy of the flock at their release from the confines of the city.

The haze of late summer made the horizon shimmer and dance, but here above the bay the air was cool. Below, in the shining water, dolphins played with the racing shadow of the Trader, leaping in and out of the dark water, hurrying to catch the elusive shadow.

Shaeli watched the islands and Great Court until they had dwindled to smudges on the horizon, and then she turned her face east.

* * *

When Purple Leaf flew from Palveron, Irinesta watched from a window in the Glade Room, tears rolling down her face.

She whispered softly, calling on every blessing she knew to send after the Trader flying above the city, following it with her eyes until the bright balloon had dwindled to a speck above the Bay of Islands. She turned back to the room where she now spent her every hour.

It was well that she loved it here, for she thought she would not leave it until after her death. She knew she *could* leave at any time, escape from her enforced seclusion, but that would alert Virrisian to the fact that there was another way out of the room, and the knowledge that Irinesta could leave the Glade Room unseen might make Virrisian think; bring back suspicions which now lay dormant. She dare not let Virrisian know there was another way out – another way besides the door where black-and-scarlet-clad guard always stood. For Irinesta's protection, it was said, yet she and Virrisian both knew that was a lie.

She walked away from the window with a sigh. She had not dared to watch the Trader leave from the balcony; that, like all of her movements, would be reported back to the queen. Queen. Irinesta closed her eyes, remembering the little faces turned up to her from the carriage. There had sat the true queen. Irinesta sighed again, and went to her desk, knowing she had taken the right course.

* * *

Virrisian, in her rooms in First Tower as Purple Leaf left Palveron, was also confident of her course. No matter how much she was urged to stray from it, she stood firm. Every argument by Sir Vulcan, Orm of the treasury, and her ministers she disregarded, smiling coolly, shrugging at their threats of unrest and uprising. Shaking her head at their efforts to make her "see reason", and "tread warily".

Finally she grew tired of their pathetic ravings and fearful predictions. She slammed her hand on the desktop, and was gratified at the instant silence.

"Enough of your preaching," she said. "The taxes stand as I have ordered them, the garrisons *will* be built. See to it my wishes are carried out. I know what is best for my kingdom." The unhidden pride and arrogance in her voice caused many to cringe and lower their eyes. "My coffers *will* be filled. The People will do as they are told."

Sir Vulcan of Conroi did not flinch from his responsibility, nor lower his eyes. "This tax will earn you no friends," he began. "The People cannot afford..."

"The People will afford what I *tell* them to, Vulcan," she interrupted. "And friends I can do without." She stood taller, her shoulders square, her chin high. She reminded Vulcan of the wilful child she had been. "Leave me now, and carry out my wishes. Unless, of course, any of you want to resign your positions?" She smiled at the silence. "No. No, I thought not." She waved her hand at them. "Then go."

They turned immediately and began to shuffle out the door, the flock of stupid sheep she always thought of them as. Except for Sir Vulcan. He stood before her still, determined to continue. She narrowed her eyes at him.

"Leave, Vulcan," she commanded. "Now."

He looked at her for a moment, and then he bowed. "As you wish, my lady," he said. "But I will not return. This is too much, and I'll not be part of it." He did not wait for her to speak, he merely turned and left the room.

She looked at his retreating back, still straight and broad for all his Winters. She shook her head; she could do without him. She turned to the only person remaining in the room. He sat in shadows by the rich satin drapes, reclining in a huge chair.

"Well?" she said, lifting an arched black brow.

"They will do as you bid."

"Of course," Virrisian said. "But…?"

"But, my dear Virrisian," said Azeron, rising from his seat and moving from the shadow into a shaft of sunlight. "But they were right, just the same." His voice was uncultured but confident, and his black eyes held no sign of kindness. They were pools of ink, cold and limitless; the eyes of a shark. "They were right about the People – the disquiet," he said slowly, moving forward until his toes touched hers. Not many men stood taller than Virrisian, but he did. "There may be uprisings. Conflicts. What then?"

"This concerns me not," she said, her lips curling. "It concerns my master-at-arms, Sir Azeron of Maxx." She leant against him, raising one arm to drape around his neck, tilting her head at him. "Does it not?"

He smiled a charming smile, but his black eyes showed none of it. "Yes," he said. "And 'tis something I'm sure I can take care of." He kissed her roughly, and grabbed a handful of her hair. "As I can take care of anything my queen desires."

She shook his hand from her head and stepped back from him. "I will join you in a moment, Azeron," she said. "I have something I must do first."

He nodded, running a rough hand up her satin gown from hip to breast as he moved past her. She waited until he had closed the door to her private chambers, then she went to a desk and unlocked it with a key that hung on a golden chain at her waist. She took out a small box and lay it upon the desk. The box opened when she pressed a hidden spring in its base, and inside there lay a half-egg-shaped stone, grey-and-black swirls patterning its dull surface. She took it out and held it in one hand; the other probed the smooth surface as they had probed the bottom of the box. She began to chant softly. The rock grew colder. The grey patterns began to shift and separate. A spark of scarlet glowed in the black heart of the rock. Virrisian smiled.

"It goes well," she said.

* * *

Azeron listened to the muffled voice through the doorway. He knew she was alone, but he also knew there were ways of speaking to those far distant, and though the queen thought his loyalty lay with her, she was mistaken. There were those on Wokk who guided him, many who waited for the right time to seize the Wokkii throne, who would wait patiently to take Zirrus; who had waited through Winterings long before he was born for just this chance, planning and readying. Virrisian knew nothing of these things, only that there were those on Wokk who supported her over their own monarch, who eyed the riches and the power of Zirrus with greed. Azeron's own father and grandfather had spoken often to him during his youth, had moulded him for just such a time as this, and he awaited the coming years with anticipation.

Something stirred in him, a needy excitement he knew he could not deny, and he thought he would satisfy his needs with the new scullery maid he had seen just this morning. Virrisian would want him to satisfy her own first, and he would do it, as he always did, yet she was so willing, so in charge of it all. He preferred his women far less compliant, far less eager. Yes, the young scullery maid would protest, struggle, cry out. Just as he liked it.

He turned away as the queen's voice stopped on the other side of the door and he threw himself down into a chair by the window, waiting until she joined him, his mind on the little maid he would seek out. Soon she would be his, trapped like a frightened fluttering bird in his hand, unwilling and exciting.

* * *

Fezzik had seen the Trader with the green and purple balloon fly from the city that morning too. He was on his way back from Palveron with Pelazarus, who had heard of a new kind of chicken which he wanted to add to his flocks, a crossbreed of the big chickens on Wokk. They had taken the small wagon from the forge, for it seemed half of Boccra had asked them to bring something back from the city, and the new chickens were packed in the tray behind them amid bundles and boxes. They had left the city early, and would spend the night at Fezzik's half-sister's, who lived beside the bay half a day's drive away.

They were in a fine mood as they drove; they had enjoyed the journey but were anxious to get home to their families. Fezzik and Verlie had a fine son, Arral, who was almost four, who they adored, yet Verlie had not conceived since. Pelazarus and Pemba were expecting their fourth child within the Moon.

There weren't many people on the road after they'd left the city. The houses grew fewer and after they passed the Royal Parklands where the Autumn's Eve Hunt was held, and they barely saw a soul as the morning passed. They were talking loudly as they wound through a copse of thick trees, the mid-morning sun slanting between the leaves.

"Aye, I think Brinn a fine name for a boy," Fezzik was saying. He sniffed at the air. "Do you smell smoke?"

Pelazarus nodded, and opened his mouth to reply, but a scream from up ahead took the words away. Around the bend ran a woman, her mouth wide in an endless wail. She saw them coming towards her, and she screamed louder.

"*Help*," she screamed. "My daughter. Her husband. Help them." She scrambled up the steps as they pulled up beside her and pointed back down the road. "Please," she cried, her lined face crumbling. "*Please*. My daughter. Her husband." And she fell upon Pelazarus, sobbing.

Fezzik slapped the horses with the reins and they took off around the bend. The smell of smoke grew stronger as the trees thinned, and around the next corner they came upon a small house. The home backed onto the bay, and there was a boat pulled up on the sand and nets drying in the yard beside an open shed. Both the shed and the house were burning.

Tied to a tree was a young man, his face bloody. Standing in a circle around him were a dozen of the queen's guard, one a ginger-haired man with a long whip in his hand, and in their midst was a young woman, standing in nothing but her petticoats. Her clothes lay scattered around her feet. A few women soldiers stood further away, watching the house burn.

"Take them off, or he gets another one," said the man with the whip.

The young man tied to the tree cried out. "No, Kora," he yelled, through his split lips. "Don't."

Kora looked at him, crying and shaking her head. She jumped as the whip cracked. The young man screamed as the tip of his ear disintegrated.

Fezzik slapped at the horses again and drove the wagon straight at the guard. Pelazarus roared as the wagon came barrelling in and the soldiers scattered. Kora saw her mother and ran towards them as Pelazarus leapt from the wagon and drew his sword. Fezzik pulled on the reins and the horses slid to a stop. He stood up and drew his own sword.

"Is this what the queen's guard are for?" Pelazarus bellowed. "Torturing her subjects?"

He aimed his sword at the one holding the whip. The soldiers pulled out their weapons and turned on Pelazarus. Fezzik thought things were going to go very badly. But still…

"This is none of your business," said the man with the whip. "The queen wants this land for a new garrison and they have to leave. You have no right to interfere."

"That may be," said Fezzik. "But I think we *will* interfere, just the same."

"Stealing someone's land does not mean torturing the owners too," said Pelazarus. "Or does it?"

The man with the whip laughed. "Queen Virrisian allows us to fulfil her wishes in whatever way we deem fit," he said. "She gives no orders for gentleness."

The guard laughed and the whip-soldier preened. Fezzik took the knife from his belt, jumped from the wagon and strode towards the tree.

"Don't touch him," said the soldier, his whip flickering along the ground. "I warn you."

The whip whistled past Fezzik's face and he stopped. He turned to look at the whip-wielder, his eyes narrowing. He gripped his sword tighter and took a step forward. The man must have seen something in Fezzik's face, for he took a step backwards, flicking his whip along the ground. The guard watched silently, some smiling, but when the whip snaked out again, Fezzik caught it in his fist and with one swift heave he yanked it out of the man's hands. The watching guard stopped smiling as the soldier howled and pulled out his sword. Fezzik leant forward, waiting for him. He thought they would do alright, though they were badly outnumbered, but a voice from behind stopped them.

A soldier was coming from the trees, a young female soldier behind him, buttoning up her blouse. She smirked at them and went to join the other women of the guard standing near the burning house. The roof collapsed as she reached them, and they jumped and laughed before turning back to watch what would happen. The dark-haired soldier strode forward, clearly unhappy.

"What's going on?" he asked.

"These men," said the one who had held the whip. "They're trying to stop us carrying out the queen's orders, sir."

The dark-haired soldier, obviously in charge, surveyed the scene. He strode past Fezzik, pulled a knife from his belt, and cut the young man from the tree. The young man collapsed with a groan, falling to his knees in the dust. Kora ran over and helped him to his feet as the head of the guard looked at the one who had held the whip.

"You've had your fun," he said, and the man lowered his eyes.

"Yes, sir," he replied.

The captain looked at Pelazarus. "If you want them so much take them," he said. "There's nothing left for them here."

Fezzik helped Kora and her husband into the back of the wagon and climbed up beside the still-sobbing mother. Pelazarus stood watching the house burn. The guard stood watching Pelazarus.

"Come on, Pel," said Fezzik, urgently. "Let's go."

"It's not right," said Pelazarus. "It's just not right."

"*Leave* it," said Fezzik. "For Merrom's sake, leave it. There's nothing more we can do."

Pelazarus sheathed his sword and went over to pick up Kora's clothes, then he walked slowly back and climbed into the wagon. Fezzik turned the horses and left, feeling the eyes of the guard on his back. Both the women were weeping, and they stopped up the road to find something to wipe the blood from the young man's face. It was covered in little welts and in a few places the flesh had been gouged away.

Fezzik drove to his sister's house where she took instant charge of the three. She bathed wounds, found clothes and food and beds, and she assured Fezzik she would find them a home. They stayed the night and left early the next morning. They travelled silently, and as Boccra came into sight, Pelazarus looked at Fezzik.

"It's just not right," he said.

"I know," Fezzik answered, and he clicked to the horses and urged them home.

* * *

CHAPTER TWENTY FOUR

Purple Leaf flew in slow bounds around the Bay, stopping at the towns and villages along the shore as autumn began to fade the Land beneath them, then the Zoi pulled them east across the plains. They spent a few days in Noresh at the bottom of the southern ranges where Eenis used to live before following the foothills north as the trees changed to bronze and gold. They crossed Meoro Pass as the first chill of the Wintering crossed the Land, and they stayed two nights in Serrat before heading up the Valley of Stones and over the Long Lea to Cave.

Eenis stood on deck as they approached the cavernous mouth, her eyes searching for a glimpse of Dari, and a changed Dari it was who met them at their Landing. His cheeks were flushed as his mother embraced him, he was taller and smiled readily, his thin arms and legs were filled out with exercise, and Shaeli was surprised when he gave her, too, a quick hug. She smiled at his happy face, remembering the sullen boy they had left at the beginning of the year.

He had spent the year down on the Lea, working in the fields and taking lessons from the old ones, but that was not the reason for his changed demeanour. Demeris and Garrit had found he had the natural aptitude required to become a Warlock; much to the surprise of everyone, including himself, he had understood the workings of simple spells, and even the book-lore interested him. Almarnoch had confirmed Dari had some talent and he believed Dari would benefit from further tuition. All through the Wintering Dari begged to be able to spend another year at Cave; Garrit was teaching him the runes and lesser incantations, and he was eager to continue. Eenis was in a dither of indecision. Magic was not one of the things she would have chosen for him and she had missed him much, but the change in Dari was so pleasing that she was loathe to deny him anything.

When they flew from Cave after the Wintering, Dari again stayed behind, this time happily waving from the ledge. Shaeli stood near her aunt, trying not to look at the tear-washed face of the staunch and harsh-voiced Eenis.

* * *

Shaeli had spent the Wintering alternating between her friends and Almarnoch. Llevvis was at the Warlock Island still, and he would return with the Fleet for the next Wintering, yet she had missed his amiable presence during the frozen Moons.

Almarnoch was pleased that she had finished the elf book. He admitted he had not expected she would, but they spent long hours discussing what she had learned. She also learnt something of the potential properties of rocks and gemstones, spending hours hovering over Almarnoch's vast collection, and Shaeli was delighted to find that some of the stones in her amulet held inherent power.

Shaeli had pondered on whether to show Almarnoch the dragon-scale bangle, and as she slept in Serrat the night before they reached Cave, Williver had come to her.

'Tis not yet time to tell the old magician of the bangle, little one, he had said when she asked him about it. They sat in a copse of sea-blue flowers, bright sunshine overhead. *When the need is strong, then you may show him.*

Alright, Williver, she replied. *But he would so love to see it.*

I know, Williver smiled. *He is one among your People who understands magic's true nature, yet now is not the time.* He had been plaiting the tiny blue blossoms together as he spoke, and he placed the flower crown upon her head. *Your heart shall tell you when it is time,* he said.

May I tell him about Nol and his family? she asked, and his smile widened.

You may, he said. *Someone must be told of your good deed, and there's no need to mention your reward. It's a story I'm sure the old one will enjoy, my friend.*

I almost gave up, she admitted. *I was looking for the house for the longest time and it was getting so late, and I knew Mam would be worried. I was about to leave, but then the locket showed me the way, and I knew you were helping.*

Williver looked puzzled. *The locket showed you?* he said, and when Shaeli told him how the locket had warmed in her hand, how the light of the World had changed, he shook his head. *It was not I who did this,* he said. *The gods must have guided you. Now sleep again, and tell the old Warlock the tale when you see him. And remember, speak to no one of what Nol gave you.*

And so she had not said anything about the bangle, though she longed to, and the secret in the battered little box Nol had given her stayed hidden between the walls with her wand – which she checked every night to ensure Dari had not touched it again. Yet her treasures remained safe, and Almarnoch did enjoy the story of Nol and his family, just as Williver said he would.

First snow had come late, and Shaeli and her friends had spent many of the short days beforehand down on the terrace. When first snow did appear – Shaeli had smelt it coming again – the blizzards set in with such fury that no one saw the sun for more than a Moon. Her thirteenth birth-day and Mid-Winter passed in a blur. She spent time exploring the small caves within Cave, sitting round the spring-pool or spotting glow worms, and when first thaw came she was almost surprised, for the Wintering had passed so quickly.

* * *

That year they traded mainly on Zirrus, but during the autumn they flew home via the Straits of Nebillonia, the west coast of Ashkanna, and back across to Meoro Pass. When they reached Cave, Llevvis was waiting to greet her, the staff of full

Warlock proudly in his hand, returned from the Warlock Island with honours, ready to serve the Fleet once more.

The next year, with a confident Dari back on board, full of his lessons and amusing little spells, they journeyed to the Starisles again. They watched the skylights on Pa'laidiz, and filled Purple Leaf with the medicinal weed that grew in the rich sea farms of the Starislanders.

Shaeli remembered that year as a quiet year. They were as busy as always trading on the Starisles, swimming in the warm seas, taking the autumn journey slowly back through Zirrus – where landingholders were increasingly prevalent. Other things, too, were changed. The faces on Zirrus seemed to Shaeli to be drawn tight, the eyes flickering about, or worse, staring dully at the ground. People in small villages gathered in fretful clumps, whispering together, yet if you walked by they would stop, stare at their feet, and as you walked away, the whispering would begin again. In the countryside, too, she noticed the change; fields lay fallow, cattle stood gauntly in dusty pastures; several times they passed over a farmhouse which had burnt to the ground. The mouths in the towns had become pursed, the faces in the cities had closed, the eyes had grown wary. Yet these things were noticed only peripherally, and Shaeli revelled in her time on the Trader; Eenis was more relaxed than she had been for a long time, for she was so happy to have Dari aboard again that lessons for the three girls were almost a pleasure, often taken on the white sands of a beach on one of the islands, or in the shade on deck. Andos, Dari and Tarkoda luxuriated in the fact they no longer had lessons; Cave year had ended their formal education, and Andos and Tarkoda had begun to take some of the responsibility of running the Trader and caring for the Zoi, and their shoulders grew broader with the work they did.

Andos was at home on deck and in the rigging, repairing snarled or fraying ropes high up on the side of the balloon, once even as they flew. Eenis had stood on the deck, her face pinched white until he stood again beside her, yet Andos had inherited the trader's gifts of natural balance and uncanny sense of direction. Both he and Tarkoda knew the paths of the moon, usual wind direction in a particular season, and the names of the stars in the night sky.

Tarkoda, sixteen that summer, a Winter younger than Andos, was often to be found standing with his father on the fore-deck. He watched Jarris as he handled the lines to the birds, learning the subtle gestures sent down through the fine line to the lead bird; gestures which signalled height and direction for the Zoi to follow. That year found Tarkoda at the control line more and more, and he was always there after a landing to unharness the birds and smooth the opalescent feathers with a rough sea sponge. The lead female in particular enjoyed the grooming, lowering her neck so Tarkoda could reach up under her chin, or holding her enormous wings out over his head so he could scratch the rainbow feathers on the underside, and when he finished she would call her thanks for his attention. All the Zoi reacted with pleasure to the careful tending of Tarkoda, flying back to the Trader at his piercing whistle, and it was plain to see the bond which grew between the boy and the graceful birds.

Dari studied still, but they were lessons set by Almarnoch or Demeris, and he amused them all with his burgeoning wizardry, producing flowers and shells from nowhere, making water spin in a cup, or creating a tiny light which hovered above his hand for small periods before fading. Shaeli told him about the young Warlocks they had seen lighting the street-lamps in Palveron, and his eyes grew bright with envy; yet though he seemed a different boy, she hid her wand and the bangle in a different place, and checked them only when she knew he wasn't on board.

When they reached Cave at the end of the year, Shaeli felt a certain sadness, a loss she could not describe. She looked back out on the Valley of Stones, loathe to leave the World behind. She sensed that her quiet time was over, and the World would change before she saw it again, or perhaps it was only *she* who would be different. This Winter she would celebrate her fifteenth birth-day, and when Purple Leaf flew out into the World after first thaw, she would not be aboard. It would be time for her Cave year.

* * *

Dari was looking forward to the Wintering. He would have more lessons, and he was eager to show Almarnoch and Demeris what he had learned. And Garrit. Garrit couldn't have been more pleased that Dari had the Warlock's gift. It seemed he had forgotten the fiasco of the wand when it became apparent Dari had some magic, and Dari hadn't dared mention it again, for he had no wish to be reminded of how angry Garrit had been. He had not spoken to Dari for a Moon afterwards. Dari had no idea how Shaeli had known he had taken it or where he had hidden it – someone must have seen him – but he had given up on the idea. Now that he had the gift of magic, Garrit could always be his friend; he need not be a trader, and he could choose to live wherever he wanted once he was a Warlock. He hoped that if he studied hard, Almarnoch would take him for apprentice. He felt sure that's what the old man intended. He had only to prove himself worthy.

* * *

On the eastern edge of the Starisles, Zeb woke from sleep in the early hours of the morning. The moon had set but the sky held a glimmer of grey to the east as he yawned and stretched, scratching his belly as he left the hut and walked down the path to where the small fire sent a beacon out into the night. He added wood to the blaze, enough to keep it bright until sunrise, and he looked west, across the beach where a low swell pushed inky waves up the sand, searching for his father's sail, yet the wind which had blown steadily the last time he'd been here had dropped to a whisper. He turned to go back to the hut and a glimmer caught his eye.

There was a light in the little bay behind the beach. The mouth of the bay opened to the south, and the outlines of several small boats were drawn against the stars. A rowboat was pulled up on the thin strip of sand, and there were a few figures on the bank above it. He grabbed a thick branch from the stack beside the fire, and crept silently down the hill. He heard voices as he went closer, and then one called out.

"Come down, Zeb," said the old woman. "I want you to meet someone."

"M'zena?" he said. He dropped the branch and walked to the edge of the light, squinting into the shadows. "What are you doing out here?"

Huddled around the light of a small lamp were M'zena, two tall elves and another, smaller figure. Zeb was not surprised to see the elves; they lived on some islands further north and often sailed by, occasionally they'd stop to talk, but he'd only ever seen drell a few times, and then only the very old woman who came to visit M'zena, and whoever escorted her. This drell was much taller than the old woman drell, though he barely reached Zeb's chest, and he was much younger, with a pleasant, open face, yet the face looked like it usually wore a much merrier expression than the sombre one upon it now.

"You know Galen and Bindi," said M'zena, and Zeb nodded at the elves. She looked at the drell, her smile gleaming in the circle of her dark face. "This is Wendll. He has come from the mountains with a few of his kindred to Winter with the elves."

Zeb nodded at the drell's greeting. "It is unusual for drell to leave their homeland, isn't it?" he asked.

"Yes, so it is," agreed Wendll. "Yet elves and drell have ever been friends." He smiled, his face falling easily into lines more suited to it, but it was clear he would offer no more explanation.

Zeb looked at Bindi. "You're out very late," he said, then he smiled. "Or very early."

"Late," Bindi said, returning his smile. She was very beautiful, her blonde hair in two long braids. "We met Wendll and his friends at Irojadis and have been escorting them to our home. The wind brought us this far before it stopped to watch the sun rise, and then M'zena signalled us."

"Did she?" said Zeb, looking down at the old woman.

"I did," she said. "I heard them lowering anchors while you were snoring, and saw the prow of Wendll's boat. Drell always have such pretty boats."

Zeb looked at her, one brow raised, but she pretended not to notice. Hearing them anchor was one thing, but seeing a prow by starlight was another. He could just see the boats and would not have known a drell craft from an elfin one. Although M'zena's eyes were keen and she had much more experience in such matters, still, he had his doubts that the visit was entirely accidental. Not a year went by that M'zena did not have an unusual visitor; elves, drell, a dignitary from the Starcluster, one of the Irikai, and, almost always, somehow she knew they were coming. He had given up being sceptical when she saw a mast and told him who it was; the only thing he did not put any credence in was when she pointed out a line of bubbles or an odd swirl of water in the bay and told him it was Ammerr, the sea people who had long since passed into legend.

"We would have come ashore at sunrise anyway," said Wendll. "My Lady Orbanna would not have forgiven me if I had not brought greetings to her old friend."

"Her greetings, and the warning you just gave me," said M'zena.

The drell looked startled, glancing at Zeb from beneath his brows, but M'zena just smiled serenely.

"Warning?" said Zeb, looking down at the drell, his own smile gone, replaced with narrowed eyes. "What warning?"

"Ah... that there will be bloodshed on Zirrus before long," said Wendll. "My Lady has seen it in the smoke, Palveron burning, its streets awash with blood." He shuddered. "She wished for M'zena to know of this, to know that…"

"It sounds like a terrible thing," M'zena interrupted, looking from a silenced Wendll to the elves. Galen nodded slightly as he met M'zena's eye.

Zeb saw the look and wondered at it, yet he relaxed. M'zena's business did not concern him, nor did far-off happenings on other Lands.

"What happens on Zirrus has little to do with us," he said.

"All Lands will be involved," Galen said, looking down at Wendll. "Isn't that what she said?"

Wendll bobbed his head as if in apology. "All Lands and all races," he said. One eye flicked to M'zena.

"Even so," said Zeb. "We are so far from anywhere, I doubt it will affect us." He looked at the grey leeching up from the eastern horizon, shivering in the pre-dawn chill. "Do you want some tezz? The wind won't be up until after sunrise."

"Our thanks," said Galen. "Tezz would be welcome, wouldn't it, Bindi?"

"Definitely," she said. "You're very kind."

She gave Zeb another dazzling smile, and he led the way up the path to the hut, past the little fire burning on its knoll above the beach. M'zena and Wendll came more slowly.

"Orbanna is sure of what she saw?" asked M'zena quietly, as Zeb and the elves went ahead.

"Oh, yes," said Wendll. "She said there can be no doubt."

"I see," M'zena said. She was silent as they walked past Zeb's beacon. "And Blenny," she said. "Has he returned home?"

Wendll shook his head. "No," he said. "He still searches."

"But Orbanna saw him there?"

"Yes," he said. "He was at the gates of Great Court. Palveron was in ruins beneath the wall."

* * *

CHAPTER TWENTY FIVE

The Wintering was harsh and first thaw came late. The traders looked every day for a sign that the blizzards were letting up, and with each day that passed with no sign of respite they grew increasingly impatient.

Shaeli was not. She was loathe for first thaw to come, and although she had looked forward to her Cave year, she realised just how much she would miss travelling beneath the balloon over the Lands and the Seas. She did not want to leave her family, and the thought of not seeing them for all the Moons of the year filled her with heartache. She spent a lot of time alone, sulking, feeling sorry for herself, and she alternated between being enormously loving and broodingly sullen. Only the thought that she would have Wyshka and Almarnoch kept her from complete depression. And Kirrit; she would also have Kirrit.

Of the friends of her childhood, Kirrit would share Cave year with her, but Driss had completed hers the previous year. Bonn and Shylo would also stay at Cave, but as the years had passed they had spent less and less time together, and were now only on nodding terms.

When first thaw finally came, the Traders left in droves. The balloons flew from the tunnel and over the Long Lea, filling the sky with splashes of colour and the melodic cries of the Zoi.

The thunderheads of the last storm lay curled far away on the southern horizon, dropping back to where Winter's fury began, the frozen wastelands across the Bastinian Ocean. A few stray storms might still lag behind the mother-cloud, but when first thaw came, the Wintering did not linger. Springtime champed at the bit of the Wintering, longing to gallop through the forests and fields, filling them with colour and life.

Purple Leaf and Red Arrow were of the last to leave. Kirrit and Shaeli had said their farewells inside, and then they walked together across the Cave and through the bolt tunnel to wave from the ledge. Halfway, Shaeli took Kirrit's hand, and Kirrit, dry-eyed, and for once with nothing to say, squeezed her hand in return.

Shaeli's eyes were rimmed with pink and shimmering still with the tears she had shed. Her father had hugged her hard when she'd said goodbye, and assured her that the time would pass quickly. He had kissed her forehead, and told her that he would miss her every day.

Jeth had kissed her, and Eenis had given her a stiff hug, thrusting a small parcel into Shaeli's hand. Shaeli had thanked her, and placed the gift into the bag sitting forlornly on the tiny Landing. The boys had hugged her too. Tarkoda had told her not to look so sad, he knew she would have a good time. She'd nodded, and tried to smile through the trembling of her lips, but she couldn't make the smile work properly. Her throat had ached with the words she did not say. Shanna and Neesha clung to her, saying what she could not.

Shanna, crying soft tears, and saying in an even softer voice, "I don't want to leave you, Shaeli. I *don't*."

And Neesha, her wails of protest opposing her lack of tears. "We're going so far away. And I'll *miss* you."

Shaeli suspected Neesha enjoyed the dramatics of the farewell, but that did not lessen her grief. She hugged both girls hard, told them to be good and careful, and she kissed their faces scores of times, "for all the kisses I'll miss". They promised to be good, and stood watching as Mareesha walked Shaeli down the stairs, both clutching tightly to Jarris, Shanna with her face against his waist.

Mareesha had held Shaeli for a long time, resting her cheek on the top of her daughter's head. The hair, thick and soft, and so like Jarris', tickled her cheek, and she marvelled at how quickly her daughter had grown. Shaeli's bowed head lay just below her chin, and she wondered at how the days and Moons had blended so quickly into the passing of time. She hugged her, and mourned the end of Shaeli's childhood.

Shaeli clung to her mother and quietly sobbed against the shawl-wrapped shoulder. When the tears had subsided Mareesha put her hand under Shaeli's chin, and lifted it to dry her eyes.

"It's true what they said, you know. The time *will* go quickly, and you *will* have fun." She smiled and Shaeli tried to smile back, but again, it didn't work very well. Mareesha stroked her cheek. "You are a strong, clever girl, Shaeli. Your spirit is as lovely as your face, and both are very dear to my heart. I know you'll have a wonderful Cave year, and when we return…" Her voice had trembled then, just a little. "When we return, we shall find you a young woman instead of our little girl."

That had made Shaeli cry again. "I'll always be your girl, Mam," she whispered. "Always."

She had hugged her mother one more time, turned away quickly and run to where Kirrit stood waiting by the spring-pool. Red Arrow was almost ready for lift, and when Purple Leaf began to untie its ropes, Shaeli and Kirrit had walked through the bolt-tunnel.

Wyshka and Olver were waiting at the mouth with Kirrit's grandmother, and they stood on the ledge as first Red Arrow, and then Purple Leaf came gliding up the tunnel. As the first Zoi flew from the shadow, the tears began again, and Wyshka put a comforting arm around Shaeli's shoulders. Red Arrow flew above them, almost close enough to touch, the crisp, white arrows on the red background seeming ready to take flight from the rippling surface of the balloon.

Purple Leaf followed. The rainbows of the Zoi's wings created a soft breeze which ruffled their hair as the birds flew over, and Shaeli looked up and saw Tarkoda on the top deck, waving down at her and grinning.

"It'll be good," he shouted down. "I promise."

Shaeli nodded and waved back, and as the Trader left the tunnel, she walked to the end of the ledge under the shadow of her home. She could see the grain in the dark wood on the bottom of the Trader, and the image blurred with tears. The spring-stream beside her seemed to murmur its condolences.

Kirrit stood beside her, waving to the many arms raised on Red Arrow, Delphi's dark head standing out among the red ones as they flew out over the Long Lea.

Purple Leaf drifted over the edge, and Shaeli looked up to see her family waving down at her. They were gathered at the rail, Jarris standing with one arm about each of the frantically waving twins, and she waved and waved until her arm ached, calling to them until her throat hurt. The last thing she heard was Neesha's strong voice echoing over the Lea.

"See you when it's cold, Shaeli," she called. "We love you."

The Zoi pulled the two balloons and their Traders along the length of the Lea, and as they dropped into the Valley of Stones, Kirrit took her arm.

"They look different from here, don't they?" she said, her voice as cracked as an old cup. "I've never seen my Trader leave before."

"I saw Purple Leaf fly away from me once," Shaeli said absently, her eyes still on the spot where the Traders had disappeared. She sniffed. "It was in a dream."

"A what?" asked Kirrit, looking at her.

"A dream, young Kirrit," said a voice from behind.

They turned and saw Almarnoch standing there, though they had not heard him approach. He smiled and looked at Shaeli from beneath his snow-white brows.

"'Tis time to tell your friend of Williver, Shaeli, and the dreams he brings."

* * *

Later, after collecting the bags that sat on the empty Landings and taking them to their grandmothers' huts, they sat sipping tezz at the table in Almarnoch's hut. The Cave outside looked strange, empty of all but three Traders, bereft of the energy that filled its space during the Wintering.

Kirrit sat staring at Shaeli, her dark eyebrows drawn together. She shook her head for what seemed to Shaeli to be the hundredth time, her deep red hair russet and gold in the light of Almarnoch's big lamp. Shaeli shifted uncomfortably and wished Kirrit would say something.

Almarnoch was of no help to her. He sat nearby, his eyes closed, as they had been the whole time she had been telling Kirrit about Williver, yet she knew he did not sleep.

Finally, after another slow shake of her head, Kirrit did speak.

"I cannot believe you've never told me this," she said. "Visits from a dream-elf." There was a long pause. "He takes you flying around Cave. He tells you *wonderful* stories..." The hurt and disbelief in her voice made Shaeli squirm. Kirrit blew out a deep breath. "And you never *told* me."

"I'm sorry, Kirrit, truly I am, but I thought no one would believe me," she said. "I tried to tell the boys once and they laughed at me." She looked over at the Warlock, then back at Kirrit. "I told Almarnoch almost by accident one day, and..." She shrugged. "And I did tell you *some* things," she finished lamely.

Almarnoch's eyes, unnoticed, cracked open.

"Like what?" Kirrit asked suspiciously.

"Like the story of Ink, the fairy who fell in love with a butterfly. And that poem about the sea-maids. And remember the story of the ugly witch, K'char?"

Almarnoch's eyes slid shut.

"The one who stole eyeballs?" Kirrit asked.

Shaeli nodded.

"And this elf told you all those stories?"

Shaeli nodded again, hopefully.

Kirrit was silent. She sat back in her chair. She pursed her lips. She studied the ceiling. Shaeli studied Kirrit.

"Do you mean to tell me," Kirrit said, after leaving Shaeli to dangle for as long as she possibly could. She sat up and leant forward, her eyes thin. "What you're *telling* me is," Kirrit said slowly, drawing the words out as if they were thick molasses, dripping with sarcasm. "What you're telling me is, that all the time we were thinking you were *so* clever and had *such* a good imagination... that last Wintering when you told that *horrible* story about K'char, and we all thought you were *so* great... all that time you were stealing this... this *Williver's* stories, letting us think you were a born storyteller, and soaking up compliments? That *is* what you're saying isn't it, Shaeli?"

Shaeli shrugged and a small, nervous giggle escaped her. "I guess you could say that, Kirrit, but..."

Kirrit stopped her with a sputter and a raised palm. She shook her head again, this time in amusement. She began to laugh. The tears welled in her eyes as she rocked with it. After a confused moment Shaeli began to laugh with her.

"You *are* something, Shaeli," Kirrit said, when she found her voice again. "'A fancy piece', my Da would say." She put on an affected voice. "Oh, Shaeli is *so* good at stories. Shaeli has such a *great* imagination. Tell us another one, Shaeli, you're *so* clever!" She laughed again.

"Stop it, Kirrit," said Shaeli, breathlessly, relieved that Kirrit was no longer angry.

"No way. I'm not letting you forget this," Kirrit grinned. "I want to know all about this Williver." She leant forward. "Everything. And wait until I tell the others."

Almarnoch spoke from his chair. "'Tis not to be spoken of, miss," he said. He opened his eyes and looked at her. "What Shaeli did *not* tell you was that I discouraged her from speaking to anyone of her dreams. I discourage *you* now in the same way. This is best kept among ourselves."

"But, why tell me?" said Kirrit.

"Because I thought you should know," Almarnoch said quietly. Then he closed his eyes again. "Now go and find your supper and your new beds. I fear you'll not sleep well tonight, but it is only the grounding, and it will pass."

They wished him goodnight, and as they closed the door behind them, Kirrit looked at Shaeli.

"What's 'the grounding'?" she whispered.

Shaeli shrugged, and they ran laughing towards the bright space around the fire-pits.

* * *

The next morning, they knew what "the grounding" was. They had spent a restless night, and as they sat blurry-eyed at one of the fire-pits next morning, Wyshka explained it to them.

"The grounding is something experienced only by Traders and sailors," she said. "It comes from the lack of movement. From sleeping close to the earth. It passes quickly."

"That's what Almarnoch said," said Shaeli. "I'm glad to hear it."

"But what about when we're moored," asked Kirrit. "We don't move then."

"Ah, but you do, lass," said her grandmother, Bydi. "There is always the shivering of the balloon above and the movement of the Zoi below." She was a big woman, and it was easy to see where her sons and grandchildren had inherited their red hair. Though scattered with many strands of white, the hair of Bydi was still a vibrant red. "And I'm not sure it passes, myself, I think you just get used to it." She sighed. "I still miss the movement."

"Is that why you sometimes sleep on Red Arrow when we're at Cave, Bydi?" asked Kirrit.

The old woman smiled. "Yes, Kirrit. Though I must say, I enjoy the quiet of my little hut after staying with your noisy family."

Kirrit laughed, and then her smile faded. "It is quiet here," she said, looking over to where Red Arrow had been moored. "*Too* quiet."

"We'll not be here long," said Bydi brightly. "Today we'll go and clean the year huts, and soon we shall move down to the Long Lea."

There was a lot to do before the move took place. After the last Traders left, each hut and store cave was cleaned, and those things that would be needed were transported down to the Lea. As the days passed, the thick snow covering the paths became brown slush with the passage of sleds and barrows.

After the cows had been led from their Wintering cave, their broad backs employed for further transportation of goods, the chickens were released too, and Wyshka said they would find their way down to the big coop on the Lea by nightfall. Then they spent what Kirrit called "a stench-filled day" raking and shovelling the huge pile of manure the animals had produced over the Wintering, transporting it down to a corner of the Lea where it could be easily collected later for use on the gardens.

When at last all was arranged, the year huts ready and the Cave clean, they gathered by the spring-pool as the fire-pits were extinguished and the shadows closed in upon them. The silence in the air was almost oppressive.

Shaeli stood in wavering candlelight, for the first time a little intimidated by the vast Cave. It was so full of warmth and light during the Wintering, so full of pattern and shape, and the murmur of many voices meant the Cave was hardly ever silent. It was so different now as they stood within a circle of thin candle-light surrounded by silent black, the flames standing straight and tall, shuddering only with the occasional breath of air that filtered down from the invisible roof.

Shaeli remembered the dream when Williver had flown her high above the Traders, and how her fingers had brushed the roof, how the space was filled with small sounds, even as the traders slept. Now, there was no sound but the tinkle of the spring-stream and the gentle voice of Sahli'en, who murmured a blessing of thanks to Ettorr and Merrom for the shelter provided by Cave for another Wintering, and when she turned, her face lit with gold from the candle held by Navez, she held her arms above her head. As she dropped them, every candle was blown out and Shaeli drew a breath as darkness enveloped the group, utterly and completely.

Almarnoch began to chant. It came out of the black, softly at first, then it began to grow louder, and suddenly two shafts of light leapt from each of his outstretched hands and flew straight up to the roof. Shaeli blinked in the brightness, dazzled after such complete darkness.

Garrit, Demeris, and Llevvis had begun to murmur too, and soon shafts of light sprung from each of their hands, though they did not reach so far, nor shine so brightly as Almarnoch's. Their chanting grew louder, and the beams of light leapt from their hands and began to ricochet around Cave as the chant gained in tempo. From the roof, to the walls, the floor, to the columns and back to the roof the lights flew, faster and faster, and where each beam touched rock, a glimmer of its light was left behind, shining in its wake.

The Warlocks' chant reached its peak and with a final cry abruptly ceased. The beams slowed, faded and disappeared – yet the darkness of Cave was now broken by hundreds of glittering lights shimmering like fairy dust, and though the light they threw was faint, it was possible to see across the length of Cave. The mouths of the main tunnel and the bolt tunnel were outlined with the tiny lights, and as they made their way back up the bolt tunnel to the ledge, Shaeli saw that here, too, the magic beams had found their way and had left enough of the tiny glimmers to make travelling the bolt tunnel an easy task.

She asked Almarnoch how long the lights would last, and he said *his* would last until the Wintering, as he had commanded them, as would old Demeris'. She could hear the pride in his voice when he said Llevvis' would also endure the whole year, now that he held the staff of a full Warlock, but the pride faded when he spoke of Garrit. He hoped his would last, for it was past the time he should have been ready to go to the Warlock Island, and creating light that endured for at least six Moons was one of the requirements. He did not mention Garrit's tantrum when his lights had begun to fade after only three Moons last year.

The next morning Shaeli was able to properly unpack her bag. While they had been up at Cave there had been little sense in taking everything out when she would only have to pack it again for the move down to the Lea, but now she was in possession of her own little room in Wyshka and Olver's year-hut, and though the grounding had worn off, the strangeness of being here had not. She was homesick for Purple Leaf and wondered constantly where they were.

Her room, Dari's before and shared by Tarkoda and Andos before that, was tiny, a walled-off square at one end of the veranda that ran round two sides of the year hut. Inside the house, there were just two rooms, a sitting room – though Wyshka said they did not sit there very much; the veranda was so much nicer in the summer – and Wyshka and Olver's room. There was a tiny bath in a curtained-off corner of the sitting room, but there was no kitchen, for all meals were taken in the big communal hall.

She liked the idea of being almost alone; she was used to a small bedroom, and there were glass windows with coloured panes in sections which she could open to catch the breeze when the weather warmed. The windows faced the clearing which was the centre of the year village, and she could see Kirrit and Bydi's hut on the far side and the big hall with the spring stream running behind it. She shivered as she sorted her clothes and books, storing them on the shelves that lined the inside wall.

In the bottom of her bag, wrapped in her old, wine-red cloak, lay her wand and Nol's box, and she wanted to find somewhere safe to keep them. As she took out the last jumble of stockings and underwear above them, a parcel dropped out. It took her a moment to remember what it was, then she pounced on it; a gift from one of the family was greatly welcome, even it was only from Eenis. When she saw what lay inside, her eyes filled with tears, and she promised herself she would never think badly of her aunt again.

It was a new pouch for her small treasures, made of thick, incredibly soft, dark leather. Like the belt made for her by Eenis Winterings ago, it was covered with tiny stars, but these were embroidered, rather than the intricate knots of the belt. There were dozens of stars scattered over the leather, sewn with expensive silver thread, some no bigger than the head of a pin, none larger than a seed of grain, falling like a shower of silver rain across the pouch. Shaeli cried softly as she undid the still-supple belt from around her waist and unthreaded the worn amulet she had been wearing for over ten Winters. She remembered then that Eenis had made the first one for her too.

The new pouch had two loops criss-crossed at the back which she threaded onto the belt, and when she opened the drawstring of the neck, she found a note.

Dear Shaeli, it read in Eenis' tiny handwriting. *I noticed your old pouch was wearing thin and hope you will think this is a good replacement. Have a safe year, love, Eenis.*

She was still sniffing and tying on the new amulet when Wyshka came to find her. She hadn't found a place for her wand and the box containing the bangle, so she left them in her bag and pushed it under the low bed beneath the windows.

***

When Wyshka, Olver and Shaeli walked down the steps of their hut, they saw the others coming from all over the little village and heading for the hall.

The hall stood beside a bend in the spring-stream, raised from the ground, with a set of broad steps on every side. Its corners were thick columns of mud-brick, as were the walls at either end, with a softly smoking chimney above each, and the long side walls were sectioned, so they could be removed altogether in the warm weather. Wide verandas, bare of any railings, ran all the way round, and a thick grape vine, bumpy with hidden buds, wound its twisted stem along beneath the eaves. Beside the hall was an enormous tree, the branches shading the building and hanging over the spring-stream behind it.

The year huts of the old ones stood in a semi-circle around the hall and the tree, and there were barns and sheds off behind the huts; even a tiny Landing edging a field behind the sheds. Wyshka and Olver's hut – Shaeli's too, now – was the last before the wide expanse of the Long Lea.

The black hole of the tunnel hung like a toothless giant's mouth, embedded faceless in the side of the mountain, and Zerrinius towered above it, blanketed by thick snow. Great white drifts still covered most of the Lea and the rugged cliffs surrounding it, and the waterfall tumbling from the ledge and first terrace sent up a shower of spray which caught the afternoon sun so that hazy rainbows hung shimmering in the crisp air. The water broke from the churning pool at the base of the cliff and curved around an outcrop, winding its way past the year village to the willow-shrouded fishing hole where the stream pooled again before running on down the southern end of the Lea and falling into the Valley of Stones.

As Shaeli watched, a lump of snow fell from the bank and swept downstream. She remembered crossing the River Zerrin on their way to Palveron, the year the twins had taken their barrel ride, and she wondered how much of that small lump of snow would reach the Sea of Aa'liu, so far away. Thinking of the twins sent a jolt of homesickness through her, and she turned away, seeking for Kirrit. She saw her with Bydi and she waved. Kirrit waved back, grinning, her hair a dark flame in the sun as the two joined them, and together they went up the stairs and into the hall.

It was dim inside, but warm. At the southern end, a fireplace large enough to burn a small tree blazed brightly; an oven of equal proportions lay at the northern end. On the far side, work-benches ranged the wall with cupboards underneath, and a deep sink was nestled in the corner. Trestle tables lay between the kitchen area and the fireplace, with low benches running beneath, and more benches, wider and thickly padded, ran along the length of the walls on the eastern side. Bright rugs lay scattered about on the floor between the tables and the benches, and Shaeli and Kirrit sat on one with the other children while the old ones sat behind them.

Shaeli looked around at the others of her Cave year. She counted nineteen, and the anticipation she felt was mirrored on the faces around her. She knew all of them, some well, others by face alone, but they would be as family to her by the end of the year. So it was said.

Jezzyn from White Star was sitting with Roxell of Four Winds and Ooli of White Moth. Ooli looked a little nervous, and sat close by Roxell, her eyes flitting around the room until she saw Shaeli looking at her and gave a thin smile. Shaeli smiled back encouragingly and then her eyes were drawn to the back of the room by a loud burst of laughter. Rhubic of Red Sun leant against the back wall near the fireplace, flanked by Davvit of Crescent Moon and Rennan of Kingfisher, all three guffawing loudly at some joke of Rhubic's. Rennan was the nephew of Renn, wife of Taffka, the Fleet leader, and he winked at Shaeli when he saw her looking at them. She blushed a little, but winked back, and then she turned forward again, conscious of Rennan's eyes still upon her. Bonn and Shylo sat nearby, their heads close together. Shylo looked from Rennan to Shaeli, whispered something in Bonn's ear, and they giggled behind their hands. Shaeli pretended not to notice.

When they were all seated, over sixty of them – old ones, the four Warlocks, and the children of Cave year – Navez, head of the Council of old ones, stood before them and spoke words of greeting. Sahli'en joined him, and between them they described what the children would experience throughout the year. There would be gardening when the ground thawed enough to dig, and then Navez spoke of archery, swordsmanship, slingshot practise, milking, forays to gather wood and the slow-burning rock used in the fire-pits. Sahli'en added to this sewing, cooking and Faunistry herb-lore, then she looked at the Warlocks, and added magic to the list. Everyone knew that if magic slept inside, it would show itself with the change into adulthood, and they looked around, wondering if any of them had the ability, if the Warlocks could waken dormant magic.

Shaeli and Kirrit looked at each other and Shaeli began to feel excitement at last, and in the days that followed, she almost forgot to be homesick.

As the snow on the slopes melted, the Long Lea began to be remade into a garden. None of the children had ever seen the Lea with anything but dry grass or thick snow covering it, and the transformation to rich green fields entranced them. The orchard at the southern end, protected by the magic of the Warlocks from freezing during the Wintering, began to prickle with colour as blossoms formed and burst forth, and their mornings were spent in the fields between the orchard and the year huts, turning over the soil and digging in the manure they had brought down from Cave.

Potatoes they planted in abundance until Shaeli was sick of the sight of them, but every herb and vegetable had its place. Flowers, too, were sown, the bulbs the first to push green, triangular points above the ground, and soon the air around the huts was filled with soft scents and the Lea was a riot of colour.

The days warmed quickly, and the stream swelled with the run-off. One day in early spring, they heard a distant rumble, and looked up to see an avalanche sliding down the side of the mountain far above, snow flying high into the air, trees and boulders disappearing under the tons of white powder, yet the thaw passed quickly, and only the top of Mount Zerrinius retained its cap of white.

Afternoons were given to archery, swordsmanship, and sling practise, and Shaeli found she was an excellent marksman. Once she had mastered the rudiments of the bow, her arrow would fly almost unerringly at the target, and she was nearly as good with a slingshot. Kirrit, too, had a good eye, and there were many contests of skill in the group during the long afternoons.

They spent the ever-warming midday hours in the shade of the meeting hall or the big tree, learning those skills that could be learned sitting still. Herb-lore bored Shaeli a little, for Mareesha had already ensured she was well versed in the art, and Bonn dominated the sessions. Sahli'en and Navez were her grandparents, and Bonn was eager to show off her skills to her grandmother, boasting over and over how she would be apprenticed to her mother, Perlis, after the year. Shaeli and Kirrit did their best to ignore her.

Cooking, Shaeli mastered tolerably well; sewing, she already knew she was not good at, but the last subject excited them all: magic.

Lessons with Almarnoch were something she had anticipated with great excitement, and she was not disappointed. Within the first few lessons she showed some talent, producing a flicker of light from the tips of two fingers, but no matter how Almarnoch and Llevvis explained it to her, she could not get the light to emerge from its proper place and hover above her palm. It burst forth only from the tips of her index fingers, her right much more brightly than her left, and though she was excited by the ability, she was frustrated by her lack of control.

Almarnoch shook his head, unable to explain it any more clearly, but he encouraged her to experiment with it, and she did. She could produce the spark at will, with little effort, and the middle fingers also began to show a gleam. After advice from Llevvis, she found she could push small objects around, or light a candle if she squinted just right. The colour at the tips of her fingers would change from clear blue to pale gold, and though she felt no heat, the candle would leap into flame.

At any other magical feat though, it seemed she could not find the knack; she could not make water spin in a cup, or revive a tired bloom, or do anything that Dari had found so easy. All she could master was the little flame which shot from her fingers, and she had to be content with that, for the ability did not signal the promise of Warlock training for her. At most it was a useful trick, so Almarnoch said, and Kirrit said at least she had that – as for herself, she was utterly hopeless at all wizardry, but it mattered little; so was everyone else. Almarnoch had found no burgeoning Warlock amongst them, yet he was not disappointed; it was rare to find one with the gift, and Shaeli's small talent amused him.

Shaeli found herself thinking less longingly of Purple Leaf. She was amazed at how beautiful the Lea had become, the fields alive with life, the colours of the plants softening the harsh bluffs and cliff faces surrounding them. Each day produced some new wonder, a fragrant flower showing its colours like a girl wearing many petticoats, or a sweet fruit, finally grown plump enough to eat, juices dripping down chins and forearms. And when they had fruit in abundance, they would begin the drying and the bottling, the beginnings of the supplies that would nourish the Fleet throughout the Wintering.

Each evening they gathered in the meeting hall, and after the meal they sat listening to stories; legends of gods and heroes; tales of traders in times gone by; or they would talk of the day past and the plans for the next. The side walls had been removed, and the night air was free to breeze through the hall, cooling them and ruffling their hair. Sometimes, ground trembling storms came thundering their way across the Lea, drowning their voices; at other times a soft rain would fall, pattering on the roof and the ground beyond the verandas, falling in lines from the roof's corrugations and dripping from thick grape leaves, catching the light and turning the droplets into showers of silver.

Shaeli's favourite spot was at the southern end of the hall, on the padded bench which used to run against a wall, but was now a thin border between the room and the veranda. She would sit with her back against the still-warm column, her legs stretched out along the bench, and from there she could survey the whole room, and see each speaker as they wove their story webs. She could also see outside, and would gaze at the star-filled sky or the silver rain-lines while listening to the storytellers. Often Rennan would sit on the other side of the column, and their eyes would meet often and not accidentally. Shaeli felt the first stirrings of attraction, and would stare curiously at Rennan when he was not looking, admiring his green-flecked brown eyes, dark blond hair and expressive hands. She, mostly, was unaware that his eyes also followed her as she walked across the compound, listened to a story, or concentrated upon some task, but Bonn and Shylo were not. Often they would come and squeeze themselves in between Shaeli and Rennan, Bonn always closest to Rennan, Shylo chatting and giggling loudly, distracting Rennan from his contemplation of Shaeli's profile.

One evening in early summer, after the meal had been eaten and was being cleared away, Shaeli sat by the column as usual, pretending to read, yet really watching Rennan through her hair as he washed up at the big sink with Bydi. It had been a long day. Wyshka's old friend, Kozett, had died the night before, and they had all taken her up and buried her on a rise overlooking the Lea, as she had wished. The afternoon was spent remembering her and there had been many tears and laughter. Their meal had been one of celebration of her long life.

Rhubic, Ooli, and Crylla of Sky Lark were drying the stack of dishes, Olver and Navez were putting them away, and Almarnoch and Sahli'en stood close by. Shaeli smiled as a joke was shared among the group. She almost wished she were on kitchen duty tonight.

She sighed, swung her legs off the bench to face the veranda, and stared out at the drizzle falling through the dusky night air. Behind her she heard the drain of the sink, and the shuffle as people found somewhere to sit. She smiled to herself as she heard the loud voice of Rhubic and the answering voice of Rennan as they took their places on the bench on the other side of the column.

She looked at Rennan over her shoulder. His eyes were upon her, though he spoke to Rhubic, and they held hers until she smiled and looked back out into the drizzle. A voice spoke in her ear.

"Rennan can't take his eyes off you," whispered Kirrit, sliding into place beside Shaeli, and swinging her legs out over the bench.

"Ssh," hissed Shaeli, glancing over shoulder. "He'll hear you."

"He looks like a cow," giggled Kirrit. "Mooning at you. Don't worry, he won't hear anything over Rhubic's voice, it's not possible," she whispered. "He's nice though, Shaeli." Her voice grew more serious. "And don't you think Bic of Yellow Star is just lovely?"

Shaeli looked at the boy sitting further down the bench with Jezzyn. Bic and Jezzyn were cousins, their grandmother had been one of the descendants of the ship from across the sea, the Irikai, and both had her dark eyes, ebony hair, and nut-brown skin. She jumped as Kirrit thumped her leg.

"Don't look," Kirrit said, and Shaeli began to giggle.

"I think he's very nice, Kirrit," she whispered. "Just don't show him the kind of affection you show me."

Shaeli rubbed her leg, and Kirrit grinned, then suddenly Kirrit's smile faded, and her eyebrows puckered.

"Who's that?" she said, her voice soft with astonishment.

Shaeli followed her gaze.

There was a man walking towards them through the evening shadows. His gait was strange, and he staggered a little as he came along the path beside the stream. Amazement drew Shaeli to her feet, and she moved across the veranda as the man reached the puddle of light around the hall.

The stranger raised his head as he neared, looking groggily at the two girls above him. The rain fell in thick drops from his hair, the cloak about his shoulders, and the pack on his back. There was a gash running from temple to hairline above his right eye, and blood dripped pale crimson from his chin. Shaeli went to the edge of the veranda and down the steps, mindless of the rain dampening her hair.

The man stopped before her, swaying slightly. He fixed her with the greenest eyes she had ever seen and they stared at each other through the rain. Kirrit was calling for Sahli'en and Almarnoch behind her, and she put out a hand to the man.

"Please come inside," she said, quietly. "You're hurt."

The stranger stared at her for a moment, and then he reached out his hand. His cold fingers brushed against Shaeli's as he fell into the mud at her feet.

* * *

CHAPTER TWENTY SIX

The stranger was carried inside, his pack removed, and he was laid upon a soft rug. A pillow was found for his head, and the traders crowded around talking excitedly, concern fighting amazement and curiosity for the right to be the strongest emotion.

Where has he come from? they asked each other. *Who is he? Is he alright?*

Sahli'en knelt and examined him, then went to the bench, prepared a poultice, poured warm water into a bowl of herbs, and came back to the stranger's side.

"Help me, Shaeli, please," she said. "Bonn, fetch some bandages. And give the man some room, everyone."

The traders obediently stepped back a pace or two, some even went to sit down again, but most stayed: curiosity had proved strongest.

Shaeli knelt beside Sahli'en, and Almarnoch knelt opposite. Llevvis and Navez stood behind him.

Bonn brought cloth and bandages, and Sahli'en bathed the wound from the bowl Shaeli held, and then she leant closer to examine the cut. It ran from just above his brow into the hairline, but it was not too deep. She applied the poultice, and Almarnoch held the man's head while she covered the wound and bound a thick bandage around it.

Sahli'en looked at Almarnoch. "Is he known to you?" she asked.

The old Warlock shook his head. "Likely some traveller who has lost his way in the mountains," he said. "A young man of good family, by the look of his clothes. Perhaps from the Starisles. He has the smell of salt about him."

Shaeli too, thought she could smell the tang of the sea in the stranger's damp hair, but Sahli'en smiled and shook her head.

"Perhaps so," she said, "but wherever he is from, 'tis lucky he found his way onto the Lea. The mountains are no place to be wandering alone."

"Should we take off his wet cloak, Sahli'en?" asked Shaeli. "He may catch a chill." She looked down at the face of the stranger. The bandage was covering much of the rich brown hair and high forehead, and his dark lashes rested on tanned cheeks above a strong square chin. She lay the backs of her fingers gently against his cheek. "He is very cold."

Before Sahli'en could answer, the lashes flickered and the eyes opened. Shaeli pulled her hand away from his cheek, but left her eyes were they were, on the stranger's face. She was again looking into those amazing green eyes; eyes a colour she had never seen before, the colour of green shadows in the ocean, just beyond the touch of sunlight. She was stunned for a moment, then she blinked, her own eyes wide and deep grey. The stranger spoke.

"I had almost thought I walked with the gods," he said, looking at Shaeli, Bonn and Sahli'en. "With three such lovely faces before me." He smiled and looked at Almarnoch. "But your face, sir, dispels the notion."

Almarnoch laughed. "Well said, young stranger. I see a blow to the head has not addled your senses." He leant forward, his long, thin beard brushing the man's chest. "Can you stand?"

The man nodded, then winced and put a hand to his head. "I think so," he said, and slowly sat up.

Sahli'en examined the man's eyes, and satisfied, she nodded her consent, and Llevvis came forward and held out his hand. The stranger took it, and Llevvis hoisted him to unsteady feet. Navez took his other arm and together they helped him to one of the tables where the wet cloak was removed. The gathered traders parted to let them through, and then closed like an incoming tide behind them, all open faces and staring eyes. The stranger smiled amicably at their curious stares.

Almarnoch sat beside him and Navez sat opposite with Sahli'en. Shaeli hovered close by. Kirrit came and slipped an arm through hers, giving it a short squeeze of excitement. They waited quietly while the man probed the bandage with long slim fingers.

Tezz was brought, and a blanket to replace the wet cloak. The young man sipped gratefully at the tezz as Almarnoch introduced himself, Sahli'en and Navez.

"Would I be right if I said this was the Long Lea of the Traders?" the stranger asked. "With Mount Zerrinius above?"

"You would, lad," agreed Almarnoch. "But you have us at a disadvantage. We are known to you, but strangers are rare on the Lea, and we are curious to know what brings you here."

"Forgive me," smiled the man. "I forget my manners in my own curiosity." His shoulders straightened, and he bowed his head formally. "I am Ishaan of Argon, and I have stupidly lost my way in my exploration of the mountains." He looked over at Navez. "I left Meoro Village to travel to Serrat by way of the mountains, and came down a thin gorge into a long valley filled with rocks and boulders of amazing shape and size."

"The Valley of Stones," Navez nodded.

"Yet you are far north of Serrat, Ishaan," said Almarnoch. "The city lies to the south of the Valley of Stones."

Ishaan turned back to the Warlock. "This I know. Yet when I determined where I was, and saw what I knew to be Zerrinius towering above, I had a need to see it closer." He smiled again, a trifle sheepishly. "And perhaps also the fabled Cave of the Traders." He shook his head. "It took me two days to travel to the base of your Lea, though I was no more than five leagues down the valley when I descended from the mountains. Time and again I had to retrace my steps after being drawn up a promising gorge, and I was almost caught in a rock-slide before I found the stream and followed it to your cliff."

"The Valley of Stones is treacherous, and you were fortunate to have travelled even that far alone," said Navez. "But how did you reach the Lea, lad? The cliff is sheer, and there are few footholds."

"There is a way beside the waterfall, close by the western edge, though it took some time to climb it after crossing the stream. 'Twas just at the last outcrop I slipped and did this." He gestured to his head. "It was luck only that caused me to fall forward and not back down to the Stone Valley. 'Twas midday when I fell, and late in the afternoon when I woke, unsure of my whereabouts. Far across the meadow before me I saw smoke, and so I came hence with all the speed I could manage."

"But your wound is freshly open, Ishaan," said Sahli'en. "How could that be?"

Ishaan looked embarrassed. "I was on the *other* side of the stream, and came to a place where I could cross. A wide pool surrounded by willows, with a fallen tree just downstream."

Many of the traders nodded; it was the fishing hole he spoke of. The tree was broad, and had bridged the spring-stream for a hundred Winters.

"I was almost across when I slipped," Ishaan continued, "and fell against the bank. It must have reopened the wound, and caused my overly dramatic entrance." He looked up at Kirrit and Shaeli. "Thankful I was when I saw these two whispering together."

Sahli'en offered the hospitality of their hut, which Ishaan accepted. He was made a brew to ease his headache, and soon after Navez and Sahli'en escorted him to their hut, Bonn carrying the wet cloak importantly behind them.

The traders also soon left for their homes – after a thorough discussion of the young stranger. Kirrit and Shaeli had to retell their first sighting of him several times; his old-fashioned speech was remarked upon, as was his handsome face. Olver said he had the biggest feet he'd ever seen anywhere; Bydi said she had not seen eyes so green in thirty Winters. The boys declared they would have to inspect the way down to the Valley of Stones and were promptly forbidden to do so. Rhubic made everyone laugh when he said that anything else after such an unusual occurrence would fall flatter than a balloon without a Lift spell, and he was right; they went to their homes, for the excitement was over.

As Shaeli was getting ready for bed, she looked over at the lights of Sahli'en's cottage across the village. Shadows moved against the glow of a lamp, and she stood for a while watching, wondering about the young stranger with the sun-flecked green eyes and the slightly crooked smile.

Before she changed into her nightgown, she checked that her bag was still safely stuffed underneath the low bed behind the jumble of shoes. She had found nowhere to keep her wand and the little box, and had decided to leave them where they were. It was as safe as anywhere; no one knew of Nol's box and she doubted if many remembered she had ever found an old wand.

She climbed into bed, knowing she should sleep, for tomorrow they went again to the gorge where the fire-rocks lay, yet her mind refused to let her sleep; it rambled on and on, no matter how much she told it to be still. Long after the last sounds of the settling traders had ceased; long after the muffled sound of Olver's snoring had begun on the other side of the hut; long after the moon had risen to the sound of night birds did she lie awake, thoughts rushing here and there, scrambling over each other in their eagerness to reach the fore, leaping from person, to place, to the past and the future; reality mixed with imaginings, fact with fantasy. When she did finally sleep, her dreams were as jumbled as her thoughts.

* * *

Wyshka woke her early the next morning, and she felt drained and groggy, the beginnings of a headache curled at the base of her skull.

She waved at Rennan as she crossed the compound – he was readying the carts with his grandfather and some others – and after breakfast she sought out Sahli'en. Shaeli explained her restless night and listless mood, and Sahli'en mixed a few herbs into freshly squeezed juice for her. Shaeli asked after Ishaan, and was told he still slept, but would have the company of those too old to gather fire-stones while they were gone.

By the time Shaeli stepped back out into the morning, she had begun to feel better. She walked over to where Kirrit stood under the big tree with Jezzyn, watching the uncooperative cows and the sullen bull being harnessed to squat two-wheeled carts.

The sun was barely risen over the shoulders of the eastern mountains, dew still sparkled atop dark shadows and only a few columns of cloud rose cotton-like into the sky, and as they walked down the Lea and through the orchards, the arrival of Ishaan was again discussed. Navez talked of the island in Nebillonia Straits where Ishaan was from. Argon lay just above Xenel Island, and though slightly larger, it was not as prosperous as Xenel, for its cliffs were high, its harbour difficult, and it was often passed by in favour of the more lively southern island. Traders sometimes stopped – Rhubic had been there a few summers before – but usually those on Argon travelled to Xenel Island to trade. Ishaan had told Navez his parents were silversmiths and sold the jewellery they made on Xenel and Ashkanna.

The fire-rocks were gathered from a thin gorge at the end of the Lea, not far from where the ground dropped abruptly into the Valley of Stones. The gorge was made up almost wholly of the stuff, and rocks lay in tumbled piles at the base. Each Wintering, the weight of the snow caused lumps to dislodge and fall to the ground, and the lumps broke into hundreds of pieces, for the rock itself was porous and weak, light enough for one person to lift large chunks, yet once the fire-pits were filled, the rocks burned smokelessly for many days with a bright and strong heat.

They returned late in the afternoon, dirty, back-sore and weary, the carts laden with fire-rocks, even the cows too tired to misbehave as the carts were propped up and their harnesses released. Unloading would wait until tomorrow, when the cows would again be harnessed and the carts taken up to Cave to store the rocks for the next Wintering.

Shaeli saw Ishaan in the shade of the tree beside the hall, and she waved at him as she walked across the clearing with Wyshka and Olver.

"Would you like some tezz, Shaeli?" Wyshka asked as they reached the veranda.

"No, thanks. I think I'll go for a swim."

Wyshka nodded, took Olver's hand and they went inside. Shaeli turned into her room, took off her shoes and gathered some clean clothes and a bar of soap.

Kirrit was walking across the clearing as Shaeli went back down the stairs, but before she noticed Shaeli, she saw the small group that had gathered about Ishaan and her steps veered sharply in that direction. Shaeli smiled; Bic was among the group. So was Rennan, and she was tempted to go and sit with them too, but she had cooking duty tonight and she needed to wash first, so she turned and followed the path beside the stream.

A short distance from the year-huts, the path and the stream began to separate, and in the space between, the passionfruit trellises flourished. Shaeli picked a couple as she passed, cracked the black skins open and sucked the sweet-tart seeds and stringy pulp from inside. On the far side of the trellises the path merged again with the stream, and the fishing hole lay just beyond.

Everyone had their favourite place to swim; the boys right behind the hall where the water was deep and a strong hemp rope dangled from a thick branch; the old ones upstream, where a gentle slope led down to a wide, slow-running section, but Shaeli preferred the wide cool water of the fishing hole where she could swim long strokes with ease.

She walked down the sloped path to the water's edge, stopping with her toes in the water. On the far side, to her right, the bank was sheer, and the roots of the willows hung down into the water, but to her left, broad flat rocks thrust themselves out into the pool, like little terraces, some below the surface, some sticking out of the bank higher above. Shaeli waded in and picked her way across several rocks with the water dragging at the bottom of her skirt. She tucked the dry bundle higher under her arm, felt with her foot for the sloping rock below and stepped down onto it, laughing as her skirt billowed up like a mushroom. She pushed her bundle up on to a higher rock, and then sank down until the water covered her shoulders, shivering with pleasure as the cold seeped through her dusty clothes. She untied her hair and sat down on a rock that was a convenient underwater seat, her skirt drifting around her weightless legs. Nothing moved save the shuffling of the willow branches and a flitting wagtail in the trees opposite.

Shaeli stood again, her clothes molding to her slim frame, her hair a sheath of brown satin. She glanced up the path and unbuttoned her dress, stripping it from her shoulders, down her hips and stepping out of it, standing in her short, thin shift. She rubbed the dress and herself with Wyshka's sweet-smelling soap, ran the dress through the water and kneaded it upon the rocks, then she hauled herself out of the water, wrung out the clean dress and lay it across a branch. She glanced up the path again, then at the sun, and dove back into the water. She came up halfway across the pool, rolled over on her back and began a lazy stroke, not stopping until she felt the hanging willow roots brush her fingertips. The little black wagtail hopped at the edge of the bank, jabbed at something in the grass and flitted off into a tree, and she swam over to where the water left the pool, edging around the spot she knew a catfish had its nest.

She looked up at the old trunk bridging the banks, wondering where Ishaan had fallen, scanning the slope until she saw a little pile of rain-washed rocks and a large sod pulled from the bank above. She swam back and hoisted herself up onto the rock beside her clothes and lay on the sun-warm stone, her hair brown strings against the grain of rock, listening to the bright song of the wagtail across the babble of the pool, then she yawned and stood up. The late afternoon sun shone on her face and she closed her eyes, tilting her face up to the light, stretching her arms luxuriously above her head. The sun shone red behind her eyelids, and she opened her eyes again, blinking in the bright light. Ishaan stood at the bottom of the path, barely a dozen paces away, staring at her.

Shaeli was horribly aware of the thin wet shift, of her arms stopped at the peak of their stretch. For an instant her startled eyes met Ishaan's, and then she dropped her eyes and her arms, pulling in vain at the hem of the shift which rode at the top of her thighs. She knew the material was threadbare, and she crossed her arms over her breasts and raised her blue-grey eyes to the sea-green ones, her cheeks hot with the rush of her embarrassment. Ishaan stared at her a moment longer, then he shook his head and turned his back.

Shaeli grabbed at her clean dress and stepped into it, fumbling with the buttons and the tie at the back. The wet shift beneath the dry dress was cool and damp against her body, yet she could still feel the warmth of Ishaan's eyes upon her. She took a deep breath, picked up the soap and her wet dress, and made her way over the rocks until her feet touched the sandy path where Ishaan stood, his back still turned. Olver was right; he did have very big feet.

"I..." she began, then started again. "You can turn around now."

He did, smiling that slightly crooked smile, and he dropped his head in a small bow. "My apologies, Shaeli," he said. "I did not see you." He paused. "At first."

Shaeli nodded, and blushed again. 'Twas certain he had seen more of her than she would have wished, and she looked back across the pool, searching for something to say.

"I always swim here," she said. "It's the only place you can swim properly." Her voice sounded strange in her ears.

"Sahli'en said the same when I asked her for the best swimming hole." He smiled. "And truly it is a beautiful spot, now that I see it by light of day."

She nodded, and smiled shyly back, feeling the pink draining from her face.

"I saw where you climbed up the bank." She looked downstream. "It was a fair fall you took," she said, looking back at him, searching her throat for a normal tone. "How is your head today?"

His hand went to the line of bandage on his forehead. "'Tis freshly dressed by your excellent Faunist, with firm advice that I not wet it." He grinned. "Advice I dare not ignore."

Shaeli laughed. "Very sensible of you," she said. "My Mam would give the same advice, but with less subtle consequences, I'm sure."

It was Ishaan's turn to laugh. "Is your mother a Faunist also, Shaeli?"

She nodded, and stopped. "How do you know my name?" she asked.

"Your friend, Kirrit, told me," he said, laughter still swimming in his eyes. "I met many of the young traders beneath the tree. Rennan, Bic, Rhubic, Roxell, Kirrit, others whose names escape me. They seem a fine group."

She nodded, and glanced at the sky. "I must go," she said. She was beginning to like Ishaan, despite the still-lingering embarrassment. "I'm on dinner duty tonight."

"I shall look forward to it," said Ishaan. "Your mountain air has given me an appetite."

"I'll see you there, then. Have a nice swim," she said. She walked up the path, then stopped and turned back. "There's a catfish nest on the far side you might want to avoid."

He looked at where she pointed, nodded, and smiled. "I thank you, Shaeli," he said, and his green eyes were suddenly serious. "And again, I apologise for my interruption."

"It's alright," she said, turning to walk up the path before he could see the pink flush which again flooded her cheeks.

His eyes followed her until she was out of sight, unreadable as a blizzard.

***

CHAPTER TWENTY SEVEN

Ishaan enjoyed dinner that night, and many more as the summer passed. He was well liked by the traders; courteous to the old ones and of endless interest to the young. Many nights he kept them enthralled with tales; he knew many dragon tales, as well as stories of elves and Ammerr, some of which even Olver had not heard. His wound healed quickly, and soon he worked beside the traders, in the fields or carrying things up to Cave for storage.

The first time he went up to Cave, his amazement was obvious. He walked around with Shaeli, Kirrit and Bic, staring about him, shaking his head and saying things like, "amazing" and "wondrous" over and over.

Jezzyn, Rhubic, Ooli and Rennan had been checking the cocoons of the glow-worms, and joined them as they took Ishaan on a tour of the storage caves, the huts and the Landings. He inspected each smaller cave with undiminished fervour, not content until he had seen everything, asking endless questions. As they passed Almarnoch's hut, Ishaan stopped and looked back

"It looks different when everyone's here," said Kirrit. "It's kind of bare without the Traders, almost like another place."

"With the fire-pits glowing and lanterns everywhere, it's much nicer," agreed Jezzyn.

"'Tis a sight I should like to see," said Ishaan. "Very much." He turned. "What lies further?" he asked.

"You can't go much further, Ishaan," said Shaeli. "There's only the Zoi cave, and we don't go there."

Ishaan turned back. "Never?"

She shook her head. "No. It is a private place for the Zoi to Winter in peace."

"May we go closer?"

"If you like," said Bic. "But there's not much to see."

They went nearer, stopping a few paces from the entrance. The hole was dark, no Warlock light had penetrated it, and a strange smell drifted from its black silence. On one side, etched into the wall, was a tiny symbol in a circle of strange shapes, but it was indistinct, faded with the passing of centuries. Ishaan asked about it, and they shrugged; nobody knew. Bic said perhaps it was an ancient symbol for the Zoi.

"So it is not known what lies within?" Ishaan said. "Or beyond."

"No one may disturb the Zoi, no," Shaeli said. "It is a sacred place for them, and no one knows what's in there." Though she said the words firmly, she had often tried to imagine what it looked like inside the Zoi cave.

"And beyond there is nothing but the roots of the mountain," said Rennan.

"Yes," said Ishaan. "Yes, I suppose that's true."

They walked back by way of the main tunnel, Ishaan marvelling at the scores of cocoons hanging above like some bizarre, giant fruit, and Rennan told him that each day someone came up to see if the cocoons had begun to open, for the sight of the creatures emerging was not to be missed.

A few days later, they all had the unique privilege of watching the glow-worms emerge.

Bonn and Shylo came bolting down from the terrace early in the morning, shouting about the winged creature which had met them inside the tunnel. Work was abandoned for the day, lunch was packed, and every member of the year village marched up the path and into the mouth of the tunnel. They walked wordlessly towards the first sweeping bend, and there, above the mouth of the animals' Wintering cave, was an enormous red moth. It clung upside-down to the tomato-red cocoon, its wings, big as a baby's blanket, still curled at the edges and shivering as they dried, its long thin legs stretching alternately out, testing the air as the traders crept past.

Many of the cocoons hung as they had throughout the spring, huge and unmoving, but among their numbers some trembled, others showed cracks, and some had moths emerging from fractured chrysalises. There were creatures with their heads straining from a tear, others pulling plump bottoms from their carapaces, still others straining to drag out oversized bodies with spindly legs. Few had their wings unfurled, and the only sign of the light which had formally illuminated the glow-worm's bodies was now reduced to a mere flicker in the two sets of feathery antennae on their heads.

At the second bend they stopped and spread blankets on the sandy floor, whispering reverently to each other as they found places to sit. Shaeli sat with her friends near the spring-stream, where a cluster of cocoons hung close together. A blue moth, its head pointing to the ground, almost had its wings open, the deeper blue of its patterns beginning to emerge as it dried. Soft light pulsed along the lacy feelers, growing stronger as its wings dried.

Close by, a crimson moth pulled its tail from a port-wine cocoon. It shook itself, danced about delicately until it found the right upside-down position, and settled itself to shiver its wings and stretch its legs one by one. Its feelers began to pulse with pink light.

They sat there all morning, spotting each new hatchling as it broke through, pointed fingers tracing the delicate patterns on the huge wings as they dried to thick velvet, then they went inside Cave to eat lunch beside the spring pool and exercise their legs and voices before creeping back through the tunnel, now full of fluttering moths, their lights blinking like hundreds of coloured stars. As the afternoon passed by unheeded outside, they watched the giant moths hatching and Navez told the children that by next day, every chrysalis would be empty.

"How long are they here, Navez?" asked Rennan.

"Barely a Moon," he answered. "They will fly soon, and use the space of Cave to stretch their wings and find a mate. The females lay their eggs back here in the tunnel, deep inside holes and crevices."

"Then what do they do?" asked Kirrit. "After they've laid their eggs?"

"No one is quite sure," Navez said, and he laughed at their puzzlement. "The moon was Full two nights ago, and somewhere near the next Full they will fly from Cave," he explained. "They cross the Lea and disappear into the Valley of Stones. No one knows where they go from there."

"Are they not seen in Serrat, or Meoro?" asked Ishaan, as interested as the children. "They must go somewhere, Navez."

"They must, indeed, but they are not seen in Serrat or Meoro, nor along the River Zerrin. And no Trader has ever seen the remains of them on our journeys along the Valley, not a sign. It is a mystery."

"The sight of them flying from Cave must be wonderful," said Shylo.

"It is, lass," smiled Navez. "A sight not to be missed."

"And after they leave we collect the cocoons?"

"Yes, Shaeli," Navez nodded.

"Collect them?" said Ishaan. "What for?"

"Didn't we tell you, Ishaan?" Shaeli smiled. "We use them for spinning and weaving. They give us the material for our balloons. That's why the colours are so bright, I'm sure." She looked up at the cocoons. "It must take so many of those to make a balloon."

"You're right," smiled Sahli'en. "Hundreds of them, and amassing enough of one colour takes many Winters." She looked at Kirrit. "Already we have begun stockpiling for a new Arrow Trader." Kirrit's eyes widened and Sahli'en laughed. "Red Arrow is already overcrowded, and your brothers will need another Trader soon."

"At *least* one," said Shaeli.

Kirrit laughed, but her face was thoughtful. "But what about the Trader part?" she asked.

"I believe we begin this Wintering," Navez answered. "In that big dead-end cavern at the far end of Cave. Many of the Fleet have been bringing in wood, and Baroz thinks we have more than enough now to make a start."

"Is that what's stored in the cave behind the landings?" asked Rennan. "The one next to the spinner's storage cave?"

Navez nodded. "It will take many Winterings to build the ship," he said. "For little can be done during the year while the Fleet is out in the World, but when it is almost complete the balloon will be sewn."

"But first we must have enough material," said Sahli'en.

Wyshka spoke from nearby. "I think there is plenty of the blue," she said. "And perhaps they would like white arrows. There is a little white, and with luck we shall have enough by the time the Trader is built. I like the name White Arrow."

"White Arrow," said Kirrit, testing the words on her tongue. "I think they might like that too."

"I haven't seen any white moths, Wyshka," said Shaeli. "Or cocoons."

"They *are* rare," her grandmother answered. "But there is usually a couple, sometimes a dozen each year."

Kirrit jumped up. "Let's look for some," she said.

"I believe I saw a white cocoon around the third bend," Almarnoch said. "Perhaps two."

The children hurried down the tunnel, and Ishaan followed them. He, too, was eager for a sight of a white moth.

As Navez had said, the giant moths moved into Cave, and often they spent an afternoon watching them dancing with each other in elaborate courtship rituals. Their dance was beautiful, each fluttering pair of wings trying its best to engage the finest mate, and when they finally paired off and began to mate, it was done in flight, the pairs embracing and flying as one through the air. They watched the females lay the eggs too, pushing their tails deep into cracks and crevices, marking spots on the roof of the tunnel in anticipation of the Wintering's glow-worms.

As the next Full Moon approached, they looked expectantly at the mouth of Cave a hundred times a day, and on the day of the Full the first moths began to fly. A cry went up and everyone came from huts and gardens and hall to stare at the side of Zerrinius.

There were only a few at first, flighty in the sunshine and looking like butterflies across the distance, but more followed, and soon the mouth of Cave was filled with wings, and then they flew towards the year village like a many-hued rain of velvet. Every face turned in wonder to the sky and was covered in the shadow as the mass of flying creatures flew overhead and blocked the sun. As the last ones flew past, the children began to run after the tail of the moth cloud, following them to the edge of the Lea and watching them fly into the Valley of Stones, waiting until they became a solid mass and then a speck in the distance, speculating about where they went. Bonn thought they found some secluded gorge in the valley, and died together romantically, but Rhubic decided they flew into another cave and were the food for some giant, deformed spider.

Ishaan greeted them upon their return, and laughed aloud when the boys told him Rhubic's theory. He was often found with the children of Cave year as the summer wore on, advising them on matters of marksmanship, for none could beat him for accuracy. He helped them collect the cocoons from the tunnel, a tricky feat which involved a knife on the end of a very long pole and children with upturned faces and open arms vying to catch the fat pillows of silk.

Ishaan spoke often with Almarnoch, revealing a passion for elf-lore and a knowledge that almost matched Almarnoch's own. Llevvis and Shaeli were sometimes part of these discussions, and one day as Ishaan and Llevvis pored over an old book, Shaeli quietly asked Almarnoch about showing

Ishaan the wand. He was thoughtful for some time, and then he looked at her, his brows drawn together. They looked like an incredibly hairy caterpillar.

"I have wondered about that myself," he said. "Our young visitor would be greatly interested, I have no doubt. It has even been on my lips to tell him of your find." He thought a moment. "Yet something stops me. Something bids me keep it secret." He sighed. "I know not why, yet I'll not go against it."

Shaeli nodded. "I had the same feeling. I like Ishaan, and know he would love to see my wand, but after all this time and when so few people remember it, I just didn't feel like bringing it out again." She looked at him. "I guess it'll stay where it is."

Almarnoch agreed. "I think it best, yet I *like* the young man. He seems of good character, open and friendly, and he knows much for the son of a small island silversmith. Perhaps too much." He looked back at her and chuckled. "It may be the fancy of an old man, but sometimes I can almost smell salt upon him still, though it is a long time since he saw the sea."

Shaeli laughed too. "Then I must have an old man's fancy too, for only yesterday, as Ishaan came back from swimming, I thought I smelt the sea upon him."

Almarnoch laughed harder. "Further from an old man than you is not possible, my friend." His face softened as he looked at her. "'Tis a very pretty woman you shall be, Shaeli, and very soon."

She smiled her thanks, and kissed the dry parchment of his cheek.

* * *

As the days passed, the fate of Ishaan was discussed many times.

It was a hard trip down to Serrat, though possible with good provision and forethought. Some were of the opinion that if he stuck close by the spring-stream, he could reach Serrat in seven or eight days, but many thought it a pointless risk when he could stay the Wintering and fly safely down with a Trader next year, or even be dropped on Argon itself. Ishaan was undecided; many times he expressed a desire to meet the Fleet and see Cave filled with the balloons and their ships, yet he often spoke longingly of his home and family.

Summer faded into autumn, leaves began to brown in the fields, grass grew between rows of harvested crops, and lessons became more intense as they moved into their final stages.

Throughout the spring and summer, each child's strengths and weaknesses had been discovered, duties delegated accordingly, encouragement and admonishment meted out with patience and wisdom. As the year crept by, more of the running of the group was given over to the young; planning of meals, care of animals, preservation and storage of produce, and, without quite realising it, the children of Cave year passed the shallows of childhood and entered the deeper waters of young adults. They drew closer to each other, came to rely on each other, and knew each other intimately. They took their responsibilities seriously, and enjoyed showing off their skills.

During that time, Shaeli saw less and less of Kirrit. Her friend spent much of her time with Bic, and while Shaeli tried not to be jealous, she sometimes felt slightly lost.

She spent time alone with Rennan, despite the best efforts of Bonn to distract him, holding his hand, and sharing her first kiss as they gathered passionfruit one golden afternoon, and Shaeli felt a curious satisfaction that he preferred her over the dimpled charms of Bonn. She was unable to keep the smug look from her face whenever Bonn was around, but she and Rennan were the best of friends, disagreeing just enough to make conversations interesting, and he and his grandfather visited often.

Ennan, father of Renn of Golden Eagle and Rennan's father, Ennell of Kingfisher, had been great friends with Povann, Jarris and Jeth's father, and Shaeli learnt a lot about her own grandfather from Rennan's. Ennan's eyes grew hazy as he talked of the Winter Purple Leaf had returned, and the big heart of Povann which had stopped beating as his feet reached the ground of Cave. He told Shaeli how Povann had died surrounded by the Fleet and the desolate voices of his Zoi, and how she had been born that very Winter, to replace her family's grief with smiles.

Ishaan also spent a lot of time in Wyshka's hut, swapping stories with Olver. They talked over endless cups of tezz, comparing stories, discussing the root of a tale, its history and the different regional interpretations, and Shaeli often went to sleep listening to the rhythm of their conversation. She liked Ishaan, and admired his inquiring mind and respectful manner. With the time he spent with the Warlocks and his talks with Olver, Shaeli was with him a great deal, until she knew the line of his jaw and the timbre of his laugh by heart. Yet, one day in early autumn, something happened that caused her to question her good opinion of him.

Late one afternoon, weary from the last gathering of the fire-rocks, they straggled home. Kirrit, Shaeli, Bic and Rennan led the way, too tired to talk, the others not far behind, clustered around the silent cattle.

Kirrit uttered one quiet word as they reached the buildings. "Swim?"

The others nodded and peeled off towards their homes. As Shaeli reached the steps she heard Bic shout something to Kirrit, and she turned in time to see Kirrit give Bic a rude gesture. She smiled and turned back to the steps. The smile froze on her face.

Ishaan stood above her, a smile on his face also, yet not his usual open, slightly-crooked smile, but a stiff, artificial smile.

Shaeli was surprised, and puzzled by his presence. More so by the look upon his face.

"Ishaan?"

His eyes flitted to the main group just entering the village and then back to Shaeli. He had been part of the work group that morning, but just after lunch he'd developed an ache behind his well-healed scar, and had returned to rest.

"You're back," he said after a moment.

"That's fairly obvious," she said, and he cringed a little at the tone in her voice. She softened it. "What are you doing here, Ishaan? Is your headache gone?"

"Headache? Oh. Yes. Thank you." His eyes flicked again at the group. "And I apologise for coming when no one was home, but I left my... pipe here last night." He looked at her, his green eyes full of shadow, his face now holding an almost genuine smile. "I did not think your grandmother would mind if I retrieved it. Do you?"

She shook her head, and tried a smile of her own. She hoped it did not look as false as his. She had heard him knocking his pipe on the veranda rail last night as he'd said goodnight to Olver.

"You startled me, that's all," she said.

He nodded, and again looked past her. "I'll go and see if I can help."

Shaeli watched him walk across the compound, then she went up the steps, into her room, and grabbed some clothes. She threw them on the bed and sat down on the floor to take off her boots, thinking about Ishaan. She was doubtful of his words, but could think of no motive apart from them. She put the boots under the bed – and then pulled them out again. She peered beneath the bed. Something was different. Something...

It took her a moment to realise what it was, and then Kirrit was banging on the wall.

"Come on, Shaeli," she yelled. "Let's go."

"I'll catch up," she shouted back. "I won't be long."

"Alright."

She waited until the sound of their voices had faded, and then she popped her head up, and looked out the window. Wyshka and Olver were still over by the carts, and she sat back on the floor and reached under her bed. She pulled out her bag and held it on her knee. She looked at one side, then the other. She opened it and studied the contents; unwrapped the wand and wrapped it again in the old velvet, lifted the lid of Nol's box. All seemed as it had been before, and yet she knew Ishaan had been in here, knew he had been looking at her things. She pushed the bag back under the bed and gathered her clothes. Outside, she turned down the path without looking at anyone, sure they would see the anger on her face.

Her bag was made from tapestry. It was her mother's old Faunist bag, well-worn, the pattern faded. But it was the pattern that had given her the clue. On one side, the pattern was unbroken, one large flower in the centre. On the other side, the material had a seam in one corner, and the flower was slightly left of the middle. Throughout the year, every time she looked under the bed, she had grown used to seeing the flower left of the middle, the seam on the far right, a little frayed around the edges. Today the flower had been in the middle.

Only Ishaan could have moved it. Wyshka seldom invaded Shaeli's privacy, Olver never, and the only reason Ishaan would have moved the bag was if he had pulled it out and looked inside.

She had known he wasn't himself as soon as he appeared at the top of the steps, for guilt had sat uncomfortably on his features. As she neared the fishing hole she could hear voices and splashes, and she shook her head, trying to throw her emotions far away from her expression. Yet questions drummed a beat inside her head. Why? What did it mean? With the *why* came other questions. Was he all he said he was, who he appeared to be? Had he searched only their hut, or had he looked in them all? Everything she believed about him was thrown into doubt. All that she knew of him could be a lie, and yet she could see he did not lie easily. And then again, maybe he did, it was just that she had surprised him.

She said nothing to the others, and though she was quiet as she swam, they were also, for they were all tired.

Throughout dinner and the talking afterwards, her preoccupation and growing misery went unnoticed. Or so she thought.

She tried to slip away quietly. She whispered to Wyshka that she was going to bed, and walked to the edge of the wide veranda. She breathed deeply. The nights were becoming chilly.

"Ah, just what is needed," said Almarnoch's voice behind her. "A strong young arm to escort a tired old Warlock home." He peered at her from beneath the wispy eyebrows, smiling, yet he was watching the frown on her face and the tight way she held her lips, as if they would tremble otherwise. "Come, my friend," he said quietly. "It seems something has happened, and I would know of it."

Shaeli nodded, but did not trust her voice. She took his arm and they descended the steps together, her thoughts racing, yet she did not speak until they were inside his hut, a mug of tezz in her hands. Then she told him everything, and asked aloud the questions that filled her mind. Almarnoch thought long before he answered her.

"I have pondered many times about our young visitor. My *inclination* is to like Ishaan, yet my *instinct* says to watch him. This I have done. He has made many friends, and talked freely about his family and home. In return, we have also talked freely about our Fleet, and our ways." He looked at Shaeli from beneath the white brows. "Harmless enough information, from what I can see, and there is no reason why anyone should *not* know it. Traders have never been secretive with the People." He frowned. "And yet something gnaws at me. The same feeling that gathers in my bones when a great storm lies beyond the horizon gathers in my *soul*, but I do not know what dark storm portends." He shook his head slowly. "Yet I cannot believe Ishaan is part of the darkness, nor why he should wish to invade your privacy." He sat thoughtfully. "Perhaps he heard rumours of the wand, some chance remark from someone, and he wished to see it."

"Yes," said Shaeli, seizing upon this explanation. "Yes, that could be it. And it would have been obvious that we were not going to tell him about it, or show it to him."

"And curiosity overcame good manners, perhaps?" Almarnoch mused.

"Well, I know how that feels," said Shaeli. "And you know he would love to see an elfin wand."

"Yes, that could be it."

"Of *course* that's it," Shaeli said. "It would explain everything. No *wonder* he looked so guilty. Oh, I feel much better." She stood up. "Thank you, Almarnoch. I can always rely on you to find an answer." She leant and kissed him.

"What? Oh, you're welcome child," he said absently, and Shaeli could see he was already thinking of something else.

"Good night, Almarnoch," she said.

"Yes, yes, dream well."

Shaeli knew he had forgotten her by the time she reached the door. She smiled to herself as she closed it behind her. She felt relieved, yet something Almarnoch said slowed her steps.

I do not know what dark storm portends, he had said.

She shivered, and walked home under the dark canopy of the sky. Behind her, Garrit stepped out from the shadows behind Almarnoch's hut, and watched her until she walked through the door.

* * *

CHAPTER TWENTY EIGHT

Autumn began to wane, and preparations were begun for the move back up to Cave. The year had passed faster than Shaeli had dreamt it could, and every day had brought her something new; fresh knowledge, another skill, a rainbow shining across the face of Mount Zerrinius. There was little left to do down on the Lea, and the days began to pass more slowly.

Shaeli had spent her spare time during the summer working on the small magical skill she possessed. The little flame now blazed strongly from her fingers, the power concentrating about her index and middle fingers, the right hand still more brightly than the left. Llevvis had worked with her on strength and control, and she could use the magic in simple, harmless ways; lighting lamps or warming forgotten cups of tezz; she had even learnt to propel the light short distances, and had found this handy for picking hard to reach fruit.

One day, she lay on her back beneath the tree beside the meeting hall. Rennan, Bic, Kirrit, Rhubic, Shylo, Bonn and Jezzyn sat on the grass nearby, watching as Shaeli sent tiny blue balls into the air. She was practising making the light-balls hover, even spin slowly, and was having some success, but she was distracted by how close Bonn was sitting to Rennan. The others called encouragement, and Rennan counted the time each hovering ball spun in the air before dissolving, but he also seemed distracted by Bonn's proximity, because he kept losing count. Shaeli took a deep breath and did her best to ignore the familiar way Bonn kept putting her hand on Rennan's knee.

She had found that if she thought about it, she could alter the shade of the light, and was pleased with the deep aqua she had just discovered. The light-ball floated above her, just beneath the tree's canopy, and she concentrated and it spun faster. She giggled, and then lost focus as the others laughed and cried out. The ball faded, and winked out. She sat up, and looked at Rennan.

"Almost a hundred, Shaeli," he grinned. "I almost lost count when it started spinning so fast. I didn't know you could do that."

"Neither did I," she said.

"I like the new colours, too," said Kirrit. "See if you can make a red one."

"I don't know," said Shaeli. "I only seem to get shades of blue, except for the gold just before I light a candle or something." She shook her hands. "And it makes my arms tired."

"'Tis the drain of the magic that tires your arms, Shaeli."

Shaeli turned and saw Ishaan coming up the path. He sat down and Shaeli smiled.

"It is only *barely* magic, Ishaan. Not real Warlock magic."

"Ah, but it *is* magic," Ishaan smiled. "Slight, pale perhaps, but real magic nonetheless. Perhaps you should try an amplifier," he said, and then he laughed as Shaeli raised her eyebrows. "A stone that holds magical properties may amplify one's talents," he explained.

"Of course," cried Shaeli. "I should have thought of that. That's what elves do, isn't it?" She pulled open the neck of her pouch, and reached inside. "Would amethyst do?"

"Very nicely," Ishaan nodded, as Shaeli pulled out the purple stone.

"I guess I just try and concentrate the light through the stone, yes?"

Ishaan shrugged. "I would imagine so. Perhaps you should ask Llevvis or Almarnoch."

"I will," she nodded. "I'll just have a little practise first."

She stood up, looked for something to aim at, and settled on the branch of a small sapling a short distance away on the bank of the spring-stream. She turned around and looked at the others, and anger bloomed in her chest when she realised Rennan wasn't even watching; he was too busy whispering with Bonn. She frowned, turned her back on them, and concentrated on the stone in her right hand, feeling the slight weight, moving the stone forward until it lay amid the tips of her fingers. She heard Bonn giggle behind her, and clamped her teeth down. She stretched out her arm, which tingled oddly, meaning to snap a twig off the tree, like picking fruit. She *pushed* from her fingers as she did when lighting a candle.

Deep purple light shot from her fingertips in an intense beam. It flew across the clearing and engulfed the entire tree with a thud. The little sapling exploded in a ball of violet flame. The beam leapt on across the spring stream, tongues of light licking the grass on the bank opposite.

Shaeli dropped her arm, her mouth hanging open as the little tree was consumed. She looked at Rennan, who had leapt to his feet, and the others sitting dumfounded on the grass, eyes goggling at the smouldering remains of the tree. Shaeli looked down at her hand and the crystal lying innocently in her palm.

"Did I do that?" she whispered.

Traders came running from all directions. They had heard the deep *whump* that had accompanied the light-ball, some had seen the blaze of purple light. They stood staring, asking questions, but Shaeli barely registered them. She looked from her hand to the thin black remains of the sapling, to the wisp of smoke curling into the sky, to Ishaan, and then at her hand again. Occasionally she broke the circuit by looking at Rennan or Kirrit instead of Ishaan, her eyes huge and blue with shock. Wyshka came, and Olver, but it was not until Almarnoch came to stand before her that she found some focus.

"What happened, Shaeli?" he asked gently, taking her shoulders in his gnarled hands.

"I'm not sure, Almarnoch," she answered, her voice unsteady. "I... I was just practising light-balls. Ishaan suggested I use a stone as an amplifier, so I got out my amethyst and aimed and..." She shrugged, and shook her head. "The little tree exploded." She looked at the rock in her hand. "I didn't *mean* to, Almarnoch," she said, looking back at him, her voice rising, tears burning the backs of her eyes. "I didn't know the amethyst would be so *strong*. It was an accident, really it was. I'm sorry. I didn't mean to."

"I know, Shaeli, calm down. It's alright," he said. He looked around as the Faunist moved through the crowd, Navez just behind her. "'Tis alright, Sahli'en. Shaeli has just discovered a new facet of her magic. There's no harm done."

"What do you mean, Almarnoch?"

"It seems she has the gift of stone channelling," he answered smoothly. "And she thought to test it on a poor unsuspecting tree."

"Did you not know the child had this talent?" Sahli'en said. "'Tis unlike you to miss such things."

"I thought her magic inclined in that direction, yes," Almarnoch replied. "I realised Shaeli had some light-talent, but had not considered the time right to try amplification with a gemstone. I thought she should learn a little more control first." Shaeli looked at her feet, and Almarnoch continued. "Light channelling has several applications but, as you know, there is little *practical* use for such things." He glanced at Shaeli with what looked suspiciously like a small grin. "There is not much call for tree-burners."

"I thought we had elves on the Lea," said Navez, with a much more obvious smirk.

There were a few titters from the crowd, and Shaeli heard Olver chuckle behind her. She started to feel better.

"But how did it happen?" Sahli'en asked, ignoring their attempts at levity.

Shaeli opened her mouth to answer, but was interrupted.

"I'm afraid it was my fault," said Ishaan. "I suggested an amplifier of some kind, but I did not foresee such amplification as this. We were all taken by surprise."

"It was an accident, truly." Kirrit came forward and took Shaeli's hand. "But it was an amazing accident. And isn't she clever?"

"I don't know about that, Kirrit," said Sahli'en. "I think it is lucky she did not aim at the hall. A little knowledge is sometimes a dangerous thing."

"I'm sorry, Sahli'en," said Shaeli. She looked around. "I'm sorry, everyone. It won't happen again."

Almarnoch spoke softly beside her. "At least not without some more knowledge, child."

Shaeli smiled gratefully at him. Now the shock of what she had done was passing, she began to be filled with a growing sense of excitement. She had no idea what her new ability meant, or what it could be used for, but the discovery was exciting, just the same.

* * *

She began to practise with the Warlocks next morning.

She attracted a small crowd, curious to see what she could do. The children were all there, along with numerous old-ones; Navez, Wyshka and Olver, Rennan's grandfather Ennan, Bydi, a few others. They crossed the spring-stream, going single file across the old tree below the fishing hole, and then back upstream until they were opposite the meeting hall. On this side of the stream, a long thin strip of land ran the length of the Lea and stone bluffs rose high above. This western field was too thin and chilly to be used for gardens, but they practised archery, slingshot, javelin and fencing here, so it was a natural place to test Shaeli's new skill.

Garrit and some of the boys stuck fallen branches in the ground a short distance away, and the spectators settled themselves on the grass overlooking the spring-stream. The Warlocks gave Shaeli final instructions.

"Feel the magic well inside you before you let fly, Shaeli," said Demeris. "The more you let it build, the brighter and stronger your light will be."

"And when you push it, keep your arm straight and your aim will be true," Llevvis added.

Shaeli looked to Almarnoch. "You're sure the amethyst will be alright? Perhaps we should try something else – one of Llevvis' quartz instead. They're lighter, he says."

"That may be so, but they are *also* Llevvis'," said Almarnoch. "The stones in your pouch are yours and have absorbed your energy; each stone gains strength the longer it is in the possession of its wielder. That is why your amethyst reacted with such power. It has been absorbing your energy for many years, and the power has lain fallow." Shaeli nodded and swallowed, and Almarnoch patted her on the shoulder. "There is nothing here you can harm, and in time we will test all your stones, and perhaps some of Llevvis' for comparison."

Shaeli thought for a moment and then stepped forward. "I'm ready," she said. "Which one shall I aim for?" She looked at the line of branches the boys had stuck in the ground. They were probably twice as far away as the small tree she had accidentally destroyed yesterday.

"Start on the left. Concentrate on feeling the power build, and when you feel the time is right, push gently towards the target," Almarnoch said.

Shaeli looked at him. "How will I know when the time is right?"

Almarnoch smiled. "'Tis impossible to describe child. You will *feel* it."

Llevvis helpfully tried a description anyway. "It's almost like pins and needles, but warm, and when the time is right, your arm will feel so full of the tingling that you will have to let it go. I'm sure it's basically the same method we use for creating light."

Shaeli nodded again and turned to face her target. The spectators called encouragement, but she tried to ignore them and the beating of her heart by concentrating on the small branch. It had leant a little in its hole, and she focused as she did while conjuring light balls. She raised her arm.

The magic built warmly as Llevvis had said, but instead of the numbness of pins and needles, she felt as if her arm had become extra sensitive; more alive than any other part of her body. Bigger somehow. She could feel each fine hair that grew on her arm; the whorls of her fingerprints as they held the cool crystal; the nails growing in their beds. And she *did* know when it was time to let it go, it became almost too much to bear that heightened sense of feeling. She took a breath and *pushed* the magic through the crystal.

Though not as dark or intense as the beam from the day before, the light that flew from her fingers was a purple thunderbolt that took out not only the small, leaning branch, but the one beside it and the grass twenty paces behind. She broke the connection by flicking her arm up to the sky and let out a breath she didn't know she held, again filled with amazement.

The crowd erupted in cheers, and she heard whistles from across the stream where more of the old ones had gathered beneath the tree beside the hall. She smiled, waved, and gave them a little curtsey, but when she turned to Almarnoch she could see he was not impressed. He shook his head, and sighed. Her smile faded.

"A little *excessive*, don't you think, Shaeli?" he said, raising one eyebrow. "You will wear yourself out very quickly if you overuse, child. You must learn control, and moderation, though your aim is fair."

Shaeli bit her lip, and looked at the targets. "Shall I try another one?"

He nodded. "But this time, think small. 'Tis only a twig that a breath of wind would knock over. Be gentle. Your magic need only ever equal its objective. Be a breath of wind, Shaeli."

She smiled, shook back her hair, and focused on the next target. The little branch would hardly reach her waist. Barely four withered leaves remained on it. It was kindling, really. Shaeli took a deep breath, and tried to lighten the magic somehow.

A breath of wind.

This time the heightened sense was less intense. It was the same, yet *softer* – like sunlight through a veil of thick lace. When the bolt flew from her fingers it went more slowly, and she could watch its progress. The little branch sighed into flame, and the beam petered out about ten paces behind. This time when she looked at Almarnoch, he was smiling.

She practised until the sun was high overhead, learning to stop the bolt at the target. She began to feel a tenuous link with the light as it flew; to have some control over it *after* it left her fingers.

When Almarnoch called a halt, she protested a little, and though she wanted to continue, she had to admit that she felt drained and her arms ached, yet she was pleased, for she had learnt some control, and she was eager to learn as much as she could about this new gift.

* * *

The time was approaching when they would move back to Cave, and soon after they could expect the first Traders to start arriving. The cap of snow on Zerrinius had grown to a cloak and cold winds had begun to whine across the Lea. The walls had been put back around the hall, and the fields lay as brown and dry as the children had seen them every Wintering of their lives, yet now they had seen the Lea in all its colours, seen it transformed into a garden and the bounty reaped from its fields. They knew that they had assured the Fleet would be fed throughout the Wintering, and were proud of the contribution they had made. They understood the integral part the old ones played in the lives of all traders, and spoke to them with greater respect. The children began to anticipate the day their families returned, and one night they sat in the meeting hall, wondering again who would arrive first. They were so caught up in their eagerness that when Ishaan spoke of his intention to leave and return to his family, they did not fully comprehend, and could only stare at him dumbly.

"Leave, Ishaan?" said Navez, at last. "But I thought you were to stay for the Wintering."

"I have thought long on the matter, Navez, and had almost decided to. Yet hearing these young people speak of their families has brought me to another conclusion. I shall leave tomorrow."

"*Tomorrow?*" Navez shook his head. "But you haven't prepared for the journey, and the Wintering is just over a Moon away. Can you make it to Serrat and down Meoro Pass by then? *And* find a boat to take you home, for all Traders will be Cave-bound."

"I believe I can, Navez," nodded Ishaan. "I have talked much with the old ones about the Valley of Stones, and they say staying close beside the stream is the only way, but I have thought of another option." He paused a moment. "The spring-stream itself. It runs mildly at this time of year. A barrel, a change of clothes, a good log to strap it to," he shrugged, as if suggesting a casual stroll down the Lea. "I think I shall make Serrat in two or three days."

"*Swim* to Serrat?" cried Olver. "You're not serious, Ishaan?"

"I am indeed, my friend. 'Tis almost too simple." Ishaan smiled. "Of course, one would not attempt it at any other time of year, but I am confident of success."

"But what of the waterfalls and rapids?" asked Navez. "There are at least six falls between here and Serrat."

"Seven, Navez, and the last the highest," said Olver. Beside him, Wyshka sat shaking her head, staring at Ishaan as if he'd just suggested riding a Zoi.

"Do you really think you can do it, Ishaan?" asked Rennan.

"I do," Ishaan nodded. "And as to waterfalls, I shall hear them coming and find a way around. The log can go over, or I'll find another downstream. Rapids, well I think they'll not be a problem."

"And you're firm in your decision, lad?" Almarnoch spoke from beside the fire where he'd sat, eyes closed, throughout the conversation. His eyes were open now, and fixed intently on Ishaan.

"I am, sir." Ishaan almost bowed.

"Then we shall have to see you are well prepared," Almarnoch said, and smiled. "I wish you good journey, and may the gods watch over you."

This time Ishaan really did bow, and his eyes took them all in as he thanked them. When he smiled and spoke of how he would miss them, his green eyes met Shaeli's.

She did not return his smile. She had been listening, hoping he would be dissuaded. She had wanted him to meet her family and Winter with them, but suddenly he would be leaving, no warning, nothing. Tomorrow he would be gone, and she realised she had badly wanted him to stay, for despite her worries over the wand, she had grown to value his company, and care for him. Some little spot inside told her she would miss him, and darkened at the thought that she would probably never see him again. The idea depressed her and she sat and watched as supplies were soon gathered and a stout barrel found and rubbed well with wax. The old ones went verbally over everything they knew of the spring-stream's course, and Ishaan listened, nodding and asking many questions. He was to leave word with Billit the baker upon his arrival in Serrat, they insisted, so they would not wonder endlessly at his fate. Plans were made to walk with him down the Lea and give him a proper farewell.

Sunrise found Shaeli wide awake, and though she tried to go back to sleep, she could not. In the end she rose and dressed, then wandered over to the meeting hall, made some tezz and went to sit with it on the step in the first pale rays of the sun. She looked up at Zerrinius as she sipped her tezz, admiring the silver on its snow cloak. Her eyes travelled down the mountain, and widened as she saw Ishaan going across the stepping stones and disappearing into the mouth of the tunnel.

She put her cup on the step and stood, puzzlement creasing her brow like a seam. She wondered what to do, and was unaware of the answer until she found herself at the foot of the path. Then she knew she must see what Ishaan was doing.

As she topped the rise above first terrace, she was greeted only by the gurgle of the stream. She crossed the stepping stones and entered the mouth, shivering in the shade of the mountain as she hurried through the bolt tunnel. Warlock lights still shone, some brighter than others – Almarnoch's, the dimmer ones belonged to Demeris and Llevvis. Garrit's had almost lasted the year, and were mere wisps of light, but even in the diminished glow there was enough light to see across Cave, yet there was no sign of Ishaan.

She stood outside the bolt tunnel, uncertain, then she went over to the storage caves and looked in each one, scanning the pools of shadow under the tiny Landings as she passed. She saw nothing and wandered back over to the silent huts of the old ones, yet they too were empty. The fire-pits lay below, piles of fire rocks stacked beside them. Only the bubble of the spring spoke.

She went down the slope and across the floor, her footfalls a whisper in the vastness, until she reached Almarnoch's cabin. She stopped beside a stalactite, mystified, and a soft scrape from behind the hut tugged at her ear. It was only a small sound, yet in the stillness of Cave it was plainly heard, and she eased herself around the rock. A tiny glimmer of light shimmered above her head, and though its glow did not reach far, it was enough to see Ishaan emerge from the dark mouth of the Zoi cave. So affronted was she that he had almost reached her before she stepped out from the shadows. She was trembling, her eyes cold grey.

Ishaan stopped when he saw her. His face paled. His eyes were the brightest thing in Cave. In his hand was a short brand, still smoking from its use as a torch. Its smell was as bitter as her disappointment.

"Shaeli. I..." he began.

"How *dare* you?" she hissed between her teeth. "You knew it was forbidden. You *knew*. We told you no one ever enters the cave of the Zoi. It is sacred, Ishaan. *Sacred*. Do you not know the meaning of the word? Or anything of honour, or loyalty to friends?" Her voice broke then, her rage covering her throat, but still she struggled on, her tirade coming in broken pieces. "When you looked at my things, I thought... I thought Almarnoch was right when he said you were just... curious. But *this*... this is not just prying into my things... this is against Cave, the whole *Fleet*."

"Shaeli, listen to me," Ishaan stammered. "Please stop."

But she did not stop. Could not have, even if she had wanted to. "What if the Zoi sense there has been an intruder? What if they think we've betrayed them. The gods, what if...?"

"Shaeli, *please*." He dropped the torch, and came towards her, hands outstretched. Shaeli leapt backwards.

"Don't touch me," she cried. Her eyes narrowed, and Ishaan winced at the hatred in her face. "What could you *want* in there, Ishaan? How can you ever explain to the old ones or Almarnoch?" Anger coursed through her, as tangible as stone. "Oh, how *could* you?"

Ishaan stood before her, his arms held out, his face stricken. "'Tis not *against* the Fleet I work, Shaeli, but *for* it.

Never would I have invaded your privacy for myself, nor the Zoi cave. But higher powers are at work..." He stopped, drew a breath and started again. "Others have seen fit to guide my hand, and I swear to you I have done no harm. Nothing has been disturbed. I touched nothing, except with my eyes. I swear to you." His eyes bored into her, willing her to believe.

Shaeli did not evade them. "I don't believe you," she said, her voice rising. "You're a *liar*."

Her hand flew up, the pointed finger daring him to disagree. As the word *liar* left her lips, a red spark shot from her finger and hit Ishaan on the cheek. He cried out and recoiled, one hand going to his cheek, his eyes widening with shock. Shaeli covered her mouth with her hands, as shocked as he. They stared at each other, her arm tingling as it did when she channelled magic through the stones, and although words of contrition were far from her mind, she could barely believe what had just happened.

She went closer and he took his hand away. A tiny burn marked his cheek, black in the middle, angry red at the edges.

"It... it's burned," she said dully.

"It's alright, Shaeli," he said. "I know you did not mean it. Your magic mirrored your feelings, that's all." He lowered his head. "I should put some water on it."

"I suppose," she said.

They went to the spring pool, and he soaked his handkerchief in the water and put it to his cheek.

"What 'higher powers'?" she said, her voice low, her eyes intent on his face. "What 'others'?"

He looked at her for a while before answering. "I cannot tell you, Shaeli," he said, at last. "Mayhap I have said too much already. But please trust me. *Please*."

She did not try to keep the suspicion from her face, though somewhere inside she wanted to trust him, just as she had a short time before. Yet she could not let it go so easily.

"But what did you want in there, Ishaan? What is there to see in the Zoi cave?" Despite herself, she was also curious.

"I wanted nothing but to look, and I have seen a wondrous sight." His eyes darted to the bolt tunnel, and he spoke more quickly. "Nothing has been harmed, believe me. There is no need to alert your elders. I would never harm your Fleet, upon my honour, and the honour of my fathers."

She looked at him, so intense, imploring her to believe, her eyes coldly suspicious still. He would not invoke the name of his fathers lightly, of that she was sure, and she nodded once, then turned and strode back across the Cave. She could hear him behind her but she did not look at him again. When they reached the ledge, she stopped, turned her face to the sun, and closed her eyes. When she opened them, Ishaan stood before her as he had that day by the pool. She felt as exposed to him now as she had then.

"I'll not promise you my silence, Ishaan, but I'll not speak to Almarnoch until you are gone." She looked down at the year huts, sitting in their half-circle around hall, tree and stream, and then back into his eyes. "It made me sad to think of you leaving, but now I must wish it. I have no trust left for you."

She saw pain in his face at that. She had tried hard to make her voice cold and friendless and she realised she had succeeded.

He nodded, lips white, the mark on his face redder in the sun. "I understand, and mourn the fact. Yet I have something I must give you."

"I don't want anything from you, Ishaan," she said.

"I am not able to leave unless you take this gift, Shaeli," he said.

Though she wondered what he meant, she did not ask; she wanted only to be rid of him. She nodded.

From inside his jacket he took a little satin-wrapped parcel and placed it in her hand. She thrust it deep into her pocket, looked into his face a moment, and then pushed past, head down. She crossed the stepping stones and ran down the path to the Lea without looking back.

* * *

When the time came for Ishaan to leave, Kirrit came to fetch her. She had thought of making some excuse, but in the end she decided to go; it would look unnatural if she did not. She had shoved the tiny parcel from Ishaan inside one of her boots, for she had no wish to see what was inside.

It seemed all of them were accompanying Ishaan to the edge of the Lea. It was almost like a party, the sun shone brightly, birds chirruped in the orchard, and if anyone noticed Shaeli's mood, it was attributed to the loss of her friend, and, in a way, they were right. At the end of the Lea, farewells were said, a safe journey hoped for, the gods asked to watch over the traveller. Sahli'en gave him a salve for the burn on his face where an ember had leapt from the fire that morning.

Ishaan showed more than his usual eloquence in his thanks to the group, but it was a short farewell and soon he lowered himself over the side. Shaeli stood looking at the sky the whole time.

The boys hung precariously over the edge, watching Ishaan's descent. The barrel was lowered by a long rope, and Ishaan found a broken stump and lashed it tightly.

A pool of tumbling water lay at the base of the falls, and Ishaan pushed the log around the edge to where the stream ran out the other side. The traders lined the cliff as Ishaan lowered himself into the water and raised an arm in final farewell. Then he let go, the current caught the log, and he was swept downstream. They waved until he was swept around a bend and out of sight.

Ishaan had gone as unusually as he had arrived.

* * *

CHAPTER TWENTY NINE

Shaeli had never seen Almarnoch so angry. His eyebrows stuck out like wire brushes. His usually mild eyes blazed. Tiny red sparks leapt from his hair and beard, crackling as they exploded. As the Warlock's anger was released in magic, for the first time since she was five Winters old, she was almost frightened of her friend.

He paced. He ranted. He thumped fist into palm, creating more crackling sparks. His voice was cold as a mid-Winter blizzard.

"The trespasser. The *scoundrel*. To abuse our trust so. To take hospitality and friendship, and repay them with lies and deceit. 'Tis too *much*." He rounded on Shaeli. "You should have told me immediately, child, instead of letting him leave as if nothing had happened. How could you let him go?"

"He said he could never harm us, Almarnoch. He said some higher power guided his hand. He swore on the name of his fathers."

"*Pah*. He was not to be trusted. You should have seen that, as surely as you saw him walk from the Zoi cave. 'Twas wrong thinking indeed, young miss, to make such a decision yourself. You take *too much* upon yourself!"

Tears welled in Shaeli's eyes. Never before had Almarnoch lost patience with her or spoken so harshly. She had never seen him speak like this to anyone, but rage blinded him to her pain, and he continued to rave at her, the little red sparks raining down upon them both.

"Ishaan should have been brought before the old ones, and held until the Fleet arrived, for Taffka to deal with. And *you*, not even finished Cave year, *you* decide to believe the intruder, and let him go free." He gave her a withering look. "How he must be laughing at you now. You will have to speak before the

Council, and justify your actions. I hope you are confident, for entering the cave of the Zoi is a grave crime and you have aided Ishaan in his escape."

"*No*, Almarnoch," she cried. "It was not like that. He swore to me he had touched nothing, and could never harm the Fleet." Her voice broke. "But you're right, I should have told you... I'm sorry, Almarnoch, truly I am. I did not think..."

"No, child, you did not *think* at all," he said in that cold voice, and he turned away. "Begone from my sight. I am ashamed of you."

Shaeli fled, the sound of Almarnoch's anger crackling in her ears. She ran home, oblivious to the curious stares that followed her across the compound. Wyshka looked up as she entered, and on seeing Shaeli's face, she opened her arms and Shaeli fell into them, sobbing.

Wyshka held her, muttering soothing words as she stroked her granddaughter's hair. Olver came to the door, eyebrows raised, and Wyshka shook her head. She knew not the answer to his unspoken question, she could only hold the child as she tried to find the cause of her grief. Only two words came unscathed through the sobs: Almarnoch and Ishaan. She spoke softly to Shaeli, urging her to try again. At length, between sobs and hitching breaths, she told the tale, beginning with Ishaan going through her things, and ending with the Warlock's reprimand.

"And now Almarnoch says I must go before the Council and explain myself. Wyshka, what can I do?"

"Perhaps he is right when he says you should have told him of Ishaan's entering the Zoi cave, for it was a terrible thing to do. Yet it is unfair of him to blame you entirely." Wyshka stood. "And I shall tell him so. Right now."

"But, Wyshka..."

"No buts, Shaeli. If you must tell the Council, or even the whole Fleet of Ishaan's treachery, then so be it. But Almarnoch has dealt with you unfairly, and I shall *tell* him so."

"Wait until tomorrow, Wyshka, please. He's so angry now, I'm sure it wouldn't do any good," Shaeli pleaded.

"Well, alright," Wyshka conceded. "But first thing in the morning, the High Warlock will hear from me."

Shaeli went to bed with the sun that night. Her head ached and her dreams were scattered and frenzied. When she woke, she went in to find her grandmother getting ready to visit Almarnoch. Olver stood silently beside the door as Wyshka kissed Shaeli.

"Wait here," she said. "And don't worry. This will not take long."

She opened the door. Llevvis stood on the veranda, hand raised to knock. He blinked and looked past her.

"Where is Shaeli?" he asked urgently. "Almarnoch needs her. Something… strange has happened. She must come."

Shaeli appeared behind Wyshka.

"What is it, Llevvis? What has happened?"

"I don't know," said Llevvis. "Yesterday, after you left – you did not see me, outside, though I called your name – I stood undecided. I heard Almarnoch cry out, and I went in and he… well, you saw him. He ordered me to leave him, and I obeyed, yet I went to check on him this morning." He shrugged, his thin, plain face wrinkled with worry. "I was concerned for him. He was still abed, and he looked terrible. He could barely speak, but he asked for you. I came straight here. Will you come?"

"Of course, Llevvis. Right away."

"I'm coming, too," said Wyshka.

"Me, too," said Olver.

"Hurry, then, I did not like the look of him. I did not want to leave him alone, but he insisted, and Garrit and Demeris are laying a final incantation upon the orchard." He practically scurried across to Almarnoch's little hut.

When they entered the room, Almarnoch was sitting on the bed.

"You look better," said Llevvis, surprised.

"Yes, yes, I am fine." He looked at Shaeli. "Fine except for the shame I feel at speaking to Shaeli as I did. I have been shown the error of my ways."

"I was coming to show them to you myself, Almarnoch," said Wyshka. "You dealt unfairly with the child."

"I know, Wyshka. I laid blame on her doorstep when I am also guilty. After Ishaan went through Shaeli's things, I should have watched him more closely, and I beg her forgiveness." He stood and crossed to Shaeli. He took her hands, contrition puckering his face. "Will you give it, Shaeli? I beg most humbly that you forgive your old friend."

"Of course, Almarnoch. Of course I forgive you. You were upset." She hugged him, relieved he was no longer angry. "But what happened? Are you alright?"

"Yes, child, and thank you. I am fine. And as to what happened, well, I'm not sure how, but last night, as I slept with my anger, your friend Williver gave me, shall we say, a short but extremely forceful dream. I woke a little... unnerved."

"You've seen Williver?"

The Warlock nodded.

"Who's Williver?" asked Wyshka.

"An elf, Wyshka. Almarnoch, what did he say?"

"Just as your grandmother did. I had done you an injustice."

"An elf, Shaeli?"

"Yes, Wyshka. He visits my dreams. Almarnoch, did he say anything else?"

"Well, just that Ishaan may not be all he seems, but that was not *your* fault. And I am to trust you. What has been done is the way it was meant to be done."

"In your *dreams*, Shaeli?"

"*Yes*, Wyshka, I'll explain later. Almarnoch, what does he mean, you must trust me? Do you not?"

"Of course, as a friend, as a member of the Fleet," he said. "But not as someone to make decisions; to know what is for the best. Forgive me, I have always had little trust in the wisdom of the young, even when I was one of them. But I must rethink. Age does not always equal wisdom, as I have so obviously shown."

"Hear, hear," said Olver, softly.

"Then it shall be as before?" Almarnoch asked, and at Shaeli's nod, he smiled. "Good," he said. Abruptly, he changed the subject. "Llevvis, Garrit's Cave lights have lasted the year. 'Tis time for him to travel to the Bay of Islands." His voice was gruff. "He shall go with Taffka at the end of the Wintering. Demeris has spoken of his desire to take on lesser duties. I wish you to become my second, if you consent."

"Thank you, Almarnoch." Llevvis was overcome, his face beaming. "I had not even begun to hope you would find me ready so soon."

"Serve well, is all the thanks I require," Almarnoch said. "I have always hoped that you would remain with the Fleet, though I'm sure you will have other, perhaps more interesting offers."

"They shall not matter. I have never anticipated working anywhere else," Llevvis said.

Almarnoch smiled. "I am happy to hear it, my boy. We are fortunate to have you."

"Come, Shaeli, it is time we finished packing the hut," Wyshka said. "Tomorrow we start taking things up to Cave. And you must tell Olver and I more of this elf."

Shaeli looked at Almarnoch and shrugged. "I'll have to tell them now," she said, and Almarnoch nodded.

Wyshka spoke again. "And I shall go with Shaeli when the Council speaks with her about this. 'Tis not fair she should have to face them alone."

"There is no need, Wyshka. I shall speak with her, and for her." Almarnoch smiled at Shaeli. "As a trusting friend should. Alright, Shaeli?"

She smiled at the old man, leftover tears filling her eyes.

As they walked back home she saw Garrit coming from the stables, heading towards Almarnoch's. She wondered how he would feel about leaving. Perhaps Almarnoch would take Dari as apprentice; she knew he would love that, and they would not see Garrit back at Cave for two years, if he came back at all. Shaeli had the feeling he wouldn't; he did not seem to love the Fleet as Llevvis did.

Later, after she'd told them about Williver – to a chorus of Wyshka tut-tutting and Olver repeating "well, I never" over and over – Wyshka asked her to pack anything she would not need in the next few days. When she pulled her bag out from under the bed, she remembered Ishaan's parting gift, found the boot she had put it in, and unravelled the cloth package. A stone fell into her lap, slipping from between the folds of blue satin, and she picked it up. Its colour was as deeply blue as the satin which had held it, the blue of the sky just before it turns night-black. The edges were dulled with age, yet the faces caught the light still. She had never seen a stone cut in such an unusual, pentagonal shape, or one so beautiful. She looked at it, pondering. It reminded her of something.

* * *

Williver came to Shaeli's dreams that night too. His visits had grown less frequent over the passing Winters, yet each time he came, it was as if no time had passed. They walked and talked together, always in some place of beauty, and he was as important to her as always.

Tonight they walked beside a lily-covered pond where the lilies opened and closed as if breathing. Pink clouds floated in the pale sky as she hugged him and thanked him for visiting Almarnoch. He smiled a trifle grimly.

'Twas no easy thing, little one, he said. *Yet so upset were you, I could not meet you in dreams, and the reason for your distress was very clear. I knew I must try to do something.*

But can't you visit whoever you want to?

No, he smiled. *Some I can reach, if I know where they are, and even though I did reach your Warlock, the dream was patchy and impossible to sustain. You are the only one I can meet in dreams with ease.*

Only me, Williver? I never realised. She thought for a moment. *But why?*

He laughed. *'Tis not for us to question, Shaeli, but to enjoy and be grateful. And I am not entirely sure myself.*

They laughed, and then she told him of her gift with the gems. He listened carefully, surprised she had a gift usually reserved for his people, then he smiled and encouraged her to keep practising. When she woke next morning she felt as if a cloud had been blown away from the sunshine in her mind.

The next days were a blur of activity. Everything but the barest of essentials was moved up to Cave, the fire-pits were stacked, candles towered in every holder, lamps were filled, storerooms overflowed with produce. The huts of the old ones both down at the year camp and at Cave were cleaned, tables scrubbed, stairs and Landings swept in anticipation of the Traders. Excitement spread like a grass fire throughout the group, and people walked about smiling for no apparent reason. The last night before they went up to Cave, the children gave the old ones a feast, and though it was a great success, there was a ripple of sadness among them; sadness that the year had, in the end, passed so quickly, and sadness because they knew it would never come again. The children would now take their places in the Fleet or the World, and, for the old ones, no year was the same, for the children were always different.

Shaeli's emotions never settled entirely in one spot. There was so much to do and think about, she was continually leaving the threads of thoughts and feelings half-unravelled. She practised with the Warlocks each day, gauging the effectiveness of the stones in her pouch, and trying out what Almarnoch called "cold" stones; stones that belonged to no one, which had no "personal essence".

Of the treasures in her amulet, many things were discarded; the silver shell, and the fossilised one, the pebble with a streak of gold, the coin, the piece of volcanic rock. These she tucked away in her bag, changing the weight of her amulet, the way it swung on her hip, for now it contained only the stones which held magic.

The amethyst proved the strongest and easiest to use, and she quickly became adept at wielding its magic, yet she never reached the kind of intensity with it as she had on that first day. The Warlocks attributed this to the pent-up energy in the stone, yet Shaeli thought differently. After burning Ishaan inside Cave, she knew what had made the beam so bright: Bonn's intimate giggle and the way she'd brushed her fingers across Rennan's thigh; she knew anger had fuelled her that day.

The squat, clear quartz crystal gave a weaker white light which held less heat, yet it left a soft white afterglow, a vapour trail which hung in the air for a short time, and which, when tested at night, was strong enough to see by.

The triangular green stone – verdena, Llevvis called it – shot tiny green streaks of light, and they thought there had been little damage done, but on closer inspection they found minute holes had been bored through the small stump she was using as a target, the edges neatly cauterised and still smoking. Almarnoch had given her a lecture on the dangers of using such magic near people or animals then, but it was hardly needed; Shaeli had already imagined what such a beam would do to a person's body. What she had done to Ishaan with only her finger and her anger was enough.

The pear-shaped amber which had come to her via the throat of a grey sea-bird on Pa'laidiz shot a thick beam of molten honey-light that coaxed fire from the target and burned with a soft gold flame. Almarnoch said he was finding her way of interpreting magic quite intriguing, or perhaps, he added as an afterthought, the magic was interpreting her. On the last morning before the move to Cave, they tried the purple-black rock.

Almarnoch had never seen the stone, and even Llevvis, who prided himself on his knowledge and had a large personal collection of gems, did not know what it was. He had pored through books of both the People and of the Elves, and had found scant reference to it, and no name to give it. He thought he had seen it once in the jewellery of a noblewoman on the streets of Palveron, but he could not be sure, so, expecting little, they had decided to try it, and no one was more surprised at the result than Almarnoch. Llevvis was suspicious of the stone, and Shaeli felt a subtle difference in the way the magic built in her arm, but Almarnoch was expecting only a mild reaction, if any. Shaeli had learned so much control that he was no longer worried about trees exploding or her magic overshooting the target.

The stone was a flattened teardrop, the thickness of two coins, and Shaeli held the pointed edge forward, feeling the silver sparkles in the stone's depths pricking strangely against her fingers like tiny needles. Her arm felt different, somehow lighter, as the magic began to build, and the feeling of heightened awareness built more quickly than with the other stones. As the climax came she pushed the energy at the target.

When the magic left her hand in a darkly purple beam, the tree stump did not explode, or burn, it merely trembled in its old roots. Shaeli flicked her arm upwards, as she had with the others to break the connection, and the stump leapt from the ground, lurching upward, grass and dirt raining down, following the path of her hand as it lifted to the sky.

Shaeli willed the light to stop, and the dusky beam ceased instantly, but purple sparks still shimmered in its trail. The tree stump stopped hanging absurdly in the air and crashed to the ground. The sparks glittered and went out.

Almarnoch was without voice for long moments. Llevvis' mouth hung slackly. The stump lay in a splintered mass in the brown grass. The spectators began to whoop and whistle.

So began another lecture on the precautions to be taken when using magic. Almarnoch gave it as much for himself as for Shaeli.

* * *

At last the move back to Cave was complete. There remained nothing else to do except wait for the Fleet to arrive. Days were filled by closing the year huts and meeting hall, shuttering the windows, and moving the last of the animal fodder up to the Wintering caves off the main tunnel. Each afternoon they would sit outside, watching as Shaeli mastered her new skill and looking out across the Lea to the Valley of Stones, waiting for the first Trader to appear.

Shaeli had showed Almarnoch the blue stone given her by Ishaan, and though his lips pursed at the mention of Ishaan's name, he admired the stone, and told her they should test it.

One crisp afternoon, they went down to first terrace. Almarnoch was taking no chances, and he had Garrit set a small branch at the edge, with nothing but air behind it.

Kirrit sat with Bic, Rennan, Jezzyn, Rhubic and a few others on the ledge above, their legs swinging down. Llevvis, Demeris and Garrit stood near Shaeli, debating the potential properties of the blue stone; azulis, Llevvis called it. It was a fairly common stone found mostly in the Starisles, but the stones were usually very small, and this was the biggest he had seen.

Shaeli tried not to be nervous, but the weight of the pentagon-shaped stone in her hand reminded her of Ishaan – and what she would say when the Council asked about him entering the Zoi cave. She shook her head, tossing the thought away, squared her shoulders, breathed deeply, and concentrated on the magic.

She marvelled at the way the magic lay curled and sleeping within a stone until she summoned it. The ability to channel energy was not unknown among the People, yet it was rare, and, as Almarnoch continually pointed out, there was not much application for such a skill. Unlike the ability to connect with plants and weave magic about them for protection, to sustain life, direct water, give Lift, or any of the other skills Warlocks utilised, the skill of gem channelling was not much used. Almarnoch told her that practical uses were few; except in times of war – and he said with a small smile that he thought it unlikely she would be called to battle.

She felt the stone's strength as soon as she began to concentrate. Her arm quivered with awareness, the blue stone felt fluid between her fingers, the tips as if they were melting into the edges of the stone. She veiled the power, and was relieved to find the sensation diminish, but she waited a moment before she raised her arm to fire. As always, her aim was good, and a clear blue beam like a strip of sea flew out at the target. The blue light covered the stick and Shaeli stopped the flow and lifted her arm – she had learnt to stop the magic *before* she raised her arm, courtesy of the unnamed purple-black stone. She moved the blue gem back to the palm of her hand, surprised at how cold it was; between her fingertips it had felt warm and almost liquefied.

The three Warlocks were exclaiming over the branch as she walked over with Almarnoch. Rhubic's booming voice came from above; they wanted to know what had happened, for they had expected the branch to burn.

Shaeli thought the branch had been unaffected by the beam, but as she got closer, she could see it was covered with a layer of thin blue light. As she neared, the branch collapsed into a pile of ash, and she turned and looked up at her friends.

"It's turned it to ash," she called.

"How do you mean?" yelled Rhubic.

"I mean dissolved it. As in burnt it to nothing."

"I'm coming down," he boomed, lifting his thick body up quickly. For all his bulk, Rhubic was not ungainly, and he was beside them in moments, the others close behind. They took turns poking at the pile of still-warm ash and exclaiming over it, and it was declared interesting, but not nearly as exciting as the purple-black light; they liked it best when Shaeli practised lifting things.

"Perhaps it's time you tried to make skylights, Shaeli," Almarnoch said casually, then he looked at Llevvis. "Don't you think it's time, Llevvis?"

Llevvis nodded. "Why, yes. Yes, I do," he smiled.

Demeris chuckled. Several mouths hung open, Shaeli's the widest.

"*Almarnoch*," she cried. "Why didn't you *tell* me?"

"I wanted to be sure of your control," Almarnoch smiled, clearly enjoying the expression on Shaeli's face. "Skylights, as I understand it, is a lesser form of light channelling, but it requires a much greater amount of connection to the beam. One must be able to contain the ball until it reaches its required position, then release it into the appropriate shape. Is that right, Llevvis?"

Llevvis nodded, barely able to contain his glee. They all knew how Shaeli loved skylights, and he grinned as he tried to explain skylight principles. While none of the Warlocks could wield this kind of magic, they relied on their own experiences which used similar principles, yet much of Shaeli's learning had come from simple trials – as shown by the lifting stone.

She listened carefully as Llevvis, Demeris and Almarnoch explained the little they knew about skylights, and she tried to do as they said, sending her beams in a series of short sharp bursts straight out over the edge. She found that if she held most of the magic back and permitted only a small, but concentrated burst of energy to fly, she could feel a connection to the light-ball, as if she held it on an invisible string. She *pulled* at the little balls as they rolled through the air, until, after dozens of tries, she could make them explode in the air at will. It was almost the same as the spinning balls, except with the right thought, the balls erupted into hundreds of tiny embers, blue sparks showering harmlessly down to the Lea. She aimed one at a twig, bursting the skylight right above the dry stick, yet it did not burn, nor did the sparks leave a mark. She had done it, real skylights, harmless and beautiful, and *she'd* made them.

She glowed with pride, and tried each of her stones in both hands. Though her right hand was still stronger than her left, each stone produced a different coloured skylight which burst above their heads, the tiny glittering sparks snuffing out before they reached the ground, and she practised until her arms ached with the effort.

"Well, that *is* a use for your gift, Shaeli," said Almarnoch. "Not very practical, perhaps, but skylights are always a welcome distraction. You shall have to give the Fleet a show, perhaps at Mid-Winter feast."

She smiled, hugely pleased with this new discovery. She was rebuking the Warlocks for not telling her of it earlier when Rhubic's voice shattered the quiet afternoon.

"Trader coming," he yelled. "Taffka, just reaching the Long Lea."

They turned and saw Golden Eagle fly up from the Valley of Stones. The lead female Zoi let out a cry that echoed across the Lea. Kirrit looked at Almarnoch.

"Shall I run up and tell them?" she asked.

"No need, they will have heard the Zoi," he said.

Kirrit nodded, and looked back across the Lea. She did a little hop and her arm flew out.

"Shaeli," she cried. "Shaeli, *look*. Purple Leaf is behind them!"

* * *

CHAPTER THIRTY

Purple Leaf came soaring up behind Golden Eagle. Shaeli smiled so broadly her cheeks hurt, and for a moment she didn't know what to do. Kirrit, as usual, had the answer.

"Up on the ledge, quick."

And they ran, the Warlocks coming up behind them and picking their way carefully across the stepping stones as the children waited impatiently on the ledge. As Purple Leaf flew over the year huts, Shaeli saw them gathered on the fore-deck. She waved with both arms, and the arms of her family raised in return. Her view was obscured as Golden Eagle reached the ledge and passed overhead, Taffka, Renn and Rafi smiling down and calling greetings, and then Golden Eagle was past and entering the tunnel mouth, and Shaeli heard Neesha's voice echo across the Lea, just as it had when they'd left.

"Shaeli. Shaeli, we're *back!*"

As the Zoi passed overhead, the female let out a cry of joy at homecoming. Another younger female joined her, their voices harmonising and echoing across the Lea, and her family's words were lost in the Zoi's cry and their own torrent. Shaeli walked beneath her home to the tunnel mouth where others had gathered with the Warlocks to greet the first Traders.

The white faces of her family peered back at her as Purple Leaf disappeared around the first bend, and she ducked into the bolt tunnel, Kirrit close behind. They began to run as they left the tunnel, down past the huts of the old ones, around the spring-pool and the cold fire-pits, to where Golden Eagle was gliding to its Landing. They waited until the Zoi came into sight and then they were away to Purple Leaf's mooring, Kirrit almost as excited as Shaeli. They bounded up the stairs, and Shaeli could see the boys readying for the landing, grinning at them. Jeth threw the hook, the birds slowed the ship and lowered their long legs, and then they were there. Her father had the gate open and Shaeli threw herself fearlessly over the gap and into his arms, tears prickling the backs of her eyes. She blinked them away as Jarris hugged her hard, and stood back to look at her.

"Hello, Da," she smiled.

"Hello, Mouse," he said, and then he hugged her to his chest again.

Jeth ruffled her hair and kissed her cheek, and then the boys were there, too, Dari and Andos smiling broadly, Tarkoda hugging her, and then, with a flurry of arms and squeals, the twins leapt upon her. She was almost knocked over as they threw themselves against her, hands scrabbling at her for purchase. Their arms went around her neck and they kissed her cheeks, saying her name over and over. She returned their kisses, exclaiming over how they had grown.

Mareesha stood behind them smiling, and she opened her arms, and Shaeli walked into them. The twins moved with her like little leeches, arms about her waist, so she was surrounded by arms, and immersed in hugs. Mareesha kissed her, held her a long moment, and then pushed her back at arm's length so she could look at her properly.

She saw her lovely Shaeli, the sun-streaked hair longer, the stubborn, pointy chin the same as always – a little taller, her figure fuller. Her eyes were the same blue-grey, tilting at the corners and black-lashed, but they held something they had not held before; some touch of maturity that had not been there before the year. That was as it should be after Cave year, yet it seemed to Mareesha that her daughter's face held something more than Cave year should have given it – a depth of sadness and knowledge that was out of place on one so young. Yet along with it was a confidence, a kind of secret excitement that gave her eyes depth and intensity. These thoughts passed quickly through Mareesha's mind, and did not register on her face; all

Shaeli saw was her mother's broad smile and approving look, and she hugged her again.

"Oh, Mam," Shaeli sighed. "How I've missed you. All of you."

"And we, you, child," Mareesha said, quietly.

Shaeli saw Eenis standing across the deck, her face as unreadable as ever, yet a smile of greeting properly upon her face. She released herself from the twins' grasp and walked over to her aunt.

"Thank you for the pouch," she said. "I love it," and she hugged Eenis with genuine warmth.

After a surprised moment, Eenis hugged briefly back, but her eyes shone as Shaeli led her back to the group.

Kirrit had been given her fair share of hugs too, and she stood talking to the boys. Others also came to greet them, and soon small knots of people stood on the deck. Shaeli stood with her arms about her sisters' shoulders, trying to listen to their prattle and answer all the questions that were asked of her. Tarkoda soon had her admitting that she'd had a wonderful year, and with a little prompting from Kirrit and Rennan, she was soon telling them about her gift with stone channelling. Dari listened a moment and then moved off to talk with Garrit.

"Dari's gone to confirm it with Garrit," Andos said. "He takes nothing on face value, especially someone else's magic." His green eyes watched his brother and the young Warlock. "He *talks* of nothing but his own skill and his wish for apprenticeship."

"He may get his wish," said Shaeli. "Almarnoch sends Garrit to The Bay of Islands after the Wintering, and Llevvis is to become Almarnoch's second."

"Good for him," said Tarkoda. "Was it Llevvis who discovered your gift with the stones?"

Kirrit laughed and Shaeli went pink.

"No," she said. "I found I could make a little magic in Almarnoch's lessons, but it only came out my fingers." She hesitated. "And then, while I was practising one day, I discovered the magic worked with my stones."

"It was an accident, really," said Kirrit.

Rennan grinned. "It happened in a flash."

"A purple flash," said Jezzyn.

Andos and Tarkoda looked puzzled as they began to laugh. Shaeli tried to explain.

"I sort of... sort of set a tree on fire," she said.

"On fire?" guffawed Rhubic. "More like blew it up."

"Blew it up?" said Tarkoda. "How?"

"It was an accident," said Shaeli, echoing Kirrit, unwilling to go into details.

"You should have seen Shaeli's face, Koda," giggled Kirrit, ignoring her friend's discomfort. "She scared herself silly."

"The poor tree didn't have a chance," said Rennan. "It just exploded. And remember the tree stump that flew into the air?" he grinned at the others. "*That* one scared the Warlocks."

"Well, that was an accident, too. We didn't know it would happen," Shaeli protested.

"Did you really set a tree on fire?" asked Reneesha.

"Yes, Neesha," she said. "But I didn't mean to."

"But *how* did you, Shaeli?" prodded Tarkoda.

"She was practising the lights one afternoon," began Kirrit. "Like she said."

"Lights?" asked Andos.

"From her fingers," said Bic, who leant against the rail with Jezzyn. "That's what she made with the first magic she learned."

"Show them, Shaeli," urged Jezzyn.

"Alright," she said and held out her hands.

Shanna cried out in amazement as the little light shot from the end of Shaeli's fingers. The spark of light rolled in the air for a moment before winking out, and Neesha looked up at her sister, awe-struck.

"How do you *do* that?" she breathed.

Shaeli smiled down at her. "I'm not sure," she said. "You just have to concentrate the right way. But I think it has to *be* there, *in* you, from the start."

Admiration shone like lamplight from both the twins' eyes — eyes which were not *quite* the same shade of green.

"So," continued Kirrit. "Shaeli was practising her lights, and Ishaan suggested she try an amplifier." She mentioned him with casual calculation.

"Who's *Ishaan?*" asked Tarkoda.

"Oh, a visitor," said Kirrit breezily, enjoying dangling the bait.

Andos and Tarkoda both stared open-mouthed and the others laughed anew. The twins stared up at them, looking from face to face.

"A visitor?" Andos took a nibble. "From where?"

"Nebillonia Straits," said Rhubic, taking a tug on Kirrit's well-baited line.

Not to be cheated of her prize, Kirrit reeled them in. "He fell at Shaeli's feet one night," she said. "He walked over the mountains and up the Valley of Stones, took one look at Shaeli and fainted."

This set up fresh waves of laughter, and fresh flushes of red into Shaeli's cheeks. She had known she would have to talk about Ishaan, though their last meeting burned in her memory as strongly as embarrassment now burned in her cheeks. To make it worse, Almarnoch had told no one but Sahli'en and Navez of Ishaan's visit to the Zoi cave, so, apart from them, Llevvis, Wyshka and Olver, nobody else knew of Ishaan's betrayal. They thought of him still as a friend, a welcome addition to their year, and she would have to let them think so, at least until Almarnoch had told Taffka and the Council and they decided what to do. Kirrit was still telling Tarkoda and Andos about Ishaan and the exploding tree when Jeth came over.

"We best go and see to the Zoi, lads," he said. "They must grow impatient for their own cave."

Tarkoda and Andos nodded and went with Jeth and Jarris down the stairs. Shaeli could see that Taffka and Rafi had already unharnessed Golden Eagle's birds, and her eyes met those of Almarnoch across the deck. He nodded imperceptibly, and her sudden panic was calmed. They had discussed the possibility of the Zoi sensing Ishaan's presence, and Almarnoch had told her that it was best not to worry over tezz that had not yet been spilled. It turned out to be good advice, for after the formal thanks from the traders and an extra scratch from Tarkoda, the Zoi flew to their cave and disappeared inside. Shaeli waited a few breathless moments, expecting them to reappear, panicked or enraged, but nothing happened.

Tarkoda and Andos called to her to come outside, for they wanted to hear more of Ishaan and Shaeli's magic. Shaeli ran over to Almarnoch.

"Can I show them a few beams and skylights, Almarnoch?" she asked.

"Yes, child," he nodded. "But out, over the edge of the terrace, where there can be no danger."

"I'll be careful," she said.

"I shall go with them," said Llevvis.

Almarnoch nodded and watched them hurry across the floor of the Cave. He could hear Neesha's voice, loudly asking if Shaeli could *really* make skylights like they did on Pa'laidiz, and Mareesha moved to his side and echoed the question. He briefly explained to a surprised Mareesha about Shaeli's power with stones.

"She has a gift, Mareesha," he said. "A wonderful gift, and it lies strongly within her. Even I am not sure of the depth of her magic." He watched the group disappear into the bolt tunnel as he spoke. "'Tis a special thing."

Mareesha was thoughtful for a moment before replying. Perhaps here was part of the reason for the change in her daughter.

"She is a special child, Almarnoch, and will carry it well," she said, at last.

"You speak with some bias," Almarnoch smiled. "Yet not wrongly. She has much to tell you of her year, I'm sure, and you will see she has grown wiser than her Winters."

"I have already seen something of that," Mareesha said. "But I'd like to hear more of her magic."

Almarnoch's smile broadened to take in Eenis, who stood nearby. "Shaeli has taken much pleasure in *your* gift, Eenis," he said.

"I'm glad of it," Eenis replied. "The old one was wearing thin, and she does dote on that amulet."

"'Tis one of the reasons her stones hold such strength." The old man's smile faded, and he spoke softly, his next words freezing the thin smile of Eenis' pleasure. "Her gift is much like elf-light, my child, though, of course without the power of the elves." He patted her hand. "I felt I should warn you, for her magic may be difficult for you to face. Her power is not without the potential for harm, yet I will guide her, and there shall be no danger to anyone, I promise you."

Almarnoch and Mareesha watched as Eenis struggled with this news. Her features tightened, the skin across her forehead puckered, her lips grew white. Then she shook her head, rubbed at the middle of her forehead, and looked back at them, forcing her lips to curve into the semblance of a smile.

"This time I know who *wields* the magic, Almarnoch," she said. "'Tis a member of my family, a loved one, not an enemy bent upon destruction. Since I lost Illen to the elves," she spat the word, stopped. Started again. "Since I lost Illen, I have had no other family but this, and I trust each of them, without question." She looked at Mareesha. "Have no doubt that I am frightened of this kind of magic, yet I know and trust the wielder." She smiled with more truth at the Warlock. "*And* her teacher. I shall endeavour to quiet my fear."

Mareesha hugged her, and Almarnoch smiled at them both and patted Eenis' shoulder.

"Bravely spoken, and you are right to trust our Shaeli, for she is worthy of it," he said. "And do not give up hope. It may be that you will see your sister again."

Eenis did not try to hide her disdain. "I have long given up hope of seeing Illen again. Those heartless elves would have returned her to me, if they had healed her as they claimed they could." She shook her head. One hair had escaped from the tightly drawn bun at her nape and waved about rebelliously. "No, Almarnoch. I believe that Illen died as a result of her ordeal, soon after she was taken from me at Noresh. Otherwise they would surely have sent word."

"Time does not run for elves as it does for us," Almarnoch said. "Do not cease to hope. Stranger things have happened."

"No, Almarnoch, I wish for no strange happenings," answered Eenis. "I pray we shall live quiet and ordinary lives. 'Tis best so."

"That may be," said Mareesha. "Yet the way things are in the World, I think we'll not have quiet times much longer." She sighed. "I fear greatly for Zirrus. So many people are unhappy."

"And rightly so," said Eenis. "Queen Virrisian is behaving appallingly."

"Are things so bad this year?" asked Almarnoch.

Mareesha nodded. "There have already been a few uprisings, though small and in isolated provinces. There are rumours of atrocities by the guard, of people disappearing, yet Taffka says people are still unwilling to talk openly of their grievances in Palveron or at Great Court, as you will no doubt hear from him this evening. I'm sure he'll speak to the Council of old ones after you light the fire-pits."

"I think I shall give that honour to Llevvis," said Almarnoch. "I am making him my second, and Garrit will go to the Bay of Islands with Taffka after the Wintering." He looked to where Dari and Garrit sat absorbed in conversation. "I have a mind to take on a new apprentice, Eenis. Shall I speak to Dari? I'm sure it would please him."

Her voiced groaned with the weight of resignation. Mareesha tried not to smile.

"I'm sure it will please him, too," Eenis sighed. "You know I would not choose for him to be a Warlock. I would much prefer he were a trader like his father and brother. Andos thankfully has no desire for anything other than the Fleet, yet Dari's heart is set upon magic, and even I can see he has some talent. He kept a vase of roses alive for almost a full Moon after they should have withered this spring. I shall speak to Jeth. If he must be apprenticed, I would rather it be to you, and here at Cave. As you knew I would." She smiled thinly at him. "You are a wise Warlock, Almarnoch, but you're also a very crafty old man."

Mareesha was astonished, but Almarnoch laughed out loud.

"You are right, child. I knew full well you would consent." His eyes twinkled. "I shall take good care of him, you know."

"I know, else I'd not leave him."

"And he will be thrilled, Eenis, you know he will," said Mareesha.

"Yes, I know that too," she said, shaking her head as if disagreeing with herself.

Almarnoch chuckled again. "He'll not be a famous Warlock, but a fair one, I think."

"If I cannot have him on the Trader, at least he shall be at Cave," Eenis said. She looked at Mareesha. "It seems we have a lot of magic in the family suddenly."

Mareesha smiled at her. "Indeed it does," she said. "Shall we go and see Shaeli's skylights?"

* * *

Dari and Garrit trailed the others outside to watch Shaeli's magic. The smile Dari had worn into Cave was gone, replaced with lowered brows and a tight mouth. Not only had his cousin robbed him of the only thing that made him special in the eyes of his family – again – but Garrit was leaving. They stood on the ledge together, looking down at the people gathered around Shaeli. Dari's arms were crossed tightly, his shoulders hunched. Garrit regarded him, one brow raised.

"They have all forgotten you again," he said. "But do not be disheartened. Her gift is of little consequence really. It is not on our level."

"Maybe," Dari said. "But they'll still make a fuss, and she'll love it."

"You're right. I have found she is interested in little apart from herself," said Garrit smoothly. "But you won't have to worry about her much longer. I suspect Almarnoch will take you for apprentice after I'm gone."

The tightness around Dari's mouth softened. "Do you think so?" he said.

"I do," Garrit nodded. "And in a few Winterings, well, who knows what will be." He looked from Dari back down at the group below. Shaeli had set off a purple skylight and they were all clapping. "Perhaps we shall meet in Palveron. I would be happy to greet an old friend." He glanced at Dari and then his eyes slid back down to settle on Shaeli.

***

That night, after Llevvis had proudly lit the fire-pits, and the first meal had been cooked and eaten beside them, the children were given leave to light all the lamps and candles. They took tapers and wandered in groups around the Cave, familiarising themselves with each light's whereabouts, for it was the responsibility of the children of Cave year to keep the lamps and candles lit throughout the frozen Moons.

Shanna and Neesha went with Shaeli and Kirrit, and they had no need of a taper, for they had Shaeli's magic, and they wandered around, searching for candelabra and hanging lamps. They lit the lamps at the bottoms of Landings, around the spring-pool, the huts of the old ones and the tunnel mouths, and then, with Llevvis, they went along the winding dark of the main tunnel. Shaeli sent short bursts of her quartz crystal ahead into the dark, and by the soft white glow it left hanging in the air, the lamps beside the spring-stream were set and lit, and would be kept burning throughout the night in case a Trader arrived. The spring stream reflected the soft cloud of Shaeli's magic, and the stronger, yellow flame of the lamps.

When they walked back through the bolt tunnel and emerged into the Cave, it was the shimmering fairyland they remembered from every other Wintering. Gone were the thick shadows that pooled around the fire-pits and the Landings, replaced with hundreds of tiny flames and coloured lamps.

"That's much better," said Neesha. "It was creepy before, wasn't it, Shanna?"

"A bit," Shanna replied. "But you're much more scared of the dark than me." She looked down at the blazing fire-pits surrounded by her family, the old ones and the gleam of candles. "It just looks more like home now."

Shaeli smiled down at her and agreed. Even the sound had changed. No longer was there an empty echo, muffled by vast space and blankets of shadow. The Cave murmured with voices, and even the spring stream seemed to speak with a merrier gurgle.

They joined the others, and Shaeli saw a cask of her mother's liqueur on one of the tables, and most of the old ones sipped upon it. Taffka also had a glass in his hand as they discussed events in the Lands. There would be more formal meetings when the whole Fleet arrived, but the old ones were eager to hear what unfolded at Great Court.

Golden Eagle spent most of each year at Palveron, organising shipments for other Traders and tending to the diplomatic side of their business. They made short trips around the Bay, or up the coast, and flew to the Faunist and Warlock Islands when they needed supplies, yet they never went far, for Taffka was called sporadically to Court.

Shaeli settled down beside her mother, who smiled and put an arm about her shoulders, and the twins sat at their feet, yawning occasionally and blinking like little owls as Taffka talked.

The queen was at last taking the advice of her ministers, he said, and appeared to have ceased her extravagant spending. Publicly she said she was finally happy with the appearance of her Court, and had no need for further renovations, but some thought the small uprisings on distant provinces and the tales of raiders on the roads had ruffled her. She had also announced there would be no further taxes for the next few Winterings, and the Land had breathed a sigh of relief. Taffka believed people would bide their time; wait and see if she kept her word. Respect for the throne was still prevalent, and though people were unhappy, they would give Queen Virrisian time to return them to former prosperity – yet he also spoke of rumours of burnings, of families being forced from ancestral homes; there were even whispers of murders by the guard. They were everywhere now, Taffka said, and their pride knew no bounds.

Shaeli sat letting the words wash over her. She heard what was said, but paid little notice. She was unconcerned with politics; things merely went on as always, the cycle of the year, the Wintering, travelling the Lands.

That night she slept aboard Purple Leaf again, on a mattress between the twins' beds, for they had refused to let her out of their sight. They chattered sleepily, telling her of their own year, and she lay contentedly listening to them, marvelling at the feel of the Trader about her, the pull of the balloon above, the almost imperceptible movement. At last, she bade them sleep, and Shanna quickly succumbed, but Neesha kept remembering something she just had to say.

"We saw acrobats at Marnissi."

"That would have been fun. Go to sleep."

Yawn. Pause. "We got sick after."

"Oh, that's no good. Have lovely dreams."

"I will." Pause. "It was from too many cream-cakes, Mam said."

"What was?"

"The sick."

"Oh, I see. Go to sleep."

"Alright."

Another pause. Another yawn. "We patted a jevvi on Ashkanna."

"How lovely. I like jevvies. Go to sleep now."

Longer pause. "Its name was Minti. It was white."

"That's nice. Sweet dreams."

A long yawn. A longer pause. "It was the princess'. Did I tell you about her?"

"Yes, Neesha. You told me you saw Princess Crissita. Now go to sleep."

"Alright," she murmured. "Koda's going to stay with them next Wintering."

"Tarkoda is?" Shaeli asked. "Why?"

But Neesha had finally gone to sleep, leaving the question hanging in the air.

* * *

Shaeli repeated the question to Tarkoda himself the next morning. He and Andos were sweeping out the Zoi space under the Trader.

"Prince Davron has offered to let me study with his paladin," he said.

Shaeli stared blankly. "Sorry?"

"His personal guard, Shaeli," said Andos.

"Oh," she nodded. "His paladin, of course." She nodded again, then shook her head, still confused. "Why would he do that?"

Koda shrugged. "I guess he took a bit of a shine to me."

Andos chuckled. "So did his daughter."

"Rubbish, Andos," protested Tarkoda, a little too quickly, his cheeks flushing. "Princess Crissita was just friendly, that's all."

Andos guffawed, and affected a high-pitched voice. "Oh, Tarkoda, would you carry my umbrella? Can I lean on your arm, you're *so* strong." He fluttered his eyelashes comically and danced away from Tarkoda's swinging broom, laughing.

"Well, don't expect it to last," said Shaeli, cynically. "She liked me once, for about half a moment."

"It doesn't matter," said Tarkoda, the red fading to the tips of his ears. "I'm there to study, and it's said Malikk is one of the best masters-at-arms in Four Lands."

"Just look out for those eyelashes," said Andos. "They flutter fast enough to blow a Trader to Wokk. Crissita's, not Malikk's. He looks like a boulder with eyes."

Shaeli giggled, but she remembered the way Tarkoda had looked at Crissita when they were children, the same way he'd looked at the knife on Wokk; the knife that was now his most precious possession.

"And the year after we're taking her to Romynn," Tarkoda added, far too casually.

"We're *what?*" Shaeli sputtered.

"Taking. Her. To. Romynn." Tarkoda spoke a word at a time, as if to a simpleton. "On the Trader."

"We're *not.*"

"Yes, Shaeli, we are," Andos answered. He studied her face. "You look like a bug with your eyes bulging like that."

Shaeli tried to make her eyes stop bulging. "Since when do we take passengers?"

"Since Da said we would," Tarkoda shrugged. "I guess in repayment for my training. Prince Davron would take no coin."

"Well, he hardly has need of coin, Koda," said Andos. "Yet a secure way of taking his daughter to Romynn is not so easy to come by. I think he has made a good bargain."

"I agree," said Shaeli. "But the gods only know how we shall manage with *that* one on board."

* * *

As Shaeli slept that first night with her family on Purple Leaf, a broken Trader slept on the ocean floor far to the south, the bodies of the still-harnessed Zoi floating in the current amid the remains of ropes and balloon. Little remained on the surface to mark its passing; a scrap of yellow material; a basket or two; the body of a woman, her belly swollen with child, her nightgown floating around her ankles, small fish already nibbling at her pale toes.

They had left Wokk a few hours before sunset for the trip home. Besca was looking forward to seeing her son after his Cave year, and they would fly through the night and see Zirrus on the horizon by morning, but they were going to fly over the island of the Qotarr before dark. She had three other sons beside the lad at Cave; the youngest, eleven-Winters Tam, and two others in their twenties – the eldest just married last spring and already his new wife was expecting their first child – and they were all eager for a sight of the giant lizards before they left Wokk.

They flew low along the coastline of the island, her husband, Vikram, circling the heads of several of the beasts they found trundling along beside the water. The sun was setting as they rounded the point of the last beach, the sky the colour of oranges.

On the beach below lay the body of a Qotarr. She wasn't dead yet, but she was groaning and her tail writhed on the sand. A huge hole, still smoking, lay under the spines on one side, entrails spilling from the wound. Other wounds were scattered along her back and sides.

Nearby, a baby Qotarr was surrounded by men with spears. It was squealing in fear, and every time it squealed its mother would try to raise herself, the wound in her side oozing blood as her life drained into the sand. The men were herding the baby towards the water where a flat barge waited. A squat ship was anchored in the bay.

Standing on a rise near the dying mother stood a tall man, a twisted staff in his hand, the stone at its tip glowing blood red in the dying sun. The Warlock looked at the Trader as they flew over, then he turned and vanished into the jungle behind the beach.

Besca met her husband's eye and saw the worry reflected there. A strange and horrible sight indeed. Vikram flicked the lead lines and the Zoi pulled them higher and out across the sea.

Later, after they'd had their meal, Besca went up to find Tam. He was, just as she had thought, with his father on the fore-deck; the others were downstairs, ready to sleep for a while until it was time to take over from their father. She took the hand of the reluctant Tam, kissed Vikram, and went down the stairs.

Something caught her eye as they reached the deck, a strange flicker of light, and she squinted into the southern sky. She saw it again, that odd light, and she called up to her husband. Vikram peered into the night, then Besca screamed as they were suddenly flooded in red light. Something approached at frightening speed, there was a whooshing sound and then all around her was on fire.

The Trader slumped in the sky and scraps of burning balloon rained down upon Tam and Besca, and as Besca understood that the balloon was shattered, the red light came again and the back of the ship exploded. Chunks of wood flew through the air and the rear of the ship was aflame, red tongues licking up the lines of rope. Besca looked up, and Vikram glanced back at her for a moment before he turned forward again, a knife in his hand. She screamed down the stairwell to her sons, gripped Tam's hand tighter, and dragged him over to the gate. As she unlatched it, there was a sensation of something rushing past, some huge thing flying at impossible speed, and as it passed she thought she saw a glimpse of a pale face looking back at her. A moment later the red light came again. Besca looked up at Vikram once more, and then she dragged Tam over the side as another boom shattered the far side of the ship.

The water came up and hit them more quickly than she expected; the Trader had fallen much further than she'd realised, and when they came up she checked Tam, said something to try and calm him, she didn't know what, and then she turned to watch the Trader hit the water.

It thudded into the sea, a flaming wreck, holed rear and side, the balloon in fiery pieces falling on top of it. Besca heard the hiss as the flames were doused by the sea, and she screamed the names of her children and her husband as the water gurgled in and sucked the ship down hungrily. The cries of the Zoi echoed across the water, and the last sight Besca had of her husband was as the birds were dragged under. He had managed to free two Zoi, and they were circling in the smoke overhead, their beautiful voices sharp with fear, but Vikram was still cutting desperately at the lines which held the other birds to the ship as the Trader was consumed. Of her sons, her new daughter-by-law, pregnant with her first grandchild, there was no sign.

It was gone too quickly. The black waves swallowed it whole. The last Zoi screamed as it went under, and Besca screamed with it. The two remaining Zoi wheeled and screamed with her. The scream had barely died in her throat when a white light came on.

It flared on the water nearby, and as it came closer, Besca again *felt* more than saw the thing that had destroyed her family. She tugged at Tam, pulling him through the water, away from the light, but it came closer and closer until its eye shone upon them. The light changed and began to pulse around them, purple and black, and Tam screeched as their bodies began to lift from the waves. Somehow they were drawn up, out of the water, their feet dripping as they left the waves, Tam's brown irises showing white all the way round as they were drawn up and up, into the light. Besca held him to her, struggling in the grip of this unseen thing, but it was useless. The waves grew further and further away and the light grew brighter, pulsing faster as they were sucked higher. Something closed around them and Besca looked up, Tam a quivering mess clutched to her breast. A shadow moved beneath them, mother and son hung in the air for a moment before the light went out and they fell onto cold metal. Weak red light filtered down.

They were surrounded by figures as squat as gargoyles, shoulders hunched, arms gripping their chairs, huge unnatural eyes staring blankly. A harsh voice began to laugh. Tam grew limp in her arms and Besca began to scream.

***

CHAPTER THIRTY ONE

Two things marred the Wintering after Shaeli's Cave year. The first was the dreaded interview with the Council about Ishaan. It turned out to be only the core of the Council, her father included, and privately done on Golden Eagle, and not *quite* as dreadful as she'd predicted. Still it was hard, answering the questions of the stern-faced men and women. Wyshka had insisted on coming, Almarnoch had been there too, and both attempted to soften the effect on Shaeli, but it was only after an agonising length of time, more than a few tears, and her continued belief that Ishaan had spoken true when he declared he had not touched anything, that they had finally let her go. They had decided that as there had been no ill-effects to the Zoi, they would leave the matter as it was, and the betrayal was not spoken of among the Fleet. Taffka thought it best to leave the Zoi cave as it had always been to the Traders: sacred and untouched. Lunn of Sky Lark was the only one who had disagreed, and he had left the meeting, enraged.

Drained of all feeling she had gone home and recited the tale to Mareesha, heard the loudness of her dismay in the long silence that followed, and then the arms of comfort around her. It had not seemed so bad after that, the silence had been half of the burden.

As awful as that ordeal had been, the second thing was much more terrible. Within ten days of Golden Eagle and Purple Leaf's arrival, all the other Traders had reached Cave. All except Yellow Star – Bic's Trader.

Fruitlessly they searched the sky as the Wintering drew its blanket over the World. Bic was outside every waking moment, his eyes fixed to the Valley of Stones, the children of his Cave year keeping him company in his vigil, and Bic continually asked Shaeli if she could smell first snow. Long after she first smelt the tang of snow the time came when she had to admit to him that she could, and he turned from the ledge, his shoulders drawn tightly, his face ashen.

The next afternoon, two Zoi flew up onto the Lea. They were grey, their feathers patched and filthy, their shoulders drooping from effort. They still wore their harnesses. The ropes had been cut raggedly, and Bic helped with the harnesses, stoically brushed the grime from their feathers, and when they had flown to their cave he went to his bed and would speak to no one. The day after, the snow came in force. It began as thick rain, forcing the watchers to withdraw back into the tunnel mouth. The sky went a sickly shade of yellow-green and the rain turned to hail that fell like gravel. Bic moaned, turned and stumbled into the tunnel, Jezzyn and Kirrit following. Shaeli buried her head in Rennan's shoulder.

Most of the Fleet gathered at the tunnel mouth, watching the hail turn to sleet and then driving snow. Of Yellow Star reaching Cave now, there was no hope. Of their other Zoi surviving outside the Cave for the Wintering, there was also none. The slim chance that the traders themselves would return, that their ship was intact somewhere, kept words of hope on some lips. Yet many walked back to Cave with tears clouding their vision.

The Wintering passed sombrely. The next year Bic was taken aboard White Star with his cousin, Jezzyn, still hoping his parents and brothers would return, but no word was ever heard from them, though every Trader inquired for them, wherever they went.

By the next Wintering the whole Fleet knew they would never see those of Yellow Star again. The last sighting of them had been as they left Wokk, half a Moon before the Wintering, plenty of time for them to fly home. It was generally thought they had encountered a storm during the crossing, and lightning had penetrated the Lift spell's protection.

Shaeli missed Tarkoda during that long Wintering – they all did – and wondered how he fared in Prince Davron's palace on Ashkanna, and whether he enjoyed training with the paladin. Yet it was a busy Winter; the skeleton of a new Trader was begun, and a new hut built to add to those of the old ones. When first thaw came they flew to Djelda and made ready for the arrival of the princess.

Tarkoda arrived swiftly, almost as soon as they moored, and he was greeted enthusiastically, a little taller, his hair longer, his shoulders broader. He informed them that the princess would come aboard next morning with her maid and wished to leave as soon as possible.

There had been much deliberation over where the princess should sleep while she was aboard. Dari was at Cave, so Andos and Tarkoda were going to put bed-rolls in the forward storage area at the turn of the stairs and give the princess their room, but Eenis declared it improper that such a lady should sleep next to the privy, so the twins were to be moved over there and the princess and her maid would occupy their room next the big room. This had initially been Tarkoda's room, but as the girls had grown, and Dari was so often away from the Trader, Koda had moved in with Andos and the girls had inherited his room – until now. Shaeli, faintly disapproving of all the fuss, was glad her room was too small to be bothered with.

Princess Crissita swept aboard next morning, a riot of bags and servants and confusion. Shaeli was sure the mound of suitcases could hold an entire lifetime of clothes – linen included.

Crissita stood amongst the chaos, directing the footmen with her luggage, declaring how exciting it all was and loudly enquiring about her room. Every now and then she would kiss the air next to her father's cheek, saying each time how much she would miss him.

Her maid, a sparrow of a woman who Shaeli judged to be not much older than the princess, shadowed Crissita's every move. She scuttled about, repeating everything Crissita said, just to make sure everyone heard, even telling Prince Davron how much her Lady would miss him, in case he hadn't been paying attention.

At last the baggage was stowed in any spare space available. Tarkoda had kept loading things into the storeroom at the turn of the stairs, saying, "we'll be right" every time someone reminded him to leave room for their bed-rolls. Shaeli thought she would be sick at the look on his face.

Crissita ordered him about, asking his advice and putting a gloved hand on his arm in such a familiar way that Shaeli made gagging motions to Andos behind their backs. He grinned, and fluttered his eyelashes. Shaeli giggled. She could see what he meant; the things fluttered like flies caught in a spider's web, except *she's* the spider, Shaeli thought, and Koda's the fly, and she could see that he was stuck fast in the princess' pretty web, for Crissita *was* beautiful, anyone could see it. The passing Winters had only enhanced the loveliness of the child, her wide blue eyes sparkled, her flawless skin covered cheekbones any girl would envy, her thickly curling blonde hair hung to her thighs and was braided with tiny crystals. The gown she wore was deep blue, cut to show her obvious advantages, and the skirt shimmered as she walked. At nineteen, Crissita was two Winters older than Shaeli, and exuded elegance more strongly than Shaeli could if she lived to be two hundred. Yes, anyone could see the Princess was beautiful, but Shaeli could only remember the cruel snub and the spiteful giggles of many Winters' before. She had not forgiven Crissita for being her friend and then wounding her the next time they'd met, yet she hid it well and was polite when the princess greeted her like an old friend, linking her arm through Shaeli's and declaring loudly what fun they should have together. She fawned over the wide-eyed twins and called them "adorable moppets", and Shaeli thought that twelve was far too old to be a "moppet", but the girls didn't seem to mind, so she smiled and extricated herself from the princess, who did not notice, and went to help the sparrow down the stairs with a particularly large bundle. The sparrow's name was S'resh, and Shaeli stifled her laughter when S'resh told her that the large bundle contained the princess' linen.

When they returned to the deck, it seemed at last they were ready. Crissita hugged Prince Davron and walked with him to the stairs, he trying his best to look moved by the occasion, and she stood at the rail as they lifted, waving her handkerchief and calling farewells. Before they had even left the square, she turned away.

"Thank the gods for that," she said. "I couldn't wait to get away from the old bore and this dreary town."

S'resh tut-tutted, and turned to watch Djelda drift past. Shaeli shook her head and went downstairs.

* * *

They flew back across Nebillonia Straits, the princess going below, complaining of the wind and the constant movement. First, though, she had asked Tarkoda was there not something that he could *do* about it. Tarkoda looked taken aback for a moment, and then apologised that no, he could do nothing. Shaeli had sweetly added that Traders, by definition, entailed wind and movement, and Koda gave Shaeli a stern look and escorted Crissita downstairs, followed closely by the scuttling sparrow-woman, S'resh.

Shaeli stayed on deck, watching the approaching mountain range, the enormous shafts of rock studding the shoreline of Zirrus, and the widening gap that was Meoro Pass. They spent the night at Meoro Village and next day they flew up the Pass, yet Crissita stayed in her room, still complaining of the movement, and she remained there for the next few days. She had S'resh scurrying about for water and pillows, making her favourite delicacies which she promptly vowed she could not eat. She tried very hard to retch – everyone heard her – and she grew petulant. They all heard that, too, and even

Koda ceased making excuses for her. She made a brief appearance at Zerrin Crossing, saying she wished to see the river that flowed from the great mountain, yet upon the appearance of the fat, lecherous Savic, whose girth swung even more pendulously than before, she had quickly retired downstairs again. Shaeli had to agree with Crissita on that one. The man was truly revolting and had taken to wearing gaudy rings on fingers like sausages.

As the days passed, Shaeli helped Eenis with the twins' lessons, taking them up on deck and listening to them read, going through the history of the Lands or devising sums for them. They had both grown a head taller since Shaeli's Cave year, and at twelve had begun to lose their babyish faces. Neesha was a little taller than her sister, her hair thick and brown, her brows black and straight, her eyes cool green. She was still boisterous, showy, and had developed an absolutely wicked sense of humour. She had trouble staying clean, her hair often resembled a bird's nest, and she found it almost impossible to speak quietly, let alone whisper. She was stubborn, had the chin to prove it, and yet still looked to her sister for emotional protection.

Shanna was happy to provide it. She was a born mother, often bringing home birds and small creatures for her mother to heal. She gave sweets and fruit to ragged children, wheedling them out of Eenis somehow, and she directed Neesha with unflinching authority. After their adventure on the barrel at Orrellis, Neesha had conceded to Shanna's more highly developed sense of survival, and looked to her to define the limits of safety. Shanna spoke quietly and never unnecessarily, but her sense of humour, dry as dust, often caused her family to collapse with laughter. She would watch them, eyes as green as wet moss, black brows riding high like twin arches, mouth tightly clamped upon her own laughter, innocently asking what was so funny. Her hair, straighter and finer than Reneesha's, was long and of a darker, richer brown, and she wore it in a single plait, often braided with ribbons. She was soft girl, loved pretty things and she always looked neat and fresh, while Neesha had difficulty staying clean and unrumpled even while sitting still. Mareesha was forever tugging at Neesha, smoothing her hair and tucking her clothes back in. Neesha did not notice what she wore; she had no dress sense, nor any desire to find some. Shanna was always immaculate; she studied stylish, well-dressed women, and wanted to make her own clothes. Eenis was thrilled, for at last she had found someone who shared her passion for sewing, and soon she was even letting Shanna help with some of the stitching on her tapestries. Eenis said she had such a neat, even stitch.

When they left Cronnus Landing early one morning, following the River Armez to Lake Marnis, Shaeli took the girls up to sit in the sun to read. As they were finishing, Crissita and S'resh came up on deck, the little maid's arms full of cushions and rugs. Crissita directed her to set them up against the rail and then noticed the sisters sitting opposite. Shaeli had promised herself she would make an effort to be pleasant, so she pulled on a smile.

"Good morning. I'm glad you're feeling better today," she called.

Crissita walked over. "Well, I'm not really," she sighed. "I just had to get out of that tiny, stuffy room." Shaeli clung to her smile as Crissita called over her shoulder to the sparrow. "Bring those things over here. I shall sit with the sisters." She turned back to Shaeli. "You don't mind do you?" the princess asked, her voice warm honey.

"Of course not," said Shaeli, striving for a tone equally as sweet. "We were just finishing lessons, weren't we?"

The twins nodded, smiling at the princess as S'resh picked up the recently arranged cushions, and carried them over. She dropped one as she came and Shanna ran over to help. Crissita didn't budge until S'resh had the cushions arranged, and then she lowered herself onto them. She delicately lifted a nostril.

"What *is* that terrible smell?" she asked.

Shaeli looked about. "Probably just the chickens," she said.

"Oh, how *revolting* to have them so near," Crissita said. "Smelly, noisy creatures." She shuddered theatrically, and Shaeli saw the look of affront on the twins' faces.

The chickens were their pets. They loved each one, and had given them all names, even the ones they knew they'd end up eating. They called the ones destined for the pot things like Soopy, Stewie, or Py, and they had one at the moment called Squish, because Mareesha said she'd probably make rissoles out of him.

Neesha was glaring openly at the princess, and Shanna's lips were tightly pursed. Shaeli sought to distract them from Crissita's snub.

"How about a few skylights?" she asked, and they nodded eagerly.

Over the last two Winters, Shaeli had begun to master the art of her lights. She could produce skylights from both hands, sending out the magic as harmless light which exploded at her chosen distance. She could create a few colours, depending on which stone she used, or have them meld to produce more colours. She was now proficient with the little light balls, but she wondered constantly how shapes were made or changed. As Almarnoch had predicted, there was not much need for the stronger version of her magic, though last Winter, she *had* been useful in clearing the tunnel mouth of debris after a small landslide, lifting rocks and pieces of smashed tree with her purple-black rock and dropping them off the edge.

They moved to the rail and Shaeli pulled two stones from the amulet; the amethyst and the purple-black stone. Crissita frowned.

"What are you doing?" she asked.

"Shaeli makes skylights," answered Neesha shortly, and she turned away. Anyone who didn't like chickens was no friend of hers.

Shaeli suppressed a smile and aimed out over the rail. The little lights shot from the stones in her fingers and exploded, falling quickly behind in the slipstream. The left-over sparks drifted in the breeze, and the twins laughed and begged her to do it again.

"Look, my lady," said S'resh. "Isn't that clever?"

Crissita stood and watched for a moment. "Yes," she yawned. "I suppose it is." She leant against the rail, watching as Shaeli made light after light. "I do like skylights," Crissita said at last, turning away and settling herself back down on the cushions. She leant back, and closed her eyes. "When they're done *well*," she added.

Neesha rolled her eyes at Shaeli, who shook her head in disgust at the veiled insult, and then the three did their best to ignore the yawning princess.

Crissita sighed and spoke loudly to S'resh. She yawned and stretched and fidgeted, and finally Neesha's lesser nature got the better of her.

"I'm amazed that you're so tired, princess," she said, looking over her shoulder and smiling sweetly. "How many days have you been in bed? Three or four?"

Crissita flared her nostrils. S'resh looked nervous.

"You wouldn't understand, child," she said, her tone implying that *child* was on par with *rodent*. "It is not tiredness that causes me to yawn, but tedium."

Neesha's smile froze at the foreign word. Her sister leapt to her rescue.

"The best cure for *tedium*," Shanna said softly, "is to get up off one's bottom and *do* something." She smiled her loveliest smile. "That's what Mam always says."

Shaeli choked back her laughter, and the three returned to their skylights, grinning at each other.

Crissita was not amused. She glared at their backs, but only S'resh was watching, so she soon stopped. She sat thinking, looking at the sisters giggling so intimately together. She was not used to being unnoticed. She motioned to S'resh, whispered in her ear, and the little woman went scurrying away down the stairs.

S'resh came back with a covered basket under her arm which she placed beside her mistress. Shaeli heard a vaguely familiar noise and turned around. On Crissita's lap sat a tiny jevvi, chittering and reaching up with one little hand, and Crissita looked over and stroked the creature invitingly, one eyebrow arched. It was too much for the twins to resist. They immediately abandoned the skylights and went to coo over the jevvi. Crissita smiled smugly over their bent heads at Shaeli, who also gave in to temptation. She knelt down and put a hand out to the little creature.

It was only a baby, and its mother popped her white head out of the basket. She checked the whereabouts of the baby, and then leapt out to sit quietly in Crissita's lap. The princess stroked the bigger jevvi and smiled.

"Is that Snowflake?" asked Shaeli, remembering Crissita's white jevvi from when they were children.

Crissita shook her head. "Minti," she said. "Snowflake's daughter. She's a present for someone on Romynn. My other jevvi are to be sent over by sea."

"We saw Minti on Ashkanna, Shaeli," said Neesha. "When you were having Cave year."

Shaeli nodded, and stroked the baby, its fur soft as velvet. It was not white like its mother, its belly, ears, and the tip of its fluffy tail were white as summer cloud, but the rest was shades of brown, like leaves on a forest floor. It had deeper, almost black patches around its eyes, huge dark orbs. Its bony hands were smaller than a fingernail, its pointed white ears covered with long fine hair. It fixed its ebony eye on Shaeli, smelt her finger with its little snub nose and promptly clambered up her arm and nestled in her hair, its long, fluffy tail hanging down like a ponytail that had been dipped in white paint. It snickered against her neck, nosed at her ear, and peeked out at the twins from under her hair. It was positively gorgeous, and the three of them sat in adoration.

Crissita became happy, and chatted amiably with them. She let the twins hold first the mother, and then the baby, and let them feed the baby small pieces of dried fruit that S'resh pulled from her voluminous pockets. The girls laughed, and appeared to forgive Crissita for denigrating their chickens and Shaeli's skylights.

Shaeli realised that Crissita *was* bored, and saw that the Trader must hold little for her to do. The princess was not really that bad, just spoilt and self-absorbed. She genuinely loved the little jevvies, and showed her generous side by giving each of the twins one of the many bangles from her arms. They all relaxed, and soon were chatting quietly and laughing together over the antics of the baby jevvi and her mother.

A kind of tentative truce was formed. Decisions were made. The three trader girls decided to accept the outsiders. Crissita decided that the trader children were rather sweet, after all. And S'resh decided that she was relieved.

* * *

They spent that afternoon at the square in Cransbey. Mareesha found many in need of Faunist treatment, and Eenis did brisk trade, much to her delight. Crissita watched with interest, and when they left it seemed that at last she was used to flying, for she ate a hearty meal and played a game with the twins and Tarkoda afterwards.

They moored late that night, and when Shaeli woke next day she looked out the tiny window. The scenery was vaguely familiar, Lake Marnis lay down a slight slope, the water fuzzy with the early morning haze, and then she remembered. It had been here that she had found her wand.

She dressed quickly, grabbed some fruit from the kitchen, and flew down the stairs of the scruffy Landing. She had long ago conquered her fear of the dreaded gap, and had learned to control the instant nausea that assailed her every time she was unfortunate enough to be somewhere high.

She ate her fruit as she walked along the shoreline, and when she found the little creek, it was just as tangled as she remembered, but the tunnel around the creek was so small she would have had to nearly crawl through it. She squatted down and peered into the dimness, squinting through her memory, amazed that she had been brave enough to go in, shaking her head at herself fighting off the jenka. Trying to find the place where she had found the wand would be impossible. The passing of twelve Winters would have rearranged the creek, and she guessed it had been rather silly to try. And what was the point? Stare at the bank for sentimental reasons? She shook her head again, and began to walk back, then broke into a run when she heard a shrill whistle: Tarkoda calling for her.

As Purple Leaf came into sight, she saw Koda on the foredeck with Crissita beside him – very close beside him. She waved at them as she ran along the thin strip of sand between the lake and the bank, and she slowed her pace a little. She put a foot up on the bank – and fell flat on her face. The clod on which she had placed her foot had broken away and she was pitched forward, falling face down, half on the bank, legs sprawled on the beach below. She clambered to her feet, heard Tarkoda and Crissita laughing faintly from above, and hoped they could see the tongue she poked out. She sat down in front of the bank where they could not see her. They could just wait while she checked her scraped shin.

What lay beside her foot took all thought of pain from her. Half buried in the fallen clod, just a stubby base showing, was what looked like a piece of quartz. She grabbed the clump of grass and released the stone from its dirt prison.

It was a wonderful find. A single, faceted piece of quartz, as long as her hand from fingertip to wrist, the width of her middle finger, and she ran down to the water's edge and washed the stone until all trace of dirt was gone. She held it up to the light, and saw it was not quite clear, but slightly smoky, and had what looked like fine hairs running through it. She turned and raced up to the Trader.

Tarkoda and Crissita stood just inside the rail.

"Good trip, Shaeli?" asked Koda.

Crissita tittered.

"Sure was," she grinned. "Look what I found." She held out her hand. "Would've missed it, but for the *trip*." So there, she thought.

Tarkoda took the quartz and whistled. "It's a beauty, Shaeli," he said. "Worth a bruise or two any day. Look." He held it out to Crissita.

Crissita took the quartz between long, slim fingers. Shaeli knew it was too much to expect them to be squat, plain hands.

"Lovely," said Crissita, handing it back.

Shaeli was unable to hide her short hands with the nails showing a generous amount of riverbank beneath them. They looked like jevvi hands beside the princess', but Crissita appeared to ignore them.

"You're very lucky. I think it's called fairy hair, the little bits inside," she explained. "Mother has a necklace full of stones like this."

"Fairy hair," repeated Shaeli. "It suits it. I'm going to show Mam, Eenis, and the girls," she said.

The girls were, as she thought, suitably impressed. Neesha wondered aloud if Shaeli would be able to make skylights with it.

"I've thought about that already," Shaeli said. "And I'm sure I could." She looked at Mareesha. "But I'll wait until we get back to Cave. I think it best that Almarnoch see it first, and be there when I try."

Mareesha smiled and nodded, and met the approving eyes of Eenis across the room.

They lifted soon after, and flew in small hops around Lake Marnis, visiting a few tiny villages before flying north across the water. A red sun went down behind the approaching city, and they flew on after dark towards the glittering lights of Marnissi, yet they did not fly to it, but straight past, to a small Landing which lay beside a village at the north-west edge of Lake Marnis.

M'Zen'sclahr Forest bordered the village on one side, the dark waters of the lake on the other, and a broad road edged its way around the perimeter of the lake running from the south into the foothills to the east, and on up to Conroi on the north coast. The forest was a silent mass, solid as a wall in the darkness of their landing.

M'Zen'sclahr Forest was fabled throughout the Four Lands and the Starisles, much discussed, seldom entered, subject of mysterious tales and shrouded in rumour. Even its name was the topic of conjecture, some believing it meant "mother of dreaming" in the old speech; others claimed it meant "dark clearing". Whatever its meaning, the name conjured up images of mystery, superstition, tales of strange lights, disappearances, and fierce creatures. It ran for leagues, vast and brooding.

To the north-east, beyond the border of the forest, were dry barren lands that stretched almost to the coast and across to the feet of the great mountain range. To the north-west, M'Zen'sclahr was bordered by steep ragged mountains that reached to the Estrellan Sea, the Drell Mountains, the ancestral home of the drell; mountains that were uninviting and largely unvisited, for strange creatures were said to roam there. To the west lay the Lakes country, and to the south the greatest lake of all, Marnis, crept almost to the roots of M'Zen'sclahr. Roads always edged the forest, never went through it, for inside the trees became impenetrable and resistant to the strongest axe.

Occasionally, some newcomer or traveller intent on felling a tree or hunting for their dinner would disappear inside the forest and the locals would nod and mumble knowingly under their breaths. Sometimes, and seemingly at random, the unfortunate person would reappear, days, Moons, or even seasons later, dazed and unsure of where they'd been, others lost their wits entirely, but most never walked in the World again.

Suffice to say that the children were interested in M'Zen'sclahr, and even Crissita's idle curiosity was roused. The twins were even more intrigued when Jarris told them next morning that this was where they had been born, here at this very Landing. The girls urged everyone to hurry, and after breakfast they went down to inspect the edges of the fabled forest, except Mareesha and Eenis, for the people of Zuen Village were already arriving for goods and Faunist services.

Zuen was an odd little village. Marnissi was close – you could see it far down on the curve of the lake – yet the inhabitants of Zuen seldom went there unless in dire need. When such a need arose, a Delegation was sent. The Delegation would gather whatever was required and return to Zuen immediately. They spoke with those in the city only as required, studiously studied the toes of their boots at all times, and they exchanged no pleasantries. They were pious, simple people, worked when the sun was up, slept when darkness came, ate four strict meals a day and never another bite. In the village square was an altar to the goddess Merrom, at whose feet a daily tribute of flowers was laid, and at any time – provided the sun was up – there was always at least one figure kneeling in prayer before the altar.

The inhabitants of the village regarded all those who resided in Marnissi as frivolous and sinful, along with anyone travelling the road. They knew any *decent* person would be at home working, and any traveller, whether they were heading to the city or away from it, must be on unwholesome business. The people of Zuen were not in the least discriminatory – they regarded everyone with equal suspicion and disdain.

They had no idea whatsoever that they were a source of amusement far and wide. If someone was reclusive, intolerant, or overly pious, people laughed and said they must have been born in Zuen. Their city neighbours chuckled at Zuen's sternness, shook their heads at the superstitions of the villagers, and made jokes at their expense. Perhaps, they said, it was having M'Zen'sclahr at their backs that made Zuen so odd. They sniggered under their worldly breaths, and looked down their noses at those from Zuen, which was a marvellous feat, as many Marnissi noses were permanently stuck in the air.

Marnissi considered itself a cultural icon, at the forefront of *anything* creative. It was filled with poets, artists, musicians, actors, and all their pretentious appendages. The taverns and restaurants along the waterfront never closed, there was always some gala, festival, or opening to attend, and though there were people *less* gaudy living in Marnissi, they were overshadowed by the cultured, fashionable set.

There was, too, a large contingent of health spas and plush retreats nestled in secluded coves along the lake for those weary of the World; scores of healers of dubious training offering obscure treatments or the secrets of youth; countless seekers looking for that intangible *thing* which would make their faces younger, their lives more complete. There were also many that preyed on the naive and gullible; pickpockets, drunkards, thieves – dirty faces with eyes hungry to find an easy way out, or up. Of all the cities on Zirrus, Marnissi partied hardest, had the most transient population, the most number of sudden marriages and unnatural deaths, and the most inflated collective ego. Queen Virrisian's guard had established a sizable barracks within the town, but in the last ten Winters,

Marnissi had become increasingly wild, and consequently more decadent in the eyes of Zuen.

Fortunately, the villagers of Zuen regarded traders as a class of their own; working and travelling with your home and family was acceptable, and if they were not exactly friendly neither were they unpleasant. The Landing was separated from the village by a wide strip of land, but there were nods and even a few smiles from the villagers who had come to trade as they made their way to the edge of the Forest, but Crissita was the recipient of many dark looks; her filmy gown was decidedly too revealing.

Crissita ignored them, her eyes on M'Zen'sclahr as they reached the first trees, a common enough variety, but beyond they could see the trunks of the huge trees which grew nowhere else in the World, except for a copse on the Island of Dead Kings. The trees were thick-trunked, their branches spreading high above and intertwining with their neighbours, creating a canopy of deep green. Here and there, the morning sun found a gap and beamed its way through to the forest floor, splashing gold onto the myriad of brown.

They were quiet for a long time, peering between the trunks, trying to see as far in as they could, then they strolled beneath the common trees on the sponge-thick grass, the darkness of M'Zen'sclahr on their right, sunshine on their left.

They rounded a bend, and before them was a tiny clearing, the sun bright upon the grass and the tiny flowers that dotted it. The twins immediately began to gather the tiny blue and pink flowers to take back to Mareesha, and the others sat down in the dappled shade. Tarkoda and Andos sprawled on the grass, Jarris and Jeth leaned against a tree, and after some hesitation and the laying down of a voluminous handkerchief, Crissita, too, sat down. S'resh hovered nearby, looking almost happy. After a moment she whispered to Crissita, who nodded, and S'resh knelt and unslung a pouch from her back. Minti appeared, her brown baby clinging tightly to her back, and

S'resh took a band from one of her pockets and slipped it over Minti's head. There was a fine chain attached to it, and Minti began to wander about, looking around and sniffing delicately at the air, huge eyes searching her surroundings.

The baby mimicked her, tiny nose lifted to the sky, poking this way and that, and then suddenly she leapt from her mother's back and dashed across to where Shaeli lay in the sun, close to the edge of M'Zen'sclahr. She leapt upon Shaeli's chest and nuzzled her cheek, and Shaeli laughed, picked her up and scratched behind the silken ears, then she rolled over and put her down.

"Back to your mam, now," she said and the baby cocked her head, chittered, and then bounded back to her mother. Minti's eyes had not left her baby, but she appeared unperturbed by its roaming.

The twins, arms laden with the sweet-smelling blossoms, lay their bouquets beside Jarris and sat near Minti, watching the antics of the two jevvies. Every now and then, the brown baby would run over to Shaeli, nuzzle her hand or cheek, or look deeply into her eyes before running back to play.

Shaeli stretched, sat up, and looked into the forest. She could not see far, the trunks became too dense, and an odd silence rolled from its depths. She looked the other way, across the meadow and the road to Marnis. The lake's surface was ruffled by a breeze, birds searched the waves for food, their cries echoing through the sunny morning, and she looked back at M'Zen'sclahr. No bird or animal called there, nothing moved between the trees, but in the shadows farther in, mist thick as cloud hovered about the trunks. She looked up into the links of branches, the leaves a shade of green belonging more to rich velvet or gemstones than leaves. The trees were still, no breeze moved the emerald leaves, yet she could hear a slight whispering, as if the touching branches spoke to each other. She stood and wandered around the edge of the little glade, keeping close by the forest, scanning for movement. When she found it, she could barely believe what her eyes told her. She focused on the flitter of movement inside the forest, amazed.

There was a tree, almost at the edge of view, in the dappled shadows where the drifts of mist began. It was smaller than the others, half the size of those nearby, its top branches just touching the canopy above, and around the unnaturally green leaves she could see fairies. Not just a few, but dozens flittered between the branches, and within the branches was the cluster itself.

She had heard of fairy clusters, most grownups had seen one or two, but of everyone she knew, only her mother and the other Faunists had ever seen a cluster up close, for there was one on the Faunist Island. She could barely believe what she was seeing.

The fairies fluttered about the cluster, wings as transparent and colourful as soap bubbles, soft clothes drifting in pastel shades or the colours of the forest, white limbs stretched lithely. They gathered around one long branch, and after a moment, Shaeli could see what they were doing. They were pulling soft, young branches together, and weaving them to create a hollow ball of living tree. More fairies came drifting through the trees, feathers and down carried amongst them, little particles of glittering light left in their wakes.

She looked behind her, caught Jarris' eye and motioned to him. He stood and she put her finger to her lips, pointed at the others, and into the trees. He understood, and soon they were all standing beside Shaeli, staring as if hypnotised into the forest, watching as the fairies built a room to add to their cluster. They appeared unaware, or at least unconcerned, by the people standing outside the forest watching them.

Crissita stood beside Shaeli. Shaeli looked at her, and Crissita smiled, her face pink with excitement, her blue eyes shining. Shaeli's returning smile faded a little as she saw Tarkoda's eyes on Crissita as much as the fairies, the enchantment of both equal.

S'resh stood slightly behind, and she gathered Minti and put her back in the pouch, but the baby evaded her and dashed over to Shaeli, put her hands on Shaeli's skirts and scrambled up, the little knuckles thick like those of an old woman. Shaeli motioned to S'resh that the baby was fine as she curled up in the crook of her arm and closed her eyes. S'resh smiled shyly, and then looked back at the cluster, her face going slack with wonder.

At last Jarris whispered they must leave. The twins were dismayed.

"But Mam will be wondering," he said.

"Eenis will already have moved on from wondering to worrying," added Jeth with a chuckle, and they all turned reluctantly back to the clearing.

Shaeli lingered a moment as the others left the clearing, and she saw one lone fairy, sitting in the crook of a branch, just inside the edge of the forest. Its gown was soft grey, shot with hints of purple, and its wings opened and closed rhythmically as it watched Shaeli. Their eyes met, and incredibly, or it seemed incredible to Shaeli, the fairy raised an arm, waved to her and grinned before it darted back to the cluster. Shaeli stood a moment longer, and then she followed the others.

When they reached the sunshine, the twins voices rose with the excitement they had held in. They gushed over how lucky they were and how clever Shaeli was to find the cluster. They gathered their flowers and walked back along the edge of the forest, Shaeli still carrying the baby jevvi curled asleep in her arms.

Shanna and Neesha dashed up the stairs to tell Mareesha the news, and they all laughed when Eenis said she'd begun to worry because they'd been so long. They took Mareesha and Eenis to see the cluster next morning before they left Zuen and for days they talked of little else.

Shaeli did not see the grey-purple fairy again, though it saw her.

* * *

They flew down to Marnissi, where Crissita insisted on being escorted on a shopping expedition, for which Tarkoda readily volunteered. They returned after dark, Tarkoda's arms laden with packages, his eyes glazed, S'resh a dishevelled mess behind. Only Crissita was invigorated by the experience, and she delighted in showing off her purchases that night as they flew west. Surprisingly, she had bought gifts for everyone, and her smile grew wide with their thanks.

They flew around the edge of the forest, stopping in many towns to trade, paying for the privilege of landing, but the villages grew scarce as the neared the Drell Mountains and they headed back across to the Lakes country.

They flew past a vast tract of empty, barren ground on their way to the green plains around the lakes. A high ridge skirted this empty land, and within its boundary the earth appeared almost scorched; the Barren Lands, Jeth called them. Jarris told them in its centre lay the Poisoned Marshes, a place forsaken by all, filled with ugly creatures and deadly bogs. He said that as the Winterings passed, the Barren Lands grew less forbidding, and the marshes within them shrank also, but this was happening very slowly. He said something terrible must have happened there, long ago, to make the land so bad.

Across the lakes they flew and at last the coast came into sight. The weather grew warmer as summer approached and they swam in the cool waters of the Sea of Aa'liu as they travelled up the coastline.

As the days passed it became plain to everyone that Tarkoda was in love with the princess. He beamed when she was near, and she in turn blossomed in his presence. They were often seen sitting side by side with their shoulders almost touching, or leaning against the rail in earnest conversation. S'resh was usually nearby, discreet, but there, attending to some task or shyly asking Andos questions about the Trader, yet as Shaeli was returning from a swim one afternoon, she came upon her brother and the princess. They stood so close to each other that Shaeli could not see space between them, and Tarkoda was curling a lock of the princess' hair around one finger. If she had not seen the gentle touch or the naked emotion on her brother's face, the sudden leap from each other and the matching blushes would have alerted her to their feelings. Yet she pretended not to notice; she merely worried quietly, and watched.

They flew up the coast, the glittering waters on one side, low hills inland, to a little town on the tip of Zirrus where the Zoi would rest for a day or two before the long flight across the sea to Romynn.

Shaeli realised that the town was Trilby when they moored at the Landing in the square. Somewhere here was Ellirra – and the other dragon scale bangle – but she did not need a dream of Williver to tell her it was not time for the bangle, and she decided to forget it. Yet the next morning, Ellirra came to the market in the square, and when she saw the Trader she came up to see them, trailed by three shy, dark-eyed girls who she proudly introduced as her daughters. She was delighted to see them again, and Mareesha invited them to come back for dinner.

When they returned, the girls were prettily dressed, their hair elaborately braided, and Ellirra had a still-warm cake in her basket. Her tall husband, Iden, appeared much the same, his voice deeper, his beard longer, and he was obviously proud of his family. Shanna and Neesha showed the three girls around, and when Tarkoda and Andos took them to see the Zoi, Crissita and S'resh followed them down. Ellirra chattered just as she had so many Winters before, her dark eyes shining as she told them of their lives since they had shared stew in Meoro Pass. Shaeli sat curled in a chair listening to the talk around the table, and Ellirra even mentioned the bangle once, but only briefly. They had been discussing the state of the

Land, and it was the only time during the afternoon that Ellirra did not smile.

"Dark times indeed, just as the old king prophesied on his deathbed. I feel the time draws near when I must give up my treasures. There will be need of them, I feel. There is a drawing together of something, change must come. And things have been seen; strange things in the sky…"

"Hush, Ellirra," said Iden. "You should not speak of such things. And the king's prophesies were only Green Fever in his brain. They mean nothing."

"They *do* mean something, Iden," Ellirra replied, her eyes flashing. "I believe King Tenelon had a vision of the future, and his words were true. And I am not the only one."

"There was no child to *be* saved," said Iden. "Queen Irinesta, the gods protect her, was delivered of a stillborn child. It could never rule as Tenelon said." He spoke patiently, but wearily, as if they had had this conversation many times before. "It holds that all else was untrue. 'Twas just the Fever, Ellirra."

Ellirra's lips pursed stubbornly. "'Twas *not* Green Fever. It was a prophecy from the king." She closed her eyes and began to recite. "'Their time is short. They will not succeed. The child will rule. The birds will rescue them. Thrice will my child be saved by its sister.' These are the words spoken by the good King Tenelon, these and more."

Shaeli shivered as Ellirra spoke, and when she looked at her mother, her face was pale, too. She'd heard of Tenelon's prophecies, yet not what they had said. Most believed, as Iden did, that it had been only Green Fever. Ellirra continued to recite.

"'The others run with the wind. Metal birds seek them. The old one knows the way in. Seek for her on Xyros.'" She opened her eyes and looked at her embarrassed husband. "'The *child will rule*,' the king said. 'There will be light after the darkness.' Well, I say that times *are* dark, and metal birds *have* been seen, and *Traders* run with the wind, as well as thousands of ships." She flung an arm out and Shaeli saw Mareesha jump. "I don't know how, but I still believe."

"Hush, Ellirra. Hush," Iden implored.

But Jarris spoke quietly. "I, too, believe, Ellirra," he said. Iden looked at him incredulously. "Yet your husband is wise when he says you should not speak openly of such things. These *are* dark times. People are unhappy and suspicious." He looked at her, his voice low. "Never speak of what you call the metal birds. I believe to do so may invite danger to you all." Ellirra looked suddenly frightened, and Jarris sought to reassure her. "You have nothing to fear from us, yet in these times it is not wise to trust many, or speak too loudly, but I would know what you know, for I have seen this 'metal bird', also."

"*You* have?" she breathed.

He nodded. "Long ago. And I believe it may have destroyed one of our Traders two Winters ago."

Shaeli drew a breath. She knew he spoke of the "dragon" they had seen when she was young, yet she was horrified when she realised the Trader he meant was Yellow Star, Bic's Trader, lost over the Bastinian Ocean. Wokk was a long way from here, thousands of leagues to the south, but the faces of her family gave a dreadful weight to her father's words. There was none of her own surprise on their faces; Jeth, Eenis, her parents, all showed in their grimness that they had discussed this before. She listened as Ellirra told what she knew.

"Rumour only have I heard. A fisherman washed ashore down the coast reported his boat had been blasted with something like elf-light. It came from a craft which flew across the waters. It is said he thought at first it was a dragon, it swooped on them from such a great height, yet the moonlight glinted strangely upon it, as it does upon an old black pot." She laughed nervously. "That's what he said, so they say, 'an old black pot'. He was the only survivor of a crew of twelve, and this is the strangest part." She stopped and looked at Jarris. "It sounds laughable, even *I* know it, but he swears, so the rumour goes, that he saw a crewmate sucked out of the water and drawn into the belly of the beast before it flew off."

Jarris did not laugh. "Where is this man?"

Ellirra looked into her lap. "It is said that madness took him soon after, and he leapt off a cliff into the sea."

"You see?" said Iden, as if justified. "It is all rumour and ravings."

Yet Jarris shook his head, thinking of Gremon, the old soldier who had also gone mad after seeing such a thing. He looked at Iden.

"Not ravings or rumour, my friend. Something worse." He looked solemnly at Mareesha. "Something far worse."

***

CHAPTER THIRTY TWO

They left Trilby before dawn the next morning, and flew all day over the Sea of Aa'liu. It was very late in the afternoon when the green shores of Romynn suddenly loomed ahead, and they landed at a small town perched on the low neck of land that ran for leagues before spreading out into the body of the Land. Here there was still no Landing tax, and they rested the Zoi for a day before heading across the garden island that was Romynn.

Grape trellises and vast orchards covered the countryside, broken by clear streams and woody forests. Here was produced the best wine in Four Lands, the best horseflesh, the best fruit. A noble and polite people, the Romynnii were renowned for their hospitality and warmth. Many of the affluent from other Lands travelled to Romynn to enjoy the gentler Wintering, and many and talented were the Warlocks here also, employed by every grower on the island to protect the precious crops.

They flew north for a few days, and then across to the eastern tip, to a province filled with trellis upon trellis of grape-laden vines. At the end of these vineyards lay the coast, and across an inlet was a large island. The distance between mainland and island was spanned by an arched bridge, and people waved at them as they flew overhead, from the vineyards, the bridge, and from the island.

The Zoi pulled them low across the island. It appeared to be almost one huge garden; row upon row of flower beds; an enormous maze, its mysteries uncovered from above; fountains; even a rainforest area with a walkway amongst the branches where several ladies waved at them, close enough to see the beading on their gowns. Past this were wide fields where prancing horses lifted their heads to stare, and beyond, against a backdrop of giant trees and the glittering sea, was the prettiest castle Shaeli had ever seen.

It was small, at least compared to Great Court, but built in the same style – soaring turrets with pointed roofs flying bright flags – yet here the windows were wide, many had small terraces with doors open to the sun, and there was no wall containing the white stone castle. A large pool covered in water lilies graced the fore-court, circled by a gravel driveway, and behind the castle the coastline drifted away, more islands dotting the blue water, the coastline of Romynn fading into a smudge on the horizon. Shaeli looked east, across the Estrellan Sea, knowing the Starisles lay there somewhere, then she turned her attention back to the castle. They were close enough now to see people in the windows and the elaborate, covered Landing on the far side, close by the eastern turret.

Jarris flew the Zoi lower, and Andos stood with the big hook at the ready. There was little breeze, they landed easily, and soon Andos and Jeth were tying them fast. Tarkoda and Andos went down to unharness the Zoi and feed them in the shade beneath the Trader, and Shaeli turned to Crissita, who had watched the approach of the castle without a word.

Crissita stood biting her lip and staring up at the castle, and she jumped when S'resh came up to tell her that she had everything in readiness. The princess nodded and asked her to bring up the jevvies' basket, and S'resh disappeared back down the stairs. When Mareesha and the twins walked to the rail to admire the Landing and the gardens below, Shaeli laid a hand on Crissita's arm. It occurred to her that she had never asked Crissita why she was going to Romynn, and she remembered how she'd felt when her family left her behind at Cave year.

"Are they nice, the people you're staying with?" she asked.

"I don't know, I believe so. They are cousins to the king of Romynn, and live here at Rezon, his summer palace," said Crissita, seemingly grateful for Shaeli's interest, or the distraction, or both.

"So, how long are you visiting? Are you going home after the Wintering?"

"No, Shaeli," she said, looking puzzled. "I thought you knew." She frowned. "I'm not going home. You didn't think I'd bring all that baggage for a mere Wintering, did you?" Crissita took a deep breath. "No, I'm to stay, and marry the man I was betrothed to twelve Winters ago." She looked at the castle. "If I want to. This is he and his mother, now, I believe. I'd better go and meet them." She moved across the deck, smoothing her nervousness into regal composure.

Shaeli tried hard to close her mouth, she really did. She managed for a moment after Crissita's news had sunk in, then, as she looked across to the Landing, it dropped open once again.

A door had opened in the wall of the castle beyond the covered Landing, and a short bridge was pushed across, complete with handrails, connecting the Landing instantly to the castle. Crossing the bridge, greeting Mareesha like an old friend – if her eyes and memory did not deceive her – was Sir Brudloc. The tall, elegant woman behind him, flanked by several maids and footmen, could only be his mother.

Could it be? Princess Crissita betrothed to Sir Brudloc? Yes. She supposed it could be, *must* be, so.

Sir Brudloc took his mother by the hand as she crossed to the Trader, and led her to Mareesha. The two shook hands and Mareesha introduced the twins. Shanna managed a curtsey, but Neesha could do no more than ogle, then Brudloc and his mother turned to greet Princess Crissita.

Crissita floated across the deck, a smile fixed upon her face, her shoulders squared. She curtsied deeply, and was kissed on both cheeks by Sir Brudloc's mother. Sir Brudloc kissed her hand.

"At last. 'Tis good to see you again," he smiled.

She saw Tarkoda at the top of the landing stairs, and the look on his face made her heart ache for him. He saw her watching him, and he turned abruptly and went down the stairs again.

S'resh came up behind Shaeli, carrying the jevvi basket, and together they walked over to join the group. S'resh stood back while Shaeli was introduced to Sir Brudloc's mother.

The Lady Bronloc was a beautiful woman, with rich olive skin, russet hair, and the loveliest eyes, a wonderful mixture of azure and pale green, and she greeted Shaeli kindly, her voice as lovely as her eyes. Shaeli dropped into an elegant curtsey that made her mother proud, then she turned to greet Sir Brudloc, wondering if he remembered her.

He did. As she began to drop into a curtsey he grabbed her hands and pulled her back to her feet.

"No need for formality among old friends, Shaeli," he smiled. Then he kissed her cheek, and studied her face. "You *have* grown into a lovely girl." Shaeli blushed, and Brudloc smiled more broadly. "As I knew you would. Anyone with eyes as pretty as yours could never be plain." He looked down at the girls. "And these two cannot be the tiny babes I saw the night you brought me tezz. Not *these* elegant young ladies."

The twins giggled.

Shaeli assured him that indeed, that was them. "And I didn't *bring* you tezz, I *spilt* it all over you," she smiled.

"A mere detail," he laughed. "And you jest. These almost-grown women make me feel old."

Shaeli thought he looked nothing of the sort. Quite the opposite. He was older, that was true, yet it sat well with him, very well. His shoulders were broader, his smile the same, his hair thicker, his manner surer.

"Hardly that," said Lady Bronloc, mirroring Shaeli's thoughts. "You were only in your seventeenth Wintering when Tenelon died, the gods rest his soul." Her eyes twinkled. "And I, of course, am only a young woman even now."

"Of course," said Mareesha. "I agree with you completely."

They laughed together, and Crissita could contain her puzzlement no longer.

"You *know* each other?" she said.

"A happy coincidence, yes," said Brudloc. "Purple Leaf was kind enough to give my horse and I a lift when I was on my way to Ashkanna the Wintering King Tenelon died."

"And Mareesha and I met once before at Great Court, many Winters ago," said Lady Bronloc. "A Spring Ball, I believe, Mareesha?"

"More Winters ago than I care to remember," agreed Mareesha.

Sir Brudloc looked about and smiled as Jeth and Jarris came over to greet them. "And where is the most kind Eenis?" he asked.

"She's downstairs," said Jeth. "She'll be up soon."

Andos came up the stairs and Jeth asked to him to fetch his mother, and he went below.

Brudloc looked back at Shaeli. "And your brother? He's here also?"

"Yes," said Shaeli, glancing at Crissita, who was studying her sleeves most intently. "He must still be seeing to the Zoi."

Eenis came across the deck with Andos, hands outstretched to greet Sir Brudloc. She smiled broadly at his mother and then asked after Rhom.

"He is well, ma'am, though he is an old horse now, and retired. He still sleeps with your quilt upon him. Refuses to settle without it."

Eenis beamed, and vowed she'd visit him in the stables. Jeth smiled and put an arm about her shoulders, and Sir Brudloc asked after Dari, and congratulated the pair when told he was apprenticed to Almarnoch. Shaeli thought she had rarely seen Eenis so happy, and marvelled at Brudloc's memory.

"S'resh," said Crissita, motioning to the little maid, who stepped closer.

S'resh stood with the basket and Crissita opened it and drew out Minti. With a small curtsey, and a short speech, Crissita presented the jevvi to Lady Bronloc, who accepted the placid creature with undisguised pleasure. She hugged Crissita, thanking her, and then Crissita turned to Shaeli.

"I want you to have the baby, Shaeli," she said.

"Sorry?" said Shaeli, her eyebrows shooting halfway up her forehead.

"It was S'resh's idea, and one I totally agree with. The baby loves you. You love the baby. And you've been very kind to us both, and we want to say thank you. Don't we, S'resh?"

"We do, m'lady," said the little woman, smiling at the traders. "A thank you to you all."

Shaeli almost missed the little sparrow's shy glance at Andos, then she looked back at Crissita.

"But won't she miss her mam? Won't Minti miss her?" she asked.

Crissita shook her head. "It is time they were separated. Jevvi do better when made independent, and Minti will have company when my other jevvies arrive. She is yours, Shaeli, a gift." She held out the basket and after a moment Shaeli took it, and hugged her.

"Thank you, Crissita," she said, tears starting in her eyes. "Thank you so much. I'll take good care of her."

"I know you will," Crissita smiled.

Shaeli turned to her parents. "Can I Mam? Da?" she asked.

"Well, I don't know…" began Jarris.

Mareesha elbowed him. "Stop teasing, Jarris. Of course you can keep the baby, Shaeli."

"Oh, thank you, thank you all," she sighed, and opened the basket. She hadn't wanted to admit to herself how much she would have missed the playful baby.

The jevvi grabbed at her hand and was soon on her shoulder, peering out from beneath her hair. The twins, almost as thrilled with the gift as Shaeli, hugged Crissita too.

Lady Bronloc decided it was time they went to the castle. Crissita whispered to S'resh, who organised the patiently waiting maids and footmen to transport the mound of baggage, while Lady Bronloc invited them all to make use of the castle baths and dine with them that evening.

The baths were huge, elaborate affairs, as wide and deep as ponds, and beside them smaller, hotter tubs, whose waters bubbled and fizzed magically, soothing tired muscles. The baths were only the beginning of the elegant surroundings at Castle Rezon, meals were taken in large, brightly-lit rooms, the courses impossible to count, the wine glasses eternally full. There were dances held in a lavish ballroom, ladies dancing like windblown flowers with charming partners, the music lilting into the sunrise hours. They took picnics in the gardens, explored the mysteries of the maze, walked amongst the treetops in the rainforest beside brightly coloured birds, and rode on gentle ponies, tutored by craggy-faced men.

They stayed almost a full Moon at Castle Rezon, enjoying the hospitality of Lady Bronloc, wandering the gardens and swimming in the cool waters of the sea, and two days before they left, the royal party arrived from the main castle in the centre of Romynn. They were introduced to King Balkus, a rotund, bewhiskered man, and his equally round, pink wife, Queen Coreta, and the king insisted on visiting the Trader, hinting so blatantly at what pleasure a lift would give him that a grinning Jarris instantly offered a trip around the island and the vineyards. Queen Coreta clapped her hands, but did not accompany her husband. Flying made her nervous, she said, but Crissita, Brudloc and Lady Bronloc joined them, and they spent an afternoon touring the king's vineyards and flying around the coast of Rezon Island.

Before lift the next day, the king sent six barrels of his best wine to Jarris in gratitude, and when they flew from Rezon the whole party gathered in front of the castle to farewell them.

Tarkoda had been quiet and brooding during the stay. He had spent time with the king's paladin, practising, he said, and wandering around the island, but he was generally absent from dinner and never went to a ball. Shaeli tried to talk to him about Crissita, but he brushed her off, and said it was no concern of his what the princess did. Shaeli knew it *did* concern him, and she tried talking to Crissita instead. She asked what she'd meant when she said she would marry Brudloc only if she wanted to. Were they not betrothed?

"Well, yes, we *are* betrothed," Crissita had said. "Yet much depends on how we like each other. Neither of our families would expect us to wed if we are not willing, and we have the Wintering to decide. If all goes well, we shall be wed this time next year." She shrugged. "I don't see much to prevent it. Brudloc seems nice enough, and I think he likes me."

"But what of love, Crissita?" Shaeli asked.

Crissita shrugged again. "If I love him, and he, me, then that will be a bonus. But an alliance such as this does not take *love* into account, Shaeli. I cannot expect it," she said, then added quietly, "yet I *do* hope for it."

"But what if," began Shaeli, "what if there were someone else you *did* love? Someone who loved you?"

Crissita looked at Shaeli for a long time before answering. At last she sighed.

"Love cannot be *all* for me, Shaeli," she said. "As a princess of Ashkanna I have responsibilities. Duties I must fulfil. I am not allowed to befriend or marry whom I chose. The whole of Ashkanna's royalty must agree with whatever match I make." She was silent again, and then she looked Shaeli in the eye. "Do you remember the time I snubbed you on the street in Djelda?"

Shaeli's eyebrows rose in surprise, and she nodded.

"You thought *I* didn't remember," Crissita went on. "Yet I did, and was embarrassed. I was with an older cousin and trying to impress her. I didn't want her to know I'd befriended common traders, so I said something nasty to amuse her. I was sorry straight away, but I couldn't take it back. I have to *live* amongst these people, to think of my position and my responsibilities. I must be diplomatic, smile at the right people, ignore those out of favour... *and* I must marry into the right family." Her eyes did not waver. "I would not be permitted to marry *below my station*," she said. She took Shaeli's hand, her eyes wide and imploring. "No matter how much I might want to, it is useless me even dreaming of such a thing. It could never happen. Do you understand?"

"Yes," said Shaeli after a moment. "Yes, I think I do."

She had not realised that being Crissita was so complicated. She hoped she could explain it to her brother sometime.

* * *

They flew leisurely back across Romynn and Zirrus through summer and autumn, and when they reached Cave they were glad of it. The Land outside seemed tense with expectation.

Shaeli greeted her friends, and then went to find Almarnoch; she missed him more every year. Llevvis was revelling in his new position, old Demeris was happy to have less responsibility, and Almarnoch was happy with Dari's progress. Dari was the only one heard to say he missed Garrit, for Garrit's rigid personality had never endeared him to the traders.

Almarnoch was impressed with Shaeli's new smoky quartz, and while the cloudy beam that flew from it was weak, she knew it would gain strength the longer it was in her amulet. The skylights it produced were wonderful, staying longer, shining brightly, even at low strength.

Tarkoda regained his even composure after a Moon or two of brooding, and took as great a pleasure from being at Cave as Shaeli did, yet it was not until the next Wintering, after another long year of trading, that she thought he was properly himself. She was delighted when she saw him flirt with the girls at Cave that next Wintering, and the open interest in his eyes.

She spent the day of her nineteenth birth-day with her friends and family, celebrating with the last barrel of wine from King Balkus of Romynn. Her jevvi, now fully grown with a thick brown coat and black eyes that followed her mistress in adoration, disgraced herself by stealing some and getting terribly drunk on the rich red wine, yet they could not help but laugh at her; she was a comical sight, stumbling about with eyes red-rimmed like those of a drell. Shaeli scolded her, and Ebony, named for her black eyes, tried to appear embarrassed – and fell flat on her face.

* * *

Far to the north, on the island at the edge of the Endless Sea, Zeb stood beside the grave he had dug for his father before the Wintering. The wasting illness that had taken him had been short and unrelenting; and when he'd died it was almost a relief to see him released from the pain. The grave was marked with a simple cairn of rocks and a small plaque Zeb had hewn himself, as close as he could make it to the one that sat at the head of his mother's grave, close beside his father's. That his father had died here was a blessing, for Zeb had always been afraid he would be lost at sea, and he would be unable to bury him beside his mother as he had promised.

He heard the tinkle of a bell, and he sighed and started walking down the hill to the hut huddled at its base. How he wished he could go out and see something of the World. That would be impossible, now.

The sun was setting when he reached the base of the hill and sullen clouds ready with the next storm were brooding on the southern horizon, so he took the cow into the lean-to beside the house before he went inside. The old woman had supper on the table when he came in, and he kissed her cheek before going to wash his hands. The wind began to whine around the house, rattling the shutters and doors. The cow stamped in the lean-to and lowed nervously.

"Another Wintering that smells of change," M'zena said, as he dried his hands. "Smelled like this, the year King Tarkon's son died, over there on Zirrus. As if the snow was curdled a bit."

"King Tenelon, you mean?" he asked absently, his mind still on the cairn on the hill.

"Aye," she said. "That's him." She carried a platter to the table. "Something's afoot out there, a change. I feel it. I can smell it, and it doesn't smell good."

"Supper does though," he answered, barely aware of what she had said.

* * *

In the Wintering Hall in the village of Boccra, no one sensed change in this year's blizzards. Their lives had changed so gradually in the last Winterings that they had barely noticed the lessening of prosperity or the sense of desperation beginning to seep into their lives, yet this Wintering something would happen that would make them take notice.

Great Court had sent out many new laws and taxes in the years after Tenelon's death, but none that affected the village of Boccra as much as the law concerning the guard. That they were to be accommodated in all things was of some concern, but what had proved most difficult was managing to be reimbursed for those things. Goods and services were not only taken freely by guard passing through, and these were numerous enough, but the demands of the garrison that had been built on the bluff beside the river above Boccra were almost too much to bear. The demands on the surrounding farms and villages grew slowly more constant too, and many times over the last few years they had heard of someone being put out of their homes because they owed money to the state for taxes. The amount owed them *by* the state for goods used by the guard was usually greater, yet this was never taken into account. Seasons or even years would go by before money would come from Court, and never what was asked for, never enough to cover what had been used, yet these things had happened so gradually that at first they had not noticed; a bag or two of flour, a few chickens or a basket of corn from one of the farms, ales at the Orange Duck Tavern, new shoes for a couple of the garrison's horses. At first, they had been paid, not speedily, but paid, and fairly, and it was a few years before things began to slip and all the while the taxes had been steadily growing. They talked about it freely, in the beginning, until one summer when the guard overheard a few of the young men complaining about the rumours of the queen's extravagance. The soldiers had taken offence, beating the young men so badly none of them could walk afterwards. Kimbel the baker said his son would never again have proper use of his right arm and the lad had been abed for a month. People began to be careful what they said around the guard.

    The year the landingholder took over the running of the Landing they began to be careful what they said amongst themselves. A chance comment from the farmer, Bort, to Pelazarus in the tavern had led to Bort's barn catching on fire, six of his best horses burnt to death, and a warning left in the shape of the queen's standard. Pelazarus said the only person standing near enough to hear Bort's disparaging remark had been the new landingholder, Qwintum, a weedy little man with a wheedling voice to match, cousin to the head guard at the garrison. He Wintered there instead of in Boccra, and these days, when the guard came to the town, they came with none of the friendly banter that they'd had when the garrison was freshly built, and they were greeted with resigned politeness by the villagers. There seemed little else they could do.

Not that Pelazarus did not keep talking about it, but he chose his moments, spoke carefully and only to those he trusted, and so Fezzik heard many of his complaints and schemes. Pelazarus had grown increasingly resentful of the guard over the years, ever since they had saved Kora and her family from the soldiers. His flocks were constantly plundered, half his eggs were collected each day, and he barely managed to raise his pheasants before they were taken to feed the soldiers. He struggled constantly to pay the taxes on his land, and had taken to raising a few birds in a pen hidden in a copse in the middle of a patch of forest at the edge of his farm, just to keep something for himself. He came often to the forge to grumble to Fedor and Fezzik, talking of challenging the guard, going to Great Court, stealing produce back from the soldiers, or even better, stealing the taxes sent regularly through Boccra on their way to the queen's coffers. The previous year he had been more sullen, but less vocal, sitting in a corner of the forge and brooding quietly to himself – that is, until one day in late summer.

Pelazarus had arrived just as Fezzik was closing up the forge, slipping soundlessly across the courtyard, and Fezzik had not seen him until he'd come in and pushed the big door shut behind him. He looked through a crack, peering back out into the street before turning to Fezzik, who grinned good naturedly.

"Are you hiding from Pemba?" Fezzik asked, yet the grin died on his face when he saw the expression on his friend's. "What is it? What's happened?"

"I need you to do something for me," said Pelazarus. His voice was low, his eyebrows the same, but there was something in his eyes that made Fezzik worry.

"If I can," said Fezzik. "But what's going on? Why all the secrecy?"

"I'll not tell you much," said Pelazarus. "The less you know the better." He dumped a pack on the bench and it jingled faintly. "I need you to hide this," he said, and he pulled open the neck of the sack.

Fezzik gasped as Pelazarus pulled out a small pouch and showed him the contents. Coin, shining dully in the weak light, filled the pouch. Pelazarus closed it and threw it back into the pack. There were at least a dozen of the small pouches in the pack. Fezzik goggled at Pelazarus.

"Where did you...?" he began. "How...?"

"Earlier today, one of the queen's tax wagons was attacked twenty leagues north of the garrison," Pelazarus said. He spoke quickly, his voice low, his eyes darting about the shadows in the forge. "Several of the guard were killed, and one of the raiders. He was a farmer from across the Clahren; a man with five children whose fields lie wasted for lack of money to buy grain, whose family ate their last horse just to stay alive. A good man." Pelazarus cleared his throat. "His wife will come here in a few days to beg that you mend her milk bucket. The cow is all that sustains her family now. She had not even the strength to shed a tear when they told her that her husband was dead." Pelazarus passed a hand across his face. "It was unsafe to leave her anything now, the guard will surely search the place, but when she comes here, will you give her one of these small pouches? And give to others who I shall send to you?"

"*You* have done this?" asked Fezzik, incredulous. "*You* have robbed the taxes, killed guard?"

"I and others, yes."

"Who else?"

"It is best you do not know."

"I cannot keep it here, Pelazarus," said Fezzik. "If the guard find out..."

"But you *must*," said Pelazarus. "You are here all day, in plain sight. No one could suspect you."

"No Pelazarus, it would bring danger to me, to my family."

"I'll do it," said a soft voice, and Fezzik turned to see Verlie at the door. She was looking at him sadly, but with her mouth set in that determined way he had grown to know so well. "We must Fezzik," she said, "just as Pelazarus says." Her forehead puckered. "That poor woman. Her children. How can we refuse?"

"But, Verlie..." began Fezzik, but she held up a hand to him.

"We cannot refuse the needs of the People, Fezzik, not when their queen abandons them so." She looked at Pelazarus. "You will tell us who has the greatest need?"

He nodded. "Yes," he said. "This is only a portion of what they had. Much has been sent to other towns where there is also need. But we must keep some aside, Verlie. There are many who need help, and there comes a time when weapons may be our only option."

Verlie looked at him closely for a long moment, and then she nodded. She started on arrowheads the next day. When the widow from across the Clahren came to the forge, she left with a lighter step and a heavier, newly repaired bucket.

It had begun then, Fezzik disapproving, but recognising the need, the lives it changed. And he found it was not just here in Boccra these things were happening. From those passing through came stories of raiders stealing stores and taxes in all corners of the Land, the guard increasing their numbers when escorting these wagons. The battles became larger, the raiders more organised. As this last year had passed, tales of the raids were whispered of in the village time and again, and by the time the Wintering began, silent support had grown for them, in Boccra, and throughout the Land, for most of the supplies and coin taken found its way back to the people. The raiders began to be called rebels in the whispered conversations.

Pelazarus was often present when these strangers arrived, talking quietly under the sound of the hammers as Fezzik shod their horses.

Fezzik was relieved when the Wintering began, for these things would be all set aside. The guard came seldom to the town, keeping to their garrison and all the comforts they had stocked it with during the year, the forge was closed, and they spent most of the time in the Wintering Hall with warmth and company. He and Verlie now had three children, a son, Arral, fair like his mother, who had had his tenth birth-day at the beginning of the Wintering, and two daughters, two and three, who had his dark curls and Verlie's brown eyes. They had thought their son was to be their only child – many Winterings had passed before Verlie fell pregnant again – and their joy at their daughter was followed by surprise just a few Moons later when Verlie found she was pregnant again. He was constantly amazed at how much he loved the girls. He thought the joy that had filled him with his son's birth could not be repeated, and yet he adored the girls unashamedly, his heart filling with warmth every time one of them put their tiny arms around his neck or took his giant gnarled hand in their own. They loved the Wintering Hall, sleeping surrounded by their friends while the blizzards raged and playing outside when the sun managed to creep through for a few hours. Arral was less happy with the confines of the Wintering, but Florry and little Zeffy thought it great fun, and their only complaint was that they could not see Pelazarus and his family until the spring.

Pelazarus and Pemba had twice as many children as Fezzik and Verlie, and another expected in early spring. Two of them were girls around the same ages as Florry and Zeffy, and they were never happier than when they were all playing together in the garden behind the forge or adoring chicks at Pelazarus' farm. While the two families were often together during the year, the Wintering kept Pelazarus and his family at their farm with their flock, and Florry and Zeffy spoke often of their friends, Sharn and Pim, as the days crept by.

One morning, when the Wintering was more than half over, the sun rose in a clear sky and the people of Boccra poured out of the Wintering Hall to feel its thin heat on their pale faces. The children raced about, building snow-castles, throwing snow at each other or piling it into people and animal shapes until the wind grew stronger and the clouds heralding the next blizzard stole the sun. By afternoon the wind was screaming around the hall, the storm was buffeting against the walls, but its fury was short-lived, and it had blown itself out by the time the sunset hours came; not that they could tell when the sun set, all light had drained from the World during the afternoon.

They had just finished their dinner when there came a pounding on the door. Koak from the tavern reached it first and drew the bolts, the door thudded open amidst a swirl of snow, and Fezzik recognised the bulk of Pelazarus, a bundle in each arm. He ran forward as Pelazarus staggered into the room, catching his arms as he stumbled and fell to his knees. He thrust the bundles towards Fezzik, his eyes red and tortured.

"The Faunist," he croaked, his voice broken and barely recognisable.

It was only then that Fezzik realised the bundles contained Sharn and Pim.

There were cries of horror as the girls were swept away to the fire, the Faunist calling directions to her apprentice and the startled villagers. Pelazarus watched them go and staggered to his feet.

"Pemba," he said in that broken voice, tugging at Fezzik's shirt.

"Where *is* she?" said Fezzik, dragging on his coat. "Where are the children? The gods, what's *happened*?"

"The forge," Pelazarus said. "Couldn't make it further." He pulled on Fezzik's sleeve again. "Hurry."

Fezzik and a dozen men followed Pelazarus to the forge, lamps held high above shocked faces. The blizzard had passed but the wind still drove the fresh snow in surly gusts down the street, and it was cold, bitterly, mind-numbingly cold. Fezzik's teeth were chattering before they'd crossed the square where the shapes the children had made that morning were once again just lumps of wind-battered snow.

They found them huddling in the corner of the courtyard outside the forge, Pemba with her arms about as many of them as she could reach. The four children hunched against their mother, faces covered against the snow, and they had to be prised from her before they could be carried back to the hall. Pemba shook as they carried her behind her children, moaning softly. Fezzik took Pelazarus' arm and helped the staggering man back to the hall where they watched as the Faunists tried to save his family. He told Fezzik and the others what had happened in that croaking, broken voice as he watched his family thaw its way back to life; as he watched the Faunist shake her head over Pim's blackened toes, Sharn's fingers; as she tried to raise his youngest son from the slumber that he shivered in. They were warmed slowly, the two eldest children sipping soup beside their tearful mother, the third child crying softly to herself amid a mound of blankets, the three younger children lost somewhere between awake and asleep. The villagers sat stunned by what Pelazarus told them, keeping vigil with him until he collapsed, utterly exhausted.

The guard had come to their farm just as the sun was topping the horizon. They had told him his farm was forfeited to the queen for taxes he had not paid. They would wait while they gathered what they could carry and escort them from the farm.

Pelazarus, of course, had told them they were mad, he would not, *could* not take his family from the farm in the middle of the Wintering, that he owed no taxes. The head of the guard had given him little choice; she had even smiled as she drew her sword. There were two score of them, swords and bows were drawn, and Pelazarus was instantly beaten, as the head of the guard had known he would be.

They had done alright at first, he said, the children had been brave, Pemba staunchly encouraging. They had been permitted no animals, no cart, and so they'd walked. They had made it to within sight of the village before the blizzard struck. It had taken the rest of the day to reach the forge.

Fezzik could not imagine what it had been like trying to keep the family together and follow the road in a blizzard. For the guard to have pushed this family out into the Wintering was viciously murderous, that they had reached Boccra a miracle, but from the look on the Faunist's face they were not saved yet. He looked at his friend's haggard face and hatred gathered like a fist in his stomach. What kind of queen ordered such things to happen? What kind of guard were they? They *looked* like ordinary men and women, but what of this? Long after the villagers went to their beds did he sit watching over Pelazarus' family, thinking, and when he finally left them to the Faunists, he stood staring down at the faces of his own children for a long time before he went to his bed to think some more.

By Winter's end, the small son of Pelazarus and Pemba was dead. Brinn never woke from the slumber that stole him that night, shivering his way through long days and nights until death finally took him. Little Sharn lost two fingers to the black ice; Pim, most of the toes on both feet. The Faunist had been worried about Green Fever, for the tiny girl was burning for days after the toes had been removed, and she and her apprentice had kept a vigil over the fever-hot girl and her shivering brother night and day.

Verlie held Pemba's hand as she sat beside her children, held her as her grief was vented when her son died, wiped her brow as her seventh child was delivered early, but safely; yet the girl was a sickly little thing, and Verlie worried with Pemba as the last blizzard swept across the World.

    Fezzik worried too. Pelazarus barely slept, ate less, and sat brooding and silent. Fezzik tried to talk to him but Pelazarus brushed aside his concern. When spring came he borrowed a cart and moved his family south, to where his sister had a farm. Fezzik went back to work, determined to keep up the things Pelazarus had started, the fist of anger still curled tightly in the pit of his stomach.

* * *

CHAPTER THIRTY THREE

First thaw came and with it came a small avalanche that blocked the path down to first terrace. It would have to be moved before the Traders could fly, for they could not leave it to the old ones and those of Cave year, and everybody set to work to clear the rubble.

The weak rays of the sun began to melt the snow into a thick sludge which coated the bodies and boots of the workers, causing scores of slips and tumbles. Shaeli was kept busy with her purple-black rock, lifting the boulders too big for the men to move, and by late afternoon most of the fall was cleared away. Only one enormous rock remained above the path, precariously balanced on a few smaller boulders. Most of the traders moved back to the other side of the spring-stream while Taffka, Jarris and Baroz remained near the fall.

Shaeli stood with Almarnoch close to the edge above first terrace, Ebony nearby on a rock. She'd spent most of the day grooming her thick Winter coat and Shaeli smiled at her; her jevvi had a strong dislike of being dirty.

In the two Winters Shaeli had had the jevvi, the animal had become part of the family. She slept in a basket that hung in a corner in Shaeli's room, ate delicately, and learned quickly to put her scraps in the bin. In fact, she learned everything quickly, and she and Shaeli communicated in numerous ways, signals and words, even eye movements, and each new trick delighted them both. Ebony would carry small things to whoever Shaeli sent her to, wherever they were on the Trader, or fetch things for her in her minute hands. She learned to balance objects on her pointy nose, pull things along in the curl of her tail, or tuck them into the tiny pouch on her belly. She loved to play with the twins, she hiding from them or they from her, or hiding small objects from each other, and Ebony was always the winner in this game, whether seeker or hider. Eenis had been initially dubious about the cleanliness of having a jevvi on the Trader, but when she saw how the little creature loved to be groomed, even complained in a loud chatter about dirt on her paws, and how she always completed her toilet scrupulously in the designated place near the chicken coop, then she, like everyone else, became very fond of the jevvi. Yet Ebony loved Shaeli best and followed her everywhere or rode on her shoulder, and on their travels Shaeli delighted children in every town with her jevvi's tricks and her little skylights. Ebony had watched the day's activities from the rocks, keeping her tail well clear of the mud.

Almarnoch dubiously asked Shaeli if she thought she could move the huge boulder that hung above the path, and though her arm ached and tiredness swarmed her body like a horde of lead ants, she nodded.

"I think at least I can move it down, so it's not balanced so dangerously," she said. "I'll push it down on to the Lea tomorrow."

Ebony chittered suddenly from the rock.

"What is it, Eb?" Shaeli asked, but the jevvi's eyes were rooted on the snow-covered mountainside.

As Shaeli and Almarnoch turned to follow the jevvi's gaze, they heard a noise from above. A small tree, high up on the side of the mountain, began to slip slowly down the slope. A rain of pebbles and rocks began to tumble into the drifts of snow.

Taffka, Baroz and Jarris turned and looked up as they heard the low tremor.

"Only a little fall," Shaeli heard Baroz say, but her eyes were fixed to the little tree. It began to slip more quickly down the slope, and then it started to lean over.

"Best move back anyway," said Jarris. "You should be alright over there," he called to Shaeli and Almarnoch.

And then Taffka was yelling, and shoving at Baroz and Jarris. He had not taken his eyes from the fall, and though it was small, as Baroz had said, and far above, its effect was disastrous.

The scree tumbled down the mountainside, dislodging rocks, lumps of icy snow and debris as it went. The tree leaned until it could lean no more, and at last it fell, tumbling over, bare roots baffled by the sunlight, dirt and rubble leaping into the air. The fall of the tree gained momentum, tumbling faster and faster down the slope, gathering more debris as it came towards them, turning the mountainside into a living thing. The tree danced at the front of the landslide, its branches cracking and snapping, slipping and sliding, then it bounced against a barrel-sized rock and the rock hurtled downward as if shot from a sling, hitting the side of the boulder hanging above the ledge. The boulder rocked from its position and began toppling towards the three men.

"Look out," yelled Taffka, and he pushed Baroz and Jarris, throwing himself to the ground as the rock covered him with its shadow.

Shaeli did not think. Her arm flew out like an arrow. She wrenched power from the stone and her hand burned as the magic struck her fingers like a thousand needles. She had never let the magic of this stone build to its full potential before, no matter how heavy the boulder, and its strength ripped through her like a tidal wave. Neither had she tried to call and fire the magic so quickly, and the force of it caused her to stagger, throwing off her aim. A dull shudder went through her body as the weight of the boulder and the force of the beam collided with an audible thud.

It was well that the target was so huge. The beam caught the boulder left of centre and for a moment she did not think she could hold it, for the boulder continued its fall, but it slowed, and she brought her left hand up to cover the right, putting every ounce of strength she possessed into the dusky-purple beam. The colour of the beam intensified almost to black, and the stone in her hand dragged at her. She felt it pulsing, the tiny prickles in her fingertips growing to red-hot needles of fire.

The huge boulder stopped, hovering a hand's breadth above Taffka's head. She strained to lift it and the effort brought her to her knees.

The rock quivered above the Fleet leader's head. Smaller rock and debris still tumbled about him, obscuring his prone form.

Shaeli pushed at the rock, but she could not move it. She would have to let it drop, but she could not. It would kill Taffka. At the edge of awareness, she saw Jarris drag Baroz clear, and knew they, at least, were safe.

Her arm trembled, and suddenly Almarnoch's hand was on her shoulder, and his strength became another source of power. She grasped at his magic with her own, pulled at it, absorbed the strength she needed and *pushed* at the giant boulder. It shivered a moment, and with a groan she sent it hurtling away, stopping the magic as soon as the boulder was past the mound of rubble that was Taffka. It thudded to the ground and she felt the tremor through her knees. The rock disappeared over the edge, roaring as it crashed over first terrace and down onto the Lea amid a cloud of snow and mud that rose high into the air.

Shaeli still had her arms out, her hands clutched into fists around the stone, her fingers slow to obey the command to relax. She studied her fingertips, sure there would be tiny burns on them, yet there was nothing, and the pain was gone.

The sparks in the air were beginning to fade as she tucked the stone back into her amulet and staggered to her feet.

* * *

Only moments had passed since the tree had begun to fall, a mere instant in time. The air still trembled with the boulder's passage and the crackle of magic, the silver and purple sparks from Shaeli's stone were still suspended in an almost solid beam in the air, but for Almarnoch, everything had changed. He sagged onto a rock, staring at Shaeli, his face white.

"My child," he breathed. "Child, I never knew."

Shaeli frowned. "Knew what, Almarnoch?" she asked, rubbing at the muscles in her right arm.

Yet he could not tell her. He shook his head. "Nothing, child. See to Taffka."

As she turned away, Almarnoch's mind crowded with questions. *How* had he been so blind? How could he not have *known*?

When he'd put his hand on Shaeli's shoulder, he had thought only to try to help her in holding the boulder until they could pull Taffka from beneath it. He had not thought it would work – power transference was rare, barely referred to in Warlock legend – yet she had not given him the chance to try. As his fingers had touched her shoulder, her magic had leapt at him and grabbed every ounce of his magic instantly. Her power had overwhelmed his and drawn the energy from him, almost all he possessed. She had literally sucked the magic from his body – *without effort*. And she did not know that such a thing was unheard of, was practically impossible. The gods help her, she had no idea what strength she possessed.

And stupidly he had continued to be blind to her, to underestimate her capabilities. For the first time in a long time, he wished he knew someone wise enough to talk to. Incredulity made his eyes round, his white caterpillar-brows into little hairy arches.

* * *

Shaeli wondered at the strange look on Almarnoch's face as she turned away, yet she did not ask. She was too tired. She hadn't felt this tired since she and Tarkoda had rescued the twins on Lake Oliss.

Silence had descended on the ledge as she stumbled over to Taffka, faintly aware that the gathered Fleet on the far side of the stream was beginning to surge forward. Jarris and Baroz had reached him already and uncovered the rubble from Taffka's head. He lay face down, one arm stretched out, the other covering his head.

Shaeli knelt beside him on legs that shook with tremors. She gently moved the arm, and brushed the dirt from his face. The closed lids flickered and she looked at her father.

"He's alive," she whispered.

Jarris smiled through his mud-encrusted face. "Thanks to you, my girl."

"I'll say," said Baroz, admiringly. "'Tis a marvel you are, child. A marvel."

He looked over his shoulder to where Rafi and Navez were dashing across the stepping stones, followed by Renn and Mareesha. Others were splashing through the water to reach the Fleet leader, the air no longer silent but filled with cries.

"He's alive," Baroz called to them, "though I'd say this leg's broken," he added quietly, as he lifted a rock from Taffka's right leg. It stuck out from his body at a strange angle.

Then the others were there, and they were surrounded by anxious traders.

Mareesha sent one of the other Faunists to prepare a bed by the fire-pits and alert Sahli'en. Some of the men ran for something to carry Taffka on. He groaned as they rolled him gently over and onto the board, his eyelids flickered again, yet he did not wake.

Renn stood close by, tears in her eyes, Rafi beside her, an arm about his mother's shoulders as Taffka was lifted and carried into Cave.

Jarris and Tarkoda helped Shaeli walk back. She sagged between them, oblivious to the open mouths and wide eyes surrounding her. Ebony was carried by a white-faced Kirrit, and the gathered Fleet parted silently to let them pass.

Dari and Llevvis supported Almarnoch behind them. The High Warlock had only recently recovered from the Lift spell, and he was as weak as though he'd just performed it again.

* * *

They carried Taffka through the bolt tunnel and over to a bed prepared near the fire-pits. Renn and Rafi stood close by as Sahli'en, Perlis and Mareesha examined him, flanked by the entire Fleet, and before he woke, the Faunists set the badly broken right leg. It was broken both above and below the knee, and it took them until nightfall to set it properly, cleanse him of his wounds, and treat every injury to ensure against Green Fever. There was a huge lump above his left eye, a red weal spreading past the eye and down his cheek, he was covered in cuts and bruises, but he would live. Shaeli waited with the others, and then went to bed after washing the mud away.

When she woke the next morning, she was still as exhausted as if she had not slept at all, and the muscles in her arms and across her shoulders ached dully. When she finally dressed and went out, she noticed people looking at her strangely – as if she'd gone purple overnight or something equally odd. Conversations stopped when she neared, people suddenly changed direction when they saw her approach. Lunn of Sky Lark gave her a withering look and whispered something to his companion as she passed. Everyone was treating her strangely, everyone but her family and the children of her Cave year. She found her friends on first terrace, near the place where the boulder had gone over the edge. There was a big gouge in the ground, and they were standing in a circle near it when Shaeli came down the path. Shylo was speaking as she came closer.

"It's just unnatural and you know it, Rennan," she was saying.

"She saved Taffka's life," said Rennan.

"That might be so," said Bonn. "But that doesn't make her any less of a freak."

She saw Shaeli coming towards them, turned her back on the others and walked across the terrace with Shylo. They both glared at her as she passed. After a moment Crylla of Sky Lark followed them, but Crylla did not meet Shaeli's eye.

"What was that about?" she asked.

"Nothing," said Rennan.

"Don't worry about them, Shaeli," said Rhubic. "It doesn't matter what they think."

Kirrit put it plainly. "Everyone was used to you doing little tricks with your magic; the skylights and even lifting things," she said. "Like watching a second-rate Warlock pull a coin from behind a kid's ear or making a wilted flower bloom again. You know, fairly ordinary. But now, *they've* seen what *we* knew you could do. Suddenly you've turned into the skylights of Pa'laidiz and a Lift spell all rolled into one." She grinned. "You've amazed them, that's all."

"And saved Taffka's life, which Kirrit has typically neglected to mention," added Rennan. "Rafi and my aunt Renn think you're just fabulous."

"Rennan here thinks you're not too shabby as well," said Rhubic, and they all laughed.

Shaeli felt better, talking to her friends, and she felt even more so when Taffka finally woke and asked for her. Jarris found her and took her to one of the old one's huts, which had been given over to him, for moving him onto Golden Eagle was impossible. Mareesha and Sahli'en were there, surrounded by the vials of their profession, and Renn and Rafi sat close by Taffka's bed.

He lay covered by blankets, the broken leg a lump beneath them, his face grey behind the bright red line of his wound and the purple bruise on his face. Shaeli could see that every movement caused him pain, and knew that Mareesha was giving him her strongest herbs, yet Taffka reached out a hand to take Shaeli's, and she looked down at it. Every knuckle was grazed, the arm a maze of bruises. She looked back at him, tears filling her eyes, and he smiled at her.

"Now, now," he said, the words slightly slurred. "No need for tears. If I could, I would celebrate. I owe you my life, Shaeli, and I give you my thanks. I'd be walking with the gods now, if not for you." He shifted and pain puckered his features. "You have a wondrous gift. You stopped a boulder the size of a cart, and you are, as Baroz keeps saying, a marvel. The Fleet is privileged to have you, and I am very grateful."

Renn put an arm about Shaeli's shoulders. "I give you my thanks also, Shaeli," she said. "We would be lost without Taffka, and 'tis to you we owe his life."

"Thank you, both," said Shaeli, blushing. "Almarnoch helped though. I don't think I could have held it without him."

"Even so, child, we will be grateful to you always." Renn looked down at her husband. "Though what we shall do for the year, I don't know."

"I have already thought on it, Renn. 'Tis obvious I shall be staying at Cave for some time, and I wish you to stay with me." Taffka smiled at his wife.

She smiled back. "They could not drag me from you," she said.

"Nor I, Da," said Rafi, who had not left his father's bedside.

Taffka smiled again. "As I thought. Then it shall be thus." He looked at Jarris and Mareesha. "Purple Leaf shall go to Great Court in my place, accompanied by Red Arrow. They will explain, and take on any duties the queen may require of them."

"But..." began Jarris.

"No buts, my friend. The Fleet must fly, and though I've not stayed here after first thaw since my Cave year, Mareesha tells me I'll be abed at least until summer. Purple Leaf will go to Great Court. The Fleet flies tomorrow."

***

CHAPTER THIRTY FOUR

Red Arrow and Purple Leaf flew to Great Court two days later. They had received instructions from Taffka before they left, and though he was still in great pain, they had all been reassured that he would recover. While Mareesha was entirely confident about Taffka healing, she was not so confident about spending half the year at Great Court, yet she worried for nothing, and by the time summer came she was even enjoying herself.

She had suffered many moments of trepidation on the journey to Palveron, yet when she had finally gone to Great Court with Jarris, Baroz and Delphi, her heart aflutter, her eyes on the tower of the Glade as they entered the inner wall, the interview had been easy and casual.

The queen, of course, remembered her from her years at Court. She had greeted the four traders courteously, surrounded by courtiers – after keeping them waiting half the day. She had sympathised momentarily with Taffka's plight, then sent them straight out on Royal Errands. Mareesha could hear the capitalisation of the letters as the queen spoke the words.

Virrisian had changed little in the many Winters since Mareesha had seen her. Her ink-black hair still hung to her waist and showed no trace of grey, her figure at fifty Winters was that of a woman half her age, and the grey of her eyes still flickered over everything and everyone with mirthful condescension. If anything she was more regal with her time as monarch; self-assurance was in every lift of her porcelain hand and every syllable of her porcelain voice. She was pleasantly cool, vastly removed, and politely dismissive.

Red Arrow was sent over the Bay of Islands to one of Virrisian's posts at the foot of the mountains with missives for her guard. Purple Leaf was sent to the Lakes country on a similar mission – and to pick up fresh spring fruits for the queen's pleasure.

On their return, Jarris and Baroz went every day from the Landing in the square at Palveron up to Great Court to present themselves, yet Virrisian found little for them to do, and their time was very much their own. Periodically, she sent the Traders on an Errand, mostly with directives for one of her guard's outposts or to pick up some delicacy, but she was distracted with many other matters of state and Baroz often complained that he was almost bored. They took to making improvements to their ships and the Zoi quarters, releasing the giant birds every day to stretch their wings in the skies above Palveron.

Andos and Tarkoda made the most of their time, and with two of Kirrit's brothers, Wez and Beren, they spent the days fishing or boating and the nights sitting in various taverns. Shaeli and Kirrit occasionally accompanied them, but found the stuffy taverns too full of smoke and strange people, and were happier to spend time with the twins and their cousin, Iyri.

Iyri provided constant amusement for the girls. She knew the best shops, picnic spots, walks and drives. She often took them out in her little carriage with two smart black horses pulling them, and Ebony would leap over to the back of one of the horses and chatter to delighted passers-by. The horses were a gift from Iyri's fiance, Meart, who accompanied them when his duties as one of Queen Virrisian's guard allowed, and it was plain to see how the two adored each other. The trader girls were impressed with Meart's cheerful personality and agreed he looked very smart in his black and scarlet uniform.

Tajindi would sometimes go with them, usually when Meart was one of the party, but most days he tagged along with his brothers and Andos and Tarkoda. Kirrit's twin brothers were constantly busy with projects of their own too, and helping their father with repairs to the Trader, while Kirrit's younger sister, Mimsy, was having her Cave year. Her eldest brother, Alvaro, and sister, Maize, had both married within the Fleet and moved to less crowded Traders, but Red Arrow was still bursting with gangly red-headed children. The frame of the new Arrow Trader being built at Cave had grown over the Winters, material was being woven for the balloon, and the young men of Red Arrow knew they would be flying their own Trader into the World in the next few years. Each Wintering found them eagerly working on the growing ship, but they were happy to spend unexpected leisure time in the city this year.

For once Delphi, Mareesha and Eenis also had leisure time; time they were unsure what to do with. There was little trading to be done in such a well-stocked city, Faunists abounded, and apart from occasionally having to attend Great Court for a function, there was little for them to do.

Mareesha made inquiries about old friends, but found few to re-visit past times with. Most of the courtiers were unknown to her, and though she occasionally spoke with Sir Vulcan of Conroi, there were few faces left from her time at Court.

She spoke with the old knight at the elaborate Spring Ball one evening, and asked after Lady Arinola, who had been away the last time they had been in Palveron. Sir Vulcan told her that she was again away from the city, at a retreat in Marnissi, but would return at the end of summer. They talked of old times together in the palace, and the changes Great Court had undergone. Mareesha marvelled at the shining ballroom, entirely refurbished since she had last been there, amazed at the chandeliers dripping crystals and lit by white-gold Warlock light; the tall bronze mirrors; the thousand candles in the gold candelabra studding the walls; the new marble floor reflecting the gaudy dresses of the ladies and the loud costumes of the gentlemen. She saw Vulcan's lips tighten when she murmured something about the cost.

They stood in a relatively quiet corner of the ballroom, there were few people nearby, and Sir Vulcan, very discreetly, gave Mareesha a much grimmer view of the country's state of affairs than was publicly discussed. He told her that in Palveron, to complain about the monarchy was to invite trouble – not obvious trouble, but discreet, unpredictable trouble. Merchants who had complained about high taxes had slowly gone out of business – missing stock, fires, strange illnesses – while those loud in their support of the queen had thrived. Courtiers had slowly been replaced with those who agreed with the queen's every edict; objectors had been "encouraged" to move to their country estates – the whereabouts of several were unknown. He had found his own position in the court impossible, and had retired a few years earlier, and now only those who answered as the queen wished served Great Court. Queen Virrisian's guard was also stocked with those staunchly in favour of the monarch, new recruits were constantly being trained, and the countryside was peppered with Tenelon's old guard, soldiers "retired" for arguing against the need for so many outposts, so many new soldiers and arms, the strain they were putting on the People. Vulcan also told Mareesha that raiders across the country were becoming increasingly prevalent, and the other Lands were demanding escorts for the transportation of their goods. She nodded her head; many towns and villages had stories of raiders – increasingly referred to as rebels – and their increasing boldness, and she asked Vulcan if he had a theory on the reason. He considered her question before answering, his straight, grey brows drawn together, then he looked at her, his eyes creased with worry.

"I believe some are displaced farmers or merchants, desperate to keep their families from starving," he said gravely. "The high taxes have forced many out of business, yet it seems there are too many raids, too well planned, for this to be always the case." He glanced at the swirling crowd before continuing. "And many of the raids seem to be aimed at the guard themselves; stores, taxes being robbed as they travel to Court." He shook his head. "I know not, yet it does not bode well for

Zirrus, nor the other Lands. What affects Zirrus affects all. There are raiders on the seas, too, and there is the..."

He clamped his mouth shut on the rest of the sentence, and Mareesha saw fear skim fleetingly across his forehead. She laid a hand upon his arm reassuringly, suddenly certain of what he had been about to say. She said it for him.

"The black ship, Vulcan?" she asked, her voice low. "The ship that flies?"

He looked shocked for the barest instant, forced a smile to his face, and glanced casually about. No one was near. He looked back at her, his countenance calm, his eyes intent.

"It is known to you?"

She nodded. "To the traders, yes."

"Do not speak of it, Mareesha," he almost implored. "To anyone."

Again she nodded. "You've heard of the fisherman on the far north-western coast?" It was his turn to nod. "And Gremon, of course?" Again the terse nod in the pleasantly masked face. Mareesha did her best to keep her own face light and carefree. "What *is* it, Vulcan?"

This time he shook his head. "I know not," he said. "Not yet."

He noticed a lady, high in the queen's favour watching them curiously, and he laughed falsely, and took Mareesha's hand. As he led her to the dance floor, he repeated his warning of silence, and she nodded imperceptibly.

They danced for a while, each struggling to muffle the question of the black ship with silence, and then Mareesha asked him about Irinesta. This time, his concern was allowed to show on his face.

"She keeps to the Glade Room," he shrugged. "I send a message to her every Moon. She replies only before every Wintering, on the anniversary of Tenelon's death. The message is invariably similar; greetings, good wishes, her continued wish to stay in seclusion." He sighed as he turned her expertly about on the floor. "If only the babe had lived, t'would all be very different. It would almost be of age," he said.

Mareesha nodded her agreement. "Almost," she murmured tightly, and quickly changed the subject.

* * *

High above on the balcony of the Glade Room, Irinesta was listening to the melodies drifting up from the ballroom. She knew Mareesha and her husband would be there, the Spring Ball was almost compulsory, and she thought back to the last Spring Ball she had shared with her husband. She sighed and wondered again what had happened to Golden Eagle, hoping that Taffka and Renn were alright. She remembered them as eager young Traders, doing a fine job of leading the Fleet after the death of Taffka's father, and she knew something drastic must have happened for the other Traders to have been sent in Golden Eagle's place. She had watched Purple Leaf fly in and out of the city, her heart going with it each time, and as the spring passed, she would spend long hours staring down at the city.

Irinesta sat there listening to the music until the last strains had drifted away into the night, and then she went inside and closed the door behind her.

* * *

Next day Mareesha woke depressed and sought distraction from too much time to think. She resolutely encompassed Delphi and Eenis in her plans.

They took to scouring the city's many used-goods shops, scouting for bargains and treasures to sell when they left the city, and they found many while satisfying their need for activity. Eenis particularly found wonderful things, most in the dingiest stores and shoddiest markets, and the day before Golden Eagle finally arrived at Palveron, she found a gem for Shaeli.

It was tiny, star-shaped, and smaller even than the green triangular stone – a cool, clear yellow. Eenis had found it in a trinket box full of cut-glass beads, and she'd had to buy the whole box, but she said she'd known it was special because it had sparkled so within the dim interior of the shop. She wondered whether it would be of use.

Shaeli was thrilled with the find and kissed her aunt's thin cheek. She tested it for skylights and found its channelling properties weak, but obviously there, and she tucked it into her amulet, knowing it would quickly gain strength. Her long smoky quartz had grown stronger over the Winters, and was now one of her most powerful stones. Almarnoch would be pleased.

She thought fondly of her old friend. She had not seen much of the Warlock before she'd left Cave, he had kept to his bed, and though she'd noticed his distracted air as she'd said good-bye, she did not attribute it to herself; Almarnoch was often distracted. Llevvis, Demeris and Dari had assured her they would care for him until he recovered, but she wondered why he was so drained – she had recovered her strength quickly – yet in the end she'd put it down to his age and the recently performed Lift spell.

* * *

Summer was half over the day Golden Eagle flew into Palveron.

The girls from Purple Leaf had just returned from lunch with their cousin, Iyri. Meart had driven them back to the square in Iyri's carriage, and they were standing on the Landing when Neesha saw Golden Eagle flying towards them, far down the Bay of Islands. She ran to fetch her father, but Jarris was standing on the top deck, and saw the Trader at the same time. He called below to Jeth, Eenis and Mareesha, and sent Neesha to tell Baroz and Delphi.

Kirrit had not accompanied them that day, she had gone on a shopping trip with Tajindi; it was their mother's birth-day in a few days. The boys were somewhere in the city with their friends too, and so missed the arrival of Golden Eagle.

They gathered to greet the Fleet leader in front of the rectangle of buildings that stood in the centre of the Landing, their excitement growing stronger as the Zoi pulled Golden Eagle over the city. Shaeli suggested sending up a skylight to greet them, and her father thought it a fine idea.

She left Ebony with Shanna, walked to the end of the Landing, and took the smoky quartz and the triangular green stone from her amulet. She grinned over her shoulder at the group dwarfed by the two Traders, and Ebony raised a tiny paw to her and she laughingly waved back; it was one of the first tricks the jevvi had learned.

Shaeli held one stone in each hand, building the magic for skylights. The energy of skylights was different from the energy of a stone for power, for lifting or burning; skylight magic was lighter, softer, the power thickly veiled, and it was harmless, but she let this one build before she let it go. She wanted it to be a big one.

When she was ready, the magic trembling from fingertips to shoulders, she raised her arms, hands together, aiming up and slightly forward. When the beam flew from her fists she was still grinning broadly. She melded the magic of the two stones together, and the beam of light which flew into the sky was green and grey and silver and arced high above. She tugged at it, and the beam erupted into a huge ball of glittering emerald-silver sparks which blossomed in the sky in a bright sphere. While the sparkling ball still hung in the air she took the amber from her pouch and fired tiny golden balls around it in celebration of Golden Eagle's arrival.

Those on the Landing cheered, and from down on the square came whoops and claps from people surprised and delighted with the unexpected show. Shaeli gave them a little curtsey before turning back to her family, and soon Golden Eagle was gliding across the square, Taffka and Renn waving to them from the fore-deck. As they landed she saw Rafi ready at the gate, and behind him, having just driven the hook into a landing post, was Rhubic.

He stood ready to leap over and secure the forward ropes, and Shaeli, astounded by his presence, opened her mouth to question him, but he flew past her and down the stairs, grinning.

"That was some welcome, Shaeli," he boomed as he passed. "Best skylight yet."

Taffka smilingly explained Rhubic's presence when he came down to greet them. The Fleet Leader limped as he crossed the deck leaning on a stout cane, the pink shadow of a scar puckered thinly above his eye, but he greeted them cheerfully, saving a special hug in which to enfold Shaeli. By the time Rhubic bounded back up the stairs they all knew he had volunteered his services to Golden Eagle for the year, knowing that they would need help on the Trader. Rennan, too, had wanted to come, but was needed on his own Trader, yet Rhubic had two older brothers and a sister, so Red Sun was not without ample support.

"Rhubic and his father cooked it up between them," Taffka was saying as Rhubic joined them. "And they'd convinced Renn before I knew anything about it."

"I didn't need much convincing Taffka," she said. "I was already worrying about how we were going to manage landings."

"I wasn't *then*, not back at the beginning of spring, but I'm glad he's with us now." Taffka smiled at Rhubic. "This leg is still stiff and Rhubic has been a great help to us."

"I noticed there is a limp, Taffka. How has it healed?" asked Mareesha.

"Very well, thanks to you and Sahli'en. But I was made to stay abed until long after the move down to the Lea. It was summer before they let me stand."

"And hard work it was, too," said Renn. "He is the most uncooperative patient I have ever had the misfortune of tending."

"I was bored, Renn," said Taffka, sheepishly, and the others laughed. "I'll make it up to you, now I've been released from my torture. Tonight we shall go wherever you want, all of us. We'll make a party of it, how's that?"

* * *

In a house high up the bluff, three figures stood on a balcony, staring down at the fading skylight and the Trader flying into the distant square. The house was beside the cliff overlooking the Bay of Islands and Great Court towered above. One of the three, a thin, anxious man, looked up at the castle.

"Do you think they saw it?" he asked.

"Bound to have," was the reply from the tall figure beside him.

"They'll make inquiries," said the thin man.

"It does not matter," said the woman who watched with them, her voice light and clear. "Does it?" She looked at the tallest of the three.

"I think not. But we shall go to the square and find the child," he said.

"She is hardly that," said the woman. "She must be a young lady by now." She sighed. "The Winters with you have passed more swiftly than I'd realised, my dear."

He took her hand and smoothed her long dark hair. "Does that sadden you?" he asked.

She smiled at him. "Yes. Yet I'd not change a thing."

"I'm glad," he said. He looked down at the thin man. "Shall we go, Flin?"

"Yes, yes. I'll ready the carriage," Flin said, and he went into the house.

The woman watched him leave, and turned again to her husband. "I'm a little nervous," she admitted. "It has been so long. What if she does not want to see me? After all this time..."

"It will be fine," he said, reassuringly. "They will welcome you. You have wanted this for many Winterings, and it is time to set her heart to rest. And I know you are as anxious to meet the child and see her gift as I."

"I am, almost as anxious as I am to see *her* again," she said. Her voice lowered, as if she feared eavesdroppers. "He said the magic lies strongly within the child, didn't he? A strength equal perhaps to one of *your* kind."

The elf beside her nodded. "Perhaps it is as he says," he replied. "And if our plans come to fruition we shall have the chance to see for ourselves."

They stood staring down at the Landing in the city for a short while, and then the elf took his wife's hand.

"Come," he said. "Let us go and meet them."

* * *

CHAPTER THIRTY FIVE

Shaeli was standing with the twins at the edge of the Landing, waving goodbye to Meart and Iyri, when she saw the carriage drive across the square. It pulled up to the Landing, the door opened, and a well-dressed man stepped down. He offered his hand to a lady who alighted behind him; a lady who had the loveliest hair Shaeli had ever seen. It fell to her knees, as shining and fluid as a waterfall of tezz. Shaeli turned to go back to the group laughing with Taffka, but Neesha's voice stopped her.

"Look, Shaeli," she cried. "An elf."

She turned back and saw her sister was right. An elf, tall and stately, had followed the two people from the ornate carriage. He took the hand of the lady and proceeded to come up the stairs, staring straight at them.

Neesha ran off to tell the others, but Shanna stayed beside Shaeli as the three reached the top of the steps. Shy as she was, Shanna had never seen an elf up close before, and she was almost as curious as Shaeli about the elfin world.

He was very tall, with the fair hair, blue eyes, and sharply pointed ears Shaeli had grown used to seeing in Williver, but this elf was older, his shoulders less broad and his lips finer than her friend's, yet it was a regal face and he held himself proudly as he walked beside the lady. She was a lady of the People, her eyes bright in a round friendly face, and Shaeli found her features oddly familiar. The man with them moved forward as they reached the top of the stairs, and he smiled at the two girls. Shanna moved closer to her sister.

"I am seeking the thrower of that wonderful skylight," he said.

He was not much taller than Shaeli, and she guessed he was only about ten or fifteen years older than herself, but his forehead was already creased with the lines of an oft-used frown. He was thin in every way – fine blonde hair brushed neatly over a thin forehead, leaf-shaped brown eyes above a thin nose, long slim fingers on slender hands – and his face was warm, if slightly anxious.

"I am Flin," he said, unabashed by their stares. "I throw a few skylights myself, and wish to meet a fellow magician."

Shaeli blushed slightly, and glanced at the other two. The green eyes of the elf were upon her, but the lady was looking past her down the Landing. Shaeli looked back at Flin, dipped her knee a little, and smiled.

"That would be me," she said.

Flin broke into a broad grin and took her hand. "Congratulations, my dear," he said, clasping her hand and pumping it. "Nicely done. Very nicely done, indeed. May I introduce my companions?" He turned to the elf and the lady, but was interrupted by a cry from across the Landing.

Shaeli turned just in time to see Eenis slump to the boards.

* * *

Eenis had been standing with the others, as calm and contained as ever, only slightly apprehensive at the proximity of an elf, but as she looked at the three newcomers, her eyes caught those of the lady. She shook her head, closed her eyes, rubbed them, and looked again. Her hand went to her throat and the colour fled from her face. She tottered towards the strangers as if pulled by an invisible cord, a trembling hand held out before her. She managed only a dozen steps before she faltered. She uttered a strangled cry as she fell.

The woman looked up at the elf, dismayed. "What should I do, Qiren?"

"Go to her, my love," he answered.

Shaeli rushed across the Landing, puzzled by their words, the lady close behind her. Shanna had already reached the group around Eenis, and for a moment Shaeli could not see her aunt between the skirts and legs of those gathered around, but then she saw that Jeth had raised her aunt's head from the deck, and was holding her as Mareesha studied her face.

"I think she's only fainted," Mareesha was saying. "She'll wake soon."

"But what caused it, Mareesha?" Jeth asked. "She was fine a moment ago, and she has not had a headache in many Moons."

The lady beside Shaeli answered him. Her voice was light and clear. "I'm afraid it's my fault," she said.

The traders swung around to look at her, surprise on every face. Shaeli caught Kirrit's eye, and shrugged. She saw her mother's brows draw together, and the questioning look on Jeth's face.

"I feared this might happen," the lady continued, "and I'm sorry. Yet there was no easy way to come. It has been many Winters since we saw each other, and I knew it would shock her."

The elf, Qiren, moved up behind her, and put a hand upon her shoulder as she spoke. Jeth looked from the lady to the elf, and his face paled, just as his wife's had moments ago.

"Are you...?" he began, but Eenis grasped at his arm.

She opened her eyes with a gasp and sat up. She looked from his startled face to the face of the lady. They stared at each other for a long time before Eenis spoke.

"It is she, Jeth," Eenis said at last, and her voice cracked. Tears began to roll down her cheeks, and yet she smiled. "It is Illen. 'Tis my sister, come home at last."

She opened her arms, and Illen dropped to her knees and fell into them.

* * *

The two women cried together for a long time, surrounded by a circle of startled traders. They stood looking down at the embracing women, wonderment on some faces, tears filling the eyes of others, until Jeth finally spoke, his own eyes shining.

"Welcome, Illen," he said. "It is good to meet you at last. Your sister has missed you."

Illen looked at him, tears streaming down her face. "As I have her," she said. She stood and they helped Eenis to her feet. "And we have much to speak of," she added, her arm around her sister's shoulders.

Eenis looked lost and ecstatic all at the same time. Her face was pink, her eyes red, and it took Shaeli a moment to realise why her aunt looked so different. She was smiling so broadly, so genuinely, that Shaeli could scarcely believe it was the same white-faced woman who had just been laying at their feet in a faint.

Neesha looked at Shaeli, her raised brows and round eyes speaking the question loud enough for Shaeli to hear, but she shrugged in reply. She had *no* idea what was going on.

Jeth was shepherding Eenis, Illen and the elf towards Purple Leaf. Mareesha was making hurried plans with Renn, Baroz and Delphi for the outing that evening. Taffka, Rhubic and Rafi went to see to the Zoi, and Jarris and the twins trailed the others down to Purple Leaf's mooring. Shaeli was left standing with Flin in the middle of an empty Landing.

"Well," he said. "That *was* a touching reunion."

Shaeli nodded, still stunned by the odd turn of events. "I didn't even know my aunt *had* a sister."

"I don't think we were properly introduced, my dear, amid the fuss and the tears," he said, and he made a small bow. "I am Flin, originally of the Starisles, now residing in Palveron."

Shaeli laughed, and curtsied back. "Shaeli, of Purple Leaf Trader," she smiled. "We should probably join the others."

Flin nodded, and as they walked he asked her how long she had been making skylights.

"A few Winters," she said, as they crossed over to the Trader's deck. "Almost five, but I wasn't very good when I started. Hopeless really. Almarnoch taught me."

"The same Warlock who once taught on the Bay of Islands?"

She nodded. "He is High Warlock at Cave, and he and Llevvis, his second, have been teaching me since Cave year." They walked across the deck, and she showed him the pouch at her waist. "I've had my stones since I was little, though. I found them, mostly, and Eenis made me a pouch to keep them in. Almarnoch says that's why they're so strong."

"That's true, Shaeli, partly at least." He stopped her with a hand on her arm outside the stairwell. "Mostly, though, it's *you*. You who supply the strength; you who have the power. The stones are merely the channel, a different thread with which to embroider the sky. We shall talk on this later, but already I can see that the magic is truly strong in you, as they said."

"As who said?" she asked.

"Oh, no one. Never mind," he said, waving the question away with a flap of his hand as they went down the stairs. "My mouth rambles with my mind at times. What I meant *is*, is that you and I have a lot to talk about. I would like to see your technique, and perhaps show you mine." He smiled almost shyly at her. "Perhaps I could teach you a few things."

"I'd love that," she said, eagerly. "How long have you been doing skylights?"

"Oh, many Winters," he said. "Over twenty."

"I've never met anyone else who can do them." Shaeli was growing excited. "Can you really show me some things? How to make something besides light balls? A flower or a bird? And what do you do with your skylights?"

"Do with them?" he cried. "I can't *supply* all that is asked of me. Marnissi alone would employ me permanently to perform at every opening, but I dislike the city intensely, and of course, I have to travel to Pa'laidiz every year or two for the festival."

"Pa'laidiz?" she said. "The skylights on Pa'laidiz are one of the most beautiful things I've ever seen. You do *those*?"

He nodded airily. "Sometimes, yes."

They had reached the bright room, yet the stunned look on Shaeli's face was not from the sudden light. Flin appeared not to notice her gaping at him as he went to introduce himself to her father.

* * *

Later that evening, Shaeli was still in a state of shock. She sat with the twins and Kirrit in a corner of the largest anteroom on the Landing. None of the ships had been big enough to hold them when they had returned from a dining room across the square, and they were using the plush interior of the room to continue the party.

Mareesha had taken her children into her room before dinner and explained about Illen, and how Eenis had lost contact with her so many Winters before. She only hinted at the things the two had had to endure at the hands of Periqol and his pillaging band, but Shaeli and Tarkoda exchanged dark looks, filling in the gaps of their mother's information for themselves, and seeing their aunt in entirely new light.

Jeth had taken Andos aside for the same reason, and he had emerged from the talk, pale and heartbroken, and had immediately gone to hug his trembling mother.

Eenis was caught in a gale of emotion. She had convinced herself she would never see her sister again; that she was dead or the elves had kept Illen from her – and yet here was Illen, as content and cheerful as she had been when they were children, married to an elven lord. The mindless, shattered girl Eenis had last seen so many Winters before in Noresh had vanished; the eyes that had stared so dully, so blankly, now shone with joy and contentment. Eenis tried to quash every nasty thought she'd had about the elves, and she began to bury the voice which had tortured her mind for twenty-five Winters. With Illen's return, Eenis at last allowed herself to let go of the past.

She began to replace resentment with hope, suspicion with confidence, and the sharp edges of her mind and her manner began to soften. At times she would forget that she was allowed to be happy, and the whining voice would creep back to whisper cruel thoughts into her mind, but now, as she sat beside her sister on the couch in the big Landing room, she felt only peace. She was so happy she was numb with it. She gazed at Illen; kept reaching out to touch her arm or stroke her hair, and then she would turn to Jeth and beam at him, so openly and proudly that he walked around with a lump caught in his throat all evening.

Jeth talked with Qiren and found him to be a calm, self-possessed person, happy to have the sisters reunited at last. He told Jeth that he had met Illen soon after she had arrived at the community where he lived. He was the brother of Rhi'aan, one of the elfin women who had ridden with the rescue party, and their father had been one of the wielders of the elf-light which had destroyed Periqol's band.

Illen had been taken into their home, and when Qiren had returned from visiting another elven community, he had found Illen sitting in their garden, silent and lovely, rocking herself with dull, sightless eyes. Qiren did not know how long it had taken her to recover, but he knew it was many Winters. Little by little Illen had returned to the World, and finding only love and kind words to greet her, she had allowed herself to be drawn slowly back into living. When that time came, Qiren was already hopelessly in love with her, and they'd married soon after. Memories of her childhood had returned slowly, and when they did, she spoke often of seeking her sister, yet, though she mercifully remembered nothing of her time with Periqol's band, it had taken her until recently to get over her fear of the World outside the safe haven which had become her home. It was known to the elves – Qiren did not say how – but it was known to them that Purple Leaf was in Palveron this year. Qiren had to visit Flin in the city, and he had persuaded

Illen to accompany him. She had not regretted her decision; she had become more cheerful with each passing league, more confident as she re-familiarised herself with her World.

Flin and Jarris joined them as they spoke, and the brothers discovered that Qiren, too, was a master of skylights. While he did not perform regularly, like Flin, the two sometimes combined their talents, or met to discuss new techniques. Flin then offered them an impromptu show.

Everyone went out onto the Landing, chatting excitedly, the boys loud and boisterous. Qiren and Flin walked out to the edge, and in moments the sky was bright with colour.

Qiren fired from a slim wand, a long finger of quartz set in white gold, and his first skylights shattered into tiny sparks, coloured like rainbows. Flin's multi-coloured skylights flew from a clear, round, many-faceted stone, and they exploded within the circle of Qiren's lights.

Flin fired almost lazily into the sky, his beams weaving ribbons of colour in and out of Qiren's rainbows. Shaeli watched, fascinated, as multiple beams of different colours flew from the stone in Flin's slender hand. Man and elf stood side by side, shattering the night sky with enormous blossoms of colour – violet-blue, orange-gold, ember-red – each bloom turning into birds, arrows, flowers, floating and flying across the sky. Shaeli was itching to know how such things were done.

Cheers and applause drifted up from below as the people around the square stared into the sky. Shaeli was enraptured, but when Flin called for her to join them, she shook her head until Kirrit and Tarkoda pushed her forward.

She joined them at the end of the Landing amid whistles and calls of encouragement, fumbling in her amulet, coming up with the triangular green stone and the amber. Self-consciously she held her fists in the air, felt the magic build, and fired tiny green bullets and honey-gold balls into the air that circled the darting birds of the other two, and when she completed the circle she sent one up high, straight overhead, melding the magic of the two stones so they ruptured into a cloud of honey-green glitter. She smiled at the whistling, cheering Traders, and turned to Flin. He grinned at her, his thin face alive, but it was Qiren who spoke.

"Excellent, Shaeli. You have the gift strongly and fire with a clear aim," he said. "With practise and guidance you will only grow better."

She thanked him, and gave them both the benefit of her dazzling smile before she ran back to the others. Jarris met them as they followed her and thanked them for the show.

"Your daughter has much talent, Jarris," said Flin. "I would like to see it developed further."

Jarris smiled. "That would please her greatly, Flin. She has never forgotten the skylights she saw on Pa'laidiz as a child. When she found it is you who helps create them, she was delighted. She told me you have offered to teach her a few things."

Flin nodded. "Most certainly," he said. "In fact, I would like to do more than that. I would like to take her as apprentice and let her take part in the skylights next year on Pa'laidiz. Do you think she would like that?"

"Like it?" Jarris asked. "She'd swim to the Starisles to do it." He looked at Shaeli, engrossed in conversation with Kirrit and the twins, and then the implications of Flin's statement sunk in. "Would that mean leaving her here in Palveron for the rest of the year?"

"Not just the year," said Flin. "The Wintering, also, and perhaps next. Think about it, Jarris. I do not offer this lightly. I can *feel* the magic in her, a strength she only suspects, I think." He turned to the elf. "Am I not right, Qiren?"

"'Tis true," Qiren nodded. "I sense it also. If I did not know better, I'd swear it was elfin magic she wields." He smiled, but his eyes were still serious. "Discuss it with Mareesha, but what she needs to learn cannot be taught by a Warlock. Illen and I will be Wintering with Flin also, and travelling to Pa'laidiz after first thaw, if that eases your mind."

"You could meet us there, perhaps, and watch your daughter perform at the festival," Flin urged.

Jarris nodded slowly. "Perhaps we could." He frowned. "I thank you for your offer, Flin, and I *will* discuss it with Mareesha." He smiled sadly. "But I know what Shaeli will say."

* * *

When they told her, she burst into tears. Mareesha moved to hug her, but Shaeli waved her away.

"It's alright, Mam," she managed to say. "I'm just happy." She cried some more. "And a bit frightened." More tears. "And... and I'll miss you," she sobbed, and then she fled to her room.

Her parents looked at each other. They had their answer. It was as they expected. What they hadn't expected was that Eenis wanted to stay too.

"Just for the rest of the year," she said. "To be with Illen. I couldn't bear to leave her so quickly. Jeth says you can pick us up on the way to Cave before the Wintering, and we can make sure that Shaeli settles in and wants to stay in Palveron."

Jarris and Mareesha looked at each other again. They looked at Jeth, and he shrugged.

"I cannot part them so soon," he said. "And we will come home to Cave for the Wintering."

Jarris and Mareesha could not help but agree. Mareesha was pleased that Shaeli would have Eenis and Jeth looking out for her, but she felt a twinge, just the same. Everything was changing, and it had happened so quickly. In the time it took for a skylight to fade from the sky.

It was the twins who were the most devastated.

"But, *Shaeli*," Neesha cried. "You *can't*."

"Why, Neesha?" Shaeli pleaded. "I have to."

Neesha looked at Shanna, distraught. "She's forgotten," she said, her sorrow tinged with disgust.

"I know she has," said Shanna mournfully.

"Forgotten *what*?" asked Shaeli, mystified.

Shanna looked at her, her eyes full of tears, her pretty face crumpled like a handkerchief.

"Next year is our Cave year, Shaeli," she said, and she ran from the room.

Neesha gave Shaeli her darkest look, and followed her sister out the door.

* * *

In the end, it was Asheen and Iyri who saved them.

A few days after they'd heard the news — and had the benefit of the twins' grief personally — Iyri and Asheen came to the Trader with a solution.

"More a compromise really," Asheen said. "We propose the girls stay here in Palveron, with us. They will be able to see Shaeli, you can pick them up when you come for Jeth and Eenis, and we would be delighted to have them."

Shaeli, Neesha and Shanna looked at their mother, breaths held in anticipation.

Mareesha looked at Jarris. The girls looked at Jarris. Jarris looked at Asheen and Iyri, and then back at Mareesha. They all looked with him.

Something happened in the moments that Mareesha and Jarris stared at each other, something that the others could not see, for at last Jarris turned back to them.

"It's going to be awfully quiet on Purple Leaf for a few Moons, isn't it?" he said.

* * *

CHAPTER THIRTY SIX

Ten days later, the three girls were preparing for the Autumn's Eve Hunt.

Purple Leaf had been gone for seven days, their parents, Andos and Tarkoda waving dolefully as they flew from the square. Red Arrow had gone the day before, flying around the bay to trade in the southern part of the Land for the rest of the year. Purple Leaf would trade up the coast and through the Lakes country, and while the girls missed them they had been so busy there had been barely time for it.

The twins were staying with Zander, Asheen and Iyri in the white house on the bay; Iyri's brothers had their own families now and lived elsewhere in the city. Shaeli was with Jeth and Eenis at Flin's house on the bluff, yet the three sisters saw each other every day and took many of their meals together.

Shaeli practised every morning and evening with Flin and Qiren in the garden beneath Flin's house. The garden was a long strip of grass, enclosed by thick shrubs and a tall fence along two sides, on the third side was a long balcony and the house, and the other side ended at the cliff's edge. The side near the cliff had no fence, only a low stone wall easily stepped over, and the scrubby grass ended in a sheer drop a few steps beyond. At first Shaeli had been emphatically nervous, for it was here that they practised skylights, throwing them, as Flin called it, into the open air above the bay. Shaeli was all too aware of the sound of the waves crashing onto the rocks below, but she was almost used to it, and when she threw skylights she could barely think of anything else. She soaked up everything Flin and Qiren told her, learning quickly how to tweak the balls into shapes, how to throw them invisibly into the air until they reached the height she wished, how to move them through the sky, and she practised until her arms ached. The making of magic was exhausting and she often found herself falling asleep in the afternoons, but when she woke her fingers itched to make more, and the evenings were her favourite, for skylights always looked more wonderful when it was dark.

Her room was above this end of the garden, a sunny room with a view of the Bay of Islands. Flin had chosen it for her because she could see Asheen and Zander's white house down the shore from the little balcony, and Shaeli had grown accustomed to the constancy of the sea's voice below. She'd had a restless few nights when she first slept in the room, and sympathised with the twins when they complained about sleeping badly too. She explained to them about "the grounding", and told them they'd experience the same thing when they started Cave year, but she would not be drawn on what else they could expect after the Wintering. While there was no rules regarding it, Cave year was spoken of sparsely to those who had yet to experience it; the mystery and anticipation was part of the adventure, and Shaeli answered few of their questions. They had to be content with hearing about her magic, and her practice sessions with Flin and Qiren. Shanna had asked what the difference was between Warlock magic and her kind, and Shaeli had to admit she didn't know. She asked Flin and Qiren about it the one morning.

Practising every day was something Flin insisted upon. Although personally he was a somewhat anxious, vain man, inclined even to peevishness at times, he was highly disciplined when it came to his art. When he threw lights he became supremely confident and his whole being seemed to grow lighter, more buoyant, his voice strong with authority and the joy of creation. Shaeli imagined his daily personality was like that of a small rooster – self-important, flighty, and conceited – while his skylight personality was that of a hawk – controlled, alert, in command. When she'd asked him about the difference between Warlock magic and their sort the day before Autumn's Eve, he had laughed.

"Magic is magic, Shaeli," he said. "It takes different forms because the gift is given to different people, and each person channels it differently. There are many forms of magical ability. Warlock magic is more prevalent, I suppose, because there are more people with the particular type of make-up which manifests itself in that most familiar way of magic; the magic wielded by Warlocks. Yet as you know, Warlock's powers are extremely varied; some never rise above simple magician, while others, like your Almarnoch, have the gift in great strength. Faunistry is also a form of magic, born within those who understand *its* art; those like your mother."

Shaeli had never thought about it like that, and was surprised to think her mother had magic too; it just came out differently. Her face grew thoughtful as Flin continued.

"Generally Faunist magic is born to women, Warlock magic to men, though there *are* instances of female Warlocks and male Faunists." He looked at Qiren. "So too is our sort of magic generally given to those in the elfin world, yet we two are clearly instances that that is not always the case." He chuckled. "'Tis not so much as the way *we* see magic, Shaeli, as the way magic sees *us*. Magic does the interpreting, not us. We are merely its channel."

She nodded. "Almarnoch said something like that once."

Flin smiled. "I would like to meet Almarnoch one day," he said. "Now let us continue our rehearsal. Tomorrow evening we have your debut, remember."

Shaeli groaned. "How could I forget."

"You will be fine, Shaeli," Qiren laughed. "Watch me for your cues, you know the melody, and you have the best aim I've seen since… for a long time."

Shaeli hoped he was right. Flin had been commissioned to perform at the Hunt, Qiren would join him, and a few days before they had persuaded her that she was ready to perform with them. She was terrified by the prospect, but it excited her as well, and in the end she had agreed, yet the next day as she was preparing for the Hunt with her sisters she felt the fluttering wings of fear.

The Autumn's Eve Hunt was held on many different levels, from the hunting of treasures by children in local parks to the hunting of pheasants in the lush forest of the Royal Parklands. They'd spent the morning roaming the streets of the city with Iyri, watching the children hunting lollies and small toys in the park, and the performers which seemed to be on almost every corner. The twins had alternated between hunting with the children, clapping at the antics of the performers, and strolling demurely behind Shaeli and Iyri, for, at almost fourteen, they were at the age where they did not know if they preferred the easy amusement of childhood or the more weighty attractions of maturity.

Iyri had dropped them at Flin's house to dress, and the twins were full of excitement. They had new dresses, and Eenis had sewn them each a velvet cape in emerald green, for the festival would run late into the night.

Shaeli was in a dither of nerves as she dressed in her best powder-blue gown, but she was determined to enjoy the hours before the skylights. She fed Ebony, giving her extra treats and attention, for she was to be left behind. She was such a tiny creature – even fully grown she was hardly bigger than a small rabbit – and she was too easily distracted, and too easy to squash. There were also many who admired the little creature – jevvi were rare on Zirrus – and Ebony was eyed enviously wherever they went. They had taken her with them that morning, Ebony riding on Shaeli's shoulder, but several times she had taken an interest in something and dashed off with her fluffy tail high in the air to inspect her find, and Shaeli was grateful she had thought to invest in a long fine chain, similar to the one used by S'resh on their journey to Romynn. Generally, Ebony came to Shaeli's whistle, but she was a stubborn creature as well as inquisitive, and would sometimes ignore the call, so Shaeli felt more at ease having her on the end of the chain. Shaeli smiled to herself as she remembered that Jarris had remarked that the jevvi's nature was not unlike her own; stubborn and curious.

She gave Ebony instructions to behave, and laughed when Ebony curled up, shut her eyes and pretended to snore.

"Alright," she giggled. "Just be good. And there could be a few nuts hidden in here, if you think you can find them."

Ebony sat up, raised a paw, and chittered softly.

"I'll be back soon," Shaeli said fondly, and closed the door behind her.

The twins were waiting for her, and as they walked out onto Flin's front porch her nerves were only a distant flitter. Qiren and Jeth stood talking at the bottom of the steps, Eenis and Illen at the top, their arms linked, as had become their new habit – or perhaps it was an old habit, fondly remembered. Flin was waiting just outside the door.

Flin's house was enormous, boasting ten bedrooms, each tastefully furnished. There were several rooms for entertainment – small private dining rooms and large ornate salons – balconies and dressing rooms; four bathrooms, each with a bath big enough to float in. He also kept a large stable and several carriages, and as they waited for the largest of these, Shaeli thought that Flin must be paid very well for what he did. It made her nerves flutter again at the small responsibility she had in the night's performance, and she was grateful for the arrival of the carriage.

It was a sleek mobile, pulled by four lively horses, with room for six in the opposing seats, and another, higher rear seat which was level with the driver's. The twins leapt into the rear seat, the others settled themselves in the main carriage and they drove down the headland to meet Zander, Asheen and Iyri, who were waiting in Iyri's carriage along the bay road, and then they joined the growing line of people leaving the city.

The roads north were bulging; every kind of conveyance, horses, ponies, people on foot, throngs of smiling faces, all heading towards the Royal Parklands on the outskirts of Palveron. The twins, while somewhat used to the masses after Moons in the city, were overwhelmed again as they reached the site of the Autumn's Eve Hunt where droves of people from every part of Palveron and the surrounding countryside were milling together.

    The Royal Parklands took in many leagues of ground, and much of it was open rolling fields, studded with shade trees and masses of flowers, with a thin stream running through it. Beyond lay a verdant forest, abundantly treed with thick-trunked monsters, where huni-deer, pheasants, and plump pigeons lived a protected life for all but one Moon of the year. For the first Moon of autumn following the Hunt festival, the People were permitted to hunt the birds and beasts of the Royal Parklands, and while this law had been generally respected, during the past few Winterings there had been many with shrivelled bellies caught poaching within its confines; many who had been caught with a pheasant or pigeon; many who had paid with their lives for defying the law. It had been at the Autumn's Eve Hunt, fourteen Winters before, that King Tenelon had sustained the wound which had eventually killed him three Moons later, on the eve of the Wintering. No one had known where the arrow had come from, but the wound had been slight and by the time Green Fever had taken hold, it had been too late – but neither the memory of Tenelon's death nor the undercurrent of unrest throughout the Land could dampen most spirits on this day. The fields were filled with tents and stalls, colourful banners streamed from hundreds of tall poles, and people walked about grinning with pleasure at the centuries-old holiday.

    There were jugglers, clowns, singers, dancers, acrobats, magicians and more; acre upon acre of festival. There were dozens of contests; tugging contests, kite-flying contests, melon-eating contests, contests for riding, archery, sheaves of wheat, cobs of corn, balancing, the prettiest baby – and there were the Hunts. Hunting for coins in the bottom of a bucket – with one's teeth. Hunting for treasure in a trough of thick mud with your toes. Hunting for beads and marbles in a tub of custard. There were hunts for golden balls in the undergrowth, for bells in the treetops, garlands in the flower-beds. A group of troubadours wandered through the crowds hunting for the prettiest girl; a gaggle of old women hunted meticulously for the handsomest man, and the two were crowned as the Hunt king and queen. And – though there were no prizes for it – attentive mothers hunted the throng for suitable husbands for their daughters and young men hunted for girls without attentive mothers.

Of course, there was the biggest hunt of all: the Hunt to bag the finest pheasant for the royal table, and the reward of a bag of coin, the choice of a horse from the royal stable, and dinner with the Queen herself.

Shaeli and the others spent the warm afternoon roaming the festival, participating in some of the hunts, laughing at others, and picnicking in the shade of a tree by the side of the stream. Afterwards they sat watching as the queen's pavilion was set up across the water and the hunters began to gather in the amphitheatre beside it, Asheen looking out for their eldest son who was taking part. Behind the amphitheatre were tiers of seats where the courtiers would sit, and beyond lay the edge of the forest.

The shadows had begun stretching long arms across the fields and the surge of the crowd had slowed from a pounding ocean to a lazy river, a slow current of late-afternoon bodies, when at last they heard the heralds trumpeting the arrival of the queen's party.

Queen Virrisian was preceded by two companies of knights on horseback – Iyri's fiance Meart one of them – and behind her came dozens of courtiers in open carriages, her personal guard on horseback, and a retinue of Warlocks and servants in long carts. Knights, carriages, and guard, even the servant's carts, were all wearing crisp scarlet-and-black colours.

The queen waved and nodded from the back of a white stallion which trotted skittishly through the crowd. She was dressed in hunting gear, elaborately decorated white leather, too soft for serious work, yet she looked a splendid sight, her black hair bound with silver and the glint of diamonds.

The crowd cheered, most of them, but Shaeli noticed a big, bearded man nearby spit on the ground as the queen passed, and the anxious look on his wife's face as she glanced about to see if anyone had noticed. Shaeli tried to pretend she hadn't, and looked at the three children with them instead – a fair-haired boy about ten, and two little girls, adorable little things with dark curls like those of their father – before she turned back to the passing spectacle.

The royal party crossed the bridge that spanned the stream and dismounted amid trumpet flourishes. Only the queen remained on her mount as the rest assembled themselves, and as the last notes from the trumpeters faded into the air, the crowd grew quiet with expectation. Queen Virrisian's voice carried easily across the water and above the heads of the people. It was a cool voice, strong and clear in its authority.

"We give thanks to the gods this day for the bounty of our Land," she proclaimed. "Celebrate with me, and bless this Land that gives us life." The crowd erupted in cheers, but when the queen raised an arm to the sky, they obediently fell silent once more. "And now, let the Hunt begin!"

The queen pulled hard on the reigns and the startled horse reared. As its feet hit the ground, she dug her heels into its sides and galloped across the field. She dragged back on the reins as the trees loomed, leaping from the horse's back as its feet dug into the turf, pulling a long bow from the saddle as her own feet hit the ground. She raised the weapon in the air and with a cry plunged into the forest. The crowd was silent for the barest instant and then they erupted as the hunters followed the queen into the trees.

Shaeli sat down on the rug-covered grass as the last of the hunters disappeared inside the forest, declining the twins offer to go and eat more candied apples. Iyri said she would go with them, and Shaeli reminded them to keep an eye out for those from Golden Eagle.

Zander and Asheen wandered off to look at a dancing contest, Flin wanted to confer with the orchestra who would accompany the skylights, and Qiren, Illen, Eenis and Jeth went with him, leaving Shaeli alone on the blanket. She was much too relaxed to go with them, and she did not want to rekindle her nerves by meeting the musicians.

The bearded man who had spat on the ground as the queen passed was now laughing jovially with his son, the dark look on his face gone as he led his family off into the crowds.

She lay back, propped up on her elbows, watching the lords and ladies settle themselves in the pavilion across the river. Occasionally she saw splashes of colour between the trees of the forest, but the plethora of food and the warm afternoon made her drowsy, and soon she rolled over and put her head on her arms.

* * *

She had barely closed her eyes when she heard Williver speak her name. She lifted her head and saw him lying on the blanket beside her. Well, not quite *on* the blanket, but floating just above it. He lay on his side, his head propped on one arm, grinning at her. She smiled.

Hello, she said, lazily.

Good afternoon, my friend, he replied, his blue eyes crinkling.

The sound of the festival had faded; even the sight of it behind Williver was fuzzy, as if the people moved behind a thick lace curtain. Shaeli was not surprised; she had always had this dream space with the elf, and had never been frightened in it with him, nor questioned its strange qualities. It was as it was: a Williver dream. She propped her head on her hand, mirroring his position.

Where have you been? she accused. *I haven't seen you in ages.*

Forgive me, he said. *'Tis only now I see you that I realise how much time has passed.* He looked her up and down. *You are grown, and I cannot call you 'little one' any more.*

He looked genuinely sad, and Shaeli laughed. *You still can if you want to,* she said. *I always liked it.*

Thank you, he said, his smile restored. *Little one.*

They grinned anew at each other.

But where have *you been, Williver? Is time so different for elves? Don't you have the Wintering, or the year to judge?*

Of course, he laughed, flicking hair from his eyes. *The World runs the same for us as it does for all creatures, yet because elves live longer, time has less meaning and it moves differently; faster, yet more leisurely.*

Is that why elves stay in their own lands most of the time?

He nodded. *Partly, yes. Three Winterings can feel almost like one in elven lands.* He grinned sheepishly. *And so it has been for me. I apologise a thousand times and beg your forgiveness.*

Despite the fact the apology was given in repose, with a flowery smile, Shaeli was surprised at the serious tone. It occurred to her he had not spoken of where he'd been or what he'd been doing, but then he seldom did. All she really knew of him was that he lived somewhere in the mountains north of Zerrinius, but she did not press him.

Of course, Williver, don't be silly, she said, reaching out to touch his hand. *I just missed you, that's all.*

And I you. He squeezed her hand, and his eyes crinkled again instantly. *Now, what has been happening in my absence?*

Oh, not much, she said, airily. *Just that I'm apprenticed to a master of skylights, I'm to stay in Palveron to Winter, I met an elf and* he's *teaching me too.* And *I'm going to perform with them tonight and at the festival on Pa'laidiz next year.* She tilted her head at him and waved her free hand in the air. *Not a lot really.*

Williver laughed heartily and Shaeli laughed with him.

Well it seems you're going to be very busy. Congratulations.

The elf's name is Qiren, and he's married to Eenis' lost sister, Illen. Do you know him?

Qiren? Williver mused. *Perhaps.* He redirected the subject. *But tell me about this master of skylights? There are few of your people who have that gift.*

He is Flin of the Starisles, she answered eagerly. *And he's so clever Williver, you should see him.*

Williver nodded. *I have heard of him, Shaeli, and you're right, he is a master. His skylights are renowned throughout all Lands, even elven ones, and you're fortunate to have someone with such strong magic to teach you.* He glanced over his shoulder before continuing. He grew serious again, and spoke quickly. *But you* also *have the magic strongly, little one, and you must learn to protect yourself, especially while you remain in Palveron. You will meet many people here, and see many things; take note of all, but trust few. You have no family, no Fleet around you, and you must learn to rely on your intuition to judge who is friend and who is not. Many people envy magic and would take advantage of you for it, and I wish you to be careful.*

But, Williver, she said, bewildered. *Surely no one will take any notice of me. I'm not anybody. My magic is only good for skylights.*

That's not quite true, my friend. You know *your magic has other properties, properties few are yet aware of, and I also know you suspect the depth of those.* Shaeli avoided his eye, and he nodded as he had before, as if confirming something already suspected. *I thought so. There's something I want you to promise me.*

She looked back up at him. *What's that?*

Remember that you are somebody, and the gods have a place for you and your magic, as they do for everything.

His eyes told her he was not joking, nor indulging her in some way; he was almost demanding she believe him, and she tried. It seemed silly, but she looked at him and nodded.

Perhaps I am a little somebody then, she said, conceding only because he wanted her to, not because she believed him. *And who knows what the gods have in mind for the future.*

No one can know, he agreed, *though some see fragments of it.*

Shaeli nodded, relieved to be able to change the subject again. *I know a drell who sees things. I've heard lots of drell see the future.*

They do, Williver said. *That is their kind of magic, though there are some of other races who also have the gift of seeing.* He looked over his shoulder again, nodding at something she could not see, and when he turned back, his face had grown sad. *I have to go now, little one.*

Already? Shaeli cried. *But you just got here.* She sighed in resignation. *Please don't take so long to visit again.*

I'll try, he smiled. *But before I go, there's one more thing.*

Yes, Williver?

Go and play in the custard. Bottom left corner. And remember your promise.

His smiling face faded as the last words left his lips. Shaeli frowned, unsure what he meant, and then she was asleep again and someone was calling her name. She struggled back from slumber and opened her eyes, but this time it was not to a dream. Neesha's nose was almost touching hers, and she was calling her name in a soft, sing-song voice. Shaeli could see each of her thick dark lashes and the handful of freckles spilling across her nose.

"Want to come and hunt in the custard?" Neesha asked. "They just dumped a whole new load of prizes in." She nodded hopefully.

"She won't want to," said Shanna's voice from somewhere above. "It looks revolting." The dusty toes of her boots sat fuzzily behind Neesha's face, the hem of her skirt above them.

"Yes, I do want to," Shaeli yawned, sitting up and smoothing her hair. "I'm going to find a treasure."

* * *

It was only a little treasure, but she found it right where Williver had said she would – in the bottom left corner of the big square tub. Shanna stood with her head shaking and her nose wrinkled as Shaeli and Neesha plunged into the gooey, yellow custard up to their elbows. Neesha came up almost at once with a string of purple glass beads, and Shaeli was only a moment behind her with a small stone that, when washed, turned out to be a gem almost identical to her verdena, except this triangle was pink instead of green. Shaeli was sure it would hold some channelling properties – why else had Williver sent her to it? – and she ran back to show Flin. The thin man admired the stone and passed it to Qiren, who nodded down at the stone as if greeting a friend.

"It is of the quartz family, Shaeli," he said. "My people call it eroscia; the rose quartz. It is a potent gem, used sometimes to bolster the strength of other gems, but powerful in its own right." He handed it back to her. "A lucky find, I'd say."

Shaeli turned to Flin. "Can we try it tomorrow?" she asked, grinning when he agreed and tucking the little stone into her amulet.

The sun had reached the western horizon and begun its fall into the plains, and the sky was brushed with feathers of gold and pink. A breeze sprang up, and a hush of expectation settled over the crowd. As the last rays faded from the sky, the torches were lit, and young Warlocks wandered through the grounds, setting lights bobbing in the trees like giant fireflies.

The Parkland put on its evening jewellery, and when the pavilion across the water exploded into light, the heralds exploded into life, proclaiming the end of the Hunt.

The hunters began to trickle from the trees, some grinning broadly and holding fat plumed birds in their fists, others with smaller birds dangling from their hands and belts. A few emerged empty-handed, but most gathered in the brightly-lit amphitheatre with their catches.

The queen was one of the last to leave the shadows of the forest, accompanied by a tall man with hair as black her own. A fine pair of birds hung from his fist, and the two walked leisurely towards the amphitheatre and settled themselves in carved chairs as the judging of the pheasants began. The brightly dressed courtiers sat behind on the tiered seats, talking loudly and drinking wine from fine-cut glassware.

Shaeli was distracted from the spectacle by a hand on her shoulder and a loud voice in her ear.

"Here you are. We've been looking for you all day."

She turned and saw Rhubic and Rafi grinning behind her, Taffka and Renn strolling towards them. They settled themselves on the rug, but Rhubic soon suggested they go over and watch the judging more closely. Shaeli, the twins, Rafi and Taffka agreed, and they left the others and walked across the bridge towards the crowd surrounding the amphitheatre. There were hundreds of people around the perimeter, but the broad shoulders and polite smiles of Rafi and Rhubic cut a path through the crowd for the limping Taffka and the three girls, and soon they stood right at the edge of the ring.

The judging was taking place amid much laughter and good-natured ribbing from the crowd. Shaeli saw her cousin in the line, and when his turn came his fat bird was pronounced unworthy, and he smilingly left the arena, the bright pheasant his only reward. Those whose birds were judged the finest were made to wait for the final appraisal, and Shaeli looked around at the crowd. Most were open, happy faces, intoxicated with the atmosphere and the anonymity of the mob, but here and there she saw faces which were closed to the festival; faces with watchful eyes and tightly held mouths who watched only the crowd and not the rowdy spectacle in the arena, and she wondered at them. The faces watching the crowd seemed strangely obvious to her, their expressions different to those of the bright-eyed revellers, as if they were searching for something Shaeli did not see. There seemed to be two different kinds of watchers, too. She didn't know how she knew this, but she did; there was just something that set them and the vast crowd apart – made them separate from the revelry, and each other. One group of faces belonged to soldiers or courtiers; the other to nondescript merchants or farmers, but both groups had one thing in common: watchful eyes.

As Shaeli watched the watchers, the multitude of happy festival faces and voices began to fade, as if something was muffling them to her eyes and ears. The other faces, the watchful faces, grew stronger and clearer as the throng paled. The sight and sound of the crowd around her faded and faded, the torches paling to distant lamplight, until those who watched the people stood out against the backdrop of the festival – stood out as if they were painted with bright oils on a canvas of pastel water-colour.

The scene around her became surreal, the mouths of the water-colour crowd opening and closing almost soundlessly; the clothing and faces of the watchers oil-bright with clarity. She closed her eyes, her heart pounding against her rib-cage, but when she opened them again, the strange, surreal landscape still surrounded her.

She studied the watching ones more closely – it was difficult not to, for she could clearly see each one down to the colour of their eyes – and it seemed to her that the watchful ones *were* two distinct groups: the people of the queen, and the nondescript Others. She knew too that they were watching for each other, and strangely, amazingly, she could see what they could not: the two groups of watchers were almost blind to each other. The watchers of the queen could not see the watchers of the Others.

She saw a knight, his eyes vigilantly searching the crowd, and two bodies away was a man with the dusty air of a farmer about him, his eyes also vigilantly searching for a danger which Shaeli could see was but two paces from him. She knew the two watchful men were watching for each other, and she also knew that the atmosphere of the festival had robbed them of the ability to see each other clearly. She examined the mob again, her heart racing, the voices around her dulled to a whispered babble, spotting dozens of the oil-bright watchers in the vast crowd.

Nearby was a well-dressed merchant, eyes everywhere but the judging in the arena, hands stuffed deep into his pockets. Just past him were a young couple who appeared to be on a happy outing, but their overbright clothes, narrow eyes, and the showy daggers in black and scarlet sheaths at their belts told her they were young soldiers in the queen's guard. She turned her head as casually as she could, scanning the press of bodies around them. Behind Rafi's shoulder stood a watcher, close enough so that she could have reached out and touched him, and she was not surprised to see it was the bearded man who had stood near them earlier, the one who had spat on the ground as the queen rode by. Of his wife and children there was no sign, but the man's arms were crossed tight across his bullish chest and his mouth was a thin line beneath his beard as he scanned the crowd. She could see the blue steel of his oil-bright eyes, the hairs on his powerful arms, and she jumped as a tortured cry echoed in her ears. It was a cry of infinite pain, and somehow she understood it was he who cried out, but it was a cry that had not yet been uttered by the bull-chested, black-bearded man. She turned away, afraid he would notice her watching him, the sound of the agonised cry still ringing in her ears.

Suddenly she knew what this meant: it was about the Land, about Zirrus. The undercurrent of unease within the realm was made clear to her by this bizarre state, and she wondered how she had not seen it before. The almost-hidden watchers within the festival crowd stood out like gaudily painted sign-posts in her mind, signs that were pointing straight at Great Court. Suddenly all the political information she had heard discussed slipped like the pieces of a puzzle into a clear picture.

The queen was extravagant, obsessed with her soldiers, and she was taxing the People harshly; it was not only traders whose lives had altered to give coin to the royal coffers. People were increasingly poorer, raiders roamed many of the roads – she had heard Taffka tell her father that even a Trader had been boarded in the southern foothills and its cargo of supplies destined for one of the queen's outposts stolen by bandits. People were unhappy; their children lacked full bellies, and the Land lacked full vitality. The queen was draining the life and the hope from the People, and Shaeli knew innately that the People would let neither life nor hope go without a fight.

Williver's words came back to her – *you must learn to rely on your intuition to judge* – and she knew her intuition, or something, was giving her an insight into the changes taking place in the World, changes she only now began to fully realise.

She had heard many times how the fortunes of Zirrus affected the fortunes of all. She knew that over the last few Winters both Wokk and Ashkanna had introduced landingholders, and her mother told Eenis it was because Virrisian had heaped tariffs on the other Lands for the privilege of trade. Her mother always called the queen by her given name, without any title.

Shaeli looked at the queen laughing on her carved chair, a jug of wine on the table before her, tiers of courtiers sitting above. A few Wokkii nobles were seated behind her; their white-blonde hair and fair skin making them obvious beside the darker Zirrus natives. One knight, his features chiselled as ice, roared at the catch entered by the latest hunter, and his goblet slopped wine over those seated nearest him, yet he did not notice, merely continued his guffawing. Behind him sat one of the watchers; a woman who stood out brightly in Shaeli's bewitched eyes amidst the intangible babble of the mob. The woman drew her eyes from watching the crowd to throw a disdainful glance at the Wokkii noble as his drink stained her gown, then she threw a brief, tight smile to someone seated below before she went back to her watching. Shaeli followed the path of the smile down to the chair beside the queen's.

The man who had caught the smile turned his head forward as Shaeli looked at him, and she saw it was the man who had accompanied the queen from the forest at the end of the Hunt. She could tell by his uniform and his position by the queen's side that he was high in the guard – perhaps master-at-arms – and she also suspected that by the way the queen possessively touched his arm to return his attention to her that their relationship went further than the professional. And, most frighteningly, she saw that the man was one of the watchers. He stood out in bold strokes against the pale wash of background, his murmur carrying across to her over the muted crowd, but most of all he stood out because this man was not like the others; this man could *see* some of the watchers, not all, but many. His eyes picked them out, just as her own did, and too many to be accidental, and as she knew this, his eyes met hers across the arena.

Shaeli caught her breath as the black eyes met hers. She tried to make herself part of the mob around her, to shrink back against Rhubic, and she dragged her eyes away from those black ones and fixed them on the hunter who stood at the judging table. When she looked back, despite telling herself not to, the eyes of the man beside the queen were still upon her, yet they did not gaze at her face. She blushed at the lewd smile and looked away again, yet once more her eyes were drawn back to him, and she was relieved when she saw that he had lost interest in her, and he had continued scanning the crowd, his eyes pausing on other girls – *and* on the watchers.

As suddenly as it had come, the strange sense of detachment dissipated – faded as if a breeze had washed the fugue from her mind. In moments she was again part of the happy mob jostling around her; the muted voices grew normal in her ears as if a door had opened, the torches brightened instantly, the pale colours of the crowd and the rich tones of the watchers balanced again and became the kaleidoscope they had been before. She saw the World as she always had; at least with her physical eyes. The view of it had changed in the eye of her mind.

She did not know where the bewitchment had come from – perhaps some leftover impression from Williver's dream – but she was grateful for it, as much as it had unnerved her. She had learnt something today; something she had known in her *head*, but not really *known*: a revelation.

Her heart began to beat in its normal rhythm; her breathing slowed with it, and while the incident had not lasted long enough to frighten her properly, it was certainly one of the most unnerving things that had ever happened to her. Only the heightened senses and bright colours she had experienced holding the locket the year she had found Nol's family could compare with it, yet the sensation subsided quickly, it was gone with the thudding of her heart, and she felt calm again – as calm as she could with the trial of the skylights still ahead.

She glanced at the others, but they were unaware of anything but the judging of the pheasants. Beside her, Shanna and Neesha laughed with Taffka, who stood protectively behind them, an arm about each of their shoulders. She could feel the reassuring weight of Rhubic at her back, and the rumble of his voice as he quietly pointed out girls in the crowd to Rafi. She caught the eye of the bearded man behind Rafi and looked quickly away, the pained cry she had heard still too fresh in her ears. She began to take an interest in the proceedings again, tucking the surreal experience away for later examination.

* * *

Fezzik stood, arms crossed, face set, scanning the crowd watching the judging of the pheasants. He knew no one here. The trip had been a reason for leaving the forge; taking the children to the Hunt festival a disguise for dropping off a crate of swords Verlie had made. They had stayed the night before at his half-sister's home on the shores of the bay and the crate had been removed from its hiding place beneath the wagon under cover of darkness. His brother Fozar would pick it up in a few days and see it was distributed.

The children were overjoyed with the unusual holiday, and they planned to visit Pelazarus, Pemba and the children on their way home. They had gone with Verlie to buy a few more trinkets, and he would meet them at the wagon where they would watch the skylights and then make the long drive back around the bay. The midnight hours would be past before they reached his sister's home, and tomorrow they would travel inland to see Pelazarus.

He had wondered constantly through spring and summer about his friend, but Fozar, who lived a short distance away, had told him that Pelazarus had regained much of himself, and had begun to take part in the harassment of the queen's guard once more. His brother had told him on his few trips to Boccra that Pelazarus was determined to continue raiding the guard's stores, but Fozar said he worried about the deeply black depressions which sometimes took Pelazarus.

Fezzik scanned the crowd again, looking over the shoulder of a young man who stood with a small group, one a pretty girl in a blue dress who did not watch the judging but the crowd, as he did. She glanced at him, but turned her eyes away when she saw him looking at her, a blush spreading across her cheeks as if he had caught her in some secret act. He shifted, and looked around. It was almost time to meet Verlie and the children.

* * *

The judging had come down to the final ten, and the judges inspected the birds again, checking wing-span, weight and plumage before finally announcing the winner. As the proud hunter came forward to take his seat at the royal table, the crowd cheered, but when the cries died away, another voice rose from the shadows.

"Wait," cried the voice. "I also have a bird for judgement."

A broad-chested man pushed through the crowd opposite where they stood. His clothes were mottled with dirt, his scruffy hair tied at the nape, and he held a huge bird out before him, its plumage brushing the ground. It was still alive, though blood dripped from its open beak.

Shaeli heard the black-bearded man behind Rafi mutter something which sounded like, "the fool", and tension gathered in her stomach.

The master of judges addressed the newcomer. "The Hunt has finished, friend, and the winner decided. A pity, for it seems you have bagged yourself a fine bird – though dead is the usual way to bring in a bird after the Hunt."

This earned him a laugh from the crowd, and his chest puffed out. The newcomer moved forward, and held the bird high for all to see. Its feathers ruffled as it tried to squawk.

"It *is* a fine bird, at that," the man said proudly. He walked closer to the royal table.

The winner of the Hunt hovered nervously above his chair, eyeing the broad man with the bird so obviously finer than his own.

"If I am too late for the judging, then I wish to present the bird to the queen as a symbol of the bounties of our Land."

The winner took his seat, confidence moulding his features once more. The queen looked pleased and nodded. The master of judges smiled benevolently.

"A loyal gesture, friend, and welcome," he said, hoping to appear magnanimous as well as witty.

The man moved closer to the royal table. He held the bird higher. Its wings fluttered against his thick forearm.

"I present this bird as a symbol of Zirrus as it was: proud, a leader above all others, glorious to behold." He waited for the cheers to die down. "And I also give this bird as a symbol of what our queen has made of our once proud Land."

There was suddenly a knife in his hand, and he slit the bird from tail to throat. Blood and guts fell from its stomach, blood and gizzards and something else, something alive, something that writhed and foamed on the red ground amid the tangle of steaming innards, something that kept writhing long after the steam melted into the air; long after the last drops of blood had fallen from the once noble bird; long after every breath had been caught in amazement and horror.

Shaeli realised that the writhing, squirming mass on the ground were maggots, hundreds of maggots, wriggling and twisting together in the tangle of gizzards and blood. As the crowd let out its drawn breath, the man dropped the dead bird and raised the knife above his head. He was but four paces from the queen's table.

"You have filled our Land with decay. Its soul is rotting with your putrid foulness. It must *end!*" he cried, and he leapt forward.

Before he had finished the stride, his eyes glazed over. He fell dead beside the pile of squirming maggots, one arm outstretched, the knife falling uselessly from his fingers. He twitched just as the pheasant had moments before. The haft of a second knife jutted from his throat.

Silence reigned as the man beside the queen walked around the table to retrieve his knife. He wiped the blade clean on the dead man's jacket before tucking it back into his boot. With a swift jerk of his head, soldiers appeared and dragged the body away. The remains of the bird and the pile of writhing maggots were swiftly removed also, and fresh sand thrown over the dark stain on the ground. Still the crowd hovered, stunned and silent. The master of judges trembled, his face a curious shade of green. He, like everyone else, was watching the queen.

If she was upset by the incident, she covered it well. Her face was paler perhaps, yet her features were as serene and cool as ever. She stood and her eyes swept the crowd.

"An unhappy occurrence indeed," she said, her voice carrying easily across the incredulous crowd. "Yet it would be foolish to let it mar our festival." There were murmurs of agreement from the courtiers at this. "Let us be *truly* grateful for the bounty of our Land and forget the ravings of one poor, wretched madman. Let us be thankful for our *own* good health and sound minds in reply to his pitiful ravings. Let the feasts begin!" The murmur grew, and then cheers began as huge barrels of wine were carried into the arena. "A gift to the People from their grateful queen," she cried, and her voice was drowned by cheers as the mob rushed forward to accept the offering.

Shaeli heard a strangled oath from behind her and turned in time to see the bearded man push his way through the crowd. She looked back at the sand covering the stain on the ground. If she had not had the strange surreal message alerting her to the state of the Land, this one brave man would have shown it to her.

* * *

Fezzik pushed his way through the mob somehow, his vision clouding, his throat knotted. He brushed a hand across his eyes, and clamped the knot in his throat to keep the grief in check, but as he reached the edge of the throng he stumbled and fell to his knees. He allowed himself a moment to bow his head and close his eyes against the image of Pelazarus lying in the dirt, blood gushing from the wound in his throat, and then he hauled himself up and went to find Verlie. His need to hold her was very strong.

* * *

The queen sat back down as hundreds of people crowded around the wine barrels. The pleasant look on her face belied the contempt in her voice as she leant towards Sir Azeron.

"So easily distracted, like children with lollies," she breathed.

"There will be some who are not so easily distracted," Azeron replied.

"Perhaps not," she said. "But you have just proven your reliability at dealing with such trivial matters. There is nothing I fear from…" She stopped and the pleasant mask dropped. The colour recently returned to her cheeks fled entirely. Her eyes were transfixed by something across the arena.

Azeron followed her gaze. "What is it, my Lady?" he asked, softly. "What did you see?"

When he touched her arm, her lids fluttered. Her eyes shifted to him, flicked back across the arena, and when they reached him again, she had control of herself. He almost thought he had been mistaken by the look he had seen on her face. It was the fear which she had been in the very act of denying.

"Nothing," she replied, shaking her head. "A fancy only." She laughed oddly. "I thought for a moment that… that Tenelon was staring at me."

Azeron looked again at where she'd fixed her eyes. He could see nothing but revellers; families; couples; a merchant of whom he was somewhat suspicious; the head trader limping off with some of his people, one the pretty girl in the blue dress he'd already admired, a couple of young men and two lasses in matching green cloaks, yet he could see no man who looked like Tenelon. Azeron had only ever seen the old king once, at a Hunt when, as a very young man, he had grazed the old king with a poisoned arrow, yet many of his portraits still hung on the walls of Great Court. He turned back to the queen.

"I can see nothing," he said, calmly.

"Neither can I, Azeron," she said, her voice growing cooler. "I told you, it was nothing but a fancy. A trick of the eyes. Forget it."

She took up her wine and drank deeply, then she turned to the winner of the Hunt, who sat bewildered and all but forgotten.

Azeron, too, drank his wine and chatted to those around him, but his black eyes remained watchful, and his mind grew wary.

* * *

Shaeli saw the queen staring across the arena at them and the black eyes that followed, and she turned to the others.

"Can we go?" she said, and Taffka nodded.

The twins stood close together, staring across at the fresh sand in front of the queen's table. Taffka put an arm around their green-cloaked shoulders and turned them away. They were silent until they were crossing the bridge, and then Shanna spoke quietly.

"It makes me think she can't be a very *good* queen," she said, sadly.

Neesha sighed and took her hand. "That's just what I was thinking," she said.

* * *

CHAPTER THIRTY SEVEN

Later that night, Shaeli stood shivering beside Qiren at the end of a dark field. The moon glinted on the stream and the lights from the festival grounds on the other side illuminated the waiting people. The festival seemed enormous from here; the crowds a multitude.

It was so different being outside looking in, she thought, and she shivered again, though she was not cold, merely terrified. Her hands clutched the amulet at her waist and she looked away from the festival to the arena down the field and the courtiers revelling in the pavilion, but the change of view did not lessen her terror, so she just shut her eyes.

She could hear Flin behind her, talking with the orchestra leader in a firm, quiet voice. He had already assumed his skylight persona and was in full control. Shaeli wished she felt the same. She daren't think about the orchestra seated further back, for when she'd seen them her knees had trembled and she'd asked Flin how many musicians there were.

"Oh, only about a hundred," he'd answered casually, failing to notice the wobble in her legs.

Luckily, Illen noticed. She'd given Shaeli a hug and words of encouragement, but now, as Shaeli stood with her eyes closed beside Qiren, she could not recall what those words had been.

Qiren's arm wrapped around her shoulders, and his breath warmed her ear.

"You'll not see the cues with your eyes shut, Shaeli," he chuckled, softly. "Don't worry, you'll be fine."

She looked at him, took a deep breath and nodded. Illen smiled, kissed her cheek and walked off to stand in the shadows. Flin came and stood before Shaeli.

"Ready?" he asked, his eyes shining and intense, and she nodded. If she wasn't now, she never would be.

Qiren and Flin stepped forward and separated, so they were in front of Shaeli and on either side, where she could see them both. When Flin was confident of her abilities she would stand beside them.

Flin raised his hands into the sky, and behind them the orchestra raised their first notes. Qiren raised his arms and more instruments joined him. Shaeli took a breath, said a silent prayer to the goddess Arrell for the strength to make it to the end, and raised her arms too. More instruments added their tones to the others, and then it began.

Afterwards, Shaeli would remember very little. She concentrated so hard on her task and the melody that she forgot all else, even the need to check her cues with Qiren. So carefully had she learned her part that it came almost without thought, and all her energy was directed into throwing colour into the sky. These skylights were different from those on Pa'laidiz; much more theatrical, the music stronger, more festive, meant to excite. Flin and Qiren created the spectacle, Shaeli merely wove details into their masterpieces.

The opening was a slow succession of huge rainbow-coloured balls which rose invisibly into the night sky. The balls blossomed accompanied by a flourish from the orchestra, and Shaeli scattered sparkles of silver around them with each flourish, her timing perfect. Each shining ball reached higher and higher into the air, the orchestra creating an accompanying crescendo.

The music picked up tempo, and long snakes of fiery red and green flew through the air. Shaeli gave them eyes with her amethyst and silver-white tails with her quartz. Next came a mass of butterflies that fluttered across the water and then a flock of birds swooped down over the mesmerised throng. Flin and Qiren created a shimmering blue pheasant in honour of the Hunt and Shaeli shot it with silver arrows, and next came the frenzied dance of spinning tops. Shaeli fell behind throwing golden balls with the amber, and she was flustered as the music changed for the next section.

As she dropped the amber back into her amulet, she had one terrible moment when she pulled out the green triangle, the verdena, only to find it was the eroscia she had found in the custard that afternoon. She did not have time to change it – she heard her next cue coming – so she pushed extra strength through the gem to compensate for its lack of her own energy. The shower of light she threw into the sky shimmered like pink raindrops falling from the stars, and even she was entranced with the spectacle. It seemed the crowd enjoyed it too, for whoops of appreciation echoed across the water.

As the orchestra wound down, the skylights were pulled into beams of light which shone on and upwards into the stars. Shaeli began to feel a warmth as she threw her last beam into the sky. It started somewhere between her stomach and her chest and spread outward, and by the time the music faded and the cries from across the water began, her body was filled with the warm glow. She was elated, floating above the ground at the rush of her accomplishment, and she let out a whoop to release it. Flin strode towards her and her grin earned her a hug, but then he held her back, and looked at her seriously.

"Missed those drums by a hair," he said, and her grin died as she nodded. "And I thought we were to have green rain?"

"I know, Flin," she said, at once contrite. "I'm sorry. I pulled out the eroscia by mistake. I would have missed my cue so I just…" she shrugged, "I just hoped for the best."

"Hmm," he looked thoughtful. "We'll have to work on that." Suddenly he laughed, picked her up and swung her around. "My dear, you were *marvellous*. Better than I'd dared hope. Qiren said I hadn't given you enough to do, but I said, 'no, she has plenty to think about'." He laughed again. "But he was right. You were *splendid*. Next time you stand beside us."

To Shaeli there was no higher praise and the warmth which had temporarily died with Flin's serious tone flared again, and her grin burned brightly with it. She walked back across the field as oblivious to the crowds as they were to the throwers of the skylights.

She regained some of her senses when they joined the others, and she smiled at their congratulations, but then Asheen said she thought she should take the twins home. She looked across to the arena where a scuffle had broken out around the queen's wine barrels, and in the bushes nearby they could hear someone retching.

Shaeli kissed the beaming, yawning twins and watched them drive off in Iyri's carriage, then they bid goodnight to Taffka, Renn, Rafi and Rhubic, and Eenis led her towards Flin's carriage, which had magically appeared on the road nearby. She gratefully tucked the blanket Eenis handed her around her knees and rested her head on Jeth's warm shoulder, and the next thing she knew, he was leading her up the stairs to her room.

Ebony greeted her almost more enthusiastically than she could cope with, and she cuddled her, murmuring quietly as she undressed and climbed into bed. She turned out the lamp and Ebony was still peering at her from the table by the bed, watching Shaeli with eyes that were pools of shadow. Shaeli blinked, meaning to say goodnight, but her eyes stayed closed.

* * *

The next morning, Shaeli lay curled beneath the blanket, warm and sleeping soundly.

Plink!

One hair was pulled delicately from her head. Shaeli scratched at the spot, and snuggled back down.

Splink!

Another hair was plucked from her head. She groaned and pulled the blanket higher.

Yet another hair went *plink,* and she finally opened one eye and squinted into the light. Ebony sat on her pillow, her tiny hand poised to pluck another hair.

"I suppose you think that's funny," Shaeli said groggily.

Ebony snatched back the hovering hand and gave Shaeli her strange, jevvi version of a smile, and Shaeli laughed, stretched and peered at the window, surprised to see the sun was already high in the sky and warm rays lay in bright puddles on the floor. Then she remembered the skylights, and she grabbed the startled jevvi and held her high above her head.

Ebony's long tail curled around Shaeli's wrist, and her pointy little face looked down, scolding until Shaeli laughingly pulled her down and snuggled her close.

"I suppose you're hungry," she said.

Ebony looked over at the table. The skins and seeds of several fruits were piled neatly beside the fruit bowl.

"Oh. Well, *I'm* hungry," she smiled, and pushed down the covers. "Wait until I'm dressed and I'll take you out into the garden." Ebony dropped her eyes. "Have you *been* out?" Shaeli asked, and Ebony looked guiltily up at a tiny round window high above the bed. It was open slightly, and the branches of a tall tree brushed against it. "Out there?" Shaeli pointed, and Ebony hung her head. "Well, I guess you needed to go," she said, and Ebony nodded so vigorously that Shaeli laughed. "I'll forgive you just this once, but you know you're not allowed to wander."

She continued talking to the jevvi as she dressed and Ebony listened to her, making little noises of agreement in all the right places. When Shaeli was dressed she picked her up and went downstairs to look for the others.

She found her uncle and Qiren eating on the sun-filled terrace above the garden. Jeth poked his fork at the laden table nearby and Shaeli found she was enormously hungry. She filled her plate and sat down beside Qiren. She asked after the others, and was told Illen and Eenis had gone down to Palveron and Flin was still in bed.

Ebony nibbled on a few things and disappeared down into the garden, and when she returned, Shaeli had finished her breakfast and was drowsing in the warm sunshine. She was surprised that she was still so tired, and said so.

Qiren laughed. "Why do you think Flin is still abed?" he asked. "Magic is tiring, you know that, performances are always more so. I'm only just up myself. It was starvation finally made me rise." He bit into another pancake to prove the point.

"And I couldn't let him eat alone," chuckled Jeth, leaning back and patting his stomach.

"I knew from practice that it's draining," said Shaeli. "That was one of the first things Almarnoch taught me. But even after we stopped that big rock at Cave, I didn't feel this tired. I guess that was because Almarnoch helped me," she mused.

"Helped you, Shaeli?" asked Qiren, suddenly looking wide awake. "Tell me about the big rock."

"Well, that's how we ended up in Palveron this year," she explained. "Before we left Cave, there was a rock fall we had to move, from a little avalanche. I helped with the bigger stones, and then there was this one big rock left. Another slide started, and a boulder hit the big rock, and it started to fall. Taffka was under it, and the stone was in my hand, so..." she shrugged, "so I tried to stop it."

"It was a sight indeed," smiled Jeth. "Our girl holding this huge boulder above Taffka's head."

Qiren did not share his amusement. "Shaeli," he said, "how did you 'help with the bigger ones'? How did you stop this boulder?"

Shaeli looked puzzled. "With one of my stones," she replied, slowly, frowning at him. She thought Qiren was being slightly dense. "The black sparkly one that makes such nice skylights. You know."

"No, Shaeli, I don't," he said. "I know the stone you mean, and its skylights. You are fortunate to have found it, but how could you stop this rock with it?"

"Well, it... it lifts things," she said, tentatively, watching his face. It did not twitch.

"Lifts things?"

"Yes, like the others can burn, or... whatever. You know, the other magic."

"The *other* magic?"

She nodded slowly.

Qiren's face was unreadable. "Show me the stone," he said.

Her hand moved to her waist. "I *must* be tired," she said. "I've left my amulet upstairs. I'll go and fetch it."

She left before Qiren could say anything else, and when she returned, tying on her amulet as she came, he was not there. She looked at Jeth.

"He went to get Flin," Jeth said.

Shaeli's face paled. "Why?" she asked.

Jeth shrugged. "It seems they were not aware of this part of your magic. They thought only the skylights were your gift." He shrugged again. "At least, that's what I *think*."

Shaeli did not have time to think, because Qiren returned, followed by a tousle-haired Flin. He yawned and rubbed at his eyes, yet those eyes were serious and alight with something Shaeli could not read.

"May we see the stone that lifts, Shaeli?" asked Qiren, and she fumbled in her pouch and handed him the gem. The silver and purple sparks in the stone's black depths glittered in the sun.

Qiren studied it, nodded, and handed it to Flin. Neither spoke as they considered the gem. Finally Qiren looked at her.

"Tell Flin about saving Taffka," he said.

Shaeli repeated the tale, with Jeth throwing in a detail or two. Flin was quiet after she'd finished, looking down at the stone in his hand.

"When you say Almarnoch helped you push it, how exactly did he help you?"

"Well," Shaeli said, nervously, "he put his hand on my shoulder, and I... I felt his magic, and sort of... sort of... *pulled* at it."

"And this helped you push the rock away from Taffka?"

She nodded. "I was having trouble holding it by myself," she said. "It was a big rock."

Flin looked at Qiren. "Power transference," he said, dryly.

Qiren raised an eyebrow. "And levitation."

"Incredible."

"*And* unwittingly, almost without training."

"More incredible," consented Flin.

"Without effort, it seems," said the elf.

"Verging on the impossible," nodded Flin. He spoke seriously, yet he seemed to grow more delighted with every word.

Shaeli could stand it no longer. "What?" she cried. "What are you *talking* about?"

Flin ignored her. "You had no idea?"

Qiren shook his head. "I thought it possible, with time and guidance, but, no, I had no idea, not even from..." he stopped. "And levitation did not occur to me. Why have we not used the stone?"

"I chose the quartz, amber, and verdena for their strength. I disregarded it. It is little known, and usually so unreliable." Flin finally turned to Shaeli. "How long have you had this extra power, this 'other magic'?"

"Always," Shaeli stammered. "I had that first, but Almarnoch said there is not much use for that sort of magic, so I was happy when I found out I could make skylights. At least there's a use for *them*. But what does it matter?" she cried. "Does it make any difference? You'll still teach me, Flin?"

He seemed surprised. "Teach you? Of course." He looked at her strangely, rather as she'd looked at Qiren a little while ago; as if she was being dense. "Shaeli, don't you *know*?"

"Know *what*?" She had passed nervous and was moving swiftly towards exasperation.

"Skylights come first," Flin said. "*Usually*, that is. The channelling for power, for *deeper* magic, that comes later. And levitation," he held Shaeli's gem between his fingers, "with *this* stone, well, that is the stuff of legend."

Luckily there was a couch behind Shaeli, for she fell onto it with a bump. Ebony leapt out from beneath her, unnoticed and indignant.

"Legend?" she squeaked.

"Yes, Shaeli, legend. Do you know what this is?"

She shook her head. Flin passed the stone to Qiren. Shaeli passed her eyes with it. Exasperation had fled. She felt dazed and a bit sick.

"There are few of these gems in the World," said Qiren, holding the stone between thumb and forefinger. "They are found only in the Drell Mountains. Small stones are sometimes cut into layers for jewellery, but there is scant reference to this stone in any books."

"We could find hardly anything about it in the Warlock's books, but Llevvis said he once saw it in a lady's necklace," Shaeli said, her voice almost a whisper.

Qiren nodded, and then continued. "My father has one, smaller than this, which wields great power. He is one of our greatest magicians." He looked at Shaeli intently, and spoke very slowly. "My father possesses great strength. He knows it is possible to lift objects with this stone, and he has sought for two hundred Winters to find its secret, but without success. He knows its properties, Shaeli, he knows what it is capable of, but he *cannot make this stone levitate.*"

Shaeli was silent as this information sunk in, and as it did, her eyes grew wider and wider. Jeth, his face a parody of amazement, came to sit beside her, taking her cold fingers in his warm hand. Shaeli looked down at it. His hand was very like her father's. When she looked back at Flin and Qiren, her eyes were filmed with tears.

"But, how…?" she began.

Qiren stopped her. "There's more, Shaeli."

"*More?*" Her voice made the squeak again.

He nodded. "This stone – we call it vistrella – this is a potent gem. Using this for levitation is rare, yet possible." He paused. "But what you did to your Warlock – transferring his power to yourself and using it as your own – this, as Flin says, is verging on the impossible. And you, a child of the People, barely grown, have done these things with ease, and without knowledge." Suddenly he began to laugh. "Oh, wait until I tell my father."

"*Now* do you understand, Shaeli?" said Flin. "Can you see now how we can learn as much from you as you can from us?"

Then he, too, began to laugh, and Jeth laughed with him, but Shaeli could not join them.

She could not believe what they said was true, found it barely possible. Yet it *was* true that she had done those things, and Qiren and Flin had no cause to lie to her. And somewhere inside, she knew it was so. She felt it. *This* is what Williver had talked of yesterday. *This* is what he'd meant.

Her next words, quietly spoken, sobered the three instantly. "You can't tell anyone," she said, and they all looked at her, sitting so small on the couch, so grave. Yet her words and the look on her face broached no refusal, and they nodded as one.

"Yes, of course, Shaeli," said Flin. "You're perfectly right. You remain my apprentice as far as anyone else is concerned, but you need not be afraid; this is a wonderful thing."

"That may be," she said, slowly. "But I know very little about it, it seems, and I'm told there are those to be wary of, if one wields magic without knowledge. I've promised to be careful." She looked at them. "I must trust you two as I trust the Fleet, and I think it best we keep this amongst ourselves." Her eyes flicked from them to Jeth. "I'm sure Almarnoch would think it best."

Jeth nodded, and she smiled at him and squeezed his hand. Qiren and Flin agreed, but Qiren's brow furrowed.

"How is it that your Warlock did not tell you something of this? He is a Warlock of high repute, is he not?"

Shaeli nodded. "Yes, but we left Cave soon after it happened, and the effort had tired him." She frowned. "But now that I think about it, he seemed a bit... distant. A bit quiet." She shrugged. "I thought he was just tired but... yes, now I'm sure he *must* have known." She sighed. "He would have told me, I'm sure, when I returned to Cave, he was just waiting for the right time. *And* he probably didn't want to frighten me." She looked accusingly at them. "Not like you two." She put a hand to her chest. "I thought I'd die of shock for a moment."

The elf and the thin man looked abashed and began to mumble apologies.

Shaeli began to laugh. Jeth chuckled beside her.

"Really, Shaeli," he said, shaking his head. "You shouldn't tease people like that."

"I'm sorry, Jeth," she giggled. "I couldn't help it. It must have been the shock."

That set her off again, and Flin and Qiren, realising they were being ridiculed, joined in. All four were laughing, watched by a still indignant Ebony, when Eenis and Illen returned.

"What's going on?" smiled Illen.

"May I tell her?" asked Qiren, and Shaeli nodded, smiling.

"Of course. Illen is part of the family," she said.

Eenis beamed at her niece, and her smile barely faltered as Qiren told his wife of Shaeli's gift. Eenis had known most of it anyway, and Illen's reaction was identical to Shaeli's.

"Of course it must be kept secret. Shaeli must be protected until she learns how to protect herself."

"Well said, Illen," said Eenis, squeezing her sisters' arm.

"But I want to see her *do* it," said Flin, petulance creeping into his voice. "And it's obvious we can't have a demonstration here. Nothing is ever secret in Palveron."

"Perhaps we shall have to start going for long drives in the country," said Qiren.

"Perhaps we shall," smiled Flin, his delight returning intact. "Perhaps even a few days in a secluded cottage might do us some good." The smile grew wider. He began to pile food onto a plate. "Yes. Yes, I can see we're all very tired after the skylights. We need a few days away."

* * *

He made plans as he ate, and by the next afternoon he had arranged to lease a house around the bay. He invited the twins too, and two days later they boarded Flin's carriage, picked the girls up at Asheen's, and set off north around the bay.

They were all excited, admiring the view and chattering endlessly, and the journey passed quickly. They stopped for lunch at a tavern along the road, chosen for the small, slightly decrepit Landing on one side of the courtyard, and the sun was halfway to the horizon when they finally reached the house Flin had leased.

It was not large, but the grounds were secluded and studded with tall trees. Private courtyards opened out in several places, and the property was bordered with a high stone wall on three sides. The fourth side was bordered by the bay itself, and sponge-thick grass ran down to meet the rippling waters.

The house was all on one level, built with the same pale stone as the walls, and the many bedrooms were small but cosy, with a fireplace in each and coloured glass in the windows. A hallway ran the length of the house from the front door to a big sitting room filled with over-padded couches and crowded bookshelves. A fireplace dominated one wall and another was panelled glass, its wide doors opening out into one of the private courtyards. There was a little turret attached to the sitting room, reached through an impossibly small door, and a narrow staircase wound up the walls to emerge at a viewing platform above the roofline. They all went up to the top where they could see the islands and the open sea to the south, Palveron and Great Court invisible down the curve of the bay, and to the north across grassy fields, a pretty little village sat on a low hill, an empty Landing on one side. Boccra, Flin called it. To the east, a river emptied into the bay – the Clahren, a tributary of the River Zerrin – yet Flin gave them little time to admire the view. He took Shaeli's hand and led her back down the staircase, through the tiny door and across the sitting room. The others trailed behind, amused by the determined look on Flin's face and the helplessness on Shaeli's as he led her out through the glass doors.

The courtyard was long, the walls unbroken except for an archway, its view of the bay hung with a lace of purple blooms. A small fountain tinkled on one side, and at the far end several stone benches were scattered on the grass beneath the trees. It was completely private, and perfect for Flin's purposes. He left Shaeli standing outside the doors, walked to the end and rummaged in the overgrowth, emerging with a long, dead branch and a rock the size of a melon.

Shaeli sighed as he put the rock on a bench and stuck the stick in the ground close by. Qiren stood nearby watching Flin set the targets. He looked at her.

"If you're tired, there's no need to do this now," he said.

"Flin will give me no peace until I show him," she said. "It was hard enough keeping him patient until now." She smiled. "I'm fine, Qiren, and it's not much different from throwing skylights really." When she saw the look on his face, she didn't know whether to laugh or be embarrassed. "I'm sorry, I didn't mean it like that."

"That's alright, Shaeli," he said, laughing. "Just don't ever say that to my father."

Flin joined them and looked at her anxiously. "The rock's not too big?" he asked.

Shaeli looked over her shoulder at the twins, Eenis, and Jeth. She lifted one eyebrow and they laughed.

"That's a rare one," cried Jeth, slapping his thigh. "'Tis like asking if an ant can move a breadcrumb."

"Stop it, Jeth," said Eenis. "He has not seen." But her face struggled to contain her own mirth as it had once struggled to contain her fear. She smiled at her niece. "Show them, Shaeli," she said, and Shaeli was warmed by the pride in her voice.

She turned around and looked at Flin. "The stick first," she said, feeling in her amulet for the amethyst.

She held the stone loosely, gauging the distance to the target, and then she raised her arm. She let the magic build, but held on to it tightly, like the reigns of a skittish horse, then she let fly with a small beam of purple which connected with the stick dead centre. It fluttered into flame with a sigh, and Shaeli disconnected the beam and looked at Flin.

"Alright?" she asked, and he nodded.

"Yes, yes, very good, but now the rock." It was almost a plea.

She smiled and dropped the amethyst back into her pouch.

The stick was crumbling into ashes as she drew out the vistrella. Qiren had told her the word meant "to touch the stars" in the old elven language, and she thought it suited it; the stone looked like tiny purple stars had been captured within its black depths. She judged the target, took aim, and waited a few moments – not because it was any more difficult, but because she had already learned something of showmanship from the thin man beside her.

She let the magic build again until it tingled down her arm, this time bridling it less tightly before letting it flow, and the slim beam ran in a straight line to its target. The rock trembled before lifting into the air, and Shaeli let it float above the bench for a moment: a stone balloon without a string.

Beside her, Flin's mouth dropped open, and Shaeli lifted the rock higher, taking it up to hover in front of the vines brushing the top of the wall. She let it hang motionless as her audience made varying noises of appreciation, and then, just to show off a bit, and to try something new, she pulled back on the beam, drawing it in, smiling to herself as the rock floated towards them.

She concentrated on contracting the beam until the rock hung in the air before Flin, and then she lowered her hand and the rock, disconnecting the magic as the rock floated before Flin's knees. It plopped onto the grass at his feet, again inanimate and weighty.

Shaeli looked at him. "Is that what you wanted to see?" she asked.

Flin looked down at the rock and poked it gingerly with his toe as if it would fly again unbidden. He looked back at her and nodded slowly.

Neesha ran over. "I haven't seen you pull them in like that before," she said, admiringly. "It was like fishing."

Shaeli shrugged. "I just made it up," she smiled.

"Good trick," said her sister.

Flin finally sputtered into life. "Trick?" he gasped. "*Trick?* It is much more than that, young lady. It is amazing, extraordinary, incredible magic."

"You're right, Flin," said Neesha, seriously. "But it's a good trick, just the same."

* * *

They spent many nights in the house by the bay after that, travelling so much between it and Palveron that the journey became familiar and the walled stone house like another home.

Most often the twins accompanied them, a few times Iyri went too, and they grew to know the small village of Boccra and the best walks and drives in the countryside around it.

They also became familiar with the tavern which had the scruffy Landing where they stopped on each trip for a meal. The tavern had a sign hanging out the front showing a fat cow sitting on a grassy knoll fishing in the waters of the bay, the rod arcing towards the water. The Fish and Field was run by Borsal and his wife, Dorkit, a rotund and jovial couple whose children had grown and left home, yet their children lived close by with their families and there was always some of them in the tavern.

Borsal was an outspoken, happy man with a beard as huge and round as his belly; his wife a red-cheeked smiling woman whose hands were never still. Dorkit was eternally filling a mug, serving a meal or wiping a bench, often with one of her many grandchildren on her hip and a joke on her lips. The twins would sit in the enormous kitchen, watching her knead bread or roll biscuit dough.

Qiren, Jeth and Flin debated every topic imaginable over an ale with Borsal and his clan, from the worsening state of the Land, to the art of fishing, to the price of grapes in Romynn.

Shaeli would often sit and listen to their thoughts on the situation in the Four Lands, for the memory of the strange fugue state which had come upon her at the Autumn's Eve Hunt was with her often. So, too, was the brave man with the pheasant in her thoughts, and she grew ever more aware of what was happening in the World around her; the empty farms, the ragged children, the abundance of guard. They passed several outposts on their journeys back and forth, one just north of the Royal Parklands where the soldiers were coarse and rowdy, always practising something; bows, swords, whips. Few people lived near these outposts, as if each one was a blight on the countryside around it.

With each journey they became closer to the family in the tavern. On one trip, Eenis heard one of the daughters bemoaning a tapestry she'd ruined, and she would not leave until the woman brought it to the tavern. Eenis inspected it, pronounced it repairable, gave instructions, and with each subsequent visit the tapestry was further inspected and talked over. Illen was also proficient with a needle, and the two sisters would talk with Dorkit and Borsal's daughters about style and technique as the sun strolled through the afternoon. Several times they stayed so long past lunch that they did not reach the house until after dark. Their return journeys included a similar stop.

Flin took few of his retinue of servants with him on these trips, just two groomsmen and his cook, a wizened little man named Yorrow, who spoke only when necessary and who smiled only at his pots. Flin told them he had poached Yorrow from a Romynnii nobleman after falling in love with Yorrow's caramel sauce, chicken stuffed with nuts, and smoked trout mousse – in that order.

Yorrow sat stiffly in the carriage on each journey, holding his bag of knives and the two pots he could not live without, his face wrinkled and unseeing. There he stayed every time they called at the tavern, staunch and unswerving, his face a mask as they ate someone else's food, only the small, pitying look he gave them as they reboarded the carriage telling them what he thought of their foolhardiness. Flin assured them of his discretion; Yorrow cared for nothing but his kitchen.

Each time they went to the house they practised skylights. Qiren and Flin both had the ability to wield the deeper magic, and while both outmatched Shaeli in throwing skylights, neither had her strength or endurance with the deeper magic, and neither could move anything with her vistrella, no matter how she tried to explain it.

While Shaeli grew prouder of her skill with these sessions, she also felt a lingering embarrassment at possessing a strength that the older, more experienced men did not. With it came a sense that she was undeserving of such a powerful gift, and a terrible mixture of elation and fear as to what it might mean. She became broody, dwelling too much on the strangeness of possessing such magic, yet she knew she must continue to explore it.

* * *

CHAPTER THIRTY EIGHT

When Purple Leaf arrived back in Palveron to collect Jeth, Eenis and the girls, Shaeli knew that she would stay. Her family were not surprised, and the days between the Trader's arrival and its inevitable departure passed quickly. She spent as much time with her family as possible, trying each time not to think about the long Wintering without them and Cave and the Fleet, and failing more often than not. At times her sight would grow hazy; seeing Purple Leaf moored with Golden Eagle at the Landing; watching the twins with the chickens; Mareesha at her Faunist bench; Tarkoda with the Zoi or yelling to Andos as he checked the rigging; her father and Jeth poring over their charts; and each time she would brush the tears from her eyes, and remind herself the Wintering would pass swiftly, just as her Cave year had, and she would see them in the Starisles in the spring.

At last they could delay no longer. Purple Leaf had stayed three days after Golden Eagle had flown from the city, and Jarris flew them all to the village of Boccra. Flin, Qiren and Illen enjoyed the trip on the Trader, marvelling at the view of Palveron and the Bay of Islands, but Shaeli was despondent and barely spoke a word the whole trip. Eenis, too, showed signs of the same malady; she was quiet and tense, her face shadowed with the old haunted look, but Illen reassured her of their meeting in spring so many times that Eenis was almost appeased.

They moored at the Landing at Boccra and walked to the stone house for a farewell dinner. Flin had arranged for his servants to travel down the day before, and they had set a table in the courtyard where Shaeli had first shown Flin her magic. Masses of candles lit the area, braziers burned brightly to stave off the autumn air, and the dinner which Yorrow served contained six courses, each more sumptuous than the last. When they had finished, they pushed back the chairs and drank rich port until weariness prodded them, and at last they had to admit the night was over. Shaeli and Illen walked the travellers out through the stone walls where they said their good-byes, for Purple Leaf would be flying at dawn, and Shaeli hugged them all as tightly as she could, trying to squeeze her love for them into each embrace. The twins, lips trembling, she held longer, for she would not see them in the spring. They would spend the year on the Long Lea, and she tried to reassure them that the time would pass quickly. She hoped it would be so for them, as well as for herself.

Illen put her arm about Shaeli's shoulders as her family disappeared into the night, and held her as she spent the tears that had been building for days. When they returned to the house she made tezz as Shaeli sniffed by the fire, drawing comfort from the only one left behind: the jevvi.

Ebony nuzzled her as Shaeli sipped her tezz, and she snuggled the animal absentmindedly, wondering what the Wintering would bring. She went to bed exhausted, but sleep evaded her. When it did come, it was in snatches, and her dreams were as tangled as her blankets.

* * *

There were others across the World who did not sleep well that night; most would rise early to contemplate the coming day, or Wintering, or year.

* * *

At Cave, Almarnoch knew he had been unwise to let Purple Leaf leave without telling them of Shaeli's enormous capacity for magic. As the year had passed, he had thought himself more and more foolhardy; magic such as hers was too incredible to go untrained, and he knew so little about the art. He awaited the Wintering with impatience.

* * *

Dari also awaited the Wintering with impatience. He had done well this year, better than he'd dared hope. Everything came so easily to him — even his Cave lights had lasted more than ten Moons — and he wanted the Wintering here so that it would pass and the next year could begin. He no longer roamed the dark hours of the night seeking food or mischief, he had not for years. His days were so full, working in the orchards with Llevvis, learning water direction with Demeris or major incantations with Almarnoch, that he had little time to brood, and found himself filled with an odd feeling. It took some time to realise the feeling was happiness. And soon he would go to Palveron and the Warlock Island to complete his training, and he would find Garrit and they would have a fine time together at his home in the city.

* * *

Dari didn't know that Garrit did not live in Palveron. Garrit lived at Great Court. He had ingratiated himself with anyone who had influence, and had secured a position at the Warlock House where he was close to the throne and the power that went with it. He spent long hours planning how to get closer to the queen's inner circle; how to become an influential member of the Court.

He thought of Dari sporadically, mostly as a means of acquiring the wand his cousin had found; it was not for nothing he had spent years grooming the boy. Once he'd almost had it, but he had not given up hope; the thing could still be his. Its riches would keep him in fine style, perhaps it would even fetch enough to be worth a house in the city.

* * *

Irinesta spent much of the night looking down on the city while E'Nith snored behind her curtain. She had watched Purple Leaf fly away that morning, and knew it may be a long time before she saw it again. Having it in Palveron most of the year had made her feel close to her daughter; she had even seen Mareesha and Jarris a few times when they came to Great

Court, though she had never watched them from the balcony again.

Another Wintering would soon begin. Tomorrow she would write her annual letter to Sir Vulcan, but she would make tezz first, and try to sleep a bit.

* * *

Queen Virrisian was up much of the night with Sir Azeron. He had proved a resourceful man in many ways, and when he finally slept she lay drowsing beside him. The Wintering would pass quickly, there were many distractions to be indulged in during the frozen Moons, and the next year she would find the rest of these so-called rebels and destroy them. She would also begin to take control of the other Lands. Wokk would be first; its king was such a weak little man, and she knew it would fall easily. *He* had promised it would be so. She thought she would take Ashkanna after that. She felt sure he would agree.

* * *

On the eastern edge of the Starisles, Zeb was up well before dawn and rowing across to a neighbouring island to bring back one of the women to stay with M'zena. A few times a year he went into Pa'laidiz with produce, and M'zena always insisted he take some time for himself. He would spend a couple of nights drinking in taverns and flirting with girls, and the days stocking up on things to take back to the island. When he'd had too much to drink he would speak longingly of sailing away from the Starisles, of sailing to all the Lands, of seeing fabled places; the burning mountains of Wokk and the famous Qotarr; the fields stretching as far as the horizon in Romynn; the dazzling scenery of Ashkanna; the city on Zirrus where the castle crowned the Land. He even boasted he would visit the elves in the mountains if given the chance.

* * *

In the village of Boccra, Fezzik pulled on his boots in the first grey light of dawn. He had not slept well, there was much on his mind, but the voices and giggles of small children wafted up through the floorboards and he smiled at the sound. Verlie's voice drifted up to him too, and then came the answering voice of Pemba, the words spoken in the same dull tone she had used since Pelazarus died.

It had been the hardest thing he had ever had to do, telling Pemba her husband was dead. Fezzik had tried to bring him back to her so she could send him to the gods fittingly, but his pleas had been ignored, the guard at the Hunt had laughed at his request, and he'd been denied the body.

They had left the Hunt as the first skylights shattered the sky, the children watching the spectacle as they drove down the dark road. Verlie had sat close beside him as he held the reins in his gnarled hands, his face wet with tears, and she had sat with him through the night as he talked of his friend and raged against the queen. The fist of hatred which had grown inside him after the eviction of Pelazarus' family had hardened into granite with his death.

Pemba had collapsed when he'd told her, and she'd begged him to take her home, to take her family back to Boccra, and he'd brought them back that day, driving the tired horses pulling the cart full of children as Pemba wept through the journey. They had built them a home beside their own, just a few rooms, but Pemba was grateful, and showed it by cooking meals and helping in the forge, learning quickly how to make those items needed most by the rebels. She poured her energy into this and the small flock of birds she kept on the flats beneath their homes; she did both in memory of Pelazarus, determined to make a small difference in his name. They hid their arrow-heads, swords and other weapons under the roosts, in a pit dug beneath the evil-smelling droppings of the birds, for the guard had become ever more vigilant, ever more suspicious. Just last night, after the children were abed and Fezzik snored by the fire, he'd woken to see Verlie and Pemba coming inside, dark shawls wrapped tightly about their heads.

He'd meant to help them take the new batch of daggers down to the pit beneath the chickens, but they'd managed without him; Verlie had said smilingly that she'd not wanted to disturb his snoring.

Fezzik had embraced the rebellion wholeheartedly since Pelazarus' death. Before, he had helped them peripherally, as a duty to be undertaken and finished as quickly as possible, but now his thoughts were always on what he could do next, who needed help most, where the guard could be attacked to most advantage. He had gone from passive underling to dedicated leader, gathering information and organising raids, keeping a vast network of spies that covered the countryside from the River Zerrin to the Royal Parklands. He did not know how such a path could help the Land, he only knew he could no longer sit by and do nothing.

The sun was almost above the horizon, its light a grey weak thing seeping through the windows when he went down to the kitchen; the thick mist which coated the morning had not yet begun to burn off. A puddle of small children sat outside the door eating breakfast, the older children were at the table, and Pemba's baby lay asleep in a basket near the warmth of the stove. She was still a tiny thing, inclined to catch a sniffle at the slightest provocation, but she was a sweet dimpled baby with Pelazarus' eyes, and they all adored her. He pulled himself up a chair and poured a mug of tezz.

He had finished his breakfast and was kissing his wife before going to the forge when it happened.

Through the window he saw soldiers on the path, more coming across the garden and the misty flats below, still more in the forge. His mother and father were being pushed out their back door, Fedor's arms gesticulating wildly; Fezzik could only guess at the words accompanying the arms. He looked at Verlie, squeezed her hand and went out onto the veranda to meet them, sending the big-eyed children scuttling inside with a jerk of his head.

The head of the guard stopped two paces from the steps. There were dozens of soldiers around the house now, all armed.

Somewhere down the hill, a chicken squawked indignantly, then another. There were shouts and oaths, some more squawks. Fezzik ignored them.

"What do you want?" he said. "Get these soldiers off my land."

The head guard ignored him. She was a tall, angular woman, her chest as flat as her cheekbones, her mouth pursed as a prune. She unrolled a short scroll and began to read in a sneeringly loud voice.

"Verlie, wife of Fezzik, and Pemba, widow of the traitor Pelazarus, are hereby taken prisoner for aiding the rebellion against the good Queen Virrisian," she said. "They are to be taken to the garrison to be held at the queen's pleasure until she decides what punishment befits this treacherous act." The woman smiled a thin slash of a smile. She rolled the scroll up again and looked at them, the smile curdling into a triumphant sneer. "Do the prisoners come freely, or do we take them?" she asked.

"Who brings these false charges?" called Fezzik. "What proof of such a thing do you have?" Though he spoke strongly, his heart had turned to ice in his chest.

Another chicken squawked.

"These are no false charges," the sneering woman said. "They were seen, last night, secreting arms. As for proof..." She looked down the slope. "Here it comes now."

As Fezzik had known they would, the guard were carrying two crates from the coops, one the box placed there last night by Verlie and Pemba, the other a long crate of swords he had put there himself three days ago in the sunrise hours. It was over and he knew it. With a roar he threw himself down the stairs.

They were ready for him, of course. Two caught his arms before he'd landed a blow, the head guard had her sword at his throat in an instant. She held it there as more soldiers came forward and grabbed Pemba and Verlie, dragging them past him and on up the path. Pemba began to cry out about the baby asleep by the stove. Verlie was calling his name over and over. Fezzik struggled. The children began to scream.

"*Mam*, where are you *going*?"
"*Da*, make them stop."
"Mam, don't go. *Mam!*"
"Fezzik, what're they doing to my Mam?"
"Help them, Da, help them."
"Let my Mam go!"
"Fezzik make them *stop!*"
"Mam. *Mam*."

But Fezzik could do nothing but struggle. The point of the sword dug into his throat and he felt the warm trickle of blood as it broke the skin, but he kept struggling. The guard, two score of them, crowded around and pushed the two women up the path and out to the courtyard. The children bobbed amongst them like corks, grabbing arms, dodging feet, their cries lost in the babble.

The courtyard and the street outside were filled with horses stamping and blowing, and amongst them was a small windowless carriage, a box on wheels, into which the two women were pushed. Fezzik, dragged behind them, saw his parents also held before sharp blades, and he struggled again, but he was held firmly, the sword pressed against his flesh as the door of the carriage was closed upon Verlie and Pemba.

He had one fleeting look at Verlie's face before they shut the door, her eyes wide and desperate, and then the door slammed and all he could see of her was her fingers coming through the thin slats. She and Pemba began calling to the children, telling them it would be alright, yet the children did not believe them. They knew well that things were not alright, they knew it very well indeed, and they milled around the carriage and the legs of the horses, screaming at the guard, pleading with them, crying.

None of the soldiers looked at them. They mounted their horses, deaf to the cries, but others had heard. Up the street people were coming from their homes, heads were poked from windows; Koak of the Orange Duck Tavern stood in his doorway, a cloth in his hand, eyes unreadable.

Further down the street, the landingholder, Qwintum, stood shadowed in a doorway. His curveless cousin, her blade at Fezzik's throat, smiled at him. Qwintum stared a moment longer, and then disappeared into the shadows. The woman looked back at Fezzik and mounted her horse, sheathing the sword and leaning back down, thrusting her face into his.

"I could have taken you too, if I'd wished," she said, her voice low. "But they want you made an example to others who might think to follow your lead." Her tongue darted in and out like a snake's. "And I can *still* have you, if you give me a reason. Remember that. And if you can't... then make a mistake," she hissed. "Just one. I dare you."

She looked past him and nodded. Fezzik did not have time to wonder at the nod before the blow came.

He knew nothing for a while, and when he opened his eyes his face was resting on cobblestones and Arral was shaking him. The hooves of many horses clattered on the stones, to one side there were the wheels of a small carriage, and he could hear the cries of children.

"Let's go," said the woman's voice somewhere above him.

The World faded and then came back.

"... the children..." came another voice.

"They'll move," said the woman. "Or not."

Fezzik moaned, put a hand to his head, and let Arral try and pull him up. The boy was shouting but Fezzik couldn't focus on the garbled words.

He regained himself as the first horses galloped away. Made it to his knees as the carriage began to move. Realised their danger as he staggered to his feet. He stumbled towards them, yelling.

Arral was beside him and the older children dodged quickly enough, one taking a glancing blow to the head from a stirrup-clad foot, but the four smaller girls had been milling about the carriage, screaming and calling to their mothers. The soldier driving it barked one meaningless word in their direction before he applied the whip to the horse's rumps. The carriage jerked forward.

Pemba's Sharn fell straight away, the hooves of a following horse just missing her, the horse after that kicking her to the side of the road where she lay screaming. Florry was pounding on the door of the carriage, Verlie yelling at her to go back, go away, when the wheel of the carriage hit her and sent her flying backwards onto the road where Fedor lunged at her and pulled her away from the horses that followed.

Little Pim, stumbling on her ruined feet near the front of the carriage, had been calling to the driver, far too close to the lofty side of a horse. His Zeffy was beside her.

Zeffy jumped at the bark from the driver; looked up as the whip cracked. As the carriage leapt forward, she grabbed Pim's arm and pulled, but too late. They were knocked by the darting hooves and fell onto the road where horses and carriage rolled over them both, the driver either not feeling or not caring about the bumps beneath his wheels. The bodies of the two tiny girls were hit by passing hooves several more times before Fezzik reached them.

They lay like broken dolls; like bundles of material discarded in the road. Pim moaned as he reached her, her breath coming in small whooping gasps, but he could see by her crushed chest that she would not live long. One of her shoes lay in the road nearby, the little foot with its two remaining toes sticking out from beneath the hem of her dress. Her other leg was twisted oddly.

His mother was there and he left Pim with her and went to his Zeffy. One look at her told him there was nothing to be done. Her little face was perfect, but the back of her head was pulpy, bloody mush. Her eyes were closed, as if she was sleeping.

He gathered her into his arms, kneeling in the road, a great howl building in his chest. His father stood nearby, Florry in his arms. There was a bruise on her forehead and she was crying, one arm held in the other. Arral stood beside them, his face grey, his mouth hanging open. Pemba's children clustered around little Sharn as she cried in the gutter. His mother hovered over the dying Pim.

The guard rode away to their garrison, the sound of the women screaming in the prison-carriage tangling with the thuds of the horse's hooves. Only one soldier looked back as they rode down into the mist laying banked like cloud below the hill; only one turned back to see the devastation left behind, a woman who bowed her head in shame before turning away.

The cry tore from Fezzik's throat in a raging flood. A great tortured, agonised cry that filled the street and the village beyond, echoing down to the guard and their prisoners. The people who had gathered around the tragedy watched as Fezzik knelt in the street cradling the body of his youngest child; watched wordlessly as he howled and howled and howled at the sky until his throat was hoarse with the force of it. It was the cry that had been heard by a young lady in a blue dress, a young lady who had stood near him as they'd watched Pelazarus die at the Autumn's Eve Hunt.

Yet when the cry had faded into the morning mists, he rose to his feet. Fezzik would not linger long in his grief. By next morning he would already be planning how he would free his wife and the widow of his dearest friend. He would also be imagining the look on the face of the head of the guard as he killed her.

* * *

    Shaeli rose in the sunrise hours and took Ebony out through the courtyard, under the archway, bare now of leaves and flowers, and down to the edge of the bay. The water was perfectly still and shrouded in mist, the silence broken only by the splash of an occasional fish. The sun was a white blur just above the horizon when she heard it, and she looked up.

    The chord from the female Zoi still resonated in the air as Purple Leaf glided silently towards her, its underside barely topping the trees. Another bird echoed the first as the Zoi flew over.

    Her family were lined up along the back rail, just as they had been when they left her for Cave year, their faces whiter spots in the white mist, their hands fluttering like handkerchiefs, but this time there was no Almarnoch, no Llevvis, no Wyshka, no Kirrit to turn to, and she waved harder, calling to her family as they flew away from her, hearing their voices even after the balloon was swallowed by the mist.

    She hugged Ebony to her, and turned back to the house.

    They were gone. She was alone.

* * *

LOOK OUT FOR

THE THROWER'S APPRENTICE

BOOK TWO OF *THE TRADERS*

ABOUT THE AUTHOR

R.L. Aiken lives on the eastern coast of Australia in a small town with the ocean out the front and kangaroos out the back. She has been writing this very big story in this very small town for a very long time, and is very happy to finally put it in your hands to be read. Thanks for holding it.

www.ingramcontent.com/pod-product-compliance
Ingram Content Group UK Ltd.
Pitfield, Milton Keynes, MK11 3LW, UK
UKHW041303180426
11947UKWH00009B/661

9 780648 568308